Friedrich Schiller, Hjalmar Hjorth Boyesen, J. G. Fischer

Schiller's works

Vol. III

Friedrich Schiller, Hjalmar Hjorth Boyesen, J. G. Fischer

Schiller's works
Vol. III

ISBN/EAN: 9783743376724

Manufactured in Europe, USA, Canada, Australia, Japa

Cover: Foto ©Andreas Hilbeck / pixelio.de

Manufactured and distributed by brebook publishing software (www.brebook.com)

Friedrich Schiller, Hjalmar Hjorth Boyesen, J. G. Fischer

Schiller's works

SCHILLER'S WORKS

ILLUSTRATED BY THE

GREATEST GERMAN ARTISTS

EDITED BY

J. G. FISCHER

WITH

BIOGRAPHICAL INTRODUCTION

BY

HJALMAR H. BOYESEN, PH.D

—

VOLUME III

PHILADELPHIA

GEORGE BARRIE, PUBLISHER

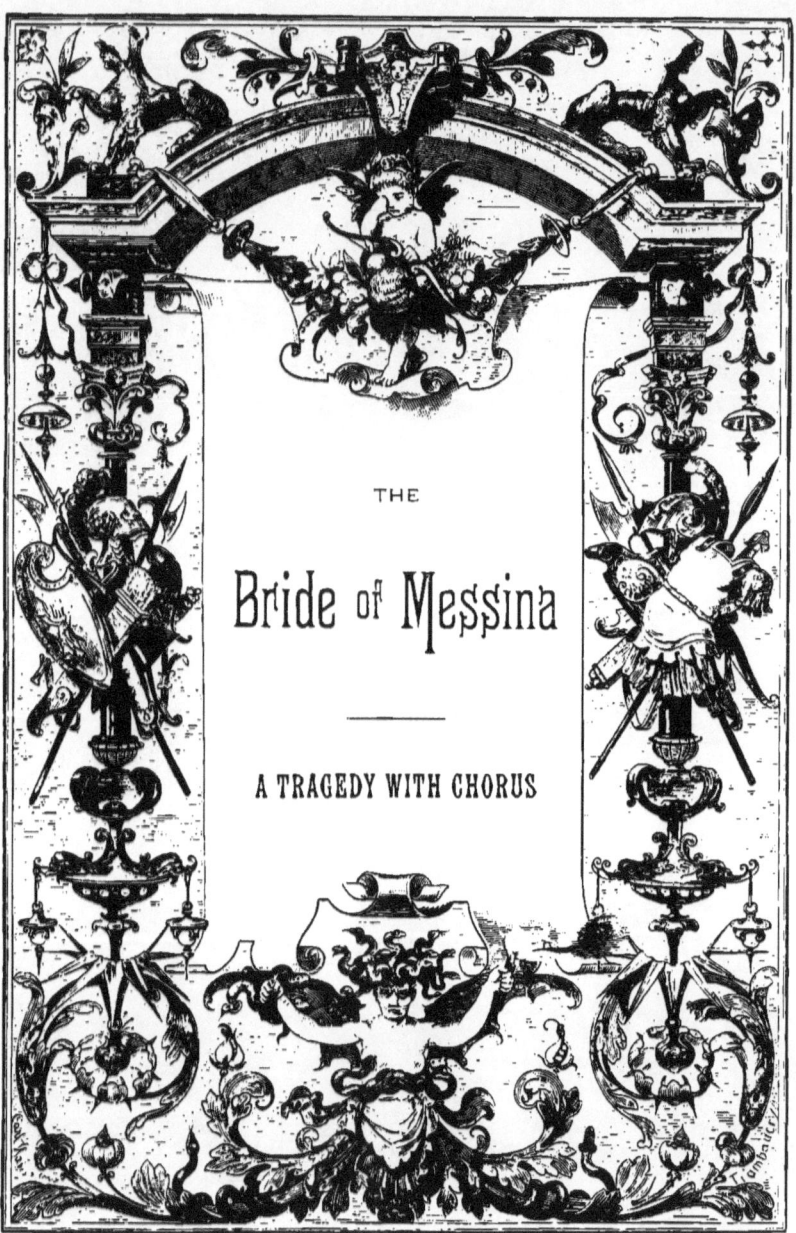

THE

Bride of Messina

A TRAGEDY WITH CHORUS

ON THE USE OF THE CHORUS IN TRAGEDY.

A POETICAL work must vindicate itself:—if the execution be defective, little aid can be derived from commentaries.

On these grounds, I might safely leave the Chorus to be its own advocate, if we had ever seen it presented in an appropriate manner. But it must be remembered that a dramatic composition first assumes the character of a whole by means of representation on the stage. The Poet supplies only the words, to which, in a lyrical tragedy, music and rhythmical motion are essential accessories. It follows, then, that if the Chorus is deprived of accompaniments appealing so powerfully to the senses, it will appear a superfluity in the economy of the drama—a mere hindrance to the development of the plot—destructive to the illusion of the scene, and wearisome to the spectators.

To do justice to the Chorus, more especially if our aims in Poetry be of a grand and elevated character, we must transport ourselves from the actual to a possible stage. It is the privilege of Art to furnish for itself whatever is requisite, and the accidental deficiency of auxiliaries ought not to confine the plastic imagination of the Poet. He aspires to whatever is most dignified, he labors to realize the ideal in his own mind—though in the execution of his purpose he must needs accommodate himself to circumstances.

The assertion so commonly made, that the Public degrades Art, is not well founded. It is the artist that brings the Public to the level of his own conceptions; and, in every age in which Art has gone to decay, it has fallen through its professors. The people need feeling alone, and feeling they possess. They take their station before the curtain with an unvoiced longing, with a multifarious capacity. They bring with them an aptitude for what is highest — they derive the greatest pleasure from what is judicious and true; and if, with these powers of appreciation, they begin to be satisfied with inferior productions, still, if they have once tasted what is excellent, they will, in the end, insist on having it supplied to them.

It is sometimes objected that the Poet may labor according to an Ideal—that the critic may judge from ideas, but that mere executive art is subject to contingencies, and depends for effect on the occasion. Managers will be obstinate; actors are bent on display—the audience is inattentive and unruly. Their object is relaxation, and they are disappointed if mental exertion be required, when they expected only amusement. But if the Theatre be made instrumental towards higher objects, the pleasure of the spectator will not be increased, but ennobled. It will be a diversion, but a poetical one. All Art is dedicated to pleasure, and there can be no higher and worthier end than to make men happy. The true Art is that which provides the highest degree of pleasure; and this consists in the abandonment of the spirit to the free play of all its faculties.

Every one expects from the imaginative arts a certain emancipation from the bounds of reality: we are willing to give a scope to Fancy, and recreate ourselves with the possible.

5

The man who expects it the least will never-theless forget his ordinary pursuits, his every-day existence and individuality, and experi-ence delight from uncommon incidents:—if he be of a serious turn of mind, he will acknowledge on the stage that moral govern-ment of the world which he fails to discover in real life. But he is, at the same time, perfectly aware that all is an empty show, and that, in a true sense, he is feeding only on dreams. When he returns from the theatre to the world of realities, he is again compressed within its narrow bounds; he is its denizen as before—for it remains what it was, and in him nothing has been changed. What, then, has he gained beyond a momentary illusive pleasure which vanished with the occasion?

It is because a passing recreation is alone desired, that a mere show of truth is thought sufficient. I mean that probability or vrai-semblance which is so highly esteemed, but which the commonest workers are able to substitute for the true.

Art has for its object not merely to afford a transient pleasure, to excite to a momentary dream of liberty; its aim is to make us abso-lutely free; and this it accomplishes by awakening, exercising, and perfecting in us a power to remove to an objective distance the sensible world (which otherwise only burdens us as rugged matter, and presses us down with a brute influence'); to transform it into the free working of our spirit, and thus acquire a dominion over the material by means of ideas. For the very reason also that true Art requires somewhat of the objective and real, it is not satisfied with a show of truth. It rears its ideal edifice on Truth itself—on the solid and deep foundations of Nature.

But how Art can be at once altogether ideal, yet in the strictest sense real;—how it can en-tirely leave the actual, and yet harmonize with Nature, is a problem to the multitude:—and hence the distorted views which prevail in regard to poetical and plastic works; for to ordinary judgments these two requisites seem to counteract each other.

It is commonly supposed that one may be attained by the sacrifice of the other:—the result is a failure to arrive at either. One to whom nature has given a true sensibility, but denied the plastic imaginative power, will be a faithful painter of the real; he will adapt casual appearances, but never catch the spirit of Nature. He will only reproduce to us the matter of the world, which, not being our

own work, the product of our creative spirit, can never have the beneficent operation of Art, of which the essence is freedom. Serious, indeed, but unpleasing, is the cast of thought with which such an artist and poet dismisses us; we feel ourselves painfully thrust back into the narrow sphere of reality by means of the very art which ought to have eman-cipated us. On the other hand, a writer endowed with a lively fancy, but destitute of warmth and individuality of feeling, will not concern himself in the least about truth; he will sport with the stuff of the world, and endeavor to surprise by whimsical com-binations; and as his whole performance is nothing but foam and glitter, he will, it is true, engage the attention for a time, but build up and confirm nothing in the understanding. His playfulness is, like the gravity of the other, thoroughly unpoetical. To string together at will fantastical images, is not to travel into the realm of the ideal; and the imitative reproduction of the actual cannot be called the representation of nature. Both requisites stand so little in contradiction to each other that they are rather one and the same thing; that Art is only true insomuch as it altogether forsakes the actual, and becomes purely ideal. Nature herself is an idea of the mind, and is never presented to the senses. She lies under the veil of appearances, but is herself never apparent. To the art of the ideal alone is lent, or rather, absolutely given, the privilege to grasp the spirit of the All, and bind it in a corporeal form.

Yet, in truth, even Art cannot present it to the senses, but by means of her creative power to the imaginative faculty alone; and it is thus that she becomes more true than all reality, and more real than all experience. It follows from these premises that the artist can use no single element taken from reality as he finds it—that his work must be ideal in all its parts, if it be designed to have, as it were, an intrinsic reality, and to harmonize with nature.

What is true of Art and Poetry, in the abstract, holds good as to their various kinds; and we may apply what has been advanced to the subject of tragedy. In this department, it is still necessary to controvert the ordinary notion of the natural, with which poetry is altogether incompatible. A certain ideality has been allowed in painting, though I fear, rather for conventional reasons, than on grounds of conviction; but in dramatic works what is desired is illusion, which, if it could be accomplished by means of the actual, would be, at least, a paltry deception. All the externals of a theatrical representation are opposed to this notion; all is merely a symbol of the real. The day itself in a theatre is an artificial one; the metrical dialogue is itself ideal; yet the conduct of the play must forsooth be real, and the general effect sacrificed to a part. Thus the French, who have utterly misconceived the spirit of the ancients, adopted on their stage the unities of time and place in the most common and empirical sense; as though there were any place but the bare ideal one, or any other time than the mere sequence of the incidents.

By the introduction of a metrical dialogue an important progress has been made towards the poetical Tragedy. A few lyrical dramas have been successful on the stage, and Poetry, by its own living energy, has triumphed over prevailing prejudices, but so long as these erroneous views are entertained little has been done—for it is not enough barely to tolerate as a poetic license that which is, in truth, the essence of all poetry. The introduction of the Chorus would be the last and decisive step; and if it only served this end, namely, to declare open and honorable warfare against naturalism in art, it would be for us a living wall which Tragedy had drawn around herself, to guard her from contact with the world of reality, and maintain her own ideal soil, her poetical freedom.

It is well known that the Greek tragedy had its origin in the Chorus; and though, in process of time, it became independent, still it may be said that poetically, and in spirit, the Chorus was the source of its existence, and that without these persevering supporters and witnessess of the incident a totally different order of poetry would have grown out of the drama. The abolition of the Chorus, and the debasement of this sensibly powerful organ into the characterless substitute of a confidant, is, by no means, such an improvement in tragedy as the French, and their imitators, would have it supposed to be.

The old Tragedy, which at first only concerned itself with gods, heroes and kings, introduced the Chorus as an essential accompaniment. The poets found it in nature, and for that reason employed it. It grew out of the poetical aspect of real life. In the new Tragedy it becomes an organ of art which aids in making the poetry prominent. The

modern poet no longer finds the Chorus in nature; he must needs create and introduce it poetically; that is, he must resolve on such an adaptation of his story as will admit of its retrocession to those primitive times, and to that simple form of life.

The Chorus thus renders more substantial service to the modern dramatist than to the old poet—and for this reason, that it transforms the commonplace actual world into the old poetical one; that it enables him to dispense with all that is repugnant to poetry, and conducts him back to the most simple, original, and genuine motives of action. The palaces of kings are in these days closed—courts of justice have been transferred from the gates of cities to the interior of buildings; writing has narrowed the province of speech; the people itself—the sensibly living mass—when it does not operate as brute force, has become a part of the civil polity, and thereby an abstract idea in our minds; the deities have returned within the bosoms of mankind. The poet must reopen the palaces—he must place courts of justice beneath the canopy of heaven—restore the gods, reproduce every extreme which the artificial fame of actual life has abolished—throw aside every factitious influence on the mind or condition of man which impedes the manifestation of his inward nature and primitive character, as the statuary rejects modern costume:—and of all external circumstances adopts nothing but what is palpable in the highest of forms—that of humanity.

But precisely as the painter throws around his figures draperies of ample volume, to fill up the space of his picture richly and gracefully, to arrange its several parts in harmonious masses, to give due play to color, which charms and refreshes the eye—and at once to envelope human forms in a spiritual veil, and make them visible—so the tragic poet inlays and entwines his rigidly contracted plot and the strong outlines of his characters with a tissue of lyrical magnificence, in which, as in flowing robes of purple, they move freely and nobly, with a sustained dignity and exalted repose.

In a higher organization, the material, or the elementary, need not be visible; the chemical color vanishes in the finer tints of the imaginative one. The material, however, has its peculiar effect, and may be included in an artistical composition. But it must deserve its place by animation, fulness and harmony, and give value to the ideal forms which it surrounds, instead of stifling them by its weight.

In respect of the pictorial art, this is obvious to ordinary apprehension, yet in poetry likewise, and in the tragical kind, which is our immediate subject, the same doctrine holds good. Whatever fascinates the senses alone, is mere matter, and the rude element of a work of art;—if it take the lead it will inevitably destroy the poetical—which lies at the exact medium between the ideal and the sensible. But man is so constituted that he is ever impatient to pass from what is fanciful to what is common; and reflection must, therefore, have its place even in tragedy. But to merit this place it must, by means of delivery, recover what it wants in actual life; for if the two elements of poetry, the ideal and the sensible, do not operate with an inward mutuality, they must at least act as allies—or poetry is out of the question. If the balance be not intrinsically perfect, the equipoise can only be maintained by an agitation of both scales.

This is what the Chorus effects in tragedy. It is, in itself, not an individual but a general conception, yet it is represented by a palpable body which appeals to the senses with an imposing grandeur. It forsakes the contracted sphere of the incidents to dilate itself over the past and the future, over distant times and nations, and general humanity, to deduce the grand results of life, and pronounces the lessons of wisdom. But all this it does with the full power of fancy—with a bold lyrical freedom which ascends, as with godlike step, to the topmost height of worldly things; and it effects it in conjunction with the whole sensible influence of melody and rhythm, in tones and movements.

The Chorus thus exercises a purifying influence on tragic poetry, insomuch as it keeps reflection apart from the incidents, and by this separation arms it with a poetical vigor; as the painter, by means of a rich drapery, changes the ordinary poverty of costume into a charm and an ornament.

But as the painter finds himself obliged to strengthen the tone of color of the living subject, in order to counterbalance the material influences—so the lyrical effusions of the Chorus impose upon the poet the necessity of a proportionate elevation of his general diction. It is the Chorus alone which entitles the poet to employ this fulness of tone, which at once charms the senses, pervades the spirit and expands the mind. This one giant form on his canvas obliges him to mount all his figures on the cothurnus, and thus impart a tragical grandeur to his picture. If the Chorus be taken away, the diction of the tragedy must generally be lowered, or what is now great and majestic will appear forced and overstrained. The old Chorus introduced into the French tragedy would present it in all its poverty, and reduce it to nothing; yet, without doubt, the same accompaniment would impart to Shakspere's tragedy its true significance.

As the Chorus gives life to the language—so also it gives repose to the action; but it is that beautiful and lofty repose which is the characteristic of a true work of art. For the mind of the spectator ought to maintain its freedom through the most impassioned scenes; it should not be the mere prey of impressions, but calmly and severely detach itself from the emotions which it suffers. The commonplace objection made to the Chorus, that it disturbs the illusion, and blunts the edge of the feelings, is what constitutes its highest recommendation; for it is this blind force of the affections which the true artist deprecates—this illusion is what he disdains to excite. If the strokes which tragedy inflicts on our bosoms followed without respite—the passion would overpower the action. We should mix ourselves up with the subject-matter, and no longer stand above it. It is by holding asunder the different parts, and stepping between the passions with its composing views, that the Chorus restores to us our freedom, which would else be lost in the tempest. The characters of the drama need this intermission in order to collect themselves; for they are no real beings who obey the impulse of the moment, and merely represent individuals—but ideal persons and representatives of their species, who enunciate the deep things of Humanity.

Thus much on my attempt to revive the old Chorus on the tragic stage. It is true that choruses are not unknown to modern tragedy; but the Chorus of the Greek drama, as I have employed it—the Chorus, as a single ideal person, furthering and accompanying the whole plot—is of an entirely distinct character; and when, in discussion on the Greek tragedy, I hear mention made of choruses, I generally suspect the speaker's ignorance of his subject.

In my view the Chorus has never been reproduced since the decline of the old tragedy.

I have divided it into two parts, and represented it in contest with itself; but this occurs where it acts as a real person, and as an unthinking multitude. As Chorus and an ideal person it is always one and entire. I have also several times dispensed with its presence on the stage. For this liberty I have the example of Æschylus, the creator of tragedy, and Sophocles, the greatest master of his art.

Another license it may be more difficult to excuse. I have blended together the Christian Religion and the Pagan Mythology, and introduced recollections of the Moorish superstition. But the scene of the drama is Messina —where these three religions either exercised a living influence, or appealed to the senses in monumental remains. Besides, I consider it a privilege of poetry to deal with different religions as a collective whole, in which everything that bears an individual character, and expresses a peculiar mode of feeling, has its place. Religion itself, the idea of a Divine Power, lies under the veil of all religions; and it must be permitted to the poet to represent it in the form which appears the most appropriate to his subject.

THE BRIDE OF MESSINA;

OR,

THE HOSTILE BROTHERS.

DRAMATIS PERSONÆ.

ISABELLA, *Princess of Messina.*

DON MANUEL ⎫
DON CÆSAR ⎭ *her Sons.*

BEATRICE.

DIEGO, *an ancient Servant.*

MESSENGERS.

THE ELDERS OF MESSINA, *mute.*

THE CHORUS, *consisting of the Followers*
of the two Princes.

SCENE I.—*A spacious hall, supported on columns, with entrances on both sides; at the
back of the stage a large folding-door leading to a chapel.*

DONNA ISABELLA, *in mourning; the* ELDERS
OF MESSINA.

ISAB.   Forth from my silent chamber's deep
    recesses,
Gray Fathers of the State, unwillingly
I come; and, shrinking from your gaze, uplift
The veil that shades my widowed brows:—
    the light
And glory of my days is fled for ever!
And best in solitude and kindred gloom
To hide these sable weeds, this grief-worn
    frame,
Beseems the mourner's heart. A mighty voice
Inexorable—duty's stern command,
Calls me to life again.——
            Not twice the moon
Has filled her orb, since to the tomb ye bore
My princely spouse, your city's lord, whose
    arm
Against a world of envious foes around
Hurled fierce defiance! Still his spirit lives

In his heroic sons, their country's pride:—
Ye marked how sweetly from their childhood's
    bloom
They grew in joyous promise to the years
Of manhood's strength;—yet in their secret
    hearts,
From some mysterious root accursed, upsprung
Unmitigable deadly hate, that spurned
All kindred ties, all youthful fond affections,
Still ripening with their thoughtful age;—not
    mine
The sweet accord of family bliss; tho' each
Awoke a mother's rapture; each alike
Smiled at my nourishing breast! for me alone
Yet lives one mutual thought, of children's
    love,
In these tempestuous souls dissevered else
By mortal strife and thirst of fierce revenge.
    While yet their father reigned, his stern
    control
Tamed their hot spirits, and with iron yoke
To awful justice bowed their stubborn will:
Obedient to his voice, to outward seeming
They calmed their wrathful mood, nor in
    array
Ere met, of hostile arms;—yet unappeased

Sat brooding malice in their bosoms' depths;
—They little reck of hidden springs, whose
power
Can quell the torrent's fury:—Scarce their
sire
In death had closed his eyes, when, as the
spark,
That long in smouldering embers sullen lay,
Shoots forth a towering flame:—so uncon-
fined
Burst the wild storm of brothers' hate, tri-
umphant
O'er nature's holiest bands. Ye saw, my
friends,
Your country's bleeding wounds, when princely
strife
Woke discord's maddening fires, and ranged
her sons
In mutual deadly conflict;—all around
Was heard the clash of arms, the din of car-
nage,
And e'en these halls were stained with kin-
dred gore.
   Torn was the state with civil rage, this heart
With pangs that mothers feel; alas! unmind-
ful
Of aught but public woes, and pitiless,
You sought my widow's chamber—there with
taunts
And fierce reproaches for your country's ills
From that polluted spring of brother's hate
Derived, invoked a parent's warning voice!
And threatening told of people's discontent
And princes' crimes! "Ill-fated land! now
wasted
By thy unnatural sons, ere long the prey
Of foeman's sword! Oh haste," you cried,
"and end
This strife! bring peace again, or soon Mes-
sina
Shall bow to other lords." Your stern decree
Prevailed; this heart, with all a mother's an-
guish
O'erlabored, owned the weight of public
cares.
I flew, and at my children's feet distracted
A suppliant lay; till to my prayers and tears
The voice of nature answered in their breasts!
   Here in the palace of their sires, unarmed,
In peaceful guise, Messina shall behold
The long inveterate foes;—this is the day!
E'en now I wait the messenger that brings
The tidings of my sons' approach: be ready
To give your princes joyful welcome home;
For dire their strife—so from this glad ac-
cord,

With thousand blessings on our happy land,
Fair Peace shall smile.

   [*The* ELDERS *retire in silence, she beckons
   to an old attendant who remains.*

                Diego!
DIEGO.   Honored Mistress!
ISAB.   Old faithful servant, thou true heart,
   come near me;
Sharer of all a mother's woes, be thine
The sweet communion of her joys:—my trea-
sure
Shrined in thy heart, my dear and holy se-
cret,
Shall pierce the envious veil, and shine trium-
phant
To cheerful day; too long by harsh decrees,
Silent and overpowered, affection yet
Shall utterance find in nature's tones of rap-
ture!
And this unprisoned heart leap to the em-
brace
Of all it holds most dear, returned to glad
My desolate halls;—
                So bend thy aged steps
To the old cloistered sanctuary that guards
The darling of my soul, whose innocence
To thy true love—(sweet pledge of happier
days!)
Trusting I gave, and asked from fortune's
storm
A resting-place and shrine: O in this hour
Of bliss, the dear reward of all thy cares.
Give to my longing arms my child again!

   [*Trumpets are heard in the distance.*

Haste! be thy footsteps winged with joy—I
hear
The trumpet's blast, that tells in warlike accents,
My sons are near :—

   [*Exit* DIEGO. *Music is heard in an opposite direction and becomes gradually
   louder.*

                Messina is awake!
Hark! how the stream of tongues hoarse mur-
muring
Rolls on the breeze,—'tis they! my mother's
heart
Feels their approach, and beats with mighty
throes
Responsive to the loud-resounding march!
They come! they come! my children! oh,
   my children!
                                [*Exit.*

12

The Chorus *enters.*

It consists of two semichoruses which enter at the same time from opposite sides, and after marching round the stage range themselves in rows, each on the side by which it entered. One semichorus consists of young knights, the other of older ones, each has its peculiar costume and ensigns. When the two choruses stand opposite each other, the march ceases, and the two leaders speak. *

First Chorus (Cajetan.)

I greet ye, glittering halls
Of olden time!
Cradle of kings! Hail! lordly roof,
In pillared majesty sublime!

Sheathed be the sword!
In chains before the portal lies
The fiend with tresses snake entwined,
Fell Discord!—Gently tread the inviolate
    floor!
      Peace to this royal dome!
Thus by the Furies' brood we swore.
And all the dark avenging Deities!

Second Chorus (Bohemund.)

I rage! I burn! and scarce refrain
To lift the glittering steel on high,
For lo! the Gorgon-visaged train
Of the detested foeman nigh:—
Shall I my swelling heart control?—
  To parley deign—or still in mortal strife
The tumult of my soul?
Dire sister, guardian of the spot, to thee
Awe-struck I bend the knee,
Nor dare with arms profane thy deep
    tranquillity!

First Chorus (Cajetan.)

Welcome the peaceful strain!
Together we adore the guardian power
Of these august abodes!
  Sacred the hour
To kindred brotherly ties
And reverend holy sympathies;—
Our hearts the genial charm shall own,
And melt awhile at friendship's soothing
    tones!—
But when in yonder plain

* The first chorus consists of Cajetan, Berengar, Manfred, Tristan and eight followers of Don Manuel. The second of Bohemund, Roger, Hippolyte and nine others of the party of Don Cæsar.

We meet—then peace away!
Come gleaming arms, and battle's deadly
    fray!

The whole Chorus.

But when in yonder plain
We meet—then peace away!
Come gleaming arms, and battle's deadly
    fray!

First Chorus (Berengar.)

I hate thee not—nor call thee foe,
My brother! this our native earth,
The land that gave our fathers birth:—
Of chief's behest the slave decreed,
The vassal draws the sword at need,
For chieftain's rage we strike the blow,
For stranger lords our kindred blood must
    flow!

Second Chorus (Bohemund.)

Hate fires their souls—we ask not why;—
At honor's call to fight and die,
Boast of the true and brave!
Unworthy of a soldier's name
Who burns not for his chieftain's fame!

The whole Chorus.

Unworthy of a soldier's name
Who burns not for his chieftain's fame!

One of the Chorus (Berengar.)

Thus spoke within my bosom's core
  The thought—as hitherward I strayed,
And pensive 'mid the waving store,
  I mused, of Autumn's yellow glade:—
These gifts of Nature's bounteous reign,—
The teeming earth, and golden grain,
Yon elms, among whose leaves entwine
The tendrils of the clustering vine;
Gay children of our sunny clime,—
Region of Spring's eternal prime!—
Each charm should woo to love and joy,
No cares the dream of bliss annoy,
And Pleasure through life's summer day
Speed every laughing Hour away.
We rage in blood,—O dire disgrace!
For this usurping, alien race;
From some far-distant land they came,
Beyond the sun's departing flame,
And owned upon our friendly shore
The welcome of our sires of yore.
Alas! their sons in thraldom pine,
The vassals of this stranger line.

13

A second (MANFRED.)

Yes! pleased, on our land, from his azure way,
The sun ever smiles with unclouded ray,
But never, fair isle, shall thy sons repose
'Mid the sweets which the faithless waves en-
    close.
On their bosom they wafted the corsair bold,
With his dreaded barks to our coast of old.
For thee was thy dower of beauty vain,
'Twas the treasure that lured the spoiler's
    train.
Oh, ne'er from these smiling vales shall rise
A sword for our vanquished liberties;
'Tis not where the laughing Ceres reigns,
And the jocund lord of the flowery plains:—
Where the iron lies hid in the mountain cave,
Is the cradle of Empire—the home of the
    brave!

[*The folding-doors at the back of the stage
are thrown open.* DONNA ISABELLA *appears between her sons,* DON MANUEL *and*
DON CÆSAR.

Both Choruses (CAJETAN.)

Lift high the notes of praise!
Behold! where like the awakening Sun,
She comes, and from her queenly brow
Shoots glad-inspiring rays.
Mistress, we bend to thee!

First Chorus.

Fair is the moon amid the starry choir
That twinkle o'er the sky,
Shining in silvery mild tranquillity;—
The mother with her sons more fair!
See! blooming at her side,
She leads the youthful royal pair;
    With gentle grace, and soft maternal
        pride,
Attempering sweet their manly fire.

Second Chorus (BERENGAR.)

From this fair stem a beauteous tree
With ever springing boughs shall smile,
And with immortal verdure shade our isle;
Mother of heroes, joy to thee!
Triumphant as the sun thy kingly race
Shall spread from clime to clime,
    And give a deathless name to rolling
        time!

ISAB. (*Comes forward with her* SONS.)
Look down! benignant Queen of Heaven,
    and still

This proud tumultuous heart, that in my
    breast
Swells with a mother's tide of ecstacy,
As blazoned in these noble youths, my image
More perfect shows;—O blissful hour! the
    first
That comprehends the fulness of my joy,
When long constrained affection dares to pour
In unison of transport from my heart
Unchecked, a parent's undivided love:
Oh! it was ever one—my sons were twain.
Say—shall I revel in the dream of bliss,
And give my soul to nature's dear emotions?
Is this warm pressure of thy brother's hand
A dagger in thy breast?   [*To* DON MANUEL.
                Or when my eyes
Feed on that brow with love's enraptured gaze,
Is it a wrong to thee? . . . [*To* DON CÆSAR.
                Trembling, I pause,
Lest e'en affection's breath should wake the
    fires
Of slumbering hate.
        [*After regarding both with inquiring looks.*
            Speak! In your secret hearts
What purpose dwells? Is it the ancient feud
Unreconciled, that in your father's halls
A moment stilled; beyond the castle gates,
Where sits infuriate War, and champs the bit
—Shall rage anew in mortal bloody conflict?

Chorus (BOHEMUND.)

Concord or strife—the Fates' decree
Is bosomed yet in dark futurity!—
What comes, we little heed to know.
Prepared for aught the hour may show

ISAB. (*Looking round.*) What mean these
    arms? this warlike dread array,
That in the palace of your sires portends
Some fearful issue? needs a mother's heart
Outpoured, this rugged witness of her joys?
Say, in these folding arms shall Treason hide
The deadly snare?—O these rude pitiless
    men,
The ministers of your wrath—trust not the
    show
Of seeming friendship; treachery in their
    breasts
Lurks to betray, and long-dissembled hate.
Ye are a race of other lands; your sires
Profaned their soil; and ne'er the invader's
    yoke
Was easy—never in the vassal's heart
Languished the hope of sweet revenge;—our
    sway
Not rooted in a people's love, but owns

14

Allegiance from their fears; with secret joy—
For conquest's ruthless sword, and thraldom's
chains
From age to age, they wait the atoning hour
Of princes' downfall; thus their bards awake
The patriot strain, and thus from sire to son
Rehearsed, the old traditionary tale
Beguiles the winter's night. False is the
world,
My sons, and light are all the specious ties
By fancy twined: Friendship—deceitful name!
Its gaudy flowers but deck our summer fortune,
To wither at the first rude breath of autumn!
So happy to whom Heaven has given a
brother;
The friend by nature signed—the true and
steadfast!
Nature alone is honest—Nature only—
When all we trusted strews the wintry shore—
On her eternal anchor lies at rest,
Nor heeds the tempest's rage.

DON M.   My mother!
DON C.   Hear me!
ISAB. (*Taking their hands.*) Be noble, and
forget the fancied wrongs
Of boyhood's age: more godlike is forgiveness
Than victory, and in your father's grave
Should sleep the ancient hate;—Oh, give your
days
Renewed henceforth in peace and holy love!
[*She recedes one or two steps, as if to give
them space to approach each other. Both
fix their eyes on the ground without re-
garding one another.*
ISAB. (*After awaiting for some time, with
suppressed emotion, a demonstration on
the part of her sons.*)
I can no more; my prayers—my tears are
vain:—
"Tis well! obey the demon in your hearts!
Fulfil your dread intent, and stain with blood
The holy altars of our household Gods;—
These halls, that gave you birth, the stage
where Murder
Shall hold his festival of mutual carnage
Beneath a mother's eye!—then, foot to foot,
Close, like the Theban pair, with maddening
gripe,
And fold each other in a last embrace!
Each press with vengeful thrust the dagger
home,
And "Victory!" be your shriek of death:—
Nor then
Shall discord rest appeased; the very flame
That lights your funeral pyre, shall tower
dissevered

In ruddy columns to the skies, and tell
With horrid image—"thus they lived and
died!"
[*She goes away: the* BROTHERS *stand as
before.*

Chorus (CAJETAN.)

How have her words with soft control
Resistless calmed the tempest of my soul!
No guilt of kindred blood be mine!
Thus with uplifted hands I pray;
Think, brothers, on the awful day,
And tremble at the wrath divine!
DON C. (*Without taking his eyes from the
ground.*) Thou art my elder—speak—
without dishonor
I yield to thee.
DON M.   One gracious word, and instant,
My tongue is rival in the strife of love!
DON C.   I am the guiltier—weaker—
DON M.   Say not so!
Who doubts thy noble heart, knows thee not
well;
Thy words were prouder, if thy soul were
mean.
DON C.   It burns indignant at the thought
of wrong;—
But thou, methinks, in passion's fiercest mood,
'Twas aught but scorn that harbored in thy
breast.
DON M.   Oh! had I known thy spirit thus
to peace
Inclined, what thousand griefs had never torn
A mother's heart!
DON C.   I find thee just and true:
Men spoke thee proud of soul.
DON M.   The curse of greatness!—
Ears ever open to the babbler's tale.
DON C.   Thou art too proud to meanness
—I to falsehood!
DON M.   We were deceived, betrayed!
DON C.   The sport of frenzy!
DON M.   And said my mother true, false
is the world?
DON C.   Believe her, false as air.
DON M.   Give me thy hand!
DON C.   And thine be ever next my heart!
[*They stand clasping each other's hands, and
regard each other in silence.*
DON M.   I gaze
Upon thy brow, and still behold my mother
In some dear lineament.
DON C.   Her image looks
From thine, and wondrous in my bosom wakes
Affection's springs.

15

Don M. And is it thou?—that smile
Benignant on thy face?—thy lips that charm
With gracious sounds of love and dear for-
giveness?
Don C. Is this my brother, this the hated
foe?
His mien all gentleness and truth—his voice—
Whose soft prevailing accents breathe of
friendship! [*After a pause.*
Don M. Shall aught divide us?
Don C. We are one for ever!
[*They rush into each other's arms.*

First Chorus, to the Second.

Why stand we thus, and coldly gaze,
While Nature's holy transports burn?
No dear embrace of happier days
The pledge — that discord never shall
return!
Brothers are they by kindred band;
We own the ties of home and native land.
[*Both* CHORUSES *embrace.*

A MESSENGER *enters.*

Second Cho. to Don C. (BOHEMUND.)
Rejoice, my Prince, thy messenger returns:—
And mark that beaming smile! the harbinger
Of happy tidings.
Mes. Health to me, and health
To this delivered state! O sight of bliss,
That lights mine eyes with rapture! I behold—
Their hands in sweet accord entwined—the
sons
Of my departed lord—the princely pair
Dissevered late by conflict's hottest rage.
Don C. Yes! from the flames of hate, a
new-born Phœnix,
Our love aspires!
Mes. I bring another joy—
My staff is green with flourishing shoots.
Don C. (*Taking him aside.*) O, tell me
Thy gladsome message.
Mes. All is happiness
On this auspicious day;—long sought, the
lost one
Is found.
Don C. Discovered! Oh, where is she?
Speak!
Mes. Within Messina's walls she lies con-
cealed.
Don M. (*Turning to the First Semichorus.*)
A ruddy glow mounts in my brother's cheek,
And pleasure dances in his sparkling eye;
Whate'er the spring, with sympathy of love
My inmost heart partakes his joy.
Don C. (*To the* MESSENGER.)

Come, lead me;
Farewell, Don Manuel—to meet again
Enfolded in a mother's arms! I fly
To cares of utmost need.
[*He is about to depart.*
Don M. Make no delay;
And happiness attend thee!
Don C. (*After a pause of reflection, he
returns.*) How thy looks
Awake my soul to transport! Yes, my brother,
We shall be friends indeed! This hour is
bright
With glad presage of ever-springing love,
That in the enlivening beam shall flourish fair,
Sweet recompense of wasted years!
Don M. The blossom
Betokens goodly fruit.
Don C. I tear myself
Reluctant from thy arms, but think not less—
If thus I break this festal hour—my heart
Thrills with a holy joy.
Don M. (*With manifest absence of mind.*)
Obey the moment!
Our lives belong to love.
Don C. What calls me hence—
Don M. Enough! thou leav'st thy heart.
Don C. No envious secret
Shall part us long; soon the last darkening
fold
Shall vanish from my breast.
[*Turning to the Chorus.*
Attend! For ever
Stilled is our strife; he is my deadliest foe,
Detested as the gates of hell who dares
To blow the fires of discord:—none may hope
To win my love, that with malicious tales
Encroach upon a brother's ear, and point,
With busy zeal of false officious friendship,
The dart of some rash angry word, escaped
From passion's heat:—it wounds not from the
lips,
But swallowed by suspicion's greedy ear,
Like a rank poisonous weed, embittered creeps,
And hangs about the heart with thousand
shoots,
Perplexing Nature's ties.
[*He embraces his brother again and goes
away, accompanied by the Second Chorus.*
Cho. (CAJETAN.) Wondering, my Prince,
I gaze, for in thy looks some mystery
Strange-seeming shows: scarce with abstracted
mien
And cold thou answered'st, when with earnest
heart
Thy brother poured the strain of dear affec-
tion.

As in a dream thou stand'st, and lost in
    thought,
As tho'—dissevered from its earthly frame—
Thy spirit roved afar. Not thine the breast
That deaf to Nature's voice, ne'er owned the
    throbs
Of kindred love :—nay more—like one en-
    tranced
In bliss, thou look'st around, and smiles of
    rapture
Play on thy cheek.
    Don M.   How shall my lips declare
The transports of my swelling heart ! My
    brother
Revels in glad surprise, and from his breast
Instinct with strange newfelt emotions, pours
The tide of joy; but mine—no hate came
    with me,

Forgot the very spring of mutual strife !
High o'er this earthly sphere, on rapture's
    wings,
My spirit floats; and in the azure sea,
Above—beneath—no track of envious night
Disturbs the deep serene ! I view these halls,
And picture to my thoughts the timid joy
Of my sweet bride, as thro' the palace gates,
In pride of queenly state, I lead her home,
She loved alone the loving one, the stranger,
And little deems that on her beauteous brow
Messina's prince shall twine the nuptial wreath.
How sweet, with unexpected pomp of great-
    ness,
To glad the darling of my soul !—too long
I brook this dull delay of crowning bliss !
Her beauty's self, that asks no borrow'd
    charm,

Shall shine refulgent, like the diamond's blaze
That wins new lustre from the circling gold!
   Cho. (CAJETAN.) Long have I marked
   thee, Prince, with curious eye,
Foreboding of some mystery deep enshrined
Within thy laboring breast. This day, impatient,
Thy lips have burst the seal; and unconstrained
Confess a lover's joy;—the gladdening chase,
The Olympian courses, and the falcon's flight,
Can charm no more:—soon as the sun declines
Beneath the ruddy west, thou hiest thee quick
To some sequestered path, of mortal eye
Unseen—not one of all our faithful train
Companion of thy solitary way.
Say, why so long concealed the blissful flame?
Stranger to fear—ill brooked thy princely heart
One thought unuttered.
   DON M.   Ever on the wing
Is mortal joy;—with silence best we guard
The fickle good?—but now, so near the goal
Of all my cherished hopes, I dare to speak.
To-morrow's sun shall see her mine! no power
Of Hell can make us twain! With timid stealth
No longer will I creep at dusky eve,
To taste the golden fruits of Cupid's tree,
And snatch a fearful, fleeting bliss: to-day
With bright to-morrow shall be one! So smooth
As runs the limpid brook, or silvery sand
That marks the flight of time, our lives shall flow
In continuity of joy!
   Cho. (CAJETAN.)   Already
Our hearts, my Prince, with silent vows have blessed
Thy happy love; and now from every tongue,
For her—the royal beauteous bride—should sound
The glad acclaim; so tell what nook unseen,
What deep umbrageous solitude, enshrines
The charmer of thy heart? With magic spells
Almost I deem she mocks our gaze, for oft
In eager chase we scour each rustic path
And forest dell; yet not a trace betrayed
The lover's haunts, ne'er were the footsteps marked
Of this mysterious fair.
   DON M.   The spell is broke!
And all shall be revealed: now list my tale:—
'Tis five months flown,—my father yet controlled

The land, and bowed our necks with iron sway;
Little I knew, but the wild joys of arms,
And mimic warfare of the chase;——
                One day,—
Long had we tracked the boar with zealous toil
On yonder woody ridge:—it chanced, pursuing
A snow-white hind, far from your train I roved
Amidst the forest maze;—the timid beast,
Along the windings of the narrow vale,
Thro' rocky cleft and thick-entangled brake,
Flew onward, scarce a moment lost, nor distant
Beyond a javelin's throw; nearer I came not
Nor took an aim; when thro' a garden's gate,
Sudden she vanished:—from my horse quick springing,
I followed:—lo! the poor scared creature lay
Stretched at the feet of a young beauteous nun,
That strove with fond caress of her fair hands
To still its throbbing heart: wondering, I gazed,
And motionless—my spear, in act to strike,
High poised—while she, with her large piteous eyes
For mercy sued—and thus we stood in silence,
Regarding one another.
             How long the pause
I know not—time itself forgot;—it seemed
Eternity of bliss: her glance of sweetness
Flew to my soul; and quick the subtle flame
Pervaded all my heart:——
              But what I spoke,
And how this blessed creature answered, none
May ask; it floats upon my thought, a dream
Of childhood's happy dawn! Soon as my sense
Returned, I felt her bosom throb responsive
To mine,—then fell melodious on my ear
The sound, as of a convent bell, that called
To vesper Song; and like some shadowy vision
That melts in air—she flitted from my sight—
And was beheld no more.
   Chorus (CAJETAN.)   Thy story thrills
My breast with pious awe! Prince, thou hast robbed
The sanctuary, and for the bride of Heaven
Burned with unholy passion! Oh, remember
The cloister's sacred vows!
   DON M.   Thenceforth one path
My footsteps wooed; the fickle train was still
Of young desires—new felt my being's aim,
My soul revealed!—and as the pilgrim turns
His wistful gaze, where, from the orient sky,
With gracious lustre beams Redemption's star;—

ARTIST: JULIUS LENGZER

THE BRIDE OF MESSINA.

DON MANUEL AND BEATRICE

So to that brightest point of Heaven, her
    presence,
My hopes and longings centered all. No sun
Sank in the western waves, but smiled farewell
To two united lovers:—thus in stillness
Our hearts were twined,—the all-seeing air
    above us
Alone the faithful witness of our joys!
O golden hours! O happy days! nor Heaven
Indignant viewed our bliss;—no vows en-
    chained
Her spotless soul; nought but the link which
    bound it
Eternally to mine!
    Cho. (CAJETAN.)   Those hallowed walls,
Perchance the calm retreat of tender youth,
No living grave?
    DON M.   In infant innocence
Consigned a holy pledge, ne'er has she left
Her cloistered home.
    Cho. (CAJETAN.) But what her royal line?
The noble only spring from noble stem.
    DON M. A secret to herself,—she ne'er
        has learned
Her name or Fatherland.
    Cho. (CAJETAN.)   And not a trace
Guides to her being's undiscovered springs?
    DON M. An old domestic, the sole mes-
        senger
Sent by her unknown mother, oft bespeaks her
Of kingly race.
    Cho. (CAJETAN.)   And hast thou won
        nought else
From garrulous age?
    DON M.   Too much I feared to peril
My secret bliss!
    Cho. (CAJETAN.)   What were his words?
        What tidings
He bore—perchance thou know'st.
    DON M.   Oft he has cheered her
With promise of a happier time, when all
Shall be revealed.
    Cho. (CAJETAN.)   O say—betokens aught
The time is near?
    DON M.   Not distant far the day
That to the arms of kindred love once more
Shall give the long-forsaken, orphaned maid—
Thus with mysterious words the aged man
Has shadowed oft what most I dread—for aught
Of change disturbs the soul supremely blest:
Nay, more; but yesterday his message spoke
The end of all my joys:—this very dawn,
He told, should smile auspicious on her fate,
And light to other scenes:—no precious hour
Delayed my quick resolves—by night I bore her
In secret to Messina.

    Cho. (CAJETAN.) Rash the deed
Of sacrilegious spoil! forgive, my Prince,
The bold rebuke; thus to unthinking youth
Old age may speak in friendship's warning
    voice.
    DON M. Hard by the convent of the Car-
        melites,
In a sequestered garden's tranquil bound,
And safe from curious eyes, I left her,—
    hastening
To meet my brother: trembling there she
    counts
The slow-paced hours, nor deems how soon
    triumphant
In queenly state, high on the throne of Fame
Messina shall behold my timid bride.
For next, encompassed by your knightly train,
With pomp of greatness in the festal show,
Her lover's form shall meet her wondering
    gaze!
Thus will I lead her to my mother; thus—
While countless thousands on her passage wait
Amid the loud acclaim—the royal bride
Shall reach my palace gates!
    Cho. (CAJETAN.)   Command us, Prince,
We live but to obey!
    DON. M.   I tore myself
Reluctant from her arms; my every thought
Shall still be hers: so come along, my friends,
To where the turbaned merchant spreads his
    store
Of fabrics gold enwrought with curious art;
And all the gathered wealth of eastern climes.
First choose the well-formed sandals—mete
    to guard
And grace her delicate feet; then for her
    robe—
The tissue, pure as Etna's snow that lies
Nearest the sun—light as the wreathy mist
At summer dawn—So playful let it float
About her airy limbs. A girdle next,
Purple with gold embroidered o'er, to bind
With witching grace the tunic that confines
Her bosom's swelling charms: of silk the
    mantle,
Gorgeous with like empurpled hues, and fixed
With clasp of gold:— remember, too, the
    bracelets
To gird her beauteous arms; nor leave the
    treasure
Of Ocean's pearly deeps and coral caves.
About her locks entwine a diadem
Of purest gems—the ruby's fiery glow
Commingling with the emerald's green. A
    veil,
From her tiara pendent to her feet

 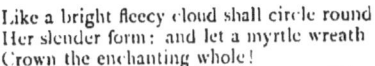

Like a bright fleecy cloud shall circle round
Her slender form: and let a myrtle wreath
Crown the enchanting whole!
   Cho. (CAJETAN.)   We haste, my Prince,
Amid the Bazar's glittering rows, to cull
Each rich adornment.
   DON M.   From my stables lead
A palfrey, milkwhite as the steeds that draw
The chariot of the Sun; purple the housings,
The bridle sparkling o'er with precious gems,
For it shall bear my Queen! Yourselves be
   ready
With trumpet's cheerful clang, in martial
   train
To lead your mistress home: let two attend
   me,
The rest await my quick return; and each
Guard well my secret purpose.

[*He goes away accompanied by two of the
Chorus.*

Chorus (CAJETAN.)

The princely strife is o'er, and say,
   What sport shall wing the slow-paced
   hours,
And cheat the tedious day?
   With hope and fear's enlivening zest
Disturb the slumber of the breast,
And wake life's dull untroubled sea
With freshening airs of gay variety.

One of the Chorus (MANFRED.)

Lovely is peace! A beauteous boy,
Couched listless by the rivulet's glassy tide,
   'Mid Nature's tranquil scene,
He views the lambs that skip with innocent joy,
   And crop the meadow's flowering pride:—
Then with his flute's enchanting sound,
He wakes the mountain echoes round,
   Or slumbers in the sunset's ruddy sheen,
   Lulled by the murmuring melody.
But War for me! my spirit's treasure,
Its stern delight, and wilder pleasure:
I love the peril and the pain,
And revel in the surge of Fortune's boisterous
   main!

A Second (BERENGAR.)

Is there not Love, and beauty's smile
That lures with soft resistless wile?
'Tis thrilling hope! 'tis rapturous fear
'Tis Heaven upon this mortal sphere;
When at her feet we bend the knee,
And own the glance of kindred ecstasy!

For ever on life's chequered way,
   'Tis Love that tints the darkening hues of
   care
With soft benignant ray:
The mirthful daughter of the wave,
   Celestial Venus ever fair,
Enchants our happy spring with Fancy's gleam,
And wakes the airy forms of Passion's golden
   dream.

First (MANFRED.)

To the wild woods away!
Quick let us follow in the train
   Of Her, chaste Huntress of the silver bow;
And from the rocks amain
   Track through the forest gloom the bound-
   ing roe,
   The war God's merry bride,
   The chase recalls the battle's fray,
     And kindles victory's pride:—
Up with the streaks of early morn,
   We scour with jocund hearts the misty vale,
Loud-echoing to the cheerful horn—
Over mountain—over dale—
And every languid sense repair,
Bathed in the rushing streams of cold reviving
   air.

A second (BERENGAR.)

Or shall we trust the ever-moving sea,
   The azure Goddess, blithe and free,
Whose face, the mirror of the cloudless sky,
   Lures to her bosom wooingly?
Quick let us build on the dancing waves
   A floating castle gay,
And merrily, merrily, swim away!
Who ploughs, with venturous keel, the brine
   Of the ocean crystaline—
   His bride is Fortune, the world his own,
For him a harvest blooms unsown:—
Here, like the wind that swift careers
   The circling bound of earth and sky,
   Flits ever-changeful Destiny!
Of airy Chance 'tis the sportive reign,
   And Hope ever broods on the boundless
   main!

A third (CAJETAN.)

Nor on the watery waste alone
   Of the tumultuous heaving sea;—
On the firm earth that sleeps secure,
   Based on the pillars of eternity.
Say, when shall mortal joy endure?
   New bodings in my anxious breast,
Waked by this sudden friendship, rise;
   Ne'er would I choose my home of rest
     On the stilled lava stream, that cold

Beneath the mountain lies:—
Not thus was Discord's flame controlled—
Too deep the rooted hate—too long
They brooded in their sullen hearts
O'er unforgotten treasured wrong.
In warning visions oft dismayed,
I read the signs of coming woe;
And now, from this mysterious maid,
My bosom tells the dreaded ills shall flow;—
Unblest, I deem, the bridal chain
Shall knit their secret loves, accurst
With holy cloisters' spoil profane.
No crooked paths to virtue lead;
Ill fruit has ever sprung from evil seed!

(BERENGAR.)

And thus to sad unhallowed rites
Of an ill-omened nuptial tie,
Too well ye know their father bore
A bride of mournful destiny,
Torn from his sire, whose awful curse has sped
Heaven's vengeance on the impious bed!
This fierce unnatural rage atones
A parent's crime—decreed by Fate,
Their mother's offspring, Strife and Hate!

The scene changes to a garden opening on the sea.

BEAT. (*Steps forward from an alcove. She
walks to and fro with an agitated air,
looking round in every direction. Suddenly
she stands still and listens.*)
No! 'tis not he: 'twas but the playful wind
Rustling the pine tops. To his ocean bed
The sun declines, and with o'erwearied heart
I count the lagging hours: an icy chill
Creeps through my frame; the very solitude
And awful silence fright my trembling soul!
Where'er I turn, nought meets my gaze—he
    leaves me
Forsaken and alone!——
And like a rushing stream the city's hum
Floats on the breeze, and dull the mighty sea
Rolls murmuring to the rocks: I shrink to
    nothing,
With horrors compassed round: and like the
    leaf,
Borne on the autumn blast, am hurried onward
Thro' boundless space.——
            Alas! that e'er I left
My peaceful cell—no cares, no fond desires
Disturbed my breast, unruffled as the stream
That glides in sunshine through the verdant
    mead;—
Nor poor in joys. Now—on the mighty surge

Of Fortune, tempest-tossed—the world enfolds
    me
With giant arms! Forgot my childhood's
    ties,
I listened to the Lover's flattering tale—
Listened, and trusted! From the sacred dome
Allured—betrayed—for sure some hell-born
    magic
Enchained my frenzied sense—I fled with him,
The invader of Religion's dread abodes!
Where art thou, my beloved? Haste—return—
With thy dear presence calm my struggling
    soul!   [*She listens.*
Hark! the sweet voice! No! 'twas the echoing
    surge
That beats upon the shore;—alas! he comes
    not.
More faintly, o'er the distant waves, the sun
Gleams with expiring ray; a deathlike shudder
Creeps to my heart, and sadder, drearier grows
E'en desolation's self.
    [*She walks to and fro, then listens again.*
            Yes! from the thicket shade
A voice resounds!—'tis he!—the loved one!
No fond illusion mocks my listening ear:
'Tis louder—nearer: to his arms I fly—
To his breast!
    [*She rushes with outstretched arms to the
    extremity of the garden.* DON CÆSAR
    meets her.

DON CÆSAR. BEATRICE.

BEAT. (*Starting back in horror.*)
What do I see!
    [*At the same moment the Chorus comes for-
    ward.*
DON C.   Angelic sweetness! fear not.
            [*To the Chorus.*
Retire! your gleaming arms and rude array
Affright the timorous maid.   [*To* BEATRICE.
            Fear nothing!—beauty
And virgin shame are sacred in my eyes.
    [*The Chorus steps aside. He approaches
    and takes her hand.*
Where hast thou been? for sure some envious
    power
Has hid thee from my gaze: long have I sought
    thee!
E'en from the hour when, 'mid the funeral rites
Of the dead Prince, like some angelic vision
Lit with celestial brightness, on my sight
Thou shon'st, no other image in my breast,
Waking or dreaming, lives;—nor to thyself
Unknown thy potent spells; my glance of fire,
My faltering accents, and my hand that lay
Trembling in thine, bespoke my ecstasy!

Aught else with solemn majesty the rite
And holy place forbade :——
⠀⠀⠀⠀⠀⠀⠀The bell proclaimed
The awful Sacrifice! With downcast eyes,
And kneeling, I adored :—soon as I rose,
And caught with eager gaze thy form again,
Sudden it vanished ; yet, with mighty magic
Of love enchained, my spirit tracked thy
⠀⠀⠀presence ;
Nor ever, with unwearied quest, I cease,
At palace gates, amid the temple's throng,
In secret paths retired, or public scenes,
Where beauteous innocence perchance might
⠀⠀⠀rove,
To mark each passing form—in vain : but,
⠀⠀⠀guided
By some propitious deity, this day
One of my train, with happy vigilance,
Espied thee in the neighboring church.

⠀⠀⠀[BEATRICE, *who has stood trembling, with
⠀⠀⠀averted eyes, here makes a gesture of terror.*
⠀⠀⠀⠀⠀⠀⠀⠀⠀⠀⠀I see thee
Once more ; and may the spirit from this
⠀⠀⠀frame
Be severed e'er we part ! Now let me snatch
This glad auspicious moment, and defy
Or chance, or envious demon's power, to shake
Henceforth my solid bliss ; here I proclaim
⠀⠀⠀thee,
Before this listening warlike train, my bride,
With pledge of knightly honors !

⠀⠀⠀⠀⠀⠀⠀⠀[*He shows her to the Chorus.*
⠀⠀⠀⠀⠀⠀⠀⠀⠀⠀⠀Who thou art,
I ask not : thou art mine ! But that thy soul
And birth are pure alike, one glance informed
My inmost heart ; and though thy lot were
⠀⠀⠀mean,
And poor thy lowly state, yet would I strain
⠀⠀⠀thee
With rapture to my arms :—no choice remains,
Thou art my love—my wife ! Know, too,
⠀⠀⠀that lifted
On fortune's height, I spurn control ; my will
Can raise thee to the pinnacle of greatness !—
Enough my name—I am Don Cæsar ! None
Is nobler in Messina !

⠀⠀⠀[BEATRICE *starts back in amazement. He
⠀⠀⠀remarks her agitation, and after a pause
⠀⠀⠀continues.*
⠀⠀⠀⠀⠀⠀⠀⠀⠀⠀⠀What a grace
Lives in thy soft surprise and modest silence !
Yes ! gentle humbleness is beauty's crown—
The Beautiful for ever hid, and shrinking
From its own lustre : but thy spirit needs

Repose, for aught of strange—e'en sudden
⠀⠀⠀joy—
Is terror-fraught. I leave thee—
⠀⠀⠀⠀⠀⠀⠀⠀[*Turning to the Chorus.*
⠀⠀⠀⠀⠀⠀⠀⠀⠀⠀⠀From this hour
She is your mistress, and my bride ; so teach
⠀⠀⠀her,
With honors due, to entertain the pomp
Of queenly state. I will return with speed,
And lead her home as fits Messina's Princess.
⠀⠀⠀⠀⠀⠀⠀⠀⠀⠀⠀[*He goes away.*

⠀⠀⠀⠀⠀BEATRICE *and the Chorus.*

⠀⠀⠀⠀⠀Chorus (BOHEMUND.)
Fair maiden—hail to thee,
⠀⠀⠀Thou lovely Queen !
Thine is the crown, and thine the victory !
Of heroes, to a distant age,
The blooming mother thou shalt shine,
Preserver of this kingly line.

⠀⠀⠀⠀⠀⠀⠀(ROGER.)
And thrice I bid thee hail,
⠀⠀⠀Thou happy fair !
Sent in auspicious hour to bless
This favored race—the gods' peculiar care.
Here twine the immortal wreaths of Fame,
And evermore, from sire to son,
Rolls on the sceptered sway,
To heirs of old renown, a race of deathless
⠀⠀⠀name !

⠀⠀⠀⠀⠀⠀(BOHEMUND.)
The household Gods exultingly
⠀⠀⠀Thy coming wait ;
The ancient, honored Sires,
That on the portals frown sedate,
⠀⠀⠀Shall smile for thee !
There blooming Hebe shall thy steps attend,
And golden Victory, that sits
By Jove's eternal throne, with waving
⠀⠀⠀plumes,
For conquest ever spread,
To welcome thee from heaven descend.

⠀⠀⠀⠀⠀⠀⠀(ROGER.)
Ne'er from this queenly bright array
⠀⠀⠀The crown of beauty fades,—
Departing to the realms of day,
Each to the next, as good and fair,
Extends the zone of feminine grace,
⠀⠀⠀And veil of purity :—
⠀⠀⠀⠀⠀O happy race !

ARTIST: JULIUS BENCZUR.

THE BRIDE OF MESSINA.

DON CESAR AND BEATRICE.

What vision glads my raptured eye!
Equal in Nature's blooming pride,
I see the mother and the virgin bride.

BEATRICE. (*Awaking from her reverie.*)

O luckless hour!
Alas! ill-fated maid!
Where shall I fly
From these rude warlike men?
Lost and betrayed!
A shudder o'er me came,
When of this race accurst—the brothers twain
—Their hands imbrued with kindred gore,
I heard the dreaded name;
Oft told, their strife and serpent hate
With terror thrilled my bosom's core:—
And now—oh, hapless fate!—
I tremble, 'mid the rage of discord thrown,
Deserted and alone!
[*She runs into the alcove.*

Chorus (BOHEMUND.)

Son of the immortal Deities,
And blest is he, the Lord of power;
His every joy the world can give;
Of all that mortals prize
He culls the flower.

(ROGER.)

For him from Ocean's azure caves
The diver bears each pearl of purest ray,
Whate'er from Nature's boundless field,
Or toil or art has won,
Obsequious at his feet we lay;
His choice is ever free;
We bow to chance, and Fortune's blind decree.

(BOHEMUND.)

But this of Princes' lot I deem,
The crowning treasure, joy supreme—
Of love the triumph and the prize,
The beauty, star of neighboring eyes!
She blooms for him alone,
He calls the fairest maid his own.

(ROGER.)

Armed for the deadly fray,
The corsair bounds upon the strand,
And drags, amid the gloom of night, away,
The shrieking captive train,
Of wild desires the hapless prey:
But ne'er his lawless hands profane
The gem—the peerless flower—
Whose charms shall deck the Sultan's bower.

(Bohemund)

Now haste and watch, with curious eye,
    These hallowed precincts round,
That no presumptuous foot come nigh
    The secret solitary ground:
Guard well the maiden fair,
Your chieftain's brightest jewel owns your
    care.
    [*The Chorus withdraws to the background.*

*The scene changes to a chamber in the interior
    of the palace.*

Donna Isabella *between* Don Manuel *and*
    Don Cæsar.

Isab. The long-expected festal day is come,
My children's hearts are twined in one, as thus
I fold their hands. Oh, blissful hour! when
    first
A mother dares to speak in nature's voice,
And no rude presence checks the tide of love.
The clang of arms affrights mine ear no more :
—And as the owls, ill-omened brood of night,
From some old shattered homestead's ruined
    walls,
Their ancient reign, fly forth a dusky swarm,
Darkening the cheerful day;—when absent
    long,
The dwellers home return with joyous shouts,
To build the pile anew;—so Hate departs
With all his grisly train—pale Envy, scowling
    Malice,
And hollow-eyed Suspicion—from our gates,
Hoarse murmuring, to the realms of night;
    while Peace,
By Concord and fair Friendship led along,
Comes smiling in his place.   [*She pauses.*
                    But not alone
This day of joy to each restores a brother;
It brings a sister! Wonderstruck you gaze!
Yet now the truth, in silence guarded long,
Bursts from my soul—attend! I have a daugh-
    ter!
A sister lives, ordained by Heaven to bind ye
With ties unknown before.
    Don. C.   We have a sister!
What hast thou said, my mother?—never told
Her being till this hour!
    Don M.   In childhood's years,
Oft of a sister we have heard, untimely
Snatched in her cradle by remorseless death ;
So ran the tale.
    Isab.   She lives!
    Don C.   And thou wert silent !

Isab. Hear how the seed was sown in early
    time,
That now shall ripen to a joyful harvest.
Ye bloomed in boyhood's tender age—e'en
    then—
By mutual deadly hate, the bitter spring
Of grief to this torn anxious heart—dissevered;
Oh, may your strife return no more! A vision,
Strange and mysterious, in your father's breast
Woke dire presage: it seemed that from his
    couch,
With branches intertwined, two laurels grew,
And in the midst a lily all in flames,
That catching swift the boughs and knotted
    stems,
Burst forth with crackling rage, and o'er the
    house
Spread in one mighty sea of fire: perplexed
By this terrific dream, my husband sought
An Arab, skilled to read the stars, and long
The trusted oracle, whose counsels swayed
His inmost purpose: thus the boding sage
Spoke Fate's decrees;—If I a daughter bore,
Destruction to his sons and all his race
From her should spring. Soon, by Heaven's
    will, this child
Of dreadful omen saw the light—your sire
Commanded instant in the waves to throw
The new-born innocent; a mother's love
Prevailed, and, aided by a faithful servant,
I snatched the babe from death.
    Don C.   Blest be the hands
The ministers of thy care! Oh, ever rich
Of counsels was a parent's love!
    Isab.   But more
Than Nature's mighty voice—a warning dream
Impelled to save my child: while yet unborn
She slumbered in my womb, sleeping, I saw
An infant, fair as of celestial kind,
That played upon the grass; soon from the
    wood
A lion rushed, and from his gory jaws,
Caressing, in the infant's lap let fall
His prey, new-caught; then thro' the air down
    swept
An eagle, and with fond caress alike
Dropt from his claws a trembling kid; and
    both
Cowered at the infant's feet, a gentle pair.
A Monk, the saintly guide whose counsels
    poured,
In every earthly need, the balm of Heaven
Upon my troubled soul, my dream resolved:—
Thus spoke the man of God:—a daughter,
    sent
To knit the warring spirits of my sons

In bonds of tender love, should recompense
A mother's pains!   Deep in my heart I
    treasured
His words, and, reckless of the Pagan Seer,
Preserved the blessed child — ordained of
    Heaven
To still your growing strife; sweet pledge of
    hope
And messenger of peace!

DON M. *(Embracing his brother.)*
                There needs no sister
To join our hearts—she shall but bind them
    closer.

ISAB.   In a lone spot obscure, by stranger
    hands
Nurtured, the secret flower has grown—to me
Denied the joy to mark each infant charm
And opening grace from that sad hour of
    parting;—
These arms ne'er clasp'd my child again!—
    her sire,
To jealousy's corroding fears a prey,
And brooding dark suspicion, restless tracked
Each day my steps.

DON C.   Yet three months flown, my father
Sleeps in the tranquil grave; say, whence de-
    layed
The joyous tidings?—Why so long concealed
The maid, nor earlier taught our hearts to glow
With brother's love?

ISAB.   The cause—your frenzied hate,
That raging unconfined, e'en on the tomb
Of your scarce buried father, lit the flames
Of mortal strife.   What! could I throw my
    daughter
Betwixt your gleaming blades?   Or mid the
    storm
Of passion would ye list a woman's counsels?
Could she, sweet pledge of peace, of all our
    hopes
The last and holy anchor, 'mid the rage
Of discord find a home?   Ye stand as brothers,
So will I give a sister to your arms!
The reconciling angel comes—each hour
I wait my messenger's return; he leads her
From her sequestered cell, to glad once more
A mother's eyes.

DON M.   .Nor her alone this day
Thy arms shall fold:—joy pours thro' all our
    gates;
Soon shall the desolate halls be full, the seat
Of every blooming Grace.—Now hear my
    secret:
A sister thou hast given, to thee I bring
A daughter—bless thy son!   My heart has
    found

Its lasting shrine; ere this day's sun has set,
Don Manuel to thy feet shall lead his bride,
The partner of his days.

ISAB.   And to my breast
With transport will I clasp the chosen maid,
That makes my first-born happy!   Joy shall
    spring
Where'er she treads, and every flower that
    blooms
Around the path of life smile in her presence!
May bliss reward the son, that for my brows
Has twined the choicest wreath a mother wears.

DON C.   Yet give not all the fulness of thy
    blessing
To him, thy eldest born.   If love be blest,
I, too, can give thee joy—I bring a daughter—
Another flower for thy most treasured garland!
The maid that in this ice-cold bosom first
Awoke the rapturous flame!   Ere yonder sun
Declines—Don Cæsar's bride shall call thee
    mother!

DON M.   Almighty Love! — thou godlike
    power—for well
We call thee sovereign of the breast!   Thy
    sway
Controls each warring element, and tunes
To soft accord; nought lives but owns thy
    greatness!
Lo! the rude soul that long defied thee, melts
At thy command!   [*He embraces* DON CÆSAR.
                Now I can trust thy heart,
And joyful strain thee to a brother's arms!
I doubt thy faith no more, for thou canst love!

ISAB.   Thrice blest the day, when every
    gloomy care
From my o'erlabored breast has flown.   I see
On steadfast columns reared our kingly race,
And with contented spirit track the stream
Of measureless time.   In these deserted halls,
Sad in my widow's veil, but yesterday
Childless I roamed—and soon, in youthful
    charms
Arrayed, three blooming daughters at my side
Shall stand!   O happiest mother!   Chief of
    women,
In bliss supreme; can aught of earthly joy
O'erbalance thine?
                But say, of royal stem,
What maidens grace our isle?   For ne'er my
    sons
Would stoop to meaner brides.

DON M.   Seek not to raise
The veil that hides my bliss; another day
Shall tell thee all.   Enough — Don Manuel's
    bride
Is worthy of thy son and thee.

ISAB. Thy sire
Speaks in thy words; thus to himself retired
For ever would he brood o'er counsels dark,
And cloak his secret purpose;—your delay
Be short, my son   [*Turning to* DON CÆSAR.
            But thou—some royal maid,
Daughter of kings, has stirred thy soul to love;
So speak—her name—
    DON C.   I have no art to veil
My thoughts with mystery's garb—my spirit
    free
And open as my brows; what thou wouldst
    know
Concerned me never. Say—what lights above
Heaven's flaming orb? Himself!—on all the
    world
He shines, and with his beaming glory tells
From light he sprung;—in her pure eyes I
    gazed,
I looked into her heart of hearts:—the bright-
    ness
Revealed the pearl. Her race—her name—
    my mother,
Ask not of me!
    ISAB.   My son, explain thy words,
For, like some voice divine, the sudden charm
Has thralled thy soul: to deeds of rash em-
    prize
Thy nature prompted, not to fantasies
Of boyish love:—tell me, what swayed thy
    choice?
    DON C. My choice? my mother! Is it
    choice when man
Obeys the might of Destiny, that brings
The awful hour?   I sought no beauteous
    bride,
No fond delusion stirred my tranquil breast,
Still as the house of death; for there, unsought,
I found the treasure of my soul. Thou know'st
That, heedless ever of the giddy race,
I looked on beauty's charms with cold disdain,
Nor deemed of womankind there lived another
Like thee—whom my idolatrous fancy decked
With heavenly graces:—
            'Twas the solemn rite
Of my dead father's obsequies; we stood
Amid the countless throng, with strange attire
Hid from each other's glance; for thus or-
    dained
Thy thoughtful care, lest with outbursting rage,
E'en by the holy place unawed, our strife
Should mar the funeral pomp.
                With sable gauze
The nave was all o'erhung; the altar round
Stood twenty giant Saints, uplifting each
A torch; and in the midst reposed on high

The coffin, with o'erspreading pall, that
    showed,
In white, Redemption's sign;—thereon were
    laid
The staff of sovereignty, the princely crown,
The golden spurs of knighthood, and the
    sword,
With diamond-studded belt:—
            And all was hushed
In silent prayer, when from the lofty choir,
Unseen, the pealing organ spoke, and loud
From hundred voices burst the choral strain!
Then, 'mid the tide of song, the coffin sank
With the descending floor beneath, for ever
Down to the world below:—but, wide out-
    spread
Above the yawning grave, the pall upheld
The gauds of earthly state, nor with the
    corse
To darkness fell; yet on the seraph wings
Of Harmony, the enfranchised spirit soared
To Heaven and mercy's throne:
                Thus to thy thought,
My mother, I have waked the scene anew,
And say, if aught of passion in my breast
Profaned the solemn hour; yet then the beams
Of mighty Love—so willed my guiding star—
First lit my soul; but how it chanced, myself
I ask in vain.
    ISAB.   I would hear all; so end
Thy tale.
    DON C. What brought her to my side, or
    whence
She came, I know not:—from her presence
    quick
Some secret all-pervading inward charm
Awoke; 'twas not the magic of a smile,
Nor playful Cupid in her cheeks, nor more,
The form of peerless grace;—'twas Beauty's
    soul,
The speaking virtue, modesty inborn,
That as with magic spells, impalpable
To sense, my being thralled. We breathed
    together
The air of Heaven:—enough!—no utterance
    asked
Of words, our spiritual converse;—in my
    heart,
Tho' strange, yet with familiar ties inwrought
She seemed, and instant spake the thought—
    'tis she!
Or none that lives!
    DON M. (*Interposing with eagerness.*)
            That is the sacred fire
From Heaven! The spark of love—that on
    the soul

Bursts like the lightning's flash and mounts
in flame,
When kindred bosoms meet! No choice re-
mains—
Who shall resist? What mortal break the
band
That Heaven has knit?—Brother, my blissful
fortune
Was echoed in thy tale—well thou hast raised
The veil that shadows yet my secret love.

ISAB. Thus destiny has marked the way-
ward course
Of my two sons: the mighty torrent sweeps
Down from the precipice; with rage he wears
His proper bed, nor heeds the channel traced
By art and prudent care. So to the powers,
That darkly sway the fortunes of our house,
Trembling I yield. One pledge of hope re-
mains;
Great as their birth—their noble souls.

ISABELLA, DON MANUEL, DON CÆSAR.
DIEGO *is seen at the door.*

ISAB. But see,
My faithful messenger returns. Come near
me,
Honest Diego. Quick! Where is she? Tell
me,
Where is my child? There is no secret here.
Oh, speak! No longer from my eyes conceal
her:
Come! we are ready for the height of joy.
[*She is about to lead him towards the door.*
What means this pause? Thou lingerest—
thou art dumb—
Thy looks are terror-fraught—a shudder creeps
Through all my frame—declare thy tidings!—
speak!
Where is she? Where is Beatrice?
[*She is about to rush from the chamber.*
DON M. (*To himself abstractedly.*)
Beatrice!
DIEGO. (*Holding back the* PRINCESS.)
Be still!
ISAB. Where is she? Anguish tears my
breast!
DIEGO. She comes not;
I bring no daughter to thy arms.
ISAB. Declare
Thy message! Speak! by all the Saints!
What has befallen?
DON M. Where is my sister? Tell us,
Thou harbinger of ill!
DIEGO. The maid is stolen

By corsairs! lost! Oh! that I ne'er had seen
This day of woe!
DON M. Compose thyself, my mother!
DON C. Be calm; list all his tale.
DIEGO. At thy command
I sought in haste the well-known path that
leads
To the old Sanctuary: — Joy winged my
footsteps;
The journey was my last!
DON C. Be brief!
DON M. Proceed!
DIEGO. Soon as I trode the convent's
court—impatient—
I ask — "Where is thy daughter?" Terror
sate
In every eye; and straight, with horror mute,
I hear the worst.
[ISABELLA *sinks, pale and trembling, upon a
chair;* DON MANUEL *is busied about her.*
DON C. Say'st thou by pirates stolen?
Who saw the band?—what tongue relates the
spoil?
DIEGO. Not far a Moorish galley was des-
cribed,
At anchor in the bay—
DON C. The refuge oft
From tempests rage; where is the bark?
DIEGO. At dawn,
With favoring breeze she stood to sea.
DON C. But never
One prey contents the Moor; say, have they
told
Of other spoil?
DIEGO. A herd that pastured near
Was dragged away.
DON C. Yet from the convent's bound
How tear the maid unseen?
DIEGO. 'Tis thought, with ladders,
They scaled the wall.
DON C. Thou know'st what jealous care
Enshrines the bride of Heaven; scarce could
their steps
Invade the secret cells.
DIEGO. Bound by no vows,
The maiden roved at will; oft would she seek,
Alone, the garden's shade. Alas! this day,
Ne'er to return!
DON C. Said'st thou—the prize of cor-
sairs?—
Perchance, at other bidding, she forsook
The sheltering dome—
ISAB. (*Rising suddenly.*)
'Twas force! 'twas savage spoil!
Ne'er has my child, reckless of honor's ties,
With vile seducer fled! My sons! Awake!

27

I thought to give a sister to your arms;
I ask a daughter from your swords! Arise!
Avenge this wrong! To arms! Launch every
  ship!
Scour all our coasts! From sea to sea pursue
  them!
O bring my daughter—haste!
Don C.   Farewell—I fly
To vengeance!   [*He goes away.*
  [Don Manuel *arouses himself from a state
  of abstraction, and turns, with an air of
  agitation, to* Diego.
Don M.   Speak! within the convent's
  walls
When first unseen—
Diego.   This day at dawn.
Don M. (*To* Isabella.)   Her name
Thou say'st, is Beatrice?
Isab.   No questions! Fly!
Don M.   Yet tell me—
Isab.   Haste! Begone! Why this delay?—
Follow thy brother.
Don M.   I conjure thee—speak—
Isab. (*Dragging him away.*)
Behold my tears!
Don M.   Where was she hid? What
  region
Concealed my sister?
Isab.   Scarce from curious eyes,
In the deep bosom of the earth more safe
My child had been!
Diego.   Oh! now a sudden horror
Starts in my breast.
Don M.   What gives thee fear?
Diego.   'Twas I
That guiltless caused this woe!
Isab.   Unhappy man!
What hast thou done?
Diego.   To spare thy mother's heart
One anxious pang, my mistress, I concealed
What now my lips shall tell:—'Twas on the
  day
When thy dead husband in the silent tomb
Was laid; from every side the unnumbered
  throng
Pressed eager to the solemn rites; thy
  daughter—
For e'en amid the cloistered shade was noised
The funeral pomp—urged me, with ceaseless
  prayers,
To lead her to the festival of Death.
In evil hour I gave consent; and, shrouded
In sable weeds of mourning, she surveyed
Her father's obsequies. With keen reproach
My bosom tells—(for through the veil her
  charms

Resistless shone)—'twas there, perchance, the
  spoiler
Lurked to betray.
Don M. (*To himself.*)
              Thrice happy words! I live!
It was another!
Isab. (*To* Diego.) Faithless! Ill betide
Thy treacherous age!
Diego.   Oh, never have I strayed
From duty's path! My mistress, in her prayers
I heard the voice of Nature;—thus from
  Heaven
Ordained, methought, the secret impulse moves
Of kindred blood, to hallow with her tears
A father's grave: the tender office owned
Thy servant's care, and thus with good intent
I wrought but ill.
Don M. (*To himself.*) Why stand I thus,
  a prey
To torturing fears! No longer will I bear
The dread suspense—I will know all!
Don C. (*Who returns.*)   Forgive me,
I follow thee.
Don M.   Away! Let no man follow!
                            [*Exit.*
Don C. (*Looking after him in surprise.*)
What means my brother? Speak—
Isab.   In wonder lost
I gaze; some mystery lurks—
Don C.   Thou mark'st, my mother,
My quick return; with eager zeal I flew
At thy command, nor asked one trace to guide
My footsteps to thy daughter. Whence was
  torn
Thy treasure? Say, what cloistered solitude
Enshrined the beauteous maid?
Isab.   'Tis consecrate
To St. Cecilia; deep in forest shades,
Beyond the woody ridge that slowly climbs
Towards Etna's towering throne, it seems a
  refuge
Of parted souls!
Don C.   Have courage, trust thy sons;
She shall be thine, tho' with unwearied quest
O'er every land and sea I track her presence
To earth's extremest bounds: one thought
  alone
Disturbs,—in stranger hands my timorous
  bride
Waits my return; to thy protecting arms
I give the pledge of all my joy! She comes;
Soon on her faithful bosom thou shalt rest,
In sweet oblivion of thy cares.   [*Exit.*
Isab. When will the ancient curse be stilled,
  that weighs

Upon our house? Some mocking demon sports
With every new-formed hope, nor envious leaves
One hour of joy. So near the haven smiled—
So smooth the treacherous main—secure I deemed
My happiness: the storm was lulled; and bright
In evening's lustre gleamed the sunny shore;
Then through the placid air the tempest sweeps,
And bears me to the roaring surge again!
[*She goes into the interior of the palace, followed by* DIEGO.

The Scene changes to the Garden.

Both Choruses, afterwards BEATRICE.

The Chorus of DON MANUEL *enters in solemn procession, adorned with garlands, and bearing the bridal ornaments above mentioned. The Chorus of* DON CÆSAR *opposes their entrance.*

First Cho. (CAJETAN.) Begone!
Second Cho. (BOHEMUND.)
                    Not at thy bidding!
CAJET.   See'st thou not
Thy presence irks?
BOHEM.   Thou hast it, then, the longer!
CAJET. My place is here! What arm repels me?
BOHEM.   Mine!
CAJET. Don Manuel sent me hither.
BOHEM.   I obey
My Lord, Don Cæsar.
CAJET.   To the eldest born
Thy master reverence owes.
BOHEM.   The world belongs
To him that wins!
CAJET. Unmannered knave, give place!
BOHEM. Our swords be measured first!
CAJET.   I find thee ever
A serpent in my path.
BOHEM.   Where'er I list,
Thus will I meet thee!
CAJET. Say, why cam'st thou hither,
To spy——?
BOHEM.   And thou to question and command?
CAJET. To parley I disdain!
BOHEM.   Too much I grace thee
By words!

CAJET. Thy hot impetuous youth should bow
To reverend age.
BOHEM.   Elder thou art—not braver.
BEAT. (*Rushing from her place of concealment.*)
Alas! What mean these warlike men?
CAJET. (*To* BOHEMUND.)   I heed not
Thy threats and lofty mien.
BOHEM.   I serve a master
Better than thine.
BEAT.   Alas! Should he appear!
CAJET. Thou liest! Don Manuel thousandfold excels.
BOHEM. In every strife the wreath of victory decks
Don Cæsar's brows!
BEAT.   Now he will come! Already
The hour is past!
CAJET. 'Tis peace, or thou shouldst know
My vengeance!
BOHEM. Fear, not peace, thy arm refrains.
BEAT. Oh! Were he thousand miles remote!
CAJET.   Thy looks
But move my scorn; the compact I obey.
BOHEM. The coward's ready shield!
CAJET.   Come on! I follow.
BOHEM. To arms!
BEAT. (*In the greatest agitation.*)
Their falchions gleam—the strife begins!
Ye heavenly powers, his steps refrain! Some snare
Throw round his feet, that in this hour of dread
He come not: all ye angels, late implored
To give him to my arms, reverse my prayers;
Far, far from hence convey the loved one!
[*She runs into the alcove. At the moment when the two Choruses are about to engage,* DON MANUEL *appears.*

DON MANUEL, *the Chorus.*

DON M.   Hold!
What do I see!
First Cho. to the Second (CAJETAN, BERENGAR, MANFRED.)
            Come on! Come on!
Second Cho. (BOHEMUND, ROGER, HIPPOLYTE.)   Down with them!
DON M. (*Stepping between them with drawn sword.*) Hold!
CAJET. 'Tis the Prince!
BOHEM.   Be still!
DON M.   I stretch him dead
Upon this verdant turf, that with one glance
Of scorn prolongs the strife, or threats his foe!

Why rage ye thus? What maddening fiend
impels
To blow the flames of ancient hate anew,
For ever reconcil'd? Say, who began
The conflict?—Speak—
    First Cho. (CAJETAN, BERENGAR.)
My Prince, we stood—
    Second Cho. (ROGER, BOHEMUND.) *inter-
    rupting them.*   They came—
    DON M. *(To the First Chorus.)*
Speak thou!
    First Cho. (CAJETAN.)
        With wreaths adorned, in festal train,
We bore the bridal gifts; no thought of ill
Disturbed our peaceful way; composed for
    ever
With holy pledge of love we deemed your strife,
And trusting came; when here in rude array
Of arms, encamped they stood, and loud de-
    fied us!
DON M. Slave! Is no refuge safe? Shall
    discord thus
Profane the bower of virgin innocence,
The home of sanctity and peace?
        [To the Second Chorus.
                Retire—
Your warlike presence ill beseems; away!
I would be private.   *[They hesitate.*
            In your master's name
I give command; our souls are one, our lips
Declare each other's thoughts; begone!
        [To the First Chorus.
                Remain—
And guard the entrance.
    BOHEM.   So! What next? Our masters
Are reconciled; that's plain; and less he wins
Of thanks than peril, that with busy zeal
In princely quarrels stirs; for when of strife
His Mightiness aweary feels, of guilt
He throws the red-dyed mantle unconcerned
On his poor follower's luckless head, and
    stands
Arrayed in virtue's robes! So let them end
E'en as they will their brawls, I hold it best
That we obey.
    *[Exit Second Chorus. The First withdraws
    to the back of the stage; at the same mo-
    ment BEATRICE rushes forward, and throws
    herself into DON MANUEL'S arms.*
    BEAT.   'Tis thou! Ah! cruel one,
Again I see thee—clasp thee—long appalled,
To thousand ills a prey, trembling I languish
For thy return: no more—in thy loved arms
I am at peace, nor think of dangers past,
Thy breast my shield from every threatening
    harm.

Quick! Let us fly! They see us not—away!
Nor lose the moment.
            Ha! Thy looks affright me!
Thy sullen cold reserve! Thou tear'st thyself
Impatient from my circling arms, I know thee
No more! Is this Don Manuel? My beloved?
My husband?
    DON M.   Beatrice!
    BEAT.   No words! The moment
Is precious! Haste.
    DON M.   Yet tell me—
    BEAT.   Quick! Away
Ere these fierce men return.
    DON M.   Be calm, for nought
Shall trouble thee of ill.
    BEAT.   Oh fly!—alas,
Thou know'st them not!
    DON M.   Protected by this arm
Canst thou fear aught?
    BEAT.   Oh! trust me; mighty men
Are here.
    DON M.   Beloved! mightier none than I!
    BEAT. And wouldst thou brave this warlike
    host alone?
    DON M. Alone! the men thou fear'st—
    BEAT.   Thou know'st them not,
Nor whom they serve.
    DON M.   Myself! I am their Lord!
    BEAT. Thou art—a shudder creeps thro'
    all my frame!
    DON M. Far other than I seemed; so learn
    at last
To know me, Beatrice. Not the poor knight
Am I, the stranger and unknown, that loving
Taught thee to love; but what I am—my
    race—
My power—
    BEAT.   And art thou not Don Manuel?
    Speak—
Who art thou?
    DON M.   Chief of all that bear the name,
I am Don Manuel, Prince of Messina!
    BEAT. Art thou Don Manuel, Don Cæsar's
    brother?
    DON M. Don Cæsar is my brother.
    BEAT.   Is thy brother!
    DON M. What means this terror? Know'st
    thou, then, Don Cæsar?
None other of my race?
    BEAT.   Art thou Don Manuel,
That with thy brother liv'st in bitter strife
Of long inveterate hate?
    DON M.   This very sun
Smiled on our glad accord! Yes, we are
    brothers!
Brothers in heart!

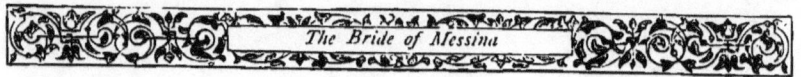

BEAT. And reconcil'd? This day?
DON M. What stirs this wild disorder?
Hast thou known
Aught but our name? Say, hast thou told
me all?
Is there no secret? Hast thou nought con-
cealed?
Nothing disguised?
BEAT. Thy words are dark; explain
What shall I tell thee?
DON M. Of thy mother nought
Hast thou e'er told; who is she? If in words
I paint her, bring her to thy sight—
BEAT. Thou know'st her!
And thou wert silent!
DON M. If I know thy mother,
Horrors betide us both!
BEAT. Oh! she is gracious
As the sun's orient beam! Yes! I behold her;
Fond memory wakes;—and from my bosom's
depths
Her godlike presence rises to my view!
I see around her snowy neck descend
The tresses of her raven hair, that shade
The form of sculptured loveliness; I see
The pale, high-thoughted brow; the darken-
ing glance
Of her large lustrous orbs; I hear the tones
Of soul-fraught sweetness!
DON M. 'Tis herself!
BEAT. This day,
Perchance, had given me to her arms, and knit
Our souls in everlasting love;—such bliss
I have renounced, yes! I have lost a mother
For thee!
DON M. Console thyself, Messina's Princess
Henceforth shall call thee daughter; to her
feet
I lead thee; come—she waits.
BEAT. What hast thou said?
Thy mother and Don Cæsar's? Never! never!
DON M. Thou shudderest! Whence this
horror? Hast thou known
My mother? Speak—
BEAT. O grief! O dire misfortune!
Alas! that e'er I lived to see this day!
DON M. What troubles thee? Thou know'st
me, thou hast found,
In the poor stranger knight, Messina's Prince.
BEAT. Give me the dear unknown again!
With him,
On earth's remotest wilds I could be blest!
DON C. *(Behind the scene.)* Away! what
rabble throng is here?
BEAT. That voice!
Oh, heavens! Where shall I fly!

DON M. Know'st thou that voice?
No! thou hast never heard it; to thine ear
'Tis strange—
BEAT. Oh, come—delay not—
DON M. Wherefore fly?
It is my brother's voice! He seeks me—how
He tracked my steps—
BEAT. By all the holy Saints!
Brave not his wrath! oh! quit this place—
avoid him—
Meet not thy brother here!
DON M. My soul! thy fears
Confound; thou hear'st me not; our strife is
o'er.
Yes! we are reconciled.
BEAT. Protect me, Heaven,
In this dread hour!
DON M. A sudden dire presage
Starts in my breast—I shudder at the thought:
If it be true! Oh, horror! Could she know
That voice! Wert thou—my tongue denies
to utter
The words of fearful import—Beatrice!
Say, wert thou present at the funeral rites
Of my dead sire?
BEAT. Alas!
DON M. Thou wert!
BEAT. Forgive me!
DON M. Unhappy woman!—
BEAT. I was present!
DON M. Horror!
BEAT. Some mighty impulse urged me to
the scene—
Oh, be not angry—to thyself I owned
The ardent fond desire; with darkening brow
Thou listenedst to my prayer, and I was silent,
But what misguiding inauspicious star
Allured, I know not; from my inmost soul
The wish, the dear emotion spoke; and vain
Aught else:— Diego gave consent—oh, par-
don me!
I disobeyed thee.

[*She advances towards him imploringly; at
the same moment* DON CÆSAR *enters, accompanied by the whole Chorus.*

BOTH BROTHERS, BOTH CHORUSES, BEATRICE.

Second Cho. (BOHEMUND) *to* DON CÆSAR.
Thou believ'st us not—
Believe thine eyes!
DON C. *(Rushes forward furiously, and at
the sight of his brother starts back with
horror.)* Some hell-born magic cheats
My senses; in her arms! Envenomed snake!

31

Is this thy love? For this thy treacherous
heart
Could lure with guise of friendship! O from
Heaven
Breathed my immortal hate! Down, down to
Hell,
Thou soul of falsehood!
[He stabs him, Don Manuel *falls.*
Don M.   Beatrice!—my brother!—
I die!
[Dies. Beatrice *sinks lifeless at his side.*
First Cho. (Cajetan.)
Help! Help! To arms! Avenge with blood
The bloody deed!
Second Cho. (Bohemund.)
                    The fortune of the day
Is ours! The strife for ever stilled:—Messina
Obeys one Lord.
First Cho. (Cajetan, Berengar, Man-
fred.)   Revenge! The murderer
Shall die! Quick offer to your master's shade
Appeasing sacrifice!
Second Cho. (Bohemund, Roger, Hippo-
lyte.)   My Prince! fear nothing,
Thy friends are true.
Don C.   *(Steps between them, looking
around.)*   Be still! The foe is slain
That practised on my trusting honest heart
With snares of brother's love! O direful shows
The deed of death! But righteous Heaven
hath judged.
First Cho. (Cajetan.)
Alas to thee, Messina! Woe for ever!
Sad city! From thy blood-stained walls this
deed
Of nameless horror taints the skies: ill fare
Thy mothers and thy children, youth and age,
And offspring yet unborn!
Don C.   Too late your grief—
Here give your help. *[Pointing to* Beatrice.
                Call her to life, and quick
Depart this scene of terror and of death.
I must away and seek my sister:—Hence!
Conduct her to my mother—
And tell her that her son, Don Cæsar, sends
her!   [*Exit.*
[The senseless Beatrice *is placed on a litter
and carried away by the Second Chorus.
The First Chorus remains with the body,
round which the boys who bear the bridal
presents range themselves in a semicircle.*

Chorus (Cajetan.)

List, how with dreaded mystery
  Was signed to my prophetic soul,
Of kindred blood the dire decree:—

Hither with noiseless giant stride
I saw the hideous Fiend of terror glide!
'Tis past!—I strive not to control
My shuddering awe—so swift of ill
The Fates the warning sign fulfil.
  Lo! to my sense dismayed,
Sudden the deed of death has shown
Whate'er my boding fears portrayed:
  The visioned thought was pain;
  The present horror curdles every vein!

One of the Chorus (Manfred.)

Sound, sound the plaint of woe!
  Beautiful Youth!
Outstretched and pale he lies,
Untimely cropped in early bloom;
The heavy night of death has sealed his eyes;—
In this glad hour of nuptial joy,
  Snatched by relentless doom,
He sleeps—while, echoing to the sky,
Of sorrow bursts the loud despairing cry!

A second (Cajetan.)

We come, we come, in festal pride,
To greet the beauteous Bride;
Behold! the nuptial gifts, the rich attire:
  The banquet waits, the guests are there;
They bid thee to the solemn rite
  Of Hymen quick repair.
Thou hear'st them not—the sportive lyre,
  The frolic dance, shall ne'er invite;
Nor wake thee from thy lowly bed,
For deep the slumber of the dead!

The whole Chorus.

No more the echoing horn shall cheer,
Nor bride with tones of sweetness charm his
  ear;
On the cold earth he lies,
In death's eternal slumber closed his eyes.

A third (Cajetan.)

What are the hopes, and fond desires
  Of mortals' transitory race?
This day, with harmony of voice and soul,
  Ye woke the long-extinguished fires
  Of brothers' love—yon flaming orb
Lit with his earliest beams your dear embrace:
  At eve, upon the gory sand
Thou liest—a reeking corse!
  Stretched by a brother's murderous hand.
Vain projects, treacherous hopes,
Child of the fleeting hour, are thine;
Fond man! thou rear'st on dust each bold
  design.

Chorus (BERENGAR.)

To thy mother I will bear
The burden of unutterable wo!
Quick shall yon cypress, blooming fair,
  Bend to the axe's murderous blow.
  Then twine the mournful bier!
For ne'er with verdant life the tree shall smile
That grew on death's devoted soil;
Ne'er in the breeze the branches play,
Nor shade the wanderer in the noontide ray;
'Twas marked to bear the fruits of doom,
Cursed to the service of the tomb.

First (CAJETAN.)

Wo to the murderer! Wo!
That sped exulting in his pride,
Behold! the parched earth drinks the crimson
    tide,

Down, down it flows, unceasingly,
  To the dim caverned halls below,
Where throned in kindred gloom the sister
    train,
  Of Themis progeny severe,
Brood in their songless silent reign!
Stern ministers of wrath's decree,
They catch in swarthy cups thy streaming gore,
And pledge with horrid rites for vengeance
    evermore!

Second (BERENGAR.)

Tho' swift of deeds the traces fade
  From earth, before the enlivening ray;
As o'er the brow the transient shade
  Of thought, the hues of fancy flit away:—
Yet in the mystic womb unseen,
Of the dark ruling Hours that sway

Our mortal lot, whate'er *has been*,
With new creative germ defies decay.
The blooming field is time,
For Nature's ever-teeming shoot,
And all is seed, and all is fruit.

[*The Chorus goes away, bearing the corpse of*
DON MANUEL *on a bier.*

SCENE.— *The Hall of Pillars. It is night.*

The stage is lighted from above by a single large
lamp.

DONNA ISABELLA *and* DIEGO *advance to the*
front.

ISAB. As yet no joyful tidings, not a trace
Found of the lost one!
DIEGO. Nothing have we heard,
My mistress; yet o'er every track, unwearied,
Thy sons pursue. Ere long the rescued maid
Shall smile at dangers past.
ISAB. Alas! Diego,
My heart is sad; 'twas I that caused this wo!
DIEGO. Vex not thy anxious bosom;
nought escaped
Thy thoughtful care.
ISAB. Oh! had I earlier shown
The hidden treasure!
DIEGO. Prudent were thy counsels,
Wisely thou left'st her in retirement's shade;
So, trust in Heaven.
ISAB. Alas! no joy is perfect—
Without this chance of ill my bliss were pure.
DIEGO. Thy happiness is but delayed; en-
joy
The concord of thy sons.
ISAB. The sight was rapture
Supreme—when, locked in one another's arms,
They glowed with brothers' love.
DIEGO. And in the heart
It burns; for ne'er their princely souls have
stooped
To mean disguise.
ISAB. Now, too, their bosoms wake
To gentler thoughts, and own the softening
sway
Of love. No more their hot impetuous youth
Revels in liberty untamed, and spurns
Restraint of Law—attempered passion's self,
With modest chaste reserve.
To thee, Diego,
I will unfold my secret heart; this hour
Of feeling's opening bloom, expected long,
Wakes boding fears: thou know'st to sudden
rage

Love stirs tumultuous breasts;—and if this
flame
With jealousy should rouse the slumbering
fires
Of ancient hate—I shudder at the thought!
If these discordant souls perchance have
thrilled
In fatal unison!—Enough—the clouds,
That black with thundering menace o'er me
hung,
Are past; some angel sped them tranquil by,
And my enfranchised spirit breathes again!
DIEGO. Rejoice, my mistress; for thy gen-
tle sense,
And soft prevailing art, more weal have
wrought
Than all thy husband's power. Be praise to
thee
And thy auspicious star!
ISAB. Yes! fortune smiled;
Nor light the task, so long with apt disguise
To veil the cherished secret of my heart,
And cheat my ever-jealous lord: more hard
To stifle mighty nature's pleading voice,
That, like a prisoned fire, for ever strove
To rend its confines.
DIEGO. All shall yet be well:
Fortune, propitious to our hopes, gave pledge
Of bliss that time will show.
ISAB. I praise not yet
My natal star, while darkening o'er my fate
This mystery hangs: too well the dire mis-
chance
Tells of the Fiend whose never slumbering
rage
Pursues our house. Now list what I have
done,
And praise or blame me as thou wilt; from
thee
My bosom guards no secret:—ill I brook
This dull repose, while swift o'er land and
sea
My sons unwearied track their sister's flight,
Yes! I have sought—Heaven counsels oft,
when vain
All mortal aid.
DIEGO. What I may know, my Mistress,
Declare.
ISAB. On Etna's solitary height
A reverend Hermit dwells;—benamed of old,
The Mountain Seer;—who to the realms of
light
More near abiding than the toilsome race
Of mortals here below, with purer air
Has cleansed each earthly grosser sense away;
And from the lofty peak of gathered years,

As from his mountain home, with downward
 glance
Surveys the crooked paths of worldy strife.
To him are known the fortunes of our house.
Oft has the holy Sage besought response
From Heaven, and many a curse with earnest
 prayer
Averted; thither at my bidding flew,
On wings of youthful haste, a messenger,
To ask some tidings of my child: each hour
I wait his homeward footsteps.

  DIEGO.   If mine eyes
Deceive me not, he comes; and well his speed
Has earned thy praise.

   MESSENGER, ISABELLA, DIEGO.

 ISAB. *(To* MESSENGER.*)*
     Now speak, and nothing hide
Of weal or woe: be Truth upon thy lips!
What tidings bear'st thou from the mountain
 Seer?

 MES. His answer, "Quick, retrace thy
  steps—the lost one
Is found."
 ISAB. Auspicious tongue! Celestial sounds
Of peace and joy! thus ever to my vows,
Thrice honored Sage, thy kindly message
 spoke!
But say, which heaven-directed brother traced
My daughter?
 MES.   'Twas thy eldest born that found
The deep-secluded maid.
 ISAB.   Is it Don Manuel
That gives her to my arms? Oh, he was ever
The child of blessing! Tell me, hast thou
 borne
My offering to the aged man?—the tapers
To burn before his Saint! for gifts, the prize
Of worldly hearts, the man of God disdains.
 MES. He took the torches from my hands
 in silence
And stepping to the altar—where the lamp
Burned to his Saint—illumed them at its fire,

35

And instant set in flames the hermit cell,
Where he has honored God these ninety years!
ISAB.   What hast thou said?   What horrors
fright my soul?
MES.   And three times shrieking "Woe!"
with downward course,
He fled; but silent with uplifted arm
Beckoned me not to follow, nor regard him!
So hither I have hastened, terror sped.
ISAB.   Oh, I am tossed amid the surge again
Of doubt and anxious fears; thy tale appals
With ominous sounds of ill.   My daughter
found—
Thou say'st; and by my eldest born, Don
Manuel?
The tidings ne'er shall bless, that heralded
This deed of woe!

MES.   My Mistress! look around,
Behold the hermit's message to thine eyes
Fulfilled.   Some charm deludes my sense, or
hither
Thy daughter comes, girt by the warlike train
Of thy two sons!

[BEATRICE *is carried in by the Second Chorus
on a litter, and placed in the front of the
stage.   She is still without perception, and
motionless.*

ISABELLA, DIEGO, MESSENGER, BEATRICE.

Chorus (BOHEMUND, ROGER, HIPPOLYTE, *and
the other nine followers of* DON CÆSAR.)

Cho. (BOHEMUND.)   Here at thy feet we lay
The maid, obedient to our Lord's command:
'Twas thus he spoke—"Conduct her to my
mother;
And tell her that her son, Don Cæsar, sends
her!"
ISAB.   *(Is advancing towards her with out-
stretched arms, and starts back in horror.)*
Heavens! she is motionless and pale!
Cho. (BOHEMUND.)   She lives,
She will awake, but give her time to rouse
From the dread shock that holds each sense
enthralled.
ISAB.   My daughter!   Child of all my cares
and pains!
And is it thus I see thee once again?
Thus thou returnest to thy father's halls!
O let my breath relume thy vital spark;
Yes! I will strain thee to a mother's arms
And hold thee fast—till, from the frost of death
Released, thy life-warm current throbs again.
                          [*To the Chorus.*

Where hast thou found her?   Speak!   What
dire mischance
Has caused this sight of wo!
Cho. (BOHEMUND.)   My lips are dumb!
Ask not of me: thy son will tell thee all—
Don Cæsar—for 'tis he that sends her.
ISAB.   Tell me,
Would'st thou not say Don Manuel!
Cho. (BOHEMUND.)   'Tis Don Cæsar
That sent her to thee.
ISAB.   *(To the* MESSENGER.*)*
                How declared the Seer?
Speak!   Was it not Don Manuel?
MES.   'Twas he!
The elder born.
ISAB.   Be blessings on his head
Whiche'er it be; to him I owe a daughter.
Alas! that in this blissful hour, so long
Expected, long implored, some envious Fiend
Should mar my joy!   Oh, I must stem the tide
Of nature's transport!   In her childhood's
home
I see my daughter; me she knows not—heeds
not—
Nor answers to a mother's voice of love!
Ope, ye dear eyelids—hands be warm—and
heave
Thou lifeless bosom with responsive throbs
To mine!   'Tis she!—Diego, look!   'tis Be-
atrice!
The long-concealed—the lost—the rescued
one!
Before the world I claim her for my own!
Cho. (BOHEMUND.)   New signs of terror to
my boding soul
Are pictured;—in amazement lost I stand!
What light shall pierce this gloom of mystery?
ISAB.   *(To the Chorus, who exhibit marks of
confusion and embarrassment.)*
O ye hard hearts!   Ye rude unpitying men!
A mother's transport from your breasts of steel
Rebounds, as from the rocks the heaving surge!
I look around your train, nor mark one glance
Of soft regard.   Where are my sons?   Oh, tell
me!
Why come they not, and from their beaming
eyes
Speak comfort to my soul?   For here environed
I stand amid the desert's raging brood,
Or monsters of the deep!
DIEGO.   She opes her eyes!
She moves!   She lives!
ISAB.   She lives!   On me be thrown
Her earliest glance!
DIEGO.   See!   They are closed again—
She shudders!

ISAN. *(To the Chorus.)* Quick! Retire—your aspect frights her.

[*Chorus steps back.*

BOHEM. Well pleased I shun her sight.

DIEGO. With outstretched eyes,
And wonderstruck, she seems to measure thee.

BEAT. Not strange those lineaments — where am I?

ISAB. Slowly
Her sense returns.

DIEGO. Behold! upon her knees
She sinks.

BEAT. O angel visage of my mother!

ISAB. Child of my heart!

BEAT. See! kneeling at thy feet
The guilty one!

ISAB. I hold thee in my arms!
Enough—forgotten all!

DIEGO. Look in my face,
Canst thou remember me?

BEAT. The reverened brows
Of honest old Diego!

ISAN. Faithful guardian
Of thy young years.

BEAT. And am I once again
With kindred?

ISAB. Nought but death shall part us more!

BEAT. Will thou ne'er send me to the stranger?

ISAB. Never!
Fate is appeased.

BEAT. And am I next thy heart?
And was it all a dream—a hideous dream?
My mother! at my feet he fell!—I know not
What brought me hither—yet 'tis well.—O bliss!
That I am safe in thy protecting arms;
They would have ta'en me to the Princess Mother—
Sooner to death!

ISAN. My daughter, calm thy fears;
Messina's Princess—

BEAT. Name her not again!
At that ill-omened sound the chill of death
Creeps through my trembling frame.

ISAB. My child! but hear me—

BEAT. She has two sons by mortal hate dissevered,
Don Manuel and Don Cæsar—

ISAB. 'Tis myself!
Behold thy mother!

BEAT. Have I heard thee? Speak!

ISAB. I am thy mother and Messina's Princess!

BEAT. Art thou Don Manuel's and Don Cæsar's mother?

ISAB. And thine! They are thy brethren
whom thou nam'st.

BEAT. O gleam of horrid light!

ISAB. What troubles thee?
Say, whence this strange emotion?

BEAT. Yes! 'twas they!
Now I remember all; no dream deceived me,
They met—'tis fearful truth! Unhappy men!
—Where have ye hid him?

[*She rushes towards the Chorus: they turn
away from her. A funeral march is
heard in the distance.*

Cho. Horror! Horror!

ISAB. Hid!
Speak—who is hid? and what is true? Ye stand
In silent dull amaze—as tho' ye fathomed
Her words of mystery!—In your faltering tones—
Your brows—I read of horrors yet unknown,
That would refrain my tongue! What is it?
Tell me!
I will know all! Why fix ye on the door
That awe-struck gaze? What mournful music
sounds? [*The march is heard nearer.*

Cho. (BOHEMUND.)
It comes! it comes! and all shall be declared
With terrible voice. My Mistress! steel thy heart,
Be firm, and bear with courage what awaits thee
—For more than woman's soul thy destined griefs
Demand.

ISAB. What comes? and what awaits me?
Hark!
With fearful tones the death-wail smites mine ear—
It echoes thro' the house! Where are my sons?

[*The first Semichorus brings in the body of
DON MANUEL on a bier, which is placed
at the side of the stage. A black pall is
spread over it.*

ISABELLA, BEATRICE, DIEGO, *both Choruses.*

First Chorus (CAJETAN.)

With Sorrow in his train,
From street to street the King of Terror glides;
With stealthy foot, and slow,
He creeps where'er the fleeting race
Of man abides!
In turn at every gate
Is heard the dreaded knock of Fate,
The message of unutterable woe!

(BERENGAR,)

When, in the sere
And Autumn leaves decayed,
The mournful forest tells how quickly fade
The glories of the year!
When in the silent tomb opprest,
Frail man, with weight of days,
Sinks to his tranquil rest;
Contented Nature but obeys
Her everlasting law,—
The general doom awakes no shuddering awe!
But, mortals, oh! prepare
For mightier ills: with ruthless hand,
Fell murder cuts the holy band—
The kindred tie: insatiate Death,
With unrelenting rage,
Bears to his bark the flower of blooming age!

(CAJETAN.)

When clouds athwart the lowering sky
Are driven—when bursts with hollow moan
The thunder's peal—our trembling bosoms
own
The might of awful Destiny!
Yet oft the lightning's glare
Darts sudden thro' the cloudless air:—
Then in thy short delusive day
Of bliss, oh! dread the treacherous snare;
Nor prize the fleeting goods and vain,
The flowers that bloom but to decay!
Nor wealth, nor joy, nor aught but pain,
Was e'er to mortal's lot secure:—
Our first best lesson—to endure!

ISAB. What shall I hear? What horrors
lurk beneath
This funeral pall?
[*She steps towards the bier, but suddenly
pauses, and stands irresolute.*
Some strange mysterious dread
Enthrals my sense. I would approach, and
sudden
The icecold grasp of terror holds me back!
[*To* BEATRICE, *who has thrown herself be-
tween her and the bier.*
Whate'er it be, I will unveil—
[*On raising the pall, she discovers the body
of* DON MANUEL.
Eternal Powers! It is my son!
[*She stands in mute horror.* BEATRICE *sinks
to the ground with a shriek of anguish near
the bier.*
Cho. Unhappy mother! 'tis thy son. Thy
lips
Have uttered what my faltering tongue denied!

ISAB. My soul! My Manuel! O eternal
grief!
And is it thus I see thee? Thus thy life
Has bought thy sister from the spoiler's rage?
Where was thy brother? Could no arm be
found
To shield thee? O—be curst the hand that dug
These gory wounds! A curse on her that bore
The murderer of my son! Ten thousand
curses
On all their race!
Cho. Woe! Woe!
ISAB. And is it thus
Ye keep your word, ye Gods? Is this your
truth?
Alas! for him that trusts with honest heart
Your soothing wiles. Why have I hoped and
trembled?
And this the issue of my prayers! Attend,
Ye terror-stricken witnesses, that feed
Your gaze upon my anguish; learn to know
How warning visions cheat, and boding seers
But mock our credulous hopes:—let none be-
lieve
The voice of Heaven!
When in my teeming womb
This daughter lay, her father, in a dream,
Saw from his nuptial couch two laurels grow,
And in the midst a lily all in flames,
That catching swift the boughs and knotted
stems,
Burst forth with crackling rage, and o'er the
house
Spread in one mighty sea of fire. Perplexed
By this terrific dream, my husband sought
The counsels of the mystic art, and thus
Pronounced the Sage—" If I a daughter bore,
The murderess of his sons, the destined spring
Of ruin to our house, the baleful child
Should see the light."
Cho. (CAJETAN *and* BOHEMUND.)
What hast thou said, my Mistress?
Woe! Woe!
ISAB. For this her ruthless father spoke
The dire behest of death. I rescued her
The innocent, the doomed one:—from my
arms
The babe was torn: to stay the curse of
Heaven,
And save my sons, the mother gave her child;
And now by robber hands her brother falls;—
My child is guiltless;—O, she slew him not!
Cho. Woe! Woe!
ISAB. No trust the fabling readers of the
stars
Have e'er deserved! Hear how another spoke

ARTIST: JULIUS BENCZUR.

THE BRIDE OF MESSINA.

BEATRICE AT THE BIER OF DON MANUEL.

With comfort to my soul, and him I deemed
Inspired to voice the secrets of the skies!
"My daughter should unite in love the hearts
Of my dissevered sons:"—and thus their tales
Of curse and blessing on her head, proclaim
Each other's falsehood. No! she ne'er has
    brought
A curse—the innocent! nor time was given
The blessed promise to fulfil! Their tongues
Were false alike—their boasted art is vain—
With trick of words they cheat our credulous
    ears
Or are themselves deceived! Nought ye may
    know
Of dark futurity, the sable streams
Of Hell the fountain of your hidden lore,
Or yon bright spring of everlasting light!

      First Chorus (CAJETAN.)

Woe! Woe! thy tongue refrain!
Oh, pause, nor thus with impious rage

The might of Heaven profane;
The holy oracles are wise—
Expect with awe thy coming destinies!

ISAB. My tongue shall speak as prompts my
    swelling heart;
My griefs shall cry to Heaven! Why do we
    lift
Our suppliant hands, and at the sacred shrines
Kneel to adore? Good easy dupes! What
    win we
From faith and pious awe?—to touch with
    prayers
The tenants of yon azure realms on high,
Were hard as with an arrow's point to pierce
The silvery moon. Hid is the womb of
    Time,
Impregnable to mortal glance, and deaf
The adamantine walls of Heaven rebound
The voice of anguish—O 'tis one whate'er
The flight of birds—the aspect of the stars!

39

The Book of Nature is a maze—a dream
The Sage's art,—and every sign a falsehood!

Second Chorus (BOHEMUND.)

Woe! Woe! Ill-fated woman, stay
Thy maddening blasphemies;
Thou but disown'st, with purblind eyes,
The flaming Orb of day!
Confess the Gods,—they dwell on high—
They circle thee with awful majesty!

All the Knights.

Confess the Gods—they dwell on high—
They circle thee with awful majesty!

BEAT. Why hast thou saved thy daughter, and defied
The curse of Heaven, that marked me in thy womb
The child of woe? Short-sighted mother!—vain
Thy little arts, to cheat the doom declared
By the all-wise interpreters, that knit
The far and near; and, with prophetic ken,
See the late harvest spring in times unborn.
O thou hast brought destruction on thy race,
Withholding from the avenging Gods their prey;
Threefold, with new embittered rage, they ask
The direful penalty; no thanks thy boon
Of life deserves—the fatal gift was sorrow!

Second Chorus (BERENGAR) *looking towards the door with signs of agitation.*

Hark to the sound of dread!
The rattling brazen din I hear!
Of hell-born snakes the hissing tones are near!
Yes—'tis the Furies' tread!

(CAJETAN.)

In crumbling ruin wide,
Fall, fall, thou roof, and sink thou trembling floor
That bear'st the dread unearthly stride!
Ye sable damps arise!
Mount from the abyss in smoky spray,
And pall the brightness of the day!
Vanish, ye guardian Powers!
They come! The avenging Deities!

DON CÆSAR, ISABELLA, BEATRICE. *The Chorus.*

On the entrance of DON CÆSAR, *the Chorus station themselves before him imploringly. He remains standing alone in the centre of the stage.*

BEAT. Alas! 'tis he—
ISAB. (*Stepping to meet him.*)
My Cæsar! O, my son!
And is it thus I meet thee? Look! Behold!
The crime of hand accurst!—
[*She leads him to the corse.*

First Chorus (CAJETAN, BERENGAR.)

Break forth once more
Ye wounds! Flow, flow, in swarthy flood,
Thou streaming gore!

ISAB. Shuddering with earnest gaze, and motionless,
Thou stand'st:—yes! there my hopes repose, and all
That earth has of thy brother; in the bud
Nipp'd is your concord's tender flower, nor ever
With beauteous fruit shall glad a mother's eyes.
DON C. Be comforted; thy sons, with honest heart,
To peace aspired, but Heaven's decree was blood!
ISAB. I know thou lovedst him well; I saw between ye,
With joy, the bands of nature sweetly twined;
Thou wouldst have borne him in thy heart of hearts
With rich atonement of long wasted years!
But see—fell Murder thwarts thy dear design,
And nought remains but vengeance!
DON C. Come, my mother,
This is no place for thee. Oh, haste and leave
This sight of woe!
[*He endeavors to drag her away.*
ISAB. (*Throwing herself into his arms.*)
Thou liv'st! I have a son!
BEAT. Alas! my mother!
DON C. On this faithful bosom
Weep out thy pains;—nor lost thy son,—his love
Shall dwell immortal in thy Cæsar's breast.

First Chorus (CAJETAN, BERENGAR, MAN-FRED.)

Break forth, ye wounds!
Dumb witnesses!—the truth proclaim;
Flow fast thou gory stream!

ISAB. (*Clasping the hands of* DON CÆSAR *and* BEATRICE.) My children!
DON C. Oh, 'tis ecstacy! my mother,
To see her in thy arms!—henceforth in love
A daughter—sister—

Isab. *(Interrupting him.)*
          Thou hast kept thy word,
My son:—to thee I owe the rescued one;
Yes, thou hast sent her—
Don C. *(In astonishment.)*
          Whom, my mother, sayst thou
That I have sent?
   Isab.   She stands before thine eyes—
Thy sister.
   Don C.   She! My sister?
   Isab.   Ay, what other?
   Don C. My sister!
   Isab.   Thou hast sent her to me!
   Don C.   Horror!
His sister, too!
   Cho.   Woe! woe!
   Beat.   Alas! my mother!
   Isab.   Speak! I am all amaze!
   Don C.   Be curst the day
When I was born!
   Isab.   Eternal powers!
   Don C.   Accurst
The womb that bore me; curst thy secret arts,
The spring of all this woe; instant to crush
   thee,
Though the dread thunder swept—ne'er should
   this arm
Refrain the bolts of death:—I slew my
   brother!
Hear it and tremble! in her arms I found
   him—
She was my love, my chosen bride;—and
   he
My brother—in her arms! Thou hast heard
   all!
If it be true—oh, if she be my sister—
And his!—then I have done a deed that
   mocks
The power of sacrifice and prayers to ope
The gates of Mercy to my soul!

Chorus (Bohemund.)

The tidings on thy heart dismayed
   Have burst, and nought remains; behold!
'Tis come, nor long delayed,
   Whate'er the warning seers foretold:
They spoke the message from on high,
   Their lips proclaimed resistless destiny!
The mortal shall the curse fulfil,
   Who seeks to turn predestined ill.

Isab. The Gods have done their worst; if
   they be true
Or false, 'tis one—for nothing they can add
To this—the measure of their rage is full.

Why should I tremble that have nought to
   fear?
My darling son lies murdered, and the living
I call my son no more. Oh! I have borne
And nourished at my breast a basilisk
That stung my best-loved child. My daugh-
   ter, haste,
And leave this house of horrors—I devote it
To the avenging Fiends!—In evil hour,
'Twas crime that brought me hither, and of
   crime
The victim I depart. Unwillingly
I came—In sorrow I have lived—despairing
I quit these halls; on me, the innocent,
Descends this weight of woe! Enough—'tis
   shown
That Heaven is just, and oracles are true!
          [Exit, followed by Diego.

Beatrice, Don Cæsar, *The Chorus.*

Don C. *(Detaining* Beatrice.*)*
My sister, wouldst thou leave me? On this
   head
A mother's curse may fall—a brother's blood
Cry with accusing voice to Heaven—all Nature
Invoke eternal vengeance on my soul—
But thou—Oh! curse me not—I cannot bear it!
    *[*Beatrice *points with averted eyes to the*
            body.
I have not slain thy lover! 'twas thy brother,
And mine, that fell beneath my sword; and
   near
As the departed one, the living owns
The ties of blood: remember, too, 'tis I
That most a sister's pity need—for pure
His spirit winged its flight, and I am guilty!
    *[*Beatrice *bursts into an agony of tears.*
Weep! I will blend my tears with thine—nay,
   more,
I will avenge thy brother; but the lover—
Weep not for him—thy passionate yearning
   tears
My inmost heart. Oh! from the boundless
   depths
Of our affliction, let me gather this,
The last and only comfort—but to know
That we are dear alike. One lot fulfilled
Has made our rights and wretchedness the
   same;
Entangled in one snare we fall together,
Three hapless victims of unpitying Fate,
And share the mournful privilege of tears.
But when I think that for the lover more
Than for the brother bursts thy sorrow's tide,
Then rage and envy mingle with my pain,

41

And Hope's last balm forsakes my withering
soul!—
Nor joyful, as beseems, can I requite
This injured Shade:—yet after him content
To Mercy's throne my contrite spirit shall fly,
Sped by this hand—if dying I may know
That in one urn our ashes shall repose,
With pious office of a sister's care.
[He throws his arms around her with pas-
sionate tenderness.
I loved thee, as I ne'er had loved before,
When thou wert strange; and that I bear the
curse
Of brother's blood, 'tis but because I loved
thee
With measureless transport: love was all my
guilt
But now thou art my sister, and I claim
Soft pity's tribute.
[He regards her with inquiring glances, and
an air of painful suspense—then turns
away with vehemence.
No! in this dread presence
I cannot bear these tears—my courage flies,
And doubt distracts my soul. Go, weep in
secret—
Leave me in error's maze—but never, never,
Behold me more: I will not look again
On thee, nor on my mother. Oh! how passion
Laid bare her secret heart! She never loved
me!
She mourned her best-loved son—that was her
cry
Of grief—and nought was mine but show of
fondness!
And thou art false as she! make no disguise—
Recoil with horror from my sight—this form
Shall never shock thee more—begone for ever!
[Exit.
[She stands irresolute in a tumult of conflict-
ing passions—then tears herself from the
spot.

Chorus (CAJETAN.)

Happy the man—his lot I prize—
That far from pomps and turmoil vain,
Child-like on Nature's bosom lies
Amid the stillness of the plain.
My heart is sad in the princely hall,
When from the towering pride of state,
I see with headlong ruin fall,
How swift! the good and great!

And he—from Fortune's storms at rest—
Smiles, in the quiet haven laid,

Who, timely warned, has owned how blest
The refuge of the cloistered shade;
To honor's race has bade farewell,
Its idle joys and empty shows;
Isatiate wishes learned to quell,
And lulled in Wisdom's calm repose:—

No more shall Passion's maddening brood
Impel the busy scenes to try,
Nor on his peaceful cell intrude
The form of sad Humanity!
'Mid crowds and strife each mortal ill
Abides—the grisly train of woe
Shuns like the Pest the breezy hill,
To haunt the smoky marts below.

BERENGAR, BOHEMUND, *and* MANFRED.

On the mountain is freedom! the breath of
decay
Never sullies the fresh flowing air;
O Nature is perfect wherever we stray;
'Tis man that deforms it with care.

The whole Chorus repeats.

On the mountain is freedom, etc., etc.

DON CÆSAR, *the Chorus.*

DON C. *(More collected.)*
I use the princely rights—'tis the last time—
To give this body to the ground, and pay
Fit honors to the dead. So mark, my friends,
My bosom's firm resolve, and quick fulfil
Your lord's behest. Fresh in your memory
lives
The mournful pomp, when to the tomb ye bore
So late my royal sire; scarce in these halls
Are stilled the echoes of the funeral wail;—
Another corse succeeds, and in the grave
Weighs down its fellow-dust — almost our
torch,
With borrowed lustre from the last, may pierce
The monumental gloom; and on the stair,
Blend in one throng confused each mourning
train.
Then in the sacred royal dome that guards
The ashes of my sire, prepare with speed
The funeral rights; unseen of mortal eye,
And noiseless be your task—let all be graced,
As then, with circumstance of kingly state.
BOHEM. My Prince, it shall be quickly
done; for still
Upreared, the gorgeous Catafalque recalls
The dread solemnity: no hand disturbed
The edifice of Death.

DON C.   The yawning grave
Amid the haunts of life?   No goodly sign
Was this: the rites fulfilled, why lingered yet
The trappings of the funeral show?
    BOHEM.   Your strife
With fresh embittered hate o'er all Messina
Woke Discord's maddening flames, and from
    the deed
Our cares withdrew—so desolate remained,
And closed the sanctuary.
    DON C.   Make no delay;
This very night fulfil your task, for well
Beseems the midnight gloom!   To-morrow's
    sun

Shall find this palace cleansed of every stain,
And light a happier race.

[*Exit the Second Chorus with the body of*
    DON MANUEL.

CAJET.   Shall I invite
The Brotherhood of monks, with rites or-
    dained
By Holy Church of old, to celebrate
The office of departed souls, and hymn
The buried one to everlasting rest?
    DON C.   Their strains above my tomb shall
        sound for ever
Amid the torches' blaze—no solemn rites

43

Beseem the day when gory murder scares
Heaven's pardoning grace.
CAJET.   Oh, let not wild despair
Tempt thee to impious rash resolve.   My
    Prince,
No mortal arm shall e'er avenge this deed;
And penance calms, with soft atoning power,
The wrath on high.
        DON C.   If for eternal justice
Earth has no minister, myself shall wield
The avenging sword; though Heaven, with
    gracious ear,
Inclines to sinners' prayers, with blood alone
Atoned is murder's guilt.
    CRJET.   To stem the tide
Of dire misfortune, that with maddening rage
Bursts o'er your house, were nobler than to
    pile
Accumulated woe.
        DON C.   The curse of old
Shall die with me!   Death self-imposed alone
Can break the chain of Fate.
    CAJET.   Thou ow'st thyself
A sovereign to this orphaned land, by thee
Robbed of its other lord!
        DON C.   The avenging Gods
Demand their prey—some other Deity
May guard the living!
    CAJET.   Wide as e'er the sun
In glory beams, the realm of Hope extends;
But—O remember!—nothing may we gain
From Death!
        DON C.   Remember thou thy vassal's
    duty;—
Remember, and be silent!   Leave to me
To follow, as I list, the Spirit of power
That leads me to the goal.   No happy one
May look into my breast:—but if thy Prince
Owns not a subject's homage, dread at least
The murderer!—the accurst!—and to the head
Of the unhappy—sacred to the Gods—
Give honors due.   The pangs that rend my
    soul—
What I have suffered—what I feel—have left
No place for earthly thoughts!

DONNA ISABELLA, DON CÆSAR, *The Chorus.*

ISAN.   *(Enters with hesitating steps, and
    looks irresolutely towards* DON CÆSAR;
    *at last she approaches, and addresses him
    with collected tones.)*
I thought mine eyes should ne'er behold thee
    more;—
Thus I had vowed despairing!   Oh, my son!
How quickly all a mother's stern resolves

Melt into air!   'Twas but the cry of rage
That stifled Nature's pleading voice; but now
What tidings of mysterious import call me
Forth from the desolate chambers of my sor-
    row?
Shall I believe it?   Is it true?—one day
Robs me of both my sons?

                Chorus.

Behold! with willing steps and free,
    Thy son prepares to tread
The paths of dark eternity—
    The silent mansions of the dead.
My prayers are vain; but thou, with power
    confest
Of nature's holiest passion, storm his breast!

    ISAB.   I call the curses back—that in the
    frenzy
Of blind despair on thy beloved head
I poured.   A mother may not curse the child
That from her nourishing breast drew life, and
    gave
Sweet recompense for all her travail past:
Heaven would not hear the impious vows;
    they fell
With quick rebound, and heavy with my tears,
Down from the flaming vault.
                    Live! live! my son!
For I may rather bear to look on thee—
The murderer of one child—than weep for
    both!
        DON C.   Heedless and vain, my mother,
    are thy prayers
For me and for thyself;—I have no place
Among the living:—if thine eyes may brook
The murderer's sight abhorred—I could not
    bear
The mute reproach of thy eternal sorrow.
    ISAB.   Silent or loud, my son, reproach
    shall never
Disturb thy breast—ne'er in these halls shall
    sound
The voice of wailing, gently on my tears
My griefs shall flow away:—the sport alike
Of pitiless Fate, togther we will mourn,
And veil the deed of blood.
        DON C. *(With a faltering voice, and taking
    her hand.)*   Thus it shall be
My mother—thus with silent, gentle woe
Thy grief shall fade: but when one common
    tomb
The murderer and his victim closes round—
When o'er our dust one monumental stone
Is rolled—the curse shall cease—thy love no
    more

Unequal bless thy sons: the precious tears
Thine eyes of beauty weep, shall sanctify
Alike our memories.   Yes!   In death are
    quenched
The fires of rage; and Hatred owns subdued,
The mighty reconciler.   Pity bends
An angel form above the funeral urn,
With weeping dear embrace.   Then to the tomb
Stay not my passage:—Oh! forbid me not,
Thus with atoning sacrifice to quell
The curse of Heaven.
    ISAB.   All Christendom is rich
In shrines of mercy, where the troubled heart
May find repose.   Oh! many a heavy burden
Have sinners in Loretto's mansion laid;
And Heaven's peculiar blessing breathes
    around
The grave that has redeemed the world!—The
    prayers
Of the devout are precious—fraught with store

Of grace, they win forgiveness from the
    skies;—
And on the soil by gory murder stained
Shall rise the purifying fane.
    DON C.   We pluck
The arrow from the wound—but the torn heart
Shall ne'er be healed.   Let him who can, drag
    on
A weary life of penance and of pain,
To cleanse the spot of everlasting guilt;—
I would not live the victim of despair;
No!   I must meet with beaming eye the smile
Of happy ones, and breathe erect the air
Of liberty and joy.   While yet alike
We shared thy love, then o'er my days of youth
Pale Envy cast his withering shade; and now,
Think'st thou my heart could brook the dearer
    ties
That bind thee in thy sorrow to the dead?
Death, in his undecaying palace throned,

45

To the pure diamond of perfect virtue
Sublimes the mortal, and with chastening fire
Each gathered stain of frail humanity
Purges and burns away: high as the stars
Tower o'er this earthly sphere, he soars above
me;
And as by ancient hate dissevered long,
Brethren and equal denizens we lived,
So now my restless soul with envy pines,
That he has won from me the glorious prize
Of immortality, and like a God
In memory marches on to times unborn!
ISAB. My sons! Why have I called you to
Messina
To find for each a grave? I brought ye hither
To calm your strife to peace. Lo! Fate has
turned
My hopes to blank despair.
    DON C.   Whate'er was spoke,
My mother, is fulfilled! Blame not the end
By Heaven ordained. We trode our father's
halls
With hopes of peace; and reconciled for ever,
Together we shall sleep in death.
    ISAB.   My son,
Live for thy mother! In the stranger's land,
Say, would'st thou leave me friendless and
alone,
To cruel scorn a prey—no filial arm
To shield my helpless age?
    DON C.   When all the world
With heartless taunts pursues thee, to our grave
For refuge fly, my mother, and invoke
Thy sons' divinity—we shall be Gods!
And we will hear thy prayers:—and as the
Twins
Of Heaven, a beaming star of comfort shine
To the lost shipman—we will hover near thee
With present help, and soothe thy troubled
soul!
    ISAB. Live—for thy mother, live, my son—
Must I lose all?
    [*She throws her arms about him with passion-*
    ate emotion. He gently disengages himself,
    and, turning his face away, extends to her
    his hand.
    DON C.   Farewell!
    ISAB.   I can no more!
Too well my tortured bosom owns how weak
A mother's prayers: a mightier voice shall
sound
Resistless on thy heart.
    [*She goes towards the entrance of the scene.*
            My daughter, come!
A brother calls him to the realms of night;
Perchance with golden hues of earthly joy

The sister, the beloved, may gently lure
The wanderer to life again.
[BEATRICE *appears at the entrance of the scene.*

    DONNA ISABELLA, DON CÆSAR, *and the*
                Chorus.

    DON C. (*On seeing her, covers his face with*
    his hands.)   My mother!
What hast thou done?
    ISAB. (*Leading* BEATRICE *forward.*)
            A mother's prayers are vain!
Kneel at his feet — conjure him — melt his
    heart!
Oh! bid him live!
    DON C.   Deceitful mother, thus
Thou triest thy son! And wouldst thou stir
    my soul
Again to passion's strife, and make the sun
Beloved once more, now when I tread the paths
Of everlasting night? See where he stands—
Angel of life!—and wondrous beautiful,
Shakes from his plenteous horn the fragrant
    store
Of golden fruits and flowers, that breathe
    around
Divinest airs of joy;—my heart awakes
In the warm sunbeam—hope returns, and life
Thrills in my breast anew.
    ISAB. (*To* BEATRICE.) Thou wilt prevail!
Or none! Implore him that he live, nor rob
The staff and comfort of our days.
    BEAT.   The loved one
A sacrifice demands. Oh, let me die
To soothe a brother's shade! Yes, I will be
The victim! Ere I saw the light forewarned
To death, I live a wrong to Heaven! The
    curse
Pursues me still :—'twas I that slew thy son—
I waked the slumbering furies of their strife—
Be mine the atoning blood!
    CAJET.   Ill-fated mother!
Impatient all thy children haste to doom,
And leave thee on the desolate waste alone
Of joyless life.
    BEAT.   Oh, spare thy precious days
For Nature's band. Thy mother needs a son ;
My brother, live for her! Light were the pang
To lose a daughter—but a moment shown,
Then snatched away!
    DON C. (*With deep emotion.*)
            'Tis one to live or die,
Blest with a sister's love!
    BEAT.   Say—dost thou envy
Thy brother's ashes?
    DON C.   In thy grief he lives
A hallowed life!—my doom is death for ever!

BEAT. My brother!
DON C. Sister! are thy tears for me?
BEAT. Live for our mother!
DON C. (*Dropping her hand, and stepping back.*) For our mother?
BEAT. (*Hiding her head in his breast.*) Live
For her and for thy sister!
Cho. (BOHEMUND.) She has won!
Resistless are her prayers. Despairing mother,
Awake to hope again—his choice is made!
Thy son shall live!
[*At this moment an anthem is heard. The folding doors are thrown open, and in the Church is seen the Catafalque erected, and the coffin surrounded with candlesticks.*
DON C. (*Turning to the coffin.*)
I will not rob thee, brother!
The sacrifice is thine:—Hark! from the tomb,
Mightier than mother's tears, or sister's love,

Thy voice resistless cries:—my arms enfold
A treasure, potent with celestial joys,
To deck this earthly sphere, and make a lot
Worthy the Gods! but shall I live in bliss,
While in the tomb thy sainted innocence
Sleeps unavenged? Thou, Ruler of our days,
All just—all wise—let not the world behold
Thy partial care! I saw her tears!—enough—
They flowed for me! I am content: my brother!
I come!
[*He stabs himself with a dagger, and falls dead at his sister's feet. She throws herself into her mother's arms.*
Cho. (CAJETAN) *after a deep silence.*
In dread amaze I stand, nor know
If I should mourn his fate. One truth revealed
Speaks in my breast;—no good supreme is life!
But of all earthly ills the chief is—Guilt!

William Tell.

Schauspiel.

WILLIAM TELL.

A PLAY.

DRAMATIS PERSONÆ.

HERMANN GESSLER, *Governor of Switz and Uri.*
WERNER, *Baron of Attinghausen, Free Noble of Switzerland.*
ULRICH VON RUDENZ, *his Nephew.*
WERNER STAUFFACHER,
CONRAD HUNN,
HANS AUF DER MAUER,
JORG IM HOFE,
ULRICH DER SCHMIDT,
JOST VON WEILER,
ITEL REDING, } *People of Schwytz*
WALTER FÜRST,
WILLIAM TELL,
RÖSSELMANN, *the Priest,*
PETERMANN, *Sacristan.*
KUONI, *Herdsman,*
WERNI, *Huntsman,*
RUODI, *Fisherman,* } *of Uri.*
ARNOLD OF MELCHTHAL,
CONRAD BAUMGARTEN,
MEYER VON SARNEN,
STRUTH VON WINKELRIED,
KLAUS VON DER FLUE,
BURKHART AM BUHEL,
ARNOLD VON SEWA, } *of Unterwald.*
PFEIFFER OF LUCERNE.
KUNZ OF GERSAU.

JENNI, *Fisherman's Son.*
SEPPI, *Herdsman's Son.*
GERTRUDE, *Stauffacher's Wife.*
HEDWIG, *Wife of Tell, Daughter of Fürst.*
BERTHA OF BRUNECK, *a rich Heiress.*
ARMGART,
MECHTHILD,
ELSBETH, } *Peasant Women.*
HILDEGARD,
WALTER,
WILLIAM, } *Tell's Sons.*
FRIESSHARDT,
LEUTHOLD, } *Soldiers.*
RUDOLPH DER HARRAS, *Gessler's Master of the Horse.*
JOHANNES PARRICIDA, *Duke of Suabia.*
STUSSI, *Overseer.*
THE MAYOR OF URI.
A COURIER.
MASTER STONEMASON, COMPANIONS, AND WORKMEN.
TASKMASTER.
A CRIER.
MONKS OF THE ORDER OF CHARITY.
HORSEMEN OF GESSLER AND LANDENBERG.
MANY PEASANTS; MEN AND WOMEN FROM THE WALDSTETTEN.

William Tell

ACT I.

SCENE. I.—*A high rocky shore of the lake of Lucerne opposite Schwytz. The lake makes a bent into the land; a hut stands at a short distance from the shore; the fisher boy is rowing about in his boat. Beyond the lake are seen the green meadows, the hamlets and farms of Schwytz, lying in the clear sunshine. On the left are observed the peaks of the Hacken, surrounded with clouds; to the right, and in the remote distance, appear the Glaciers. The Ranz des Vaches, and the tinkling of cattle bells, continue for some time after the rising of the curtain.*

FISHER BOY. *(Sings in his boat.)*

Melody of the Ranz des Vaches.

The clear smiling lake woo'd to bathe in its
    deep,
A boy on its green shore had laid him to sleep;
    Then heard he a melody
      Flowing and soft,
    And sweet, as when angels
      Are singing aloft.

And as thrilling with pleasure he wakes from
    his rest,
The waters are murmuring over his breast;
    And a voice from the deep cries,
      "With me thou must go,
    I charm the young shepherd,
      I lure him below."

HERDSMAN. *(On the mountains.)*

Air.—Variation of the Ranz des Vaches.

    Farewell, ye green meadows,
      Farewell, sunny shore,
    The herdsman must leave you,
      The summer is o'er.
We go to the hills, but you'll see us again,
    When the cuckoo is calling, and woodnotes
      are gay,
When flow'rets are blooming in dingle and
      plain,
    And the brooks sparkle up in the sunshine
      of May.
    Farewell, ye green meadows,
      Farewell, sunny shore,

The herdsman must leave you,
The summer is o'er.

CHAMOIS HUNTER. *(Appearing on the top of a cliff.)*

Second variation of the Ranz des Vaches.

On the heights peals the thunder, and trembles
  the bridge,
The huntsman bounds on by the dizzying
  ridge.
Undaunted he hies him
  O'er ice-covered wild,
Where leaf never budded,
  Nor Spring ever smiled,
And beneath him an ocean of mist, where
  his eye
No longer the dwellings of man can espy;
  Through the parting clouds only
The earth can be seen,
  Far down 'neath the vapor
The meadows of green.

[*A change comes over the landscape. A rumbling, crackling noise is heard among the mountains. Shadows of clouds sweep across the scene.*

[RUODI, *the fisherman, comes out of his cottage.* WERNI, *the huntsman, descends from the rocks.* KUONI, *the shepherd, enters, with a milkpail on his shoulders, followed by* SEPPI, *his assistant.*

RUODI. Bestir thee, Jenni, haul the boat
  on shore.
The grizzly Vale-King comes, the Glaciers
  moan,
The lofty Mytenstein draws on his hood,
And from the Stormcleft chilly blows the
  wind;
The storm will burst, before we are prepared.
KUONI. 'Twill rain ere long; my sheep
  browse eagerly,
And Watcher there is scraping up the earth.
WERNI. The fish are leaping, and the
  water-hen
Dives up and down. A storm is coming on.
KUONI. *(To his boy.)*
Look, Seppi, if the cattle are not straying.
SEPPI. There goes brown Liesel, I can
  hear her bells.
KUONI. Then all are safe; she ever ranges
  farthest.
RUODI. You've a fine yoke of bells there,
  master herdsman.
WERNI. And likely cattle, too. Are they
  your own?

KUONI. I'm not so rich. They are the
  noble lord's
Of Attinghaus, and trusted to my care.
RUODI. How gracefully yon heifer bears
  her ribbon!
KUONI. Ay, well she knows she's leader of
  the herd,
And, take it from her, she'd refuse to feed.
RUODI. You're joking now. A beast de-
  void of reason——
WERNI. That's easy said. But beasts have
  reason, too,—
And that we know, we men that hunt the
  chamois:
They never turn to feed—sagacious creatures!
Till they have placed a sentinel ahead,
Who pricks his ears when ever we approach,
And gives alarm with clear and piercing pipe.
RUODI. *(To the shepherd.)*
Are you for home?
KUONI.   The Alp is grazed quite bare.
WERNI. A safe return, my friend!
KUONI.   The same to you!
Men come not always back from tracks like
  yours.
RUODI. But who comes here, running at
  topmost speed?
WERNI. I know the man; 'tis Baumgart
  of Alzellen.
CONRAD BAUMGARTEN. *(Rushing in breath-
less.)* For God's sake, ferryman, your boat!
RUODI.   How now?
Why all this haste?
BAUM.   Cast off! My life's at stake!
Set me across!
KUONI.   Why, what's the matter, friend?
WERNI. Who are pursuing you? First tell
  us that.
BAUM. *(To the fisherman.)*
Quick, quick, e'en now they're close upon
  my heels!
The Viceroy's horsemen are in hot pursuit!
I'm a lost man should they lay hands upon me.
RUODI. Why are the troopers in pursuit
  of you?
BAUM. First save my life, and then I'll
  tell you all.
WERNI. There's blood upon your gar-
  ments—how is this?
BAUM. The imperial Seneschal, who dwelt
  at Rossberg——
KUONI. How! What! The Wolfshot?
  Is it he pursues you?
BAUM. He'll ne'er hurt man again; I've
  settled him.

ALL. *(Starting back.)* Now, God forgive you, what is this you've done!

BAUM. What every free man in my place had done.
I have but used mine own good household right
'Gainst him that would have wrong'd my wife
—my honor.

KUONI. And has he wrong'd you in your honor, then?

BAUM. That he did not fulfil his foul desire,
Is due to God and to my trusty axe.

WERNI. You've cleft his skull, then, have you, with your axe?

KUONI. O, tell us all! You've time enough, before
The boat can be unfastened from its moorings.

BAUM. When I was in the forest felling timber,
My wife came running out in mortal fear.
"The Seneschal," she said, "was in my house,
Had order'd her to get a bath prepared,
And thereupon had ta'en unseemly freedoms,
From which she rid herself, and flew to me."
Arm'd as I was, I sought him, and my axe
Has given his bath a bloody benediction.

WERNI. And you did well; no man can blame the deed.

KUONI. The tyrant! Now he has his just reward!
We men of Unterwald have owed it long.

BAUM. The deed got wind, and now they're in pursuit.
Heavens! whilst we speak, the time is flying fast. [*It begins to thunder.*

KUONI. Quick, ferryman, and set the good man over.

RUODI. Impossible! a storm is close at hand,
Wait till it pass! You must.

BAUM. Almighty heavens!
I cannot wait; the least delay is death.

KUONI. *(To the fisherman.)*
Push out—God with you! We should help our neighbors;
The like misfortune may betide us all.
[*Thunder and the roaring of the wind.*

RUODI. The South wind's up! See how the lake is rising!
I cannot steer against both storm and wave.

BAUM. *(Clasping him by the knees.)*
God so help you, as now you pity me!

WERNI. His life's at stake. Have pity on him, man!

KUONI. He is a father: has a wife and children. [*Repeated peals of thunder.*

RUODI. What! and have I not, then, a life to lose,
A wife and child at home as well as he?
See, how the breakers foam, and toss, and whirl,
And the lake eddies up from all its depths!
Right gladly would I save the worthy man
But 'tis impossible, as you must see.

BAUM. *(Still kneeling.)*
Then must I fall into the tyrant's hands,
And with the port of safety close in sight!
Yonder it lies! My eyes can measure it,
My very voice can echo to its shores.
There is the boat to carry me across,
Yet must I lie here helpless and forlorn.

KUONI. Look! who comes here?

RUODI. 'Tis Tell, brave Tell, of Bürglen.
[*Enter* TELL *with a crossbow.*

TELL. Who is the man that here implores for aid?

KUONI. He is from Alzellan, and to guard his honor
From touch of foulest shame, has slain the Wolfshot,
The Imperial Seneschal, who dwelt at Rossberg.
The Viceroy's troopers are upon his heels;
He begs the boatman here to take him over,
But he, in terror of the storm, refuses.

RUODI. Well, there is Tell can steer as well as I,
He'll be my judge, if it be possible.
[*Violent peals of thunder—the lake becomes more tempestuous.*
Am I to plunge into the jaws of hell?
I should be mad to dare the desperate act.

TELL. The brave man thinks upon himself the last.
Put trust in God, and help him in his need!

RUODI. Safe in the port, 'tis easy to advise.
There is the boat, and there the lake! Try you!

TELL. The lake may pity, but the Viceroy will not.
Come, venture, man!

SHEPHERD *and* HUNTSMAN.
　　　　O save him! save him! save him!

RUODI. Though 'twere my brother, or my darling child,
I would not go. It is St. Simon's day,
The lake is up, and calling for its victim.

TELL. Nought's to be done with idle talking here.
Time presses on—the man must be assisted.
Say, boatman, will you venture?

RUODI. 　　　　　　　No; not I.

TELL. In God's name, then, give me the
boat! I will,
With my poor strength, see what is to be done!
KUONI. Ha, noble Tell!
WERNI. That's like a gallant huntsman!
BAUM. You are my angel, my preserver,
Tell.
TELL. I may preserve you from the Vice-
roy's power,
But from the tempest's rage another must.
Yet you had better fall into God's hands,
Than into those of men. [*To the herdsman.*
Herdsman, do thou
Console my wife, should aught of ill befall me.
I do but what I may not leave undone.
[*He leaps into the boat.*
KUONI. (*To the fisherman.*)
A pretty man to be a boatman, truly!
What Tell could risk, you dared not venture on.
RUODI. Far better men than I would not
ape Tell.
There does not live his fellow 'mong the moun-
tains.
WERNI. (*Who has ascended a rock.*)
He pushes off. God help thee now, brave
sailor!
Look how his bark is reeling on the waves!
KUONI. (*On the shore.*)
The surge has swept clean over it. And now
'Tis out of sight. Yet stay, there 'tis again!
Stoutly he stems the breakers, noble fellow!
SEPPI. Here come the troopers hard as
they can ride!
KUONI. Heavens! so they do! Why, that
was help, indeed.
[*Enter a troop of horsemen.*
FIRST HORSEMAN. Give up the murderer!
You have him here!
SECOND HORSEMAN. This way he came!
'Tis useless to conceal him!
RUODI *and* KUONI. Whom do you mean?
FIRST H. (*discovering the boat.*)
The devil! What do I see!
WERNI. (*From above,*)
Is't he in yonder boat ye seek? Ride on,
If you lay to, you may o'ertake him yet.
SECOND H. Curse on you, he's escaped!
FIRST H. (*To the shepherd and fisherman.*)
You help'd him off,
And you shall pay for it. Fall on their herds!
Down with the cottage! burn it! beat it down!
[*They rush off.*
SEPPI. (*Hurrying after them.*)
Oh my poor lambs!
KUONI. (*following him.*)
Unhappy me, my herds!

WERNI. The tyrants!
RUODI. (*Wringing his hands.*)
Righteous Heaven!
Oh, when will come
Deliverance to this devoted land?
[*Exeunt severally.*

———

SCENE II.—*A lime tree in front of* STAUFF-
ACHER'S *house at Steinen, in Schwytz,
upon the public road, near a bridge.*
WERNER STAUFFACHER *and* PFEIFFER OF LU-
CERNE *enter into conversation.*

PFEIF. Ay, ay, friend Stauffacher, as I
have said,
Swear not to Austria, if you can help it.
Hold by the Empire stoutly as of yore,
And God preserve you in your ancient free-
dom!
[*Presses his hand warmly and is going.*
STAUF. Wait till my mistress comes. Now
do! You are
My guest in Schwytz—I in Lucerne am yours.
PFEIF. Thanks! thanks! But I must reach
Gersau to-day.
Whatever grievances your rulers' pride
And grasping avarice may yet inflict,
Bear them in patience—soon a change may
come.
Another emperor may mount the throne.
But Austria's once, and you are hers for ever.
[*Exit.*
[STAUFFACHER *sits down sorrowfully upon a
bench under the lime tree.* GERTRUDE,
*his wife, enters, and finds him in this
posture. She places herself near him, and
looks at him for some time in silence.*
GERT. So sad, my love! I scarcely know
thee now.
For many a day in silence I have mark'd
A moody sorrow furrowing thy brow.
Some silent grief is weighing on thy heart.
Trust it to me. I am thy faithful wife,
And I demand my half of all thy cares.
[STAUFFACHER *gives her his hand and is silent.*
Tell me what can oppress thy spirits thus?
Thy toil is blest—the world goes well with
thee—
Our barns are full—our cattle, many a score;
Our handsome team of sleek and well-fed
steeds
Brought from the mountain pastures safely
home,

ARTIST: A. BAUR.

WILLIAM TELL.

ACT 1, SCENE 1.

To winter in their comfortable stalls.
There stands thy house—no nobleman's more
    fair!
'Tis newly built with timber of the best,
All grooved and fitted with the nicest skill;
Its many glistening windows tell of comfort!
'Tis quarter'd o'er with 'scutcheons of all hues,
And proverbs sage, which passing travellers
Linger to read, and ponder o'er their meaning.
    STAUF. The house is strongly built, and
        handsomely,
But, ah! the ground on which we built it
    totters.
    GERT. Tell me, dear Werner, what you
        mean by that?
    STAUF. No later since than yesterday, I sat
Beneath this linden, thinking with delight,
How fairly all was finished, when from Küss-
    nacht,
The Viceroy and his men came riding by.
Before this house he halted in surprise:
At once I rose, and, as beseemed his rank,
Advanced respectfully to greet the lord,
To whom the Emperor delegates his power,
As judge supreme within our Canton here.
"Who is the owner of this house?" he asked,

With mischief in his thoughts, for well he knew.
With prompt decision, thus I answered him:
"The Emperor, your grace—my lord and
    yours,
And held by me in fief." On this he an-
    swered,
"I am the Emperor's viceregent here,
And will not that each peasant churl should
    build
At his own pleasure, bearing him as freely
As though he were the master in the land.
I shall make bold to put a stop to this!"
So saying, he, with menaces, rode off,
And left me musing with a heavy heart,
On the fell purpose that his words betray'd.
    GERT. Mine own dear lord and husband!
        Wilt thou take
A word of honest counsel from thy wife?
I boast to be the noble Iberg's child,
A man of wide experience. Many a time,
As we sat spinning in the winter nights,
My sisters and myself, the people's chiefs
Were wont to gather round our father's hearth,
To read the old imperial charters, and
To hold sage converse on the country's weal.
Then heedfully I listened, marking well

What or the wise man thought, or good man
   wished
And garner'd up their wisdom in my heart.
Hear, then, and mark me well; for thou wilt
   see,
I long have known the grief that weighs thee
   down.
The Viceroy hates thee, fain would injure thee,
For thou hast cross'd his wish to bend the
   Swiss
In homage to this upstart house of princes,
And kept them staunch, like their good sires
   of old,
In true allegiance to the Empire.   Say,
Is't not so, Werner? Tell me, am I wrong?
   STAUF.   'Tis even so. For this doth Gessler
   hate me.
   GERT.   He burns with envy, too, to see
   thee living
Happy and free on thine inheritance,
For he has none.   From the Emperor himself
Thou hold'st in fief the lands thy fathers left
   thee.
There's not a prince i'the Empire that can show
A better title to his heritage;
For thou hast over thee no lord but one.
And he the mightiest of all Christian kings.
Gessler, we know, is but a younger son,
His only wealth the knightly cloak he wears:
He therefore views an honest man's good
   fortune
With a malignant and a jealous eye.
Long has he sworn to compass thy destruction.
As yet thou art uninjured.   Wilt thou wait,
Till he may safely give his malice scope?
A wise man would anticipate the blow.
   STAUF.   What's to be done?
   GERT.   Now hear what I advise.
Thou knowest well, how here with us in
   Schwytz
All worthy men are groaning underneath
This Gessler's grasping, grinding tyranny.
Doubt not the men of Unterwald as well,
And Uri, too, are chafing like ourselves,
At this oppressive and heart-wearying yoke.
For there, across the lake, the Landenberg
Wields the same iron rule as Gessler here—
No fishing-boat comes over to our side,
But brings the tidings of some new encroach-
   ment,
Some outrage fresh, more grievous than the
   last.
Then it were well, that some of you—true
   men—
Men sound at heart, should secretly devise,
How best to shake this hateful thraldom off.

Well do I know; that God would not desert
   you,
But lend his favor to the righteous cause.
Hast thou no friend in Uri, say, to whom
Thou frankly may'st unbosom all thy thoughts?
   STAUF.   I know full many a gallant fellow
   there,
And nobles, too,—great men of high repute,
In whom I can repose unbounded trust.
                                                   [Rising.
Wife! what a storm of wild and perilous
   thoughts
Hast thou stirr'd up within my tranquil breast?
The darkest musings of my bosom thou
Hast dragg'd to light, and placed them full
   before me,
And what I scarce dared harbor e'en in
   thought,
Thou speakest plainly out, with fearless tongue.
But hast thou weigh'd well what thou urgest
   thus?
Discord will come, and the fierce clang of
   arms,
To scare this valley's long unbroken peace,
If we, a feeble shepherd race, shall dare
Him to the fight, that lords it o'er the world.
E'en now they only wait some fair pretext
For setting loose their savage warrior hordes,
To scourge and ravage this devoted land,
To lord it o'er us with the victor's rights,
And, 'neath the show of lawful chastisement,
Despoil us of our chartered liberties.
   GERT.   You, too, are men; can wield a
   battle axe
As well as they.   God ne'er deserts the brave.
   STAUF.   Oh, wife! a horrid, ruthless fiend
   is war,
That strikes at once the shepherd and his
   flock.
   GERT.   Whate'er great Heaven inflicts, we
   must endure;
No heart of noble temper brooks injustice.
   STAUF.   This house—thy pride—war, un-
   relenting war,
Will burn it down.
   GERT.   And did I think this heart
Enslaved and fettered to the things of earth,
With my own hand I'd hurl the kindling
   torch.
   STAUF.   Thou hast faith in human kind-
   ness, wife; but war
Spares not the tender infant in its cradle.
   GERT.   There is a friend to innocence in
   heaven!
Look forward, Werner—not behind you,
   now!

STAUF. We men may perish bravely, sword in hand;
But oh, what fate, my Gertrude, may be thine?
GERT. None are so weak, but one last choice is left.
A spring from yonder bridge, and I am free!
STAUF. *(Embracing her.)* Well may he fight for hearth and home, that clasps
A heart so rare as thine against his own!
What are the hosts of Emperors to him?
Gertrude, farewell! I will to Uri straight.
There lives my worthy comrade, Walter Fürst;
His thoughts and mine upon these times are one.
There, too, resides the noble Banneret

Of Attinghaus. High though of blood he be,
He loves the people, honors their old customs.
With both of these I will take counsel, how
To rid us bravely of our country's foe.
Farewell! and while I am away, bear thou
A watchful eye in management at home.
The pilgrim, journeying to the house of God,
And pious monk collecting for the cloister,
To these give liberally from purse and garner.
Stauffacher's house would not be hid. Right out
Upon the public way it stands, and offers
To all that pass an hospitable roof.
[*While they are retiring,* TELL *enters with* BAUMGARTEN.

57

TELL. Now, then, you have no further need of me.
Enter yon house. 'Tis Werner Stauffacher's,
A man that is a father to distress.
See, there he is, himself! Come, follow me.
[*They retire up. Scene changes.*

SCENE III.—*A common near Altdorf. On an eminence in the back-ground a Castle in progress of erection, and so far advanced that the outline of the whole may be distinguished. The back part is finished; men are working at the front. Scaffolding, on which the workmen are going up and down. A slater is seen upon the highest part of the roof. All is bustle and activity.*

TASKMASTER, MASON, WORKMEN *and* LABORERS.

TASK. (*With a stick, urging on the workmen.*)
Up, up! You've rested long enough. To work!
The stones here! Now the mortar, and the lime!
And let his lordship see the work advanced,
When next he comes. These fellows crawl like snails! [*To two laborers, with loads.*
What! call ye that a load? Go, double it.
Is this the way ye earn your wages, laggards?
FIRST W. 'Tis very hard that we must bear the stones,
To make a keep and dungeon for ourselves!
TASK. What's that you mutter? 'Tis a worthless race,
And fit for nothing but to milk their cows,
And saunter idly up and down the mountains.
OLD MAN. (*Sinks down exhausted.*)
I can no more.
TASK. (*Shaking him.*)
          Up, up, old man, to work!
FIRST W. Have you no bowels of compassion, thus
To press so hard upon a poor old man,
That can scarce drag his feeble limbs along?
MAS. M. *and* WORK. Shame, shame upon you—shame! It cries to heaven!
TASK. Mind your own business. I but do my duty.
FIRST W. Pray, master, what's to be the name of this
Same castle, when 'tis built?
TASK.   The Keep of Uri;
For by it we shall keep you in subjection.

WORK. The Keep of Uri?
TASK.   Well, why laugh at that?
SECOND W. So you'll keep Uri with this paltry place!
FIRST W. How many molehills such as that must first
Be piled above each other, ere you make
A mountain equal to the least in Uri?
[TASKMASTER *retires up the stage.*
MAS. M. I'll drown the mallet in the deepest lake,
That served my hand on this accursed pile.
[*Enter* TELL *and* STAUFFACHER.
STAUF. O, that I had not lived to see this sight!
TELL. Here 'tis not good to be. Let us proceed.
STAUF. Am I in Uri, in the land of freedom?
MAS. M. O, sir, if you could only see the vaults
Beneath these towers. The man that tenants them
Will never hear the cock crow more.
STAUF.   O God!
MASON. Look at these ramparts and these buttresses,
That seem as they were built to last for ever.
TELL. Hands can destroy whatever hands have rear'd. [*Pointing to the mountains.*
That house of freedom God hath built for us.
[*A drum is heard. People enter bearing a cap upon a pole, followed by a Crier. Women and children thronging tumultuously after them.*
FIRST W. What means the drum? Give heed!
MASON. Why, here's a mumming!
And look, the cap—what can they mean by that?
CRIER. In the Emperor's name, give ear!
WORK.   Hush! silence! hush!
CRIER. Ye men of Uri, ye do see this cap!
It will be set upon a lofty pole
In Altdorf, in the market place: and this
Is the Lord Governor's good will and pleasure,
The cap shall have like honor as himself,
And all shall reverence it with bended knee,
And head uncovered; thus the king will know
Who are his true and loyal subjects here;
His life and goods are forfeit to the crown,
That shall refuse obedience to the order.
[*The people burst out into laughter. The drum beats, and the procession passes on.*
FIRST W. A strange device to fall upon, indeed!

58

Do reverence to a cap! A pretty farce!
Heard ever mortal anything like this?

MAS. M. Down to a cap on bended knee,
forsooth!

Rare jesting this with men of sober sense!

FIRST W. Nay, were it but the imperial
crown, indeed!

But 'tis the cap of Austria! I've seen it
Hanging above the throne in Gessler's hall.

MASON. The cap of Austria? Mark that!
A snare
To get us into Austria's power, by Heaven!

WORK. No freeborn man will stoop to such
disgrace.

MAS. M. Come—to our comrades, and advise with them! [*They retire up.*

TELL. (*To* STAUFFACHER.)
You see how matters stand. Farewell, my
friend!

STAUF. Whither away? Oh, leave us not
so soon.

TELL. They look for me at home. So fare
ye well.

STAUF. My heart's so full, and has so much
to tell you.

TELL. Words will not make a heart that's
heavy light.

STAUF. Yet words may possibly conduct to
deeds.

TELL. All we can do is to endure in silence.

STAUF. But shall we bear what is not to be
borne?

TELL. Impetuous rulers have the shortest
reigns.
When the fierce south wind rises from his
chasms,
Men cover up their fires, the ships in haste
Make for the harbour, and the mighty spirit
Sweeps o'er the earth, and leaves no trace be-
hind.
Let every man live quietly at home;
Peace to the peaceful rarely is denied.

STAUF. And is it thus you view our grievances?

TELL. The serpent stings not, till it is pro-
voked.
Let them alone; they'll weary of themselves,
Whene'er they see we are not to be roused.

STAUF. Much might be done—did we stand
fast together.

TELL. When the ship founders, he will best
escape,
Who seeks no other's safety but his own.

STAUF. And you desert the common cause
so coldly?

TELL. A man can safely count but on himself!

STAUF. Nay, even the weak grow strong
by union.

TELL. But the strong man is strongest when
alone.

STAUF. Your country, then, cannot rely
on you,
If in despair she rise against her foes?

TELL. Tell rescues the lost sheep from
yawning gulfs.
Is he a man, then, to desert his friends?
Yet, whatsoe'er you do, spare me from council!
I was not born to ponder and select;
But when your course of action is resolved,
Then call on Tell; you shall not find him fail.

[*Exeunt severally. A sudden tumult is heard
around the scaffolding.*

MASON. (*Running in.*) What's wrong?

FIRST W. (*Running forward.*)
The slater's fallen from the roof.

BERTHA (*Rushing in.*)
Is he dashed to pieces? Run—save him, help!
If help be possible, save him! Here is gold.

[*Throws her trinkets among the people.*

MASON. Hence with your gold,—your uni-
versal charm,
And remedy for ill! When you have torn
Fathers from children, husbands from their
wives,
And scattered woe and wail throughout the
land,
You think with gold to compensate for all.
Hence! Till we saw you, we were happy men;
With you came misery and dark despair.

BER. (*To the* TASKMASTER, *who has re-
turned.*)
Lives he? [TASKMASTER *shakes his head.*
Ill-fated towers, with curses built,
And doomed with curses to be tenanted!

[*Exit.*

———

SCENE IV.—*The House of* WALTER FÜRST.

WALTER FÜRST *and* ARNOLD VON MELCHTHAL
enter simultaneously at different sides.

MELCH. Good Walter Fürst.

FÜRST. If we should be surprised!
Stay where you are. We are beset with spies.

MELCH. Have you no news for me from
Unterwald?
What of my father? 'Tis not to be borne,
Thus to be pent up like a felon here!

59

What have I done of such a heinous stamp,
To skulk and hide me like a murderer?
I only laid my staff across the fingers
Of the pert varlet, when before my eyes,
By order of the governor, he tried
To drive away my handsome team of oxen.
FÜRST. You are too rash by far. He did
no more
Than what the governor had ordered him.
You had transgress'd, and therefore should
have paid
The penalty, however hard, in silence.
MELCH. Was I to brook the fellow's saucy
words?
"That if the peasant must have bread to eat,
Why, let him go and draw the plough him-
self!"
It cut me to the very soul to see
My oxen, noble creatures, when the knave
Unyoked them from the plough. As though
they felt
The wrong, they lowed and butted with their
horns.
On this I could contain myself no longer,
And, overcome by passion, struck him down.
FÜRST. O, we old men can scarce command
ourselves!
And can we wonder youth should break its
bounds?
MELCH. I'm only sorry for my father's
sake!
To be away from him, that needs so much
My fostering care! The governor detests him,
Because he hath, whene'er occasion served,
Stood stoutly up for right and liberty.
Therefore they'll bear him hard—the poor old
man!
And there is none to shield him from their
gripe.
Come what come may, I must go home again.
FÜRST. Compose yourself, and wait in pa-
tience till
We get some tidings o'er from Unterwald.
Away! away! I hear a knock! Perhaps
A message from the Viceroy! Get thee in!
You are not safe from Landenberger's arm
In Uri, for these tyrants pull together.
MELCH. They teach us Switzers what *we*
ought to do.
FÜRST. Away! I'll call you when the coast
is clear.   [MELCHTHAL *retires.*
Unhappy youth! I dare not tell him all
The evil that my boding heart predicts!
Who's there? The door ne'er opens, but I
look
For tidings of mishap. Suspicion lurks

With darkling treachery in every nook.
Even to our inmost rooms they force their
way,
These myrmidons of power; and soon we'll
need
To fasten bolts and bars upon our doors.
[*He opens the door, and steps back in sur-
prise as* WERNER STAUFFACHER *enters.*
What do I see? You, Werner? Now, by
Heaven!
A valued guest, indeed. No man e'er set
His foot across this threshold, more esteem'd.
Welcome! thrice welcome, Werner, to my
roof!
What brings you here? What seek you here
in Uri?
STAUF. (*Shakes* FÜRST *by the hand.*)
The olden times and olden Switzerland.
FÜRST. You bring them with you. See how
I'm rejoiced,
My heart leaps at the very sight of you.
Sit down—sit down, and tell me how you left
Your charming wife, fair Gertrude? Iberg's
child,
And clever as her father. Not a man,
That wends from Germany, by Meinrad's Cell,
To Italy, but praises far and wide
Your house's hospitality. But say,
Have you come here direct from Flüelen,
And have you noticed nothing on your way,
Before you halted at my door?
STAUF. (*Sits down.*)   I saw
A work in progress, as I came along.
I little thought to see—that likes me ill.
FÜRST. O friend! you've lighted on my
thought at once.
STAUF. Such things in Uri ne'er were
known before.
Never was prison here in man's remembrance,
Nor ever any stronghold but the grave.
FÜRST. You name it well. It is the grave
of freedom.
STAUF. Friend, Walter Fürst, I will be
plain with you.
No idle curiosity it is
That brings me here, but heavy cares. I left
Thraldom at home, and thraldom meets me
here.
Our wrongs e'en now, are more than we can
bear,
And who shall tell us where they are to end?
From eldest time the Switzer has been free,
Accustom'd only to the mildest rule.
Such things as now we suffer, ne'er were
known,
Since herdsman first drove cattle to the hills.

FÜRST. Yes, our oppressions are unparal-
lel'd!
Why even our own good lord of Attinghaus,
Who lived in olden times, himself declares,
They are no longer to be tamely borne.
STAUF. In Unterwalden yonder 'tis the
same;
And bloody has the retribution been.
The imperial Seneschal, the Wolfshot, who
At Rossberg dwelt, long'd for forbidden fruit
—Baumgarten's wife, that lives at Alzellen,
He wished to overcome in shameful sort,
On which the husband slew him with his axe.
FÜRST. Oh, Heaven is just in all its judg-
ments still!
Baumgarten, say you? A most worthy man.
Has he escaped, and is he safely hid?
STAUF. Your son-in-law conveyed him o'er
the lake,
And he lies hidden in my house at Steinen,
He brought the tidings with him of a thing
That has been done at Sarnen, worse than all,
A thing to make the very heart run blood!
FÜRST. (Attentively.) Say on; what is it?
STAUF. There dwells in Melchthal, then,
Just as you enter by the road from Kerns,
An upright man, named Henry of the Halden,
A man of weight and influence in the Diet.
FÜRST. Who knows him not? But what
of him? Proceed.
STAUF. The Landenberg, to punish some
offence,
Committed by the old man's son, it seems,
Had given command to take the youth's best
pair
Of oxen from his plough; on which the lad
Struck down the messenger and took to flight.
FÜRST. But the old father—tell me, what
of him?
STAUF. The Landenberg sent for him, and
required
He should produce his son upon the spot;
And when th' old man protested, and with
truth,
That he knew nothing of the fugitive,
The tyrant call'd his torturers.
FÜRST. (Springs up and tries to lead him to
the other side.) Hush, no more!
STAUF. (With increasing warmth.)
"And tho' thy son," he cried, "has 'scaped
me now,
I have thee fast, and thou shalt feel my ven-
geance."
With that they flung the old man to the earth,
And plunged the pointed steel into his eyes.
FÜRST. Merciful Heaven!

MELCH. (Rushing out.) Into his eyes, his
eyes?
STAUF. (Addressing himself in astonishment
to WALTER FÜRST.) Who is this youth?
MELCH. (Grasping him convulsively.)
Into his eyes? Speak, speak!
FÜRST. Oh, miserable hour!
STAUF. Who is it, tell me?
[STAUFFACHER makes a sign to him.
It is his son! All righteous Heaven!
MELCH. And I
Must be from thence! What! into both his
eyes?
FÜRST. Be calm, be calm; and bear it
like a man!
MELCH. And all for me—for my mad wil-
ful folly!
Blind, did you say? Quite blind—and both
his eyes?
STAUF. E'en so. The fountain of his
sight's dried up:
He ne'er will see the blessed sunshine more.
FÜRST. Oh, spare his anguish!
MELCH. Never, never more!
[Presses his hands upon his eyes and is silent
for some moments; then turning from one
to the other, speaks in a subdued tone,
broken by sobs.
O the eye's light, of all the gifts of Heaven,
The dearest, best! From light all beings live—
Each fair created thing—the very plants
Turn with a joyful transport to the light,
And he—he must drag on through all his days
In endless darkness! Never more for him
The sunny meads shall glow, the flow'rets
bloom;
Nor shall he more behold the roseate tints
Of the iced mountain top! To die is nothing,
But to have life, and not have sight,—oh, that
Is misery indeed! Why do you look
So piteously at me? I have two eyes,
Yet to my poor blind father can give neither!
No, not one gleam of that great sea of light,
That with its dazzling splendor floods my gaze.
STAUF. Ah, I must swell the measure of
your grief,
Instead of soothing it. The worst, alas!
Remains to tell. They've stripp'd him of his
all;
Nought have they left him, save his staff, on
which,
Blind, and in rags, he moves from door to
door.
MELCH. Nought but his staff to the old
eyeless man!
Stripp'd of his all—even of the light of day,

The common blessing of the meanest wretch.
Tell me no more of patience, of concealment!
Oh, what a base and coward thing am I,
That on mine own security I thought,
And took no care of thine! Thy precious head
Left as a pledge within the tyrant's grasp!
Hence, craven-hearted prudence, hence! And
    all
My thoughts be vengeance, and the despot's
    blood!
I'll seek him straight—no power shall stay me
    now—
And at his hands demand my father's eyes.
I'll beard him 'mid a thousand myrmidons!
What's life to me, if in his heart's best blood
I cool the fever of this mighty anguish.
                            [*He is going.*
FÜRST. Stay, this is madness, Melchthal!
    What avails
Your single arm against his power? He sits
At Sarnen high within his lordly keep,
And, safe within its battlemented walls,
May laugh to scorn your unavailing rage.
    MELCH. And though he sat within the icy
        domes
Of yon far Schreckhorn—ay, or higher, where
Veil'd since eternity, the Jungfrau soars,
Still to the tyrant would I make my way;
With twenty comrades minded like myself,
I'd lay his fastness level with the earth!
And if none follow me, and if you all,
In terror for your homesteads and your herds,
Bow in submission to the tyrant's yoke,
I'll call the herdsmen on the hills around me,
And there beneath heaven's free and boundless
    roof,
Where men still feel as men, and hearts are
    true,
Proclaim aloud this foul enormity!
    STAUF. (*To* FÜRST.)
'Tis at its height—and are we then to wait
Till some extremity——
    MELCH.   What extremity
Remains for apprehension, when men's eyes
Have ceased to be secure within their sockets?
Are we defenceless? Wherefore did we learn
To bend the cross-bow,—wield the battle-
    axe?
What living creature, but in its despair,
Finds for itself a weapon of defence?
The baited stag will turn, and with the show
Of his dread antlers hold the hounds at bay;
The chamois drags the huntsman down th'
    abyss;
The very ox, the partner of man's toil,
The sharer of his roof, that meekly bends

The strength of his huge neck beneath the
    yoke,
Springs up, if he's provoked, whets his strong
    horn,
And tosses his tormentor to the clouds.
    FÜRST. If the three Cantons thought as
        we three do,
Something might, then, be done, with good
    effect.
    STAUF. When Uri calls, when Unterwald
        replies,
Schwytz will be mindful of her ancient league.
    MELCH. I've many friends in Unterwald,
        and none
That would not gladly venture life and limb,
If fairly back'd and aided by the rest.
Oh, sage and reverend fathers of this land,
Here do I stand before your riper years,
An unskill'd youth, whose voice must in the
    Diet
Still be subdued into respectful silence.
Do not, because that I am young, and want
Experience, slight my counsel and my words.
'Tis not the wantonness of youthful blood
That fires my spirit; but a pang so deep
That e'en the flinty rocks must pity me.
You, too, are fathers, heads of families,
And you must wish to have a virtuous son,
To reverence your gray hairs, and shield your
    eyes
With pious and affectionate regard.
Do not, I pray, because in limb and fortune
You still are unassail'd, and still your eyes
Revolve undimm'd and sparkling in their
    spheres;
Oh, do not, therefore, disregard our wrongs!
Above you, too, doth hang the tyrant's sword.
You, too, have striven to alienate the land
From Austria. This was all my father's crime:
You share his guilt, and may his punishment.
    STAUF. (*To* FÜRST.)
Do thou resolve! I am prepared to follow.
    FÜRST. First let us learn, what steps the
        noble lords
Von Sillinen and Attinghaus propose.
Their names would rally thousands in the
    cause.
    MELCH. Is there a name within the Forest
        Mountains
That carries more respect than thine — and
    thine?
To names like these the people cling for help
With confidence—such names are household
    words.
Rich was your heritage of manly virtue,
And richly have you added to its stores.

What need of nobles? Let us do the work
Ourselves.   Although we stood alone, me-
    thinks,
We should be able to maintain our rights.
    STAUF.   The nobles' wrongs are not so great
        as ours.
The torrent, that lays waste the lower grounds,
Hath not ascended to the uplands yet.
But let them see the country once in arms,
They'll not refuse to lend a helping hand
    FÜRST.   Were there an umpire 'twixt our-
        selves and Austria,
Justice and law might then decide our quarrel.
But our oppressor is our Emperor, too,
And judge supreme.   'Tis God must help us,
    then,

And our own arm!   Be yours the task to rouse
The men of Schwytz; I'll rally friends in Uri.
But whom are we to send to Unterwald?
    MELCH.   Thither send me.   Whom should
        it more concern?
    FÜRST.   No, Melchthal, no; thou art my
        guest, and I
Must answer for thy safety.
    MELCH.   Let me go,
I know each forest track and mountain pass;
Friends too I'll find, be sure, on every hand,
To give me willing shelter from the foe.
    STAUF.   Nay, let him go; no traitors har-
        bor there:
For tyranny is so abhorred in Unterwald,
No minions can be found to work her will.

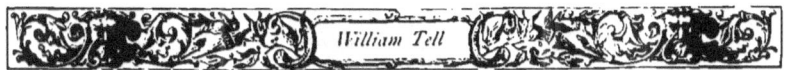

In the low valleys, too, the Alzeller
Will gain confederates, and rouse the country.
MELCH. But how shall we communicate,
and not
Awaken the suspicion of the tyrants?
STAUF. Might we not meet at Brunnen or
at Treib,
Hard by the spot where merchant vessels
land?
FÜRST. We must not go so openly to work.
Hear my opinion. On the lake's left bank,
As we sail hence to Brunnen, right against
The Mytenstein, deep-hidden in the wood
A meadow lies, by shepherds called the
Rootli,
Because the wood has been uprooted there.
'Tis where our Canton bound'ries verge on
yours;— [*To* MELCHTHAL.
Your boat will carry you across from Schwytz.
[*To* STAUFFACHER.
Thither by lonely by-paths let us wend
At midnight, and deliberate o'er our plans.
Let each bring with him there ten trusty men,
All one at heart with us; and then we may

Consult together for the general weal,
And, with God's guidance, fix our onward
course.
STAUF. So let it be. And now your true
right hand!
Yours, too, young man! and as we now three
men
Among ourselves thus knit our hands together
In all sincerity and truth, e'en so
Shall we three Cantons, too, together stand
In victory and defeat, in life and death.
FÜRST *and* MELCH. In life and death.
[*They hold their hands clasped together for
some moments in silence.*
MELCH. Alas, my old blind father!
Thou canst no more behold the day of free-
dom;
But thou shalt hear it. When from Alp to Alp
The beacon fires throw up their flaming signs,
And the proud castles of the tyrants fall,
Into thy cottage shall the Switzer burst,
Bear the glad tidings to thine ear, and o'er
Thy darken'd way shall Freedom's radiance
pour.

ACT II.

SCENE I.—*The Mansion of the* BARON OF
ATTINGHAUSEN. *A Gothic Hall, decorated
with escutcheons and helmets. The* BARON, *a
gray-headed man, eighty-five years old, tall
and of a commanding mien, clad in a furred
pelisse, and leaning on a staff tipped with
chamois horn.* KUONI *and six hinds standing round him with rakes and scythes.*

ULRICH OF RUDENZ *enters in the costume of
a Knight.*

RUD. Uncle, I'm here! Your will?
ATT. First let me share,
After the ancient custom of our house,
The morning cup, with these my faithful ser-
vants!
[*He drinks from a cup, which is then passed
round.*
Time was, I stood myself in field and wood,
With mine own eyes directing all their toil,
Even as my banner led them in the fight,
Now I am only fit to play the steward;

And, if the genial sun come not to me,
I can no longer seek it on the mountains.
Thus slowly, in an ever narrowing sphere,
I move on to the narrowest and the last,
Where all life's pulses cease. I now am but
The shadow of my former self, and that
Is fading fast—'twill soon be but a name.

KUO. (*Offering* RUDENZ *the cup.*)
A pledge, young master!
[RUDENZ *hesitates to take the cup.*
Nay, Sir, drink it off!
One cup, one heart! You know our proverb,
Sir?

ATT. Go, children, and at eve, when work
is done,
We'll meet and talk the country's business
over. [*Exeunt servants.*
Belted and plumed, and all thy bravery on!
Thou art for Altdorf—for the castle, boy?

RUD. Yes, uncle. Longer may I not delay—

65

ATT. *(Sitting down.)* Why in such haste?
Say, are thy youthful hours
Doled in such niggard measure, that thou must
Be chary of them to thy aged uncle?
RUD. I see, my presence is not needed
here,
I am but as a stranger in this house.
ATT. *(Gazes fixedly at him for a consider-
able time.)*
Alas, thou art indeed! Alas, that home
To thee has grown so strange! Oh, Uly!
Uly!
I scarce do know thee now, thus deck'd in
silks,
The peacock's feather flaunting in thy cap,
And purple mantle round thy shoulders flung;
Thou look'st upon the peasant with disdain,
And takest with a blush his honest greeting.
RUD. All honor due to him I gladly pay,
But must deny the right he would usurp.
ATT. The sore displeasure of the king is
resting
Upon the land, and every true man's heart
Is full of sadness for the grievous wrongs
We suffer from our tyrants. Thou alone
Art all unmoved amid the general grief
Abandoning thy friends, thou tak'st thy stand
Beside thy country's foes, and, as in scorn
Of our distress, pursuest giddy joys,
Courting the smiles of princes, all the while
Thy country bleeds beneath their cruel scourge.
RUD. The land is sore oppress'd, I know
it, uncle.
But why? Who plunged it into this distress?
A word, one little easy word, might buy
Instant deliverance from such dire oppression,
And win the good will of the Emperor.
Woe unto those, who seal the people's eyes,
And make them adverse to their country's
good—
The men, who, for their own vile selfish ends,
Are seeking to prevent the Forest States
From swearing fealty to Austria's House,
As all the countries round about have done.
It fits their humor well, to take their seats
Amid the nobles on the Herrenbank;
They'll have the Cæsar for their lord, for-
sooth,—
That is to say, they'll have no lord at all.
ATT. Must I hear this, and from thy lips,
rash boy!
RUD. You urged me to this answer. Hear
me out.
What, uncle, is the character you've stoop'd
To fill contentedly through life? Have you
No higher pride, than in these lonely wilds

To be the Landamman or Banneret,
The petty chieftain of a shepherd race?
How! Were it not a far more glorious choice,
To bend in homage to our royal lord,
And swell the princely splendors of his court,
Than sit at home, the peer of your own vassals,
And share the judgment-seat with vulgar
clowns?
ATT. Ah, Uly, Uly; all too well I see,
The tempter's voice has caught thy willing
ear,
And pour'd its subtle poison in thy heart.
RUD. Yes, I conceal it not. It doth offend
My inmost soul, to hear the stranger's gibes,
That taunt us with the name of "Peasant No-
bles!"
Think you the heart that's stirring here can
brook,
While all the young nobility around
Are reaping honor under Hapsburg's banner,
That I should loiter, in inglorious ease,
Here on the heritage my fathers left,
And, in the dull routine of vulgar toil,
Lose all life's glorious spring? In other lands
Deeds are achieved. A world of fair renown
Beyond these mountains stirs in martial pomp.
My helm and shield are rusting in the hall;
The martial trumpet's spirit-stirring blast,
The herald's call, inviting to the lists,
Rouse not the echoes of these vales, where
nought,
Save cowherd's horn and cattle bell, is heard,
In one unvarying dull monotony.
ATT. Deluded boy, seduced by empty
show!
Despise the land that gave thee birth! Ashamed
Of the good ancient customs of thy sires!
The day will come, when thou, with burning
tears,
Wilt long for home, and for thy native hills,
And that dear melody of tuneful herds,
Which now, in proud disgust, thou dost de-
spise!
A day when thou wilt drink its tones in
sadness,
Hearing their music in a foreign land.
Oh! potent is the spell that binds to home!
No, no, the cold, false world is not for thee.
At the proud court, with thy true heart, thou
wilt
For ever feel a stranger among strangers.
The world asks virtues of far other stamp
Than thou hast learned within these simple
vales.
But go—go thither,—barter thy free soul,
Take land in fief, become a prince's vassal,

Where thou might'st be lord paramount, and
   prince
Of all thine own unburden'd heritage!
Oh, Uly, Uly, stay among thy people!
Go not to Altdorf. Oh, abandon not
The sacred cause of thy wrong'd native land!
I am the last of all my race. My name
Ends with me. Yonder hang my helm and
   shield;
They will be buried with me in the grave.
And must I think, when yielding up my breath,
That thou but wait'st the closing of mine eyes,
To stoop thy knee to this new feudal court,
And take in vassalage from Austria's hands
The noble lands, which I from God received,
Free and unfetter'd as the mountain air!
   RUD.   'Tis vain for us to strive against the
   king.
The world pertains to him:—shall we alone,
In mad presumptuous obstinacy, strive
To break that mighty chain of lands, which he
Hath drawn around us with his giant grasp.
His are the markets, his the courts,—his too
The highways: nay, the very carrier's horse,
That traffics on the Gotthardt, pays him toll.
By his dominions, as within a net,
We are enclosed, and girded round about.
—And will the Empire shield us? Say, can it
Protect itself 'gainst Austria's growing power?
To God, and not to emperors must we look!
What store can on their promises be placed,
When they, to meet their own necessities,
Can pawn, and even alienate the towns
That flee for shelter 'neath the Eagle's wings?
No, uncle! It is wise and wholesome prudence?
In times like these, when faction's all abroad,
To own attachment to some mighty chief.
The imperial crown's transferred from line to
   line.
It has no memory for faithful service:
But to secure the favor of these great
Hereditary masters, were to sow
Seed for a future harvest.
   ATT.   Art so wise?
Wilt thou see clearer than thy noble sires,
Who battled for fair freedom's costly gem,
With life, and fortune, and heroic arm?
Sail down the lake to Lucerne, there inquire,
How Austria's rule doth weigh the Cantons
   down.
Soon she will come to count our sheep, our
   cattle,
To portion out the Alps, e'en to their summits,
And in our own free woods to hinder us
From striking down the eagle or the stag;
To set her tolls on every bridge and gate,

Impoverish us, to swell her lust of sway,
And drain our dearest blood to feed her wars.
No, if our blood must flow, let it be shed
In our own cause! We purchase liberty
More cheaply far than bondage.
   RUD.   What can we,
A shepherd race, against great Albert's hosts?
   ATT. Learn, foolish boy, to know this shep-
   herd race!
I know them, I have led them on in fight,—
I saw them in the battle at Favenz.
Austria will try, forsooth, to force on us
A yoke we are determined not to bear!
Oh, learn to feel from what a race thou'rt
   sprung!
Cast not, for tinsel trash and idle show,
The precious jewel of thy worth away.
To be the chieftain of a free born race,
Bound to thee only by their unbought love,
Ready to stand—to fight—to die with thee,
Be that thy pride, be that thy noblest boast!
Knit to thy heart the ties of kindred—home—
Cling to the land, the dear land of thy sires,
Grapple to that with thy whole heart and soul!
Thy power is rooted deep and strongly here,
But in yon stranger world thou'lt stand alone,
A trembling reed beat down by every blast.
Oh, come! 'tis long since we have seen thee,
   Uly!
Tarry but this one day. Only to-day
Go not to Altdorf. Wilt thou? Not to-day!
For this one day, bestow thee on thy friends
                        [*Takes his hand.*
   RUD. I gave my word. Unhand me! I
   am bound.
   ATT. (*Drops his hand and says sternly.*)
Bound, didst thou say? Oh, yes, unhappy boy,
Thou art indeed. But not by word or oath.
'Tis by the silken mesh of love thou'rt bound.
                        [RUDENZ *turns away.*
Ay, hide thee, as thou wilt. 'Tis she, I know,
Bertha of Bruneck, draws thee to the court;
'Tis she that chains thee to the Emperor's ser-
   vice,
Thou think'st to win the noble knightly maid
By thy apostacy. Be not deceived.
She is held out before thee as a lure;
But never meant for innocence like thine.
   RUD. No more, I've heard enough. So
   fare you well.   [*Exit.*
   ATT. Stay, Uly! Stay! Rash boy, he's
   gone! I can
Nor hold him back, nor save him from destruc-
   tion.
And so the Wolfshot has deserted us;—
Others will follow his example soon.

This foreign witchery, sweeping o'er our hills,
Tears with its potent spell our youth away!
O, luckless hour! when men and manners
    strange
Into these calm and happy valleys came,
To warp our primitive and guileless ways.
The new is pressing on with might. The old,
The good, the simple, fleeteth fast away.
New times come on. A race is springing up,
That think not as their fathers thought be-
    fore!
What do I here? All, all are in the grave
With whom erewhile I moved, and held con-
    verse;
My age has long been laid beneath the sod:
Happy the man, who may not live to see
What shall be done by those that follow me!

——

SCENE II.—*A meadow surrounded by high
rocks and wooded ground. On the rocks are
tracks, with rails and ladders, by which the
peasants are afterwards seen descending. In
the back-ground the lake is observed, and over
it a moon rainbow in the early part of the
scene. The prospect is closed by lofty mountains, with glaciers rising behind them. The
stage is dark; but the lake and glaciers glisten
in the moonlight.*

MELCHTHAL, BAUMGARTEN, WINKELRIED,
MEYER VON SARNEN, BURKHART AM BUHEL,
ARNOLD VON SEWA, KLAUS VON DER FLUE,
and four other peasants, all armed.

MELCH. *(Behind the scenes.)*
The mountain pass is open. Follow me!
I see the rock, and little cross upon it:
This is the spot; here is the Rootli.
                [*They enter with torches.*
WIN.   Hark!
SEWA.   The coast is clear.
MEYER.   None of our comrades come?
We are the first, the Unterwaldeners.
MELCH.   How far is't i' the night?
BAUM.   The beacon watch
Upon the Selisberg has just called two.
                [*A bell is heard at a distance.*
MEYER.   Hush! Hark!
BUHEL.   The forest chapel's matin bell
Chimes clearly o'er the lake from Switzerland.
FLUE.   The air is clear, and bears the sound
so far.

MELCH.   Go, you and you, and light some
    broken boughs,
Let's bid them welcome with a cheerful blaze.
                [*Two peasants exeunt.*
SEWA.   The moon shines fair to-night.
    Beneath its beams
The lake reposes, bright as burnish'd steel
BUHEL.   They'll have an easy passage.
WIN. *(Pointing to the lake.)*
                            Ha! look there!
See you nothing?
MEYER.   What is it? Ay, indeed!
A rainbow in the middle of the night.
MELCH.   Formed by the bright reflection
    of the moon!
FLUE.   A sign most strange and wonderful,
    indeed!
Many there be, who ne'er have seen the like.
SEWA.   'Tis doubled, see, a paler one above!
BAUM.   A boat is gliding yonder right be-
    neath it.
MELCH.   That must be Werner Stauffacher!
    I knew
The worthy patriot would not tarry long.
            [*Goes with* BAUMGARTEN *towards the shore.*
MEYER.   The Uri men are like to be the last.
BUEL.   They're forced to take a winding
    circuit through
The mountains; for the Viceroy's spies are out.
            [*In the meanwhile the two peasants have
            kindled a fire in the centre of the stage.*
MELCH. *(On the shore.)*
Who's there? The word?
STAUF. *(From below.)*
                    Friends of the country.
    [*All retire up the stage, towards the party
    landing from the boat. Enter* STAUFFA-
    CHER, ITEL REDING, HANS AUF DER
    MAUER, JORG IM HOFE, CONRAD HUNN,
    ULRICH DER SCHMIDT, JOST VON WEILER,
    and three other peasants, armed.
ALL.   Welcome!
    [*While the rest remain behind exchanging
    greetings,* MELCHTHAL *comes forward with*
    STAUFFACHER.
MELCH.   Oh, worthy Stauffacher, I've look'd
    but now
On him, who could not look on me again.
I've laid my hands upon his rayless eyes,
And on their vacant orbits sworn a vow
Of vengeance, only to be cool'd in blood.
STAUF.   Speak not of vengeance. We are
    here, to meet
The threatened evil, not to avenge the past.
Now tell me what you've done, and what
    secured,

ARTIST: A. BAUR.

WILLIAM TELL.

ACT II, SCENE II.

To aid the common cause in Unterwald,
How stand the peasantry disposed, and how
Yourself escaped the wiles of treachery?
    MELCH.   Through the Surenen's fearful
    mountain chain,
Where dreary ice-fields stretch on every side,
And sound is none, save the hoarse vulture's
    cry,
I reach'd the Alpine pasture, where the herds
From Uri and from Engelberg resort,
And turn their cattle forth to graze in comnion.
Still as I went along, I slaked my thirst
With the coarse oozings of the lofty glacier,
That thro' the crevices come foaming down,
And turned to rest me in the herdsmen's cots,

Where I was host and guest, until I gain'd
The cheerful homes and social haunts of men.
Already through these distant vales had spread
The rumor of this last atrocity;
And wheresoe'er I went, at every door,
Kind words and gentle looks were there to
    greet me.
I found these simple spirits all in arms
Against our rulers' tyrannous encroachments.
For as their Alps through each succeeding year
Yield the same roots,—their streams flow ever
    on
In the same channels,—nay, the clouds and
    winds
The selfsame course unalterably pursue,

So have old customs there, from sire to son,
Been handed down, unchanging and un-
changed;
Nor will they brook to swerve or turn aside
From the fixed even tenor of their life.
With grasp of their hard hands they welcomed
me,—
Took from the walls their rusty falchion's
down,—
And from their eyes the soul of valor flash'd
With joyful lustre, as I spoke those names,
Sacred to every peasant in the mountains,
Your own and Walter Fürst's. Whate'er your
voice
Should dictate as the right, they swore to do;
And you they swore to follow e'en to death.
—So sped I on from house to house, secure
In the guest's sacred privilege;—and when
I reached at last the valley of my home,
Where dwell my kinsmen, scatter'd far and
near—
And when I found my father, stript and blind,
Upon the stranger's straw, fed by the alms
Of charity——
   STAUF.   Great Heaven!
   MELCH.   Yet wept I not!
No—not in weak and unavailing tears
Spent I the force of my fierce burning an-
guish;
Deep in my bosom, like some precious treasure,
I lock'd it fast, and thought on deeds alone.
Through every winding of the hills I crept,—
No valley so remote but I explored it;
Nay, even at the glacier's ice-clad base,
I sought and found the homes of living men;
And still, where'er my wandering footsteps
turn'd,
The selfsame hatred of these tyrants met me.
For even there, at vegetation's verge,
Where the numb'd earth is barren of all fruits,
Their grasping hands had been stretch'd forth
for plunder.
Into the hearts of all this honest race,
The story of my wrongs struck deep, and now
They, to a man, are ours; both heart and hand.
   STAUF. Great things, indeed, you've wrought
in little time.
   MELCH. I did still more than this. The
fortresses,
Rossberg and Sarnen, are the country's dread;
For from behind their rocky walls the foe
Swoops, as the eagle from his eyrie, down,
And, safe himself, spreads havoc o'er the land.
With my own eyes I wish'd to weigh its
strength,
So went to Sarnen, and explored the castle.

   STAUF. How! Risk thyself e'en in the
tiger's den?
   MELCH. Disguised in pilgrim's weeds I
entered it;
I saw the Viceroy feasting at his board—
Judge if I'm master of myself or no!
I saw the tyrant, and I slew him not!
   STAUF. Fortune, indeed, has smiled upon
your boldness.
   [*Meanwhile the others have arrived and
join* MELCHTHAL *and* STAUFFACHER.
Yet tell me now, I pray, who are the friends,
The worthy men, who came along with you?
Make me acquainted with them, that we may
Speak frankly, man to man, and heart to heart.
   MEYER. In the three Cantons, who, sir,
knows not you?
Meyer of Sarnen is my name; and this
Is Struth of Winkelried, my sister's son.
   STAUF. No unknown name. A Winkelried
it was,
Who slew the dragon in the fen at Weiler,
And lost his life in the encounter, too.
   WIN. That, Master Stauffacher, was my
grandfather.
   MELCH. (*Pointing to two peasants.*)
These two are men belonging to the convent
Of Engelberg, and live behind the forest.
You'll not think ill of them because they're
serfs,
And sit not free upon the soil, like us.
They love the land, and bear a good repute.
   STAUF. (*To them.*) Give me your hands.
He has good cause for thanks,
That unto no man owes his body's service.
But worth is worth, no matter where 'tis found.
   HUNN. That is Herr Reding, sir, our old
Landamman.
   MEYER. I know him well. There is a
suit between us,
About a piece of ancient heritage.
Herr Reding, we are enemies in court,
Here we are one.   [*Shakes his hand.*
   STAUF. That's well and bravely said.
   WIN. Listen! They come. Hark to the
horn of Uri!
   [*On the right and left armed men are seen
descending the rocks with torches.*
   MAUER. Look, is not that God's pious
servant there?
A worthy priest! The terrors of the night,
And the way's pains and perils scare not him.
A faithful shepherd caring for his flock.
   BAUM. The Sacrist follows him, and Walter
Fürst.
But where is Tell? I do not see him there.

[WALTER FÜRST, RÖSSELMANN *the Pastor,*
PETERMANN *the Sacrist,* KUONI *the Shep-
herd,* WERNI *the Huntsman,* RUODI *the
Fisherman, and five other countrymen.
Thirty-three in all, advance and take their
places round the fire.*

FÜRST. Thus must we, on the soil our
fathers left us,
Creep forth by stealth to meet like murderers,
And in the night, that should her mantle lend
Only to crime and black conspiracy,
Assert our own good rights, which yet are clear
As is the radiance of the noonday sun.

MELCH. So be it. What is woven in gloom
of night
Shall free and boldly meet the morning light.

RÖSS. Confederates! listen to the words
which God
Inspires my heart withal. Here we are met,
To represent the general weal. In us
Are all the people of the land convened.
Then let us hold the Diet, as of old,
And as we're wont in peaceful times to do.
The time's necessity be our excuse,
If there be aught informal in this meeting.
Still, wheresoe'er men strike for justice, there
Is God, and now beneath his heav'n we stand.

STAUF. 'Tis well advised.—Let us, then,
hold the Diet,
According to our ancient usages.—
Though it be night, there's sunshine in our
cause.

MELCH. Few though our numbers be, the
hearts are here
Of the whole people; here the BEST are met.

HUNN. The ancient books may not be
near at hand,
Yet are they graven in our inmost hearts.

RÖSS. 'Tis well. And now, then, let a
ring be formed,
And plant the swords of power within the
ground.

MAUER. Let the Landamman step into his
place,
And by his side his secretaries stand.

PETER. There are three Cantons here.
Which hath the right
To give the head to the united Council?
Schwytz may contest that dignity with Uri,
We Unterwald'ners enter not the field.

MELCH. We stand aside. We are but
suppliants here,
Invoking aid from our more potent friends.

STAUF. Let Uri have the sword. Her
banner takes,
In battle, the precedence of our own.

FÜRST. Schwytz, then, must share the
honor of the sword;
For she's the honored ancestor of all.

RÖSS. Let me arrange this generous con-
troversy.
Uri shall lead in battle—Schwytz in Council.

FÜRST. *(Gives* STAUFFACHER *his hand.)*
Then take your place.

STAUF. Not I. Some older man.

HOFE. Ulrich, the Smith, is the most aged
here.

MAUER. A worthy man, but he is not a
freeman;
—No bondman can be judge in Switzerland.

STAUF. Is not Herr Reding here, our old
Landamman?
Where can we find a worthier man than he?

FÜRST. Let him be Amman and the Diet's
chief!
You that agree with me, hold up your hands!
[*All hold up their right hands.*

RED. *(Stepping into the centre.)*
I cannot lay my hands upon the books;
But by yon everlasting stars I swear,
Never to swerve from justice and the right.
[*The two swords are placed before him, and
a circle formed; Schwytz in the centre,
Uri on his right, Unterwald on his left.*

RED. *(Resting on his battle-sword.)*
Why, at the hour when spirits walk the earth,
Meet the three Cantons of the mountains here,
Upon the lake's inhospitable shore?
And what the purport of the new alliance
We here contract beneath the starry Heaven?

STAUF. *(Entering the circle.)*
No new alliance do we now contract,
But one our fathers framed, in ancient times,
We purpose to renew! For know, confederates,
Though mountain ridge and lake divide our
bounds
And every Canton's ruled by its own laws,
Yet are we but one race, born of one blood,
And all are children of one common home.

WIN. Then is the burden of our legends
true,
That we came hither from a distant land?
Oh, tell us what you know, that our new league
May reap fresh vigor from the leagues of old.

STAUF. Hear, then, what aged herdsmen
tell. There dwelt
A mighty people in the land that lies
Back to the north. The scourge of famine
came;
And in this strait 'twas publicly resolved,
That each tenth man, on whom the lot might
fall,

Should leave the country. They obey'd—and
forth,
With loud lamentings, men and women went,
A mighty host; and to the south moved on,
Cutting their way through Germany by the
sword,
Until they gained these pine-clad hills of ours;
Nor stopp'd they ever on their forward course,
Till at the shaggy dell they halted, where
The Müta flows through its luxuriant meads.
No trace of human creature met their eye,
Save one poor hut upon the desert shore,
Where dwelt a lonely man, and kept the ferry.
A tempest raged—the lake rose mountains high
And barr'd their further progress. Thereupon
They view'd the country—found it rich in
wood,
Discover'd goodly springs, and felt as they
Were in their own dear native land once more.
Then they resolved to settle on the spot;
Erected there the ancient town of Schwytz;
And many a day of toil had they to clear
The tangled brake and forest's spreading roots.
Meanwhile their numbers grew, the soil became
Unequal to sustain them, and they cross'd
To the black mountain, far as Weissland,
where,
Conceal'd behind eternal walls of ice,
Another people speak another tongue.
They built the village Stanz, beside the Kern-
wald;
The village Altdorf, in the vale of Reuss;
Yet, ever mindful of their parent stem,
The men of Schwytz, from all the stranger race,
That since that time have settled in the land,
Each other recognize. Their hearts still know,
And beat fraternally to kindred blood.
       [Extends his hand right and left.
Mauer. Ay, we are all one heart, one
blood, one race!
All. *(Joining hands.)*
We are one people, and will act as one.
Stauf. The nations round us bear a foreign
yoke;
For they have yielded to the conqueror.
Nay, e'en within our frontiers may be found
Some, that owe villein service to a lord,
A race of bonded serfs from sire to son.
But we, the genuine race of ancient Swiss,
Have kept our freedom from the first till now.
Never to princes have we bow'd the knee;
Freely we sought protection of the Empire.
Röss. Freely we sought it—freely it was
given.
'Tis so set down in Emperor Frederick's char-
ter.

Stauf. For the most free have still some
feudal lord,
There must be still a chief, a judge supreme,
To whom appeal may lie, in case of strife.
And therefore was it, that our sires allow'd,
For what they had recover'd from the waste,
This honor to the Emperor, the lord
Of all the German and Italian soil;
And, like the other free men of his realm,
Engaged to aid him with their swords in war;
And this alone should be the free man's duty,
To guard the Empire that keeps guard for
him.
Melch. He's but a slave that would ac-
knowledge more.
Stauf. They followed, when the Heribann
went forth,
The imperial standard, and they fought its
battles!
To Italy they march'd in arms, to place
The Cæsars' crown upon the Emperor's head.
But still at home they ruled themselves in
peace,
By their own laws and ancient usages.
The Emperor's only right was to adjudge
The penalty of death; he therefore named
Some mighty noble as his delegate,
That had no stake nor interest in the land.
He was call'd in when doom was to be pass'd,
And, in the face of day, pronounced decree,
Clear and distinctly, fearing no man's hate.
What traces here that we are bondsmen?
Speak,
If there be any can gainsay my words!
Hofe. No! you have spoken but the sim-
ple truth;
We never stoop'd beneath a tyrant's yoke.
Stauf. Even to the Emperor we refused
obedience,
When he gave judgment in the church's favor;
For when the Abbey of Einsiedlen claimed
The Alp our fathers and ourselves had grazed,
And showed an ancient charter, which be-
stowed
The land on them as being ownerless—
For our existence there had been concealed—
What was our answer? This: "The grant is
void,
No Emperor can bestow what is our own:
And if the Empire shall deny us justice,
We can, within our mountains, right our-
selves!"
Thus spake our fathers! And shall we endure
The shame and infamy of this new yoke,
And from the vassal brook what never king
Dared, in the fulness of his power, attempt?

This soil we have created for ourselves,
By the hard labor of our hands; we've changed
The giant forest, that was erst the haunt
Of savage bears, into a home for man;
Extirpated the dragon's brood, that wont
To rise, distent with venom, from the swamps;
Rent the thick misty canopy that hung
Its blighting vapors on the dreary waste;
Blasted the solid rock; o'er the abyss
Thrown the firm bridge for the wayfaring
man;
By the possession of a thousand years
The soil is ours. And shall an alien lord,
Himself a vassal, dare to venture here,
On our own hearths insult us,—and attempt
To forge the chains of bondage for our
hands,
And do us shame on our own proper soil?
Is there no help against such wrong as this?
[*Great sensation among the people.*
Yes! there's a limit to the despot's power!
When the oppress'd looks round in vain for
justice,
When his sore burden may no more be borne,
With fearless heart he makes appeal to Hea-
ven,
And thence brings down his everlasting rights,
Which there abide, inalienably his,
And indestructible as are the stars.
Nature's primæval state returns again,
Where man stands hostile to his fellow man;
And if all other means shall fail his need,
One last resource remains—his own good
sword.
Our dearest treasures call to us for aid,
Against the oppressor's violence; we stand
For country, home, for wives, for children
here!
ALL. (*Clashing their swords.*)
Here stand we for our homes, our wives, and
children.
RÖSS. (*Stepping into the circle.*)
Bethink ye well, before ye draw the sword.
Some peaceful compromise may yet be made;
Speak but one word, and at your feet you'll
see
The men who now oppress you. Take the
terms
That have been often tendered you; renounce
The Empire, and to Austria swear allegiance!
MAUER. What says the priest? To Austria
allegiance?
BUHEL. Hearken not to him!
WIN. 'Tis a traitor's counsel,
His country's foe!
RED. Peace, peace, confederates!

SER. Homage to Austria, after wrongs like
these!
FLUE. Shall Austria extort from us by
force,
What we denied to kindness and entreaty?
MEYER. Then should we all be slaves, de-
servedly.
MAUER. Yes! Let him forfeit all a Switzer's
rights,
Who talks of yielding to the yoke of Austria!
I stand on this, Landamman. Let this be
The foremost of our laws!
MELCH. Even so! Whoe'er
Shall talk of tamely bearing Austria's yoke,
Let him be stripp'd of all his rights and honors;
And no man hence receive him at his hearth!
ALL. (*Raising their right hands.*)
Agreed! Be this the law!
RED. (*After a pause.*) The law it is.
RÖSS. Now you are free—by this law you
are free.
Never shall Austria obtain by force
What she has fail'd to gain by friendly suit.
WEILER. On with the order of the day!
Proceed!
RED. Confederates! Have all gentler means
been tried?
Perchance the Emp'ror knows not of our
wrongs;
It may not be his will that thus we suffer:
Were it not well to make one last attempt,
And lay our grievances before the throne,
Ere we unsheath the sword? Force is at best
A fearful thing e'en in a righteous cause;
God only helps, when man can help no more.
STAUF. (*To* CONRAD HUNN.)
Here you can give us information. Speak!
HUNN. I was at Rheinfeld, at the Em-
peror's palace,
Deputed by the Cantons to complain
Of the oppressions of these governors,
And claim the charter of our ancient freedom,
Which each new king till now has ratified.
I found the envoys there of many a town,
From Suabia and the valley of the Rhine,
Who all received their parchments as they
wish'd,
And straight went home again with merry
heart.
They sent for me. your envoy, to the council,
Where I was soon dismiss'd with empty com-
fort;
"The Emperor at present was engaged;
Some other time he would attend to us!"
I turn'd away, and passing through the hall,
With heavy heart, in a recess I saw

The Grand Duke John in tears, and by his
    side
The noble lords of Wart and Tegerfeld,
Who beckon'd me, and said, "Redress your-
    selves.
Expect not justice from the Emperor.
Does he not plunder his own brother's child,
And keep from him his just inheritance?
The Duke claims his maternal property,
Urging he's now of age, and 'tis full time
That he should rule his people and dominions;
What is the answer made to him? The king
Places a chaplet on his head; 'Behold
The fitting ornament,' he cries, 'of youth!'"
    MAUER. You hear. Expect not from the
    Emperor
Or right or justice! Then redress yourselves!
    REI. No other course is left us. Now,
    advise
What plan most likely to ensure success.
    FÜRST. To shake a thraldom off that we
    abhor,
To keep our ancient rights inviolate,
As we received them from our fathers,—this,
Not lawless innovation, is our aim.

Let Cæsar still retain what is his due;
And he that is a vassal, let him pay
The service he is sworn to faithfully.
    MEYER. I hold my land of Austria in fief.
    FÜRST. Continue, then, to pay your feudal
    service.
    WEILER. I'm tenant of the lords of Rap-
    persweil.
    FÜRST. Continue, then, to pay them rent
    and tithe.
    RÖSS. Of Zurich's Lady I'm the humble
    vassal.
    FÜRST. Give to the cloister, what the
    cloister claims.
    STAUF. The Empire only is my feudal lord.
    FÜRST. What needs must be, we'll do, but
    nothing further.
We'll drive these tyrants and their minions
    hence,
And raze their towering strongholds to the
    ground,
Yet shed, if possible, no drop of blood.
Let the Emperor see, that we were driven to
    cast
The sacred duties of respect away;

And when he finds we keep within our bounds,
His wrath, belike, may yield to policy;
For truly is that nation to be fear'd,
That, when in arms, is temp'rate in its wrath.
RED.   But prithee tell us how may this be
done?
The enemy is arm'd as well as we,
And, rest assured, he will not yield in peace.
STAUF.   He will, whene'er he sees us up in
arms;
We shall surprise him, ere he is prepared.
MEYER.   'Tis easily said, but not so easily
done.
Two fortresses of strength command the coun-
try—
They shield the foe, and should the King in-
vade us,
The task would then be dangerous indeed.
Rossberg and Sarnen both must be secured,
Before a sword is drawn in either Canton.
STAUF.   Should we delay the foe will soon
be warned;
We are too numerous for secrecy.
MEYER.   There is no traitor in the Forest
States.
RÖSS.   But even zeal may heedlessly be-
tray.
FÜRST.   Delay it longer, and the keep at
Altdorf
Will be complete,—the governor secure.
MEYER.   You think but of yourselves.
PETER.   You are unjust!
MEYER.   Unjust! said you? Dares Uri taunt
us so?
RED.   Peace, on your oath!
MEYER.   If Schwytz be leagued with Uri,
Why, then, indeed, we must perforce be silent.
RED.   And let me tell you, in the Diet's
name,
Your hasty spirit much disturbs the peace.
Stand we not all for the same common cause?
WIN.   What, if we delay till Christmas? 'Tis
then
The custom for the serfs to throng the castle,
Bringing the governor their annual gifts.
Thus may some ten or twelve selected men
Assemble unobserved, within its walls,
Bearing about their persons pikes of steel,
Which may be quickly mounted upon staves,
For arms are not admitted to the fort.
The rest can fill the neighb'ring wood, pre-
pared
To sally forth upon a trumpet's blast,
Whene'er their comrades have secured the
gate;
And thus the castle will be ours with ease.

MELCH.   The Rossberg I will undertake to
scale,
I have a sweetheart in the garrison,
Whom with some tender words I could per-
suade
To lower me at night a hempen ladder.
Once up, my friends will not be long behind.
RED.   Are all resolved in favor of delay?
                    [*The majority raise their hands.*
STAUF.   (*Counting them.*)
Twenty to twelve is the majority.
FÜRST.   If on the appointed day the castles
fall,
From mountain on to mountain we shall pass
The fiery signal: in the capital
Of every Canton quickly rouse the Landsturm.
Then, when these tyrants see our martial front,
Believe me, they will never make so bold
As risk the conflict, but will gladly take
Safe conduct forth beyond our boundaries.
STAUF.   Not so with Gessler. He will make
a stand.
Surrounded with his dread array of horse.
Blood will be shed before he quits the field,
And even expell'd he'd still be terrible.
'Tis hard, indeed 'tis dangerous, to spare him.
BAUM.   Place me where'er a life is to be
lost;
I owe my life to Tell, and cheerfully
Will pledge it for my country. I have clear'd
My honor, and my heart is now at rest.
RED.   Counsel will come with circumstance.
Be patient!
Something must still be trusted to the moment.
Yet, while by night we hold our Diet here,
The morning, see, has on the mountain tops
Kindled her glowing beacon. Let us part,
Ere the broad sun surprise us.
FÜRST.   Do not fear.
The night wanes slowly from these vales of
ours.
[*All have involuntarily taken off their caps,
and contemplate the breaking of day, ab-
sorbed in silence.*
RÖSS.   By this fair light which greeteth us,
before
Those other nations, that, beneath us far,
In noisome cities pent, draw painful breath,
Swear we the oath of our confederacy!
We swear to be a nation of true brothers,
Never to part in danger or in death!
[*They repeat his words with three fingers
raised.*
We swear we will be free, as were our sires,
And sooner die than live in slavery!
[*All repeat as before.*

75

We swear to put our trust in God Most High,
And not to quail before the might of man !

    [*All repeat as before, and embrace each
        other.*

STAUF.   Now every man pursue his several
   way
Back to his friends, his kindred, and his home.
Let the herd winter up his flock, and gain,
In silence, friends for our confederacy !
What for a time must be endured, endure,
And let the reckoning of the tyrants grow,
Till the great day arrive, when they shall pay

The general and particular debt at once.
Let every man control his own just rage,
And nurse his vengeance for the public
   wrongs:
For he whom selfish interests now engage,
Defrauds the general weal of what to it be-
   longs.

    [*As they are going off in profound silence, in
      three different directions, the orchestra
      plays a solemn air. The empty scene re-
      mains open for some time, showing the
      rays of the sun rising over the Glaciers.*

ACT III.

SCENE I.—*Court before* TELL'S *house.* TELL
with an axe. HEDWIG *engaged in her do-*
mestic duties. WALTER *and* WILLIAM *in the*
back-ground, playing with a little cross-bow.

WALTER *sings.*

With his cross-bow, and his quiver,
  The huntsman speeds his way,

Over mountain, dale, and river,
  At the dawning of the day,

As the eagle, on wild pinion,
  Is the king in realms of air,
So the hunter claims dominion
  Over crag and forest lair.

Far as ever bow can carry,
'Thro' the trackless airy space,
All he sees he makes his quarry,
Soaring bird and beast of chase.

WILLIAM. *(Runs forward.)* My string has
snapt? Wilt mend it for me, father?
TELL. Not I; a true-born archer helps
himself. *[Boys retire.*
HED. The boys begin to use the bow be-
times.
TELL. 'Tis early practice only makes the
master.
HED. Ah! Would to Heaven they never
learnt the art!
TELL. But they shall learn it, wife, in all
its points.
Whoe'er would carve an independent way
Through life, must learn to ward or plant a
blow.
HED. Alas, alas! and they will never rest
Contentedly at home.
TELL. No more can I!
I was not framed by nature for a shepherd.
Restless I must pursue a changing course;
I only feel the flush and joy of life,
In starting some fresh quarry every day.
HED. Heedless the while of all your wife's
alarms,
As she sits watching through long hours at
home
For my soul sinks with terror at the tales
The servants tell about your wild adventures.
Whene'er we part, my trembling heart fore-
bodes,
That you will ne'er come back to me again.
I see you on the frozen mountain steeps,
Missing, perchance, your leap from cliff to cliff.
I see the chamois, with a wild rebound,
Drag you down with him o'er the precipice.
I see the avalanche close o'er your head,—
The treacherous ice give way, and you sink
down
Intombed alive within its hideous gulf.
Ah! in a hundred varying forms does death
Pursue the Alpine huntsman on his course.
That way of life can surely ne'er be blessed,
Where life and limb are perill'd every hour.
TELL. The man that bears a quick and
steady eye,
And trusts to God, and his own lusty sinews,
Passes, with scarce a scar, through every dan-
ger.
The mountain cannot awe the mountain child.
*[Having finished his work, he lays aside his
tools.*

And now, methinks, the door will hold
awhile.—
The axe at home oft saves the carpenter.
[Takes his cap.
HED. Whither away?
TELL. To Altdorf, to your father,
Hed. You have some dangerous enterprise
in view?
Confess!
TELL. Why think you so?
HED. Some scheme's on foot,
Against the governors. There was a Diet
Held on the Rootli—that I know—and you
Are one of the confederacy, I'm sure.
TELL. I was not there. Yet will I not
hold back,
When e'er my country calls me to her aid.
HED. Wherever danger is, will you be
placed.
On you, as ever, will the burden fall.
TELL. Each man shall have the post that
fits his powers.
HED. You took—ay, 'mid the thickest of
the storm—
The man of Unterwald across the lake.
'Tis a marvel you escaped. Had you no
thought
Of wife and children, then?
TELL. Dear wife, I had;
And therefore saved the father for his children.
HED. To brave the lake in all its wrath!
'Twas not
To put your trust in God! 'Twas tempting
him.
TELL. The man that's over cautious will
do little.
HED. Yes, you've a kind and helping
hand for all;
But be in straits, and who will lend you aid?
TELL. God grant I ne'er may stand in
need of it!
[Takes up his crossbow and arrows.
HED. Why take your crossbow with you?
Leave it here.
TELL. I want my right hand, when I want
my bow. *[The boys return.*
WALTER. Where, father, are you going?
TELL. To grand-dad, boy—
WALTER. Ay, that I will!
HED. The Viceroy's there just now. Go
not to Altdorf!
TELL. He leaves to-day.
HED. Then let him first be gone.
Cross not his path.—You know he bears us
grudge.

TELL. His ill-will cannot greatly injure me.
I do what's right, and care for no man's hate.
HED. 'Tis those who do what's right, whom most he hates.
TELL. Because he cannot reach them. Me, I ween,
His knightship will be glad to leave in peace.
HED. Ay!—Are you sure of that?
TELL. Not long ago,
As I was hunting through the wild ravines
Of Shechenthal, untrod by mortal foot,—
There, as I took my solitary way
Along a shelving ledge of rocks, where 'twas
Impossible to step on either side;
For high above rose, like a giant wall,
The precipice's side, and far below
The Shechen thunder'd o'er its rifted bed;—
[*The boys press towards him, looking upon him with excited curiosity.*
There, face to face, I met the Viceroy. He
Alone with me—and I myself alone—
Mere man to man, and near us the abyss.
And when his lordship had perused my face,
And knew the man he had severely fined
On some most trivial ground, not long before;
And saw me, with my sturdy bow in hand,
Come striding t'wards him, then his cheek grew pale,
His knees refused their office, and I thought
He would have sunk against the mountain side.

Then, touch'd with pity for him, I advanced,
Respectfully, and said, "'Tis I, my lord."
But ne'er a sound could he compel his lips
To frame in answer. Only with his hand
He beckoned me in silence to proceed.
So I pass'd on, and sent his train to seek him.
HED. He trembled, then, before you? Woe the while
You saw his weakness; that he'll ne'er forgive.
TELL. I shun him, therefore, and he'll not seek me.
HED. But stay away to-day. Go hunting rather!
TELL. What do you fear?
HED. I am uneasy. Stay.
TELL. Why thus distress yourself without a cause?
HED. Because there is no cause. Tell, Tell! stay here!
TELL. Dear wife, I gave my promise I would go.
HED. Must you,—then go. But leave the boys with me.
WALTER. No, mother dear, I'm going with my father.
HED. How, Walter! will you leave your mother then?
WALTER. I'll bring you pretty things from grandpapa. [*Exit with his father.*
WILLIAM. Mother, I'll stay with you!

79

HED. (*Embracing him.*) Yes, yes! thou art My own dear child. Thou'rt all that's left to me.

[*She goes to the gate of the court, and looks anxiously after* TELL *and her son for a considerable time.*]

SCENE II.—*A retired part of the Forest.— Brooks dashing in spray over the rocks.*

Enter BERTHA *in a hunting dress. Immediately afterwards* RUDENZ.

BER. He follows me. Now to explain myself!

RUD. (*Entering hastily.*) At length, dear lady, we have met alone. In this wild dell, with rocks on every side, No jealous eye can watch our interview. Now let my heart throw off this weary silence. BER. But are you sure they will not follow us?

RUD. See, yonder goes the chase. Now, then, or never! I must avail me of the precious moment,— Must hear my doom decided by thy lips, Though it should part me from thy side for ever. Oh, do not arm that gentle face of thine With looks so stern and harsh! Who—who am I, That dare aspire so high, as unto thee? Fame hath not stamp'd me yet; nor may I take My place amid the courtly throng of knights, That, crown'd with glory's lustre, woo thy smiles. Nothing have I to offer, but a heart That overflows with truth and love for thee. BER. (*Sternly and with severity.*) And dare you speak to me of love—of truth? You, that are faithless to your nearest ties! You, that are Austria's slave—bartered and sold To her—an alien, and your country's tyrant! RUD. How! This reproach from thee! Whom do I seek, On Austria's side, my own beloved, but thee? BER. Think you to find me in the traitor's ranks? Now, as I live, I'd rather give my hand To Gessler's self, all despot though he be, Than the Switzer who forgets his birth, And stoops to be the minion of a tyrant. RUD. Oh, heaven, what must I hear! BER. Say, what can lie

Nearer the good man's heart, than friends and kindred? What dearer duty to a noble soul, Than to protect weak, suffering innocence, And vindicate the rights of the oppress'd? My very soul bleeds for your countrymen. I suffer with them, for I needs must love them; They are so gentle, yet so full of power; They draw my whole heart to them. Every day I look upon them with increased esteem. But you, whom nature and your knightly vow, Have given them as their natural protector, Yet who desert them and abet their foes, In forging shackles for your native land, You—you it is, that deeply grieve and wound me. I must constrain my heart, or I shall hate you. RUD. Is not my country's welfare all my wish? What seek I for her, but to purchase peace 'Neath Austria's potent sceptre? BER. Bondage, rather. You would drive freedom from the last stronghold That yet remains for her upon the earth. The people know their own true int'rests better; Their simple natures are not warp'd by show. But round your head a tangling net is wound. RUD. Bertha, you hate me—you despise me! BER. Nay! And if I did, 'twere better for my peace. But to see him despised and despicable,— The man whom one might love— RUD. Oh, Bertha! You Show me the pinnacle of heavenly bliss, Then, in a moment, hurl me to despair! BER. No, no! the noble is not all extinct Within you. It but slumbers,—I will rouse it. It must have cost you many a fiery struggle, To crush the virtues of your race within you. But, Heaven be praised, 'tis mightier than yourself, And you are noble in your own despite! RUD. You trust me, then? Oh, Bertha, with thy love What might I not become! BER. Be only that For which your own high nature destin'd you. Fill the position you were born to fill;— Stand by your people and your native land— And battle for your sacred rights! RUD. Alas! How can I hope to win you—to possess you, If I take arms against the Emperor?

ARTIST; A. BAUR

WILLIAM TELL.

ACT III, SCENE II

Will not your potent kinsmen interpose,
To dictate the disposal of your hand?
BER. All my estates lie in the Forest Can-
tons;
And I am free, when Switzerland is free.
RUD. Oh! what a prospect, Bertha, hast
thou shown me!
BER. Hope not to win my hand by Austria's
favor;
Fain would they lay their grasp on my estates,
To swell the vast domains which now they hold.
The selfsame lust of conquest, that would rob
You of your liberty, endangers mine.
Oh, friend, I'm mark'd for sacrifice;—to be
The guerdon of some parasite, perchance!
They'll drag me hence to the Imperial court,
That hateful haunt of falsehood and intrigue;
There do detested marriage bonds await me.
Love, love alone,—your love can rescue me.
RUD. And thou couldst be content, love,
to live here,
In my own native land to be my own?
Oh, Bertha, all the yearnings of my soul
For this great world and its tumultuous strife,
What were they, but a yearning after thee
In glory's path I sought for thee alone,
And all my thirst of fame was only love.
But if in this calm vale thou canst abide
With me, and bid earth's pomps and pride
adieu,
Then is the goal of my ambition won;
And the rough tide of the tempestuous world
May dash and rave around these firm-set hills!
No wandering wishes more have I to send
Forth to the busy scene that stirs beyond.
Then may these rocks, that girdle us, extend
Their giant walls impenetrably round,
And this sequestered happy vale alone
Look up to Heaven, and be my paradise!
BER. Now art thou all my fancy dream'd
of thee.
My trust has not been given to thee in vain.
RUD. Away, ye idle phantoms of my folly!
In mine own home I'll find my happiness.
Here, where the gladsome boy to manhood
grew,
Where ev'ry brook, and tree, and mountain
peak,
Teems with remembrances of happy hours,
In mine own native land thou wilt be mine.
Ah, I have ever loved it well, I feel
How poor without it were all earthly joys.
BER. Where should we look for happiness
on earth,
If not in this dear land of innocence?
Here, where old truth hath its familiar home,

Where fraud and guile are strangers, envy ne'er
Shall dim the sparkling fountain of our bliss,
And ever bright the hours shall o'er us glide.
There do I see thee, in true manly worth,
The foremost of the free and of thy peers,
Revered with homage pure and unconstrain'd
Wielding a power that kings might envy thee.
RUD. And thee I see, thy sex's crowning
gem,
With thy sweet woman grace and wakeful love.
Building a heaven for me within my home,
And, as the spring-time scatters forth her flow-
ers,
Adorning with thy charms my path of life,
And spreading joy and sunshine all around.
BER. And this it was, dear friend, that
caused my grief,
To see thee blast this life's supremest bliss,
With thine own hand. Ah! what had been
my fate,
Had I been forced to follow some proud lord,
Some ruthless despot, to his gloomy castle!
Here are no castles, here no bastion'd walls
Divide me from a people I can bless.
RUD. Yet, how to free myself; to loose the
coils
Which I have madly twined around my head?
BER. Tear them asunder with a man's re-
solve.
Whatever the event, stand by thy people.
It is thy post by birth.
[*Hunting horns are heard in the distance.*
But hark! The chase!
Farewell,—'tis needful we should part—away!
Fight for thy land; thou fightest for thy love.
One foe fills all our souls with dread; the blow
That makes one free, emancipates us all.
[*Exeunt severally.*

———

SCENE III.—*A meadow near Altdorf. Trees
in the fore-ground. At the back of the stage
a cap upon a pole. The prospect is bounded
by the Bannberg, which is surmounted by a
snow-capped mountain.*

FRIESSHARDT *and* LEUTHOLD *on guard.*

FRIESS. We keep our watch in vain. There's
not a soul
Will pass, and do obeisance to the cap.
But yesterday the place swarm'd like a fair;
Now the whole green looks like a very desert,
Since yonder scarecrow hung upon the pole.

LEUTH. Only the vilest rabble show themselves,
And wave their tattered caps in mockery at us.
All honest citizens would sooner make
A tedious circuit over half the town,
Than bend their backs before our master's cap.
FRIESS. They were obliged to pass this way at noon,
As they were coming from the Council House.
I counted then upon a famous catch,
For no one thought of bowing to the cap.
But Rösselmann, the priest, was even with me:
Coming just then from some sick penitent,
He stands before the pole,—raises the Host—
The Sacrist, too, must tinkle with his bell,—
When down they dropp'd on knee—myself and all
In reverence to the Host, but not the cap.
LEUTH. Hark ye, companion, I've a shrewd suspicion,
Our post's no better than the pillory.
It is a burning shame, a trooper should
Stand sentinel before an empty cap,
And every honest fellow must despise us.
To do obeisance to a cap, too! Faith,
I never heard an order so absurd!
FRIESS. Why not, an't please thee, to an empty cap?
Thou'st duck'd, I'm sure, to many an empty sconce.
[HILDEGARD, MECHTHILD, and ELSBETH enter with their children, and station themselves around the pole.
LEUTH. And thou art an officious sneaking knave,
That's fond of bringing honest folks to trouble.
For my part, he that likes, may pass the cap:—
I'll shut my eyes and take no note of him.
MECH. There hangs the Viceroy! Your obeisance, children!
ELSB. I would to God he'd go, and leave his cap!
The country would be none the worse for it.
FRIESS. (Driving them away.)
Out of the way! Confounded pack of gossips!
Who sent for you? Go, send your husbands here,
If they have courage to defy the order.
[TELL enters with his crossbow, leading his son WALTER by the hand. They pass the hat without noticing it, and advance to the front of the stage.
WALTER. (Pointing to the Bannberg.)
Father, is't true, that on the mountain there,
The trees, if wounded with a hatchet, bleed?
TELL. Who says so, boy?

WAL. The master herdsman, father!
He tells us, there's a charm upon the trees,
And if a man shall injure them, the hand
That struck the blow will grow from out the grave.
TELL. There is a charm about them—that's the truth.
Dost see those glaciers yonder—those white horns—
That seem to melt away into the sky?
WAL. They are the peaks that thunder so at night,
And send the avalanches down upon us.
TELL. They are; and Altdorf long ago had been
Submerged beneath these avalanches' weight,
Did not the forest there above the town
Stand like a bulwark to arrest their fall.
WAL. (After musing a little.) And are there
countries with no mountains, father?
TELL. Yes, if we travel downwards from our heights,
And keep descending in the rivers' courses,
We reach a wide and level county, where
Our mountain torrents brawl and foam no more,
And fair large rivers glide serenely on.
All quarters of the heaven may there be scann'd
Without impediment. The corn grows there
In broad and lovely fields, and all the land
Is fair as any garden to the view.
WAL. But, father, tell me, wherefore haste we not
Away to this delightful land, instead
Of toiling here, and struggling as we do?
TELL. The land is fair and bountiful as Heaven;
But they who till it, never may enjoy
The fruits of what they sow.
WAL. Live they not free,
As you do, on the land their fathers left them?
TELL. The fields are all the bishop's or the king's.
WAL. But they may freely hunt among the woods?
TELL. The game is all the monarch's—bird and beast.
WAL. But they, at least, may surely fish the streams?
TELL. Stream, lake, and sea, all to the king belong.
WAL. Who is this king, of whom they're so afraid?
TELL. He is the man who fosters and protects them.

WAL. Have they not courage to protect themselves?

TELL. The neighbor there dare not his neighbor trust.

WAL. I should want breathing room in such a land.
I'd rather dwell beneath the avalanches.

TELL. 'Tis better, child, to have these glacier peaks
Behind ones back, than evil-minded men!

[They are about to pass on.

WAL. See, father, see the cap on yonder pole!

TELL. What is the cap to us? Come let's be gone

[As he is going, FRIESSHARDT, presenting his pike, stops him.

FRIESS. Stand, I command you, in the Emperor's name!

TELL. (Seizing the pike.) What would ye? Wherefore do ye stop my path?

FRIESS. You've broke the mandate, and must go with us.

LEUTH. You have not done obeisance to the cap.

TELL. Friend, let me go.

FRIESS. Away, away to prison!

WAL. Father to prison! Help!

[Calling to the side scene.
This way, you men!
Good people, help! They're dragging him to prison!

[RÖSSELMAN the Priest, and the SACRISTAN, with three other men, enter.

PETER. What's here amiss?

RÖSS. Why do you seize this man?

FRIESS. He is an enemy of the King—a traitor.

TELL. (Seizing him with violence.)
A traitor, I!

RÖSS. Friend, thou art wrong. 'Tis Tell.
An honest man, and worthy citizen.

WAL. (Deserts FÜRST and runs up to him.)
Grandfather, help, they want to seize my father!

FRIESS. Away to prison!

FÜRST (Running in.) Stay, I offer bail,
For God's sake, Tell, what is the matter here!

[MELCHTHAL and STAUFFACHER enter.

83

LEUTH. He has contemn'd the Viceroy's sovereign power,
Refusing flatly to acknowledge it.
STAUF. Has Tell done this?
MELCH. Villain, thou knowest 'tis false!
LEUTH. He has not made obeisance to the cap.
FÜRST, And shall for this to prison? Come, my friend,
Take my security, and let him go.
FRIESS. Keep your security for yourself—you'll need it.
We only do our duty. Hence with him.
MELCH. *(To the country people.)*
This is too bad—shall we stand by, and see them
Drag him away before our very eyes?
PETER. We are the strongest. Don't endure it, friends.
Our countrymen will back us to a man.
FRIESS. Who dares resist the governor's commands?
OTHER THREE PEASANTS. *(Running in.)*
We'll help you. What's the matter? Down with them!
[HILDEGARD, MECHTHILD *and* ELSBETH *return.*
TELL. Go, go, good people, I can help myself.
Think you, had I a mind to use my strength,
These pikes of theirs should daunt me?
MELCH. *(To* FRIESSHARDT,*)* Only try—
Try, if you dare, to force him from amongst us.
FÜRST *and* STAUFFACHER.
Peace, peace, friends!
FRIESS. *(Loudly.)* Riot! Insurrection, ho!
[*Hunting horns without.*
WOMEN. The Governor!
FRIESS. *(Raising his voice.)*
Rebellion! Mutiny!
STAUF. Roar, till you burst, knave!
RÖSSELMANN *and* MELCHTHAL.
Will you hold your tongue?
FRIESS. *(Calling still louder,)*
Help, help, I say, the servants of the law!
FÜRST. The Viceroy here! Then we shall smart for this!
[*Enter* GESSLER *on horseback, with a falcon on his wrist*; RUDOLPH DER HARRAS, BERTHA, *and* RUDENZ, *and a numerous train of armed attendants, who form a circle of lances round the whole stage.*
HAR. Room for the Viceroy!
GES. Drive the clowns apart.
Why throng the people thus? Who calls for help? [*General silence.*
Who was it! I will know.
[FRIESSHARDT *steps forward.*

And who art thou?
And why hast thou this man in custody?
[*Gives his falcon to an attendant.*
FRIESS. Dread sir, I am a soldier of your guard,
And station'd sentinel beside the cap;
This man I apprehended in the act
Of passing it without obeisance due,
So I arrested him, as you gave order,
Whereon the people tried to rescue him.
GES. *(After a pause.)*
And do you, Tell, so lightly hold your king,
And me, who act as his vicegerent here,
That you refuse the greeting to the cap
I hung aloft to test your loyalty?
I read in this a disaffected spirit.
TELL. Pardon me, good my lord! The action sprung
From inadvertence,—not from disrespect.
Were I discreet, I were not William Tell:
Forgive me now—I'll not offend again.
GES. *(After a pause.)*
I hear, Tell, you're a master with the bow,—
And bear the palm away from every rival.
WAL. That must be true, sir! At a hundred yards
He'll shoot an apple for you off the tree.
GES. Is that boy thine, Tell?
TELL. Yes, my gracious lord.
GES. Hast any more of them?
TELL. Two boys, my lord.
GES. And, of the two, which dost thou love the most?
TELL. Sir, both the boys are dear to me alike.
GES. Then, Tell, since at a hundred yards thou canst
Bring down the apple from the tree, thou shalt
Approve thy skill before me. Take thy bow—
Thou hast it there at hand—and make thee ready
To shoot an apple from the stripling's head!
But take this counsel,—look well to thine aim,
See, that thou hitt'st the apple at the first,
For, shouldst thou miss, thy head shall pay the forfeit. [*All give signs of horror.*
TELL. What monstrous thing, my lord, is that you ask?
That I, from the head of mine own child!—
No, no!
It cannot be, kind sir, you meant not that—
God, in His grace, forbid! You could not ask
A father seriously to do that thing!
GES. Thou art to shoot an apple from his head!
I do desire—command it so.

TELL.   What I!
Level my crossbow at the darling head
Of mine own child? No—rather let me die!
GES. Or thou must shoot, or with thee dies
the boy.
TELL. Shall I become the murd'rer of my
child!
You have no children, sir—you do not know
The tender throbbings of a father's heart.
GES. How now, Tell, so discreet upon a
sudden.
I had been told thou wert a visionary,—
A wanderer from the paths of common men.
Thou lov'st the marvellous. So have I now
Cull'd out for thee a task of special daring.
Another man might pause and hesitate;—
Thou dashest at it, heart and soul, at once.
BER. Oh, do not jest, my lord, with these
poor souls!
See, how they tremble, and how pale they look,
So little used are they to hear thee jest.
GES. Who tells thee, that I jest?
          [*Grasping a branch above his head.*
                              Here is the apple.
Room there, I say! And let him take his
distance—
Just eighty paces,—as the custom is,—
Not an inch more or less! It was his boast,
That at a hundred he could hit his man.
Now, archer, to your task, and look you miss
not!
HAR. Heavens! this grows serious—down,
boy, on your knees,
And beg the governor to spare your life.
FÜRST. (*Aside to* MELCHTHAL, *who can
scarcely restrain his impatience.*)
Command yourself,—be calm, I beg of you!
BER. (*To the governor.*)
Let this suffice you, sir! It is inhuman
To trifle with a father's anguish thus.
Although this wretched man had forfeited
Both life and limb for such a slight offence,
Already has he suffer'd tenfold death.
Send him away uninjured to his home;
He'll know thee well in future; and this hour
He and his children will remember.
GES. Open a way there—quick! Why
this delay?
Thy life is forfeited; I might despatch thee,
And see I graciously repose thy fate
Upon the skill of thine own practis'd hand.
No cause has he to say his doom is harsh,
Who's made the master of his destiny.
Thou boastest of thy steady eye. 'Tis well!
Now is a fitting time to show thy skill.
The mark is worthy, and the prize is great.

To hit the bull's eye in the target;—that
Can many another do as well as thou;
But he, methinks, is master of his craft,
Who can at all times on his skill rely,
Nor let's his heart disturb or eye or hand.
FÜRST. My lord, we bow to your authority;
But oh, let justice yield to mercy here.
Take half my property, nay, take it all,
But spare a father this unnatural doom!
WAL. Grandfather, do not kneel to that
bad man!
Say, where am I to stand? I do not fear;
My father strikes the bird upon the wing,
And will not miss now when 'twould harm his
boy!
STAUF. Does the child's innocence not
touch your heart!
RÖSS. Bethink you, sir, there is a God in
heaven,
To whom you must account for all your deeds.
GES. (*Pointing to the boy.*)
Bind him to yonder lime tree straight!
WAL.   Bind me?
No, I will not be bound! I will be still,
Still as a lamb—nor even draw my breath!
But if you bind me, I can not be still.
Then I shall writhe and struggle with my
bonds.
HAR. But let your eyes at least be band-
aged, boy!
WALTER. And why my eyes? No! Do
you think I fear
An arrow from my father's hand? Not I!
I'll wait it firmly, nor so much as wink!
Quick, father, show them that thou art an
archer!
He doubts thy skill—he thinks to ruin us.
Shoot then, and hit, though but to spite the
tyrant!
          [*He goes to the lime tree, and an apple is
          placed on his head.*
MELCH. (*To the country people.*)
What! Is this outrage to be perpetrated
Before our very eyes? Where is our oath?
STAUF. 'Tis all in vain. We have no wea-
pons here;
And see the wood of lances that surrounds us!
MELCH. Oh! would to Heaven that we had
struck at once!
God pardon those, who counsell'd the delay!
GES. (*To* TELL.)
Now, to thy task! Men bear not arms for
nought.
'Tis dangerous to carry deadly weapons,
And on the archer oft his shaft recoils.
This right, these haughty peasant churls assume,

85

Trenches upon their master's privileges.
None should be armed, but those who bear
command.
It pleases you to wear the bow and bolt;—
Well,—be it so. I will provide the mark.
TELL. *(Bends the bow, and fixes the arrow.)*
A lane there! Room!
STAUF. What, Tell? You would—no, no!
You shake—your hand's unsteady—your knees
tremble.
TELL. *(Letting the bow sink down.)*
There's something swims before mine eyes!
WOMEN.   Great Heaven!
TELL. Release me from this shot! Here
   is my heart!   [*Tears open his breast.*
Summon your troopers—let them strike me
down!
GES. I do not want thy life, Tell, but the
shot.
Thy talent's universal! Nothing daunts thee!
Thou canst direct the rudder like the bow!
Storms fright not thee, when there's a life at
stake.
Now, saviour, help thyself,—thou savest all!
   [*TELL stands fearfully agitated by contending
   emotions, his hands moving convulsively,
   and his eyes turning alternately to the
   governor and Heaven. Suddenly he takes
   a second arrow from his quiver, and sticks
   it in his belt. The governor watches all
   these motions.*
WAL. *(Beneath the lime tree.)* Come, father,
   shoot! I'm not afraid.
TELL.   It must be!
   [*Collects himself and levels the bow.*
RUD. *(Who all the while has been standing
   in a state of violent excitement, and has
   with difficulty restrained himself, ad-
   vances.)*
My lord, you will not urge this matter further.
You will not. It was surely but a test.
You've gained your object. Rigor push'd too
   far
Is sure to miss its aim, however good,
As snaps the bow that's all too straightly bent.
GES. Peace, till your counsel's ask'd for!
RUD.   I will speak!
Ay, and I dare! I reverence my king!
But acts like these must make his name ab-
   horr'd.
He sanctions not this cruelty. I dare
Avouch the fact. And you outstep your
   powers
In handling thus an unoffending people.
GES. Ha! thou grow'st bold, methinks!
RUD.   I have been dumb

To all the oppressions I was doom'd to see,
I've closed my eyes, that they might not be-
   hold them,
Bade my rebellious, swelling heart be still,
And pent its struggles down within my breast.
But to be silent longer, were to be
A traitor to my king and country both.
   BER. *(Casting herself between him and the
   governor.)*
Oh, Heavens! you but exasperate his rage!
   RUD. My people I forsook—renounced
   my kindred—
Broke all the ties of nature, that I might
Attach myself to you. I madly thought,
That I should best advance the general weal,
By adding sinews to the Emperor's power.
The scales have fallen from mine eyes—I see
The fearful precipice on which I stand.
You've led my youthful judgment far astray,—
Deceived my honest heart. With best intent,
I had well nigh achieved my country's ruin.
   GES. Audacious boy, this language to thy
   lord?
   RUD. The Emperor is my lord, not you!
   I'm free
As you by birth, and I can cope with you
In every virtue that beseems a knight,
And if you stood not here in that King's name
Which I respect e'en where 'tis most abused,
I'd throw my gauntlet down, and you should
   give
An answer to my gage in knightly fashion.
Ay, beckon to your troopers! Here I stand;
But not like these—   [*Pointing to the people.*
   unarmed. I have a sword,
And he that stirs one step——
   STAUF. *(Exclaims.)*   The apple's down!
   [*While the attention of the crowd had been
   directed to the spot where BERTHA has cast
   herself between RUDENZ and GESSLER,
   TELL has shot.*
RÖSS. The boy's alive!
MANY VOICES. The apple has been struck!
   [*WALTER FÜRST staggers, and is about to
   fall, BERTHA supports him.*
GES. *(Astonished.)* How? Has he shot?
The madman!
   BER.   Worthy father!
Pray you, compose yourself. The boy's alive.
   WALTER. *(Runs in with the apple.)*
Here is the apple, father! Well I knew,
You would not harm your boy.
   [*TELL stands with his body bent forwards,
   as though he would follow the arrow. His
   bow drops from his hand. When he sees
   the boy advancing, he hastens to meet him

with open arms, and embracing him passion-
ately sinks down with him quite exhausted.
All crowd round them deeply affected.
BER. Oh, ye kind Heavens!
FÜRST. *(To father and son.)*
My children, my dear children!
STAUF. God be praised!
LEUTH. Almighty powers! That was a
shot indeed;
It will be talked of to the end of time.
HAR. This feat of Tell, the archer, will
be told
While yonder mountains stand upon their
base. [*Hands the apple to* GESSLER.
GES. By Heaven! the apple's cleft right
through the core.
It was a master shot, I must allow.
RÖSS. The shot was good. But woe to
him, who drove
The man to tempt his God by such a feat!
STAUF. Cheer up, Tell, rise! You've no-
bly freed yourself,
And now may go in quiet to your home.
RÖSS. Come, to the mother let us bear her
son! [*They are about to lead him off.*

GES. A word, Tell.
TELL. Sir, your pleasure?
GES. Thou didst place
A second arrow in thy belt—nay, nay!
I saw it well—what was thy purpose with it?
TELL. *(Confused.)* It is a custom with all
archers, Sir.
GES. No, Tell, I cannot let that answer
pass.
There was some other motive, well I know,
Frankly and cheerfully confess the truth;—
Whate'er it be, I promise thee thy life,
Wherefore the second arrow?
TELL. Well, my Lord.
Since you have promised not to take my life,
I will, without reserve, declare the truth.
[*He draws the arrow from his belt, and fixes
his eyes sternly upon the governor.*
If that my hand had struck my darling child,
This second arrow I had aimed at you,
And, be assured, I should not then have
miss'd.
GES. Well, Tell, I promised thou shouldst
have thy life;
I gave my knightly word, and I will keep it.

87

Yet, as I know the malice of thy thoughts,
I will remove thee hence to sure confinement,
Where neither sun nor moon shall reach thine
    eyes,
Thus from thy arrows I shall be secure.
Seize on him, guards, and bind him;
                [*They bind him.*
  STAUF.   How, my lord—
How can you treat in such a way a man,
On whom God's hand has plainly been re-
    veal'd?
  GES. Well, let us see if it will save him
    twice!
Remove him to my ship; I'll follow straight.
In person I will see him lodged at Küssnacht.
  RÖSS. You dare not do't. Nor durst the
    Emperor's self
So violate our dearest chartered rights.
  GES. Where are they? Has the Emp'ror
    confirm'd them?
He never has. And only by obedience
Need you expect to win that favor from him.
You are all rebels 'gainst the Emp'ror's power,
—And bear a desperate and rebellious spirit.
I know you all—I see you through and through.
Him do I single from amongst you now,
But in his guilt you all participate.
The wise will study silence and obedience.

[*Exit, followed by* BERTHA, RUDENZ, HAR-
  RAS, *and attendants.* FRIESSHARDT *and*
  LEUTHOLD *remain.*
  FÜRST. (*In violent anguish.*)
All's over now! He is resolved, to bring
Destruction on myself and all my house.
  STAUF. (*To* TELL.)
Oh, why did you provoke the tyrant's rage?
  TELL. Let him be calm who feels the
    pangs I felt.
  STAUF. Alas! alas! Our every hope is gone.
With you we all are fettered and enchain'd.
  COUNTRY PEOPLE. (*Surrounding* TELL.)
Our last remaining comfort goes with you!
  LEUTH. (*Approaching him.*)
I'm sorry for you, Tell, but must obey.
  TELL.   Farewell!
  WALTER. (*Clinging to him in great agony.*)
Oh, father, father, my dear father!
  TELL. (*Pointing to Heaven.*)
Thy father is on high, appeal to him!
  STAUF. Hast thou no message, Tell, to
    send thy wife?
  TELL. (*Clasping the boy passionately to his
    breast.*) The boy's uninjured; God will
    succor me!
    [*Tears himself suddenly away, and follows
        the soldiers of the guard.*

WILLIAM TELL.

ACT III, SCENE III

ACT IV.

SCENE I. — *Eastern shore of the Lake of Lucerne; rugged and singularly shaped rocks close the prospect to the west. The lake is agitated, violent roaring and rushing of wind, with thunder and lightning at intervals.*

KUNZ OF GERSAU, FISHERMAN *and* BOY.

KUNZ. I saw it with these eyes! Believe me, friend,
It happen'd all precisely as I've said.
FISH. Tell made a prisoner and borne off to Küssnacht?
The best man in the land, the bravest arm,
Had we resolved to strike for liberty!
KUNZ. The Viceroy takes him up the lake in person:
They were about to go on board, as I
Left Flüelen; but still the gathering storm,
That drove me here to land so suddenly,
Perchance has hindered their abrupt departure.
FISH. Our Tell in chains, and in the Viceroy's power!
O, trust me, Gessler will entomb him, where
He never more shall see the light of day;
For, Tell once free, the tyrant well might dread
The just revenge of one so deep incensed.
KUNZ. The old Landamman, too — von Attinghaus—
They say, is lying at the point of death.
FISH. Then the last anchor of our hopes gives way!
He was the only man that dared to raise
His voice in favor of the people's rights.
KUNZ. The storm grows worse and worse.
So, fare ye well!
I'll go and seek out quarters in the village.
There's not a chance of getting off to-day.
[*Exit.*
FISH. Tell dragg'd to prison, and the Baron dead!
Now, tyranny, exalt thy insolent front,—
Throw shame aside! The voice of truth is silenced,
The eye that watch'd for us, in darkness closed.
The arm that should have struck thee down, in chains!

89

Boy. 'Tis hailing hard—come, let us to the cottage!
This is no weather to be out in, father!
Fish. Rage on, ye winds! Ye lightnings, flash your fires!
Burst, ye swollen clouds! Ye cataracts of Heaven,
Descend, and drown the country! In the germ,
Destroy the generations yet unborn!
Ye savage elements, be lords of all!
Return, ye bears; ye ancient wolves, return
To this wide howling waste! The land is yours
Who would live here, when liberty is gone!
Boy. Hark! How the wind whistles, and the whirlpool roars,
I never saw a storm so fierce as this!
Fish. To level at the head of his own child!
Never had father such command before.
And shall not nature, rising in wild wrath,
Revolt against the deed? I should not marvel,
Though to the lake these rocks should bow their heads,
Though yonder pinnacles, yon towers of ice,
That, since creation's dawn, have known no thaw,
Should, from their lofty summits, melt away,—
Though yonder mountains, yon primeval cliffs,
Should topple down, and a new deluge whelm
Beneath its waves all living men's abodes!
[*Bells heard.*
Boy. Hark, they are ringing on the mountain, yonder!
They surely see some vessel in distress,
And toll the bell that we may pray for it.
[*Ascends a rock.*
Fish. Woe to the bark that now pursues its course,
Rock'd in the cradle of these storm-tost waves!
Nor helm nor steersman here can aught avail;
The storm is master. Man is like a ball,
Toss'd 'twixt the winds and billows. Far or near,
No haven offers him its friendly shelter!
Without one ledge to grasp, the sheer smooth rocks
Look down inhospitably on his despair,
And only tender him their flinty breasts.
Boy. (*Calling from above.*)
Father, a ship; and bearing down from Flüelen.
Fish. Heaven pity the poor wretches!
When the storm
Is once entangled in this strait of ours,
It rages like some savage beast of prey,
Struggling against its cage's iron bars!

Howling, it seeks an outlet—all in vain;
For the rocks hedge it round on every side,
Walling the narrow pass as high as Heaven.
[*He ascends a cliff.*
Boy. It is the Governor of Uri's ship;
By its red poop I know it, and the flag.
Fish. Judgments of Heaven! Yes, it is he himself.
It is the Governor! Yonder he sails,
And with him bears the burden of his crimes!
Soon has the arm of the avenger found him;
Now over him he knows a mightier lord.
These waves yield no obedience to his voice,
These rocks bow not their heads before his cap.
Boy, do not pray; stay not the Judge's arm!
Boy. I pray not for the governor—I pray
For Tell, who is on board the ship with him.
Fish. Alas, ye blind, unreasoning elements!
Must ye, in punishing one guilty head,
Destroy the vessel and the pilot too?
Boy. See, see, they've clear'd the Buggisgrat; but now
The blast, rebounding from the Devil's Minster,
Has driven them back on the Great Axemberg.
I cannot see them now.
Fish. The Hakmesser
Is there, that's founder'd many a gallant ship.
If they should fail to double that with skill,
Their bark will go to pieces on the rocks,
That hide their jagged peaks below the lake.
They have on board the very best of pilots.
If any man can save them, Tell is he;
But he is manacled both hand and foot.
[*Enter* William Tell, *with his crossbow. He enters precipitately, looks wildly round, and testifies the most violent agitation. When he reaches the centre of the stage, he throws himself upon his knees, and stretches out his hands, first towards the earth, then towards Heaven.*
Boy. (*Observing him.*) See, father! Who is that man, kneeling yonder?
Fish. He clutches at the earth with both his hands,
And looks as though he were beside himself.
Boy. (*Advancing.*)
What do I see? Father, come here, and look!
Fish. (*Approaches.*) Who is it? God in Heaven! What! William Tell!
How came you hither? Speak, Tell!
Boy. Were you not
In yonder ship, a prisoner, and in chains?
Fish. Were they not bearing you away to Küssnacht?
Tell. (*Rising.*) I am released.

FISH. *and* BOY. Released, oh miracle!
BOY. Whence came you here?
TELL. From yonder vessel!
FISH. What!
BOY. Where is the Viceroy?
TELL. Drifting on the waves.
FISH. Is't possible? But you! How are
you here?
How 'scaped you from your fetters and the
storm?
TELL. By God's most gracious providence.
Attend.
FISH. *and* BOY. Say on, say on!
TELL. You know what passed at Altdorf?
FISH. I do—say on!
TELL. How I was seized and bound,
And order'd by the governor to Küssnacht.
FISH. And how with you at Flüelen he em-
barked.
All this we know. Say, how have you escaped?
TELL. I lay on deck, fast bound with cords,
disarm'd,
In utter hopelessness. I did not think
Again to see the gladsome light of day,
Nor the dear faces of my wife and children,
And eyed disconsolate the waste of waters.—
FISH. Oh, wretched man!
TELL. Then we put forth; the Viceroy,
Rudolph der Harras, and their suite. My bow
And quiver lay astern beside the helm;
And just as we had reached the corner, near
The Little Axen, Heaven ordain'd it so,
That from the Gotthardt's gorge, a hurricane
Swept down upon us with such headlong force,
That every rower's heart within him sank,
And all on board look'd for a watery grave.
Then heard I one of the attendant train,
Turning to Gessler, in this strain accost him:
"You see our danger, and your own, my lord,
And that we hover on the verge of death.
The boatmen there are powerless from fear,
Nor are they confident what course to take;—
Now, here is Tell, a stout and fearless man,
And knows to steer with more than common
skill.
How if we should avail ourselves of him
In this emergency?" The Viceroy then
Address'd me thus: "If thou wilt undertake
To bring us through this tempest safely, Tell,
I might consent to free thee from thy bonds."
I answer'd, "Yes, my lord, with God's as-
sistance,
I'll see what can be done, and help us,
Heaven!"
On this they loosed me from my bonds, and I
Stood by the helm and fairly steer'd along;

Yet ever eyed my shooting gear askance,
And kept a watchful eye upon the shore,
To find some point where I might leap to land:
And when I had descried a shelving crag,
That jutted, smooth atop, into the lake—
FISH. I know it. 'Tis at foot of the Great
Axen;
But looks so steep, I never could have dreamt
'Twere possible to leap it from the boat.
TELL. I bade the men put forth their ut-
most might,
Until we came before the shelving crag.
For there, I said, the danger will be passed!
Stoutly they pull'd, and soon we neared the
point;
One prayer to God for his assisting grace,
And straining every muscle, I brought round
The vessel's stern close to the rocky wall;
Then snatching up my weapons, with a bound
I swung myself upon the flattened shelf,
And with my feet thrust off, with all my might,
The puny bark into the hell of waters.
There let it drift about, as Heaven ordains!
Thus am I here, delivered from the might
Of the dread storm, and man, more dreadful
still.
FISH. Tell, Tell, the Lord has manifestly
wrought
A miracle in thy behalf! I scarce
Can credit my own eyes. But tell me, now,
Whither you purpose to betake yourself?
For you will be in peril, should the Viceroy
Chance to escape this tempest with his life.
TELL. I heard him say, as I lay bound on
board,
His purpose was to disembark at Brunnen;
And, crossing Schwytz, convey me to his
castle.
FISH. Means he to go by land?
TELL. So he intends.
FISH. Oh, then, conceal yourself without
delay!
Not twice will heaven release you from his
grasp.
TELL. Which is the nearest way to Arth
and Küssnacht?
FISH. The public road leads by the way of
Steinen,
But there's a nearer road, and more retired,
That goes by Lowerz, which my boy can show
you.
TELL. (*Gives him his hand.*) May Heaven
reward your kindness! Fare ye well.
[*As he is going, he comes back.*
Did you not also take the oath at Rootli?
I heard your name, methinks.

FISH. Yes, I was there,
And took the oath of the confederacy.
TELL. Then do me this one favor: speed
to Bürglen—
My wife is anxious at my absence—tell her
That I am free, and in secure concealment.
FISH. But whither shall I tell her you have
fled?
TELL. You'll find her father with her, and
some more,
Who took the oath with you upon the Rootli;
Bid them be resolute, and strong of heart,—
For Tell is free and master of his arm;
They shall hear further news of me ere long.
FISH. What have you, then, in view?
Come, tell me frankly!
TELL. When once 'tis *done*, 'twill be in
every mouth. [*Exit.*
FISH. Show him the way, boy. Heaven
be his support!
Whate'er he has resolved, he'll execute.
[*Exit.*

———

SCENE II.—*Baronial mansion of Attinghausen. The* BARON *upon a couch, dying.*
WALTER FÜRST, STAUFFACHER, MELCHTHAL,
and BAUMGARTEN *attending round him.*
WALTER TELL *kneeling before the dying man.*

FÜRST. All now is over with him. He is
gone.
STAUF. He lies not like one dead. The
feather, see,
Moves on his lips! His sleep is very calm,
And on his features plays a placid smile.
[BAUMGARTEN *goes to the door and speaks
with some one.*
FÜRST. Who's there?
BAUM. (*Returning.*) Tell's wife, your
daughter, she insists
That she must speak with you, and see her boy,
[WALTER TELL *rises.*
FÜRST. I who need comfort, can I comfort
her?
Does every sorrow centre on my head?
HEDWIG. (*Forcing her way in.*)
Where is my child? Unhand me! I must see
him.
STAUF. Be calm! Reflect you're in the
house of death!
HED. (*Falling upon her boy's neck.*)
My Walter! Oh, he yet is mine!
WAL. Dear mother!

HED. And is it surely so? Art thou un-
hurt?
[*Gazing at him with anxious tenderness.*
And is it possible he aim'd at thee?
How could he do it? Oh, he has no heart—
And he could wing an arrow at his child!
FÜRST. His soul was rack'd with anguish
when he did it.
No choice was left him, but to shoot or die!
HED. Oh, if he had a father's heart, he
would
Have sooner perished by a thousand deaths!
STAUF. You should be grateful for God's
gracious care,
That ordered things so well.
HED. Can I forget
What might have been the issue. God of
Heaven!
Were I to live for centuries, I still
Should see my boy tied up,—his father's
mark,—
And still the shaft would quiver in my breast!
MELCH. You know not how the Viceroy
taunted him!
HED. Oh, ruthless heart of man! Offend
his pride,
And reason in his breast forsakes her seat;
In his blind wrath he'll stake upon a cast
A child's existence, and a mother's heart!
BAUM. Is then your husband's fate not
hard enough,
That you embitter it by such reproaches?
Have you no feeling for his sufferings?
HED. (*Turning to him and gazing full upon
him.*) Hast thou tears only for thy
friend's distress?
Say, where were you when he—my noble Tell,
Was bound in chains! Where was your friend-
ship then?
The shameful wrong was done before your
eyes;
Patient you stood, and let your friend be
dragg'd,
Ay, from your very hands. Did ever Tell
Act thus to you? Did he stand whining by
When on your heels the Viceroy's horsemen
press'd,
And full before you roared the storm-toss'd
lake?
Oh! not with idle tears he show'd his pity;
Into the boat he sprung, forgot his home,
His wife, his children, and delivered thee!
FÜRST. It had been madness to attempt his
rescue,
Unarm'd, and few in numbers as we were?
HED. (*Casting herself upon his bosom.*)

ARTIST A. BAUR.

WILLIAM TELL.

ACT IV, SCENE II.

Oh, father, and thou, too, hast lost my Tell!
The country—all have lost him! All lament
His loss; and, oh, how he must pine for us!
Heaven keep his soul from sinking to despair!
No friend's consoling voice can penetrate
His dreary dungeon walls. Should he fall sick!
Ah! In the vapors of the murky vault
He must fall sick. Even as the Alpine rose
Grows pale and withers in the swampy air,
There is no life for him, but in the sun,
And in the balm of Heaven's refreshing
    breeze.
Imprison'd! Liberty to him is breath;
He cannot live in the rank dungeon air!
    STAUF. Pray you be calm! And hand in
hand, we'll all
Combine to burst his prison doors.
    HED.   Without him,
What have you power to do? While Tell was
    free,
There still, indeed, was hope—weak innocence
Had still a friend, and the oppress'd a stay.
Tell saved you all! You cannot all combined
Release him from his cruel prison bonds.
               [*The* BARON *wakes.*
    BAUM. Hush, hush! He starts!
    ATT. (*Sitting up.*)   Where is he?
    STAUF.   Who?
    ATT.   He leaves me,
—In my last moments he abandons me.
    STAUF. He means his nephew. Have they
sent for him?
    FÜRST. He has been summoned. Cheerly
sir! Take comfort!
He has found his heart at last, and is our own.
    ATT. Say, has he spoken for his native land?
    STAUF. Ay, like a hero!
    ATT.   Wherefore comes he not,
That he may take my blessing ere I die?
I feel my life fast ebbing to a close.
    STAUF. Nay, talk not thus, dear sir! This
last short sleep
Has much refresh'd you, and your eye is bright.
    ATT. Life is but pain, and even that has left
me;
My sufferings, like my hopes, have pass'd away.
              [*Observing the boy.*
What boy is that?
    FÜRST.   Bless him. Oh, good my lord!
He is my grandson, and is fatherless.
    [HEDWIG *kneels with the boy before the dying*
               man.
    ATT. And fatherless—I leave you all, ay all!
Oh, wretched fate, that these old eyes should
    see
My country's ruin, as they close in death!

Must I attain the utmost verge of life,
To feel my hopes go with me to the grave?
    STAUF. (*To* FÜRST.) Shall he depart 'mid
    grief and gloom like this?
Shall not his parting moments be illumed
By hope's delightful beams? My noble lord,
Raise up your drooping spirit! We are not
Forsaken quite—past all deliverance.
    ATT. Who shall deliver you?
    FÜRST.   Ourselves. For know
The Cantons three are to each other pledged,
To hunt the tyrants from the land. The
    league
Has been concluded, and a sacred oath
Confirms our union. Ere another year
Begins its circling course—the blow shall fall.
In a free land your ashes shall repose.
    ATT. The league concluded! Is it really
    so?
    MELCH. On one day shall the Cantons rise
together.
All is prepared to strike—and to this hour
The secret closely kept, though hundreds share
    it.
The ground is hollow 'neath the tyrants' feet;
Their days of rule are number'd, and ere
    long
No trace of their dominion shall remain.
    ATT. Ay, but their castles, how to master
    them?
    MELCH. On the same day they, too, are
    doom'd to fall.
    ATT. And are the nobles parties to this
    league?
    STAUF. We trust to their assistance should
    we need it;
As yet the peasantry alone have sworn.
    ATT. (*Raising himself up, in great astonish-*
    ment.) And have the peasantry dared
    such a charge
On their own charge, without the nobles' aid—
Relied so much on their own proper strength?
Nay then, indeed, they want our help no more;
We may go down to death cheer'd by the
    thought,
That after us the majesty of man
Will live, and be maintain'd by other hands.
    [*He lays his hand upon the head of the child,*
    who is kneeling before him.
From this boy's head, whereon the apple lay,
Your new and better liberty shall spring:
The old is crumbling down — the times are
    changing—
And from the ruins blooms a fairer life.
    STAUF. (*To* FÜRST.) See, see, what splen-
    dor streams around his eye!

This is not Nature's last expiring flame,
It is the beam of renovated life.
ATT. From their old towers the nobles are
    descending,
And swearing in the towns the civic oath.
In Uechtland and Thurgau the work's begun;
The noble Bern lifts her commanding head,
And Freyburg is a stronghold of the free;
The stirring Zurich calls her guilds to arms;—
And now, behold!—the ancient might of kings
Is shiver'd gainst her everlasting walls.
    [*He speaks what follows with a prophetic*
    tone; his utterance rising into enthusiasm.
I see the princes and their haughty peers,
Clad all in steel, come striding on to crush
A harmless shepherd race with mailed hand.
Desp'rate the conflict; 'tis for life or death;
And many a pass will tell to after years
Of glorious victories sealed in foemen's blood.
The peasant throws himself with naked breast,
A willing victim on their serried lances.
They yield—the flower of chivalry's cut down,
And freedom waves her conquering banner
    high!
    [*Grasps the hands of* WALTER FÜRST *and*
        STAUFFACHER.
Hold fast together, then,—for ever fast!
Let freedom's haunts be one in heart and
    mind!
Set watches on your mountain tops, that league
May answer league, when comes the hour to
    strike.
Be one—be one—be one——
    [*He falls back upon the cushion. His lifeless*
    hands continue to grasp those of FÜRST *and*
    STAUFFACHER, *who regard him for some*
    moments in silence, and then retire, over-
    come with sorrow. Meanwhile the servants
    have quietly pressed into the chamber,
    testifying different degrees of grief. Some
    kneel down beside him and weep on his
    body; while this scene is passing, the castle
    bell tolls.
RUDENZ. (*Entering hurriedly.*) Lives he?
    Oh, say, can he still hear my voice?
FÜRST. (*Averting his face.*)
You are our seignior and protector now;
Henceforth this castle bears another name.
RUD. (*Gazing at the body with deep emotion.*)
Oh, God! Is my repentance, then, too late?
Could he not live some few brief moments
    more,
To see the change that has come o'er my heart?
Oh, I was deaf to his true counselling voice
While yet he walked on earth. Now he is
    gone,—

Gone, and for ever,—leaving me the debt—
The heavy debt I owe him—undischarged!
Oh, tell me! did he part in anger with me?
    STAUF. When dying, he was told what you
    had done,
And bless'd the valor that inspired your words!
    RUD. (*Kneeling down beside the dead body.*)
Yes, sacred relics of a man beloved!
Thou lifeless corpse! Here, on thy death-cold
    hand,
Do I abjure all foreign ties for ever!
And to my country's cause devote myself.
I am a Switzer, and will act as one,
With my whole heart and soul.   [*Rises.*
                Mourn for our friend,
Our common parent, yet be not dismay'd!
'Tis not alone his lands that I inherit,—
His heart—his spirit, have devolved on me;
And my young arm shall execute the task,
For which his hoary age remain'd your debtor.
Give me your hands, ye venerable fathers!
Thine, Melchthal, too! Nay, do not hesitate,
Nor from me turn distrustfully away.
Accept my plighted vow—my knightly oath!
    FÜRST. Give him your hands, my friends!
    A heart like his,
That sees and owns its error, claims our trust.
    MELCH. You ever held the peasantry in
    scorn,
What surety have we, that you mean us fair?
    RUD. Oh, think not of the error of my
    youth!
    STAUF. (*To* MELCHTHAL.)
Be one! They were our father's latest words.
See they be not forgotten!
    MELCH.   Take my hand,—
A peasant's hand,—and with it, noble sir,
The gage and the assurance of a man!
Without us, sir, what would the nobles be?
Our order is more ancient, too, than yours!
    RUD. I honor it, and with my sword will
    shield it!
    MELCH. The arm, my lord, that tames the
    stubborn earth,
And makes its bosom blossom with increase,
Can also shield a man's defenceless breast.
    RUD. Then you shall shield my breast, and
    I will yours;
Thus each be strengthen'd by the other's aid!
Yet wherefore talk we, while our native land
Is still to alien tyranny a prey?
First let us sweep the foeman from the soil,
Then reconcile our difference in peace!
                [*After a moment's pause.*
How! You are silent! Not a word for me?
And have I yet no title to your trust?—

Then must I force my way, despite your will,
Into the League you secretly have form'd.
You've held a Diet on the Rootli,—I
Know this,—know all that was transacted
    there!
And though I was not trusted with your secret,
I still have kept it like a sacred pledge.
Trust me, I never was my country's foe,
Nor would I e'er have ranged myself against
    you!
Yet you did wrong—to put your rising off.
Time presses! We must strike, and swiftly
    too!
Already Tell has fallen a sacrifice
To your delay.
    STAUF.   We swore to wait till Christmas.
    RUD.   I was not there,—I did not take the
    oath.
If you delay, I will not!
    MELCH.   What! You would——
    RUD.   I count me now among the country's
    fathers,
And to protect you is my foremost duty.
    FÜRST.   Within the earth to lay these dear
    remains,
That is your nearest and most sacred duty.

RUD.   When we have set the country free,
    we'll place
Our fresh victorious wreaths upon his bier.
Oh, my dear friends, 'tis not your cause alone!
—I have a cause to battle with the tyrants,
That more concerns myself.   Know, that my
    Bertha
Has disappear'd,—been carried off by stealth,
—Stolen from amongst us by their ruffian
    hands!
    STAUF.   And has the tyrant dared so fell an
    outrage
Against a lady free and nobly born?
    RUD.   Alas! my friends, I promised help
    to you,
And I must first implore it for myself!
She that I love, is stolen—is forced away.
And who knows where the tyrant has conceal'd
    her,
Or with what outrages his ruffian crew
May force her into nuptials she detests?
Forsake me not!—Oh, help me to her rescue.
She loves you! Well, oh well, has she de-
    served,
That all should rush to arms in her behalf!
    STAUF.   What course do you propose?

95

Rud.   Alas! I know not.
In the dark mystery that shrouds her fate,—
In the dread agony of this suspense,—
Where I can grasp at nought of certainty,—
One single ray of comfort beams upon me.
From out the ruins of the tyrant's power
Alone can she be rescued from the grave.
Their strongholds must be levell'd! every one,
Ere we can pierce into her gloomy prison.
    Melch.   Come, lead us on! We follow!
        Why defer
Until to-morrow, what to-day may do?
Tell's arm was free when we at Rootli swore,
This foul enormity was yet undone.
And change of circumstance brings change of
    law;
Who such a coward as to waver still?
    Rud. *(To* Walter Forst.*)*
Meanwhile to arms, and wait in readiness
The fiery signal on the mountain tops.
For swifter than a boat can scour the lake
Shall you have tidings of our victory;
And when you see the welcome flames ascend,
Then, like the lightning, swoop upon the foe,
And lay the despots and their creatures low!

———

SCENE III.—*The pass near Küssnacht, slop-*
ing down from behind, with rocks on either
side. The travelers are visible upon the
heights, before they appear on the stage.
Rocks all round the stage. Upon one of the
foremost a projecting cliff overgrown with
brushwood.

    Tell. *(Enters with his crossbow.)*
Here thro' this deep defile he needs must pass;
There leads no other road to Küssnacht:—here
I'll do it:—the opportunity is good.
Yon alder tree stands well for my concealment,
Thence my avenging shaft will surely reach
    him;
The straightness of the path forbids pursuit.
Now, Gessler, balance thine account with
    Heaven!
Thou must away from earth,—thy sand is run.

I led a peaceful inoffensive life;—
My bow was bent on forest game alone,
And my pure soul was free from thoughts of
    murder—
But thou hast scared me from my dream of
    peace;
The milk of human kindness thou hast turn'd
To rankling poison in my breast; and made

Appalling deeds familiar to my soul.
He who could make his own child's head his
    mark,
Can speed his arrow to his foeman's heart.

My children dear, my lov'd and faithful
    wife,
Must be protected, tyrant, from thy fury!—
When last I drew my bow — with trembling
    hand—
And thou, with murderous joy, a father forced
To level at his child—when, all in vain,
Writhing before thee, I implored thy mercy—
Then in the agony of my soul, I vow'd
A fearful oath, which met God's ear alone,
That when my bow next wing'd an arrow's
    flight,
Its aim should be thy heart.—The vow I made,
Amid the hellish torments of that moment,
I hold a sacred debt, and I will pay it.

Thou art my lord, my Emperor's delegate;
Yet would the Emperor not have stretch'd his
    power
So far as thou. — He sent thee to these Can-
    tons
To deal forth law — stern law — for he is an-
    ger'd;
But not to wanton with unbridled will
In every cruelty, with fiend-like joy:—
There is a God to punish and avenge.

Come forth, thou bringer once of bitter
    pangs,
My precious jewel now,—my chiefest treasure
A mark I'll set thee, which the cry of grief
Could never penetrate,—but thou shalt pierce
    it.—
And thou, my trusty bowstring, that so oft
Has served me faithfully in sportive scenes,
Desert me not in this most serious hour—
Only be true this once, my own good cord,
That hast so often wing'd the biting shaft:—
For shouldst thou fly successless from my hand,
I have no second to send after thee.
        [*Travelers pass over the stage.*

I'll sit me down upon this bench of stone,
Hewn for the way-worn traveler's brief repose
—For here there is no home.—Each hurries by
The other, with quick step and careless look,
Nor stays to question of his grief.—Here goes
The merchant, full of care.—the pilgrim next,
With slender scrip,—and then the pious monk,
The scowling robber, and the jovial player,
The carrier with his heavy-laden horse,

ARTIST: A. BAUR.

WILLIAM TELL.

ACT IV, SCENE III.

That comes to us from the far haunts of men;
For every road conducts to the world's end.
They all push onwards—every man intent
On his own several business—mine is murder.
　　　　　　　　　　　　　　　[Sits down.

Time was, my dearest children, when with
　　joy
You hail'd your father's safe return to home
From his long mountain toils; for, when he
　　came,
He ever brought some little present with him.
A lovely Alpine flower—a curious bird—
Or elf-boat, found by wanderer on the hills.—
But now he goes in quest of other game:
In the wild pass he sits, and broods on mur-
　　der;
And watches for the life-blood of his foe.—
But still his thoughts are fixed on you alone,
Dear children.—'Tis to guard your innocence,
To shield you from the tyrant's fell revenge,
He bends his bow to do a deed of blood!
　　　　　　　　　　　　　　　[Rises.

Well—I am watching for a noble prey—
Does not the huntsman, with severest toil,
Roam for whole days, amid the winter's cold,
Leap with a daring bound from rock to rock,—
And climb the jagged, slippery steeps, to which
His limbs are glued by his own streaming
　　blood—
And all this but to gain a wretched chamois;
A far more precious prize is now my aim—
The heart of that dire foe, who would destroy
me.

*[Sprightly music heard in the distance, which
　comes gradually nearer.*

From my first years of boyhood I have used
The bow—been practised in the archer's feats;
The bull's eye many a time my shafts have hit,
And many a goodly prize have I brought home,
Won in the games of skill.—This day I'll make
My master-shot, and win the highest prize
Within the whole circumference of the moun-
tains.

*[A marriage train passes over the stage, and
goes up the pass. TELL gazes at it, leaning on his bow. He is joined by STUSSI
the Ranger.*

STUS.　There goes the bridal party of the
steward
Of Mörlischachen's cloister.　He is rich!
And has some ten good pastures on the Alps.
He goes to fetch his bride from Imisee,
There will be revelry to-night at Küssnacht.
Come with us—ev'ry honest man's invited.

TELL.　A gloomy guest fits not a wedding
feast.
STUS.　If grief oppress you, dash it from
your heart!
Bear with your lot.　The times are heavy now,
And we must snatch at pleasure while we can.
Here 'tis a bridal, there a burial.
TELL.　And oft the one treads close upon
the other.
STUS.　So runs the world at present.
　　　　Everywhere
We meet with woe and misery enough.
There's been a slide of earth in Glarus, and
A whole side of the Glärnisch has fallen in.
TELL.　Strange! And do even the hills
begin to totter?
There is stability for nought on earth.
STUS.　Strange tidings, too, we hear from
other parts.
I spoke with one but now, that came from
Baden,
Who said a knight was on his way to court,
And, as he rode along a swarm of wasps
Surrounded him, and settling on his horse,
So fiercely stung the beast, that it fell dead,
And he proceeded to the court on foot.
TELL.　Even the weak are furnish'd with a
sting.
*[ARMGART enters with several children, and
places herself at the entrance of the pass.*
STUS.　'Tis thought to bode disaster to the
country,—
Some horrid deed against the course of nature.
TELL.　Why, every day brings forth such
fearful deeds;
There needs no miracle to tell their coming.
STUS.　Too true! He's bless'd, who tills
his field in peace,
And sits untroubled by his own fireside.
TELL.　The very meekest cannot rest in
quiet,
Unless it suits with his ill neighbor's humor.
*[TELL looks frequently with restless expecta-
tion towards the top of the pass.*
STUS.　So fare you well! You're waiting
some one here?
TELL.　I am.
STUS.　　　A pleasant meeting with your
friends!
You are from Uri, are you not? His grace
The governor's expected thence to-day.
TRAVELER.　*(Entering.)*
Look not to see the governor to-day,
The streams are flooded by the heavy rains,
And all the bridges have been swept away.
　　　　　　　　　　　　　　　[TELL rises.

97

ARM. (*Coming forward.*) The Viceroy not arrived?

STUS. And do you seek him?

ARM. Alas, I do!

STUS. But why thus place yourself Where you obstruct his passage down the pass! ARM. Here he cannot escape me. He *must* hear me.

FRIESSHARDT. (*Coming hastily down the pass, and calls upon the stage.*) Make way, make way! My lord, the governor, Is coming down on horseback close behind me.

[*Exit* TELL.

ARM. (*With animation.*) The Viceroy comes!

[*She goes towards the pass with her children.* GESSLER *and* RUDOLPH DER HARRAS *appear upon the heights on horseback.*

STUS. (*To* FRIESSHARDT.) How got ye through the stream, When all the bridges have been carried down? FRIESS. We've battled with the billows; and, my friend, An Alpine torrent's nothing after that.

STUS. How! Were you out, then, in that dreadful storm?

FRIESS. Ay, that we were! I shall not soon forget it.

STUS. Stay, speak—

FRIESS. I cannot. I must to the castle, And tell them, that the governor's at hand.

[*Exit.*

STUS. If honest men, now, had been in the ship, It had gone down with every soul on board :— Some folks are proof 'gainst fire and water both. [*Looking round.* Where has the huntsman gone, with whom I spoke? [*Exit.*

Enter GESSLER *and* RUDOLPH DER HARRAS *on horseback.*

GESS. Say what you please; I am the Emperor's servant, And my first care must be to do his pleasure. He did not send me here to fawn and cringe And coax these boors into good humor. No! Obedience he must have. We soon shall see, If king or peasant is to lord it here?

ARM. Now is the moment! Now for my petition!

GESS. 'Twas not in sport that I set up the cap In Altdorf—or to try the people's hearts— All this I knew before. I set it up

That they might learn to bend those stubborn necks They carry far too proudly—and I placed What well I knew their eyes could never brook Full in the road, which they perforce must pass, That, when their eye fell on it, they might call That lord to mind whom they too much forget.

HAR. But surely, sir, the people have some rights—

GESS. This is no time to settle what they are. Great projects are at work, and hatching now. The Imperial house seeks to extend its power. Those vast designs of conquest, which the sire Has gloriously begun, the son will end. This petty nation is a stumbling-block— One way or other it must be subjected.

[*They are about to pass on.* ARMGART *throws herself down before* GESSLER.

ARM. Mercy, lord governor! Oh, pardon, pardon!

GESS. Why do you cross me on the public road? Stand back, I say.

ARM. My husband lies in prison; My wretched orphans cry for bread. Have pity, Pity, my lord, upon our sore distress!

HAR. Who are you, woman; and who is your husband!

ARM. A poor wild-hay-man of the Rigiberg, Kind sir, who on the brow of the abyss, Mows down the grass from steep and craggy shelves, To which the very cattle dare not climb.

HAR. (*To* GESSLER.) By Heaven! a sad and miserable life! I prithee, give the wretched man his freedom. How great soever his offence may be, His horrid trade is punishment enough.

[*To* ARMGART. You shall have justice. To the castle bring Your suit. This is no place to deal with it.

ARM. No, no, I will not stir from where I stand, Until your grace restore my husband to me. Six months already has he been in prison, And waits the sentence of a judge in vain.

GESS. How! would you force me, woman? Hence! Begone!

ARM. Justice, my lord! Ay, justice! Thou art judge: The deputy of the Emperor—of Heaven. Then do thy duty,—as thou hopest for justice From him who rules above, show it to us!

Gess. Hence, drive this daring rabble from my sight!

Arm. *(Seizing his horse's reins.)* No, no, by Heaven, I've nothing more to lose.— Thou stirr'st not, Viceroy, from this spot, until Thou dost me fullest justice. Knit thy brows, And roll thy eyes—I fear not. Our distress Is so extreme, so boundless, that we care No longer for thine anger.

Gess. Woman, hence! Give way, I say, or I will ride thee down.

Arm. Well, do so—there— *[Throws her children and herself upon the ground before him.*

Here on the ground I lie, I and my children. Let the wretched orphans Be trodden by thy horse into the dust! It will not be the worst, that thou hast done.

Har. Are you mad, woman?

Arm. *(Continuing with vehemence.)* Many a day thou hast Trampled the Emperor's lands beneath thy feet. Oh, I am but a woman! Were I man, I'd find some better thing to do, than here Lie grovelling in the dust. *[The music of the wedding party is again heard from the top of the pass, but more softly.*

Gess. Where are my knaves? Drag her away, lest I forget myself, And do some deed I may repent hereafter.

Har. My lord, the servants cannot force a passage; The pass is block'd up by a marriage party.

Gess. Too mild a ruler am I to this people, Their tongues are all too bold—nor have they yet Been tamed to due submission, as they shall be. I must take order for the remedy; I will subdue this stubborn mood of theirs, And crush the Soul of Liberty within them. I'll publish a new law throughout the land; I will— *[An arrow pierces him,—he puts his hand on his heart, and is about to sink—with a feeble voice,*

Oh God, have mercy on my soul!

Har. My lord! my lord! Oh God! What's this? Whence came it?

Arm. *(Starts up.)* Dead, dead! He reels, he falls! 'Tis in his heart!

Har. *(Springs from his horse,)* This is most horrible! Oh Heaven! Sir Knight, Address yourself to God and pray for mercy, —You are a dying man.

Gess. That shot was Tell's. *[He slides from his horse into the arms of* Rudolph der Harras, *who lays him down upon the bench.* Tell *appears above upon the rocks.*

Tell. Thou know'st the archer, seek no other hand. Our cottages are free, and innocence Secure from thee: thou'lt be our curse no more. *[*Tell *disappears. People rush in.*

Stus. What is the matter? Tell me what has happen'd!

Arm. The governor is shot,—kill'd by an arrow!

People. *(Running in.)* Who has been shot? *[While the foremost of the marriage party are coming on the stage, the hindmost are still upon the heights. The music continues.*

Har. He's bleeding fast to death. Away, for help—pursue the murderer! Unhappy man, is't thus that thou must die? Thou wouldst not heed the warnings that I gave thee!

Stus. By Heaven, his cheek is pale! His life ebbs fast.

Many Voices. Who did the deed?

Har. What! Are the people mad, That they make music to a murder? Silence! *[Music breaks off suddenly. People continue to flock in.*

Speak, if thou canst, my lord. Hast thou no charge To intrust me with? *[*Gessler *makes signs with his hand, which he repeats with vehemence, when he finds they are not understood.*

What would you have me do? Shall I to Küssnacht? I can't guess your meaning. Do not give way to this impatience. Leave All thoughts of earth, and make your peace with Heaven. *[The whole marriage party gather round the dying man.*

Stus. See there! how pale he grows! Death's gathering now About his heart:—his eyes grow dim and glazed.

Arm. *(Holds up a child.)* Look, children, how a tyrant dies!·

Har. Mad hag! Have you no touch of feeling, that you look On horrors such as these, without a shudder? Help me—take hold. What, will not one assist To pull the torturing arrow from his breast?

WOMEN. We touch the man whom God's own hand has struck?

HAR. All curses light on you!
[*Draws his sword.*

STUS. (*Seizes his arm.*) Gently, sir knight! Your power is at an end. 'Twere best forbear. Our country's foe is fallen. We will brook No further violence. We are free men.

ALL. The country's free!

HAR. And is it come to this? Fear and obedience at an end so soon?
[*To the soldiers of the guard, who are thronging in.*
You see, my friends, the bloody piece of work They've acted here. 'Tis now too late for help, And to pursue the murderer were vain. New duties claim our care. Set on to Küssnacht,
And let us save that fortress for the king!

For in an hour like this, all ties of order, Fealty and faith, are scatter'd to the winds. No man's fidelity is to be trusted.
[*As he is going out with the soldiers, six* FRATRES MISERICORDIÆ *appear.*
ARM. Here come the brotherhood of mercy. Room!

STUS. The victim's slain, and now the ravens stoop.

BROTHERS OF MERCY. (*Form a semicircle round the body, and sing in solemn tones.*)
With hasty step death presses on,
Nor grants to man a moment's stay,
He falls ere half his race be run,
In manhood's pride is swept away.
Prepar'd, or unprepar'd to die,
He stands before his Judge on high.
[*While they are repeating the last two lines, the curtain falls.*

ACT V.

SCENE I.—*A common near Altdorf. In the background to the right the Keep of Uri, with the scaffold still standing, as in the Third Scene of the first Act. To the left, the view opens upon numerous mountains, on all of which signal fires are burning. Day is breaking, and bells are heard ringing from various distances.*

RUODI, KUONI, WERNI, MASTER MASON, *and many other country people, also women and children.*

RUODI. Look at the fiery signals on the mountains!

MAS. M. Hark to the bells above the forest there!

RUODI. The enemy's expelled.

MAS. M.   The forts are taken.

RUODI. And we of Uri, do we still endure
Upon our native soil, the tyrant's Keep?
Are we the last to strike for liberty?

MAS. M. Shall the yoke stand, that was to bow our necks?

Up! Tear it to the ground!

ALL.   Down, down with it!

RUODI. Where is the Stier of Uri?

URI.   Here. What would ye?

RUODI. Up to your tower, and wind us such a blast,
As shall resound afar, from hill to hill;
Rousing the echoes of each peak and glen,
And call the mountain men in haste together!

[*Exit* STIER OF URI—*enter* WALTER FÜRST.

FÜRST. Stay, stay, my friends! As yet we have not learn'd
What has been done in Unterwald and Schwytz.
Let's wait till we receive intelligence!
RUODI. Wait, wait for what? The accursed tyrant's dead,
And the bright day of liberty has dawn'd!
MAS. M. How! Do these flaming signals not suffice,
That blaze on every mountain top around?
RUODI. Come all, fall to—come, men and women, all!
Destroy the scaffold! Tear the arches down!
Down with the walls, let not a stone remain!
MAS. M. Come, comrades, come! We built it, and we know
How best to hurl it down.
ALL. Come! Down with it!
[*They fall upon the building at every side.*
FÜRST. The floodgate's burst. They're not to be restrained.
[*Enter* MELCHTHAL *and* BAUMGARTEN.
MELCH. What! Stands the fortress still, when Sarnen lies
In ashes, and when Rossberg is a ruin?
FÜRST. You, Melchthal, here? D'ye bring us liberty?
Say, have you freed the country of the foe?
MELCH. We've swept them from the soil.
Rejoice, my friend;
Now, at this very moment, while we speak,
There's not a tyrant left in Switzerland!
FÜRST. How did you get the forts into your power?
MELCH. Rudenz it was who with a gallant arm,
And manly daring, took the keep at Sarnen.
The Rossberg I had storm'd the night before.
But hear, what chanced. Scarce had we driven the foe
Forth from the keep, and given it to the flames,
That now rose crackling upwards to the skies,
When from the blaze rush'd Diethelm, Gessler's page,
Exclaiming, "Lady Bertha will be burnt!"
FÜRST. Good heavens!
[*The beams of the scaffold are heard falling.*
MELCH. 'Twas she herself. Here had she been
Immured in secret by the Viceroy's orders.
Rudenz sprang up in frenzy. For we heard
The beams and massive pillars crashing down,
And through the volumed smoke the piteous shrieks
Of the unhappy lady.

FÜRST. Is she saved?
MELCH. Here was a time for promptness and decision!
Had he been nothing but our baron, then
We should have been most chary of our lives;
But he was our confederate, and Bertha
Honor'd the people. So, without a thought,
We risk'd the worst, and rushed into the flames.
FÜRST. But is she saved?
MELCH. She is. Rudenz and I
Bore her between us from the blazing pile,
With crashing timbers toppling all around.
And when she had revived, the danger past,
And raised her eyes to meet the light of heaven,
The baron fell upon my breast; and then
A silent vow of friendship pass'd between us—
A vow that, tempered in yon furnace heat,
Will last through ev'ry shock of time and fate.
FÜRST. Where is the Landenberg?
MELCH. Across the Brünig.
No fault of mine it was, that he, who quench'd
My father's eyesight, should go hence unharm'd.
He fled—I followed—overtook and seized him,
And dragg'd him to my father's feet. The sword
Already quiver'd o'er the caitiff's head,
When at the entreaty of the blind old man,
I spared the life for which he basely pray'd.
He swore URPHEDE, never to return:
He'll keep his oath, for he has felt our arm.
FÜRST. Thank God, our victory's unstain'd by blood!
CHILDREN. (*Running across the stage with fragments of wood.*) Liberty! Liberty!
Hurrah, we're free!
FÜRST. Oh! what a joyous scene! These children will,
E'en to their latest day, remember it.
[*Girls bring in the cap upon a pole. The whole stage is filled with people.*
RUODI. Here is the cap, to which we were to bow!
BAUM. Command us, how we shall dispose of it.
FÜRST. Heavens! 'Twas beneath this cap my grandson stood!
SEVERAL VOICES. Destroy the emblem of the tyrant's power!
Let it be burnt!
FÜRST. No. Rather be preserved!
'Twas once the instrument of despots—now
'Twill be a lasting symbol of our freedom.

[*Peasants, men, women, and children, some
standing, others sitting upon the beams of
the shattered scaffold, all picturesquely
grouped, in a large semicircle.*

MELCH. Thus now, my friends, with light
and merry hearts,
We stand upon the wreck of tyranny;
And gallantly have we fulfill'd the oath,
Which we at Rootli swore, Confederates!
FÜRST. The work is but begun. We must
be firm.
For, be assured, the king will make all speed,
To avenge his Viceroy's death, and reinstate,
By force of arms, the tyrant we've expell'd.
MELCH. Why let him come, with all his
armaments!
The foe within has fled before our arms;
We'll give him welcome warmly from without!
RUODI. The passes to the country are but
few;
And these we'll boldly cover with our bodies.
BAUM. We are bound by an indissoluble
league,
And all his armies shall not make us quail.
        [*Enter* RÖSSELMANN *and* STAUFFACHER.
RÖSS. (*Speaking as he enters.*)
These are the awful judgments of the Lord!

PEASANT. What is the matter?
RÖSS.   In what times we live!
FÜRST. Say on, what is't? Ha. Werner,
is it you?
What tidings?
PEASANT. What's the matter?
RÖSS.   Hear and wonder!
STAUF. We are released from one great
cause of dread.
RÖSS. The Emperor is murdered.
FÜRST.   Gracious Heaven!
[*Peasants rise up and throng round* STAUF-
FACHER.
ALL. Murder'd the Emp'ror? What! The
Emp'ror! Hear!
MELCH. Impossible! How came you by
the news?
STAUF. 'Tis true! Near Bruck, by the
assassin's hand,
King Albert fell. A most trustworthy man,
John Müller, from Schaffhausen, brought the
news.
FÜRST. Who dared commit so horrible a
deed?
STAUF. The doer makes the deed more
dreadful still;

It was his nephew, his own brother's child,
Duke John of Austria, who struck the blow.
  MELCH. What drove him to so dire a
    parricide?
  STAUF. The Emp'ror kept his patrimony
    back,
Despite his urgent importunities;
'Twas said, indeed, he never meant to give it,
But with a mitre to appease the duke.
However this may be, the duke gave ear
To the ill counsel of his friends in arms;
And with the noble lords, Von Eschenbach,
Von Tegerfeld, Von Wart and Palm, resolved,
Since his demands for justice were despised,
With his own hands to take revenge at least.
  FÜRST. But say, how compass'd he the
    dreadful deed?
  STAUF. The king was riding down from
    Stein to Baden,
Upon his way to join the court at Rheinfeld,
—With him a train of high-born gentlemen,
And the young princes John and Leopold,
And when they'd reach'd the ferry of the Reuss,
The assassins forced their way into the boat,
To separate the Emperor from his suite.
His highness landed, and was riding on
Across a fresh plough'd field—where once,
    they say,
A mighty city stood in Pagan times—
With Habsburg's ancient turrets full in sight,
Where all the grandeur of his line had birth—
When Duke John plunged a dagger in his
    throat,
Palm ran him thro' the body with his lance,
Eschenbach cleft his skull at one fell blow,
And down he sank, all weltering in his blood,
On his own soil, by his own kinsmen slain.
Those on the opposite bank, who saw the deed,
Being parted by the stream. could only raise
An unavailing cry of loud lament.
But a poor woman, sitting by the way,
Raised him, and on her breast he bled to death.
  MELCH. Thus has he dug his own untimely
    grave,
Who sought insatiably to grasp at all.
  STAUF. The country round is fill'd with
    dire alarm.
The mountain passes are blockaded all,
And sentinels on ev'ry frontier set;
E'en ancient Zurich barricades her gates,
That for these thirty years have open stood,
Dreading the murd'rers, and th' avengers more.
For cruel Agnes comes, the Hungarian queen,
To all her sex's tenderness a stranger,
Arm'd with the thunders of the church, to
    wreak

Dire vengeance for her parent's royal blood,
On the whole race of those that murder'd
    him,—
Upon their servants, children, children's chil-
    dren,—
Nay, on the stones that build their castle walls.
Deep has she sworn a vow to immolate
Whole generations on her father's tomb,
And bathe in blood as in the dew of May.
  MELCH. Know you which way the mur-
    derers have fled?
  STAUF. No sooner had they done the deed,
    than they
Took flight, each following a different route,
And parted, ne'er to see each other more.
Duke John must still be wand'ring in the
    mountains.
  FÜRST. And thus their crime has yielded
    them no fruits.
Revenge is barren. Of itself it makes
The dreadful food it feeds on; its delight
Is murder—its satiety despair.
  STAUF. The assassins reap no profit by their
    crime;
But we shall pluck with unpolluted hands
The teeming fruits of their most bloody deed.
For we are ransomed from our heaviest fear;
The direst foe of liberty has fallen,
And, 'tis reported, that the crown will pass
From Habsburg's house into another line;
The Empire is determined to assert
Its old prerogative of choice, I hear,
  FÜRST *and several others.*
Has any one been named to you?
  STAUF.   The Count
Of Luxembourg is widely named already.—
  FÜRST. 'Tis well we stood so staunchly by
    the Empire!
Now we may hope for justice, and with cause.
  STAUF. The Emperor will need some valiant
    friends.
And he will shelter us from Austria's ven-
    geance.
  [*The peasantry embrace. Enter* SACRIST
    with imperial messenger.
  SACRIST. Here are the worthy chiefs of
    Switzerland!
  RÖSS. *and several others.*
Sacrist, what news?
  SACRIST.   A courier brings this letter.
  ALL. (*To* WALTER FÜRST.)
Open and read it.
  FÜRST. (*Reading.*) "To the worthy men
Of Uri, Schwytz, and Unterwald, the Queen
Elizabeth sends grace and all good wishes!

MANY VOICES. What wants the Queen with us? Her reign is done.

FÜRST. (Reads.)
" In the great grief and doleful widowhood,
In which the bloody exit of her lord
Has plunged her majesty, she still remembers
The ancient faith and love of Switzerland."

MELCH. She ne'er did that, in her prosperity.

RÖSS. Hush, let us hear!

FÜRST. (Reads.) "And she is well assured,
Her people will in due abhorrence hold
The perpetrators of this damned deed.
On the three Cantons, therefore, she relies,
That they in nowise lend the murderers aid;
But rather, that they loyally assist,
To give them up to the avenger's hand.
Remembering the love and grace which they
Of old received from Rudolph's princely house."

[Symptoms of dissatisfaction among the peasantry.

MANY VOICES. The love and grace!

STAUF. Grace from the father we, indeed, received,
But what have we to boast of from the son?
Did he confirm the charter of our freedom,
As all preceding emperors had done?
Did he judge righteous judgment, or afford
Shelter, or stay, to innocence oppress'd?
Nay, did he e'en give audience to the envoys
We sent, to lay our grievances before him?
Not one of all these things e'er did the king.
And had we not ourselves achieved our rights
By resolute valor, our necessities
Had never touch'd him. Gratitude to him!
Within these vales he sowed not gratitude;
He stood upon an eminence—he might;
Have been a very father to his people,
But all his aim and pleasure was to raise
Himself and his own house: and now may those
Whom he has aggrandized, lament for him!

FÜRST. We will not triumph in his fall, nor now
Recall to mind the wrongs we have endured,
Far be't from us! Yet, that we should avenge
The sovereign's death, who never did us good,
And hunt down those who ne'er molested us,
Becomes us not, nor is our duty. Love
Must bring its offerings free, and unconstrain'd;
From all enforced duties death absolves—
And unto him we are no longer bound.

MELCH. And if the queen laments within her bower,

Accusing Heaven in sorrow's wild despair;
Here see a people from its anguish freed,
To that same Heav'n send up its thankful praise.
For who would reap regrets, must sow affection. [Exit the Imperial Courier.

STAUF. (To the people.) But where is Tell?
Shall he, our freedom's founder,
Alone be absent from our festival?
He did the most—endured the worst of all.
Come—to his dwelling let us all repair,
And bid the saviour of our country hail!
[Exeunt omnes.

———

SCENE II.—Interior of TELL'S cottage. A fire burning on the hearth. The open door shows the scene outside.

HEDWIG, WALTER, and WILLIAM.

HED. Boys, dearest boys! your father comes to-day;
He lives, is free, and we, and we all are free!
The country owes its liberty to him!

WAL. And I, too, mother, bore my part in it;
I shall be named with him. My father's shaft
Went closely by my life, but yet I shook not!

HED. (Embracing him.)
Yes, yes, thou art restored to me again!
Twice have I given thee birth,—twice suffer'd all
A mother's agonies for thee, my child!
But this is past—I have you both, boys, both!
And your dear father will be back to-day.
[A MONK appears at the door.

WILL. See, mother, yonder stands a holy friar;
He's asking alms, no doubt.

HED. Go lead him in,
That we may give him cheer, and make him feel
That he has come into the house of joy.
[Exit, and returns immediately with a cup.

WILL. (To the MONK.) Come in, good man. Mother will give you food!

WAL. Come in and rest, then go refresh'd away!

MONK. (Glancing round in terror, with unquiet looks.) Where am I? In what country?

WAL. Have you lost
Your way, that you are ignorant of this?
You are at Brüglen, in the land of Uri,
Just at the entrance of the Sheckenthal.

105

MONK. *(To* HEDWIG.*)*
Are you alone? Your husband, is he here?
HED. I momently expect him. But what
 ails you?
You look as one whose soul is ill at ease.
Whoe'er you be, you are in want—take that.
 [Offers him the cup.
MONK. Howe'er my sinking heart may
 yearn for food.
I will taste nothing till you've promised me—
HED. Touch not my dress, nor yet ad-
 vance one step.
Stand off, I say, if you would have me hear
 you.
MONK. Oh, by this hearth's bright hos-
 pitable blaze,
By your dear children's heads, which I em-
 brace— *[Grasps the boys.*
HED. Stand back, I say! What is your
 purpose, man?
Back from my boys! You are no monk,—no,
 no.
Beneath that robe content and peace should
 dwell,
But neither lives within that face of thine.
MONK. I am the veriest wretch that breathes
 on earth.
HED. The heart is never deaf to wretch-
 edness;
But thy look freezes up my inmost soul.
WAL. *(Springs up.)* Mother, my father!
HED. Oh, my God!
 [Is about to follow, trembles and stops.
WILL. *(Running after his brother.)*
 My father!
WAL. *(Without.)* Thou'rt here once more!
WILL. *(Without.)*
 My father, my dear father!
TELL. *(Without.)* Yes, here I am once
 more! Where is your mother?
 [They enter.
WAL. There at the door she stands, and
 can no further,
She trembles so with terror and with joy.
TELL. Oh! Hedwig, Hedwig,! mother of
 my children!
God has been kind and helpful in our woes.
No tyrant's hand shall e'er divide us more.
HED. *(Falling on his neck.)* O, Tell, what
 have I suffer'd for thy sake!
 [MONK becomes attentive.
TELL. Forget it now, and live for joy
 alone!
I'm here again with you! This is my cot!
I stand again on mine own hearth!

WILL. But, father,
Where is your crossbow left? I see it not.
TELL. Nor shalt thou ever see it more, my
 boy.
It is suspended in a holy place,
And in the chase shall ne'er be used again.
HED. Oh, Tell! Tell!
 [Steps back, dropping his hand.
TELL. What alarms thee, dearest wife?
HED. How—how dost thou return to me?
 This hand—
Dare I take hold of it? This hand—Oh God!
TELL. *(With firmness and animation.)*
Has shielded you and set my country free;
Freely I raise it in the face of Heaven.
 [MONK gives a sudden start—he looks at him.
Who is this friar here?
HED. Ah, I forgot him.
Speak thou with him; I shudder at his presence.
MONK. *(Stepping nearer.)*
Are you that Tell that slew the governor?
TELL. Yes, I am he. I hide the fact from
 no man.
MONK. You are that Tell! Ah! it is God's
 own hand
That hath conducted me beneath your roof.
TELL. *(Examining him closely.)*
You are no monk. Who are you?
MONK. You have slain
The governor, who did you wrong. I, too,
Have slain a foe, who late denied me justice.
He was no less your enemy than mine.
I've rid the land of him.
TELL. *(Drawing back.)*
 Thou art—oh, horror!
In—children, children—in without a word.
Go, my dear wife! Go! Go! Unhappy man,
Thou shouldst be——
HED. Heav'ns, who is it?
TELL. Do not ask.
Away! away! the children must not hear it.
Out of the house—away! Thou must not rest
'Neath the same roof with this unhappy man!
HED. Alas! What is it? Come!
 [Exit with the children.
TELL. *(To the* MONK.*)* Thou art the Duke
Of Austria—I know it. Thou hast slain
The Emperor, thy uncle, and liege lord.
JOHN. He robb'd me of my patrimony.
TELL. How!
Slain him—thy king, thy uncle! And the
 earth
Still bears thee! And the sun still shines on
 thee!
JOHN. Tell, hear me, ere you——
TELL. Reeking with the blood

ARTIST: A. BAUR.

WILLIAM TELL.

ACT V, SCENE II.

Of him that was thy Emperor, and kinsman,
Durst thou set foot within my spotless house?
Show thy fell visage to a virtuous man,
And claim the rites of hospitality?
   JOHN. I hoped to find compassion at your
    hands,
You also took revenge upon your foe!
   TELL. Unhappy man! And dar'st thou
    thus confound
Ambition's bloody crime, with the dread act
To which a father's direful need impell'd him?
Hadst thou to shield thy children's darling
   heads?
To guard thy fireside's sanctuary—ward off
The last, worst doom from all that thou didst
   love?
To Heaven I raise my unpolluted hands,
To curse thine act and thee! I have avenged
That holy nature which thou hast profaned.

I have no part with thee. Thou art a mur-
   derer;
I've shielded all that was most dear to me.
   JOHN. You cast me off to comfortless des-
    pair!
   TELL. My blood runs cold ev'n while I
    talk with thee.
Away! Pursue thine awful course! Nor longer
Pollute the cot where innocence abides!
            [JOHN *turns to depart.*
   JOHN. I cannot live, and will no longer
    thus!
   TELL. And yet my soul bleeds for thee—
    gracious Heaven!
So young, of such a noble line, the grandson
Of Rudolph, once my lord and emperor,
An outcast—murderer—standing at my door,
The poor man's door—a suppliant, in despair!
            [*Covers his face.*

JOHN. If thou hast power to weep, oh let
my fate
Move your compassion—it is horrible.
I am—say, rather was—a prince. I might
Have been most happy, had I only curb'd
Th' impatience of my passionate desires.
But envy gnaw'd my heart—I saw the youth
Of mine own cousin Leopold endow'd
With honor, and enrich'd with broad domains,
The while myself, that was in years his equal,
Was kept in abject and disgraceful nonage.
TELL. Unhappy man, thy uncle knew thee
well,
When he withheld both land and subjects from
thee.
Thou, by thy mad and desperate act hast set
A fearful seal upon his sage resolve.
JOHN. Where'er the demon of revenge has
borne them;
I have not seen them since the luckless deed.
TELL. Know's thou the Empire's ban is
out,—that thou
Art interdicted to thy friends, and given
An outlaw'd victim to thine enemies!
JOHN. Therefore I shun all public thor-
oughfares
And venture not to knock at any door—
I turn my footsteps to the wilds, and through
The mountains roam, a terror to myself.
From mine own self I shrink with horror back,
Should a chance brook reflect my ill-starr'd
form.
If thou hast pity for a fellow mortal——
[Falls down before him.
TELL. Stand up, stand up!
JOHN. Not till thou shalt extend
Thy hand in promise of assistance to me.
TELL. Can I assist thee? Can a sinful
man?
Yet get thee up — how black soe'er thy
crime,—
Thou art a man. I, too, am one. From Tell
Shall no one part uncomforted. I will
Do all that lies within my power.
JOHN. (Springs up and grasps him ardently
by the hand.) Oh, Tell,
You save me from the terrors of despair!
TELL. Let go my hand! Thou must away.
Thou canst not
Remain here undiscover'd, and discover'd,
Thou canst not count on succor. Which way,
then,
Wilt bend thy steps? Where dost thou hope
to find
A place of rest?

JOHN. Alas! alas! I know not.
TELL. Hear, then, what Heaven suggesteth
to my heart,
Thou must to Italy,—to Saint Peter's City—
There cast thyself at the Pope's feet,—confess
Thy guilt to him, and ease thy laden soul!
JOHN. But will he not surrender me to
vengeance?
TELL. Whate'er he does, receive as God's
decree.
JOHN. But how am I to reach that unknown
land?
I have no knowledge of the way, and dare not
Attach myself to other travelers.
TELL. I will describe the road, and mark
me well!
You must ascend, keeping along the Reuss,
Which from the mountains dashes wildly down.
JOHN. (In alarm.) What! See the Reuss?
The witness of my deed!
TELL. The road you take lies through the
river's gorge,
And many a cross proclaims where travelers
Have perish'd 'neath the avalanche's fall.
JOHN. I have no fear for nature's terrors,
so
I can appease the torments of my soul.
TELL. At every cross, kneel down and
expiate
Your crime with burning penitential tears—
And if you 'scape the perils of the pass,
And are not whelm'd beneath the drifted
snows,
That from the frozen peaks come sweeping
down.
You'll reach the bridge, that hangs in drizzling
spray;
Then if it yield not 'neath your heavy guilt,
When you have left it safely in your rear,
Before you frowns the gloomy Gate of Rocks,
Where never sun did shine. Proceed through
this
And you will reach a bright and gladsome vale.
Yet must you hurry on with hasty steps,
For in the haunts of peace you must not
linger.
JOHN. Oh, Rudolph, Rudolph, royal grand-
sire! thus
Thy grandson first sets foot within thy realms!
TELL. Ascending still, you gain the Gott-
hardt's heights,
On which the everlasting lakes repose,
That from the streams of Heaven itself are
fed,
There to the German soil you bid farewell;

And thence, with rapid course, another stream
Leads you to Italy, your promised land.
   [*Ranz des Vaches sounded on Alp-horns is
     heard without.*
But I hear voices! Hence!
  HED. *(Hurrying in.)* Where art thou, Tell?
Our father comes, and in exulting bands
All the confederates approach.
  JOHN. *(Covering himself.)*   Woe's me!
I dare not tarry 'mid this happiness!
  TELL. Go, dearest wife, and give this man
    to eat.
Spare not your bounty. For his road is long,
And one where shelter will be hard to find.
Quick! they approach.
  HED.   Who is he?
  TELL.   Do not ask!
And when he quits thee, turn thine eyes away,
That they may not behold the road he takes.
  [*DUKE JOHN advances hastily towards TELL.,
   but he beckons him aside and exit. When
   both have left the stage, the scene changes
   and discloses in*

SCENE III. — *The whole valley before TELL's
house, the heights which enclose it occupied
by peasants, grouped into tableaux. Some
are seen crossing a lofty bridge, which crosses*

*the Shechen. WALTER FÜRST with the two
boys. WERNER and STAUFFACHER come for-
ward. Others throng after them. When
TELL appears, all receive him with loud
cheers.*
  ALL. Long live brave Tell, our shield, our
    liberator.
  [*While those in front are crowding round
   TELL, and embracing him, RUDENZ and
   BERTHA appear. The former salutes the
   peasantry, the latter embraces HEDWIG.
   The music from the mountains continues to
   play. When it has stopped, BERTHA steps
   into the centre of the crowd.*
  BER. Peasants! Confederates! Into your
    league
Receive me here, that happily am the first
To find protection in the land of freedom.
To your brave hands I now entrust my rights.
Will you protect me as your citizen?
  PEASANT. Ay, that we will, with life and
    fortune both!
  BER. 'Tis well! And to this youth I give
    my hand.
A free Swiss maiden to a free Swiss man!
  RUD. And from this moment all my serfs
    are free! [*Music, and the curtain falls.*

DEDICATED TO HER IMPERIAL HIGHNESS,

THE CROWN PRINCESS OF WEIMAR, MARIA PAULOWNA,

GRAND DUCHESS OF RUSSIA.

REPRESENTED AT THE COURT THEATRE, WEIMAR, NOVEMBER 12, 1804.

DRAMATIS PERSONÆ.

FATHER.	MAIDEN.
MOTHER.	CHORUS OF PEASANTS.
YOUTH.	GENIUS.

THE SEVEN ARTS.

THE SCENE is in the open country. In the middle an orange tree loaded with fruit and decorated with garlands. Peasants are engaged in planting it in the earth, while maidens and children support it, on each side, by chains of flowers.

FATHER. Wax and flourish, thou blooming tree,
With thy golden coronet of fruit,
Which we transplant from thy foreign zone
Into the fair fields of home!
Let full crops of sweet fruit
Bend down thy evergreen boughs!
PEASANTS. Wax and flourish, thou blooming tree,
Ever striving upwards towards the expanse of heaven.
YOUTH. May thy golden fruit answer the promise
Of thy beauteous fragrant blossoms!
Mayst thou stand aloft in the storm of the years,
Endure through the flight of time!
MOTHER. Receive it graciously, holy Earth;
Take the tender stranger in!
Leader of the spotted herds,
Glorious flower-god, care for it!
MAIDENS. Care for it, ye gentle Dryads!
Protect it, guard it, Father Pan!
And ye free Oreads,
Chain up the ruthless storms,
That no tempest may ever scathe it!

ALL. Care for it, ye gentle Dryads!
Protect it, guard it, Father Pan!
YOUTH. May the warm Ether from on high
Smile upon thee, ever clear, ever blue!
Sun, shed on it thy genial rays!
Earth, nourish it with thy richest dew!
FATHER. Joy, joy and quickened life
Mayst thou to every wanderer give;
For joy it was that planted thee here.
May thy nectar-gifts refresh
Our latest children's children,
And, refreshed, may they bless thee!
ALL. Joy, joy and quickened life
Mayst thou to every wanderer give;
For joy it was that planted thee here.

[They dance around the tree, hand in hand. The music of the orchestra accompanies them, and gradually swells into a nobler strain, while GENIUS and the SEVEN GODDESSES are seen to arise in the back-ground. The peasantry arrange themselves on both sides of the stage, while GENIUS steps into the middle; the three plastic ARTS taking place to its right, the four ARTS of language and music, on its left.

CHORUS OF ARTS. We come from afar,
We wander and pass
From people to people,
From age to age.
We seek on earth an abiding home
There ever to rest
On peaceful thrones,

In busy tranquillity,
In true productiveness.
We wander and search, but nowhere find a
    home.
YOUTH. See! who are these that approach?
A godlike band!
Forms such as we never saw before:
They seize my heart powerfully.
GENIUS. Where weapons clash
With iron clang,
Where hate and fury lash the heart to turmoil,
Where mankind wander for ever in error—
Thence turn we quick away with hurrying
    steps.
CHORUS OF ARTS. We hate the false,
The contemners of the gods;
We search out among mankind
The upright races;
Where childlike dispositions
Give us kindly welcome.
There build we our homes,
There we settle in peace.
MAIDEN. What strange, new feeling pos-
    sesses my soul?
What rapture fills my breast?
They draw me to them with mysterious power:
To me they seem as well-known, beloved
    forms,
And yet I have never seen them before.
ALL THE PEASANTS. What strange, new
    feeling possesses our souls?
What rapture fills our breasts?
GENIUS. Still! I see human beings,
And they seem in high enjoyment.
Richly with ribbons and with garlands
In festive manner is the tree adorned.
Are these not the marks of joy?
Say, what is being done here?
FATHER. Shepherds are we of these plains,
And we celebrate a festival.
GENIUS. What festival? Oh, let us learn!
MOTHER. In honor of our queen,
The exalted, the truly gracious,
Who from her halls of imperial splendor,
Has descended into our peaceful vale,
Bringing with her blessings for us.
YOUTH. She it is whom every charm adorns,
Generous, as the sun's own blessed rays.
GENIUS. Wherefore do you plant this tree?
YOUTH. Alas! She comes from a far land,
And her heart turns yet back to her distant
    home.
Gladly would we bind her here,
To this her new-found Fatherland.
GENIUS. And therefore you bury the cling-
    ing roots

Of this fair tree deep in your native earth—
Emblem that she, the high-born lady, will
    find a home
In this her new-found Fatherland?
MAIDEN. Alas! so many and so tender ties
Draw her back to the home of her youth!
All that she there left behind her—
The paradise of her early childhood,
The holy bosom of her mother,
The magnanimous souls of her brothers,
The tender hearts of her sisters—
For these can we ever compensate her?
For such joys, such treasures,
Can Nature's simple pleasures e'er repay her?
GENIUS. Love roots too in a foreign soil;
Love is chained to no one spot.
As the flame burns none the less strong
When another, kindling itself at its glow,
Leaps up with ever brightening gleam,
So what of dearest she there possessed
Awaits her here still all unlost:
Though she has left love behind her,
She finds new and equal love here.
MOTHER. Alas! she comes from marble
    halls,
From halls rich with golden magnificence.
Will the exalted lady here content her—
Here, where o'er our free and open meads,
Only the golden sun sheds his gladsome smile?
GENIUS. Shepherds, to you it is not granted
Into a pure and beauteous heart to pry.
Know, then, that a truly elevated soul
Places true greatness in the real life,
And seeks it not in splendors such as these.
YOUTH. Oh, lovely stranger, teach us how
    to bind her!
Oh, teach us how we best may meet her wish!
Gladly will we the fragrant garlands wreathe,
And gladly welcome her to our humble cots.
GENIUS. A beauteous heart finds easily a
    home,
And, stilly working, shapes its own true world.
And as the tree winds deep into the earth
With all its fibre-power, and there roots fast;
So knits herself, the noble, the illustrious,
With her good deeds to very life itself.
Quick knit themselves the tender bands of
    love.
Where'er we bless, there find we Fatherland.
ALL THE PEASANTS. Oh, beauteous stranger!
Say, how shall we bind her—
The nobly-born—to these our peaceful fields?
GENIUS. Soon is it found—that tender
    band you crave.
Not all is strange to her in this new land.
Me will she know and all my fair attendants,

113

When we disclose ourselves and speak our names.

[*Here* GENIUS *advances to the proscenium. The* SEVEN GODDESSES *do the same, so that the whole form a half-circle. At the moment they advance, they display their attributes, which till now they had kept concealed under their robes.*]

I'm the creative Genius of the beautiful,
And those who follow are the Arts' fair band.
'Tis we who crown all works of mortal man,
We beautify the palace and the altar.
Long dwelt we with thy grandly royal race,
And she, the noble one, who gave thee birth
Fed with her own pure hand the altar-fire,
That burned for us in our loved shrine, thy home.
Sent by thy mother's care, we follow thee,
For all true joy is perfected by us.

ARCHITECTURE. (*With a mural crown on her head and a golden ship in her hand.*)
Me, saw'st thou throned upon the Neva stream!
Thy great forefather called me to the North,
And there I reared for him a second Rome ;
Through me it has become a Kaiser-seat.
A paradise of glory and of grandeur
Rose at the stroke of my strange magic wand.
Now storms the noisy rush of lusty life
Where erstwhile only gloomy clouds sat throned.
The banners floating from his ships' high masts
Strike terror to old Belt in his sea-palace.

SCULPTURE. (*With a Victoria in her hand.*)
Me also—Sculptress of the ancient gods—
Hast thou with wonder often looked upon.
On a strong rock—for ever shall it stand—
Have I the glorious hero-form enfixed,
And this, proud Victory's figure, shaped by me
[*Showing Victoria.*]
Thy great-souled brother sways in mightier hand.
It flies abroad before his conquering arms,
For ever he has bound it to his host.
I can from clay but lifeless forms evoke ;
He, greater, calls a people into being,
Which, ere he spoke, were dead in savagery.

PAINTING. Me too, Illustrious, thou wilt not disown,
The pleasing limner of deceptive forms.
From out my canvas glances life itself,
While color lends its charm and bright effects.
The soul I know to seize, by fair deceit,
And through the eyes I cheat the very heart.
Through the dear lineaments deftly reproduced,

I sweeten oft deep longing's bitter pain :
When friends part—one to the North, another to the South—
They call on my aid and are not entirely separated.

POESY. Me holds no bond : me limits no fixed bound.
Free fly I forth through all the realm of space ;
My limitless domain is that of thought.
My wingéd instrument is the mighty Word.
What lives and moves in Heaven or on Earth,
What Nature in her hidden caverns shapes,
To me stands forth unveiled and all unsealed ;
Naught circumscribes my freedom and my power.
Yet naught more beautiful, how long I search,
Find I in nature than the beauteous form
In which enshrined, breathes the more beauteous soul.

MUSIC. The power of sound that wells from out the chords,
Thou knowest it well, for thou canst it control.
The deep forebodings that the bosom fill
Find fit expression only in my tones.
A gentler charm plays ever round thy soul
When I pour forth my stream of harmonies,
In sweeter sadness will the heart dissolve,
And from the lips the very soul flows forth :
And when I raise my scale to loftier tones
Then raise I thee to loftiest beauty's pitch.

DANCING. (*With the cymbals.*) The highest
Godlike rests in earnest silence ;
By the still spirit will it be discovered.
In conscious fullness of voluptuous power
Life moves with high enjoyment. Wanton Youth
Must have expression, claims its need of pleasure.
Joy, which the bounds of measure would overstep,
By beauty's gentle bridle I restrain.
To heavy frames I give the Zephyr's wings,
And on the dance's step impose due measure ;
With my fine staff I rule whatever moves ;
Grace is the beauteous gift which I confer.

DRAMATIC ART. (*With a double mask.*)
In Janus-form I stand now here before thee :
This face shows pleasure ; this expresses pain.
Man fluctuates ever between joy and tears,
And with the earnest mates itself the jibe.
With all its heights and depths do I unfold,
For thy inspection, very life itself.
When thou, through me, hast seen the world's great game,
Return'st thou richer back to thine own self.

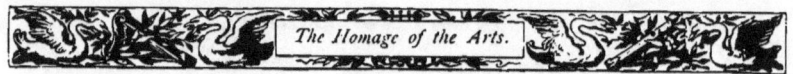
For who his mind keeps on the whole
  directed,
To him the breast's keen strife is calmed and
  soothed.
  GENIUS. And all, who here before thy pres-
    ence stand,
The sacred god-circle of higher arts—
We all are ready, Princess, thee to serve.
Do thou but order; quick, at thy command,
Like the proud walls of Thebes at the lyre's
  tone,
The senseless stone is quickened into life,
A world of beauty opens to thy sight.
  ARCHITECTURE. Columns, at once, shall
    range themselves with columns.
  SCULPTURE. Marble shall waste under the
    mallet's strokes.
  PAINTING. For thee fresh life shall breathe
    from out the canvas.

MUSIC. The stream of harmonies shall flow
  for thee.
DANCING. Light-footed dance shall wind
  its joyous rounds.
DRAMATIC ART. The world itself shall on
  this stage be mirrored.
POESY. Imagination on her mighty wings
Shall thee transport to the blest fields of
  Heaven.
  PAINTING. And as the rainbow's beauteous
    color-form
Builds itself up from the sun's brilliant rays,
We seven, the elements of highest beauty,
Shall weave for thee, with fine harmonious
  striving,
Illustrious one, the carpet-web of life.
  ALL THE ARTS. For from the power of fine
    harmonious striving,
Arises, first the true, the perfect life.

DRAMATIS PERSONÆ.

MARGARET OF YORK, *Duchess of Burgundy.*

ADELAIDE, *Princess of Bretagne.*

ERICH, *Prince of Gothland.*

WARBECK *(pretended* RICHARD, *Duke of York).*

SIMNEL *(pretended* EDWARD, *Duke of Clarence).*

EDWARD PLANTAGENET, *the true Duke of Clarence.*

EARL OF HEREFORD, *an exiled English Peer.*

His five sons.

SIR WILLIAM STANLEY, *Ambassador from Henry VII. of England.*

Earl of Kildare.

BELMONT, *Bishop of Ypres.*

SIR RICHARD BLOUNT, *Ambassador of the false* EDWARD.

Citizens of Brussels.

Servants in the Court of Margaret.

ACT I.

LORD HEREFORD, a partizan of the house of York, has, with his five sons, left England, on the report that Richard Duke of York, second son of Edward IV (who was believed to have been murdered while a boy) was alive in Brussels and claimed restitution of his birthright. The acknowledgment of the Pretender by his aunt, Margaret Duchess of Burgundy, by France and Portugal, as well as by the public voice were sufficient grounds to Hereford for renouncing allegiance to Henry VII and staking all his possessions and all his hopes on the issue. He enters the palace of Margaret and finds there exposed the portrait of the alleged York, and expresses his joy in being in a country where he can manifest his favor for the house of York with safety.

Lord Stanley, Henry Seventh's Ambassador at the court of Margaret, meets him here, and, in vain, endeavors to open his eyes to the imposture which is on foot. Both lose their temper, and the strife of the two roses renews itself in the entrance-hall of Margaret's court.

The Bishop of Ypres, the trusted counsellor of Margaret, interposes and separates them. He lauds the pious fidelity of Margaret to the cause of the oppressed party and her defenceless relative, and explains in detail why Margaret deserves to be loved and respected.

Burghers of Brussels and their wives fill the hall, awaiting the coming of the Duchess with the Duke of York. Stanley upbraids them for, and ridicules, their delusion. They are roused to such a pitch of fury by the insults he heaps on their adored Prince, that they threaten to rend him to pieces. Trumpets are heard announcing the approach of York.

Richard intervenes, rescues the ambassador, harangues and pacifies the people. While he is speaking, Margaret enters with the Prince of Gothland, the Princess of Bretagne and other grandees.—Hereford is convinced and overcome by the sight of Richard. He casts himself on his knees before him and does him homage as the son of his King. Margaret now speaks and expresses herself with all the tenderness of a mother regarding her nephew. She calls on the Prince to receive the Earl into his favor.

Richard embraces him and expresses himself with feeling and, at the same time, with princely dignity. Hereford is more and more captivated by him and now asks the Prince to relate to him his history.

This, Richard endeavors to evade. The Duchess excuses the Prince and undertakes the task.

Now follows the mythical narrative of Richard's history, which makes a deep impression on the hearers and is often interrupted by their emotional cries.

Stanley once more protests against the whole thing, and leaves the hall without having convinced any one. Richard's noble declarations make his words of no effect.

Hereford strengthens his assurances of support and promises Duke Richard that adherents will flock to him in England. Richard recalls with emotion his former ignorance of his rank and rights, and compares his previous condition of happy ignorance and freedom from care with that in which he now finds himself. It is a heavy duty and no happiness to him that he must now vindicate his rights. He seems once more to propose the question to himself, and to the Duchess as well, whether he ought to enter into the bloody war-game which is to destroy the peace of two lands.

She encourages him to the hazard, however painful the separation, and the thought that she is exposing him to the perils of war may be to herself.—Lively attestations of her tender affection for him.—

She then speaks of the two objects that lie nearest her heart—the restitution of her nephew's rights and the marriage of Adelaide,

ARTIST: H. KNADFUS?.

WARBECK.

which is shortly to be celebrated with the Prince of Gothland.

Prince Erich of Gothland remains in the background alone with the Princess of Bretagne, and jeers at what is being enacted before them. Adelaide's feelings are still in a state of high excitement and she manifests how she is wounded by Erich's unfeeling coldness. He mocks her, and speaks of the Duke of York with contempt. She warmly takes the part of Warbeck, of whose genuineness and honesty she does not entertain a doubt, and institutes a comparison between him and Erich, much to the disadvantage of the latter. Her tender feelings for the alleged York betray themselves. Erich demonstrates to her from Warbeck's demeanor, that he can be no true Prince, and adduces evidence such as proves his own low estimate of what beseems a Prince. Adelaide conceals her contempt for him, but in her heart sets him far below the Yorkist Prince.

Erich has perceived that Adelaide regards York tenderly, but the enjoyment he has in indulging his malice outweighs even his jealousy. He feels a malicious pleasure in the fact that they love each other hopelessly, while he himself shall enjoy the Princess. Possession, he thinks, will compensate for all, and it gives him sweet delight to think that he shall snatch from Warbeck the object of his affections.

Adelaide in a soliloquy, expresses her love and compassion for Warbeck, and the suffering she endures in her own position in the court of Margaret. She finds much similarity between Richard's fate and her own. Both are the helpless victims of violence and live on the bounty of a proud, arrogant relative.

ACT II.

THE first act showed Warbeck in his public relations; now we are to see him in his private. The brilliantly deceptive veil falls; he comes now before us neglected and unworthily treated by the servants Margaret has placed around him. Some of these doubt whether he is the genuine personage; others, while believing him to be the true Prince, treat him with small respect because he is poor and lives on the charity of his relative. Twofold misery—that, namely, of an impostor who is playing the part of a Prince, and that of a true Prince destitute of means accumulates itself on his head at one and the same time. He suffers for want of common necessaries, and misses in his princely station the happiness and plenty of his former private condition.

Warbeck plays his rôle with grave earnestness, not without dignity, and with a strange peculiar kind of faith. So long as he represents Richard, he *is* Richard. He acts his part in some measure for himself, but also for his accomplice in the imposture. His assumption of the princely character has nothing theatrical about it: it is an office which he has taken on himself to fill and with which he identifies himself, rather than a mask he has assumed. After taking the first decisive step he has, once and for all, renounced his former personality. All that followed on this he adopted on making his decision. After taking the whole on himself he considers no longer about individual details. A certain poetical mystery of which he is dimly conscious in regard to himself and the rôle he is playing, an over-faith—a sort of frenzy, in short—helps to rescue him from the charge of immorality. What in the eyes of the Duchess makes him little better than a fool serves, in reality, as a palliation of his acts.

He did not deign to utter complaints till love has, at length, melted him. Mortifications he endures with suppressed emotion, he does kind acts from a sort of native greatness of soul and without ulterior views, but with a

lofty condescension and a cold reserve eminently unsentimental and realistic, and this out of a greatness of soul natural to him, and in no respect allied to calculation.

It must be made clear how natural it is that tender sympathy for the alleged Richard should discover itself in the heart of the Princess and there wax to perfect love—an effect of the imposture of which no one thought and yet which flowed from it so naturally. It is tragical to observe how a fine mind may through humane sympathy become entangled in an unfortunate relation, how a beautiful life may try to develop itself where man has sown only the pernicious.

The Princess is a simple maiden with nothing princely about her—her birth, her station appear to her only hindrances restraining and operating against the development of her beautiful nature. Greatness has for her no charm ; her desire is only for that happiness which is of the heart, and she recalls her exalted birth only when she speaks with a certain enthusiasm of the simple station in life, which presents itself to her in a light all the more poetical that she has no experience of it and sees it only from afar.

Adelaide's mind is far more occupied with her love to Warbeck than with his to her. She is of a resigned nature and has been brought up to be a sacrifice. She dares not raise her hopes towards the object of her love ; she envies only the happy woman who shall, one day, call him hers. He must marry a rich or mighty king's daughter ; she is only a poor orphan living on the charity of a relation.

Warbeck—a nature striving after self-reliant independence—is in the power of a false, arrogant, powerful, implacable woman, as if in the wiles of an evil spirit. He has sold himself to her. His relation to her is humiliating and deadly mortifying. In vain he tries to ameliorate it. She sees in him only a tool—the counterfeit York, the impostor—and she makes her demands on him without the slightest delicacy or regard for his feeling of honor. In vain does he strive to raise himself to a higher level. She ever keeps him in mind of their ignominious relation which he would so gladly forget ; nay, which he must forget if he is to play his part properly. In public, she honors and caresses him ; in private, she is a tyranness. She dictates to him what he must profess to wish and not to wish in the presence of the public, commanding this, forbidding that. In public she acts as if his wishes were to her orders, and counsels him to do what she has most strictly prohibited. Woe to him if he presume to take a single step of his own accord ! In spite of all this, he does occasionally act independently ; hence her disfavor and aversion.

— —

Adelaide is aware of the humiliating and constrained position occupied by Warbeck and seeks to better it. Although he does not at once accept the boon offered by her magnanimity, not the less this avowal of her love makes him happy.

Erich concocts and endeavors to carry through a malicious plot against Warbeck in order to disgrace him. He uses as his tool a worthless man whose statements are most derogatory to Warbeck. Warbeck bears himself firmly and nobly. The treachery is unveiled and Erich exposed to shame.

The Duchess is at once informed of the occurrence by Belmont, and comes in person to reconcile the princes to each other. She wills that Warbeck shall offer his hand to his enemy, and when he hesitates, she gives him to understand that she will have it so. She lays emphasis on the fact that Erich is a prince, and gives Warbeck to feel, although in a way perceptible only to himself, his dependence on her and utter nothingness.

An adventurer comes professing to be ambassador of Edward Duke of Clarence, and begs for that (alleged) prince a safeguard to Brussels, that he may present himself to his aunt, and lay before her the evidence of his birth. The ambassador gives out that the Prince has escaped from the Tower of London and comes to make good his claim to the English throne.

Margaret is not in a moment's doubt in regard to the fraud that is being practised, but it meets her views to favor it. She shows herself inclined, therefore, to offer her aid, but Warbeck, with much warmth, counsels to the contrary. Margaret, in her own arrogant way, directs him to keep within his proper limits, and makes him feel that he has no voice here. Warbeck must bear all in silence; but he goes off with the declaration that Clarence shall answer to him with the sword.

Margaret is now alone with Belmont, and remarks with haughty displeasure that Warbeck is beginning to presume to some extent in opposition to her wishes. She has long had a dislike to him; now his assumptions begin to inflame this into hate. She finds him, not only not submissive enough; the fraud itself, which she has long practised through him as her tool, has become burdensome and distasteful to her, and his existence as York, and her nephew, is derogatory to her princely pride.

In this unfavorable mood she is found by Adelaide, who comes in a state of great emotion to beg that she may be relieved from receiving the addresses of the Prince of Gothland. She, at the same time, betrays her tender interest in Warbeck, and, in consequence, inflames the mind of the Duchess still more against him. She is dismissed harshly, and ordered to think no more of Warbeck, but to regard Gothland as her husband. The marriage is resolved on for the earliest possible moment and Adelaide finds herself in the bitterest distress.

ACT III.

—

An open space—A throne for the Duchess— Barriers have been erected — Arrangements for a judicial duel—Spectators fill the background of the scene.

———

Edward Plantagenet inquires from one of the bystanders what these preparations import. — Exposition of the question of right between Simnel and Warbeck, which is to be decided according to law by single combat. Edward receives the information with the highest astonishment, and his questions, which display at once deep ignorance of the latest news and the highest interest in the affair, arouse the wonder of the other.

The English ambassador is also present and the strange youth has strongly attracted his attention. He seems to recognize him and to be horrified.

— - —

Simnel presents himself with his retinue and harangues the people. He speaks of his family and his escape from the tower, and the multitude divides into two parties in regard to him. The English ambassador makes up to Edward and endeavors to find out who he is. He finds him exceedingly shy and distrustful and is, thereby, confirmed in his suspicions.

— —

The Duchess arrives with her court. Erich and Adelaide accompany her. Trumpets sound, and Margaret seats herself on the throne.

In the meantime Warbeck has a short interview with Adelaide, wherein she expresses the indignation and pain which the scene before them occasions her, while he lets it be seen that he regards the coming contest with cheerful courage.

The herald advances, and after declaring the occasion of this solemnity, summons both combatants into the lists. First he calls on Simnel, who affirms himself to be Edward Plantagenet and expounds his claims; thereafter on Warbeck, who asserts Simnel's pretences to be false and criminal and declares himself ready to maintain his assertion by the sword. Both combatants appeal to the judgment of Heaven. The ordinary formalities

123

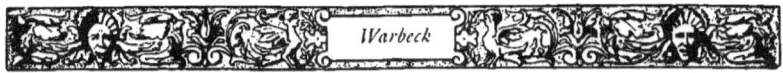

are gone through, and the two claimants with-draw to fight it out in the lists.

_____

While the usual preparations are being made the young Plantagenet, by his extreme excite-ment and striking figure, has attracted the no-tice of the Duchess and Princess.

The former addresses some questions to him, to which he gives ingenious answers and mani-fests some degree of emotion in his demeanor towards the Duchess. Before she has time to satisfy her curiosity in regard to the interesting youth, the trumpets sound as a signal for the combat.

_____

The fight—Simnel is overcome and falls—All is in excitement; the barriers are broken down and the people crowd in with loud cries. Simnel dying confesses his fraud and names the instigator to it. He acknowledges War-beck to be the true York and asks his forgive-ness. Joy of the people.

_____

Warbeck, as conqueror and acknowledged Duke, seizes the moment to declare publicly his love for the Princess and to beg the Duchess for her consent.

—   —

The English interest themselves in the mat-ter and support his prayer. Erich is wild with rage, the Duchess gnashes her teeth, calls on the Princess to follow her and goes off with furious looks.

—   —

The lords now gather round their Duke, swear fealty to him and promise support, accompanying him in triumph to his house.

_____

Plantagenet alone feels himself deserted, his personality lost, and himself without sup-port: he has nothing now but his right. He decides, notwithstanding, to approach the Duchess. Stanley comes up to him and en-deavors to frighten him away.

ACT IV.

___

THE Duchess comes home full of rage and malice. Her hate to Warbeck is in-creased by his good fortune and bravery. The news of the escape of the true Plantagenet from the tower makes the impostor superfluous to her. She determines to drop him, and be-gins by harshly forbidding the Princess, who had followed her, to so much as think of him, suggesting at the same time a doubt as to his genuineness. Warbeck is announced. She dismisses the Princess from her presence in tears, although she had begged to be allowed to remain.

_____

Warbeck and the Duchess. Warbeck em-boldened by his success and relying on his following, at the same time exalted by the power of love, and resolved to put an end to the intolerable state of matters, assumes a bold tone to the Duchess and dares to call her to account for her unfriendly treatment to him. She is amazed at his daring and treats him with the deepest contempt. The more she endeavors to humble him, the more he opposes to her a firm independence. He appeals to the fact that it was she who called him from the private position, in which he was happy, and placed him in that he now occupies, and declares that she is bound in honor to main-tain his cause, affirming that she has no right to play with his happiness.

Her answers reveal her unfeeling pride of place and haughtiness, as well as her cold ego-istic soul; she has never troubled herself about his happiness or misery, he is nothing to her

but a tool for executing her designs—a tool she will throw away so soon as it is no longer of use to her. But this tool is self-reliant, and just the very quality that adapted him for playing the prince, gives him strength to withdraw from a humiliating dependence. In the end the Duchess sees herself compelled to conceal the wrath in her heart, and leaves him, apparently reconciled to him, but with revenge and deadly hate fixed in her soul.

Dread of a hated union and utter hopelessness of having anything to expect from the goodness of the Duchess co-operate powerfully to throw the Princess into the arms of the impostor. In full confidence of his genuineness she comes to him and proposes that he shall carry her off. She manifests to him all the tenderness of her affection and without a shade of suspicion trusts herself to his honor and his love. She suggests the Earl of Kildare—a man venerable alike for age and honor and an old friend of the House of York—as the person to whom they should flee together. She gives over to him all the jewels and valuables she possesses. The more confidence she manifests, the more torturing to himself becomes the feeling of his treachery. He cannot accept the hand that is offered to him, and still less risk a confession of the truth. The conflict he wages with himself is frightful. He leaves her in despair.

She remains overcome with amazement at his conduct; and reproaches herself that probably she had gone too far, but excuses herself on the grounds of the danger and of her love.

Plantagenet enters, looking around him, suspicious and alarmed. He greets the dear soil yet left to a member of his family with painful emotion. On recognizing the York family-pictures, he kneels before them, and sheds tears over the fate of his race and of himself.

Warbeck comes back resolved to declare to the Princess the whole truth. He perceives

the kneeling Plantagenet, is transfixed with astonishment, detains him and enters into conversation with him. What he hears and sees increases his terror and astonishment.

At last he has no longer any doubt that he has the true York before him. Plantagenet retires expressing himself nobly and in words of high import, leaving Warbeck full of consternation behind.

Scarcely had he begun to give utterance to his forebodings and his terror before the English ambassador enters and begs speech with him. The ambassador has his suspicions at once confirmed and proposes to Warbeck an arrangement with the English king, provided Warbeck will help in getting the true York out of the way. Both have a common interest in removing this rightful claimant to the crown. Warbeck feels the whole danger of his situation; still his hate for Lancaster and his better nature prevail, and he orders the tempter to leave him.

But the matter must be dealt with. The true York is there and he may demand his rights. The Duchess will gladly recognize him and strip the false York of his foreign plumage. All is at stake. The Princess is lost to him forever if the true York is not got rid of. Now the unhappy man feels that treachery can only be maintained by a succession of crimes. He curses his first step; he wishes he had never been born.

The Duchess appears with her council. They learn that the Earl of Kildare is on his way to Brussels in the hope that he shall there find the young Plantagenet who had communicated to him that he meant to hurry thither. The Duchess is at once happy and embarrassed over his arrival; embarrassed in regard to Warbeck, although she is firmly resolved to offer him up as a sacrifice as soon as the true Plantagenet is found.—But where is this dear nephew? Kildare writes that he is on his way to Brussels; it is possible that he is already there.—She recalls the unknown youth.—A

handkerchief is noticed on the floor.—She recognizes it for one she had presented to Edward nine years before.—Full of astonishment she asks who had come into the chamber. She is told, no one but Warbeck. This penetrates her like a lightning flash. She sends for the unknown youth and for Warbeck.

ACT V.

THE Duchess, Her Council, the Princess, Lords—All inquiries after Edward are fruitless; he is nowhere to be found. The Duchess has a horrible suspicion— She dispatches a messenger for Warbeck.

———

Erich and the ambassador tell of a murder that must have been perpetrated. They had heard cries for help, had hurried to the spot, and found blood upon the ground. The Duchess and Princess are in a state of terrible excitement.

———

Warbeck arrives. The Duchess receives him with the words: "Where is my nephew? Where have you disposed of him?" On his hesitating to answer, she denounces him plainly as a murderer. The word strikes the lords with consternation. She repeats it with increased vehemence. They remonstrate with her for bringing such a hideous charge against the Duke, her nephew. Fury extorts her secret from her. "Duke!" she cries: "A York!! He my nephew!!!" She then in a few words discovers the whole plot. The Princess totters and is on the point of falling. Warbeck advances to support her. She throws herself into the arms of the Duchess. Warbeck now turns himself to the lords. They shrink back from him in horror. At this moment the dreaded Earl of Kildare is announced. The Duchess says: "He comes at the right time. I have not desired his arrival, but now he is welcome. He knows my nephews. He brought them up as children." She turns then to Warbeck: "Dissemble now if thou canst. See whether thou wilt maintain your pretences in the face of this witness also."

Kildare enters. Warbeck stands as far from him as possible, with his eyes fixed on the ground.—The Duchess goes to meet Kildare. "You come to embrace a York! Unhappy man! You find none," and so on. Before Kildare makes answer he looks around the circle and observes Warbeck. He advances towards him, stops, stands amazed, and exclaims: "What do I see!" At these words Warbeck erects himself, looks the Earl in the face and cries out: "My Father!" Kildare in like manner exclaims: "My Son!"—"His Son!" all repeat with astonishment. Warbeck rushes to throw himself on his father's breast. Kildare stands amazed, and knows not what to say. He begs the bystanders to leave him alone with Warbeck for an instant. They do so out of respect for Kildare. At the same moment it is announced that the two murderers have been brought in. The Duchess hurries off to see them.

———

Warbeck remains with Kildare, who is thunder-struck to find, in the pretended York, his own son. Warbeck tells him all in a few words. Kildare apostrophizes Providence and praises its ways. He declares to Warbeck that he is not his son; that he had been robbed of the name that truly belonged to him. He is a natural son of Edward IV, a born York. The riddle of his mysterious feelings is now solved. The involved clue of his fate at once unravels itself. In unspeakable joy he casts the whole burden of the torture she has hitherto borne from his shoulders: he begs Kildare to permit him to retire for an instant.

Kildare and the lords. They are in despair over the game of treachery which has been played and bewail their lost lives and shattered hopes.

In the meantime Warbeck appears leading in Plantagenet by the hand. All are amazed. Kildare recognizes the young Prince. The latter cannot understand what it all means, till Warbeck explains the whole mystery to him, and ends by doing homage to him as his liege lord, and embracing him as his cousin. Warbeck had found the Plantagenet lying asleep before the monument of the York family and rescued him from two murderers who were about to kill him. Joy of the lords; magnanimity of Plantagenet.

The Duchess comes upon the scene. She embraces her nephew and clasps him to her heart. The lords desire that she shall do the same by Warbeck. Noble declaration of Warbeck, who falls at her feet as her nephew. She is moved and shows her gracious disposition by going off to bring the Princess.

Business during the interval of her absence. The murderous design of Erich and the ambassador comes to light. They are forgiven, and they stand there disgraced. Warbeck shows himself to the ambassador in the attitude of embracing Plantagenet, and dismisses him to his king (Lancaster) with the declaration that they both will make good their claims on the throne in unison.

The Duchess returns leading in the Princess.

FRAGMENTS OF THE FIRST SCENE OF ACT I.

Court of the DUCHESS MARGARET *at Brussels.*
A great hall.

SCENE I.—*Enter the Earl of Hereford, with his five sons. Sir William Stanley stands on the side of the proscenium and observes him.*

HEREFORD. This is the sacred hearth to which we flee,
My sons! This is the hospitable palace
Where Margaret, who here wields princely sway
O'er the rich Netherlands, a noble woman,
Mindful of her right royal ancestors,
Still shelters and protects the constant friends
Of that oppressed and ancient kingly race,
Offering the exile here a place of refuge.
Look all round! Like friendly household
gods

Receive you — — — — — —
The noble figures of the glorious Yorks.
Know ye them — — — — —
The white rose shows right fair in every hand
— — — — — — — —
With these dear emblems, that now with joy
We fix upon our caps — — — — — —
— — — — — — — —

SCENE II.—BELMONT. *The preceding.*

BELMONT. Let peace be kept,
My lords, to peace this house is sacred.
HEREFORD. Hither I flew — — — —
And, right here on the threshold, must I see
A hated follower of a hated race
Boldly presume to show his brazen brow?

STANLEY.   Traitor I name thee loud,
  where'er I find thee.
BELMONT.   No further, noble lords — —
The princely dame who here holds sway
— — — — — —
And here at Brussels opens she her court
To all contending parties,
For mediation is her highest glory.
STANLEY.   Enough! Here is he aye a wel-
  come guest
Who against England weaves the basest plots.
BELMONT.   She is the sister to two English
  kings
Of Yorkist blood — — — —
And kind to all as well her birth beseems,
Never can she forget that princely race
Which evil times' mishaps have brought so
  low.
Where can it find, on this unfriendly earth,
Shelter save here, by her most peaceful hearth?
Even to the foe she shows herself upright,
And in the person of this noble lord
Honors the ambassador — — — —
— — — — — — —

SCENE IV.

— — — — — — —
— — — — — — —
HEREFORD.   Hither! my sons. Come all!
  O, quickly come!
A voice within my heart speaks loud and clear:
He is our king! These are King Edward's
  features,
This the noble countenance of my liege,
The accents of his voice I hear once more.
                    [Casting himself at his feet.
O Richard! Richard! Son of my dead king!

WARBECK.   Arise, my lord! Not there is
  your just place,
Come to my heart! — — — — —
— — — — — — —
HEREFORD. — — — — How escaped you
The murderers' hands? Speak! Where con-
  cealed you
The rescuing hand of Heaven — — —
To show us now in this most happy hour

128

Thy presence so thrice welcome?
WARBECK. — — Not now — — Let me
Draw a dark veil over the wretched past.
It is now bygone — — Here am I among
  you.
I see myself surrounded by my friends.
O, fate has led me in a wondrous way.
— — — — — — —
— — — — — — —

MARGARET. — — — — — —
— — — — — — —
Richard of Gloster mounted England's throne;
His brother's sons he shut within the tower,
This is the truth; he wished the world to
  think
That Tyrrel in their blood imbrued his hands.
Nay, even the very spot report points out
Where their remains lie buried — —

Long night and darkness that could not be
  pierced,
Enshrouded in deep gloom the barbarous deed
Within the tower — Only later times
Withdrew the veil and let us know the truth.
'Tis true the murderer Tyrrel was dispatched
The princes to assassin; a strict behest
From Richard's self he showed to this effect.
The Prince of Wales died by the traitor's steel;
His brothers to a similar fate were doomed:
Whether it were that this barbarian's con-
  science
Awoke within him, or the children's prayers
Melted his iron heart within his bosom—
One other, but uncertain, blow he drew,
Then, shuddering before the frightful deed,
He fled — — — — — —
— — — — — —

The Maltese

MALTA is besieged by the whole power of Soliman, who has sworn the destruction of the Order. With the Turkish commanders Mustapha and Pialy, are associated the Corsairs Muzzialy and Dragut, and the Algerines Hascem and Candelissa. The Turkish fleet invests both the harbors, and, without risking a battle with it, no relief can reach the island. By land the enemy has attacked the fort of St. Elmo, and already has carried several important points of vantage. The possession of this fort makes the enemy masters of the two harbors, and puts him in a position to assault, with success, St. Ange, St. Michael and Il Borgo, in which places the whole force of the Order is concentrated.

La Valette is grand-master of the Order at Malta. He has expected the attack of the Turks, and prepared himself to meet it. The Knights have been summoned to the island, and have responded in great numbers. Besides these, he has still about ten thousand men at his disposal. There is no lack either of munitions of war or provisions, and the works are in excellent condition. Notwithstanding, a reinforcement from Sicily is anxiously expected, for the enemy, in virtue of his numbers and obstinate perseverance, must at length reduce the works to ruin and annihilate the defenders.

La Vallette had every reason to expect aid from Sicily, for the subjection of Malta would expose the States of the King of Spain to the greatest danger. Philip II. had therefore pledged every assistance, and had given orders to his Viceroy in Sicily. His fleet lay fully equipped in the harbors of this island; many Knights and other warriors had flocked hither, with the view of embarking for Malta. The emissaries of the grand-master are unwearied in their exhortations to the Viceroy to hurry the departure of the fleet.

But the policy of Spain is too selfish to risk much, even for this great cause. The great force of the Turks intimidates the Spaniards, and they desire to gain time till the enemy is weakened. This result they hope for from the bravery of the Knights of the Order, and await, accordingly, either the raising of the siege, or, at least, an easier victory. It is to them a matter of indifference whether the power of the Order should be weakened by this dilatory policy; only they are resolved that it shall not utterly perish. The Viceroy of Spain, therefore, promises help from time to time, but he does nothing.

Meanwhile the fort of St. Elmo is ever

closer pressed by the enemy. Of itself, on account of its narrow bounds, on which no sufficient works can be erected, it is by no means an easily tenable place, and affords accommodation for only a limited number of defenders. The Turks have already got possession of some of the outworks; their artillery commands the walls, and already they have effected some considerable breaches. The defenders are not protected by the works, and with all their bravery fall easy victims to the guns of the enemy.

Under these circumstances, the Knights, to whom the holding of this post is entrusted, beg the grand-master to transfer them to a place more capable of defence, as there is no hope of maintaining St. Elmo. The other Knights represent also to the master that he is sacrificing the Knights in St. Elmo to no purpose; that it is not good policy to gradually weaken the power of the Order by a protracted defence of an untenable place; and that it would be better to concentrate his whole strength in the main work.

These reasons are very plausible, but the grand-master does not concur in them. Although perfectly convinced that St. Elmo cannot be maintained, and deploring bitterly the fate of the Knights who must there be sacrificed, two reasons operate to prevent him from consenting to give up the fort. First, everything lies in defending St. Elmo as long as possible, in order to give time for the arrival of the auxiliary fleet from Sicily; for if this fort falls into the hands of the enemy, it is then in a position to close both harbors, and relief becomes more difficult. In such a contingency, the Spaniards would, indeed, sail home as they had threatened. Next, the force of the Turks will be weakened physically and morally if they are necessitated to take St. Elmo by storm. Their loss by such an eventuality would make it more difficult for them to attack the main work, while such an example of desperate defence would give them

such an idea of the heroism of the Christians that they would begin to doubt as to the certainty of victory, and be less ready for new efforts.

The grand-master has thus preponderating reasons for offering up a portion of his knighthood—the defenders, namely, of St. Elmo—for the good of the whole. Such a procedure is in perfect conformity with the rules of the Order, for every Knight has bound himself, on his acceptance into the Order, to sacrifice his life in blind obedience for the good of religion. But to a proper compliance with this rule it is necessary the sacrifice should be made in the pure spirit of order—such a deed must be executed " from within outwards," and not be forced on the members by outside compulsion.

But this pure spirit of order, so essential at this conjuncture, is awanting. Bold and heroic are the Knights, but they wish to show these qualities in their own way, and not to submit themselves to the rule with blind resignation. The moment demands minds truly spiritual; theirs are worldly. They have degenerated from the spirit that dictated the original constitution of the Order; they love things other than duty; they are heroes, but no longer Christian heroes. Love, riches, ambition, national pride and similar motives influence their hearts.

The disorders in the Order have, at the moment when the siege was commenced, reached their highest pitch. Many Knights have openly given themselves over to excesses, and defy censure on the ground that war and danger justify license. La Valette had been hitherto indulgent, partly from his liberal mode of thinking, partly because he knew himself to be by no means free from human frailties. Now, however, he sees himself compelled to endeavor to bring back the Order to its former state of purity, and to constitute it, as it were, anew.

ARTIST: FR. PECHT.

THE MALTESE.

FRAGMENT OF THE FIRST SCENE.

An open hall, which commands a view of the harbor.

ROMEGAS *and* BIRON *are in strife over a Grecian captive. The latter has laid hold of her, the former insists on taking possession of her.*

ROMEGAS. Hold! Insolent! Wouldst thou rob me of my slave
Whom I have seized, and for my own declared?
BIRON. To freedom I restore her. Let her choose,
Herself, the man whom she would rather follow.
ROMEGAS. Mine is she by the right and use of war;
Upon the Corsair's ship I won my claim.
BIRON. Who wishes to propitiate the free heart
Contemns the Corsairs' barbarous usages.
ROMEGAS. Fair woman's beauty is the brave man's prize.
BIRON. And woman's honor shields the brave knight's sword.
ROMEGAS. Defend Saint Elmo. There is thy place.
BIRON. There is the fight and here the combat's prize.
ROMEGAS. Much safer is it women here to steal,
Than there, with manly heart, to front the Turk.
BIRON. Of the hot fight that rages on the breach
'Tis pleasant to discourse in the still cloister.
ROMEGAS. Hear thy commander's voice! Back to thy post.
BIRON. Upon thy fleet thou may'st command; not here.
ROMEGAS. Respect, at least, the great cross on this breast.
BIRON. The small one here covers as great a heart.
ROMEGAS. O, boastful ever is the Provence tongue.
BIRON. But sharper is its sword.

ROMEGAS. — — —

KNIGHTS. *(Interfering).* The Spaniard has the right—the arrogance
Of the Provençal must be sharply chastised.
OTHER KNIGHTS. *(Coming from the other side.)*
Three swords 'gainst one! — — —
At the Castilian! Courage, my brave brother!
We stand by thee, as will the whole French langue.
KNIGHT. Down with the Provençals.
OTHER KNIGHTS. — — — Down
With every Spaniard!

More knights of both parties come to the scene of the quarrel. The choir enters and parts the combatants. It consists of sixteen spiritual Knights, in the long robes of the Order, who surround the others in two rows. The choir reproaches the Knights for quarreling amongst themselves at such a moment. Description of the great peril and cause for anxiety, based both on the dangers threatening from without and the internal condition of the Order. Over confidence of the knights, who reckon on Sicily for help.

La Valette appears with Miranda, an ambassador from Sicily. The grand-master calls on the Knights not to look for earthly help but to trust in heaven and their own courage. Miranda declares that from Spain nothing is to be hoped. That St. Elmo must be maintained: even if the Sicilian fleet should appear, it would sail back if, on its arrival, this fort were found to be in the hands of the Turks. Murmurs of the Knights over the policy of Spain. Miranda decides of his own free motion to abide on the island and share the fate of the Order.

An old Christian slave is brought by the Knight Montalto to the grand-master. He has been sent by the Turkish commander, under the pretext of entering into negotia-

133

tions in regard to Fort St. Elmo, but in reality to initiate an interchange of letters with a traitor. The grand-master will hear of no terms between the Knights and the infidels, and threatens to behead every future herald. To the Christian slave, who bewails his hard fate, permission is given to remain in Malta. He prefers to return to captivity, because he is persuaded Malta cannot hold out. Before he leaves he lets a hint as to treachery escape him.

—

Two delegates from the garrison of St. Elmo now appear. This garrison had not been selected by the grand-master, but had been appointed, without any suggestion on his part, in accordance with the established usage. A Knight named St. Priest, of only twenty years of age, beloved by all, and especially distinguished by the master, is among the defenders of St. Elmo. In figure and daring he resembles the youthful Rinaldo. He is a scourge of the Turks, and much as every one seeks to spare him, he is foremost in every fight. But in the midst of death and danger he remains still unscathed : his very glance appears to disarm the foe, or guardian angels seem to surround and watch over him. Crequi, another young Knight of keen courage, is attached to him with a passionate, but pure and honorable, affection. The deputies depict the condition of St. Elmo, the advances of the foe, the untenability of the work, and beg that the garrison may be permitted to withdraw to another post. The younger Knights, especially Crequi, support the prayer with urgency; but the grand-master declines to grant it. He lets his sympathy for the fate of the defenders be clearly known, but he declares earnestly and conclusively, that St. Elmo must be defended, and withdraws with the older Knights.

Murmurs against the grand-master among the younger Knights. Crequi enquires anxiously after St. Priest, and learns from the deputies with what especial forwardness he exposes himself to danger. Montalto returns from accompanying the Christian slave, and encourages the bitterness against the master, through malicious hints in regard to his unfeeling hardness and arbitrary temper.

—

The discontented Knights retire; the choir remains behind. It bewails the decay of the order and its injustice to the grand-master, whose merits it recognizes. Reminiscences from the history of the order.

La Valette, the choir. The grand-master shows himself to be human. He fears that he has not strength enough to remain firm to what necessity requires. The sacrifice of the brave defenders of St. Elmo pains him deeply. He is troubled, moreover, over the abuses so prevalent in the Order. The choir points out to him the consequences of his over-indulgence, and reminds him of the strife over the Greek captive. La Valette acknowledges his errors, and promises his uttermost endeavors to effect a reform of the order. The Greek he has already caused to be sent away.

————

Romegas, Biron and the foregoing. Both Knights complain of the removal of the Greek. La Valette reminds the Knights of their vows. They maintain that the present conjuncture gives them a claim on his indulgence. Their wild nature shows itself by breaking down all barriers in this time of the highest danger. This present moment will they enjoy; the next hour, probably, they may never see. The brave man, whose services are needed, believes he can set laws at defiance. The grand-master speaks to them earnestly, as their commander, and withdraws.

————

Romegas and Biron embittered to the last degree, become reconciled, and combine against the grand-master. Romegas holds him, for other reasons, his enemy.

— —

Crequi comes up and speaks without reserve of the stern severity of the master. The conversation is interrupted by Montalto, who announces new delegates from St. Elmo. The circumstances have become worse and worse. The Turks have gained possession of an important outwork. The defenders again urge their petition for permission to retreat, otherwise they will go to meet certain death in a sortie. Among the deputies is St. Priest, through whom it was hoped they might prevail on the master. La Valette refuses to

speak with him. This apparent hardness stirs
the Knights to yet greater rage, although it is,
in reality, due to his softness, for he is not
confident that he possesses sufficient firmness
to see, in such circumstances, a youth so dear
to him. St. Priest is his natural son, but no
one knows of this save La Valette himself.

———

The deputies withdraw, accompanied by
several Knights, who loudly express their indignation at the master. St. Priest himself
says nothing, but Crequi indulges in the
warmest outbursts of passion. Romegas and
Biron concur with him. Montalto avails himself of the moment to instigate the Knights
against the master. In vain does the choir
remind them most impressively of their duty.
A terrible confederacy against the grand-
master is originated.

———

La Valette gives the Engineer Castriotto a commission to investigate the condition of St. Elmo.

La Valette has suspicions of Montalto, and causes him to be narrowly observed. He speaks to him in private, with the view of warning him with all possible gentleness; but without effect. Montalto denies all obstinately and confidently, and falls back on his own dignity as a commander.

After his withdrawal, St. Priest appears before La Valette. The youth is of far different mind from the other deputies from St. Elmo. He does not wish to be recalled from his post, and comes now to the master, with childlike open confidence, to discover to him the mutiny of the Knights. With difficulty can La Valette dissemble his feelings. He speaks still to St. Priest as grand-master, and dismisses him with charges. Fresh inspiration of the youth for duty and devotion for the person of the master.

Enter Romegas, Biron, Crequi and several of their partisans. They begin with forcible representations relative to the garrison of St. Elmo, and of the grand-master's refusal they speak as mutineers. Crequi is the most violent of all. To the reproach that La Valette, by his obstinacy, is leading the Order to destruction, he (La Valette) answers that it is already ruined, is at the present moment no longer in existence; and that not through the power of the enemy, but through internal corruption and decay. He withdraws with dignity, ordering the Knights to await his orders.

The Knights are shaken by this last speech of the grand-master, and some of them begin to see the wrong of which they have been guilty. A Knight brings the news that, despite La Valette's threat that he would put every emissary of the enemy to death, a renegade has been seized bearing commissions from the Turkish commander. On his person letters for Montalto have been found, containing great promises. Montalto himself has escaped to the enemy. The Knights reflect that it was he who chiefly fostered the bitterness against the master.

Enter Miranda, the Spanish ambassador, after him the young Knights, then some of the oldest Knights and the choir, all armed. The grand-master, with Castriotto, follows. The engineer receives a command to make his report concerning the state of St. Elmo before the whole assemblage. He maintains that it is still possible to defend St. Elmo for a considerable time. The grand-master now asks the youngest and the oldest Knights, then the choir and Miranda, if they are willing to undertake the defence under his leading. All are ready; the grand-master now grants the prayer of the garrison, that it be allowed to withdraw from the post, dismisses the mutinous Knights and orders only Romegas to remain.

La Valette speaks to him as a dying man who explains his last wishes. Only Romegas, who has brought the Order nearly to ruin, is in a position to rescue it. He (La Valette) has chosen him for his successor, and gained for him the weightiest voices. Romegas is now placed on the standpoint of a prince, a position he is capable of occupying, and recognizes now how objectionable his previous conduct has been. Ashamed to the uttermost by the magnanimity of a man whom he had so thoroughly misunderstood, he withdraws with purpose of showing by his acts that he is not unworthy of the confidence that has been placed in him.

St. Priest appears to take leave of the grand-master. La Valette is most deeply moved. He discovers himself as his father, and says to him that he will go with him to meet death in the breach of St. Elmo. The choir is present.

Romegas advances with the mutinous Knights and the deputies from St. Elmo. All repent their past errors, and every one is ready to offer himself up in St. Elmo for the preservation of the order. The choir deepens the Knights' feelings of shame by discovering to them that St. Priest is the son of the grand-master, and that even him he has devoted to death. La Valette at first refuses to depart from his first resolution, till he is convinced of the total change of spirit that has come over the Knights. At length he consents that the defenders of St. Elmo may still maintain the defence of this post, and, in the necessity

of the present critical circumstances, devotes himself to maintaining the Order. All urge him not to separate himself from his son. Every one is ready to fill the place of the admirable youth. St. Priest rejects the offer and remains immovable. His whole demeanor expresses the loftiest enthusiasm. La Valette, also, will listen to no personal considerations. St. Priest takes leave of the grand-master and Crequi.

—

The choir alone, in its state of highest dignity, inspired by all that elevates man—feeling of duty, knightly spirit, religion.

—

News from St. Elmo. The fort is being stormed. Crequi has flown to St. Elmo to die with his friend. La Valette enters in a state of extreme distress. He deeply feels what he has offered up.

———

St. Elmo is taken. A Greek, Laskaris, of a race that once sat on the Greek throne, escapes, at imminent peril of his life, from the Turkish host, where he occupied a high position, to the Maltese, whose heroism he admires, and to whose religion the earliest impressions of his childhood attach him. He gives a detailed account of the incredible deeds of the defenders of St. Elmo, of the enormous loss of the Turks, of their amazement and horror when they became aware of the condition of the fort and the smallness of the number of its defenders, of the especially weighty loss of the enemy in the person of their highest and most experienced commander, Dragut, Bey of Tripoli, who fell during the siege. From Montalto's treachery nothing more is to be dreaded. He was confronted by St. Priest in the storming, and had met his reward.

———

The body of St. Priest has been rescued from the waves. It is brought in, and the Knights accompany it in mute grief. La Valette rises above himself. He praises the lofty determination of his illustrious son, sees sons in all the Knights, and confides firmly in the strength of the Order, which now stands without restriction and for all time. Through a great sacrifice the victory is as good as secured, as it was in the Persian war by the death of Leonidas. Success had justified his confidence and faith.

PREFACE.

THE idea of a dramatic delineation of the police of Paris under Louis XIV had occupied Schiller's mind for a considerable time. Over the many-hued crowd and tumult of the multitudinous figures of every description constituting the Parisian world the police was to be depicted as hovering like a being of some higher nature, whose glance sweeps over an immeasurable field and penetrates into the most secret recesses, just as if nothing is beyond the reach of its comprehensive arm.

"Paris appears in its totality. The utmost extremes of social circumstances and moral conditions, in their most conspicuous features and most characteristic aspects, enter into the representation—the most simple innocence as well as the most unnatural vileness, idyllic peacefulness as well as gloomy despair."

"A most highly complicated crime, involving many families, which in the progress of investigation becomes ever more involved and ever brings out new revelations is the cardinal point of the plot. It is like some enormous tree which has intertwined its branches with those of other trees wide around it, and to uproot which one requires to dig up a whole tract. So is Paris excavated, and every variety of existence in the course of the procedure brought successively to light."

"The case is apparently insoluble, but Argenson—at the head of the police, after causing certain data to be given him, promises, in confidence in his power, a successful issue and gives his agents their commissions forthwith."

"After long following-up he loses the trail of the chase, and sees himself in danger of not being able to keep the promise so confidently given. But at this conjuncture destiny itself comes into play and drives the murderer into the hands of justice."

"Argenson has seen mankind too frequently on its worst side to be able to have an elevated conception of human nature. He has become more sceptical in regard to the good in it, but more tolerant to the evil; still he has not lost his feeling for the beautiful, and wherever he meets it unequivocally, he is, on that account, affected all the more sensibly. He comes on a case of this kind and does homage to proved virtue."

"In the course of the piece he appears as a private man. Here he shows himself in quite a different character—jovial and ready to oblige, deserving of good will and respect, not only as an agreeable companion, but as a man of heart and intellect. In point of fact he does find a heart to love him, and his admirable conduct earns for him a wife worthy of his love."

"The minister of police, like a father-confessor, becomes acquainted with the weak points and failings in many families, and, therefore, has need, like the latter, to be a man of the highest discretion—A case occurs, where every one is equally amazed and terrified by reason of his apparent omniscience, but wherein he shows himself a forbearing friend."

"Scene showing Argenson with a philosopher and an author. It contains a comparison of the ideal with the real, wherein is shown the superiority of the realist over the theorizer."

"Occasionally Argenson warns innocence as well as guilt. He causes spies to track, not the criminal only, but also such unfortunates as are liable to become criminal through despair. An individual of this class comes before him in utter desperation, to whom the police shows itself in the character of a rescuing Providence."

"The dark side also of police administration must be shown. It can employ deceit to gain its ends, the innocent can suffer through

138

it; it is often compelled to make use of base tools and to employ base means. Even the crimes of its own officials enjoy a certain impunity."

Of the further carrying out of these ideas in all their comprehensiveness we find no trace in Schiller's papers, but on the contrary the plan of a drama of which only a very small portion of the above material constitutes the groundwork. It was a characteristic of Schiller that his first thoughts never became contracted in the progress of execution, but, on the contrary, expanded themselves—We must therefore believe that the following scheme of a drama had an earlier origin—probably from the reading of the *Causes célèbres* of Pitaval—and was given up because it led him up to these ideas that offered such a wealth of characters and situations.

Narbonne is a rich and respected private gentleman in a French provincial town—Bordeaux, Lyons or Nantes,—a man in the prime of life, between 40 and 50. He enjoys universal esteem, and the favorable disposition which people had to his deceased brother, Pierre Narbonne, has followed the name. He is the sole survivor of the house; for his brother left no heirs. Two of the latter's children perished in a fire through carelessness of the servants.

After Pierre's death Louis was sole heir. He was absent at the time of the death, but came back thereon to take up his permanent abode in the town.

Ten years have elapsed since these events, and Narbonne is on the eve of his marriage which is to perpetuate the race. His affections are fixed on a beautiful, noble and rich young lady, Victoire de Pontis, whose parents feel themselves honored by the proposal, and gladly promise him their daughter.

Six years before a young man, by name Saint-Foix, had been received into Narbonne's house as a helpless orphan, and had received many acts of kindness, especially a good education, from him. He lived with him, not on the footing of a servant but of a poor relation, and the whole town admired Narbonne's generosity to the young man, whom people soon began to envy.

Saint-Foix made rapid progress in the education afforded him by Narbonne. He showed an admirable disposition both of head and heart; at the same time, however, he manifested a certain aristocratic pride, which was scarcely becoming in a poor, adopted orphan. He was full of grateful reverence for his benefactor, but evidenced otherwise no sign of a feeling of subserviency or humiliation; he appeared, rather, when he accepted Narbonne's benefits to avail himself only of what was his by right. His spirit showed itself often in arrogance, and a certain naïveté and lightheartedness was liable to border on frivolity. He was extravagant, free and jealous of his honor.

Victoire had often had opportunities of seeing this Saint-Foix, and soon felt an affection for him which, however, appeared to be hopeless. The solicitation of her hand by Narbonne, for whom she had a peculiar aversion, strengthened, more and more, her feeling for Saint-Foix, who was often, in the circumstances, sent to her by Narbonne himself. Saint-Foix adored Victoire from the first instant he saw her, but he dared not raise his hopes to her.

He had learned to know another maiden, who like himself was parentless, and to whom he had done a great service. For her he had a tender friendship, his heart being divided between her and Victoire; but he discriminated very easily between his feelings for the two—

By the numerous household of Narbonne (among whom a single old servant of Pierre Narbonne, named Thierry, maintained his place), Saint-Foix was partly hated, partly envied; only one female among them had a favorable disposition towards him, and cherished views on his hand. She was much older than he, and had no other claim on him than the little fortune she could share with him, and which had not been earned in the most honorable way. Her name was Madelon.

So were matters circumstanced at the opening of the piece.

Madelon has returned from a little pilgrimage in which she had sought consolation for her disquietude. A bygone unrighteous act troubles her conscience; she brings no consolation back.

She finds Narbonne contented, in high spirits and secure; everything seems to be going

according to his wish. He is only disturbed over the disappearance of a trinket which he meant to present to his bride, and he purposes to set the law agoing in regard to it.

Madelon is alarmed. Let the law rest! says she. " Accept the little loss cheerfully !" " It is no little loss." " Take it then as a compensation ! The unbroken continuance of your prosperity has long troubled me." " I will pursue my right." " Your right !" sighs Madelon.

Madelon exhibits still greater uneasiness, when she hears that a gypsy is in the house, who is under suspicion in regard to the jewel. She laments sorely that she had not been here. " Ah, while I was on that fruitless pilgrimage in order to gain rest for my heart, I have missed the only opportunity of freeing myself from my long sorrow."

Monsieur de Pontis, bailiff of the place, and future father-in-law of Narbonne, comes to institute inquiries in regard to the disappearance of the trinket. This is gone about with all formality and with the assistance of an actuary. The jewel is described, the household examined one by one, and, on the occasion, a part of the history of the house is brought to light. The account of Saint-Foix is especially remarkable. His history is narrated and shows Narbonne in the light of a benefactor. He seems to indulge no suspicion of Saint-Foix.

After the transaction of these official matters, the marriage is spoken of. Pontis shows how much he and the whole town honor Narbonne, and is happy in the thought of a closer relation with him.

Saint-Foix in conversation with the old Thierry. The young man manifests a strange nervous unrest ; he finds the house too narrow for him ; he must out into the wider world ; he has, moreover, on his mind something secret, something that gives him a feeling of

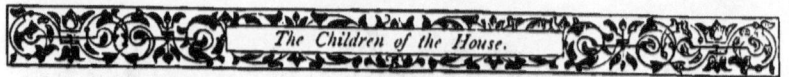

insecurity, that shuns the light and oppresses him—something, in fact, that looks like trouble of conscience. Especially he seems to accuse himself of great ingratitude towards Narbonne. When the marriage of the latter is referred to his uneasiness becomes extreme.

His scene with Thierry seems like a final leave-taking. He takes farewell even of the lifeless objects, and tears himself away in a state of the highest excitement.

Thierry shakes his head, and seems to struggle against a suspicion arising in his mind. In his soliloquy he tells how it was in the house in old times, and how it is now.

Saint-Foix with Adelaide. Traces of an innocent affection, gratitude of the girl, sympathy of the youth. She details her lot ; he, his. Adelaide has escaped from a dangerous gypsy woman, who tyrannized over and wished to lead her into wickedness. Saint-Foix had found her in a helpless condition and brought her to good people, with whom she still remains in secret.

From poverty she offers for sale the only valuable she has, a precious piece of jewelry ; the goldsmith, to whom she brought it, recognizes it for his own work which he had executed for the wife of Narbonne, gives information to this effect, and this causes Adelaide to be arrested.

The police officers appear and order Adelaide to follow them to the bailiff. Saint-Foix opposes this in vain.

Victoire and her mother. Victoire shows her abhorrence for Narbonne's addresses, on account of which the whole world envies her. One can detect in her, independently of her aversion to the person of Narbonne, a secret but hopeless regard for some one else.

Pontis comes and tells that they are on the track of the stolen ornament.

Adelaide is brought in and as Pontis proceeds to hear her, Saint-Foix comes to Victoire in great excitement to call on her for aid to, and intercession in behalf of Adelaide. A most affecting scene between the two which leads to the discovery of their mutual love.

Narbonne enters during this scene and discovers Saint-Foix his rival.

Pontis enters after the hearing is concluded and declares Saint-Foix an accomplice. Narbonne hears that a portion of the stolen jewelry has been found ; but when he sees the jewel referred to he is utterly confounded.

Scene between Pontis and Narbonne. The latter affects generosity, wishes a stop to be put to the investigation, and that both the suspected persons be shipped off to the colonies. Pontis insists on the closest investigation. While they are still together, it is reported to the bailiff that the gypsy woman has been brought in, and that Adelaide on seeing her had betrayed extreme terror.

Madelon and Narbonne. Madelon has recognized the gypsy as the woman to whom she had given over both the children of Pierre Narbonne, when she made her escape by springing from the burning house, giving out that they had both perished in the flames. It is now discovered that Adelaide is the daughter, but the fate of the boy is still a mystery.

Pontis enters and announces that Adelaide and Saint-Foix have recognized each other as brother and sister, and that the gypsy had received them fifteen years previously. Saint-Foix spent only five years with her, having escaped when he was in his tenth year.

Narbonne wishes now to interfere and check any further investigation ; Pontis, on the other hand, insists that the parents of the children must be discovered and bethinks himself of the jewel.

Narbonne advises Saint-Foix and Adelaide to escape secretly, but they both refuse to do so.

Narbonne and Madelon. Madelon has recognized the children and urges on Narbonne to adopt them as his own and make them his heirs. Narbonne is in the utmost perplexity; he knows of no way out of his difficulties but through the death of Madelon, and murders her.

The children of the house are recognized and brought in triumph by a crowd to Narbonne.

The murderer of Pierre Narbonne knows of a secret door admitting to Louis Narbonne's chamber; he has entered by this way, discovered the jewel lying there, and gone off with it. He leaves behind a few lines addressed to Narbonne, wherein he shows that he must now go into the wide world, being compelled to flee on account of a murder. He is arrested in the course of his flight, a consequence of the police arrangements.

Narbonne finds in his chamber traces of the murderer.

Pontis announces triumphantly the discovery of the jewel.

Narbonne, in vain, endeavors to escape. He and the murderer are confronted with each other. An attempt he makes to kill himself is frustrated. He is completely unmasked and given over to justice. Saint-Foix rescues the hand of Victoire.

ACT I.

THE DIET AT CRACOW.

SCENE I.—*On the rising of the curtain, the Polish Diet is discovered, seated in the great Senate Hall. On a raised platform, elevated by three steps, and surmounted by a canopy, is the imperial throne; the escutcheons of Poland and Lithuania suspended on each side. The* KING *seated upon the throne; on his right and left hand his ten royal officers standing on the platform. Below the platform the* BISHOPS, PALATINES, *and* CASTELLANS *seated on each side of the stage. Opposite to these stand the Provincial* DEPUTIES, *in a double line, uncovered. All armed. The* ARCHBISHOP OF GNESEN, *as the Primate of the kingdom, is seated next the Proscenium; his Chaplain behind him, bearing a golden cross.*

ARCHBISHOP OF GNESEN. Thus, then, hath
   this tempestuous Diet been
Conducted safely to a prosperous close ;
And king and commons part as cordial friends.
The nobles have consented to disarm,
And straight disband the dangerous Rocoss * ;
Whilst our good king his sacred word has
   pledged,
That every just complaint shall have redress.

And now that all is peace at home, we may
Look to the things that claim our care abroad.

* An insurrectionary muster of the nobles.

Is it the will of the most High Estates,
That Prince Demetrius, who hath advanced
A claim to Russia's crown, as Ivan's son,
Should at their bar appear, and in the face
Of this august assembly prove his right ?
   CASTELLAN OF CRACOW. Honor and justice
      both demand he should ;
It were unseemly to refuse his prayer.
   BISHOP OF WERMELAND. The documents
      on which he rests have been
Examined, and are found authentic. We
May give him audience.
   SEVERAL DEPUTIES. Nay ! We must, we
      must !
LEO SAPIEHA. To hear is to admit his right.
ODOWALSKY.   And not
   To hear is to reject his claims unheard.
ARCHBISHOP OF GNESEN. Is it your will
   that he have audience ?
I ask it for the second time—and third.
   IMPERIAL CHANCELLOR. Let him stand forth
      before our throne !
   SENATORS.   And speak !
   DEPUTIES. Yes, yes ! Let him be heard !

[*The Imperial* GRAND MARSHAL *beckons with his baton to the door-keeper, who goes out.*

SAPIEHA (*to the* CHANCELLOR). Write down,
   my lord,
That here I do protest against this step,
And all that may ensue therefrom, to mar
The peace of Poland's state, and Moscow's
   crown.

[*Enter* DEMETRIUS. *Advances some steps
towards the throne, and makes three bows,
with his head uncovered, first to the* KING,
next to the SENATORS, *and then to the*
DEPUTIES, *who all severally answer with
an inclination of the head. He then takes
up his position so as to keep within his eye
a great proportion of the assemblage, and
yet not to turn his back upon the throne.*
ARCHBISHOP OF GNESEN. Prince Dmitri,
 son of Ivan! if the pomp
Of this great Diet scare thee, or a sight
So noble and majestic chain thy tongue,
Thou may'st — for this the Senate have al-
 low'd —
Choose thee a proxy, wheresoe'er thou list,
And do thy mission by another's lips.
 DEMETRIUS. My Lord Archbishop, I stand
 here to claim
A kingdom, and the state of royalty.
'Twould ill beseem me, should I quake before
A noble people, and its king and senate.
I ne'er have view'd a circle so august,
But the sight swells my heart within my breast,
And not appals me. The more worthy ye,
To me ye are welcome ; I can ne'er
Address my claim to nobler auditory.
 ARCHBISHOP OF GNESEN. — — The au-
 gust Republic
Is favorably bent. — — — — — —
 DEMETRIUS. Most puissant king! Most
 worthy and most potent
Bishops and palatines, and my good lords,
The deputies of the august Republic!
It gives me pause and wonder, to behold
Myself, Czar Ivan's son, now stand before
The Polish people in their Diet here.
Both realms were sunder'd by a bloody hate,
And, whilst my father lived, no peace might be.
Yet now hath Heaven so order'd these events,
That I, his blood, who with my nurse's milk
Imbibed the ancestral hate, appear before you,
A fugitive, compelled to seek my rights
Even here, in Poland's heart. Then, ere I
 speak,
Forget magnanimously all rancours past,
And that the Czar, whose son I own myself,
Roll'd war's red billows to your very homes
I stand before you, sirs, a prince despoil'd.
I ask protection. The oppressed may urge
A sacred claim on every noble breast.
And who in all earth's circuit shall be just,
If not a people great and valiant,—one
In plenitude of power so free, it needs
To render 'count but to itself alone,
And may, unchallenged, lend an open ear

And aiding hand to fair humanity.
 ARCHBISHOP OF GNESEN. You do allege
 you are Czar Ivan's son,
And, truly, nor your bearing nor your speech
Gainsays the lofty title that you urge.
But shows us that you are indeed his son,
And you shall find that the Republic bears
A generous spirit. She has never quail'd
To Russia in the field ! She loves, alike,
To be a noble foe—a cordial friend.
 DEMETRIUS. Ivan Wasilowitch, the mighty
 Czar
Of Moscow, took five spouses to his bed,
In the long years that spared him to the throne.
The first, a lady of the heroic line
Of Romanoff, bore him Feodor, who reign'd
After his father's death. One only son,
Dmitri, the last blossom of his strength,
And a mere infant when his father died,
Was born of Marfa, of Nagori's line.
Czar Feodor, a youth, alike effeminate
In mind and body, left the reins of power
To his chief equerry, Boris Godunow,
Who ruled his master with most crafty skill.
Feodor was childless, and his barren bride
Denied all prospect of an heir. Thus, when
The wily Boiar, by his fawning arts,
Had coil'd himself into the people's favor,
His wishes soar'd as high as to the throne.
Between him and his haughty hopes there stood
A youthful prince, the young Demetrius
I Iwanowitsch, who with his mother lived
At Uglitsch, where her widowhood was passed.
 Now, when his fatal purpose was matured,
He sent to Uglitsch ruffians, charged to put
The Czarowitsch to death. — — —
One night, when all was hush'd, the castle's
 wing
Where the young prince, apart from all the
 rest,
With his attendants lay, was found on fire.
The raging flames engulph'd the pile—the
 prince,
Unseen, unheard. was spirited away,
And all the world lamented him as dead.
All Moscow knows these things to be the truth.
 ARCHBISHOP OF GNESEN. Yes. these are
 facts familiar to us all.
The rumor ran abroad, both far and near,
That Prince Demetrius perished in the flames.
When Uglitsch was destroy'd. And, as his
 death
Raised to the throne the Czar who fills it now,
Fame did not hesitate to charge on him
This murder foul and pitiless. But yet,
His death is not the business now in hand !

This prince is living still!   He lives in you!
So runs your plea.   Now bring us to the proofs!
Whereby do you attest that you are he?
What are the signs by which you shall be
    known?
How 'scaped you those were sent to hunt you
    down,
And now, when sixteen years are passed, and
    you
Well nigh forgot, emerge to light once more?
DEMETRIUS.   'Tis scarce a year since I
    have known myself;
I lived a secret to myself till then,
Surmising nought of my imperial birth.
I was a monk with monks, close pent within
The cloister's precincts, when I first began
To waken to consciousness of self.
My impetuous spirit chafed against the bars,
And the high blood of princes 'gan to course
In strange unbidden moods along my veins.
At length I flung the monkish cowl aside,
And fled to Poland, where the noble Prince
Of Sendomir, the generous, the good,
Took me as guest into his princely house,
And train'd me up to noble deeds of arms.
    ARCHBISHOP OF GNESEN.   How? You still
        ignorant of what you were?
Yet ran the rumor then on every side,
That Prince Demetrius was still alive.
Czar Boris trembled on his throne, and sent

His sassafs to the frontiers, to keep
Sharp watch on every traveller that stirr'd.
Had not the tale its origin with you?
Did you not give the rumor birth yourself?
Had you not named to any that you were
Demetrius?
    DEMETRIUS.   I relate that which I know.
If a report went forth I was alive,
Then had some god been busy with the fame.
Myself I knew not.   In the prince's house,
And in the throng of his retainers lost,
I spent the pleasant springtime of my youth.
— — — — In silent homage
My heart was vow'd to his most lovely daughter;
Yet in those days it never dreamt to raise
Its wildest thoughts to happiness so high.
My passion gave offence to her betrothed,
The Castellan of Lemberg.   He with taunts
Chafed me, and in the blindness of his rage
Forgot himself so wholly as to strike me.
Thus savagely provoked, I drew my sword;
He, blind with fury, rushed upon the blade,
And perished there by my unwitting hand.
    MEISCHEK.   Yes, it was even so. — — —
    DEMETRIUS.   Mine was the worst mischance!
        A nameless youth,
A Russian and a stranger, I had slain
A grandee of the empire—in the house
Of my kind patron done a deed of blood,
And sent to death his son-in-law and friend

145

My innocence avail'd not; not the pity
Of all his household, nor his kindness—his,
The noble Palatine's,—could save my life;
For it was forfeit to the law, that is,
Though lenient to the Poles, to strangers stern.
Judgment was pass'd on me—that judgment
    death.
I knelt upon the scaffold, by the block;
To the fell headsman's sword I bared my throat,
And in the act disclosed a cross of gold,
Studded with precious gems, which had been
    hung
About my neck at the baptismal font.
This sacred pledge of Christian redemption
I had, as is the custom with my people,
Worn on my neck conceal'd, where'er I went.
From my first hours of infancy; and now,
When from sweet life I was compell'd to part,
I grasped it as my only stay, and press'd it
With passionate devotion to my lips.—
    [*The Poles intimate their sympathy by dumb*
    show.
The jewel was observed; its sheen and worth
Awaken'd curiosity and wonder.
They set me free, and questioned me; yet still
I could not call to memory a time
I had not worn the jewel on my person.
Now it so happened, that three Boiars, who
Had fled from the resentment of their Czar,
Were on a visit to my lord at Sambor.
They saw the trinket,—recognized it, by
Nine emeralds, alternately inlaid
With amethysts, to be the very cross
Which Ivan Westislowsky at the font
Hung on the neck of the Czar's youngest son.
They scrutinized me closer, and were struck
To find me marked with one of nature's freaks,
For my right arm is shorter than my left.
Now, being closely plied with questions, I
Bethought me of a little psalter, which
I carried from the cloister when I fled.
Within this book were certain words in Greek,
Inscribed there by the Igumen himself.
What they imported was unknown to me,
Being ignorant of the language. Well, the
    psalter
Was sent for, brought, and the inscription read.
It bore, that Brother Wasili Philaret,
(Such was my cloister-name,) who own'd the
    book,
Was Prince Demetrius, Ivan's youngest son,
By Andrei, an honest Diak, saved
By stealth in that red night of massacre.
Proofs of the fact lay carefully preserved
Within two convents, which were pointed out.
On this the Boiars at my feet fell down,

Won by the force of these resistless proofs,
And hail'd me as the offspring of their Czar.
So, from the yawning gulphs of black despair,
Fate raised me up to Fortune's topmost heights.
ARCHBISHOP OF GNESEN. — — — —
DEMETRIUS. And now the mists cleared
    off, and all at once
Memories on memories started into life,
In the remotest back-ground of the past.
And, like some city's spires, that gleam afar
In golden sunshine when nought else is seen,
So in my soul two images grew bright,
The loftiest sun-peaks in the shadowy past.
I saw myself escaping one dark night,
And a red lurid flame lit up the gloom
Of midnight darkness as I looked behind me.
A memory 'twas of very earliest youth,
For what preceded or came after it
In the long distance utterly was lost.
In solitary brightness there it stood,
A ghastly beacon light on memory's waste.
Yet I remember'd how, in later years,
One of my comrades called me, in his wrath,
Son of the Czar. I took it as a jest,
And with a blow avenged it at the time.
All this now flash'd like lightning on my soul,
And told with dazzling certainty, that I
Was the Czar's son, so long reputed dead.
With this one word the clouds that had per-
    plexed
My strange and troubled life were cleared
    away.
Nor merely by these signs, for such deceive;
But in my soul, in my proud throbbing heart,
I felt within me coursed the blood of kings;
And sooner will I drain it drop by drop,
Than bate one jot my title to the crown.
ARCHBISHOP OF GNESEN. And shall we
    trust a scroll, which might have found
Its way by merest chance into your hands,
Back'd by the tale of some poor runagates?
Forgive me, noble youth! Your tone, I grant,
And bearing, are not those of one who lies;
Still you in this may be yourself deceived.
Well may the heart be pardoned, that beguiles
Itself in playing for so high a stake.
What hostage do you tender for your word?
DEMETRIUS. I tender fifty, who will give
    their oaths,—
All Piasts to a man, and free-born Poles
Of spotless reputation,—each of whom
Is ready to enforce what I have urged.
There sits the noble Prince of Sendomir,
And at his side the Castellan of Lublin;
Let them declare, if I have spoke the truth.
— — — — — —

ARCHBISHOP OF GNESEN. How seem these things to the august Estates?
To the enforcement of such numerous proofs
Doubt and mistrust, methinks, must needs give way.
Long has a creeping rumor fill'd the world,
That Dmitri, Ivan's son, is still alive.
The Czar himself confirms it by his fears.
—Before us stands a youth, in age and mien,
Even to the very freak that nature play'd,
The lost heir's counterpart, and of a soul
Whose noble stamp keeps rank with his high claims.
He left the cloister's precincts, urged by strange
Mysterious promptings; and this monk-train'd boy
Was straight distinguish'd for his knightly feats.
He shows a trinket which the Czarowitsch
Once wore, and one that never left his side;
A written witness, too, by pious hands,
Gives us assurance of his princely birth;
And, stronger still, from his unvarnish'd speech
And open brow Truth makes his best appeal.
Such traits as these Deceit doth never don;
It masks its subtle soul in vaunting words,
And in the high-gloss'd ornaments of speech.
No longer then can I withhold the title,
Which he with circumstance and justice claims;
And, in the exercise of my old right,
I now, as Primate, give him the first voice.
ARCHBISHOP OF LEMBERG. My voice goes with the Primate's.
SEVERAL VOICES. So does mine.
SEVERAL PALATINES. And mine!
ODOWALSKY. And mine!
DEPUTIES. And all!
SAPIEHA. My gracious sirs!
Weigh well ere you decide! Be not so hasty!
It is not meet, the council of the realm
Be hurried on to — — —
ODOWALSKY. There is nothing here
For us to weigh; all has been fully weigh'd.
The proofs demonstrate incontestably.
This is not Moscow, sirs! No despot here
Keeps our free souls in manacles. Here Truth
May walk by day or night with brow erect.
I will not think, my lords, in Cracow here,
Here in the very Diet of the Poles,
That Moscow's Czar should have obsequious slaves.
DEMETRIUS. Oh, take my thanks, ye reverend senators!

That ye have lent your credence to these proofs;
And if I be indeed the man whom I
Protest myself, oh then, endure not this
Audacious robber should usurp my seat,
Or longer desecrate that sceptre, which
To me, as the true Czarowitsch, belongs.
— — — — — — —
Yes, justice lies within me,—you have the power
'Tis the most dear concern of every state
And throne, that right should everywhere prevail,
And all men in the world possess their own.
For there, where Justice holds uncumber'd sway,
There each enjoys his heritage secure,
And over every house and every throne
Law, truth, and order keep their angel watch.

It is the key-stone of the world's wide arch,
The one sustaining and sustained by all,
Which, if it fall, brings all in ruin down.
— — — — — — —
(Answers of SENATORS, giving assent to DEME-
TRIUS.)
DEMETRIUS. Oh look on me, renowned Sigismund!
Great king, on thine own bosom turn thine eyes,
And in my destiny behold thine own.
Thou, too, hast known the rude assaults of Fate;
Within a prison camest thou to the world;
Thy earliest glances fell on dungeon walls.
Thou, too, hadst need of friends to set thee free,
And raise thee from a prison to a throne.
These didst thou find. The noble kindness thou
Didst reap from them, oh, testify to me!
— — — — — — —
And you, ye grave and honor'd councillors,
Most reverend bishops, pillars of the church,
Ye palatines and castellans of fame,
The moment has arrived, by one high deed
To reconcile two nations long estranged.
Yours be the glorious boast, that Poland's power
Hath given the Moscovites their Czar, and in
The neighbour, who oppress'd you as a foe,
Secure an ever-grateful friend. And you,
The deputies of the august Republic,
Saddle your steeds of fire! Leap to your seats!
To you expand high fortune's golden gates;
I will divide the foeman's spoil with you.

147

Moscow is rich in plunder; measureless
In gold and gems, the treasures of the Czar;
I can give royal guerdons to my friends,
And I will give them too. When I, as Czar,
Set foot within the Kremlin, then, I swear,
The poorest of you all, that follows me,
Shall robe himself in velvet and in sables;
With costly pearls his housings shall he deck,
And silver be the metal of least worth,
That he shall shoe his horses' hoofs withal.
[*Great commotion among the* DEPUTIES.
KORELA, *Hetman of the Cossacks, declares
himself ready to put himself at the head of
an army.*
ODOWALSKY. How! shall we leave the
Cossack to despoil us
At once of glory and of booty both?
— — — — — — — — — —
We've made a truce with Tartar and with Turk,
And from the Swedish power have nought to
fear.
Our martial spirit has been wasting long
In slothful peace; our swords are red with rust.
Up! and invade the kingdom of the Czar,
And win a grateful and true-plighted friend,
Whilst we augment our country's might and
glory.
MANY DEPUTIES. War! War with Moscow!
OTHERS.   Be it so resolved!
On to the votes at once!
SAPIEHA (*rises*).   Grand Marshal, please
To order silence! I desire to speak.
A CROWD OF VOICES.   War! War with
Moscow!
SAPIEHA.   Nay, I will be heard.
Ho, Marshal, do your duty!
[*Great tumult within and outside the hall.*
GRAND MARSHAL.   'Tis, you see,
Quite fruitless.
SAPIEHA.   What? The Marshal's self
suborn'd?
Is this our Diet, then, no longer free?
Throw down your staff, and bid this brawling
cease!
I charge you, on your office, to obey!
[*The* GRAND MARSHAL *casts his baton into
the centre of the hall; the tumult abates.*
What whirling thoughts, what mad resolves
are these?
Stand we not now at peace with Moscow's
Czar?
Myself, as your imperial envoy, made
A treaty to endure for twenty years;
I raised this right hand, that you see, aloft,
In solemn pledge, within the Kremlin's walls;
And fairly hath the Czar maintain'd his word.

What is sworn faith—what compacts, treaties,
when
A solemn Diet tramples on them all?
DEMETRIUS.   Prince Leo Sapieha! You
concluded
A bond of peace, you say, with Moscow's
Czar?
That did you not; for I, I am that Czar.
In me is Moscow's majesty; I am
The son of Ivan, and his rightful heir.
Would the Poles treat with Russia for a peace,
Then must they treat with me! Your compact's
null,
As being made with one whose title's null.
ODOWALSKY.   What reck we of your treaty?
So we will'd
When it was made—our wills are changed to-
day.
SAPIEHA.   Is it, then, come to this? If none
beside
Will stand for justice, then, at least, will I.
I'll rend the woof of cunning into shreds,
And lay its falsehoods open to the day.
Most reverend Primate! art thou, canst thou
be
So simple-soul'd, or canst thou so dissemble?
Are ye so credulous, my lords? My liege,
Art thou so weak? Ye know not—will not
know,
Ye are the puppets of the wily Waywode
Of Sendomir, who rear'd this spurious Czar,
Whose measureless ambition, while we speak,
Clutches in thought the spoils of Moscow's
wealth.
Is't left for me to tell you, that even now
The league is made and sworn betwixt the
twain,—
The pledge the Waywode's youngest daughter's
hand?
And shall our great Republic blindly rush
Into the perils of an unjust war,
To aggrandize the Waywode, and to crown
His daughter as the Empress of the Czar?
There's not a man he has not bribed and
bought.
He means to rule the Diet, well I know;
I see his faction rampant in this hall,
And, as 'twere not enough that he controll'd
The SEYM WALMY by a majority,
He's girt the Diet with three thousand horse,
And all Cracow is swarming like a hive
With his sworn feudal vassals. Even now
They throng the halls and chamber where we
sit,
To hold our liberty of speech in awe.
Yet stirs no fear in my undaunted heart;

And while the blood keeps current in my veins,
I will maintain the freedom of my voice!
Let those who think like men come stand by
    me!
Whilst I have life, shall no resolve be pass'd
That is at war with justice and with reason.
'Twas I that ratified the peace with Moscow,
And I will hazard life to see it kept.
    ODOWALSKY. Give him no further hearing!
Take the votes!
    [*The* BISHOPS OF CRACOW *and* WILNA *rise,*
    and descend each to his own side, to collect
    the votes
MANY. War, war with Moscow!
ARCHBISHOP OF GNESEN (*to* SAPIEHA). Noble
sir, give way!
You see the mass are hostile to your views;
Then do not force a profitless division!
    IMPERIAL HIGH CHANCELLOR (*descends from*
    the throne, to SAPIEHA).

The king entreats you will not press the point,
Sir Waywode, to division in the Diet.
    DOORKEEPER (*aside to* ODOWALSKY).
Keep a bold front, and fearless—summon
    those
That wait without. All Cracow stands by
    you.
    IMPERIAL HIGH CHANCELLOR (*to* SAPIEHA).
Such excellent decrees have passed before:
Oh, cease, and for their sake, so fraught with
    good,
Unite your voice with the majority!
    BISHOP OF CRACOW (*has collected the votes on*
    his side).
On this right bench are all unanimous.
    SAPIEHA. And let them, to a man!—Yet I
    say, No!
I urge my veto—I break up the Diet.
Stay further progress! Null and void are all
The resolutions pass'd——

149

[*General commotion; the* KING *descends from the throne, the barriers are broken down, and there arises a tumultuous uproar.* DEPUTIES *draw their swords, and threaten* SAPIEHA *with them. The* BISHOPS *interpose, and protect him with their stoles.*
Majority?
What is it? The majority is madness;
Reason has still rank'd only with few.
What cares he for the general weal, that's poor?
Has the lean beggar choice, or liberty?
To the great lords of earth, that hold the purse,
He must for bread and raiment sell his voice.
'Twere meet that voices should be weigh'd, not counted
Sooner or later must the State be wreck'd,
Where numbers sway, and ignorance decides.
ODOWALSKY. Hark to the traitor!——
DEPUTIES. Hew him into shreds!
Down with him!
ARCHBISHOP OF GNESEN (*snatches the crucifix out of his Chaplain's hand, and interposes*).
Peace, peace!
Shall native blood be in the Diet shed?
Prince Sapieha! be advised! [*To the* BISHOPS.
Bring him away,
And interpose your bosoms as his shield!
Through this side door remove him quietly,
Or the wild mob will tear him limb from limb!
[SAPIEHA, *still casting looks of defiance, is forced away by the* BISHOPS, *whilst the* ARCHBISHOPS OF GNESEN *and* LEMBERG *keep the* DEPUTIES *at bay. Amidst violent tumult and clashing of arms, the hall is emptied of all but* DEMETRIUS, MEISCHEK, ODOWALSKY, *and the Hetman of the Cossacks.*
ODOWALSKY. That point miscarried,—
Yet shall you not lack aid because of this;
If the Republic holds the peace with Moscow,
At our own charges we shall push your claims.
KORELA. Who ever could have dreamt, that he alone
Would hold his ground against the assembled Diet?
MEISCHEK. The king! the king!
[*Enter* KING SIGISMUND, *attended by the* LORD HIGH CHANCELLOR, *the* GRAND MARSHALL, *and several* BISHOPS.
KING. Let me embrace you, prince!
At length the high republic does you justice;
My heart has done so long, and many a day.
Your fate doth move me deeply, as, indeed,
What monarch's heart but must be moved by it?

DEMETRIUS. The past, with all its sorrows,
is forgot;
Here on your breast I feel new life begin.
KING. I love not many words; yet what a king
May offer, who has vassals richer far
Than his poor self, that do I offer you.
You have been witness of an untoward scene,
But deem not ill of Poland's realm, because
A tempest jars the vessel of the state.
MEISCHEK. When winds are wild the steersman backs his helm,
And makes for port with all the speed he may.
KING. The diet is dissolved. Although I wish'd,
I could not break the treaty with the Czar.
But you have powerful friends; and if the Pole,
At his own risk, take arms on your behalf,
Or if the Cossack choose to venture war,
They are free men, I cannot say them nay.
MEISCHEK. The whole Rocoss is under arms already.
Please it but you, my liege, the angry stream
That raved against your sovereignty may turn
Its wrath on Moscow, leaving you unscathed.
KING. The best of weapons Russia's self will give thee;
Thy surest buckler is the people's heart.
By Russia only Russia will be vanquish'd.
Even as the Diet heard thee speak to-day,
Speak thou at Moscow to thy subjects, prince.
So chain their hearts, and thou wilt be their king.
In Sweden I by right of birth ascended
The throne of my inheritance in peace;
Yet did I lose the kingdom of my sires,
Because my people's hearts were not with me.
Enter MARINA.

MEISCHEK. My gracious liege, here, kneeling at your feet,
Behold Marina, youngest of my daughters;
The prince of Moscow offers her his heart.
Thou art the stay and pillar of our house,
And only from thy royal hand 'tis meet
That she receive her spouse and sovereign.
[MARINA *kneels to the* KING.
KING. Well, if you wish it, cousin, gladly I
Will do the father's office to the Czar.
[*To* DEMETRIUS, *giving him* MARINA'S *hand.*
Thus do I bring you, in this lovely pledge,
High Fortune's blooming goddess; and may these
Old eyes be spared to see this gracious pair
Sit in imperial state on Moscow's throne.

MARINA. My liege, I humbly thank your grace, and shall
Esteem me still your slave, where'er I be.
KING. Rise up, Czaritza! This is not a place
For you, the plighted bride-mate of the Czar;
For you, the daughter of my foremost Way-wode.
You are the youngest of your sisters; yet
Your spirit wings a high and glorious course,
And nobly grasps the top of sovereignty.
DEMETRIUS. Be thou, great monarch, wit-ness of my oath,
As, prince to prince, I pledge it here to you!
This noble lady's hand I do accept
As fortune's dearest pledge, and swear that, soon
As on my father's throne I take my seat,
I'll lead her home in triumph as my bride,
With all the state that fits a mighty queen.
And, for a dowry, to my bride I give
The principalities Plaskow and Great Neugart,
With all towns, hamlets, and in-dwellers there,
With all the rights and powers of sovereignty,
In absolute possession evermore;
And this, my gift, will I as Czar confirm
In my free city, Moscow. Furthermore,
As compensation to her noble sire
For present charges, I engage to pay
A million ducats, Polish currency.
— — — — — —
So help me God, and all his saints, as I
Have truly sworn this oath, and shall fulfil it.
KING. You will do so; you never will for-get
For what you are the noble Waywode's debtor;
Who, for your wishes, perils his sure wealth,
And, for your hopes, a child his heart adores.
A friend so rare is to be rarely prized!
Then, when your hopes are crown'd, forget not ever
The steps by which you mounted to the throne,
Nor with your garments let your heart be changed!
Think, that in Poland first you knew yourself,—
That this land gave you birth a second time.
DEMETRIUS. I have been nurtured in ad-versity;
And learned to reverence the beauteous bond
Which links mankind with sympathies of love.
KING. But now you enter on a realm where all—
Use, custom, morals—are untried and strange
In Poland here reigns freedom absolute;
The king himself, although in pomp supreme,

Must oftime be the serf of his noblesse;
But there the father's sacred power prevails,
And in the subject finds a passive slave.
DEMETRIUS. That glorious freedom, which surrounds me here,
I will transplant into my native land,
And turn these bond-serfs into glad-soul'd men;
Not o'er the souls of slaves will I bear rule.
KING. Do nought in haste; but by the time be led!
Prince, ere we part, three lessons take from me,
And truly follow them when thou art king.
It is a king that gives them, old and tried,
And they may prove of profit to thy youth.
DEMETRIUS. Oh, share thy wisdom with me! Thou hast won
The reverence of a free and mighty people;
What must I do to earn so fair a prize?
KING. — — You come from a strange land,
Borne on the weapons of a foreign foe;
This first felt wrong thou hast to wash away.
Then bear thee like a genuine son of Mos-cow,
With reverence due to all her usages.
Keep promise with the Poles, and value them,
For thou hast need of friends on thy new throne;
The arm that placed thee there can hurl thee down
Esteem them honourably, yet ape them not;
Strange customs thrive not in a foreign soil.
— — — — — —
And, whatsoe'er thou dost, revere thy mother—
You'll find a mother——
DEMETRIUS. Oh, my liege!
KING. High claim
Hath she upon thy filial reverence.
Do not ever honour.—'Twixt thy subjects and
Thyself she stands, a sacred, precious link.
No human law o'errides the imperial power;
Nothing but nature may command its awe;
Nor can thy people own a surer pledge,
That thou art gentle, than thy filial love.
I say no more. Much yet is to be done,
Ere thou mak'st booty of the golden fleece
Expect no easy victory! — — —
Czar Boris rules with strong and skilful hand;
You take the field against no common man.
He that by merit hath achieved the throne,
Is not puff'd from his seat by popular breath;
His deeds do serve to him for ancestors.
To your good fortune I commend you now;
Already twice, as by a miracle,

151

Hath it redeem'd you from the grasp of death;
'Twill put the finish on its work, and crown
   you.
[*Exeunt Omnes but* MARINA *and* ODOWALSKY.
ODOWALSKY. Say, lady, how have I fulfill'd
   my charge?
Truly and well, and wilt thou laud my zeal?
   MARINA. 'Tis, Odowalsky, well we are
   alone;
Matters of weight have we to canvass, which
'Tis meet the prince know nothing of. May he
Pursue the voice divine that goads him on !
If in himself he have belief, the world
Will catch the flame, and give him credence
   too.
He must be kept in that vague, shadowing mist,
Which is a fruitful mother of great deeds,
While we see clear, and act in certainty.
He lends the name—the inspiration ; we
Must bear the brain, the shaping thought, for
   him ;
And when, by art and craft, we have insured
The needful levies, let him still dream on,
And think they dropt, to aid him, from the
   clouds.
   ODOWALSKY.   Give thy commands ; I live
   but for thy service.
Think'st thou this Moscovite or his affairs
Concern my thoughts? 'Tis thou, thou and
   thy glory
For which I will adventure life and all.
For me no fortune blossoms; friendless, land-
   less,
I dare not let my hopes aspire to thee.
Thy grace I may not win, but I'll deserve it.
To make thee great be my one only aim;
Then, though another should possess thee,
   still
Thou wilt be mine,—being what I have made
   thee.
   MARINA. Therefore my whole heart do I
   pledge to thee ;
To thee I trust the acting of my thoughts.
The king doth mean us false. I read him
   through.
'Twas a concerted farce with Sapieha,
A juggle, all ! 'Twould please him well, be-
   like,
To see my father's power, which he dreads
   deeply,
Enfeebled in this enterprise—the league
Of the noblesse, which shook his heart with
   fear,
Drawn off in this campaign on foreign bounds,
While he himself sits neutral in the fray.
He thinks to share our fortune, if we win ;

And if we lose, he hopes with greater ease
To fix on us the bondage of his yoke
We stand alone. The die is cast. If he
Cares for himself, we shall be selfish too.

You lead the troops to Kioff. There let them
   swear
Allegiance to the prince, and unto me ;—
Mark you, to *me !* 'Tis needful for our ends
— — — — — — —
   ODOWALSKY.   — — — — — — —
   MARINA.   I want your eye, and not your
   arm alone.
   ODOWALSKY.   Command me—speak—
   MARINA.   You lead the Czarowitsch.
Keep your eye on him ; stir not from his side,
Render me 'count of every step he makes.
   ODOWALSKY.   Rely on me, he'll never cast
   us off.
   MARINA.   No man is grateful. Once his
   throne is sure,
He'll not be slow to cast our bonds aside.
— — — — — —
The Russian hates the Pole—must hate him
   ever ;
No bond of amity can link their hearts.
— — — — — —

[*Enter* OPALINSKY, BIELSKY, *and several
   Polish Noblemen.*
   OPALINSKY.   Fair patron, get us gold, and
   we march with you,
This lengthened Diet has consumed our all.
Let us have gold, we'll make thee Russia's
   queen.
   MARINA.   The Bishop of Kaminieck and
   Culm
Lends money on the pawn of land and serfs.
Sell, barter, pledge the hamlets of your boors,
Turn all to silver, horses, means of war !
War is the best of chapmen. He transmutes
Iron into gold. Whate'er you now may lose,
You'll find in Moscow twenty-fold again.
   BIELSKY.   Two hundred more wait in the
   tavern yonder ;
If you will show yourself, and drain a cup
With them, they're yours, all yours—I know
   them well.
   MARINA.   Expect me ! You shall introduce
   me to them.
   OPALINSKY.   — — — — — —
'Tis plain that you were born to be a queen.
   MARINA.   I was, and therefore I must be a
   queen.
   BIELSKY.   Ay, mount the snow-white steed,
   thine armor on,

And so, a second Vanda, lead thy troops,
Inspired by thee, to certain victory.
MARINA. My spirit leads you. War is not
for women.
The rendezvous's in Kioff. Thither my father
Will lead a levy of three thousand horse.
My sister's husband gives two thousand more,
And the Don sends a Cossack host in aid.
Do you all swear you will be true to me?
ALL. All, all—we swear!
(Draw their swords)
Vivat Marina, Russiæ Regina!
[MARINA *tears her veil in pieces, and divides
it among them. Exeunt omnes but* MARINA.

Enter MEISCHEK.
MARINA. Wherefore so sad, when fortune
smiles on us,
When every step thrives to our utmost wish,
And all around are arming in our cause?
MEISCHEK. 'Tis even because of this, my
child! All, all
Is staked upon the cast. Thy father's means
Are in these warlike preparations swamp'd.
I have much cause to ponder seriously;
Fortune is false, uncertain the result.

MARINA. — — — — — — —
MEISCHEK. Mad, venturous girl, what hast
thou brought me to?
What a weak father have I been, that I
Did not withstand thy importunities!
I am the richest Waywode of the empire,
The next in honor to the king. Had we
But been content to be so, and enjoy'd
Our stately fortunes with a tranquil soul!
Thy hopes soar'd higher—not for thee sufficed
The moderate station which thy sisters won.
Thou wouldst attain the loftiest mark that can
By mortals be achieved, and wear a crown.
I, thy fond, foolish father, long'd to heap
On thee, my darling one, all glorious gains,
So by thy prayers I let myself be fool'd,
And peril my sure fortunes on a chance.
MARINA. How? My dear father, dost thou
rue thy goodness?
Who with the meaner prize can live content,
When o'er his head the noblest courts his
grasp?
MEISCHEK. Thy sisters wear no crowns,
yet they are happy.

MARINA. What happiness is that, to leave
the home
Of the Waywode, my father, for the house

Of some count palatine, a grateful bride?
What do I gain of new from such a change?
And can I joy in looking to the morrow,
When it brings naught but what was stale to-
day?
Oh, tasteless round and petty, worn pursuits!
Oh, wearisome monotony of life!
Are they a guerdon for high hopes, high aims?
Or love or greatness I must have; all else
Are unto me alike indifferent.
MEISCHEK. — — — — —
MARINA. Smooth off the trouble from thy
brow, dear father!
Let's trust the stream that bears us on its breast,
Think not upon the sacrifice thou makest,
Think on the prize, the goal that's to be won—
When thou shalt see thy daughter robed in
state,
In regal state, aloft on Moscow's throne,
And thy son's sons the rulers of the world!
MEISCHEK. I think of nought, see nought,
but thee, my child
Girt with the splendors of the imperial crown.
Thou'rt bent to have it; I cannot gainsay thee.
MARINA. Yet one request, my dearest, best
of fathers,
I pray you grant me!
MEISCHEK. Name thy wish, my child
MARINA. Shall I remain shut up at Sambor,
with
The fires of boundless longing in my breast?
Beyond the Dnieper will my die be cast,—
While boundless space divides me from the
spot;
Can I endure it? Oh, the impatient spirit
Will lie upon the rack of expectation,
And measure out this monstrous length of space
With groans and anxious throbbings of the
heart.
MEISCHEK. What dost thou wish? What
is it thou wouldst have?
MARINA. Let me abide the issue in Kioff!
There I can gather tidings at their source.
There on the frontier of both kingdoms — —
MEISCHEK. Thy spirit's over-bold. Re-
strain it, child!
MARINA. Yes, thou dost yield,—thou'lt
take me with thee, then?
MEISCHEK. *Thou* rulest me. *Must* I not
do thy will?
MARINA. My own dear father, when I am
Moscow's queen,
Kioff, you know, must be our boundary.
Kioff must then be mine, and thou shalt rule it.
MEISCHEK. Thou dreamest, girl! Already
the great Moscow

Is for thy soul too narrow ; thou, to grasp
Domains, wilt strip them from thy native
   land.
  MARINA. Kioff belong'd not to our native
   land.
There the Varegers ruled in days of yore.
I have the ancient chronicles by heart—

'Twas from the Russian empire wrenched by
   force.
I will restore it to its former crown.
  MEISCHEK. Hush, hush! The waywode
   must not hear such talk.
                    [*Trumpet without.*
They're breaking up. — — —

ACT II.

—

SCENE I.—*A Greek Convent in a bleak district near the Sea Belozero. A train of Nuns, in black robes and veils, passes over the back of the Stage.* MARFA, *in a white veil, stands apart from the others, leaning on a tombstone.* OLGA *steps out from the train, remains gazing at her for a time, and then advances to her.*

OLGA. And does thy heart not urge thee forth with us,
To taste reviving nature's opening sweets?
The glad sun comes, the long, long night retires,
The ice melts in the streams, and soon the sledge
Will to the boat give place and summer swallow.
The world awakes once more, and the new joy
Woos all to leave their narrow cloister cells,
For the bright air and freshening breath of spring.

And wilt thou only, sunk in lasting grief,
Refuse to share the general exultation?
MARFA. On with the rest, and leave me to myself!
Let those rejoice who still have power to hope.
The time that puts fresh youth in all the world
Brings nought to me; to me the past is all,
My hopes, my joys are with the things that were.
OLGA. Dost thou still mourn thy son— still, still lament
The sovereignty which thou hast lost? Does time,
Which pours a balm on every wounded heart,
Lose all its potency with thee alone?
Thou wert the empress of this mighty realm,
The mother of a blooming son. He was
Snatch'd from thee by a dreadful destiny;
Into this dreary convent wert thou thrust,
Here on the verge of habitable earth.

155

Full sixteen times since that disastrous day
The face of nature hath renew'd its youth;
Still have I seen no change come over thine,
That look'd a grave amid a blooming world.
Thou'rt like some moveless image, carved in
  stone
By sculptor's chisel, that doth ever keep
The selfsame fixed unalterable mien.
  MARFA. Yes, Time, fell Time, hath sign'd
  and set me up
As a memorial of my dreadful fate.
I will not be at peace, will not forget.
That soul must be of poor and shallow stamp,
Which takes a cure from time—a recompense
For what can never be compensated!
Nothing shall buy my sorrow from me. No,
As heaven's vault still goes with the wanderer,
Girds and environs him with boundless grasp,
Turn where he will, by sea or land, so goes
My anguish with me, wheresoe'er I turn;
It hems me round, like an unbounded sea;
My ceaseless tears have failed to drain its
  depths
  OLGA. Oh, see! what news can yonder
  boy have brought,
The sisters round him throng so eagerly?
He comes from distant shores, where homes
  abound,
And brings us tidings from the land of men.
The sea is clear, the highways free once more.
Art thou not curious to learn his news?
Though to the world we are as good as dead,
Yet of its changes willingly we hear,
And, safe upon the shore, with wonder mark
The roar and ferment of the trampling waves.
  [*Nuns come down the Stage with a* FISHER BOY.
  XENIA—HELENA. Speak, speak, and tell
  us all the news you bring.
  ALEXIA. Relate what's passing in the world
  beyond.
  FISHER BOY. Good pious ladies, give me
  time to speak!
  XENIA. Is't war—or peace?
  ALEXIA. Who's now upon the throne?
  FISHER BOY. A ship is to Archangel just
  come in,
From the north pole, where everything is ice.
  OLGA. How came a vessel into that wild
  sea?
  FISHER BOY. It is an English merchant-
  man, and it
Has found a new way out to get to us.
  ALEXIA. What will not man adventure for
  his gain?
  XENIA. And so the world is nowhere to be
  barr'd!

  FISHER BOY. But that's the very smallest
  of the news.
'Tis something very different moves the world.
  ALEXIA. Oh speak, and tell us!
  OLGA.   Say, what has occurr'd!
  FISHER BOY. We live to hear strange mar-
  vels now-a-days:
The dead rise up, and come to life again.
  OLGA. Explain yourself.
  FISHER BOY.   Prince Dmitri, Ivan's son,
Whom we have mourn'd for dead these sixteen
  years,
Is now alive, and has appear'd in Poland.
  OLGA. The Prince alive?
  MARFA (*starting*).   My son!
  OLGA.   Compose thyself!
Calm down thy heart, till we have learn'd the
  whole.
  ALEXIA. How can this possibly be so,
  when he
Was kill'd, and perish'd in the flames at
  Uglitsch?
  FISHER BOY.   He managed somehow to
  escape the fire,
And found protection in a monastery.
There he grew up in secrecy, until
His time was come to publish who he was.
  OLGA (*to* MARFA). You tremble, Princess!
  You grow pale!
  MARFA.   I know
That it must be delusion, yet so little
Is my heart steel'd 'gainst fear and hope e'en
  now,
That in my breast it flutters like a bird.
  OLGA. Why should it be delusion? Mark
  his words!
How could this rumor spread without good
  cause?
  FISHER BOY. Without good cause? The
  Lithuanians
And Poles are all in arms upon his side.
The Czar himself quakes in his capital.
  [MARFA *is compelled, by her emotion, to lean
  upon* OLGA *and* ALEXIA.
  XENIA. Speak on, speak, tell us everything
  you know.
  ALEXIA. And tell us, too, of whom you
  stole the news.
  FISHER BOY. I stole the news? A letter
  has gone forth
To every town and province from the Czar.
This letter the Posadnik of our town
Read to us all, in open market-place.
It bore, that busy schemers were abroad,
And that we should not lend their tales belief.
But this made us believe them; for, had they

Been false, the Czar would have despised the
   lie.
MARFA.   Is this the calm I thought I had
   achieved?
And clings my heart so close to temporal
   things,
That a mere word can shake my inward soul?
For sixteen years have I bewail'd my son,
And yet at once believe that still he lives.
   OLGA.   Sixteen long years thou'st mourn'd
   for him as dead,
And yet his ashes thou hast never seen!
Nought countervails the truth of the report.
Nay, does not Providence watch o'er the fate
Of kings and monarchies?   Then welcome
   hope!
More things befall than thou canst compre-
   hend.
Who can set limits to the Almighty's power?
   MARFA.   Shall I turn back to look again
   on life,
To which long since I spoke a sad farewell?
— — — — — —
It was not with the dead my hopes abode.
Oh, say no more of this.   Let not my heart
Hang on this phantom hope!   Let me not lose
My darling son a second time!   Alas,
My peace of mind is gone,—my dream of
   peace!
I cannot trust these tidings,—yet, alas,
I can no longer dash them from my soul!
Woe's me, I never lost my son till now.
Oh, now I can no longer tell, if I
Shall seek him 'mongst the living or the dead,
Toss'd on the rock of never ending doubt.
   [*A bell sounds,—the sister* PORTERESS *enters.*
   OLGA.   Why has the bell been sounded,
   sister, say?
PORTERESS.   The Lord Archbishop waits
   without; he brings
A message from the Czar, and craves an au-
   dience.
   OLGA.   Does the archbishop stand without
   our gates?
What strange occurrence can have brought
   him here?
   XENIA.   Come all, and give him greeting
   as befits.
   [*They advance towards the gates, as the*
   ARCHBISHOP *enters; they all kneel before
   him, and he makes the sign of the Greek
   cross over them.*
Iob.   The kiss of peace I bring you in the
   name
Of Father, Son, and of the Holy Ghost,
Proceeding from the Father!

OLGA.   Sir, we kiss
In humblest reverence thy paternal hand! ·
— — — —   Command thy daughters!
   IOB.   My mission is addressed to sister
   Marfa.
   OLGA.   See, here she stands, and waits to
   know thy will.
                   [*All the* NUNS *withdraw.*

———

IOB.   It is the mighty prince who sends me
   here;
Upon his distant throne he thinks of thee;
For as the sun, with his great eye of flame,
Sheds light and plenty all abroad the world,
So sweeps the sovereign's eye on every side;
Even to the farthest limits of his realm
His care is wakeful and his glance is keen.
   MARFA.   How far his arm can strike I know
   too well.
   IOB.   He knows the lofty spirit fills thy
   soul,
And therefore feels indignantly the wrong
A bold-faced villain dares to offer thee.
   MARFA.   — — — — — — —
   IOB.   Learn then, in Poland, an audacious
   churl,
A renegade, who broke his monkish vows,
Laid down his habit, and renounced his God,
Doth use the name and title of thy son,
Whom death snatch'd from thee in his in-
   fancy.
The shameless varlet boasts him of thy blood,
And doth affect to be Czar Ivan's son;
A Waywode breaks the peace,—from Poland
   leads
This spurious monarch, whom himself created,
Across our frontiers with an armed power:
So he beguiles the Russian's faithful hearts,
And lures them on to treason and revolt.
— — — — — —   The Czar,
With pure paternal feeling, sends me to thee.
—Thou hold'st the manes of thy son in
   honour;
Nor wilt permit a bold adventurer
To steal his name and title from the tomb,
And with audacious hand usurp his rights.
Thou wilt proclaim aloud to all the world, ·
That thou dost own him for no son of thine.
Thou wilt not nurse a bastard's alien blood
Upon thy heart, that beats so nobly—never!
Thou wilt,—and this the Czar expects from
   thee,—
Give the vile counterfeit the lie, with all
The righteous indignation it deserves.

Demetrius.

MARFA (*who has during the last speech subdued the most violent emotion*). What do I hear, Archbishop? Can it be? Oh tell me, by what signs and marks of proof This bold-faced trickster doth uphold himself As Ivan's son, whom we bewail'd as dead?

IOB. By some faint shadowy likeness to the Czar, By documents which chance threw in his way, And a precious trinket, which he shows, He cheats the credulous and wondering mob.

MARFA. What is the trinket? Oh, pray, tell me what?

IOB. A golden cross, gemm'd with nine emeralds, Which Ivan Westislowsky, so he says, Hung round his neck at the baptismal font.

MARFA. What do you say?—He shows this trinket, this?

[*With forced composure.* And how does he allege he came by it?

IOB. A faithful servant and Diak, he says, Preserved him from the assassins and the flames, And bore him to Smolenskow privily.

MARFA. But where was he brought up— where, gives he forth, Was he conceal'd and foster'd until now?

IOB. In Tschudow's monastery he was rear'd, Unknowing who he was; from thence he fled To Lithuania and Poland, where He served the Prince of Sendomir, until An accident reveal'd his origin.

MARFA. With such a tale as this can he find friends, To peril life and fortune in his cause?

IOB. Oh, madam, false, false-hearted is the Pole, And enviously he eyes our country's wealth. He welcomes every pretext that may serve To light the flames of war within our bounds!

MARFA. And were there credulous spirits even in Moscow, Could by this juggle be so lightly stirr'd?

IOB. Oh, fickle, princess, is the people's heart! They doat on alteration, and expect To reap advantage from a change of rulers. The bold assurance of the falsehood charms; The marvellous finds favour and belief. Therefore the Czar is anxious thou shouldst quell This mad delusion, as thou only canst. A word from thee annihilates the traitor That falsely claims the title of thy son.

It joys me thus to see thee moved. I see, The audacious juggle rouses all thy pride, And with a noble anger paints thy cheek.

MARFA. And where—where, tell me, does he tarry now, Who dares usurp the title of my son?

IOB. E'en now he's moving on to Tscherinsko; His camp at Kioff has broke up, 'tis rumoured; And, with a force of mounted Polish troops And Don Cossacks, he comes to push his claims.

MARFA. Oh, God Almighty, thanks, thanks, thanks, that thou Has sent me rescue and revenge at last!

IOB. How, Marfa, how am I to construe this?

MARFA. Oh, heavenly powers, conduct him safely here! Hover, oh all ye angels, round his banners!

IOB. Can it be so? The traitor, canst thou trust——

MARFA. He is my son. Yes! by these signs alone I recognize him. By thy Czar's alarm I recognize him. Yes!—He lives!—He comes! Down, tyrant, from thy throne, and shake with fear! There still doth live a shoot from Rurik's stem; The genuine Czar—the rightful heir draws nigh, He comes to claim a reckoning for his own.

IOB. Dost thou bethink thee what thou say'st? 'Tis madness!

MARFA. At length—at length has dawn'd the day of vengeance,— Of restoration. Innocence is dragg'd To light by Heav'n from the grave's midnight gloom. The haughty Godunow, my deadly foe, Must crouch and sue for mercy at my feet; Oh, now my burning wishes are fulfill'd!

IOB. Can hate and rancourous malice blind you so?

MARFA. Can terror blind your monarch so, that he Should hope deliverance from me—from me— Whom he hath done immeasurable wrong?

— — — — — — — —

I shall, forsooth, deny the son whom Heav'n Restores me by a miracle from the grave, And to please him, the butcher of my house, Who piled upon me woes unspeakable? Yes, thrust from me the succour God has sent

158

In the sad evening of my heavy anguish?
Ion. — — — — — — —
MARFA. No, thou escap'st me not. No!
thou shalt hear me.
I have thee fast, I will not let thee free.
Oh, I can ease my bosom's load at last!
At last launch forth against mine enemy
The long-pent anger of my inmost soul!
— — — — Who was it, who,
That shut me up within this living tomb,
In all the strength and freshness of my youth,
With all its feelings glowing in my breast?
Who from my bosom rent my darling son,
And chartered ruffian hands to take his life?
Oh, words can never tell what I have suffered,
When, with a yearning that would not be
still,
I watch'd throughout the long, long starry
nights,
And noted with my tears the hours elapse!
The day of succour comes, and of revenge;
I see the mighty glorying in his might.
Ion. You think the Czar would dread you
—you mistake.
MARFA. He's in my power—one little word
from me,
One only, sets the seal upon his fate!
It was for this thy master sent thee here!
The eyes of Russia and of Poland now
Are closely bent upon me. If I own
The Czarowitsch as Ivan's son and mine,
Then all will do him homage; his the throne.
If I disown him, then he is undone;
For who will credit, that his rightful mother,
A mother wrong'd, so foully wrong'd as I,
Could from her heart repulse its darling
child,
To league with the despoilers of her house?
I need but speak one word, and all the world
Deserts him as a traitor. Is't not so?
This word you wish from me.—That mighty
service,
Confess, I can perform for Godunow!
Ion. Thou wouldst perform it for thy coun-
try, and
Avert the dread calamities of war,
Shouldst thou do homage to the truth. Thy-
self,
Ay, thou hast ne'er a doubt thy son is dead;
And couldst thou testify against thy con-
science?
MARFA. These sixteen years I've mourn'd
his death; but yet
I ne'er have seen his ashes. I believed
His death, there trusting to the general voice
And my sad heart—I now believe he lives,

Trusting the general voice and my strong
hope.
'Twere impious, with audacious doubts, to
seek
To set a bound to the Almighty's will;
And even were he not my heart's dear son,
Yet should he be the son of my revenge.
In my child's room I take him to my breast,
Whom Heav'n has sent to me to avenge my
wrongs.
Ion. Unhappy one, dost thou defy the
strong?
From his far-reaching arm thou art not safe,
Even in the convent's distant solitude.
MARFA. Kill me he may, and stifle in the
grave,
Or dungeon's gloom, my woman's voice,
that it
Shall not reverberate throughout the world.
This he may do; but force me to speak
aught
Against my will, that can he not; though
back'd
By all thy craft—no, he has miss'd his aim!
Ion. Is this thy final purpose? Ponder
well!
Hast thou no gentler message for the Czar?
MARFA. Tell him to hope for Heaven, if
so he dare,
And for his people's love, if so he can.
Ion. Enough! thou'rt bent on thy de-
struction.
Thou lean'st upon a reed, will break beneath
thee;
One common ruin will o'erwhelm ye both.
— — [*Exit.*

MARFA. It is my son, I cannot doubt 'tis
he.
E'en the wild hordes of the uncultured wastes
Take arms upon his side; the haughty Pole,
The Palatine, doth stake his noble daughter
On the pure gold of his most righteous
cause,
And I alone reject him,—I, his mother?
I, only I, shook not beneath the storm
Of joy, that lifts all hearts with dizzying
whirl,
And scatters turmoil widely o'er the earth.
He is my son—I must, will trust in him,
And grasp with living confidence the hand,
Which heaven hath sent for my deliverance.
'Tis he, he comes with his embattled hosts,
To set me free, and to avenge my shame!
Hark to his drums, his martial trumpets'
clang!

Ye nations, come—come from the east and
  south,
Forth from your steppes, your immemorial
  woods !
Of every tongue, of every raiment come !
Bridle the steed, the reindeer, and the camel !
Sweep hither, countless as the ocean waves,
And throng around the banners of your king !
Oh, wherefore am I mew'd and fetter'd here,
A prison'd soul with longings infinite !
Thou deathless sun, that circlest earth's huge
  ball,
Be thou the messenger of my desires !
The all-pervading chainless breeze, that
  sweep'st
With lightning speed to earth's remotest
  bound,
Oh, bear to him the yearnings of my heart.
My pray'rs are all I have to give ; but these
I pour all glowing from my inmost soul,
And send them up to heav'n on wings of flame,
Like armed hosts, I send them forth to hail
  him !

———————

SCENE II.—*A height crowned with trees.*

*A wide and smiling landscape occupies the back
ground, which is traversed by a beautiful
river, and enlivened by the budding green of
spring. At various points the towers of several towns are visible. Drums and martial
music without. Enter* ODOWALSKY, *and
other officers; and immediately afterwards*
DEMETRIUS.

ODOWALSKY. Go, lead the army downward
  by the wood,
Whilst we look round us here upon the height.
          [*Exeunt some of the Officers.*
          Enter DEMETRIUS.
DEMETRIUS (*starting back*). Ha ! what a
  prospect !
ODOWALSKY. Sire, thou see'st thy king-
  dom
Spread out before thee. That is Russian land.
RAZIN. Why e'en this pillar here bears
  Moscow's arms ;
Here terminates the empire of the Poles.
DEMETRIUS. Is that the Dnieper, rolls its
  quiet stream
Along these meadows ?
ODOWALSKY. That, sire, is the Desna ;
See, yonder rise the towers of Tschernizow !
RARIN. Yon gleam you see upon the far
  horizon,
Is from the roofs of Sewerisch Novgorod.

DEMETRIUS. What a rich prospect ! What
  fair meadow lands !
ODOWALSKY. The spring has deck'd them
  with her trim array :
A teeming harvest clothes the fruitful soil.
DEMETRIUS. The view is lost in limitless
  expanse.
RAZIN. Yet is this but a small beginning,
  sire,
Of Russia's mighty empire. For it spreads
Towards the east to confines unexplored,
And on the north has ne'er a boundary,
Save the productive energy of earth.
— — — — — —
RAZIN. Behold, our Czar is quite absorb'd
  in thought.
DEMETRIUS. On these fair meads dwells
  peace, unbroken peace,
And with war's terrible array I come,
To scatter havoc, like a listed foe !
ODOWALSKY. Hereafter 'twill be time to
  think of that.
DEMETRIUS. Thou feelest as a Pole, I am
  Moscow's son.
It is the land to which I owe my life ;
Forgive me, thou dear soil, land of my home,
Thou sacred boundary-pillar, which I clasp,
Whereon my sire his broad-spread eagle
  graved,
That I, thy son, with foreign foemen's arms,
Invade the tranquil temple of thy peace.
'Tis to reclaim my heritage I come,
And the proud name that has been stolen from
  me
Here the Varegers, my forefathers, ruled,
In lengthen'd line, for thirty generations ;
I am the last of all their lineage, snatch'd
From murder by God's special providence.
— — — — — —

———————

SCENE III.

*A Russian Village. An open square before a
church. The tocsin is heard.* GLEB, ILIA,
and TIMOSKA *rush in, armed with hatchets.*

GLEB (*entering from a house*). Why are they
  running ?
ILIA (*entering from another house*). Who has
  toll'd the bell.
TIMOSKA. Neighbours, come forth ! Come
  all, to council come !
[*Enter* OLEG *and* IZOR, *with many other
  Peasants, Women, and Children, who
  carry bundles.*

GLEB. Whence come ye hither with your
wives and children?
IGOR. Fly, fly! The Pole has fallen upon
the land
At Maromesk, and slaughters all he finds.
OLEG. Fly into the interior—to strong
towns!
We've fired our cottages, there's not a soul
Left in the village, and we're making now
Up country for the army of the Czar.
TIMOSKA. Here comes another troop of
fugitives.
[IWANSKA *and* PETRUSCHKA, *with armed
Peasantry enter on different sides.*
IWANSKA. Long live the Czar! The mighty
Prince Dmitri!
GLEB. How! What is this!
ILIA. What do-you mean?
TIMOSKA. Who are you?
PETRUSCHKA. Join all, who're loyal to our
princely line!
TIMOSKA. What means all this? There a
whole village flies
Up country, to escape the Poles, while you
Make for the very point whence these have
fled,
To join the standard of the country's foe!
PETRUSCHKA. What foe? It is no foe that
comes; it is
The people's friend, the emperor's rightful
heir.

The POSADMIK (the village judge) enters, to
read a manifesto by Demetrius. Vacillation
of the inhabitants of the village between the
two parties. The peasant women are the first
to be won over to Demetrius, and turn the
scale.

Camp of DEMETRIUS. He is worsted in the
first action, but the army of Czar Boris con-
quers in a manner against its will, and does
not follow up its advantages. Demetrius, in
despair, is about to destroy himself, and is
with difficulty prevented from doing so by
Korela and Odowalsky. Overbearing demeanour of the Cossacks, even to Demetrius.

Camp of the army of the CZAR BORIS. He

is absent himself, and this injures his cause, as
he is feared, but not loved. His army is strong,
but not to be relied on. The leaders are not
unanimous, and partly incline to the side of
Demetrius, from a variety of motives. One
of their number, Soltikow, declares for him
from conviction. His adherence is attended
with the most important results; a large portion of the army deserts to Demetrius.

BORIS in Moscow. He still maintains his
position as absolute ruler, and has faithful servants around him; but already he is discom-
posed by evil tidings. He is withheld from
joining the army by apprehension of rebellion
in Moscow. He is also ashamed, as Czar, to
enter the field in person against a traitor.
Scene between him and the Archbishop.

Bad news pours in from all sides, and Boris's
danger grows momently more imminent. He
hears of the revolt of the peasantry and the
provincial towns—of the inactivity and mutiny of the army—of the commotions in Moscow—of the advance of Demetrius. Romanow, whom he has deeply wronged, arrives
in Moscow. This gives rise to new apprehensions. Now come the tidings that the
Boiars are flying to the camp of Demetrius,
and that the whole army has gone over to him.

BORIS and AXINIA. The Czar appears in a
touching aspect as father, and in the dialogue
with his daughter unfolds his inmost nature.

BORIS has made his way to the throne by
crime, but undertaken and fulfilled all the
duties of a monarch; to the country he is a
valuable prince, and a true father of his people.
It is only in his personal dealings with individuals that he is cunning, revengeful, and
cruel. His spirit, as well as his rank, elevates

him above all that surround him. The long possession of supreme power, the habit of ruling over men, and the despotic form of government, have so nursed his pride, that it is impossible for him to outlive his greatness. He sees clearly what awaits him ; but still he is Czar, and not degraded, though he resolves to die.

He believes in forewarnings, and in his present mood things appear to him of significance, which, on other occasions, he had despised. A particular circumstance, in which he seems to hear the voice of destiny, decides him.

Shortly before his death his nature changes ; he grows milder, even towards the messengers of evil, and is ashamed of the bursts of rage with which he had received them before. He permits the worst to be told to him, and even rewards the narrator.

So soon as he learns the misfortune that seals his fate, he leaves the stage without further explanation with composure and resignation. Shortly afterwards he returns in the habit of a monk, and removes his daughter from the sight of his last moments. She is to seek protection from insult in a cloister ; his son, Feodor, as a child, will perhaps have less to fear. He takes poison, and enters a retired chamber to die in peace.

General confusion at the tidings of the Czar's death. The Boiars form an Imperial Council, and rule in the Kremlin. Romanow (afterwards Czar, and founder of the now ruling house) enters at the head of an armed force, swears, on the bosom of the Czar, an oath of allegiance to his son Feodor, and compels the Boiars to follow his example. Revenge and ambition are far from his soul ; he pursues

only justice. He loves Axinia without hope, and is, without knowing it, beloved by her in return.

Romanow hastens to the army, to secure it for the young Czar. Insurrection in Moscow, brought about by the adherents of Demetrius. The people drag the Boiars from their houses, make themselves masters of Feodor and Axinia—put them in prison, and send delegates to Demetrius.

Demetrius in Tula, at the pinnacle of success. The army is his own ; the keys of numerous towns are brought to him. Moscow alone appears to offer resistance. He is mild and amiable, testifies a noble emotion at the intelligence of the death of Boris ; pardons a detected conspiracy against his life ; despises the servile adulations of the Russians, and is for sending them away. The Poles, on the other hand, by whom he is surrounded, are rude and violent, and treat the Russians with contempt. Demetrius longs for a meeting with his mother, and sends a messenger to Marina.

Among the multitude of Russians who throng around Demetrius, in Tula, appears a man, whom he at once recognizes ; he is greatly delighted to see him. He bids all the rest withdraw, and so soon as he is alone with this man, he thanks him, with full heart, as his preserver and benefactor. This person hints that Demetrius is under special obligations to him, and to a greater extent than he is himself aware. Demetrius urges him to explain, and the assassin of the genuine Demetrius thereupon discloses the real facts of the case. For this murder he had received no recompense, but, on the contrary, had nothing but death to anticipate from Boris. Thirsting for revenge, he stumbled upon a boy, whose resemblance to the Czar Ivan struck him ! This circumstance must be turned to account. He seized the boy, fled with him from Uglitsch, brought him to a monk, whom he succeeded in gaining over for his ends, and delivered to him the trinket which he had himself taken

from the murdered Demetrius. By means of
this boy, whom he had never lost sight of,
and whose steps he had attended upon all
occasions, without being observed, he is now
revenged. His tool, the false Demetrius,
rules over Russia in Boris's room.

———————

During this narration a mighty change
comes over Demetrius. His silence is awful.
In the moment of the highest rage and despair, the assassin drives him to the extreme
of endurance, when with a defying and insolent air he demands his reward. Demetrius
strikes him to the earth.

———————

Soliloquy of Demetrius. Internal conflict;
but the feeling of the necessity for maintaining
his position as Czar is triumphant.

———————

The delegates from Moscow arrive, and
submit themselves to Demetrius. They are
received gloomily, and with a menacing demeanour. Among them is the Patriarch.
Demetrius deposes him from his dignity, and
soon afterwards sentences to death a Russian
of rank, who had questioned the authenticity
of his birth.

———————

MARFA and OLGA await Demetrius under a

magnificent tent. Marfa speaks of the approaching interview with more doubt and fear than hope, and trembles as the moment draws near which should assure her highest happiness. Olga speaks to her, herself without faith. During the long journey they have both had time to recall the whole circumstances; the first exultation had given place to reflection. The gloomy silence and the repulsive glances of the guards, who surround the tent, serve still further to augment their despondency.

———

The trumpets sound. Marfa is irresolute whether she shall advance to meet Demetrius. Now he stands before her, alone. The little that was left of hope in her heart altogether vanishes on seeing him. An unknown something steps between them—Nature does not speak—they are separated for ever. The first impulse is an endeavour to approach; Marfa is the first to make a movement to recede. Demetrius observes it, and remains for a moment paralyzed. Significant silence.

DEMETRIUS. Does thy heart say nothing? Dost thou not recognize thy blood in me?

MARFA *(is silent)*.

DEMETRIUS. The voice of nature is holy and free; I will neither constrain nor belie it. Had thy heart spoken at the first glance, then had mine answered it; thou shouldst have found a pious loving son in me. The claim of duty would have concurred with inclination and heartfelt affection. But if thou dost not feel as a mother for me, then, think as a princess, command thyself as a queen! Fate unexpectedly gave me to thee as a son; accept me as a gift of heaven. Though even I were not thy son, which I now appear to be, still I rob thy son of nothing. I stripped it from thy foe. Thee and thy blood have I avenged; I have delivered thee from the grave in which thou wert entombed alive, and led thee back into the royal seat. That thy destiny is linked with mine, thou know'st. With me thou standest, and with me must fall. All the people's eyes are upon us. I hate deception, and what I do not feel I may not show; but I do really feel a reverence for thee, and this feeling, which bends my knee before thee, comes from my heart.

[*Dumb show of* MARFA, *to indicate her internal emotion.*

DEMETRIUS. Make thy resolve! Let that which nature will not prompt be the free act of thy will! I ask no hypocrisy—no falsehood, from thee; I ask genuine feelings. Do not seem to be my mother, but be so. Throw the past from thee—grasp the present with thy whole heart! If I am not thy son, yet I am the Czar—I have power and success upon my side. He who lies in his grave is dust; he has no heart to love thee, no eye to smile upon thee. Turn to the living.

[MARFA *bursts into tears.*

DEMETRIUS. Oh, these golden drops are welcome to me. Let them flow! Show thyself thus to the people!

[*At a signal from* DEMETRIUS *the tent is thrown open, and the assembled Russians become spectators of this scene.*

———

Entrance of Demetrius into Moscow. Great splendour, but of a military kind. Poles and Cossacks compose the procession. Gloom and terror mingle with the demonstrations of joy. Distrust and misfortune surround the whole.

———

Romanow, who came to the army too late, has returned to Moscow to protect Feodor and Axinia. It is all in vain; he is himself thrown into prison. Axinia flies to Marfa, and at her feet implores protection against the Poles. Here Demetrius sees her and a violent and irresistible passion is kindled in his breast. Axinia detests him.

———

DEMETRIUS as Czar. A fearful element sustains him, but he does not control it; he is urged on by the force of strange passions. His inward consciousness betokens a general distrust; he has no friend on whom he can rely. Poles and Cossacks, by their insolent licentiousness, injure him in the popular opinion. Even that which is creditable to him—his popular manners, simplicity, and contempt of stiff ceremonial, occasions dissatisfaction. Occasionally he offends, through inadvertency. the usages of the country. He persecutes the monks, because he suffered severely under them. Moreover, he is not exempt from despotic caprices in the moments of offended pride. Odowalsky knows how to make himself at all times indispensable to him, removes the Russians to a distance, and maintains his overruling influence.

———

DEMETRIUS meditates inconstancy to Marina. He confers upon the point with the Archbishop Iob, who, in order to get rid of the Poles, falls in with his desire, and puts before him an exalted picture of the imperial power.

———

MARINA appears, with a vast retinue, in Moscow. Meeting with Demetrius. Hollow and cold meeting on both sides; she, however, wears her disguise with greater skill. She urges an immediate marriage. Preparations are made for a magnificent festival.

———

By the orders of Marina, a cup of poison is brought to Axinia. Death is welcome to her: she was afraid of being forced to the altar with the Czar.

———

Violent grief of Demetrius. With a broken heart he goes to the betrothal with Marina.

———

After the marriage, Marina discloses to him that she does not consider him to be the true Demetrius, and never did. She then coldly leaves him in a state of extreme anguish and dismay.

———

Meanwhile SCHINSKOI, one of the former generals of the Czar BORIS, avails himself of

the growing discontent of the people, and becomes the head of a conspiracy against Demetrius.

———

ROMANOW, in prison, is comforted by a supernatural apparition. Axinia's spirit stands before him, opens to him a prospect of happier times in store, and enjoins him calmly to allow destiny to ripen, and to stain himself with blood. ROMANOW receives a hint that he may himself be called to the throne. Soon afterwards he is solicited to take part in the conspiracy, but declines.

———

SOLTIKOW reproaches himself bitterly for having betrayed his country to Demetrius. But he will not be a second time a traitor, and adheres, from principle and against his feelings, to the party which he has once adopted. As the misfortune has happened, he seeks at least to alleviate it, and to enfeeble the power of the Poles. He pays for this effort with his life; but he accepts death as a merited punishment, and confesses this, when dying, to Demetrius himself.

———

CASIMIR, a brother of LODOISKA, a young Polish lady, who has been secretly and hopelessly attached to Demetrius, in the house of the Waywode of Sendomir, has, at his sister's request, accompanied Demetrius in the campaign, and in every encounter defended him bravely. In the moment of danger, when all the other retainers of Demetrius think only of their personal safety, Casimir alone remains faithful to him, and sacrifices life in his defence.

———

The conspiracy breaks out. Demetrius is with Marfa when the leading conspirators

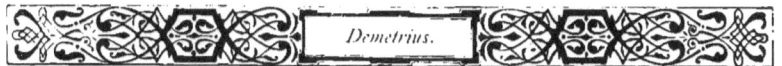

force their way into the room. The dignity and courage of Demetrius have a momentary effect upon the rebels. He nearly succeeds in disarming them, by a promise to place the Poles at their disposal. But at this point Schinskoi rushes in with an infuriated band. An explicit declaration is demanded from the ex-Empress; she is required to swear, upon the cross, that Demetrius is her son. To testify against her conscience in a manner so solemn is impossible. She turns from Demetrius in silence, and is about to withdraw. " Is she silent?" exclaims the tumultuous throng. "Does she disown him?" "Then, traitor, die!" and Demetrius falls, pierced by their swords, at Marfa's feet.

Prosaic Writings.

THE CRIMINAL
FROM LOST HONOR

IN the whole history of man, no chapter is more instructive for heart and mind than that comprising the annals of his errors. In the case of every great crime a proportionately great force was in action. If the mysterious operations of the power of desire lie half-hidden in the dim light shed on them when actuated by ordinary emotions, all the more prominently do they show themselves, more colossal, and more clearly defined, when called into action by the more violent passions. The more subtle analyst of human nature, who understands how far we may calculate on the mechanism of the ordinary freedom of the will, and how far we are justified in drawing conclusions from analogy, will be able to bring many experiences from this province in aid of his study of psychology and to utilize them for the improvement of man's moral nature.

The heart of man is something so simple and yet so complicated! One and the same faculty or desire can operate in a thousand different forms and directions, can produce a thousand contradictory phenomena, and may appear in the same character in a thousand different combinations, and thousands of unlike characters and operations be elaborated from the same disposition, even though the individual who is the subject of all may be utterly unconscious of the existing relationship. If a Linnæus should ever undertake to do for the human race what he effected for the other kingdoms of nature, and classify mankind according to its instincts and appetencies, how we would be astonished at the number we should find whose vices, though now choked in their narrow burgher-sphere and hedged in by the contracted limits allowed them by law, entitle them to be classified in the same order with the monster Borgia!

Observed from this point of view, much might be objected to the ordinary mode of treating history, and herein lies, I think, the obstacle by reason of which the study must ever remain fruitless to common everyday life. Between the vehement emotions of the men who are shown us in action, and the tranquil mental disposition of the reader, to whom the action is presented, there exists so irreconcilable a contrast, so wide an interval, that it is difficult for the latter to apprehend that he and they have any relation to each other. There exists such a gap between the historical subject and the reader, that all possibility of comparison between them or of personal application, is entirely precluded, and instead of the narrative exciting that salutary terror which would act as a warning to his own proud security, it produces only an unsympathetic shake of the head. We see in the unfortunate—who, even in the very hour when he perpetrated his deed of violence, as well as in that in which he expiated it—a man of like nature with ourselves, a being of a species altogether alien to ours, whose blood circulates in quite different fashion from ours, whose will obeys altogether different rules; his fate moves us little, for emotion bases itself only on a dim consciousness of a similar danger, and we are far removed from even dreaming of such a relationship. Instruction is lost when no relationship is appreciated, and the story, instead of being to us a school of moral culture, must content itself with furnishing only a wretched gratification to our curiosity. If it is to be more to us and attain its high object, we must of necessity choose between these two methods—either the reader must raise himself to the temperature of the hero, or the hero must cool down to that of the reader.

I am aware that many among our best historians, of modern times as well as of antiquity, have made choice of the former method and have moved the hearts and biased the judgments of their readers by an intense and overpowering eloquence. But this style is a usurpation on the part of the author, and an offence against the republican freedom of his reader, whose province it is, himself to sit in judgment; it is besides a trespass on the limits prescribed by right and justice, for this method belongs exclusively and properly to the orator and poet. To the historian, therefore, is left only the other method. The hero must be exhibited as cool as the reader, or, what comes to the same thing, we must get thoroughly acquainted with him, before we see him in action; we must see him not only accomplishing his acts, but also inspiring them. His thoughts interest us far more than his deeds; and still more the springs of these thoughts than the consequences of his acts. Man has explored the soil of Vesuvius to discover the origin of its outbreaks; wherefore does he give less attention to a moral phenomenon than to a physical? Why does he not with equal care scan the condition and character of the circumstances by which such a man was surrounded, till the accumulated fiery material in his nature burst out into flame? The strange and adventurous in such a phenomenon captivates the dreamer; the lover of truth seeks a mother for these forlorn children. He seeks her in the immutable structure of the human soul, and in the ever-changing circumstances; that is, inquires what gave birth to such anomalous moral phenomena which conditioned it from without, and in these two conditions he finds her without fail. It no longer surprises him to see the noxious hemlock flourish in the very plot where in other circumstances wholesome plants alone would be blooming; to find wisdom and folly, vice and virtue, sleeping together in the same cradle.

Although I do not here bring into the calculation any of the advantages which psychology might derive from treating history in this manner, still it, and it alone, has this advantage, that it eradicates that cruel scorn and proud consciousness of security with which untried and self-righteous virtue commonly looks down upon a fallen fellow-mortal; because it disseminates that soft spirit of forbearance without which no fugitive returns, no reconciliation of the law with its transgressor can find place, no infected member of society can be rescued from total corruption.

Had the criminal, of whom I am now to speak, a right to appeal to this spirit of forbearance? Was he indeed lost to the body politic without hope of deliverance? I will not anticipate the reader's decision. Our charity is no longer of avail to him, for he died by the hand of the executioner; but the autopsy of his vices may probably instruct humanity—it is possible even justice herself.

Christian Wolf was the son of an innkeeper in a country town (the name, for reasons that will manifest themselves in the sequel, we cannot give), and helped his mother in keeping the inn, for his father was dead. Business was but indifferent, and Wolf had often unemployed hours. Already at school he had been known as a mischievous boy. Grown-up girls brought complaints of his impudent forwardness, while the youths honoured him for his inventive head. Nature had neglected his body. A little, ungainly figure, coarse curly hair of an unpleasantly black hue, a flattened nose and a swollen overlip (which had been knocked further out of shape by a kick from a horse), gave a repulsiveness to his appearance which scared every woman away from him, and offered to his comrades a rich subject for their wit.

He resolved to extort what was refused him, because he naturally displeased every one he

set himself more resolutely to please. He was fanciful and persuaded himself he was in love. The maiden whom he chose for his sweetheart used him badly; he had reason for fearing that his rivals were more fortunate than he; but the girl was poor. A heart which remained closed to his caresses would probably open itself to his gifts; but he himself suffered for want, and his vain endeavours to give an effective appearance to his own outer man swallowed up the little he could earn from the poor inn. Too indolent and too ignorant to make an effort to help his wretched circumstances by speculation; too vain, and at the same time too weak to exchange the position of Herr (half-gentleman) which he had hitherto occupied for that of a peasant, and so renounce his much-valued freedom, he saw but one resource open to him—namely, that, of frankly stealing. His native town bordered on one of the seigneurial forests; he became a poacher, and the proceeds of his plunder found their way faithfully to the hands of his beloved.

Among Hannchen's lovers was Robert, one of the assistant gamekeepers in the forest. Very soon this young man perceived the advantage which his rival's openhandedness won for him over himself, and with envious jealousy set himself to discover the sources of this change. He showed himself more frequently in the "Sun" (this was the device on the inn), and his watchful eye, sharpened by jealousy and envy, soon discovered whence the gold flowed. Not long before a strong edict against poaching had been revived, which condemned the transgressor to the house of correction. Robert was unwearied in dogging his enemy in his secret excursions, and at length he succeeded in seizing him unawares in the very deed. Wolf was arrested, and only by the sacrifice of all his little property, was he able with great pains to convert the penalty attached to his offence into a fine. Robert triumphed. His rival was beaten out of the field, and Hannchen's favour for the beggar was a thing of the past. Wolf knew his enemy; and this enemy was the happy man who enjoyed his Joan. A humiliating feeling of poverty associated itself with that of injured pride. Need and jealousy contend with each other in his heart; hunger would drive him into the wide world; revenge and passion detain him where he is. He again takes to poaching, but Robert's redoubled watchfulness outwits him a second time. This time he experiences the law's full severity. Having no funds, and deprived of

his property, in a few weeks he was delivered over to the penitentiary.

His year's imprisonment has come to an end, his passion has been strengthened by absence, and his spite become exaggerated under the weight of ill fortune. No sooner does he gain his freedom than he sets off to his native town to show himself to his Joan.

peasant will trust his swine to such a good-for-nothing. Disappointed in all his plans, rejected wherever he offered himself, he becomes poacher for the third time, and for the third time has the misfortune to fall into the hands of his watchful enemy.

This second relapse into crime adds to the weight of his punishment. The judges looked

He appears; everyone shuns him. Urgent want has at length bowed his proud spirit and overcome his aversion for work—he offers himself to the people of good circumstances in the place, and will work for day's wages.

The farmer shrugs his shoulder over the effeminate weakling. The coarse-boned build of his robust competitors beats him out of the field with such a feelingless patron. He ventures a last attempt. One office is still vacant; the most forlorn post of honest name —he offers himself as town-herd, but no

into the statute-book of the law, but not into the mental condition of the prisoner. The edict against poaching called for a solemn and exemplary punishment, and Wolf was condemned to have the figure of the gallows branded on his neck and to three years' labor in the fortress.

This period, too, came to an end, and he left the fortress—but a very different man from what he was when he entered it. Here begins a new epoch in his life. Let us hear what he himself said when, later, he made his con-

fession to his spiritual adviser and before the court of justice. "I entered the fortress," said he, "a misguided man; I left it a worthless villain. I had always had something in the world that was dear to me, and my pride writhed under my weight of infamy. When I was brought to the fortress, I was shut in along with twenty-three prisoners, of whom two were murderers, and the rest, without exception, notorious thieves and vagabonds. They mocked me when I spoke of God, and tried to get me to utter shameless blasphemies against the Saviour. They sang lewd songs before me, which I, loose as I had been, heard with disgust and horror; but what I saw them practice revolted my sense of shame still more. No day passed in which some scandalous lifehistory was not narrated, some wicked design concocted. At first I shunned these people and shrunk from conversation with them so far as I was able; but I needed some creature, and the barbarity of my guards had refused me even my dog. The work was hard, and enforced tyranically; my body was sickly; I was in need of assistance, and, since I must honestly confess it, I craved for sympathy, and for these I required to barter the last remains of conscience. So with time I accustomed myself to whatever was most revolting, and in the last quarter of a year I surpassed my teachers.

From this time on I longed for the day of my liberation, because I was thirsting for revenge. I felt that all men had injured me, for all were better and happier than I. I regarded myself as a martyr for the natural rights of man, and a victim of the law. Gnashing my teeth I fretted my chains whenever the sun rose from behind my prison hill; a wide prospect is a twofold hell for a prisoner. The free breeze that whistled through the airholes of my tower, and the swallows that alighted on the iron bar of my grated window seemed to taunt me with their freedom, and made my imprisonment so much the more hateful. Then and there I vowed implacable burning hate against all that bears semblance of man; and what I then vowed I have faithfully adhered to.

My first thought, so soon as I saw myself free, was of my native town. All the less that I had there anything to hope for as a future means of support, by so much the more I promised to satisfy my hunger after revenge.

My heart beat wilder as the church-tower rose afar before me out of the surrounding foliage. It was no longer the heartfelt satisfaction that I experienced on my return from my first pilgrimage—the thought of all the sufferings, all the persecutions that I had endured, awoke me at once as out of a dreadful death-sleep; all my wounds bled anew, all my scars opened afresh. I redoubled my steps, for it animated me, even in anticipation, to think how I would set my enemies in terror by my sudden appearance, and I thirsted for still further humilia-

tions as much as previously I had quaked before them.

The bells sounded for Vesper as I stood in the middle of the market-place. The people were crowding to church. I was instantly recognized; every one who chanced to approach me shrank back as if from fear. In old times I had ever cherished a real love for the little children, and even yet this feeling was so powerful within me that I offered a groschen to a boy who was skipping past me. The boy stared fixedly at me for a moment, and then threw the groschen in my face. If my blood had been somewhat cooler than it was, I might have remembered that the beard which I brought with me from the fortress, gave a hideous expression to my features; but

ARTIST: F. PILOTY.

THE CRIMINAL.

my wicked heart poisoned my reason. Tears, such as I never shed before, coursed down my checks.

"The boy knows neither who I am nor whence I come," said I half-aloud to myself, "and yet he avoids me like a noxious animal. Do I bear a brand on my forehead, or have I ceased to present the appearance of a man, since I feel that I can no longer cherish any regard for my race?" The contempt of this boy pained me more keenly than thirty years in confinement would have done, for I had tried to do him a kind act, and could accuse him of no personal hate.

I sat down on a log in a carpenter's yard opposite the church. What I really meant to do, I cannot tell; yet this I know that I rose to my feet with bitterness in my heart, for of all my acquaintances that passed me while sitting there, not one deigned to greet me—not so much as one. With a heart burning with indignation I left the place to look out for quarters. As I turned the corner of a street I ran up against my old sweetheart Joan. "Landlord of the Sun!" she cried out loudly, and made a motion as if to embrace me. "Thou back again, dear host! God be praised that thou art back again!" Hunger and misery expressed themselves in her appearance and clothing; a shameful disease disfigured her countenance; her whole appearance, in short, proclaimed her to be the worthless creature to which she had become degraded. I concluded at once what had befallen her. I had just met a party of dragoons in the street, and this fact led me to infer that a garrison lay in the town. "Soldiers' strumpet!" cried I, and with a jeering laugh turned my back on her. It pleased me to think that there existed one being, lower even than I, in the ranks of the living. I never loved her.

My mother was dead; my creditors had sold my little house to satisfy their claims. I now had nobody and nothing. All the world fled from me as a venomous reptile, but I had, at length, unlearned all sense of shame. Formerly I had withdrawn from the view of men, for contempt was intolerable to me. Now I forced myself on their notice and gloried in scaring them away. I was pleased that I had nothing more to lose, and nothing more to care for. I stood no longer in need of good qualities, for men gave me credit for none.

The whole world lay open before me. I might, perhaps, in some province where I was unknown have passed for an honest man; but I had lost all spirit, all desire, even, to appear such. Despair and shame had driven me to this state of mind. My sole resource now was to dispense with respect, for I could no longer lay claim to it. Had my vanity and my pride survived my humiliation, I must have put an end to my existence.

What particular course I had now resolved on was still almost unknown to myself. I determined to do something wicked; so much I can obscurely remember, I would deserve my fate. Laws, thought I, are benefits to the world, therefore I took the resolution to violate them. Hitherto I had transgressed through necessity and thoughtlessness; now I did so from free choice and for my own pleasure.

My first step was to recommence poaching. Step by step the chase had grown to be an overmastering passion with me, and besides this, I must live. But this was not all; it gratified me to show contempt for the princely edict and to do all the injury I could to my sovereign. I no longer dreaded detection and arrest, for I had now a bullet ready for my captor, and I knew that my shot would never miss its man. I killed all the game that I came on; only a small portion I exchanged on the frontiers for gold; the most I left to rot on the ground. I lived sparingly in order to meet the outlay for lead and powder. The devastation I worked among the greater game was notorious, but suspicion no longer troubled me. My concealment extinguished it. My name was forgotten.

This mode of life I followed for several months. One morning I had, according to my wont, roved through the wood, following the track of a deer. Two hours long had I wearied myself in vain, and now I began to give up the chase as bootless, when instantly I saw the animal within easy reach of my gun. I was taking aim and on the point of firing, when suddenly the sight of a hat lying on the ground a few steps from me alarmed me. I examined closer and recognized the hunter Robert, who from behind the thick trunk of an oak was taking aim at the game which I designed to shoot. At this discovery a deathly coldness penetrated my members. There before me was the man whom of all mortals I hated most deadly, and this man was given over to the power of my bullet. In this single moment it seemed to me as if the whole world lay in one shot of my gun, and the hate of my

whole life concentrated itself in the finger-point with which I should give the murderous pressure. An unseen, frightful hand seemed to wave over me; the dial-plate of my fate pointed irrevocably to this black moment. My arm shook, while I allowed to my gun, as it were, the selection; my teeth chattered, and my breath seemed to be choked in my lungs. Some seconds the barrel of my gun wavered uncertainly between the man and the deer—this moment pointed in one direction; the next, in the other. Revenge and conscience struggled obstinately and with dubious result; but revenge conquered, and the huntsman lay on the ground—dead.

With the shot, my gun fell from my hands. . . . "Murderer!" . . . I stammered slowly. The wood was still as a churchyard—I heard distinctly that I said "Murderer!" As I crept nearer, the man expired. Long stood I speechless before the dead. A shrill burst of laughter at last gave vent to my feelings. "Will you now keep a clean tongue, my good friend?" said I, as I stepped quickly up, while at the same time I turned the face of the murdered man outwards. His eyes stood wide open. I became earnest, and was suddenly still. Everything began to be strange to me.

Up to this time I had committed misdemeanours only, as an equivalent for the wrongs I had suffered; now I had done a deed which I had not expiated beforehand. One hour before I believe that no one could have convinced me that anything baser than myself existed under heaven; now I began to realize that an hour previously I was a man to be envied.

God's judgments did not enter my mind, or at most only one—a strange, confused recollection of rope and sword, and the execution of a child-murderess of which I had been witness when a schoolboy. Something especially terrible lay for me in the thought that henceforward my life was forfeited. Of many things I have no clear remembrance. Instantly on the deed I wished he were alive again. I compelled myself to recall in the most lively manner I could all the evil he had ever worked me, but strange! my memory was as if dead. I could no longer recall one of all his acts, which a quarter of an hour before had driven me frantic. I could not comprehend, how I had come to this murderous deed.

I stood before the body, and was still standing, when the crack of a whip and the grating of the wheels of a wagon that was passing through the wood recalled me to myself. It was scarcely a quarter of a mile from the highway that the deed had been done. I must think of my safety. Involuntarily I buried myself deeper in the wood. On the way it occurred to me that the deceased formerly possessed a watch. I needed money in order to reach the frontier—and yet my courage failed me to turn back to the place where the corpse was lying. Here thoughts of the devil and of the omnipresence of God struck me with terror. I collected all my fortitude; and, determined to fight it out with all hell, returned to the spot. I found what I was looking for, and in a green purse a little over a dollar in money. Even when I was about putting both in my pocket, I stopped suddenly and reflected. It was no sudden fit of shame, neither was it fear to aggravate my crime by robbery —defiant pride I believe it was that caused me to throw the watch from me, and retain

only half the money. I would be held for a personal enemy of the murdered man, not for his plunderer.

Now I fled deeper into the wood. I knew that the forest extended four German miles north, and there touched the frontier of the country. Till noon I pushed on breathless. The very hurry of my flight operated as a distraction to my anguish of mind; but it returned more terrible than before, as my strength became more and more exhausted. A thousand hideous figures passed before my eyes, and seemed to sheathe their cruel knives in my breast. Only a dreadful choice was left me between a life full of restless dread of death, and voluntary death by violence, and choose I must. I had not the heart to leave the world by self-murder, and was terrified at the prospect of remaining in it. Hemmed in between the certain torments of life, and the uncertain dread of eternity, alike unfit for living and dying, I completed the sixth hour of my flight—an hour full of agony such as no living man is capable of expressing.

With my thoughts turned in on myself, and with slow steps, my hat unconsciously pressed deep down over my face (as if this would conceal me from the eye of lifeless nature), I had, unnoticed by myself, followed a narrow foot-path which led me through the thickest of the forest. Suddenly a harsh, commanding voice right in my way called out "Halt!" The voice was quite near; the distraction of my thoughts and my down-pressed hat had prevented me from looking around. I raised my eyes and saw a wild-looking man come towards me, carrying a large knotty club. His figure approached the gigantic—my first consternation at least made me believe so— and his skin was of a yellow mulatto darkness, against which the white of one squinting eye showed with hideous effect. Instead of a girdle he had a thick rope tied twice round a green woollen coat, wherein were stuck a butcher's knife and a pistol. The call was repeated, and a strong arm held me fast. The sound of a human voice had struck me with terror, but the sight of a rogue gave me courage. In the circumstances in which I now was, I had reason to tremble before every honest man, but no longer cause to do so before a robber.

"Who goes there?" demanded this apparition.

"A man like yourself," was my answer,

"if you are, indeed, what your appearance speaks."

"There is no thoroughfare in this direction. What are you seeking here?"

"What right have you to ask?" answered I, defiantly. The man scanned me twice from head to foot. It seemed as if he would compare my figure with his own, and my answer with my figure. "You speak insolently, like a beggar," said he, at length.

"That may be; I was one yesterday."

The man laughed: "One might take his oath on that," cried he; "even yet you would not pass for anything better."

"For something worse, then"—I was about to continue.

"Softly, friend! What hounds you on so? What's all the hurry?"

I bethought myself an instant. I know not how the words came to my tongue. "Life is short," said I, slowly, "and hell endures for ever."

He looked at me with a wild stare. "I will be damned," said he, at length, "if you have not been rubbing shoulders with the gallows."

"That may well come yet. To our better acquaintance, comrade!"

"Done, comrade!" cried he, while he produced a tin flask from his hunting-pocket, took a hearty pull at it and then handed it to me. Flight and anxiety had exhausted my strength, and during all this terrible day nothing had passed my lips. Already I began to fear I should perish from want in this forest, wherein for three German miles round, neither bite nor sup was to be hoped for. It may easily be conceived then, how gladly I pledged him in this offered cordial. New strength permeated my limbs as I drank, fresh courage pervaded my heart, fresh hope and love of life. I began to believe that I was not entirely wretched; such influence did this welcome drought produce on me. Yes, I confess it, my condition bordered again on happiness, for, after a thousand disappointed hopes, I had found a creature who appeared like myself. In the state to which I was sunk, I would have drank "good-fellowship" with the spirits of the pit, in order to have a comrade I could rely on.

The man had stretched himself on the grass: I did the same.

"Thy drink has done me good," I said. "We must get better acquainted."

He struck fire to light his pipe.

"Hast thou been at this work long?"

He looked fixedly at me. "What dost thou mean by that question?"

"Has this been often bloody?" I drew the knife out of his girdle.

"Who art thou?" said he, as if alarmed, and laid the pipe out of his mouth.

"A murderer, like thyself—but yet only a beginner."

The man looked at me unmoved and resumed his pipe.

"Thou dost not live here?" said he, at length.

"Three miles from here. I am the host of the 'Sun' in L—— if thou hast heard of me."

The man sprang up like a person possessed. "The poacher Wolf?" cried he, eagerly.

"The same."

"Welcome, comrade, welcome!" cried he, and shook my hand warmly. This is glorious, that I have thee at last, my host of the 'Sun'! For years have I been scheming how I could secure thee. I know thee right well. I know all about thee. I have long counted on thee."

"Counted on me? For what, then?"

"The whole country is full of thee. Thou hast enemies. An official has oppressed thee, Wolf. The law has brought thee to ruin. The wrongs thou hast endured cry heaven-high."

The man waxed warm. "Because thou hast shot a boar or two that the prince fattens on our acres, they have doomed thee to long years of bondage in the prison and fortress; they have made thee a beggar. Is it come to this, my brother, that a man is of no more account than a hare? Are we nothing better than the cattle in the fields? And a brave man like thee can tolerate this!"

"Can I, in any way, alter matters?"

"That we will soon see. But tell me now, whence dost thou come and what are thy designs?"

I told him my whole history. The man, without waiting till I concluded, sprang up with joyful impatience, and drew me to him. "Come, brother Sun-host," said he, "now thou art ripe; now I have thee just as I wanted thee. I will gain honour by thee. Follow me."

"Wither wilt thou lead me?"

"Don't stay asking questions. Follow!" He drew me forcibly forward.

We had gone but a short quarter of a mile. The forest became ever more declivi-

tous, more difficult of passage and wilder; neither of us spoke a word, till a whistle from my leader startled me out of my reflections. I raised my eyes and saw that we stood on the edge of a rugged precipice of a rock that opened out below into a deep caverned chasm. A second whistle responded from the innermost recess of the rock, and a ladder came up, as if by self-motion, slowly out of the depth. My guide began to descend first, calling on me to wait where I was till he returned. "I must first cause the dog to be chained," added he; "you are here unknown, and the beast would tear you to pieces." With these words he disappeared.

I stood now alone by the edge of the abyss, and was perfectly alive to the fact that I was alone. The want of foresight in my guide did not escape my notice. It would have cost me only a bold resolution to draw up the ladder; then I was free and my escape insured. I confess I thought seriously of the matter. I peered down into the chasm, which was about to swallow me. It reminded me dimly of the abyss of Hell, whence there is no redemption. I began to shudder as I thought of the course of life on which I was about to enter, and from which only immediate and rapid flight could rescue me.—Determined on this flight—already I had stretched out my arm to draw up the ladder—when in the instant it was thundered into my ears "What has a murderer to risk?" while all around there resounded as it were the derisive laughter of Hell. My arm fell as if paralyzed. My calculation was made. The time for repentance was past. The murder I had perpetrated lay piled up like rock behind me, and cut off my return for ever. At the same moment my guide re-appeared and told me to follow him. I had no longer any choice. I descended into the depths.

We had got but a few steps under the rock-wall, when the ground widened itself, and some huts became visible, in the centre of which, on a circular open place covered with grass, a band of from eighteen to twenty persons lay stretched around a charcoal fire. "Here, comrades!" said my leader, and took his place in the middle of the circle, "our host of the Sun! Bid him welcome!" "The host of the Sun!" exclaimed they all together, and every one—men and women—sprang up and pressed around me. Shall I confess it? Their joy was without dissimulation and from the heart. Respect and trust expressed themselves on every countenance.

This one pressed my hand, that one shook me in a friendly way by the clothes. The whole scene was like the meeting with an old acquaintance, dear and valued. My arrival had interrupted the carousal, which had just begun. It was at once resumed and I was compelled to drink a reciprocal welcome to them. Game of all sorts was on the table, and the wine-flask travelled unweariedly from neighbour to neighbour. Pleasure and harmony seemed to animate every heart, and they emulated each other in demonstrating in the most unrestrained way their joy at receiving me.

They had assigned me my place between two women, which seemed to be the seat of honor at the table. I expected to see in them only the outcasts of their sex, but how great was my surprise to discover among this shameless crew two of the most beautiful forms it has ever been my fortune to behold. Margaret, the older and more strikingly beautiful of the two, might still be named young, being scarcely yet twenty-five years of age. She expressed herself without modesty, and her gestures said yet more. Mary, the younger, had been married, but had fled from a husband who misused her. She was of finer form, but somewhat pale and thin, and less readily took the eye as compared with her more ardent neighbour. Both were emulous to enkindle my appetite; the beauteous Margaret anticipated my diffidence by wanton jests, but the shyer Mary made my heart a prisoner for ever.

"You see, brother Sun-host," said now the man who had brought me here, "you see how we live with each other, and every day resembles this. Is it not so, comrades?"

"Every day is like this" echoed the whole band. "If you can make up your mind to find pleasure in a life like this, then join our band and be our leader. Hitherto I have held that post but I will yield it to you. Does this please you, comrades?"

A joyous "Yes" was the response from every throat. My head was as if on fire, my brain was dazed. My blood boiled from wine and passion. The world had cast me out as if plague-stricken; here I found brotherly welcome, pleasure, honor. Whichever choice I made death awaited me; here, however, I could at least sell my life for a higher price. Love of the fair sex was my strongest passion; hitherto the sex had met my advances only with contempt; here favor and unbridled gratification awaited me. It cost me little thought to make up my mind. "I remain with you, comrades," I cried with decision, and advanced into the middle of the band : "I remain with you," I cried a second time, "if you yield to me my beautiful neighbour." All concurred in granting me my desire ; I was the declared owner of a ——, and captain of a band of robbers."

The succeeding portion of the above history we pass entirely over; the purely hideous has nothing instructive for the reader. An unfortunate, who has sunk to such a depth, must end his career by allowing himself every indulgence that can stir man's lower nature, but a second murder he never perpetrated, as he himself testified with the halter round his neck.

The evil repute of this man soon spread itself over the entire province. The highways became unsafe, nightly burglaries kept the burghers in a state of constant dread, the name of the host of the Sun became the terror of the country-people; justice endeavoured to lay hold of him, and a reward was set on his head. He was fortunate enough to frustrate every attempt on his liberty, and artful enough to utilize the superstition of the credulous boors for his own security. His confederates spread a report that he had made a league with the devil and could bewitch people. The district, within which he played his rôle, belonged then, even less than now, to the enlightened part of Germany; people believed these reports and no one felt secure. No one showed any desire to combat the dangerous man who had the devil at his call.

A year long had he pursued this miserable business when it began to become unendurable to him. The gang, of which he had taken the leadership, by no means fulfilled his brilliant expectations. A deceitful outside had dazzled him when excited with wine ; now he recognized with horror how terribly he had been deceived. Hunger and want came in place of the abundance with which he had been initiated ; very often he had to risk his life for a single meal which was scarcely sufficient to preserve him from actual starvation. The delusive picture of brotherly harmony was dissolved ; envy, suspicion, jealousy raged in the hearts of the members of this worthless band. Justice had promised to any one who would deliver him up, a reward ; and, if he were an accomplice in his crimes, a solemnly ratified pardon—a mighty tempta-

tion to these outcasts of the earth. The unhappy man knew his danger. The honour of wretches who were false alike to man and to God, was but a slight pledge for the security of his life. Sleep henceforward left his eyes; everlasting disquietude destroyed his rest ; the hideous spectre, suspicion, dogged his footsteps wherever he fled, tormented him when he awoke, shared his bed when he went to sleep, and terrified him with frightful dreams. His deadened conscience regained, at the same time, its voice ; the sleeping viper of remorse, in this universal storm, was awakened in his bosom. The whole force of his hate was diverted from mankind and turned its keenest edge against himself. He now forgave all nature, and found no one to execrate save himself.

Vice had completed the education of the unhappy man ; his naturally good understanding at length gained the victory over miserable deception. Now he felt how deep he had fallen ; a more tranquil melancholy came in place of maddening despair. With tears he wished he could recall the past, for now he knew he would re-live it in quite other fashion. He began to hope he might yet become upright, for he felt within himself that he had the ability to live an honest life. In the very extremity of his degradation he was probably nearer to goodness than he was when he took the first wrong step.

Just at this time the Seven Years' War had broken out, and recruiting was exceedingly active. The unfortunate man conceived hopes from this, and wrote a letter to his sovereign, from which we make the following extract :

"If your princely grace is not hindered by disgust from stooping so low as to me ; if a criminal of my species does not lie beyond the scope of your mercy, so, my most illustrious liege lord, grant me a hearing. I am a murderer and thief, the law condemns me to death, the courts of justice seek to seize me, and I offer to deliver myself up of my own free will. But I bring at the same time a strange request before your throne. I despise life and fear not to die, but it is frightful for me to die without ever having lived. I would gladly live to make amends for a part, at least, of my past crimes ; I wish to live to make expiation to the state which I have offended. My execution would be an example for the world, but no compensation for my deeds. I abhor vice and long earnestly after honesty and virtue. I have shown my ability to make

myself terrible to my fatherland; I hope that I have yet some power remaining to enable me to be of use to it.

"I know I am desiring something unheard of. My life is forfeited, and it little befits me to make conditions with justice. But I do not appear before you in bonds or chains; as yet I am free, and fear has the least share in urging this prayer.

"It is grace I pray for. Even if I had any claim on justice I would not venture to make it of avail. Still of one thing I might put my judges in remembrance. My career as a criminal dates from the hour when the first sentence was pronounced against me, that ruined my honour for ever. Had equity not then been denied me, probably to-day I should not be suing for mercy.

"Let mercy take the place of strict justice, my prince! If it stands within your princely power to prevail with justice in my behalf, then grant me my life. It shall from this hour on be devoted to your service. If you can grant my prayer, be pleased to let me learn your most gracious will through the public papers, and in reliance on your princely word I will render myself up in the capital. Should you have otherwise decided, then let justice do her part; I must do mine."

The petition remained unanswered, as well as a second and third, wherein the supplicant begged for the position of a horse-soldier in the service of the prince. All hope of pardon was utterly extinguished, and he took the resolution to escape out of the land and to die as a brave soldier in the service of the King of Prussia.

He succeeded in eluding the band and set out on his journey. His way led him through a little country town where he meant to pass the night. A short time previously a stringent mandate had been promulgated over the whole land, enjoining the strictest scrutiny of all travellers, as the sovereign—an electoral prince—had taken part in the war. Such an order had come to the hands of the gate-ward of this town, who was sitting on a bench before the postern as the Sun-host rode up. The appearance of the man had something grotesque, and at the same time threatening and savage about it. The lean jade he rode, and the fantastic *ensemble* presented by the various articles of his dress (in the collection of which taste, apparently, had had less to do than the chronological order in which they were acquired), contrasted strongly enough with a countenance whereon traces of so many furious passions lay outspread like the mutilated bodies of the dead on a field of battle. The gate-ward was startled by the look of this strange-looking wanderer. He had grown gray at his post, and forty years' experience in duty had developed him into an infallible physiognomist in regard to all vagabonds. The eagle-glance of this detective was not at fault in the case before him. He at once drew the bar of the gate and demanded from the rider his pass, while he laid hold on his bridle. Wolf was prepared for such an eventuality and carried a pass with him, which, in point of fact, he had taken from a plundered merchant. But this unsupported evidence was not enough to invalidate forty years' experience and move the oracle of the gate to a revocation of his suspicions. He had more confidence in his own eyes than in this piece of paper, and Wolf was under the necessity of accompanying him to the courthouse.

There, the chief magistrate of the place examined the pass and declared it in form. This man was possessed by a strong thirst for news, and loved, above all things, to discuss the contents of the newspapers over a bottle. The pass informed him that its possessor had come directly from the hostile country which was the theatre of the present campaign. He hoped to extract from its hearer private information regarding what was going on abroad, and sent his secretary back to Wolf with the pass, and at the same time extended him an invitation to share a flask of wine with his principal.

In the meantime Wolf was halting in front of the courthouse and affording an amusing spectacle to the riff-raff of the place who had gathered round him in crowds. They whispered each other in the ear, and pointed alternately to the horse and its rider; the sauciness of the rabble increased ultimately till it culminated in a noisy uproar. Unfortunately the horse, to which their attention was specially directed, was a stolen one; and Wolf conceived that it must have been described in hue-and-cry placards and so recognized. The unexpected hospitality of the magistrate converted his suspicion into conviction. He now held it for certain that the fraudulency of the pass had been detected, and that this invitation was a snare to seize him alive and without resistance. An evil conscience deprived him, for the moment, of his cooler judgment, and, without making a word of answer, he gave his horse the spur and rode off at speed.

This sudden flight was the signal for a tumultuous chase. "A thief!" shouted every one and set off in pursuit. For the robber the matter was one of life and death. He had a considerable start, and his pursuers panted breathlessly after him. He is near deliverance—but a heavy hand pressed unseen against him; the hour of his destiny had struck, the inexorable Nemesis seizes her debtour. The street in which he confided was a *cul-de-sac*; he must turn back and face his persecutors. The noise and hubbub had in the meantime set the whole town in uproar, crowd joins itself to crowd, all the streets are blocked, a host of enemies advance against him. He draws a pistol—the people give away—and in his desperation he determines to force his way through the mass by violence.

"The foolhardy man," cried he, "who

shall dare to lay hands on me, this bullet will—." Fear commands a universal halt and pause, till a courageous locksmith seizes him from behind, catches the finger wherewith the furious man would discharge the weapon, and dislocates it. The pistol falls, and the man, now unarmed, was torn down from his horse and dragged back to the courthouse in triumph.

"Who are you?" demanded the judge in a somewhat brutal tone.

"A man resolved to answer no questions till they are asked in a more courteous way."

"Who are you?"

"I am what I gave myself out to be. I have travelled over all Germany, and nowhere have I experienced such shameless treatment as I have received here."

"Your hurried flight renders you very suspicious. Why did you flee?"

"Because I was weary of serving as a butt for the jeers of your rabble."

"You threatened to fire on the people."

"My pistol was not loaded."

The pistol was examined and no bullet found in it.

"Why do you carry concealed weapons on your person?"

"Because I have with me articles of considerable value, and I had been warned to be on my guard against a certain Sun-host, who with his band infests this district."

"Your answers testify abundantly to your confidence, but not to your good faith. I give you till to-morrow morning to reflect whether you will disclose the simple truth."

"I will stand to what I have said."

"Conduct him to the tower."

"To the tower? Your honour, I trust there is yet justice in this land. I will demand satisfaction."

"I will give it to you as soon as you are cleared of suspicion." Next morning the magistrate reflected that it was quite possible the stranger might be an innocent man; an imperious style would avail nothing against his stubborness, it would therefore be probably better to treat him more temperately and respectfully. He caused the jurymen of the place to be summoned, and the prisoner to be brought before them.

"Pardon the first roughness, my good sir, if I expressed myself somewhat harshly towards you yesterday."

"With pleasure, when you take me in this way."

"Our laws are severe, and your conduct gave occasion for uproar. I cannot give you your freedom, without violating my duty. Appearances are against you. I wish you could say something whereby these might be confuted."

"What if I wished to say nothing?"

"Then I must report the case to government, and in the meantime you must remain in confinement."

"And then?"

"Then you run the risk of being whipped over the border as a vagabond, or, if the government should deal mercifully with you, of falling into the hands of the recruiting sergeant."

He was silent for some minutes and seemed as if maintaining a severe struggle with himself; then turning quickly round to the judge, said:

"Can I see you for a quarter of an hour in private?"

The jurymen looked at each other dubiously; but withdrew on receiving a signal to that effect from their superior.

"Now, what do you desire of me?"

"Your demeanour of yesterday, your honour, would never have brought me to a confession, for I defy compulsion. The moderation with which you have treated me to-day has won for you my confidence and respect. I believe you to be an honourable man."

"What have you to say to me?"

"I see you are an honourable man. I have long wished to meet with a man like you. Suffer me to take your right hand."

"What does all this mean?"

"Your head is gray and venerable. You have lived long in the world—have probably had your share of troubles—is it not so?—and have thereby learned to sympathize with others?"

"Sir—whither does all this tend?"

"You stand but a step's length from eternity—soon will you need mercy from God; and yet you will deny it to a fellow-mortal? With whom think you, you are speaking?"

"What is all this?—You terrify me."

"Fear nothing—write to your prince how you found me, and that I, of my own free will, betrayed myself. Say that God will in His own time show such mercy to him as he will show to me now. Intercede for me, old man, and let a tear drop on your report: I am the Host of the Sun."

The Sport of Destiny

A FRAGMENT OF TRUE HISTORY

ALOYSIUS VON G—— was the son of a citizen of distinction, in the service of——, and the germs of his fertile genius had been early developed by a liberal education. While yet very young, but already well grounded in the principles of knowledge, he entered the military service of his sovereign, to whom he soon made himself known as a young man of great merit, and still greater promise. G—— was now in the full glow of youth, so also was the prince. G—— was ardent and enterprising; the prince, of a similar disposition, loved such characters. Endued with brilliant wit, and a rich fund of information, G—— possessed the art of ingratiating himself with all around him; he enlivened every circle in which he moved, by his felicitous humour, and infused life and spirit into every subject that came before him. The prince had discernment enough to appreciate in another those virtues which he himself possessed in an eminent degree. Everything which G—— undertook, even to his very sports, had an air of grandeur; no difficulties could daunt him, no failures vanquish his perseverance. The value of these qualities was increased by an attractive person, the perfect image of blooming health and herculean strength, and heightened by the eloquent expression natural to an active mind; to these was added a certain native and unaffected dignity, chastened and subdued by a noble modesty. If the prince was charmed with the intellectual attractions of his young companion, his fascinating exterior irresistibly captivated his senses. Similarity of age, of tastes, and of character, soon produced an intimacy between them, which pos-

sessed all the strength of friendship, and all the warmth and fervour of the most passionate love. G—— rose with rapidity from one promotion to another; but, whatever the extent of favours conferred, they still seemed in the estimation of the prince to fall short of his deserts. His fortune advanced with gigantic strides, for the author of his greatness was his devoted admirer and his warmest friend. Not yet twenty-two years of age, he already saw himself placed on an eminence hitherto attained only by the most fortunate at the close of their career. But his active spirit was incapable of reposing long in the lap of indolent vanity, or of contenting itself with the glittering pomp of an elevated office, to perform the behests of which he was conscious of possessing both the requisite courage and the abilities. Whilst the prince was engaged in rounds of pleasure, his young favourite buried himself among archives and books, and devoted himself with laborious assiduity to affairs of state, in which he at length became so expert that every matter of importance passed through his hands. From the companion of his pleasures, he soon became first councillor and minister, and finally the ruler of his sovereign. In a short time there was no road to the prince's favour but through him. He disposed of all offices and dignities; all rewards were received from his hands.

G—— had attained his vast influence at too early an age, and had risen by too rapid strides, to enjoy his power with moderation. The eminence on which he beheld himself made his ambition dizzy, and no sooner was his final object of his wishes attained than his modesty forsook him. The respectful

deference shown him by the first nobles of the land, by all who, in birth, fortune, and reputation, so far surpassed him, and which was even paid to him, youth as he was, by the oldest senators, intoxicated his pride, while his unlimited power served to develope a certain harshness which had been latent in his character, and which, throughout all vicissitudes of his fortune, remained. There was no service, however considerable or toilsome, which his friends might not safely ask at his hands;—but his enemies might well tremble! for in proportion as he was extravagant in rewards, so was he implacable in revenge. He made less use of his influence to enrich himself than to render happy a number of beings who should pay homage to him as the author of their prosperity; but caprice alone, and not justice, dictated the choice of his subjects. By a haughty imperious demeanour he alienated the hearts even of those whom he had most benefitted; while at the same time he converted his rivals and secret enviers into deadly enemies.

Amongst those who watched all his movements with jealousy and envy, who were silently preparing instruments for his destruction, was Joseph Martinengo, a Piedmontese count, belonging to the prince's suite, whom G—— himself had formerly promoted, as an inoffensive creature, devoted to his interests, for the purpose of supplying his own place in attending upon the pleasures of the prince —an office which he began to find irksome, and which he willingly exchanged for more useful employment. Viewing this man merely as the work of his own hands, whom he might at any period consign to his former insignificance, he felt assured of the fidelity of his creature, from motives of fear no less than of gratitude. He thus fell into the very error committed by Richelieu, when he made over to Louis XIII., as a sort of plaything, the young Le Grand. Without Richelieu's sagacity, however, to repair his error, he had to deal with a far more wily enemy than fell to the lot of the French minister. Instead of boasting of his good fortune, or allowing his benefactor to feel that he could now dispense with his patronage, Martinengo was, on the contrary, the more cautious to maintain a show of dependence, and with studied humility affected to attach himself more and more closely to the author of his prosperity. Meanwhile, he did not omit to avail himself, to its fullest extent, of the opportunities

afforded him by his office, of being continually about the prince's person, to make himself daily more useful, and eventually indispensable to him. In a short time he had fathomed the prince's sentiments thoroughly, had discovered all the avenues to his confidence, and imperceptibly stolen himself into his favour. All those arts which a noble pride, and a natural elevation of character, had taught the minister to disdain, were brought into play by the Italian, who scrupled not to avail himself of the most despicable means of attaining his object. Well aware that man never stands so much in need of a guide and assistant as in the paths of vice, and that nothing gives a stronger title to bold familiarity than a participation in secret indiscretions, he took measures for exciting passions in the prince which had hitherto lain dormant, and then obtruded himself upon him as a confidant and an accomplice. He plunged him especially into those excesses which least of all endure witnesses, and imperceptibly accustomed the prince to make him the depository of secrets to which no third person was admitted. Upon the degradation of the prince's character he now began to found his infamous schemes of aggrandizement, and, as he had made secrecy a means of success, he had obtained entire possession of his master's heart before G—— even allowed to suspect that he shared it with another.

It may appear singular that so important a change should escape the minister's notice; but G—— was too well assured of his own worth, ever to think of a man like Martinengo in the light of a competitor; while the latter was far too wily, and too much on his guard, to commit the least error which might tend to rouse his enemy from his fatal security. That which has caused thousands of his predecessors to stumble on the slippery path of royal favour was also the cause of G——'s fall—immoderate self-confidence. The secret intimacy between his creature Martinengo and his royal master gave him no uneasiness; he readily resigned a privilege which he despised, and which had never been the object of his ambition. It was only because it smoothed his way to power that he had ever valued the prince's friendship, and he inconsiderately threw down the ladder by which he had risen, as soon as he had attained the wished-for eminence.

Martinengo was not the man to rest satisfied

with so subordinate a part. At each step which he advanced in the prince's favour his hopes rose higher, and his ambition began to grasp at a more substantial gratification. The deceitful humility which he had hitherto found it necessary to maintain towards his benefactor became daily more irksome to him, in proportion as the growth of his reputation awakened his pride. On the other hand, the minister's deportment towards him by no means improved with his marked progress in the prince's favour, but was often too visibly directed to rebuke his growing pride by reminding him of his humble origin. This forced and unnatural position having become quite insupportable, he at length formed the determination of putting an end to it by the destruction of his rival. Under an impenetrable veil of dissimulation he brought his plan to maturity. He dared not venture as

yet to come into open conflict with his rival; for, although the first glow of the minister's favour was at end, it had commenced too early, and struck root too deeply in the bosom of the prince, to be torn from it abruptly. The slightest circumstance might restore it to all its former vigour; and therefore Martinengo well understood that the blow which he was about to strike must be a mortal one. Whatever ground G—— might have lost in the prince's affections, he had gained in his respect. The more the prince withdrew himself from the affairs of state, the less could he dispense with the services of a man, who with the most conscientious devotion and fidelity had consulted his master's interests, even at the expense of the country; and G—— was now as indispensable to him as a minister as he had formerly been dear to him as a friend.

By what means the Italian accomplished his purpose has remained a secret between those on whom the blow fell and those who directed it. It was reported that he laid before the prince the original draughts of a secret and very suspicious correspondence, which G—— is said to have carried on with a neighbouring court; but opinions differ as to whether the letters were authentic or spurious. Whatever degree of truth there may have been in the accusation, it is but too certain that it fearfully accomplished the end in view. In the eyes of the prince G—— appeared the most ungrateful and vilest of traitors, whose treasonable practices were so thoroughly proved, as to warrant the severest measures without further investigation. The whole affair was arranged with the most profound secrecy between Martinengo and his master, so that G—— had not the most distant presentment of the impending storm. He continued wrapped in this fatal security, until the dreadful moment in which he was destined, from being the object of universal homage and envy, to become that of the deepest commiseration.

When the decisive day arrived, G—— appeared, according to custom, upon the parade. He had risen, in a few years, from the rank of ensign to that of colonel; and even this was only a modest name for that of prime minister, which he virtually filled, and which placed him above the foremost of the land. The parade was the place where his pride was greeted with universal homage, and where he enjoyed, for one short hour, the dignity for which he endured a whole day of toil and privation. Those of the highest rank approached him with reverential deference, and those who were not assured of his favour, with fear and trembling. Even the prince, whenever he visited the parade, saw himself neglected by the side of the vizier, inasmuch as it was far more dangerous to incur the displeasure of the latter than profitable to gain the friendship of the former. This very place, where he was wont to be adored as a god, had been selected for the dreadful theatre of his humiliation.

With a careless step he entered the well-known circle of courtiers, who, as unsuspicious as himself of what was to follow, paid their usual homage, awaiting his commands. After a short interval appeared Martinengo, accompanied by two adjutants, no longer the supple, cringing, smiling courtier, but overbearing and insolent, like a lacquey suddenly raised to the rank of a gentleman. With insolence and effrontery he strutted up to the prime minister, and, confronting him with his head covered, demanded his sword in the prince's name. This was handed to him with a look of silent consternation; Martinengo resting the naked point on the ground, snapped it in two with his foot, and threw the fragments at G——'s feet. At this signal the two adjutants seized him; the other pulled off his epaulettes, the facings of his uniform, and even the badge and plume of feathers from his hat. During the whole of this appalling operation, which was conducted with incredible speed, not a sound nor a respiration was heard from more than five hundred persons who were present; but all, with blanched faces and palpitating hearts, stood in death-like silence around the victim, who in this strange disarray—a rare spectacle of the melancholy and the ridiculous—underwent a moment of agony which could only be equalled by feelings engendered on the scaffold. Thousands there are who in his situation would have been stretched senseless on the ground by the first shock; but his firm nerves, and unflinching spirit, sustained him through this bitter trial, and enabled him to drain the cup of bitterness to its dregs.

When this procedure was ended, he was conducted, through rows of thronging spectators, to the extremity of the parade, where a covered carriage was in waiting. He was motioned to ascend, an escort of hussars being ready mounted to attend him. Meanwhile, the report of this event spread through the whole city; every window was flung open, every street lined with throngs of curious spectators, who pursued the carriage, shouting his name, amid cries of scorn and malicious exultation, or of commiseration more bitter to bear than either. At length he cleared the town, but here a no less fearful trial awaited him. The carriage turned out of the high road into a narrow, unfrequented path—a path which led to the gibbet, and alongside which, by command of the prince, he was borne at a slow pace. After he had suffered all the torture of anticipated execution, the carriage turned off into the public road. Exposed to the sultry summer-heat, without refreshment or human consolation, he passed seven dreadful hours in journeying to the place of destination—a prison fortress. It was nightfall before he arrived; when, bereft

of all consciousness, more dead than alive, his giant strength having at length yielded to twelve hours' fast and consuming thirst, he was dragged from the carriage; and—on regaining his senses—found himself in a horrible subterraneous vault. The first object that presented itself to his gaze was a horrible dungeon wall, feebly illuminated by a few rays of the moon, which forced their way through narrow crevices, to a depth of nineteen fathoms. At his side he found a coarse loaf, a jug of water, and a bundle of straw for his couch. He endured this situation until noon the ensuing day, when an iron wicket in the centre of the tower was opened, and two hands were seen lowering a basket, containing food like that he had found the preceding night. For the first time since the terrible change in his fortunes did

pain and suspense extort from him a question or two—Why was he brought hither? What offence had he committed? But he received no answer; the hands disappeared; and the sash was closed. Here, without beholding the face, or hearing the voice of a fellow-creature; without the least clue to his terrible destiny; fearful doubts and misgivings overhanging alike the past and the future; cheered by no rays of the sun, and soothed by no refreshing breeze; remote alike from human aid and human compassion;—here, in this frightful abode of misery, he numbered four hundred and ninety long and mournful days, which he counted by the wretched loaves that, day after day, with dreary monotony, were let down into his dungeon. But a discovery which he one day made early in his confinement, filled

up the measure of his affliction. He recognized the place. It was the same which he himself, in a fit of unworthy vengeance against a deserving officer, who had the misfortune to displease him, had ordered to be constructed only a few months before. With inventive cruelty, he had even suggested the means by which the horrors of captivity might be aggravated; and it was but recently that he had made a journey hither in order personally to inspect the place, and hasten its completion. What added the last bitter sting to his punishment was, that the same officer for whom he had prepared the dungeon, an aged and meritorious colonel, had just succeeded the late commandant of the fortress, recently deceased, and, from having been the victim of his vengeance, had become the master of his fate. He was thus deprived of the last melancholy solace, the right of compassionating himself, and of accusing destiny, hardly as it might use him, of injustice. To the acuteness of his other suffering was now added a bitter self-contempt, and the pain which to a sensitive mind is the severest—dependence upon the generosity of a foe to whom he had shown none.

But that upright man was too noble-minded to take a mean revenge. It pained him deeply to enforce the severities which his instructions enjoined; but as an old soldier, accustomed to fulfil his orders to the letter with blind fidelity, he could do no more than pity, compassionate. The unhappy man found a more active assistant in the chaplain of the garrison, who, touched by the sufferings of the prisoner, which had but just reached his ears, and then only through vague and confused reports, instantly took a firm resolution to do something to alleviate them. This excellent man, whose name I unwillingly suppress, believed he could in no way better fulfil his holy vocation, than by bestowing his spiritual support and consolation upon a wretch being deprived of all other hopes of mercy.

As he could not obtain permission from the commandant himself to visit him, he repaired in person to the capital, in order to urge his suit personally with the prince. He fell at his feet, and implored mercy for the unhappy man, who, shut out from the consolations of Christianity, a privilege from which even the greatest crime ought not to debar him, was pining in solitude, and perhaps on the brink of despair. With all the intrepidity and dignity which the conscious discharge of duty inspires, he entreated, nay demanded, free access to the prisoner, whom he claimed as a penitent for whose soul he was responsible to heaven. The good cause in which he spoke made him eloquent, and time had already somewhat softened the prince's anger. He granted him permission to visit the prisoner, and administer to his spiritual wants.

After a lapse of sixteen months, the first human face which the unhappy G—— beheld was that of his new benefactor. The only friend he had in the world he owed to his misfortunes—all his prosperity had gained him none. The good pastor's visit was like the appearance of an angel—it would be impossible to describe his feelings—but from that day forth his tears flowed more kindly, for he had found one human being who sympathized with and compassionated him.

The pastor was filled with horror on entering the frightful vault. His eyes sought a human form, but beheld, creeping towards him from a corner opposite, which resembled rather the lair of a wild beast than the abode of anything human, a monster, the sight of which made his blood run cold. A ghastly deathlike skeleton—all the hue of life perished from a face on which grief and despair had traced deep furrows—his beard and nails, from long neglect, grown to a frightful length—his clothes rotten and hanging about him in tatters; and the air he breathed, for want of ventilation and cleansing, foul, fetid, and infectious. In this state he found the favourite of fortune;—his iron frame had stood proof against it all! Seized with horror at the sight, the pastor hurried back to the governor, in order to solicit a second indulgence for the poor wretch, without which the first would prove of no avail.

As the governor again excused himself by pleading the imperative nature of his instructions, the pastor nobly resolved on a second journey to the capital, again to supplicate the prince's mercy.—There he protested solemnly that, without violating the sacred character of the sacrament, he could not administer it to the prisoner until some resemblance of the human form was restored to him. This prayer was also granted; and, from that day forward, the unfortunate man might be said to begin a new existence.

Several long years were spent by him in the fortress, but in a much more supportable condition, after the short summer of the new favorite's reign had passed, and others suc-

ceeded in his place, who either possessed
more humanity, or no motive of revenge.
At length, after ten years of captivity, the
hour of his delivery arrived, but without any
judicial investigation, or formal acquittal.
He was presented with his freedom as a boon
of mercy, and was, at the same time, ordered
to quit his native country for ever.

Here the oral traditions which I have been
able to collect respecting his history begin to
fail; and I find myself compelled to pass in
silence over a period of about twenty years.
During the interval G—— entered anew upon
his military career, in a foreign service;
which eventually brought him to a pitch of
greatness quite equal to that from which he
had, in his native country, been so awfully
precipitated. At length, time, that friend
of the unfortunate, who works a slow but
inevitable retribution, took into his hands
the winding up of this affair. The prince's
days of passion were over; humanity gradually resumed its sway over him as his hair
whitened with age. At the brink of the
grave he felt a yearning towards the friend
of his early youth. In order to repay, as far
as possible, the gray-headed old man for the
injuries which had been heaped upon the
youth, the prince, with friendly expressions,
invited the exile to revisit his native land,
towards which, for some time past, G——'s
heart has secretly yearned. The meeting was
extremely trying, though apparently warm
and cordial, as if they had only separated a
few days before. The prince looked earnestly
at his favorite, as if trying to recall features
so well known to him, and yet so strange;
he appeared as if numbering the deep furrows
which he had himself so cruelly traced there.
He looked searchingly in the old man's face
for the beloved features of the youth, but
found not what he sought. The welcome,
and the look of mutual confidence, were
evidently forced on both sides; shame on
one side, and dread on the other, had for
ever separated their hearts. A sight which
brought back to the prince's soul the full
sense of his guilty precipitancy could not be
gratifying to him; while G—— felt that he
could no longer love the author of his misfortunes. Comforted, nevertheless, and in
tranquillity, he looked back upon the past as
the remembrance of a fearful dream.

In a short time G—— was reinstated in all
his former dignities, and the prince smothered
his feelings of secret repugnance by showering
upon him the most splendid favors, as some
indemnification for the past. But could he
also restore to him the heart which he had
for ever untuned for the enjoyment of life?
Could he restore his years of hope? or make
even a shadow of reparation to the stricken
old man for what he had stolen from him in
the days of his youth?

For nineteen years G—— continued to enjoy this clear, unruffled evening of his days. Neither misfortune nor age had been able to quench in him the fire of passion, nor wholly to obscure the genial humor of his character. In his seventieth year, he was still in pursuit of the shadow of a happiness which he had actually possessed in his twentieth. He at length died governor of the fortress ——, where state prisoners are con-fined. One would naturally have expected that towards these he would have exercised a humanity, the value of which he had been so thoroughly taught to appreciate in his own person; but he treated them with harshness and caprice; and a paroxysm of rage, in which he broke out against one of his prisoners, laid him in his coffin, in his eightieth year.

THE GHOST-SEER

FROM THE PAPERS OF THE COUNT OF O.

FIRST BOOK

I AM about to relate an adventure, which to many will appear incredible, but of which I was in great part an eye-witness. The few who are acquainted with a certain political event will, if indeed these pages should happen to find them alive, receive a welcome solution thereof. And, even to the rest of my readers, it will be, perhaps, important as a contribution to the history of the deception and aberrations of the human intellect. The boldness of the schemes which malice is able to contemplate and to carry out must excite astonishment, as must also the means of which it can avail itself to accomplish its aims. Clear unvarnished truth shall guide my pen; for, when these pages come before the public, I shall be no more, and shall therefore never learn their fate.

On my return to Courland in the year 17—, about the time of the Carnival, I visited the Prince of —— at Venice. We had been acquainted in the —— service, and we here renewed an intimacy which, by the restoration of peace, had been interrupted. As I wished to see the curiosities of this city, and as the Prince was waiting only for the arrival of remittances to return to his native country, he easily prevailed on me to tarry till his departure. We agreed not to separate during the time of our residence at Venice, and the Prince was kind enough to accommodate me at his lodgings at the Moor Hotel.

As the Prince wished to enjoy himself, and his small revenues did not permit him to maintain the dignity of his rank, he lived at Venice in the strictest *incognito*. Two noblemen, in whom he had entire confidence, and a few faithful servants, composed all his retinue. He shunned expenditure, more, however, from inclination than economy. He avoided all kinds of dissipation, and up to the age of thirty-five years had resisted the numerous allurements of this voluptuous city. To the charms of the fair sex he was wholly indifferent. A settled gravity and an enthusiastic melancholy were the prominent features of his character. His affections were tranquil, but obstinate to excess. He formed his attachments with caution and timidity, but when once formed they were cordial and permanent. In the midst of a tumultuous crowd he walked in solitude. Wrapped in his own visionary ideas, he was often a stranger to the world about him; and, sensible of his own deficiency in the knowledge of mankind, he scarcely ever ventured an opinion of his own, and was apt to pay an unwarrantable deference to the judgment of others. Though far from being weak, no man was more liable to be governed; but, when conviction had once entered his mind, he became firm and decisive; equally courageous to combat an acknowledged prejudice, or to die for a new one.

As he was the third prince of his house, he had no likely prospect of succeeding to the sovereignty. His ambition had never been awakened; his passions had taken another direction. Contented to find himself independent of the will of others, he never enforced his own as a law; his utmost wishes did not soar beyond the peaceful quietude of a private life, free from care. He read much, but without discrimination. As his education had been neglected, and as he had early entered the career of arms, his understanding had never been fully matured. Hence the knowledge he afterwards acquired served but to increase the chaos of his ideas, because it was built on an unstable foundation.

He was a Protestant, as all his family had been, by birth, but not by investigation, which he had never attempted, although at one period of his life he had been an enthusiast in its cause. He had never, so far as came to my knowledge, been a freemason.

*   *   *   *   *

One evening we were, as usual, walking by ourselves, well masked, in the Square of St. Mark.—It was growing late, and the crowd was dispersing, when the Prince observed a mask which followed us everywhere. This mask was an Armenian, and walked alone. We quickened our steps, and endeavored to baffle him by repeatedly altering our course. It was in vain, the mask was always close behind us.—"You have had no intrigue here, I hope," said the Prince at last, "the husbands of Venice are dangerous."—"I do not know a single lady in the place," was my answer.—"Let us sit down here, and speak German," said he; "I fancy we are mistaken for some other persons." We sat down upon a stone bench, and expected the mask would have passed by. He came directly up to us, and took his seat by the side of the Prince.

The latter took out his watch, and, rising at the same time, addressed me thus in a loud voice in French: "It is past nine. Come, we forget that we are waited for at *the Louvre*." This speech he only invented in order to deceive the mask as to our route.— "Nine!" repeated the latter in the same language, in a slow and expressive voice, "Congratulate yourself, my Prince" (calling him by his real name); "he died at nine." In saying this, he arose and went away.

We looked at each other in amazement.— "Who is dead?" said the Prince at length, after a long silence.—"Let us follow him," replied I, "and demand an explanation." We searched every corner of the place; the mask was nowhere to be found. We returned to our hotel disappointed. The Prince spoke not a word to me the whole way; he walked apart by himself, and appeared to be greatly agitated, which he afterwards confessed to me was the case.—Having reached home, he began at length to speak: "Is it not laughable," said he, "that a madman should have the power thus to disturb a man's tranquillity by two or three words?" We wished each other a good night; and, as soon as I was in my own apartment, I noted down in my pocket-book the day and the hour when this adventure happened. It was on a Thursday.

The next evening the Prince said to me, "Suppose we go to the Square of St. Mark, and seek for our mysterious Armenian? I long to see this comedy unraveled." I consented. We walked in the square till eleven. The Armenian was nowhere to be seen. We repeated our walk the four following evenings, and each time with the same bad success.

On the sixth evening, as we went out of the hotel, it occurred to me, whether designedly or otherwise I cannot recollect, to tell the servants where we might be found in case we should be inquired for. The Prince remarked my precaution, and approved of it with a smile. We found the Square of St. Mark very much crowded.—Scarcely had we advanced thirty steps, when I perceived the Armenian, who was pressing rapidly through the crowd, and seemed to be in search of some one. We were just approaching him, when Baron F——, one of the Prince's retinue, came up to us quite breathless, and delivered to the Prince a letter: "It is sealed with black," said he, "and we supposed from this that it might contain matters of importance." I was struck as with a thunderbolt. The Prince

went near a torch, and began to read. "My cousin is dead!" exclaimed he.—"When?" inquired I anxiously, interrupting him. He looked again into the letter. "Last Thursday night at nine."

We had not recovered from our surprise when the Armenian stood before us. "You are known here, my Prince!" said he. "Hasten to your hotel. You will find there the deputies from the Senate. Do not hesitate to accept the honor they intend to offer you. Baron F—— forgot to tell you that your remittances are arrived."—He disappeared among the crowd.

We hastened to our hotel, and found every thing as the Armenian had told us. Three noblemen of the republic were waiting to pay their respects to the Prince, and to escort him in state to the Assembly, where the first nobility of the city were ready to receive him. He had hardly time enough to give me a hint to sit up for him till his return.

About eleven o'clock at night he returned. On entering the room, he appeared grave and thoughtful. Having dismissed the servants, he took me by the hand, and said, in the words of Hamlet, "Count—

"'There are more things in heav'n and earth
Than are dreamt of in your philosophy.'"

"Gracious Prince!" replied I, "you seem to forget that you are retiring to your pillow greatly enriched in prospect." The deceased was the hereditary prince.

"Do not remind me of it," said the Prince; "for, should I even have acquired a crown, I am now too much engaged to occupy myself with such a trifle. If that Armenian has not merely guessed by chance——"

"How can that be, my Prince?" interrupted I.

"Then will I resign to you all my hopes of royalty in exchange for a monk's cowl."

I have mentioned this purposely to show how far every ambitious idea was then distant from his thoughts.

The following evening we went earlier than usual to the Square of St. Mark. A sudden shower of rain obliged us to take shelter in a coffee-house, where we found a party engaged at cards. The Prince took his place behind the chair of a Spaniard to observe the game. I went into an adjacent chamber to read the newspapers. A short time afterwards I heard a noise in the card-room. Previously to the entrance of the Prince, the Spaniard had been constantly losing, but since then he had won upon every card. The fortune of the game was reversed in a striking manner, and the bank was in danger of being challenged by the pointeur, whom this lucky change of fortune had rendered more adventurous. A Venetian, who kept the bank, told the Prince in a very rude manner that his presence interrupted the fortune of the game, and desired him to quit the table. The latter looked coldly at him, remained in his place, and preserved the same countenance, when the Venetian repeated his insulting demand in French. He thought the Prince understood neither French nor Italian; and, addressing himself with a contemptuous laugh to the company, said, "Pray, gentlemen, tell me how I must make myself understood to this fool." At the same time he rose and prepared to seize the Prince by the arm. His patience forsook the latter; he grasped the Venetian with a strong hand, and threw him violently on the ground. The company rose up in confusion. Hearing the noise, I hastily entered the room and unguardedly called the Prince by his name. "Take care," said I, imprudently; "we are in Venice." The name of the Prince caused a general silence, which ended in a whispering which appeared to me to have a dangerous tendency. All the Italians present divided into parties, and kept aloof. One after the other left the room, so that we soon found ourselves alone with the Spaniard and a few Frenchmen. "You are

lost, Prince," said they, "if you do not leave the city immediately. The Venetian whom you handled so roughly is rich enough to hire a *bravo*. It costs him but fifty zechins to be revenged by your death." The Spaniard offered, for the security of the Prince, to go for the guards, and even to accompany us home himself. The Frenchmen proposed to do the same. We were still deliberating what to do, when the door suddenly opened, and some officers of the Inquisition entered the room. They produced an order of government, which charged us both to follow them immediately. They conducted us under a strong escort to the canal, where a gondola was waiting for us, in which we were ordered to embark. We were blindfolded before we landed. They led us up a large stone staircase, and through a long winding passage over vaults, as I judged from the echoes that resounded under our feet. At length we came to another staircase, and, having descended a flight of steps, we entered a hall, where the bandage was removed from our eyes. We found ourselves in a circle of venerable old men, all dressed in black; the hall was hung round with black, and dimly lighted. A dead silence reigned in the assembly, which inspired us with a feeling of awe. One of the old men, who appeared to be the principal Inquisitor, approached the Prince with a solemn countenance, and said, pointing to the Venetian, who was led forward:

"Do you recognize this man as the same who offended you at the coffee-house?"

"I do," answered the Prince.

Then addressing the prisoner: "Is this the same person whom you meant to have assassinated to-night?"

The prisoner replied: "Yes."

In the same instant the circle opened, and we saw with horror the head of the Venetian severed from his body.

"Are you content with this satisfaction?" said the Inquisitor. The Prince had fainted in the arms of his attendants. "Go" added the Inquisitor, turning to me with a terrible voice, "Go; and in future judge less hastily of the administration of justice in Venice."

Who the unknown friend was who had thus saved us from inevitable death, by interposing in our behalf the active arm of justice, we could not conjecture. Filled with terror we reached our hotel. It was past midnight. The Chamberlain Z—— was waiting anxiously for us at the door.

"How fortunate it was that you sent us a message!" said he to the Prince as he lighted us up the staircase. "The news which Baron F—— soon after brought us respecting you, from the Square of St. Mark would otherwise have given us the greatest uneasiness."

"I sent you a message!" said the Prince. "When? I know nothing of it."

"This evening after eight, you sent us word that we must not be alarmed if you should come home later to-night than usual."

The Prince looked at me. "Perhaps you have taken this precaution without mentioning it to me?"

I knew nothing of it.

"It must be so, however," replied the chamberlain, "since here is your repeating watch, which you sent me as a mark of authenticity."

The Prince put his hand to his watch-pocket. It was empty, and he recognized the watch which the chamberlain held as his own.

"Who brought it?" said he in amazement.

"An unknown mask in an Armenian dress, who disappeared immediately."

We stood looking at each other. "What do you think of this?" said the Prince, at last, after a long silence. "I have a secret guardian here in Venice."

The frightful transaction of this night threw the Prince into a fever, which confined him to his room for a week. During this time our hotel was crowded with Venetians and strangers, who visited the Prince from a deference to his newly discovered rank. They vied with each other in offers of service, and it was not a little entertaining to observe that the last visitor seldom failed to hint some suspicion derogatory to the character of the preceding one. *Billets doux* and nostrums poured in upon us from all quarters. Every one endeavored to recommend himself in his own way. Our adventure with the Inquisition was no more mentioned. The Court of —— wishing the Prince to delay his departure from Venice for some time, orders were sent to several bankers to pay him considerable sums of money. He was thus, against his will, compelled to protract his residence in Italy; and, at his request, I also resolved to postpone my departure for some time longer.

As soon as the Prince had recovered strength enough to quit his chamber, he was advised by his physician to take an airing in a gondola

upon the Brenta, for the benefit of the air, to which, as the weather was serene, he readily consented. Just as the Prince was about to step into the boat he missed the key of a little chest in which some very valuable papers were inclosed. We immediately turned back to search for it. He very distinctly remembered that he had locked the chest the day before, and he had never left the room in the interval. As our endeavors to find it proved ineffectual, we were obliged to relinquish the search in order to avoid being too late. The Prince, whose soul was above suspicion, gave up the key as lost, and desired that it might not be mentioned any more.

Our little voyage was exceedingly delightful. A picturesque country, which at every winding of the river seemed to increase in richness and beauty; the serenity of the sky, which formed a May day in the middle of February; the charming gardens and elegant country-seats which adorned the banks of the Brenta; the majestic city of Venice behind us, with its lofty spires, and a forest of masts rising as it were out of the waves; all this afforded us one of the most splendid prospects in the world. We wholly abandoned ourselves to the enchantment of Nature's luxuriant scenery, our minds shared the hilarity of the day, even the Prince himself lost his wonted gravity, and vied with us in merry jests and diversions. On landing about two Italian miles from the city, we heard the sound of sprightly music; it came from a small village, at a little distance from the Brenta, where there was at that time a fair. The place was crowded with company of every description. A troop of young girls and boys, dressed in theatrical habits, welcomed us with a pantomimical dance. The invention was novel; animation and grace attended their every movement. Before the dance was quite concluded, the principal actress, who represented a Queen, stopped suddenly as if arrested by an invisible arm. Herself and those around her were motionless. The music ceased. The assembly was silent. Not a breath was to be heard, and the queen stood with her eyes fixed on the ground in deep abstraction. On a sudden she started from her reverie, with the fury of one inspired, and looked wildly around her: "A king is among us!" she exclaimed, taking her crown from her head, and laying it at the feet of the Prince. Every one present cast their eyes upon him, and doubted for some time whether there was any meaning in this farce;

so much were they deceived by the impressive seriousness of the actress. This silence was at length broken by a general clapping of hands, as a mark of approbation. I looked at the Prince. I noticed that he appeared not a little disconcerted, and endeavored to escape the inquisitive glances of the spectators. He threw money to the players, and hastened to extricate himself from the crowd.

We had advanced but a few steps, when a venerable bare-footed friar, pressing through the crowd, placed himself in the Prince's path. "My lord!" said he, "give the holy Virgin part of your gold. You will want her prayers." He uttered these words in a tone of voice which startled us extremely, and then disappeared in the throng.

In the meantime our company had increased. An English Lord, whom the Prince had seen before at Nice, some merchants of Leghorn, a German Prebendary, a French *Abbé* with some ladies, and a Russian officer, attached themselves to our party. The physiognomy of the latter had something so uncommon as to attract our particular attention. Never in my life did I see such various features, and so little expression; so much attractive benevolence, and such forbidding coldness in the same face. Each passion seemed, by turns, to have exercised its ravages on it, and to have successively abandoned it. Nothing remained but the calm piercing look of a person deeply skilled in the knowledge of mankind; but it was a look that abashed every one on whom it was directed. This extraordinary man followed us at a distance, and seemed apparently to take but little interest in what was passing.

We came to a booth where there was a lottery. The ladies bought shares. We followed their example, and the Prince himself purchased a ticket. He won a snuff-box. As he opened it, I saw him turn pale and start back.—It contained his lost key.

"How is this?" said he to me, as we were left for a moment alone. "A superior power attends me, Omniscience surrounds me. An invisible Being, whom I cannot escape, watches over my steps. I must seek for the Armenian, and obtain an explanation from him."

The sun was setting when we arrived at the pleasure house, where a supper had been prepared for us. The Prince's name had augmented our company to sixteen. Besides the above-mentioned persons, there was a virtuoso from Rome; several Swiss gentlemen, and an adventurer from Palermo in regimentals, who gave himself out for a Captain. We resolved to spend the evening where we were, and to return home by torch-light. The conversation at table was lively. The Prince could not forbear relating his adventure of the key, which excited general astonishment. A warm dispute on the subject presently took place. Most of the company positively maintained that the pretended occult sciences were nothing better than juggling tricks. The French *Abbé*, who had drunk rather too much wine, challenged the whole tribe of Ghosts; the English Lord uttered blasphemies, and the musician made a cross to exorcise the devil. Some few of the company, amongst whom was the Prince, contended, that opinions respecting such matters ought to be kept to oneself. In the meantime the Russian officer discoursed with the ladies, and did not seem to pay attention to any part of the conversation. In the heat of the dispute, no one observed that the Sicilian had left the room. In less than half an hour he returned, wrapt in a cloak, and placed himself behind the chair of the Frenchman. "A few moments ago," said he, "you had the temerity to challenge the whole tribe of Ghosts. Would you wish to make a trial with one of them?"

"I will," answered the *Abbé*, "if you will take upon yourself to introduce one."—

"That I am ready to do," replied the Sicilian, turning to us, "as soon as these ladies and gentlemen have left us."—

"Why only then?" exclaimed the Englishman. "A courageous Ghost will surely not be afraid of a cheerful company."

"I would not answer for the consequences," said the Sicilian.—

"For heaven's sake, no!" cried the ladies, starting affrighted from their chairs.—

"Call your Ghost," said the *Abbé*, in a tone of defiance, "but warn him before-hand, that there are sharp-pointed weapons here." At the same time he asked one of the company for a sword.—

"If you preserve the same intention in his presence," answered the Sicilian, cooly, "you may then act as you please." He then turned towards the Prince: "Your Highness," said he, "asserts that your key has been in the hands of a stranger; can you conjecture in whose?"

"No."—

"Have you no suspicion?"—

"It certainly occurred to me that—"

"Should you know the person if you saw him?"—

"Undoubtedly."

The Sicilian, throwing back his cloak, took out a looking-glass and held it before the Prince. "Is this the man?"—

The Prince drew back with affright.

"Whom have you seen?" I inquired.

"The Armenian."

The Sicilian concealed his looking-glass under his cloak.

"Is it the person whom you thought of?" demanded the whole company.—

"The same."—

A sudden change manifested itself on every face; no more laughter was to be heard. All eyes were fixed with curiosity on the Sicilian. "*Monsieur l'Abbé!* The matter grows serious," said the Englishman. "I advise you to think of beating a retreat."—

"The fellow is in league with the devil," exclaimed the Frenchman, and rushed out of the house.—The ladies ran shrieking from the room. The Virtuoso followed them.—The German Prebendary was snoring in a chair.—The Russian officer continued sitting in his place as before, perfectly indifferent to what was passing.

"Perhaps your attention was only to raise a laugh at the expense of that boaster," said the Prince, after they were gone, "or would you indeed fulfil your promise to us?"—

"It is true," replied the Sicilian; "I was but jesting with the *Abbé*. I took him at his word, because I knew very well that the coward would not suffer me to proceed to extremities. The matter itself is however too serious to serve merely as a jest."—

"You grant, then, that it is in your power?"

The Sorcerer maintained a long silence, and kept his look fixed steadily on the Prince, as if to examine him.

"It is!" answered he at last.

The Prince's curiosity was now raised to the highest pitch. A fondness for the marvellous had ever been his prevailing weakness. His improved understanding, and a proper course of reading, had for some time dissipated every idea of this kind; but the appearance of the Armenian had revived them. He stept aside with the Sicilian, and I heard them in very earnest conversation.

"You see in me," said the Prince, "a man who burns with impatience to be convinced on this momentous subject. I would embrace

as a benefactor, I would cherish as my best friend, him who could dissipate my doubts, and remove the veil from my eyes.—Would you render me this important service?''—

"What is your request?'' inquired the Sicilian, hesitating.

"For the present I only beg some proof of your art. Let me see an apparition.''—

"To what will this lead?''

"After a more intimate acquaintance with me, you may be able to judge whether I deserve further instruction.''—

"I have the greatest esteem for your Highness, gracious Prince. A secret power in your countenance, of which you yourself are as yet ignorant, drew me at first sight irresistibly towards you. You are more powerful than you are yourself aware. You may command me to the utmost extent of my power, but—''

"Then let me see an apparition.''—

"But I must first be certain that you do not require it from mere curiosity. Though the invisible powers are in some degree at my command, it is on the sacred condition that I do not abuse my authority.''

"My intentions are most pure. I want truth.''

They left their places, and moved to a distant window, where I could no longer hear them. The English lord, who had likewise overheard this conversation, took me aside. ' Your prince has a noble mind. I am sorry for him. I will pledge my salvation that he has to do with a rascal.''—

"Everything depends on the manner in which the Sorcerer will extricate himself from this business.''—

"Listen to me. The poor devil is now pretending to be scrupulous. He will not show his tricks, unless he hears the sound of gold. There are nine of us. Let us make a collection. That will spoil his scheme, and perhaps open the eyes of the Prince.''

"I am content.'' The Englishman threw six guineas upon a plate, and went round gathering subscriptions. Each of us contributed some louis d'ors. The Russian officer was particularly pleased with our proposal; he laid a bank note of one hundred zechins on the plate; a piece of extravagance which startled the Englishman. We brought the collection to the Prince. "Be so kind,'' said the English lord, '' as to entreat this gentleman in our names to let us see a specimen of his art, and to accept of this small token of our gratitude.'' The Prince added a ring of

value, and offered the whole to the Sicilian. He hesitated a few moments. "Gentlemen,'' answered he, "I am humbled by this generosity, but I yield to your request. Your wishes shall be gratified.''—At the same time he rung the bell.—"As for this money,'' continued he, " to which I have no right myself, permit me to send it to the next monastery, to be applied to pious uses. I shall only keep this ring as a precious memorial of the worthiest of princes.''

Here the landlord entered; and the Sicilian handed him over the money.—" He is a rascal notwithstanding,'' whispered the Englishman to me. " He refuses the money because at present his designs are chiefly on the Prince.''

"Whom do you wish to see?'' asked the Sorcerer.

The Prince considered for a moment.— " We may as well have a great man at once,'' said the Englishman. "Ask for Pope Ganganelli. It can make no difference to this gentleman.''

The Sicilian bit his lips. " I dare not call one of the Lord's anointed.''

" That is a pity !'' replied the English lord ; " perhaps we might have heard from him what disorder he died of.''

" The *Marquis de Lanoy*,'' began the Prince, " was a French brigadier in the late war, and my most intimate friend.—Having received a mortal wound in the battle of *Hastinbeck*, he was carried to my tent, where he soon after died in my arms. In his last agony he made a sign for me to approach. Prince, said he to me, I shall never again behold my native land, I must, therefore, acquaint you with a secret known to none but myself. In a convent on the frontiers of Flanders lives a ———. He expired. Death cut short the thread of his discourse. I wish to see my friend to hear the remainder.''

" You ask much,'' exclaimed the Englishman with an oath. " I proclaim you the greatest sorcerer on earth, if you can solve this ' problem,'' continued he, turning to the Sicilian.—We admired the wise choice of the Prince, and unanimously gave our approval to the proposition. In the mean time the Sorcerer paced up and down the room with hasty steps, apparently struggling with himself.

" This was all that the dying Marquis communicated to you ?''

" It is all.''

THE GHOST-SEER.

"Did you make no further inquiries about the matter in his native country?"

"I did, but they all proved fruitless."

"Had the Marquis de Lanoy led an irreproachable life? I dare not call up every shade indiscriminately."—

"He died, repenting the excesses of his youth."—

"Do you carry with you any token of his?"—

"I do."——(The Prince had really a snuffbox, with the Marquis's portrait enamelled in miniature on the lid, which he had placed upon the table near his plate during the time of supper).

"I do not want to know what it is. If you will leave me, you shall see the deceased."—

He requested us to wait in the other pavilion until he should call us. At the same time he caused all the furniture to be removed from the room, the windows to be taken out, and the shutters to be bolted. He ordered the inn-keeper, with whom he appeared to be intimately connected, to bring a vessel with burning coals, and carefully to extinguish every fire in the house. Previous to our leaving the room, he obliged us separately to pledge our honor that we would maintain an everlasting silence respecting every thing we should see and hear. All the doors of the pavilion we were in were bolted behind us when we left it.

It was past eleven, and a dead silence reigned throughout the whole house. As we were retiring from the saloon, the Russian officer asked me whether we had loaded pistols. "For what purpose?" asked I.—"They may possibly be of some use," replied he. "Wait a moment. I will provide some." He went away; the Baron F—— and I opened a window opposite the pavilion we had left; we fancied we heard two persons whispering to each other, and a noise like that of a ladder applied to one of the windows. This was, however, a mere conjecture, and I did not dare affirm it as a fact. The Russian officer came back with a brace of pistols, after having been absent half an hour. We saw him load them with powder and ball. It was almost two o'clock in the morning when the Sorcerer came, and announced that all was prepared. Before we entered the room, he desired us to take off our shoes, and to appear in our shirts, stockings, and under-garments. He bolted the doors after us as before.

We found in the middle of the room a large black circle, drawn with charcoal, the space within which was capable of containing us all very easily. The planks of the chamber floor next to the wall were taken up, all round the room, so that we stood, as it were, upon an island. An altar, covered with black cloth, was placed in the centre upon a carpet of red satin. A Chaldee Bible was laid open, together with a skull; and a silver crucifix was fastened upon the altar. Instead of candles some spirits of wine were burning in a silver vessel. A thick smoke of frankincense darkened the room, and almost extinguished the lights. The Sorcerer was undressed like ourselves, but bare-footed; about his bare neck he wore an amulet*, suspended by a chain of human hair; round his middle was a white apron, marked with cabalistic characters and symbolical figures. He desired us to join hands, and to observe profound silence; above all, he ordered us not to ask the apparition any question. He desired the Englishman and myself, whom he seemed to mistrust the most, constantly to hold two naked swords crossways, an inch above his head, as long as the conjuration should last. We formed a half moon round him; the Russian officer placed himself close to the English lord, and was the nearest to the altar. The Sorcerer stood upon the satin carpet with his face turned to the East. He sprinkled holy water in the direction of the four cardinal points of the compass, and bowed three times before the Bible. The *formula* of the conjuration, of which we did not understand a word, lasted for the space of seven or eight minutes; at the end of which he made a sign to those who stood close behind to seize him firmly by the hair. Amid the most violent convulsions he called the deceased three times by his name, and the third time he

* AMULET is a charm or preservative against mischief, witchcraft, or diseases. Amulets were made of stone, metal, simples, animals, and every thing which fancy or caprice suggested; and sometimes they consisted of words, characters, and sentences, ranged in a particular order, and engraved upon wood, and worn about the neck, or some other part of the body. At other times they were neither written nor engraved, but prepared with many superstitious ceremonies, great regard being usually paid to the influence of the stars. The Arabians have given to this species of amulets the name of TAI. ISMANS. All nations have been fond of amulets. The Jews are extremely superstitious in the use of them (drive away diseases; and, even amongst the Christian. of the early times, amulets were made of the wood of the Cross, or ribands, with a text of Scripture written in them, as preservatives against diseases.

stretched forth his hand towards the crucifix.

On a sudden we all felt, at the same instant, a stroke as of a flash of lightning, so powerful that it obliged us to quit each other's hands; a terrible thunder shook the house; the locks jarred; the doors creaked; the cover of the silver box fell down, and extinguished the light; and on the opposite wall, over the chimney-piece, appeared a human figure, in a bloody shirt, with the paleness of death on its countenance.

"Who calls me?" said a hollow, hardly intelligible voice.

"Thy friend," answered the Sorcerer, "who respects thy memory, and prays for thy soul." —He named the prince.

The answers of the apparition were always given at very long intervals.

"What does he want with me?" continued the voice.

"He wants to hear the remainder of the confession, which thou hadst begun to impart to him in thy dying hour, but did not finish.

"In a convent on the frontiers of Flanders lives a——"

The house again trembled; a dreadful thunder rolled; a flash of lightning illuminated the room; the doors flew open, and another human figure, bloody and pale as the first, but more terrible, appeared on the threshold. The spirit in the box began to burn again by itself, and the hall was light as before.

"Who is amongst us?" exclaimed the Sorcerer, terrified, casting a look of horror on the assemblage; "I did not want thee."—The figure advanced with noiseless and majestic steps directly up to the altar, stood on the satin carpet over against us, and touched the crucifix. The first apparition was seen no more.

"Who calls me?" demanded the second apparition.

The Sorcerer began to tremble. Terror and amazement kept us motionless for some time.—I seized a pistol. The Sorcerer snatched it out of my hand, and fired it at the altar, and the figure emerged unaltered from the smoke. The Sorcerer fell senseless on the ground.

"What is this?" exclaimed the Englishman, in astonishment, aiming a blow at the ghost with a sword. The figure touched his arm, and the weapon fell to the ground. The perspiration stood on my brow with horror.—

Baron F—— afterwards confessed to me that he had prayed silently.

During all this time the Prince stood fearless and tranquil, his eyes riveted on the second apparition. "Yes, I know thee," said he at length, with emotion. "Thou art *Lanoy;* thou art my friend. Whence comest thou?" "Eternity is mute. Ask me concerning my past life."

"Who is it that lives in the convent which thou mentionedst to me in thy last moments?" "My daughter."

"How? Hast thou been a father?" "Woe is me that I was not!"

"Art thou not happy, *Lanoy?*" "God has judged."

"Can I render thee any further service in this world?" "None, but to think of thyself."

"How must I do that?" "Thou wilt learn at Rome."

The thunder again rolled—a black cloud of smoke filled the room; when it had dispersed, the figure was no longer visible. I forced open one of the window-shutters. It was daylight.

The Sorcerer now recovered from his swoon. "Where are we?" asked he, seeing the daylight. The Russian officer stood close behind him, and looked over his shoulder: "Juggler!" said he to him, with a terrible countenance, "thou shalt summon no more ghosts."

The Sicilian turned round, looked steadfastly in his face, uttered a loud shriek, and threw himself at his feet.

We looked all at once at the pretended Russian. The Prince instantly recognized the features of the Armenian, and the words he was about to utter expired on his tongue. We were all, as it were, petrified with fear and amazement. Silent and motionless, our eyes were fixed on this mysterious being, who beheld us with a calm but penetrating look of grandeur and superiority. A minute elapsed in this awful silence, another succeeded; not a breath was to be heard.

A violent battering against the door roused us at last from this stupor. The door fell in pieces into the room, and several officers of justice, with a guard, rushed in. "Here they are, all together!" said the leader to his followers—Then addressing himself to us—"In the name of the government," continued he, "I arrest you!" We had no time to recollect ourselves; in a few moments we were surrounded. The Russian officer, whom I shall

again call the Armenian, took the chief officer aside, and, as far as I in my confusion could notice, I observed him whisper a few words to the latter, and show him a written paper. The officer, bowing respectfully, immediately quitted him, turned to us, and, taking off his hat, said: "Gentlemen, I humbly beg your pardon for having confounded you with this impostor. I shall not inquire who you are, as this gentleman assures me you are men of honor." At the same time he gave his companions a sign to leave us at liberty. He ordered the Sicilian to be bound and strictly guarded. "The fellow is ripe for punishment," added he; "we have been searching for him these seven months."

The wretched Sorcerer was really an object of pity. The terror caused by the second apparition, and by this unexpected arrest, had together overpowered his senses. Helpless as a child, he suffered himself to be bound without resistance. His eyes were wide open and immovable; his face was pale as death; his lips quivered convulsively, but he was unable to utter a sound. Every moment we expected he would fall into a fit. The Prince was moved by the situation in which he saw him. He undertook to procure his discharge from the leader of the police, to whom he discovered his rank. "Do you know, gracious Prince," said the officer, "for whom your highness is so generously interceding? The juggling tricks by which he endeavored to deceive you are the least of his crimes. We have secured his accomplices; they depose terrible facts against him. He may think himself fortunate if he is only punished with the galleys."

In the mean time we saw the inn-keeper and his family led bound through the yard. "This man too?" said the Prince; "and what is his crime?"—"He was his comrade and accomplice," answered the officer. "He assisted him in his deceptions and robberies, and shared the booty with him. Your highness shall be convinced of it presently." "Search the house," continued he, turning to his followers, "and bring me immediate notice of what you find."

The Prince looked around for the Armenian, but he had disappeared. In the confusion occasioned by the arrival of the watch, he had found means to steal away unperceived. The Prince was inconsolable; he declared he would send all his servants, and would himself go in search of this mysterious man; and he wished me to go with him. I hastened to the window;

the house was surrounded by a great number of idlers, whom the account of this event had attracted to the spot. It was impossible to get through the crowd. I represented this to the Prince. "If," said I, "it is the Armenian's intention to conceal himself from us, he is doubtless better acquainted with the intricacies of the place than we, and all our inquiries would prove fruitless. Let us rather remain here a little longer, gracious Prince," added I. "This officer, to whom, if I observed right, he discovered himself, may perhaps give us some information respecting him."

We now, for the first time, recollected that we were still undressed. We hastened to the other pavilion, and put on our clothes as quickly as possible. When we returned, they had finished searching the house.

On removing the altar and some of the boards of the floor, a spacious vault was discovered. It was high enough, for a man might sit upright in it with ease, and was separated from the cellar by a door and a narrow staircase. In this vault they found an electrical machine, a clock, and a little silver bell, which, as well as the electrical machine, was in communication with the altar and the crucifix that was fastened upon it. A hole had been made in the window-shutter, opposite the chimney, which opened and shut with a slide. In this hole, as we learned afterwards, was fixed a magic-lantern, from which the figure of the ghost had been reflected on the opposite wall, over the chimney. From the garret and the cellar they brought several drums, to which large leaden bullets were fastened by strings; these had probably been used to imitate the roaring of thunder which we had heard.

On searching the Sicilian's clothes, they found in a case different powders, genuine mercury in vials and boxes, phosphorus in a glass bottle, and a ring, which we immediately knew to be magnetic, because it adhered to a steel button that by accident had been placed near it. In his coat-pockets were found a rosary, a Jew's beard, a dagger, and a brace of pocket-pistols. "Let us see whether they are loaded," said one of the watch, and fired up the chimney.

"Jesus Maria!" cried a hollow voice, which we knew to be that of the first apparition, and at the same instant a bleeding person came tumbling down the chimney. "What! not yet laid, poor ghost?" cried the Englishman, while we started back in affright. "Home to thy grave! Thou hast appeared what thou

wert not; now thou wilt become what thou didst but seem."

"Jesus Maria! I am wounded," repeated the man in the chimney. The ball had fractured his right leg. Care was immediately taken to have the wound dressed.

"But who art thou?" said the English lord; "and what evil spirit brought thee here?"

"I am a poor mendicant friar," answered the wounded man; "a strange gentleman gave me a zechin to— "

"Repeat a speech. And why didst thou not withdraw as soon as thy task was finished?"

"I was waiting for a signal which we had agreed on to continue my speech; but, as this signal was not given, I was endeavoring to get away, when I found the ladder had been removed."

"And what was the formula he taught thee?"

The wounded man fainted away; nothing more could be got from him. In the mean time the Prince turned towards the principal officer of the watch, giving him at the same time some pieces of gold. "You have rescued us," said he, "from the hands of an impostor, and done us justice without even knowing who we were; would you increase our gratitude by telling us the name of the stranger who, by speaking only a few words, was able to procure us our liberty."

"Whom do you mean?" inquired the party addressed, with an air which plainly showed that the question was useless.

"The gentleman in a Russian uniform, who took you aside, showed you a written paper, and whispered a few words, in consequence of which you immediately set us free."

"Do you not know the gentleman? Was he not one of your company?"

"No," answered the Prince; "and I have very important reasons for wishing to be more intimately acquainted with him."

"I know very little of him myself. Even his name is unknown to me, and I saw him to-day for the first time in my life."

"How? And was he in so short a time, and by using only a few words, able to convince you both of our innocence and his own?"

"Undoubtedly, with a single word."

"And this was?—I confess I wish to know it."

"This stranger, my Prince!" said the officer, weighing the zechins in his hand: "You have been too generous for me to make a secret of it any longer; this stranger is an officer of the Inquisition."

"Of the Inquisition? This man?"

"He is indeed, gracious Prince. I was convinced of it by the paper which he showed to me."

"This man, did you say? That cannot be."

"I will tell your highness more. It was upon his information that I have been sent here to arrest the Sorcerer."

We looked at each other in the utmost astonishment.

"Now we know," said the English lord, at length, "why the poor devil of a Sorcerer started in such terror when he looked more closely into his face. He knew him to be a spy, and that is why he uttered that shriek, and fell down before him."—

"No!" interrupted the Prince. "This man is whatever he wishes to be, and whatever the moment requires him to be. No mortal ever knew what he really was. Did you not see the knees of the Sicilian sink under him, when he said, with that terrible voice: 'Thou shalt summon no more ghosts?' There is something inexplicable in this matter. No person can persuade me that one man should be thus alarmed at the sight of another."

"The Sorcerer himself will probably explain it the best," said the English lord, "if

that gentleman," pointing to the officer, "will afford us an opportunity of speaking with his prisoner."

The officer consented to it, and, having agreed with the Englishman to visit the Sicilian in the morning, we returned to Venice.*

Lord Seymour (this was the name of the Englishman) called upon us very early in the forenoon, and was soon after followed by a confidential person whom the officer had intrusted with the care of conducting us to the prison. I forgot to mention that one of the Prince's domestics, a native of Bremen, who had served him many years with the strictest fidelity, and had entirely gained his confidence, had been missing for several days. Whether he had met with any accident, whether he had been kidnapped, or had voluntarily absented himself, was a secret to every one. The last supposition was extremely improbable, as his conduct had always been quiet and regular, and nobody had ever found fault with him. All that his companions could recollect was, that he had been for some time very melancholy, and that, whenever he had a moment's leisure, he used to visit a certain monastery in the *Giudecca*, where he had formed an acquaintance with some monks. This induced us to suppose that he might have fallen into the hands of the priests, and had been persuaded to turn Catholic; and, as the Prince was very tolerant, or rather indifferent about matters of this kind, and the few inquiries he caused to be made proved unsuccessful, he gave up the search. He, however, regretted the loss of this man, who had constantly attended him in his campaigns, had always been faithfully attached to him, and whom it was therefore difficult to replace in a foreign country. The very same day the Prince's banker, whom he had commissioned to provide him with another servant, was announced at the moment we were going out. He presented to the Prince a middle-aged man, well dressed, and of good appearance, who had been

* Count O——, whose narrative I have thus far literally copied, describes minutely the various effects of this adventure upon the mind of the Prince, and of his companions, and recounts a variety of tales and apparitions, which this event gave occasion to introduce. I shall omit giving them to the reader, on the supposition that he is as curious as myself to know the conclusion of the adventure, and its effects on the conduct of the Prince. I shall only add, that the Prince got no sleep the remainder of the night, and that he waited with impatience for the moment which was to disclose this incomprehensible mystery.—*Note of the German Editor.*

for a long time secretary to a *Procurator*. spoke French, and a little German, and was besides furnished with the best recommendations. The Prince was pleased with the man's physiognomy; and, as he declared that he would be satisfied with such wages as his service should be found to merit, the Prince engaged him immediately.

We found the Sicilian in a private prison, where, as the officer assured us, he had been lodged for the present, to accommodate the Prince, before being removed to the lead roofs, to which there is no access. These lead roofs are the most terrible prisons in Venice. They are situated on the top of the palace of St. Mark, and the miserable criminals suffer so dreadfully from the heat of the leads, occasioned by the burning rays of the sun descending directly upon them, that they frequently become delirious. The Sicilian had recovered from his yesterday's terror, and rose respectfully on seeing the Prince enter. He had fetters on one hand and one leg, but was able to walk about the room at liberty. The sentinel at the door withdrew as soon as we had entered.

"I come," said the Prince, "to request an explanation of you on two subjects. You owe me the one, and it shall not be to your disadvantage if you grant me the other."

"My part is now acted," replied the Sicilian, "my destiny is in your hands."

"Your sincerity alone can mitigate your punishment."

"Speak, honored Prince, I am ready to answer you. I have nothing now to lose."

"You showed me the face of the Armenian in a looking-glass. How was this affected?"

"What you saw was no looking-glass. A portrait in crayons behind a glass, representing a man in an Armenian dress, deceived you. My quickness, the twilight, and your astonishment favored the deception. The picture itself must have been found among the other things seized at the inn."

"But how could you read my thoughts so accurately as to hit upon the Armenian?"

"This was not difficult, your highness. You must frequently have mentioned your adventure with the Armenian at table in the presence of your domestics. One of my accomplices accidentally got acquainted with one of your domestics in the *Giudecca*, and learned from him gradually as much as I wished to know."

"Where is this man?" asked the Prince;

"I have missed him, and doubtless you know of his desertion."

"I swear to your honor, sir, that I know not a syllable about it. I have never seen him myself, nor had any other concern with him than the one before mentioned."

"Proceed with your story," said the Prince.

"By this means, also, I received the first information of your residence, and of your adventures at Venice; and I resolved immediately to profit by them. You see, Prince, I am sincere. I was apprised of your intended excursion on the *Brenta*. I prepared for it, and a key that dropped by chance from your pocket afforded me the first opportunity of trying my art upon you."

"How! Have I been mistaken? The adventure of the key was then a trick of yours, and not of the Armenian? You say this key fell from my pocket?"

"You accidentally dropped it in taking out your purse, and I seized an opportunity, when no one noticed me, to cover it with my foot. The person of whom you bought the lottery-ticket acted in concert with me. He caused you to draw it from a box where there was no blank, and the key had been in the snuff-box long before it came into your possession."

"I understand you. And the monk who stopped me in my way, and addressed me in a manner so solemn—"

"Was the same who, as I hear, has been wounded in the chimney. He is one of my accomplices, and under that disguise has rendered me many important services."

"But what purpose was this intended to answer?"

"To render you thoughtful; to inspire you with such a train of ideas as should be favorable to the wonders I intended afterwards to show you."

"The pantomimical dance, which ended in a manner so extraordinary, was at least none of your contrivance?"

"I had taught the girl who represented the Queen. Her performance was the result of my instructions. I supposed that your highness would not be a little astonished to find yourself known in this place, and (I entreat your pardon, Prince) your adventure with the Armenian gave me reason to hope that you were already disposed to reject natural interpretations, and to attribute so marvellous an occurrence to supernatural agency."

"Indeed," exclaimed the Prince, at once

angry and amazed, and casting upon me a significant look. "Indeed, I did not expect this." *

"But, continued he after a long silence, "how did you produce the figure which appeared on the wall over the chimney?"

"By means of a magic-lantern that was fixed in the opposite window-shutter, in which you have undoubtedly observed an opening."

"But how did it happen that not one of us perceived the lantern?" asked Lord Seymour.

"You remember, my lord, that on your re-entering the room, it was darkened by a thick smoke of frankincense. I likewise took the precaution to place the boards which had been taken up from the floor upright against the wall near the window. By these means I prevented the shutter from immediately attracting observation. Moreover, the lantern remained covered by a slide until you had taken your places, and there was no further reason to apprehend that you would institute any examination of the saloon."

"As I looked out of the window in the other pavilion," said I, "I fancied I heard a noise like that of a person placing a ladder against the side of the house. Was I right?"

"Exactly; it was the ladder upon which my assistant stood to direct the magic-lantern."

"The apparition," continued the Prince, "had really a superficial likeness to my de-

*Neither did probably the greater number of my readers. The circumstance of the crown deposited at the feet of the Prince, in a manner so solemn and un-expected, and the former prediction of the Armenian, seem so naturally and so obviously to aim at the same object, that at the first reading of these memoirs I immediately remembered the deceitful speech of the Witches in Macbeth:—

"Hail to thee, Thane of Glamis!
All hail, Macbeth! that shalt be king hereafter!"

and probably the same thing has occurred to many of my readers.

When a certain conviction has taken hold upon a man's mind in a solemn and extraordinary manner, it is sure to follow, that all subsequent ideas, which are in any way capable of being associated with this conviction, should attach themselves to, and in some degree seem to be consequent upon it. The Sicilian who seems to have had no other motive for his whole scheme than to astonish the Prince by showing him that his rank was discovered, played, without being himself aware of it, the very game which most furthered the view of the Armenian; but, however much of its interest this adventure will lose, if I take away the higher motive which at first seemed to influence these actions, I must by no means infringe upon historical truth, but must relate the facts exactly as they occurred.—*Note of the German Editor.*

ceased friend, and what was particularly striking, his hair, which was of a very light color, was exactly imitated. Was this mere chance, or how did you come by such a resemblance?"

"Your highness must recollect that you had at table a snuff-box by your plate, with an enamelled portrait of an officer in a . . . uniform. I asked whether you had anything about you as a memento of your friend, and as your highness answered in the affirmative, I conjectured that it might be the box. I had attentively examined the picture during supper, and being very expert in drawing, and not less happy in taking likenesses, I had no difficulty in giving to my shade the superficial resemblance you have perceived, the more so as the Marquis's features are very marked."

"But the figure seemed to move?"

"It appeared so, yet it was not the figure that moved, but the smoke on which the light was reflected."

"And the man who fell down the chimney spoke for the apparition?"

"He did."

"But he could not hear your questions distinctly."

"There was no occasion for it. Your highness will recollect that I cautioned you all very strictly not to propose any question to the apparition yourselves. My inquiries and his answers were preconcerted between us; and, that no mistake might happen, I caused him to speak at long intervals, which he counted by the beating of a watch."

"You ordered the innkeeper carefully to extinguish every fire in the house with water; this was undoubtedly—"

"To save the man in the chimney from the danger of being suffocated; because the chimneys in the house communicate with each other, and I did not think myself very secure from your retinue."

"How did it happen," asked Lord Seymour, "that your ghost appeared neither sooner nor later than you wished him?"

"The ghost was in the room for some time before I called him, but, while the room was lighted, the shade was too faint to be perceived. When the formula of the conjuration was finished, I caused the cover of the box, in which the spirit was burning, to drop down, the saloon was darkened, and it was not till then that the figure on the wall could be distinctly seen, although it had been reflected there a considerable time before."—

"When the ghost appeared, we all felt an electric shock. How was that managed?"

"You have discovered the machine under the altar. You have also seen, that I was standing upon a silk carpet. I directed you to form a half moon around me, and to take each other's hands. When the crisis approached, I gave a sign to one of you to seize me by the hair. The silver crucifix was the conductor, and you felt the electric shock when I touched it with my hand."

"You ordered Count O—— and myself," continued Lord Seymour, "to hold two naked swords crossways over your head, during the whole time of the conjuration—for what purpose?"

"For no other than to engage your attention during the operation; because I distrusted you two the most. You remember, that I expressly commanded you to hold the sword one inch above my head; by confining you exactly to this distance, I prevented you from looking where I did not wish you. I had not then perceived my principal enemy."

"I own," cried Lord Seymour, "you acted with due precaution;—but why were we obliged to appear undressed?"

"Merely to give a greater solemnity to the scene, and to excite your imaginations by the strangeness of the proceeding."

"The second apparition prevented your ghost from speaking," said the Prince. "What should we have learned from him?"

"Nearly the same as what you heard afterwards. It was not without design that I asked your highness whether you had told me everything that the deceased communicated to you, and whether you had made any further inquiries on this subject in his country. I thought this was necessary, in order to prevent the deposition of the ghost from being contradicted by facts with which you were previously acquainted. Knowing likewise that every man in his youth is liable to error, I inquired whether the life of your friend had been irreproachable, and on your answer I founded that of the ghost."

"Your explanation of this matter is satisfactory," resumed the Prince, after a short silence; "but there remains a principal circumstance which I must ask you to clear up."

"If it be in my power, and—"

"No conditions! Justice, in whose hands you now are, might perhaps not interrogate you with so much delicacy. Who was this unknown at whose feet we saw you fall?

What do you know of him? How did you get acquainted with him? And in what way was he connected with the appearance of the second apparition?"

"Your highness—"

"On looking at him more attentively, you gave a loud scream, and fell at his feet. What are we to understand by that?"

"This man, your highness . . . . ." He stopped, grew visibly perplexed, and with an embarrassed countenance looked around him.

"Yes, Prince, by all that is sacred, this unknown is a terrible being."

"What do you know of him? What connection have you with him? Do not hope to conceal the truth from us."

"I shall take care not to do so;—for who will warrant that he is not among us at this very moment?"

"Where? Who?" exclaimed we altogether, half amused, half startled, looking about the room. "That is impossible."

"Oh! to this man, or whatever he may be, things still more incomprehensible are possible?"

"But who is he? Whence comes he? Is he an Armenian or a Russian? Of the characters he assumes, which is his real one?"

"He is nothing of what he appears to be. There are few conditions or countries of which he has not worn the mask. No person knows who he is, whence he comes, or whither he goes. That he has been for a long time in Egypt, as many pretend, and that he has brought from thence, out of a catacomb, his occult sciences, I will neither affirm nor deny. Here we only know him by the name of the *Incomprehensible*. How old, for instance, do you suppose he is?"

"To judge from his appearance, he can scarcely have passed forty."

"And of what age do you suppose I am?"

"Not far from fifty."

"Quite right; and I must tell you, that I was but a boy of seventeen, when my grandfather spoke to me of this marvellous man, whom he had seen at *Famagusta;* at which time he appeared nearly of the same age as he does at present."

"This is exaggerated, ridiculous, and incredible."

"By no means. Were I not prevented by these fetters, I could produce vouchers, whose dignity and respectability should leave you no room for doubt. There are several credible persons, who remember having seen him, each

at the same time, in different parts of the globe. No sword can wound, no poison can hurt, no fire can burn him; no vessel in which he embarks can be wrecked. Time itself seems to lose its power over him. Years do not affect his constitution, nor age whiten his hair. Never was he seen to take any food. Never did he approach a woman. No sleep closes his eyes. Of the twenty-four hours in the day, there is only one which he cannot command; during which no person ever saw him, and during which he never was employed in any terrestrial occupation."

"And this hour is?"

"The twelfth in the night. When the clock strikes twelve at midnight he ceases to belong to the living. In whatever place he is, he must immediately be gone; whatever business he is engaged in, he must instantly leave it. The terrible sound of the hour of midnight tears him from the arms of friendship, wrests him from the altar, and would drag him away even in the agonies of death. Whither he then goes, or in what he is then engaged, is a secret to every one. No person ventures to interrogate, still less to follow him. His features, at this dreadful hour, assume a sternness of expression so gloomy and terrifying, that no person has courage sufficient to look him in the face, or to speak a word to him. However lively the conversation may have been, a dead silence immediately succeeds it, and all around wait for his return in respectful silence, without venturing to quit their seats, or to open the door through which he has passed."

"Does nothing extraordinary appear in his person when he returns?" inquired one of our party.

"Nothing, except that he seems pale and exhausted, like a man who has just suffered a painful operation, or received some disastrous intelligence. Some pretend to have seen drops of blood on his linen, but with what degree of veracity I cannot affirm."

"Did no person ever attempt to conceal the approach of this hour from him, or endeavor to preoccupy his mind in such a manner as to make him forget it?"

"Once only, it is said, he missed the appointed time. The company was numerous and remained together late in the night. All the clocks and watches were purposely set wrong, and the warmth of conversation carried him away. When the stated hour arrived, he suddenly became silent and motionless; his limbs continued in the position in which this instant had arrested them; his eyes were fixed; his pulse ceased to beat. All the means employed to awake him proved fruitless, and this situation endured till the hour had elapsed. He then revived on a sudden without any assistance, opened his eyes, and reassumed his speech at the very syllable which he was pronouncing at the moment of interruption. The general consternation discovered to him what had happened, and he declared, with an awful solemnity, that they ought to think themselves happy in having escaped with the fright alone. The same night he quitted for ever the city where this circumstance had occurred. The common opinion is that during this mysterious hour he converses with his genius. Some even suppose him to be one of the departed, who is allowed to pass twenty-three hours of the day among the living, and that in the twenty-fourth his soul is obliged to return to the infernal regions, to suffer its punishment. Some believe him to be the famous *Apollonius of Tyana*; and others, the disciple of *John*, of whom it is said—*he shall remain until the last judgment.*"

"A character so wonderful," replied the Prince, "cannot fail to give rise to whimsical conjectures. But all this you profess to know only by hearsay, and yet his behavior to you, and yours to him, seemed to indicate a more intimate acquaintance. Is it not founded upon some particular event in which you have yourself been concerned? Conceal nothing from us."

The Sicilian looked at us doubtingly and remained silent.

"If it concerns something," continued the Prince, "that you do not wish to be made known, I promise you, in the name of these two gentlemen, the most inviolable secrecy. But speak candidly and without reserve."

"Could I hope," answered the prisoner after a long silence, "that you would not make use of what I am going to relate as evidence against me, I would tell you a remarkable adventure of this Armenian, of which I myself was witness, and which will leave you no doubt of his supernatural powers. But I beg leave to conceal some of the names."

"Cannot you do it without this condition?"

"No, your highness. There is a family concerned in it, whom I have reason to respect."

"Let us hear your story."

"It is about five years ago," began the Sicilian, "that at Naples, where I was practising my art with tolerable success, I became acquainted with a person of the name of Lorenzo del M——, Chevalier of the order of St. Stephen, a young and rich nobleman, of one of the first families in the kingdom, who loaded me with kindnesses, and seemed to have a great esteem for my occult knowledge. He told me that the Marquis del M——nte, his father, was a zealous admirer of the Cabala, and would think himself happy in having a philosopher like myself (for such he was pleased to call me) under his roof. The Marquis lived in one of his country seats on the sea-shore, about seven miles from Naples. There, almost entirely secluded from the world, he bewailed the loss of a beloved son, of whom he had been deprived by a terrible calamity. The Chevalier gave me to understand, that he and his family might perhaps have occasion to employ me on a matter of the most grave importance, in the hope of gaining through my secret science some information, to procure which all natural means had been tried in vain. He added, with a very significant look, that he himself might, perhaps at some future period, have reason to look upon me as the restorer of his tranquillity, and of all his earthly happiness. The affair was as follows:

" This Lorenzo was the younger son of the Marquis, and for that reason had been destined for the church ; the family estates were to descend to the eldest. Jeronymo, which was the name of the latter, had spent many years on his travels, and had returned to his country about seven years prior to the event, which I am about to relate, in order to celebrate his marriage with the only daughter of the neighboring Count C——tti. This marriage had been determined on by the parents during the infancy of the children, in order to unite the large fortunes of the two houses. But though this agreement was made by the two families, without consulting the hearts of the parties concerned, the latter had mutually pledged their faith to each other in secret. Jeronymo del M—— and Antonia C—— had been brought up together, and the little constraint imposed on the two children, whom their parents were already accustomed to regard as destined for each other, soon produced between them a connection of the tenderest kind ; the congeniality of their tempers cemented this intimacy; and in later years it ripened insensibly into love. An absence of four years, far from cooling this passion, had only served to inflame it ; and

Jeronymo returned to the arms of his intended bride, as faithful and as ardent as if they had never been separated.

" The raptures occasioned by his return had not yet subsided, and the preparations for the happy day were advancing with the utmost zeal and activity, when the bridegroom disappeared. He used frequently to pass whole afternoons in a summer-house which commanded a prospect of the sea, and was accustomed to take the diversion of sailing on the water. One day, on an evening spent in this manner, it was observed that he remained absent a much longer time than usual, and his friends began to be very uneasy on his account. Messengers were despatched after him, vessels were sent to sea in quest of him ; no person had seen him. None of his servants were missed ; he must, therefore, have gone alone.—Night came on, and he did not appear. The next morning dawned ; the day passed, the evening succeeded ; Jeronymo came not. Already they had begun to give themselves up to the most melancholy conjectures, when the news arrived, that an Algerine pirate had landed the preceding day on that coast, and carried off several of the inhabitants. Two galleys, which were ready for sea, were immediately manned ; the old Marquis himself embarked in one of them, to attempt the deliverance of his son at the peril of his own life. On the third morning they perceived the corsair. They had the advantage of the wind ; they were just about to overtake the pirate, and had even approached so near that Lorenzo, who was in one of the galleys, fancied that he saw, upon the deck of the adversary's ship, a signal made by his brother, when a sudden storm separated the vessels. Hardly could the damaged galleys sustain the fury of the tempest. The pirate in the mean time had disappeared, and the distressed state of the other vessels obliged them to land at Malta. The affliction of the family knew no bounds. The distracted old Marquis tore his gray hairs in the utmost violence of grief ; and fears were entertained for the life of the young Countess. Five years were consumed in fruitless inquiries. Diligent search was made along all the coast of Barbary ; immense sums were offered for the ransom of the young Marquis, but no person came forward to claim them. The only probable conjecture which remained for the family to form was, that the same storm which had separated the galleys from the pirate had de-

stroyed the latter, and that the whole ship's company had perished in the waves.

"But, however this supposition might be, it did not by any means amount to a certainty, and could not authorize the family altogether to renounce the hope that the lost Jeronymo might again appear. In case, however, that he was really dead, either the family must become extinct, or the younger son must relinquish the church, and assume the rights of the elder. As justice, on one hand, seemed to oppose the latter measure, so, on the other hand, the necessity of preserving the family from annihilation required that the scruple should not be carried too far. In the mean time, through grief, and the infirmities of age, the old Marquis was fast sinking to his grave; every unsuccessful attempt diminished the hope of finding his lost son; he saw the danger of his family's becoming extinct, which might be obviated by a trifling injustice on his part, in consenting to favor his younger son at the expense of the elder. The consummation of his alliance with the house of Count C——tti required only that a name should be changed, for the object of the two families was equally accomplished, whether Antonia became the wife of Lorenzo or of Jeronymo. The faint probability of the latter's appearing again, weighed but little against the certain and pressing danger of the total extinction of the family, and the old Marquis, who felt the approach of death every day more and more, ardently wished at least to die free from this inquietude.

"Lorenzo, however, who was to be principally benefited by this measure, opposed it with the greatest obstinacy. Alike unmoved by the allurements of an immense fortune, and the attractions of the beautiful and accomplished being whom his family were about to deliver into his arms, he refused, on principles the most generous and conscientious, to invade the rights of a brother, who perhaps was still alive, and might some day return to claim his own. 'Is not the lot of my dear Jeronymo,' said he, 'made sufficiently miserable by the horrors of a long captivity, that I should yet add bitterness to his cup of grief by stealing from him all that he holds most dear? With what conscience could I supplicate heaven for his return, when his wife is in my arms? With what countenance could I hasten to meet him, should he at last be restored to us by some miracle? And even supposing that he is torn from us for ever,

how can we better honor his memory than by keeping constantly open the chasm which his death has caused in our circle? Can we better show our respect to him than by sacrificing our dearest hopes upon his tomb, and keeping untouched, as a sacred deposit, what was peculiarly his own?'

"But all the arguments which fraternal delicacy could adduce were insufficient to reconcile the old Marquis to the idea of being obliged to witness the extinction of a pedigree which nine centuries had beheld flourishing. All that Lorenzo could obtain was a respite of two years before leading the affianced bride of his brother to the altar. During this period they continued their inquiries with the utmost diligence. Lorenzo himself made several voyages, and exposed his person to many dangers. No trouble, no expense was spared to recover the lost Jeronymo. These two years, however, like those which preceded them, were consumed in vain."

"And the Countess Antonia?" said the Prince. "You tell us nothing of her. Could she so calmly submit to her fate? I cannot suppose it."

"Antonia," answered the Sicilian, "experienced the most violent struggle between duty and inclination, between hate and admiration. The disinterested generosity of a brother's love affected her; she felt herself forced to esteem a person whom she could never love. Her heart was torn by conflicting sentiments. But her repugnance to the Chevalier seemed to increase in the same degree as his claims upon her esteem augmented. Lorenzo perceived with heartfelt sorrow the grief that consumed her youth. A tender compassion insensibly assumed the place of that indifference with which, till then, he had been accustomed to regard her; but this treacherous sentiment quickly deceived him, and an ungovernable passion by degrees to shake the steadiness of his virtue—a virtue which, till then, had been unequalled.

"He, however, still obeyed the dictates of generosity, though at the expense of his love. By his efforts alone was the unfortunate victim protected against the arbitrary proceedings of the rest of the family. But his endeavors were ineffectual. Every victory he gained over his passion rendered him more worthy of Antonia; and the disinterestedness with which he refused her, left her no excuse for resistance.

"'This was the state of affairs when the Chevalier engaged me to visit him at his father's villa. The earnest recommendation of my patron procured me a reception which exceeded my most sanguine hopes. I must not forget to mention, that by some remarkable operations, I had previously rendered my name famous in different lodges of Freemasons, which circumstance may, perhaps, have contributed to strengthen the old Marquis's confidence in me, and to heighten his expectations. I beg you will excuse me from describing particularly the lengths I went with him, and the means which I employed; you may judge of them from what I have already confessed to you. Profiting by the mystic books which I found in his very extensive library, I was soon able to converse with him in his own language, and to adorn my system of the invisible world with the most extraordinary inventions. In a short time I could make him believe whatever I pleased, and he would have sworn as readily as upon an article in the canon. Moreover, as he was very devout, and was by nature somewhat credulous, my fables received credence the more readily, and in a short time I had so completely surrounded and hemmed him in with mystery, that he cared for nothing that was not supernatural. In short I became the patron saint of the house. The usual subject of my lectures was the exaltation of human nature, and the intercourse of men with superior beings; the infallible Count Gabalis* was my oracle. The young Countess, whose mind since the loss of her lover had been more occupied in the world of spirits than in that of nature, and who had, moreover, a strong shade of melancholy in her composition, caught my hints with a fearful satisfaction. Even the servants contrived to have some business in the room when I was speaking, and seizing now and then one of my expressions, joined the fragments together in their own way.

"'Two months were passed in this manner at the Marquis's villa, when the Chevalier one morning entered my apartment. A deep sorrow was painted on his countenance, his features were convulsed, he threw himself into a chair, with gestures of despair.

"''Captain,' said he, 'it is all over with

---

* A mystical work of that title, written in French in 1670, by the Abbé de Villars, and translated into English in 1680. Pope is said to have borrowed from it the machinery of his Rape of the Lock.

me, I must begone; I can remain here no longer.'

"''What is the matter, Chevalier? What ails you?'

"''Oh! this fatal passion!' said he, starting frantically from his chair. 'I have combated it like a man; I can resist no longer.'

"''And whose fault is it but yours, my dear Chevalier? Are they not all in your favor? Your father, your relations—'

"''My father, my relations! What are they to me? I want not a forced union, but one of inclination. Have not I a rival? Alas! and what a rival! Perhaps among the dead! Oh! let me go! Let me go to the end of the world,—I must find my brother.'

"''What! after so many unsuccessful attempts, can you still cherish hope?'

"''Hope!' replied the Chevalier. 'Alas, no! It has long since vanished from my heart, but it has not from hers. Of what consequence are my sentiments? Can I be happy while there remains a gleam of hope in Antonia's heart? Two words, my friend, would end my torments. But it is in vain. My destiny must continue to be miserable till eternity shall break its long silence, and the grave shall speak in my behalf.'

"''Is it then a state of certainty that would render you happy?'

"''Happy! Alas! I doubt whether I can ever again be happy. But uncertainty is of all others the most dreadful pain.'

"After a short interval of silence, he suppressed his emotion, and continued mournfully: 'If he could but see my torments! Surely a constancy which renders his brother miserable cannot add to his happiness! Can it be just that the living should suffer so much for the sake of the dead, who can no longer enjoy earthly felicity. If he knew the pangs I suffer,' continued he, hiding his face on my shoulder, while the tears streamed from his eyes, 'yes, perhaps he himself would conduct her to my arms.'

"''But is there no possibility of gratifying your wishes?'

"He started. 'What do you say, my friend?'

"''Less important occasions than the present,' said I, 'have disturbed the repose of the dead for the sake of the living. Is not the whole earthly happiness of a man, of a brother—'

"''The whole earthly happiness! Ah! my

friend, I feel what you say is but too true—
my entire felicity.'

"'And the tranquillity of a distressed
family, are not these sufficient to justify such
a measure? Undoubtedly. If any sublunary
concern can authorize us to interrupt the
peace of the blessed, to make use of a
power—'

"'For God's sake, my friend!' said he, interrupting me, 'no more of this. Once, I
avow it, I had such a thought; I think I mentioned it to you; but I have long since rejected it as horrid and abominable.'

"You will have conjectured already," continued the Sicilian, "to what this conversation led us. I endeavored to overcome the
scruples of the Chevalier, and at last succeeded. We resolved to summon the spirit
of the deceased Jeronymo. I only stipulated
for the delay of a fortnight, in order, as I
pretended, to prepare myself in a suitable
manner for so solemn an act. The time being
expired, and my machinery in readiness, I
took advantage of a very gloomy day, when
we were all assembled as usual, to obtain the
consent of the family, or rather, gradually to
lead them to the subject, so that they themselves requested it of me. The most difficult
part of the task was to obtain the approbation
of Antonia, whose presence was most essential. My endeavors were, however, greatly
assisted by the melancholy turn of her mind,
and perhaps still more so by a faint hope that
Jeronymo might still be living, and therefore
would not appear. A want of confidence in
the thing itself, or a doubt of my ability, was
the only obstacle which I had not to contend
with.

"Having obtained the consent of the
family, the third day was fixed on for the
operation. I prepared them for the solemn
transaction by mystical instruction, by fast-
ing, solitude and prayers, which I ordered to
be continued till late in the night. Much use
was also made of a certain musical instrument, unknown till that time, and which, in
such cases, has often been found very powerful. The effect of these artifices was so much
beyond my expectation, that the enthusiasm
to which on this occasion I was obliged to
force myself, was infinitely heightened by
that of my audience. The anxiously expected
hour at last arrived."

"I guess," said the Prince, "whom you
are now going to introduce. But go on, go
on."

"No, your highness. The incantation succeeded according to my wishes."

"How? Where is the Armenian?"

"Do not fear, your highness. He will appear but too soon. I omit the description of
the farce itself, as it would lead me to too
great a length. Be it sufficient to say, that
it answered my utmost expectations. The
old Marquis, the young Countess, her mother,
Lorenzo, and a few others of the family, were
present. You may imagine that during my
long residence in this house, I had not wanted
opportunities of gathering information respecting everything that concerned the deceased. Several portraits of him enabled me
to give the apparition the most striking likeness, and as I suffered the ghost to speak only
by signs, the sound of his voice could excite
no suspicion.

"The departed Jeronymo appeared in the
dress of a Moorish slave, with a deep wound
in his neck. You observe that in this respect
I was counteracting the general supposition
that he had perished in the waves, for I had
reason to hope that the unexpectedness of this
circumstance would heighten their belief in
the apparition itself, while, on the other hand,
nothing appeared to me more dangerous than
to keep too strictly to what was natural."

"I think you judged rightly," said the
Prince. "In whatever respects apparitions,
the most probable is the least acceptable. If
their communications are easily compre-
hended, we undervalue the channel by which
they are obtained. Nay, we even suspect the
reality of the miracle, if the discoveries which
it brings to light are such as might easily have
been imagined. Why should we disturb the repose of a spirit, if it is to inform us of nothing
more than the ordinary powers of the intellect
are capable of teaching us? But, on the
other hand, if the intelligence which we receive is extraordinary and unexpected, it confirms in some degree the miracle by which it
is obtained; for who can doubt an operation
to be supernatural, when its effect could not
be produced by natural means?—I interrupt
you," added the Prince. "Proceed in your
narrative."

"I asked the ghost whether there was anything in this world which he still considered
as his own," continued the Sicilian, "and
whether he had left anything behind that was
particularly dear to him? The ghost shook
his head three times, and lifted up his hand
towards heaven. Previous to his retiring he

dropped a ring from his finger, which was found on the floor after he had disappeared. Antonia took it, and looked at it attentively. She knew it to be the ring she had given her intended husband on their betrothal."

"The ring!" exclaimed the Prince, surprised. "How did you get it?"

"Who?—I!—It was not the true one, your highness!—I got it!—It was only a counterfeit."

"A counterfeit!" repeated the Prince. "But in order to counterfeit you required the true one. How did you come by it? Surely the deceased never went without it."

"That is true," replied the Sicilian, with symptoms of confusion. "But from a description which was given me of the genuine ring—"

"A description which was given you! By whom?"

"Long before that time. It was a plain gold ring, and had, I believe, the name of the young Countess engraved on it. But you made me lose the connection."

"What happened farther?" said the Prince, with a very dissatisfied countenance.

"The family felt convinced that Jeronymo was no more. From that day forward they publicly announced his death, and went into mourning. The circumstance of the ring left no doubt even in the mind of Antonia, and added a considerable weight to the addresses of the Chevalier.

"In the mean time, the violent shock which the young Countess had received from the sight of the apparition, brought on her a disorder so dangerous, that the hopes of Lorenzo were very near being destroyed for ever. On her recovery she insisted upon taking the veil; and it was only at the most serious remonstrances of her confessor, in whom she placed implicit confidence, that she was induced to abandon her project. At length the united solicitations of the family, and of the confessor, forced from her a reluctant consent. The last day of mourning was fixed on for the day of marriage, and the old Marquis determined to add to the solemnity of the occasion by making over all his estates to his lawful heir.

"The day arrived, and Lorenzo received his trembling bride at the altar. In the evening a splendid banquet was prepared for the cheerful guests, in a hall superbly illuminated, and the most lively and delightful music contributed to increase the general gladness.

The happy old Marquis wished all the world to participate in his joy. All the entrances of the palace were thrown open, and every one who sympathized in his happiness was joyfully welcomed. In the midst of the throng—"

The Sicilian paused. A trembling expectation suspended our breath.

"In the midst of the throng," continued the prisoner, "appeared a Franciscan monk, to whom my attention was directed by the person who sat next to me at table. He was standing motionless like a marble pillar. His shape was tall and thin; his face pale and ghastly; his eyes were fixed with a grave and mournful expression on the new-married couple. The joy which beamed on the face of every one present appeared not on his. His countenance never once varied. He seemed like a statue among the living. Such an object, appearing amidst the general joy, struck me more forcibly from its contrast with everything around. It left on my mind so indelible an impression, that from it alone I have been enabled (which would otherwise have been impossible) to recollect the features of this Franciscan monk in the Russian officer; for without doubt, you must have already conceived that the person I have described was no other than your Armenian.

"I frequently attempted to withdraw my eyes from this terrible figure, but they wandered back involuntarily, and found his countenance unaltered. I pointed him out to the person who sat nearest to me on the other side, and he did the same to the person next to him. In a few minutes a general curiosity and astonishment pervaded the whole company. The conversation languished; a general silence succeeded; the monk did not heed it. He continued motionless as before; his grave and mournful looks constantly fixed upon the new-married couple: his appearance struck every one with terror. The young Countess alone, who found the transcript of her own sorrow in the face of the stranger, beheld with a melancholy satisfaction the only object that seemed to understand and to sympathize her sufferings. The crowd insensibly diminished. It was past midnight; the music became fainter and more languid; the tapers grew dim, and many of them went out. The conversation declining by degrees, lost itself at last in secret murmurs, and the faintly illuminated hall was nearly deserted. The monk, in the mean time, continued motionless, with the same grave and mournful look still fixed on the new-married couple. The company at length rose from the table; the guests dispersed; the family assembled in a separate group, and the monk, though uninvited, continued near them. How it happened that no person spoke to him, I cannot conceive.

The female friends now surrounded the trembling bride, who cast a supplicating and distressed look on the venerable stranger; he did not answer it. The gentlemen assembled in the same manner around the bridegroom. A solemn and anxious silence prevailed among them. 'That we should be so happy here together,' began at length the old Marquis, who alone seemed not to behold the stranger, or at least seemed to behold him without dismay—'that we should be so happy here together, and my son Jeronymo cannot be with us!'

"'Have you invited him, and has he failed to come?' asked the monk. It was the first time he had spoken. We looked at him in alarm.

"'Alas! he is gone to a place from whence there is no return,' answered the old man. 'Reverend father! you misunderstood me. My son Jeronymo is dead.'

"'Perhaps he only fears to appear in this company,' replied the monk. 'Who knows how your son Jeronymo may be situated? Let him now hear the voice which he heard the last. Desire your son Lorenzo to call him.'

"'What means he?' whispered the company to one another. Lorenzo changed color. I will not deny that my own hair began to stand on end.

"In the mean time the monk approached a sideboard; he took a glass of wine and carried it to his lips—'To the memory of our dear Jeronymo!' said he. 'Let every one who loved the deceased follow my example.'

"'Be you who you may, reverend father!' exclaimed the old Marquis, 'you have pronounced a name dear to us all, and you are heartily welcome here;'—then turning to us, he offered us full glasses. 'Come, my friends!' continued he, 'let us not be surpassed by a stranger. The memory of my son Jeronymo!'

"Never, I believe, was any toast less heartily received.

"'There is one glass still unemptied.' said the Marquis. 'Why does my son Lorenzo refuse to drink this friendly toast?'

"Lorenzo, trembling, received the glass from the hands of the monk; tremblingly he put it to his lips. 'To my dearly beloved brother Jeronymo!' he stammered out, and replaced the glass with a shudder.

"'That was my murderer's voice!' exclaimed a terrible figure, which appeared suddenly in the midst of us, covered with blood, and disfigured with horrible wounds.

"Do not ask me the rest," added the Sicilian, with every symptom of horror in his countenance. "I lost my senses the moment I looked at this apparition. The same happened to every one present. When we recovered, the monk and the ghost had disappeared; Lorenzo was writhing in the agonies of death. He was carried to bed in the most dreadful convulsions. No person attended him but his confessor and the sorrowful old Marquis, in whose presence he expired. The Marquis died a few weeks after him. Lorenzo's secret is locked in the bosom of the priest who received his last confession; no person ever learned what it was.

"Soon after this event, a well was cleaned in the farmyard of the Marquis's villa. It had been disused many years, and was almost closed up by shrubs and old trees. On digging away the rubbish, a human skeleton was found. The house where this happened is now no more; the family del M——nte is extinct, and Antonia's tomb may be seen in a convent not far from Salerno."

"You see," continued the Sicilian, seeing us all stand silent and thoughtful, "you see how my acquaintance with this Russian officer, Armenian, or Franciscan friar, originated. Judge now whether I had not good cause to tremble at the sight of a being who has twice placed himself in my way in a manner so terrible."

"I beg you will answer me one question more," said the Prince, rising from his seat. "Have you been always sincere in your account of everything relating to the Chevalier?"

"To the best of my knowledge I have," replied the Sicilian.

"You really believe him to be an honest man?"

"I did; by Heaven! I did." answered he again.

"Even at the time that he gave you the ring?"

"How! He gave me no ring. I did not say that he gave me the ring."

"Very well!" said the Prince, pulling the bell, and preparing to depart. "And you believe." (going back to the prisoner) "that the ghost of the Marquis de Lanoy, which the Russian officer introduced after your apparition, was a true and real ghost?"

"I cannot think otherwise."

"Let us go!" said the Prince, addressing himself to us. The gaoler came in. "We have done," said the Prince to him. "You, sir," turning to the prisoner, "you shall hear farther from me."

"I am tempted to ask your highness the last question you proposed to the sorcerer," said I to the Prince, when we were alone. "Do you believe the second ghost to have been a real and true one?"

"I believe it! No, not now, most assuredly."

"Not now? Then you did once believe it."

"I confess I was tempted for a moment to believe it something more than the contrivance of a juggler."

"And I could wish to see the man who under similar circumstances would not have had the same impression. But what reasons have you for retracting your opinion? What the prisoner has related of the Armenian ought to increase rather than diminish your belief in his supernatural powers."

"What this wretch has related of him," said the Prince, interrupting me very gravely. "I hope," continued he, "you have now no doubt but that we have had to do with a villain."

"No; but must his evidence on that account—"

"The evidence of a villain, even supposing I had no other reason for doubt, can have no weight against common sense and established truth. Does a man who has already deceived me several times, and whose trade it is to deceive, does he deserve to be heard in a cause in which the unsupported testimony of even the most sincere adherent to truth could not be received? Ought we to believe a man who perhaps never once spoke truth for its own sake? Does such a man deserve credit, when he appears as evidence against human reason and the eternal laws of nature? Would it not be as absurd as to admit the accusation of a person notoriously infamous, against unblemished and irreproachable innocence?"

"But what motives could he have for giving so great a character to a man whom he has so many reasons to hate?"

"I am not to conclude that he can have no motives for doing this because I am unable to comprehend them. Do I know who has bribed him to deceive me? I confess I cannot penetrate the whole contexture of his plan; but he has certainly done a material injury to the cause he advocates, by proving himself to be at least an impostor, and perhaps something worse."

"The circumstance of the ring, I allow, appears somewhat suspicious."

"It is more than suspicious," answered the Prince; "it is decisive. He received this ring from the murderer; and at the moment he received it he must have been certain that it was from the murderer. Who but the assassin could have taken from the finger of the deceased a ring which he undoubtedly never took off himself? Throughout the whole of his narration the Sicilian had labored to persuade us, that while he was endeavoring to deceive Lorenzo, Lorenzo was in reality deceiving him. Would he have had recourse to this subterfuge, if he had not been sensible how much he should lose in our estimation by confessing himself an accomplice with the assassin? The whole story is visibly nothing but a series of impostures, invented merely to connect the few truths he has thought proper to give us. Ought I, then, to hesitate in disbelieving the eleventh assertion of a person who has already deceived me ten times, rather than admit a violation of the fundamental laws of nature, which I have ever found in the most perfect harmony?"

"I have nothing to reply to all this,—but the apparition we saw yesterday is to me not the less incomprehensible."

"It is also incomprehensible to me, although I have been tempted to believe that I have found a key to it."

"How so?" asked I.

"Do not you recollect that the second apparition, as soon as he entered, walked directly up to the altar, took the crucifix in his hand, and placed himself upon the carpet?"

"It appeared so to me."

"And this crucifix, according to the Sicilian's confession, was a conductor. You see that the apparition hastened to make himself electrical. Thus the blow which Lord Seymour struck him with a sword was of course ineffectual; the electric stroke disabled his arm."

"This is true with respect to the sword. But the pistol fired by the Sicilian, the ball of which we heard roll slowly upon the altar?"

"Are you convinced that this was the same ball which was fired from the pistol?" replied the Prince. "Not to mention that the puppet, or the man who represented the ghost, may have been so well accoutred as to be invulnerable by sword or bullet; but consider who it was that loaded the pistols."

"True," said I, and a sudden light broke upon my mind; "the Russian officer had loaded them, but it was in our presence. How could he have deceived us?"

"Why should he not have deceived us? Did you suspect him sufficiently to observe him? Did you examine the ball before it was put into the pistol? May it not have been one of quicksilver or clay? Did you take notice whether the Russian officer really put it into the barrel, or dropped it into his other hand? But supposing that he actually loaded the pistols, what is to convince you that he really took the loaded ones into the room where the ghost appeared, and did not change them for another pair, which he might have done the more easily, as nobody ever thought of noticing him, and we were besides occupied in undressing? And could not the figure, at the moment when we were prevented from seeing it by the smoke of the pistol, have dropped another ball, with which it had been beforehand provided, on the altar? Which of these conjectures is impossible?"

"You are right. But that striking resemblance to your deceased friend! I have often seen him with you, and I immediately recognized him in the apparition."

"I did the same, and I must confess the illusion was complete. But if the juggler, from a few stolen glances at my snuff-box, was able to give his apparition a resemblance, what was to prevent the Russian officer, who had used the box during the whole time of supper, who had had liberty to observe the picture unnoticed, and to whom I had discovered in confidence whom it represented, what was to prevent him from doing the same? Add to this what has been before observed by the Sicilian, that the prominent features of the Marquis were so striking as to be easily imitated; what is there so inexplicable in this second ghost?"

"But the words he uttered? The information he gave you about your friend?"

"What?" said the Prince. "Did not the Sicilian assure us, that from the little which

he had learned from me he had composed a similar story? Does not this prove that the invention was obvious and natural? Besides, the answers of the ghost, were so obscure, that he was in no danger of being detected in a falsehood. If the man who personated the ghost possessed sagacity and presence of mind, and knew ever so little of the affair on which he was consulted, to what length might not he have carried the deception?"

"Pray consider, your highness, how much preparation such a complicated artifice would have required from the Armenian; how much time it takes to paint a face with sufficient exactness; how much time would have been requisite to instruct the pretended ghost, so as to guard him against gross errors; what a degree of minute attention to regulate every minor attendant or adventitious circumstance, which must be answered in some manner, lest they should prove detrimental! And remember that the Russian officer was absent but half an hour. Was that short space of time sufficient to make even such arrangements as were most indispensable? Surely, my Prince, not even a dramatic writer, who has the least desire to preserve the three terrible unities of Aristotle, durst not venture to load the interval between one act and another with such a variety of action, or to presume upon such a facility of belief in his audience."

"What! You think it absolutely impossible that every necessary preparation should have been made in the space of half an hour?"

"Indeed, I look upon it as almost impossible."

"I do not understand this expression. Does it militate against the physical laws of time and space, or of matter and motion, that a man so ingenious and expert as this Armenian must undoubtedly be, assisted by agents whose dexterity and acuteness are probably not inferior to his own; favored by the time of night, and watched by no one, provided with such means and instruments as a man of this profession is never without—is it impossible that such a man, favored by such circumstances, should be able to effect so much in so short a time? Is it ridiculous or absurd to suppose, that by a very small number of words or signs he can convey to his assistants very extensive commissions, and direct very complex operations?—Nothing ought to be admitted that is contrary to the established laws of nature, unless it is something with which these laws are absolutely incompatible. Would you rather give credit to a miracle than admit an improbability? Would you solve a difficulty rather by overturning the powers of nature than by believing an artful and uncommon combination of them?"

"Though the fact will not justify a conclusion such as you have condemned, you must, however, grant that it is far beyond our conception."

"I am almost tempted to dispute even this," said the Prince, with a quiet smile. "What would you say, my dear Count, if it should be proved, for instance, that the operations of the Armenian were prepared and carried out on, not only during the half hour that he was absent from us, not only in haste and incidentally, but during the whole evening and the whole night? You recollect that the Sicilian employed nearly three hours in preparation."

"The Sicilian? Yes, my Prince."

"And how will you convince me that this juggler had not as much concern in the second apparition as in the first?"

"How so, your highness?"

"That he was not the principal assistant of the Armenian? In a word, how will you convince me that they did not co-operate?"

"It would be a difficult task to prove that," exclaimed I, with no little surprise.

"Not so difficult, my dear Count, as you imagine. What! Could it have happened by mere chance that these two men should form a design so extraordinary and so complicated upon the same person, at the same time, and in the same place? Could mere chance have produced such an exact harmony between their operations, that one of them should play so exactly the game of the other? Suppose for a moment that the Armenian intended to heighten the effect of his deception, by introducing it after a less refined one—that he created a Hector to make himself his Achilles. Suppose that he has done all this to discover what degree of credulity he could expect to find in me, to examine the readiest way to gain my confidence, to familiarize himself with his subject by an attempt that might have miscarried without any prejudice to his plan; in a word, to tune the instrument on which he intended to play. Suppose he did this with the view of exciting my suspicions on one subject, in order to divert my attention from another more important to his design. Lastly, suppose he wishes to have some in-

direct methods of information, which he had himself occasion to practice, imputed to the Sorcerer, in order to divert suspicion from the true channel."

"How do you mean?" said I.

"Suppose for instance that he may have bribed some of my servants, to give him secret intelligence, or, perhaps, even some papers which may serve his purpose. I have missed one of my domestics. What reason have I to think that the Armenian is not concerned in his leaving me? Such a connection, however, if it existed, may be accidentally discovered; a letter may be intercepted; a servant, who is in the secret, may betray his trust. Now all the consequence of the Armenian is destroyed, if I detect the source of his omniscience. He therefore introduces this Sorcerer, who must be supposed to have some design upon me. He takes care to give me early notice of him, and his intentions, so that whatever I may hereafter discover, my suspicions must necessarily rest upon the Sicilian. This is the puppet with which he amuses me, whilst himself, unobserved and unsuspected, is entangling me in invisible snares."

"We will allow this. But is it consistent with the Armenian's plan that he himself should destroy the illusion which he has created, and disclose the mysteries of his science to the eyes of the uninitiated?"

"What mysteries does he disclose? None, surely, which he intends to practice on me. He therefore loses nothing by the discovery. But, on the other hand, what an advantage will he gain, if this pretended victory over juggling and deception should render me secure and unsuspecting; if he succeeds in diverting my attention from the right quarter, and in fixing my wavering suspicions on an object the most remote from the real one! He could naturally expect that, sooner or later, either from my own doubts, or at the suggestion of another, I should be tempted to seek a key to his mysterious wonders, in the mere art of a juggler; how could he better provide against such an inquiry than by contrasting his prodigies with juggling tricks. By confining the latter within artificial limits, and by delivering, as it were, into my hands a scale by which to appreciate them, he naturally exalts and perplexes my ideas of the former. How many suspicions he precludes by this single contrivance! How many methods of accounting for his miracles, which

might afterwards have occurred to me, does he refute beforehand!''

"But in exposing such a finished deception, he has acted very much against his own interest, both by quickening the penetration of those whom he meant to impose upon, and by staggering their belief in miracles in general. Your highness's self is the best proof of the insufficiency of his plan, if indeed he ever had one."

"Perhaps he has been mistaken in respect to myself," said the Prince; "but his conclusions have nevertheless been well founded. Could he foresee that I should exactly notice the very circumstance which threatens to become the key to the whole artifice? Was it in his plan that the creature he employed should render himself thus vulnerable? Are we certain that the Sicilian has not far exceeded his commission? He has undoubtedly done so with respect to the ring, and yet it is chiefly this single circumstance which determined my distrust in him. How easily may a plan, whose contexture is most artful and refined, be spoiled in the execution by an awkward instrument! It certainly was not the Armenian's intention that the Sorcerer should trumpet his fame to us in the style of a mountebank, that he should endeavor to impose upon us such fables as are too gross to bear the least reflection. For instance, with what countenance could this impostor affirm, that the miraculous being he spoke of must renounce all commerce with mankind at twelve in the night? Did we not see him among us at that very hour?''

"That is true," cried I. "He must have forgotten it."

"It often happens, to people of this description, that they overact their parts; and, by aiming at too much, mar the effects which well-managed deception is calculated to produce."

"I cannot, however, yet prevail on myself to look upon the whole as a mere preconcerted scheme. What! the Sicilian's terror—his convulsive fits—his swoon—the deplorable situation in which we saw him, and which was even such as to move our pity—were all these nothing more than a studied part? I allow that a skilful performer may carry imitation to a very high pitch, but he certainly has no power over the organs of life."

"As for that, my friend," replied the Prince, "I have seen Richard the Third performed by Garrick. But were we at that moment sufficiently cool to be capable of

observing dispassionately? Could we judge of the emotion of the Sicilian, when we were almost overcome by our own? Besides, the decisive crisis even of a deception is so momentous to the deceiver himself, that excessive anxiety may produce in him symptoms as violent as those which surprise excites in the deceived. Add to this the unexpected entrance of the watch.''

"I am glad you remind me of that, Prince. Would the Armenian have ventured to discover such a dangerous scheme to the eye of justice; to expose the fidelity of his creature to so severe a test? And for what purpose?''

"Leave that matter to him; he is no doubt acquainted with the people he employs. Do we know what secret crimes may have secured him the silence of this man? You have been informed of the office he holds in Venice; what difficulty will he find in saving a man of whom he himself is the only accuser?''

[This suggestion of the Prince was but too well justified by the event. For, some days after, on inquiring after the prisoner, we were told that he had escaped, and had not since been heard of.]

"You ask what could be his motives for delivering this man into the hands of justice?'' continued the Prince. "By what other method, except this violent one, could he have wrested from the Sicilian such an infamous and improbable confession, which, however, was so material to the success of his plan? Who but a man whose case is desperate, and who has nothing to lose, would consent to give so humiliating an account of himself? Under what other circumstances could we have believed such a confession?''

"I grant all this, my Prince. That the two apparitions were mere contrivances of art; that the Sicilian has imposed upon us a tale which the Armenian, his master, had previously taught him; that the efforts of both have been directed to the same end, and, from this mutual intelligence, all the wonderful incidents which have astonished us in this adventure, may be easily explained. But the prophecy in the Square of St. Mark, that first miracle, which, as it were, opened the door to all the rest, still remains unexplained; and of what use is the key to all his other wonders, if we despair of resolving this single one?''

"Rather invert the proposition, my dear Count," answered the Prince. "and say, what do all these wonders prove, if I can demon-

strate that a single one among them is a jug-gling trick? The prediction, I own, is totally beyond my conception. If it stood alone; if the Armenian had closed the scene with it, instead of beginning it, I confess I do not know how far I might have been carried. But, in the base alloy with which it is mixed, it is certainly rather suspicious. Time may explain, or not explain it; but believe me, my friend!" added the Prince, taking my hand, with a grave countenance—"a man, who can command supernatural powers has no occasion to employ the arts of a juggler; he despises them."

"Thus," says Count O——, "ended a con-versation which I have related word for word, because it shows the difficulties which were to be overcome before the Prince could be effec-tually imposed upon; and I hope it may free his memory from the imputation of having blindly and inconsiderately thrown himself into a snare, which was spread for his destruc-tion, by the most unexampled and diabolical wickedness. Not all," continues Count O——, "who, at the moment I am writing. smile con-temptuously at the Prince's credulity, and, in the fancied superiority of their own yet un-tempted understanding, unconditionally con-demn him; not all of these, I apprehend, would have stood his first trial so courageously. If afterwards, notwithstanding this providen-tial warning, we witness his downfall; if we see that the black design against which, at the very outset, he was thus cautioned, is finally successful, we shall be less inclined to ridicule his weakness, than to be astonished at the infamous ingenuity of a plot which could seduce an understanding so fully pre-pared. Considerations of worldly interest can have no influence upon my testimony; he, who alone would be thankful for it, is now no more. His dreadful destiny is accom-plished; his soul has long since been purified before the throne of truth, where mine will likewise have appeared before these passages meet the eyes of the world. His was a noble character, and would have adorned a throne which, seduced by the most atrocious artifice, he attempted to ascend by the commission of crime.

SECOND BOOK.

"NOT long after these events," continues Count O——, in his narrative, "I began to observe an extraordinary alteration in the disposition of the Prince, which was partly the immediate consequence of the last event, and partly produced by the concurrence of many adventitious circumstances. Hitherto he had avoided every severe trial of his faith, and contented himself with purifying the rude and abstract notions of religion, in which he had been educated, by those more rational ideas upon this subject which forced themselves upon his attention, or comparing the many discordant opinions with each other, without inquiring into the foundations of his faith. Religious subjects, he has many times confessed to me, always appeared to him like an enchanted castle, into which one does not set one's foot without horror, and that they act therefore much the wiser part, who pass it in respectful silence, without exposing themselves to the danger of being bewildered in its labyrinths. A servile and bigoted education was the source of this dread: this had impressed frightful images upon his tender brain, which, during the remainder of his life, he was never able wholly to obliterate. Religious melancholy was an hereditary disorder in his family. The education which he and his brothers had received was calculated to produce it; and the men to whose care they were intrusted, selected with this object, were also either enthusiasts or hypocrites.

"To stifle all the sprightliness of the boy, by a gloomy restraint of his mental faculties, was the only method of securing to themselves the highest approbation of his royal parents. The whole of our Prince's childhood wore a dark and gloomy aspect; mirth was banished even from his amusements. All his ideas of religion were accompanied by some frightful image, and the representations of terror and severity were those which first took hold of his lively imagination, and which the longest retained their empire over it. His God was an object of terror, a being whose occupation is to chastise; and the adoration

he paid him, was either slavish fear, or a blind submission which stifled all his energies. In all his youthful propensities, which a vigorous growth and a fine constitution naturally excited to break out with the greater violence, religion stood in his way; it opposed everything upon which his young heart was bent; he learned to consider it not as a friend, but as the scourge of his passions; so that a silent indignation was gradually kindled against it in his heart, which, together with a bigoted faith and a blind fear, produced an incongruous mixture of feelings, and an abhorrence of a ruler before whom he trembled.

"It is no wonder, therefore, that he took the first opportunity of escaping from so galling a yoke—but he fled from it as a bond-slave who, escaping from his rigorous master, drags along with him a sense of his servitude, even in the midst of freedom; for, as he did not renounce the faith of his earlier years from a deliberate conviction, and did not wait till the maturity and improvement of his reasoning had weaned him from it, but escaped from it like a fugitive, upon whose person the rights of his master are still in force, so was he obliged, even after his widest separation, to return to it at last. He had escaped with his chain, and for that reason must necessarily become the prey of any one who should discover it, and know how to make use of the discovery. That such a one presented himself, the sequel of this history will prove; most likely the reader has already surmised it.

"The confessions of the Sicilian left a deeper impression upon his mind than they ought, considering the circumstances; and the small victory which his reason had thence gained over this weak imposture, remarkably increased his reliance upon his own powers. The facility with which he had been able to unravel this deception, appeared to have surprised him. Truth and error were not yet so accurately distinguished from each other in his mind, but that he often mistook the arguments which were in favor of the one for those in favor of the other. Thence it arose, that the same blow which destroyed his faith in wonders, made the whole edifice of it totter. In this instance, he fell into the same error as an inexperienced man who has been deceived in love or friendship, because he happened to make a bad choice, and who denies the existence of these sensations, because he takes the occasional exceptions for distinguishing features. The unmasking of a deception made even truth suspicious to him, because he had unfortunately discovered truth by false reasoning.

"This imaginary triumph pleased him in proportion to the magnitude of the oppression from which it seemed to deliver him. From this instant there arose in his mind a skepticism which did not spare even the most sacred objects.

"Many circumstances concurred to encourage, and still more to confirm, him in this turn of mind. He now quitted the retirement in which he had hitherto lived, and gave way to a more dissipated mode of life. His rank was discovered; attentions which he was obliged to return, etiquettes for which he was indebted to his rank, drew him imperceptibly within the vortex of the great world. His rank, as well as his personal attractions, opened to him the circles of all the *beaux esprits* in Venice, and he soon found himself on terms of intimacy with the most enlightened persons in the republic, men of learning as well as politicians. This obliged him to enlarge the monotonous and limited circle to which his understanding had hitherto been confined. He began to perceive the poverty and feebleness of his ideas, and to feel the want of more elevated impressions. The old-fashioned turn of his understanding, in spite of the many advantages with which it was accompanied, formed an unpleasing contrast with the current ideas of society; his ignorance of the commonest things frequently exposed him to ridicule, than which he dreaded nothing more. The unfortunate prejudice which attached to his native country appeared to him a challenge to overcome it in his own person. Besides this, there was a peculiarity in his character; he was offended with every attention that he thought was paid him on account of his rank, rather than his personal qualities. He felt this humiliation principally in the company of persons who shone by their abilities, and triumphed, as it were, over their birth by their merit. To perceive himself distinguished as a prince, in such a society, was always a deep humiliation to him, because he

unfortunately fancied himself excluded by his rank from all competition. These circumstances convinced him of the necessity of cultivating his mind, in order to raise it to a level with the thinking part of the world, from which he had hitherto been so separated; and for that purpose he chose the most modern books, and applied himself to them with all the ardor with which he was accustomed to pursue every object to which he devoted himself. But the unskilful hand that directed his choice always prompted him to select such as were little calculated to improve either his heart or his reason; besides that, he was influenced by a propensity which rendered everything irresistible which was incomprehensible. He had neither attention nor memory for anything that was not of that character, and both his reason and his heart remained untouched, while he was filling the vacuities of his brain with confused ideas. The dazzling style of some writers captivated his imagination, while the subtlety of others ensnared his reason. Together, they easily took possession of a mind which became the prey of whatever was obtruded upon it with a certain degree of dogmatism. A course of reading, which had been continued with ardor for more than a year, had scarcely enriched him with one benevolent idea, but had filled his head with doubts, which as a natural consequence with such a character, had almost found an unfortunate road to his heart. In a word, he had entered this labyrinth as a credulous enthusiast, had left it as a skeptic, and at length became a perfect free-thinker.

"Among the circles into which he had been introduced, there was a private society called the Bucentauro, which, under the mask of a noble and rational liberality of sentiment, encouraged the most unbridled licentiousness of manners and opinion. As it enumerated many of the clergy among its members, and could even boast of some cardinals at its head, the Prince was the more easily induced to join it. He thought that certain dangerous truths, which reason discovers, could be nowhere better preserved than in the hands of such persons, whose rank compelled them to moderation, and who had the advantage of hearing and examining the other side of the question. The Prince did not recollect that licentiousness of sentiment and manners takes so much the stronger hold among persons of this rank, inasmuch as they for that reason feel one curb less; and this was the case with the

Bucentauro; most of whose members, through an execrable philosophy, and manners worthy of such a guide, were not only a disgrace to their own rank, but even to human nature itself. The society had its secret degrees; and I will believe, for the credit of the Prince, that they never thought him worthy of admission into the inmost sanctuary. Every one who entered this society was obliged, at least so long as he continued to be a member of it, to lay aside all distinctions arising from rank, nation, or religion; in short, every general mark or distinction whatever, and to submit himself to the condition of universal equality. To be elected a member was indeed a difficult matter, as superiority of understanding alone paved the way to it. The society boasted of the highest ton and the most cultivated taste, and such indeed was its fame throughout all Venice. This, as well as the appearance of equality which predominated in it, attracted the Prince irresistibly. Sensible conversations, set off by the most admirable humor, instructive amusements, and the flower of the learned and political world, which were all attracted to this point as to their common centre, concealed from him for a long time the danger of this connection. As he by degrees discovered, through its mask, the spirit of the institution, as they grew tired of being any longer on their guard before him, to recede was dangerous, and false shame and anxiety for his safety obliged him to conceal the displeasure he felt. But he already began, merely from familiarity with men of this class and their sentiments, though they did not excite him to imitation, to lose the pure and charming simplicity of his character, and the delicacy of his moral feelings. His understanding, supported by real knowledge, could not, without foreign assistance, solve the fallacious sophisms with which he had been here ensnared; and this fatal poison had already destroyed all, or nearly all, the basis on which his morality rested. He surrendered the natural and indispensable safeguards of his happiness for sophisms which deserted him at the critical moment, and he was consequently left to the operation of any specious argument which came in his way.

"Perhaps the hand of a friend might yet have been in time to extricate him from this abyss; but, acquainted with the real character of the Bucentauro till long after the evil had taken place, an urgent circumstance called me away

from Venice just at the beginning of this period. Lord Seymour, too, a valuable acquaintance of the Prince's, whose cool understanding was proof against every species of deception, and who would have infallibly been a secure support to him, left us at this time in order to return to his native country. Those in whose hands I left the Prince were indeed worthy men, but inexperienced, excessively narrow in their religious opinions, deficient in their perception of the evil, and wanting in credit with the Prince. They had nothing to oppose to his captious sophisms, except the maxims of a blind and uninquiring faith, which either irritated him or excited his ridicule. He saw through them too easily, and his superior reason soon silenced those weak defenders of the good cause, as will be clearly evinced from an instance which I shall introduce in the sequel. Those who, subsequent to this, possessed themselves of his confidence, were much more interested in plunging him deeper into error. When I returned to Venice in the following year how great a change had already taken place in everything!

"The influence of this new philosophy soon showed itself in the Prince's conduct. The more openly he pursued pleasure, and acquired new friends, the more did he lose in the estimation of his old ones. He pleased me less and less every day; we saw each other more seldom, and indeed he was seldom accessible. He had launched out into the torrent of the great world. His threshold was eternally thronged when he was at home. Amusements, banquets, and galas followed each other in rapid succession. He was the idol whom every one courted—the great attraction of every circle. In proportion as he in his secluded life had fancied living in society to be difficult, did he to his astonishment find it easy. Everything met his wishes. Whatever he uttered was admirable, and when he remained silent it was like committing a robbery upon the company. They understood the art of drawing his thoughts insensibly from his soul, and then with a little delicate management to surprise him with them. This happiness, which accompanied him everywhere, and this universal success, raised him indeed too much in his own ideas, because it gave him too much confidence and too much reliance upon himself.

"The heightened opinion which he thus acquired of his own worth, made him credit the excessive and almost idolatrous adoration

223

that was paid to his understanding; which, but for this increased self complacency, must have necessarily recalled him from his aberrations. For the present, however, this universal voice was only a confirmation of what his complacent vanity whispered in his ear—a tribute which he felt entitled to by right. He would have infallibly disengaged himself from this snare, had they allowed him to take breath —had they granted him a moment of uninterrupted leisure to compare his real merit with the picture that was exhibited to him in this seducing mirror; but his existence was a continued state of intoxication, a whirl of excitement. The higher he had been elevated, the more difficulty had he to support himself in this elevation. This incessant exertion slowly undermined him—rest had forsaken even his slumbers. His weakness had been discovered, and the passion kindled in his breast turned to good account.

"His worthy attendants soon found to their cost that their lord had become a wit. That anxious sensibility, those glorious truths which his heart once embraced with the greatest enthusiasm, now began to be the objects of his ridicule. He revenged himself on the great truths of religion for the oppression which he had so long suffered from misconception. But, since from too true a voice his heart combated the intoxication of his head, there was more of acrimony than of humor in his jests. His disposition began to alter, and caprice to exhibit itself. The most beautiful ornament of his character, his modesty, vanished—parasites had poisoned his excellent heart. That tender delicacy of address which frequently made his attendants forget that he was their lord, now gave place to a decisive and despotic tone, which made the more sensible impression, because it was not founded upon distinction of rank, for the want of which they could have consoled themselves, but upon an arrogant estimation of his own superior merit. When at home, he was attacked by reflections, that seldom made their appearance in the bustle of company; his own people scarcely ever saw him otherwise than gloomy, peevish and unhappy, whilst elsewhere a forced vivacity made him the soul of every circle. With the sincerest sorrow did we behold him treading this dangerous path, but in the vortex in which he was involved the feeble voice of friendship was no longer heard, and he was too much intoxicated to understand it.

"Just at the beginning of this epoch, an affair of the greatest consequence required my presence in the court of my sovereign, which I dared not postpone even for the dearest interests of friendship. An invisible hand, the agency of which I did not discover till long afterwards, had contrived to derange my affairs, and to spread reports concerning me which I was obliged to contradict by my presence. The parting from the Prince was painful to me, but did not affect him. The ties which united us had been severed for some time, but his fate had awakened all my anxiety: I, on that account, prevailed on the Baron von F—— to inform me by letter of every event, which he has done in the most conscientious manner. As I was, for a considerable time, no longer an eye-witness of these events, it will be allowable for me to introduce the Baron von F—— in my stead, and to fill up the gap in my narrative by the contents of his letters. Notwithstanding that the representation of my friend F—— is not always what I should have given, I would not alter any of his expressions, so that the reader will be enabled to discover the truth with very little trouble."

LETTER I.

Baron von F—— to Count von O——.

May 17.

I thank you, my most honored friend, for the permission you have given me to continue in your absence that confidential intercourse with you, which during your stay here formed my greatest pleasure. You must be aware that there is no one here with whom I can venture to open my heart on certain private matters. Whatever you may urge to the contrary, I detest the people here. Since the Prince has become one of them, and since we have lost your society, I feel solitary in the midst of this populous city. Z—— takes it less to heart, and the fair ones of Venice manage to make him forget the mortifications he is compelled to share with me at home. And why should he make himself unhappy? He desires nothing more in the Prince than a master, whom he could also find elsewhere— But I!—you know how deep an interest I feel in our Prince's weal and woe, and how much cause I have for doing so; I have now lived with him sixteen years, and seem to exist only

for his sake. As a boy of nine years old I first entered his service, and since that time we have never been separated. I have grown up under his eye—a long intercourse has insensibly attached me more and more to him—I have borne a part in all his adventures, great and small. Until this last unhappy year, I had been accustomed to look upon him in the light of a friend, or of an elder brother—I have basked in his smile as in the sunshine of a summer's day—no cloud hung over my happiness!—and all this must now go to ruin in this unlucky Venice!

Since your departure several changes have taken place in our establishment. The Prince of —d— arrived here last week, with a numerous and brilliant retinue, and has caused a new and tumultuous life in our circle. As he is so nearly related to our Prince, and as they are moreover at present upon pretty good terms, they will be very little apart during his sojourn, which I hear is to last until after the feast of the Ascension. A good beginning has already been made; for the last ten days our Prince has hardly had time to breathe. The Prince of —d— has all along been living in a very expensive way, which was excusable in him, as he will soon take his departure; but the worst of the business is that he has inoculated our Prince with his extravagance, because he could not well withdraw himself from his company, and, in the peculiar relation which exists between the two houses, thought it incumbent upon himself to assert the dignity of his own. We shall, moreover, depart from Venice in a few weeks, which will relieve the Prince from the necessity of continuing for any length of time this extraordinary expenditure.

The Prince of —d—, it is reported, is here on business of the —— order, in which he imagines that he plays an important part. That he has taken advantage of all the acquaintances of our Prince, you may readily imagine. He has been introduced with distinguished honor into the society of the Bucentauro, as he is pleased to consider himself a wit, and a man of great genius, and allows himself to be styled in his correspondences, which he keeps up throughout all parts of the world, the "Prince philosophique." I do not know whether you have ever had the pleasure of meeting him. He displays a promising exterior, piercing eyes, a countenance full of expression, much show of reading, much acquired naturalness (if I may be allowed the expression), joined to a princely condescension towards the human race, a large amount of confidence in himself, and an eloquence which talks down all opposition. Who could refuse to pay homage to such splendid qualities in a "Royal Highness?" But to what advantage the quiet and sterling worth of our Prince will appear, when contrasted with these dazzling accomplishments, the event must show.

In the arrangement of our establishment, various and important changes have taken place. We have rented a new and magnificent house opposite the new Procuracy, because the lodging at the Moor Hotel became too confined for the Prince. Our suit has been augmented by twelve persons, pages, Moors, guards, etc. During your stay here you complained of unnecessary expense—you should see us now!

Our internal arrangements remain the same as of old, except that the Prince, no longer held in check by your presence, is, if possible, more reserved and distant towards us than ever; we see very little of him, except while dressing or undressing him. Under the pretext that we speak the French language very badly, and the Italian not at all, he has found means to exclude us from most of his entertainments, which to me personally is not a very great grievance; but I believe I know the true reason of it—he is ashamed of us: and this hurts me, for we have not deserved it of him.

As you wish to know all our minor affairs, I must tell you, that of all his attendants, the Prince almost exclusively employs Biondello, whom he took into his service, as you will recollect, on the disappearance of his huntsman, and who, in his new mode of life, has become quite indispensable to him. This man knows Venice thoroughly, and turns everything to some account. It is as though he had a thousand eyes, and could set a thousand hands in motion at once. This he accomplishes, as he says, by the help of the gondoliers. To the Prince he renders himself very useful by making him acquainted with all the strange faces that present themselves at his assemblies, and the private information he gives his highness has always proved to be correct. Besides this, he speaks and writes both Italian and French excellently, and has in consequence already risen to be the Prince's secretary. I must, however, relate to you an instance of fidelity in him which is rarely found among

people of his station. The other day, a merchant of good standing from Rimini requested an audience of the Prince. The object of his visit was an extraordinary complaint concerning Biondello. The Procurator, his former master, who must have been rather an odd fellow, had lived in irreconcilable enmity with his relations; this enmity he wished if possible to continue even after his death. Biondello possessed his entire confidence, and was the repository of all his secrets; while on his death-bed, he obliged him to swear that he would keep them inviolably, and would never disclose them for the benefit of his relations; a handsome legacy was to be the reward of his silence. When the deceased Procurator's will was opened, and his papers inspected, many blanks and irregularities were found, to which Biondello alone could furnish a key. He persisted in denying that he knew anything about it, gave up his very handsome legacy to the heirs, and kept his secrets to himself. Large offers were made to him by the relations, but all in vain; at length, in order to escape from their importunities and their threats of legally prosecuting him, he entered the service of the Prince. The merchant, who was the chief heir, now applied to the Prince, and made larger offers than before, if Biondello would alter his determination. But even the persuasions of the Prince were fruitless. He admitted that secrets of consequence had really been confided to him; he did not deny that the deceased had perhaps carried his enmity towards his relations too far; but, added he, he was my dear master and benefactor, and died with a firm belief in my integrity. I was the only friend he had left in the world, and will therefore never prove myself unworthy of his confidence. At the same time, he hinted that the avowals they wished him to make would not tend to the honor of the deceased. Was not that acting nobly and delicately? You may easily imagine that the Prince did not renew his endeavors to shake so praiseworthy a determination. The extraordinary fidelity which he has shown towards his deceased master has procured him the unlimited confidence of his present one!

Farewell, my dear friend. How I sigh for the quiet life we led when first you came amongst us, for the stillness of which your society so agreeably indemnified us. I fear my happy days in Venice are over, and shall be glad if the same remark does not also apply

to the Prince. The element in which he now lives is not calculated to render him permanently happy, or my sixteen years' experience has deceived me.

LETTER II.

BARON VON F—— TO COUNT VON O——.

June 4th.

I should never have thought that our stay at Venice would have been productive of any good consequences. It has been the means of saving a man's life, and I am reconciled to it.

Some few evenings ago the Prince was being carried home, late at night, from the Bucentauro; two domestics, of whom Biondello was one, accompanied him. By some accident it happened that the sedan, which had been hired in haste, broke down, and the Prince was obliged to proceed the remainder of the way on foot. Biondello walked in front; their course lay through several dark, retired streets, and, as daybreak was at hand, the lamps were either burning dimly or had gone out altogether. They had proceeded about a quarter of an hour, when Biondello discovered that he had lost his way. The similarity of the bridges had deceived him, and, instead of crossing that of St. Mark, they found themselves in Sestiere di Castello. It was in a by-street, and not a soul was stirring; they were obliged to turn back, in order to gain a main street by which to set themselves right. They had proceeded but a few paces when they heard cries of "Murder" in a neighboring street. With his usual determined courage, the Prince, unarmed as he was, snatched a stick from one of his attendants, and rushed forward in the direction whence the sound came. Three ruffianly-looking fellows were just about to assassinate a man, who with his companion was feebly defending himself; the Prince appeared just in time to arrest the fatal blow. The voices of the Prince and his followers alarmed the murderers, who did not expect any interruption in so lonely a place; after inflicting a few slight wounds with their daggers, they abandoned their victim and took to their heels. Exhausted with the unequal combat, the wounded man sunk half fainting into the arms of the Prince; his companion informed my master that the man whose life he had

saved was the Marquis Civitella, a nephew of the Cardinal A——i. As the Marquis's wounds bled freely, Biondello acted as surgeon, to the best of his ability, and the Prince took care to have him conveyed to the palace of his uncle, which was near at hand, and whither he himself accompanied him. This done, he left the house without revealing his name.

This, however, was discovered by a servant who had recognized Biondello. Already on the following morning, the Cardinal, an old acquaintance from the Bucentauro, waited upon the Prince. The interview lasted an hour; the Cardinal was much moved; tears stood in his eyes when they parted; the Prince, too, was affected. The same evening a visit was paid the sick man, of whose case the surgeon gives a very favorable report; the mantle in which he was wrapped had rendered the thrusts unsteady, and weakened their force. Since this event not a day has passed without the Prince's paying a visit at the Cardinal's, or receiving one from him, and a close intimacy has begun to exist between him and the Cardinal's family.

The Cardinal is a venerable man of sixty, with a majestic aspect, but full of gayety and good health. He is said to be the richest prelate throughout all the dominions of the republic. He is reported to manage his immense fortune in a very liberal manner, and, although prudently economical, to despise none of the joys of this life. This nephew, who is his sole heir, is not always on the best of terms with his uncle. For, although the Cardinal is anything but an enemy to youthful pleasures, the conduct of the nephew must exhaust the utmost tolerance. His loose principles and dissipated manner of living, aided unhappily by all the attractions which can make vice tempting, and excite sensuality, have rendered him the terror of all fathers, and the bane of all husbands; this last attack also was said to have been caused by an intrigue he had begun with the wife of the —— Ambassador, without speaking of other serious broils from which the power and the money of the Cardinal could scarcely extricate him. But for this the Cardinal would be the happiest man in Italy, for he possesses everything that can make life agreeable; but by this one domestic misfortune all the gifts of fortune are annulled, and the enjoyment of his wealth is embittered to the Cardinal, by the continual fear of finding nobody to inherit it.

The whole of this information I have obtained from Biondello. The Prince has found in this man a real treasure. Every day he becomes more indispensable, and we are continually discovering in him some new talent. Some days ago the Prince felt feverish and could not sleep; the night-lamp was extinguished, and all his ringing failed to arouse the valet-de-chambre, who had gone to sleep out of the house with an opera-dancer. At length the Prince determined to rise himself, and to rouse one of his people. He had not proceeded far, when a strain of delicious melody met his ear. Like one enchanted, he followed the sound, and found Biondello in his room playing the flute, with his fellow-servants assembled around him. The Prince could hardly believe his senses, and commanded him to proceed. With a surprising degree of facility he began to vary a touching adagio air with some fine extempore variations, which he executed with all the taste of a virtuoso. The Prince, who, as you know, is a judge of music, says that he might play with confidence in the finest choir in Italy.

"I must dismiss this man," said he to me next morning, "for I am unable to reward him according to his merits." Biondello, who had overheard these words, came forward. "If you dismiss me, gracious Prince," said he, "you deprive me of my best reward."

"You are born to something better than to serve," answered my master. "I must not stand in the way of your fortune."

"Do not press upon me any better fortune, gracious sir, than that which I have chosen for myself."

"To neglect talent like yours——No! I can never permit it."

"Then permit me, gracious sir, sometimes to exercise it in your presence."

Preparations were immediately made for carrying this proposition into effect. Biondello had a room assigned to him next the apartment of the Prince, so that he can lull him to sleep with his strains, and wake him in the same manner. The Prince wished to double his salary, but Biondello declined, requesting that this intended boon should be retained in his master's hands as a capital of which he might some day wish to avail himself. The Prince expects that he will soon come to ask a favor at his hands; and whatever it may be, it is granted beforehand.

Farewell, dearest friend. I am waiting with impatience for tidings from K——n.

LETTER III.

BARON VON F—— TO COUNT VON O——.

June 4th.

The Marquis of Civitella, who is now entirely recovered from his wounds, was last week introduced to the Prince by his uncle the Cardinal, and since then he has followed him like his shadow. Biondello cannot have told me the truth respecting this Marquis, or at any rate his account must be greatly exaggerated. His mien is highly engaging, and his manners irresistibly winning. It is impossible to be out of humor with him; the first sight of him has disarmed me. Imagine a man of the most enchanting figure, none of that contemptuous pride, none of that solemn starchness, which we disliked so much in all the other nobles. His whole being is redolent of youthful joyousness, benevolence and warmth of feeling. His excesses must have been much exaggerated; I never saw a more perfect picture of health. If he is really so wholly abandoned as Biondello represents him, he is a syren whom none can resist.

Towards me he behaved with much frankness. He confessed with the most pleasing sincerity that he was by no means on the best of terms with his uncle the Cardinal, and that it was his own fault. But he was seriously resolved to amend his life, and the merit would be entirely the Prince's. At the same time, he hoped through his instrumentality to be reconciled to his uncle, as the Prince's influence with the Cardinal was unbounded. The only thing he had wanted, till now, was a friend and a guide, and he trusted he should find both in the person of the Prince.

The Prince has now assumed the authority of a preceptor towards him, and treats him with all the watchfulness and strictness of a Mentor. But this intimacy also gives the Marquis a certain degree of influence, of

which he well knows how to avail himself. He hardly stirs from his side; he is present at all parties where the Prince is one of the guests; for the Bucentauro alone he is fortunately as yet too young. Wherever he appears in public with the Prince, he manages to draw him away from the rest of the company, by the pleasing manner in which he engages him in conversation, and arrests his attention. Nobody, they say, has yet been able to reclaim him, and the Prince will deserve to be immortalized in an epic, should he accomplish such an Herculean task. I am much afraid, however, that the tables may be turned, and the guide be led away by the pupil, of which, in fact, there seems to be every prospect.

The Prince of —d— has taken his departure, much to the satisfaction of us all, my master not excepted. What I predicted, my dear O——, has come to pass. Two characters so widely opposed must inevitably clash together, and cannot maintain a good understanding for any length of time. The Prince of —d— had not been long in Venice before a terrible schism took place in the intellectual world, which threatened to deprive our Prince of one-half of his admirers. Wherever he went he was crossed by this rival, who possessed exactly the requisite amount of small cunning to avail himself of every little advantage he gained. As he besides never scrupled to make use of any petty manœuvres to increase his consequence, he in a short time drew all the weak-minded of the community on his side, and shone at the head of a company of parasites worthy of such a leader.* The wiser course would certainly have been, not to enter into competition at all with an adversary of this description, and a few months back this is the part which the Prince would have taken. But now he has launched too far into the stream easily to regain the shore. These trifles have, perhaps by the circumstances in which he is placed, acquired a certain degree of importance in his eyes, and had he even despised them, his pride would

not have allowed him to retire at a moment when his yielding would have been looked upon less as a voluntary act, than as a confession of inferiority. Added to this, an unlucky revival of forgotten satirical speeches had taken place; and the spirit of rivalry which took possession of his followers had affected the Prince himself. In order, therefore, to maintain that position in society, which public opinion had now assigned him, he deemed it advisable to seize every possible opportunity of display and of increasing the number of his admirers; but this could only be affected by the most princely expenditure; he was, therefore, eternally giving feasts, entertainments, and expensive concerts, making costly presents, and playing high. As this strange madness, moreover, had also infected the Prince's retinue, who are generally much more punctilious in respect to what they deem "the honor of the family" than their masters, the Prince was obliged to assist the zeal of his followers by his liberality. Here, then, is a whole catalogue of ills, all irremediable consequences of a sufficiently excusable weakness, to which the Prince, in an unguarded moment, gave way!

We have, it is true, got rid of our rival, but the harm he has done will not so soon be remedied. The finances of the Prince are exhausted; all that he had saved by the wise economy of years is spent; and he must hasten from Venice, if he would escape plunging into debt, which till now he has most scrupulously avoided. It is decisively settled that we leave as soon as fresh remittances arrive.

I should not have minded all this splendor if the Prince had but reaped the least real satisfaction from it. But he was never less happy than at present! He feels that he is not what he formerly was—he seeks to regain his self-respect—he is dissatisfied with himself, and launches into fresh dissipation, in order to drown the recollection of the last. One new acquaintance follows another, and each involves him more deeply. I know not where this will end. We must away—there is no other chance of safety—we must away from Venice.

But, my dear friend, I have not yet received a single line from you! How am I to interpret this long and obstinate silence?

* The harsh judgment which Baron F—— (both here and in some passages of his first letter) pronounces upon this talented Prince, will be found exaggerated by every one who has the good fortune to be acquainted with him, and must be attributed to the prejudiced views of the young observer.—*Note of the Count von O——.*

LETTER IV.

BARON VON F—— TO COUNT VON O——.

June 12th.

I thank you, my dear friend, for the token of your remembrance which young B——hl brought me. But what is it you say about letters I ought to have received? I have received no letter from you; not a single line. What a circuitous route must they have taken! In future, dear O——, when you honor me with an epistle, despatch it, viâ Trent, under cover to the Prince, my master.

We have at length been compelled, my dear friend, to resort to a measure which till now we had so happily avoided. Our remittances have failed to arrive—failed, for the first time, in this pressing emergency, and we have been obliged to have recourse to a usurer, as the Prince is willing to pay handsomely to keep the affair secret. The worst of this disagreeable occurrence is, that it retards our departure. On this affair the Prince and I have had an explanation. The whole transaction had been arranged by Biondello, and the son of Israel was there, before I had any suspicion of the fact. It grieved me to the heart to see the Prince reduced to such an extremity, and revived all my recollections of the past and fears for the future, and I suppose I may have looked rather sorrowful and gloomy when the usurer left the room. The Prince, whom the foregoing scene had left in not the happiest frame of mind, was pacing angrily up and down the room; the rouleaus of gold were still lying on the table; I stood at the window counting the panes of glass in the procurator's house opposite. There was a long pause. At length the Prince broke silence. "F——!" he began, "I cannot bear to see dismal faces about me."

I remained silent.

"Why do you not answer me? Do I not perceive that your heart is almost bursting to vent some of its vexation? I insist on your speaking, otherwise you will begin to fancy that you are keeping some terrible momentous secret."

"If I am gloomy, gracious sir," replied I, "it is only because I do not see you cheerful."

"I know," continued he, "that you have been dissatisfied with me for some time past— that you disapprove of every step I take—that —what does Count O—— say in his letters?"

"Count O—— has not written to me."

"Not written? Why do you deny it? You keep up a confidential correspondence together, you and the Count; I am quite aware of that. Come, you may confess it, for I have no wish to pry into your secrets."

"Count O——," replied I, "has not yet answered any of the three letters which I have written to him."

"I have done wrong," continued he; "don't you think so?" (taking up one of the rouleaus) "I should not have done this?"

"I see that it was necessary."

"I ought not to have reduced myself to such a necessity?"

I did not answer.

"Oh, of course! I ought never to have indulged my wishes, but have grown gray in the same dull manner in which I was brought up! Because I once venture a step beyond the drear monotony of my past life, and look around me, to see whether there be not some new source of enjoyment in store for me— because I—"

"If it was but a trial, gracious sir, I have no more to say; for the experience you have gained would not be dearly bought at three times the price it has cost. It grieves me, I confess, to think that the opinion of the world should be concerned in determining the question—how you are to choose your own happiness."

"It is well for you that you can afford to despise the world's opinion," replied he; "I am its creature, I must be its slave. What are we princes but opinion? With us it is everything. Public opinion is our nurse and preceptor in infancy, our oracle and idol in riper years, our staff in old age. Take from us what we derive from the opinion of the world, and the poorest of the humblest class is in a better position than we, for his fate has taught him a lesson of philosophy which enables him to bear it. But a prince who laughs at the world's opinion destroys himself, like the priest who denies the existence of a God."

"And yet, gracious Prince—"

"I see what you would say; I can break through the circle which my birth has drawn around me. But can I also eradicate from my memory all the false impressions which education and early habit have implanted, and which a hundred thousand fools have been continually laboring to impress more and more firmly? Everybody naturally wishes

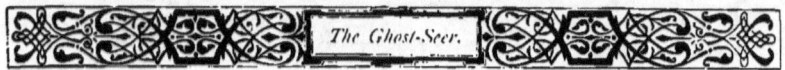

whole aim of a prince's existence is to APPEAR
HAPPY. If we cannot be happy after your
fashion, is that any reason why we should
discard all other means of happiness, and not
be happy at all? If we cannot drink of joy
pure from the fountain head, can there be any
reason why we should not beguile ourselves
with artificial pleasure—nay, even be content
to accept a sorry substitute from the very hand
that robs us of the higher boon?"

"You were wont to look for this compensation in your own heart."

"But if I no longer find it there?—Oh,
how came we to fall on this subject? Why
did you revive these recollections in me? I
had recourse to this tumult of the senses in
order to stifle an inward voice, which embit-
ters my whole life—in order to lull to rest
this inquisitive reason, which, like a sharp
sickle, moves to and fro in my brain, at each
new research lopping off another branch of
my happiness!"

"My dearest Prince!"—He had risen and
was pacing up and down the room in unusual
agitation.*

"When everything gives way before me
and behind me—when the past lies in the distance in dreary monotony, like a city of the
dead—when the future offers me nought—
when I see my whole being enclosed within
the narrow circle of the present—who can
blame me if I clasp this niggardly present
of time in my arms with fiery eagerness, as
though it were a friend whom I was embracing
for the last time? Oh, I have learned to
value the present moment! The present
moment is our mother—let us love it as
such!"

"Gracious sir, you were wont to believe in
a more lasting good."

"Do but make the enchantment last, and
fervently will I embrace it. But what pleasure can it give to me to render beings happy

* I have endeavored, dearest O——, to relate to you
this remarkable conversation exactly as it occurred;
but this I found impossible, although I sat down to
write it the evening of the day it took place. In order
to assist my memory, I was obliged to transpose the
observation of the Prince, and thus this compound of a
conversation and a philosophical lecture, which is, in
some respects, better, and in others worse, than the
source from which I took it, arose; but I assure you
that I have rather omitted some of the Prince's words
than ascribe to him any of my own; all that is mine is
the arrangement, and a few observations, whose owner-
ship you will easily recognize by their stupidity.—Note
of the Baron von F——.

who to-morrow will have passed away like
myself? Is not everything passing away
around me? Each one bustles and pushes
his neighbor aside hastily to catch a few drops
from the fountain of life, and then departs
thirsting. At this very moment, while I am
rejoicing in my strength, some being is waiting to start into life at my dissolution. Show
me one being who will endure, and I will become a virtuous man."

"But what then has become of those benevolent sentiments which used to be the joy
and the rule of your life? To sow seeds for
the future, to assist in carrying out the designs
of a high and eternal providence—"

"Future! eternal providence!—If you take
away from man all that he derives from his
own heart, all that he associates with the idea
of a Godhead, and all that belongs to the law
of nature,—what then do you leave him?"

"What has already happened to me, and
what may still follow, I look upon as two
black impenetrable curtains hanging over the
two extremities of human life, and which no
mortal has ever yet drawn aside. Many hundred generations have stood before the second
of these curtains, casting the light of their
torches upon its folds, speculating and guess-
ing as to what it may conceal. Many have
beheld themselves, in the magnified image of
their passions, reflected upon the curtain which
hides futurity from their gaze, and have turned
away shuddering from their own shadows.
Poets, philosophers and statesmen have painted
their fancies on the curtain, in brighter or
more sombre colors, according as their own
prospects were bright or gloomy. Many a
juggler has also taken advantage of the universal curiosity, and by well-managed deceptions led astray the excited imagination. A
deep silence reigns behind this curtain; no
one who passes beyond it answers any questions; all the reply is an empty echo, like
the sound yielded by a vault. Sooner or later
all must go behind this curtain, and they approach it with fear and trembling, in doubt
who may be waiting there behind to receive
them; quid sit id, quod tantum morituri vident.
There have been infidels who asserted that
this curtain only deluded mankind, and that
we saw nothing behind it, because there was
nothing there to see; but, to convince them,
they were quickly sent behind it themselves."

"It was, indeed a rash conclusion," said I,
"if they had no better ground for it than that
they saw nothing themselves."

"You see, my dear friend, I am modest enough not to wish to look behind this curtain, and the wisest course will doubtless be, to abstain from all curiosity. But while I draw this impassable circle around me, and confine myself within the bounds of present existence, this small point of time, which I was in danger of neglecting in useless researches, becomes the more important to me. What you call the chief end and aim of my existence concerns me no longer. I cannot escape my destiny; I cannot promote its consummation; but I know, and firmly believe, that I am here to accomplish some end, and that I do accomplish it. But the means which nature has chosen to fulfil my destiny are so much the more sacred to me—to me it is everything—my morality, my happiness. All the rest I shall never learn. I am like a messenger who carries a sealed letter to its place of destination. What the letter contains is indifferent to him—his business is only to earn his fee for carrying it."

"Alas!" said I, "how poor a thing you would leave me!"

"But in what a labyrinth have we lost ourselves!" exclaimed the Prince, looking with a smile at the table on which the rouleaus lay. "After all perhaps not far from the mark," continued he; "you will now no doubt understand my reasons for this new mode of life. I could not so suddenly tear myself away from my fancied wealth, could not so readily separate the props of my morality and happiness from the pleasing dream with which everything within me was so closely bound up. I longed for the frivolity which seems to render the existence of most of those about me endurable to themselves. Everything which precluded reflection was welcome to me. Shall I confess it to you? I wished to lower myself, in order to destroy this source of my griefs, by deadening the power of reflection."

Here we were interrupted by a visit. In my next I shall have to communicate to you a piece of news, which, from the tenor of a conversation like the one of to-day, you would scarcely have anticipated.

LETTER V.

BARON VON F—— TO COUNT VON O——.

As the time of our departure from Venice is now approaching with rapid steps, this week was to be devoted to seeing everything worthy of notice in pictures and public edifices; a task which, when one intends making a long stay in a place, is always delayed till the last moment.

The "Marriage at Cana," by Paul Veronese, which is to be seen in a Benedictine convent in the island of St. George, was in particular mentioned to us in high terms. Do not expect me to give you a description of this extraordinary work of art, which, on the whole, made a very surprising, but not equally pleasing, impression on me. We should have required as many hours as we had minutes to study a composition of one hundred and twenty figures, upon a ground thirty feet broad. What human eye is capable of grasping so complicated a whole, or at once to enjoy all the beauty which the artist has everywhere lavished upon it! It is, however, to be lamented, that a work of so much merit, which if exhibited in some public place, would command the admiration of every one, should be destined merely to ornament the refectory of a few monks. The church of the monastery is no less worthy of admiration, being one of the finest in the whole city. Towards evening we went in a gondola to the Guidecca, in order to spend the pleasant hours of evening in its charming garden. Our party, which was not very numerous, soon dispersed in various directions; and Civitella, who had been waiting all day for an opportunity of speaking to me privately, took me aside into an arbor.

"You are a friend of the Prince," he began, "from whom he is accustomed to keep no secrets, as I know from very good authority. As I entered his hotel to-day, I met a man coming out, whose occupation is well known to me, and when I entered the room, the Prince's brow was clouded."—I wished to interrupt him—"You cannot deny it," continued he; "I knew the man, I looked at him well. And is it possible that the Prince should have a friend in Venice—a friend who owes his life to him, and yet be reduced on an emergency to make use of such creatures?

"Tell me frankly, Baron! Is the Prince in difficulties? It is in vain you strive to conceal it from me. What! you refuse to tell me! I can easily learn from one who would sell any secret for gold."

"My good Marquis—"

"Pardon me! I must appear intrusive, in order not to be ungrateful. To the Prince I

am indebted for life, and, what is still more, for a reasonable use of it. Shall I stand idly by, and see him take steps which, besides being inconvenient to him, are beneath his dignity? Shall I feel it in my power to assist him, and hesitate for a moment to step forward?"

"The Prince," replied I, "is not in difficulties. Some remittances which we expected *via* Trent have not yet arrived, most likely either by accident, or because not feeling certain whether he had not already left Venice, they waited for a communication from him. This has now been done, and until their arrival—"

Civitella shook his head. "Do not mistake my motive," said he; "in this there can be no question as to diminishing the extent of my obligations towards the Prince, which all my uncle's wealth would be insufficient to cancel. My object is simply to spare him a few unpleasant moments. My uncle possesses a large fortune, which I can command as freely as though it were my own. A fortunate circumstance occurs, which enables me to avail myself of the only means by which I can possibly be of the slightest use to your master. I know," continued he, "how much delicacy the Prince possesses, but the feeling is mutual, and it would be noble on his part to afford me this slight gratification, were it only to make me appear to feel less heavily the load of obligation under which I labor."

He continued to urge his request, until I had pledged my word to assist him to the utmost of my ability. I knew the Prince's character, and had but small hopes of success. The Marquis promised to agree to any conditions the Prince might impose, but added, that it would deeply wound him to be regarded in the light of a stranger.

In the heat of our conversation we had strayed far away from the rest of our company, and were returning, when Z—— came to meet us.

"I am in search of the Prince," he cried; "is he not with you?"

"We were just going to him," was our reply. "We thought to find him with the rest of the party."

"The company is altogether, but he is nowhere to be found, I cannot imagine how we lost sight of him."

It now occurred to Civitella that he might have gone to look at the adjoining church, which had a short time before attracted his attention. We immediately went to look for him there. As we approached, we found Biondello waiting in the porch. On coming nearer, we saw the Prince emerge hastily from a side door; his countenance was flushed, and he looked anxiously round for Biondello, whom he called. He seemed to be giving him very particular instructions for the execution of some commission, while his eyes continued constantly fixed on the church door, which had remained open. Biondello hastened into the church. The Prince, without perceiving us, passed through the crowd, and went back to his party, which he reached before us.

We resolved to sup in an open pavilion of the garden, where the Marquis had, without our knowledge, arranged a little concert, which was quite first-rate. There was a young singer in particular, whose delicious voice and charming figure excited general admiration. Nothing, however, seemed to make an impression on the Prince; he spoke little, and gave confused answers to our questions; his eyes were anxiously fixed in the direction whence he expected Biondello; and he seemed much agitated. Civitella asked him what he thought of the church; he was unable to give any description of it. Some beautiful pictures, which rendered the church remarkable, were spoken of; the Prince had not noticed them. We perceived that our questions annoyed him, and therefore discontinued them. Hour after hour rolled on, and still Biondello returned not. The Prince could no longer conceal his impatience; he rose from the table, and paced alone, with rapid strides, up and down a retired walk. Nobody could imagine what had happened to him. I did not venture to ask him the reason of so remarkable a change in his demeanor; I have for some time past resigned my former place in his confidence. It was, therefore, with the utmost impatience that I awaited the return of Biondello to explain this riddle to me.

It was past ten o'clock when he made his appearance. The tidings he brought did not make the Prince more communicative. He returned in an ill-humor to the company, the gondola was ordered, and we returned home.

During the remainder of that evening I could find no opportunity of speaking to Biondello, and was therefore obliged to retire to my pillow with my curiosity unsatisfied. The Prince had dismissed us early, but a

thousand reflections flitted across my brain, and kept me awake. For a long time I could hear him pacing up and down his room ; at length sleep overcame me. Late at midnight I was awakened by a voice, and I felt a hand passed across my face ; I opened my eyes, and saw the Prince standing at my bedside, with a lamp in his hand. He told me he was unable to sleep, and begged me to keep him company through the night. I was going to dress myself, but he told me to stay where I was, and seated himself at my bedside.

" Something has happened to me, to-day," he began, " the impression of which will never be effaced from my soul. I left you, as you know, to see the —— church, respecting which Civitella had raised my curiosity, and which had already attracted my attention. As neither you nor he were at hand, I walked the short distance alone, and ordered Biondello to wait for me at the door. The church was quite empty ; a dim and solemn light surrounded me as I entered, from the blazing sultry day without. I stood alone in the spacious building, throughout which there reigned the stillness of the grave. I placed myself in the centre of the church, and gave myself up to the feelings which the sight was calculated to produce ; by degrees, the grand proportions of this majestic building expanded to my gaze, and I stood wrapt in deep and pleasing contemplation. Above me, the evening bell was tolling ; its tones died softly away in the aisles, and found an echo in my heart. Some altar-pieces at a distance attracted my attention. I approached to look at them ; unconsciously I had wandered through one side of the church, and was now standing at the opposite end. Here, a few steps raised round a pillar, led into a little chapel, containing several small altars, with statues of saints in the niches above them. On entering the chapel on the right, I heard a whispering, as though some one near me was speaking in a low voice. I turned towards the spot whence the sound proceeded, and saw before me a female form. No ! I cannot describe to you the beauty of this form. My first feeling was one of awe, which, however, soon gave place to ravishing surprise."

" But this figure, your highness ? Are you certain that it was something living, something real, and not perhaps a picture, or an illusion of your fancy ?"

" Hear me further. It was a lady. Surely, till that moment, I have never seen her sex in its full perfection ! All around was sombre ; the setting sun shone through a single window into the chapel, and its rays rested upon her figure. With inexpressible grace, half kneeling, half lying, she was stretched before an altar ;—one of the most striking, most lovely, and picturesque objects in all nature. Her dress was of black moreen, fitting tightly to her slender waist and beautifully-formed arms, the skirts spreading around her, like a Spanish robe ; her long, light-colored hair was divided into two broad plaits, which, apparently from their own weight, had escaped from under her veil, and flowed in charming disorder down her back. One of her hands grasped the crucifix, and her head rested gracefully upon the other. But, where shall I find words to describe to you the angelic beauty of her countenance, in which the charms of a seraph seemed displayed. The setting sun shone full upon her face, and its golden beams seemed to surround it, as with a glory. Can you recall to your mind the Madonna of our Florentine painter ?—She was here personified, even to those few deviations from the studied costume, which so powerfully, so irresistibly attracted me in the picture."

With regard to the Madonna, of whom the Prince spoke, the case is this :—Shortly after your departure, he made the acquaintance of a Florentine painter, who had been summoned to Venice, to paint an altar-piece for some church, the name of which I do not recollect. He had brought with him three paintings, which had been intended for the gallery in the Cornari palace. They consisted of a Madonna, a Heloise, and a Venus, very lightly apparelled. All three were of great beauty ; and, although the subjects were quite different, they were so intrinsically equal, that it seemed almost impossible to determine which to prefer. The Prince alone did not hesitate for a moment. As soon as the pictures were placed before him, the Madonna absorbed his whole attention ; in the two others, he admired the painter's genius—but in this, he forgot the artist and his art, his whole soul being absorbed in the contemplation of the work. He was quite moved, and could scarcely tear himself away from it. We could easily see, by the artist's countenance, that in his heart he coincided with the Prince's judgment ; he obstinately refused to separate the pictures, and demanded 1500 zechins for the three. The Prince offered him half that sum for the Madonna alone, but in vain. The artist insisted

THE GHOST-SEER.

THE FAIR GREEK AT PRAYER.

on his first demand, and who knows what might have been the result if a ready purchaser had not stepped forward. Two hours afterwards all three pictures were sold, and we never saw them again. It was this Madonna which now recurred to the Prince's mind.

"I stood," continued he. "gazing at her in silent admiration. She did not observe me; my arrival did not disturb her, so completely was she absorbed in her devotion. She prayed to her Deity, and I prayed to her—yes, I adored her!—All the pictures of saints, all the altars and the burning tapers around me, had failed to remind me of what now for the first time burst upon me, that I was in a sacred place. Shall I confess it to you? In that moment I believed firmly in Him, whose image was clasped in her beautiful hand. I read in her eyes that he answered her prayers. Thanks be to her charming devotion, it had revealed Him to me.—I wandered with her through all the paradise of prayer.

"She rose, and I recollected myself. I stepped aside, confused; but the noise I made in moving discovered me. I thought that the unexpected presence of a man might alarm, that my boldness would offend her; but neither of these feelings were expressed in the look with which she regarded me. Peace, benign peace, was portrayed in her countenance, and a cheerful smile played upon her lips. She was descending from her heaven—and I was the first happy mortal who met her benevolent look. Her mind was still wrapt in her concluding prayer—she had not yet come in contact with earth.

"I now heard something stir in the opposite corner of the chapel. It was an elderly lady, who rose from a cushion close behind me. Till now I had not observed her. She had been distant only a few steps from me, and must have seen my every motion. This confused me. I cast my eyes to the earth, and both the ladies passed by me."

On this last point I thought myself able to console the Prince.

"Strange." continued he, after a long silence, "that there should be something which one has never known—never missed; and that yet, on a sudden, one should seem to live and breathe for that alone! Can one single moment so completely metamorphose a human being? It would now be as impossible for me to indulge in the wishes, or enjoy the pleasures of yesterday, as it would be to return to the toys of my childhood; and all this since I have seen this object, which lives and rules in the inmost recesses of my soul. It seems to say that I can love nothing else, and that nothing else in this world can produce an impression on me."

"But consider, gracious Prince," said I, "the excitable mood you were in, when this apparition surprised you, and how all the circumstances conspired to inflame your imagination. Quitting the dazzling light of day, and the busy throng of men, you were suddenly surrounded by twilight and repose. You confess that you had quite given yourself up to those solemn emotions which the majesty of the place was calculated to awaken—the contemplation of fine works of art had rendered you more susceptible to the impressions of beauty in any form. You supposed yourself alone—when you saw a maiden, who, I will readily allow, may have been very beautiful, and whose charms were heightened by a favorable illumination of the setting sun, a graceful attitude, and an expression of fervent devotion—what is more natural than that your vivid fancy should look upon such a form as something supernaturally perfect?"

"Can the imagination give what it never received?" replied he. "In the whole range of my fancy, there is nothing which I can compare with that image. It is impressed on my mind distinctly and vividly as in the moment when I beheld it. I can think of nothing but that picture—but you might offer me whole worlds for it in vain."

"My gracious Prince, this is love."

"Must the sensation which makes me happy necessarily have a name? Love! Do not degrade my feeling by giving it a name, which is so often misapplied by the weak-minded. Who ever felt before what I do now? Such a being never before existed; how then can the name be admitted before the emotion which it is meant to express? Mine is a novel and peculiar feeling, connected only with this being, and capable of being applied to her alone. Love! From love I am secure!"

"You sent away Biondello, no doubt, to follow in the steps of these strangers, and to make inquiries concerning them? What news did he bring you?"

"Biondello discovered nothing; or, at least, as good as nothing. An aged, respectably dressed man, who looked more like a citizen than a servant, came to conduct them to their gondola. A number of poor people placed themselves in a row, and quitted her, apparently well satisfied. Biondello said he saw one of her hands, which was ornamented with several precious stones. She spoke a few words, which Biondello could not comprehend, to her companion; he says it was Greek. As she had some distance to walk to the canal, the people began to throng together, attracted by the strangeness of her appearance. Nobody knew her—but beauty seems born to rule. All made way for her, in a respectful manner. She let fall a black veil, that covered half of her person, over her face, and hastened into the gondola. Along the whole Guidecca, Biondello managed to keep the boat in view, but the crowd prevented his following it further."

"But surely he took notice of the gondolier, so as to be able to recognize him again."

"He has undertaken to find out the gondolier, but he is not one of those with whom he associates. The mendicants, whom he questioned, could give him no further information than that the Signora had come to the church for the last few Saturdays, and had each time divided a gold piece among them. It was a Dutch ducat, which Biondello changed for them, and brought to me."

"It appears, then, that she is a Greek—most likely of rank; at any rate, rich and charitable. That is as much as we dare venture to conclude at present, gracious sir; perhaps too much. But a Greek lady in a Catholic church?"

"Why not? She may have changed her religion. But there is certainly some mystery in the affair. Why should she go only once a week? Why always on Saturday, on which day, as Biondello tells me, the church is generally deserted. Next Saturday, at the latest, must decide this question. Till then, dearest friend, you must help me to while away the hours. But it is in vain. They will go their lingering pace, though my soul is burning with expectation!"

"And when this day at length arrives—what then, gracious Prince? What do you purpose doing?"

"What do I purpose doing? I shall see her. I will discover where she lives, and who she is. But to what does all this tend? I hear you ask. What I saw made me happy; I therefore now know wherein my happiness consists!"

"And our departure from Venice, which is fixed for next Monday?"

"How could I know that Venice still contained such a treasure for me? You ask me questions of my past life. I tell you that from this day forward I will begin a new existence."

"I thought that now was the opportunity to keep my word to the Marquis. I explained to the Prince that a protracted stay in Venice was altogether incompatible with the exhausted state of his finances, and that, if he extended his sojourn here beyond the appointed time, he could not reckon on receiving funds from his court. On this occasion, I learned what had hitherto been a secret to me, namely, that the Prince had, without the knowledge of his other brothers, received from his sister, the reigning —— of ——, considerable loans, which she would gladly double, if his court left him in the lurch. This sister, who, as you know, is a pious enthusiast, thinks that the large savings which she makes at a very economical court, cannot be deposited in better hands than in those of a brother whose wise benevolence she well knows, and whose character she warmly honors. I have, indeed, known for some time that a very close intercourse has been kept up between the two, and that many letters have been exchanged; but, as the Prince's own resources have hitherto always been sufficient to cover his expenditure, I had never guessed at this hidden channel. It is clear, therefore, that the Prince must have had some expenses which have been and still are unknown to me; but if I can judge of them by his general character, they will certainly not be of such a description as to tend to his disgrace. And yet I thought I understood him thoroughly. After this disclosure, I of course did not hesitate to make known to him the Marquis's offer, which, to my no small surprise, he immediately accepted. He gave me the authority to transact the business with the Marquis in whatever way I thought most advisable, and then immediately to settle the account with the usurer. To his sister he proposed to write without delay.

It was morning when we separated. However disagreeable this affair is to me for more than one reason, the worst of it is, that it seems to threaten a longer residence in Venice. From the Prince's passion, I rather augur good than evil. It is, perhaps, the most powerful method of withdrawing him from his meta-

physical dreams to the concerns and feelings of real life. It will have its crisis, and, like an illness produced by artificial means, will eradicate the natural disorder.

Farewell, my dear friend. I have written down these incidents immediately upon their occurrence. The post starts immediately; you will receive this letter on the same day as my last.

LETTER VI.

BARON VON F—— TO COUNT VON O——.

June 20th.

This Civitella is certainly one of the most obliging personages in the world. The Prince had scarcely left me the other day, before I received a note from the Marquis, enforcing his former offers with renewed earnestness. I instantly forwarded him, in the Prince's name, a bond for 6000 zechins; in less than half an hour it was returned, with double the sum required, in notes and gold. The Prince at length assented to this increase, but insisted that the bond, which was drawn only for six weeks, should be accepted.

The whole of the present week has been consumed in inquiries after the mysterious Greek. Biondello set all his engines to work, but until now in vain. He certainly discovered the gondolier; but from him he could learn nothing, save that the ladies had disembarked on the island of Murano, where they entered two sedan chairs which were waiting for them. He supposed them to be English because they spoke a foreign language, and had paid him in gold. He did not even know their guide, but believed him to be a glass manufacturer from Murano. We were now, at least, certain that we must not look for her in the Guidecca, and that in all probability she lived in the island of Murano; but, unluckily, the description the Prince gave of her was not such as to make her recognizable by a third party. The passionate interest with which he had regarded her had hindered him from observing her minutely; for all the minor details, which other people would not have failed to notice, had escaped his observation; from his description, one would have sooner expected to find her prototype in the works of Ariosto or Tasso than on a Venetian island. Besides, our inquiries had to be conducted with the utmost caution, in order not to become prejudicial to the lady,

or to excite undue attention. As Biondello was the only man besides the Prince who had seen her, even through her veil, and could therefore recognize her, he strove to be as much as possible in all the places where she was likely to appear; the life of the poor man, during the whole week, was on a continual race through all the streets of Venice. In the Greek church, particularly, every inquiry was made, but always with the same ill success; and the Prince, whose impatience increased with every successive failure, was at last obliged to wait till Saturday, with what patience he might. His restlessness was excessive. Nothing interested him, nothing could fix his attention. He was in constant feverish excitement; he fled from society, but the evil increased in solitude. He had never been so much besieged by visitors as in this week. His approaching departure had been announced, and everybody crowded to see him. It was necessary to occupy the attention of the people in order to lull their suspicions, and to amuse the Prince with the view of diverting his mind from its all engrossing object. In this emergency Civitella hit upon play; and, for the purpose of driving away most of the visitors, proposed that the stakes should be high. He hoped by awakening in the Prince a transient liking for play, from which it would afterwards be easy to wean him, to destroy the romantic bent of his passion. "The cards," said Civitella, "have saved me from many a folly which I had intended to commit, and repaired many which I had already perpetrated. At the faro table I have often recovered my tranquillity of mind, of which a pair of bright eyes had robbed me, and women never had more power over me than when I had not money enough to play."

I will not enter into a discussion as to how far Civitella was right; but the remedy we had hit upon soon began to be worse than the disease it was intended to cure. The Prince, who could only make the game at all interesting to himself by staking extremely high, soon overstepped all bounds. He was quite out of his element. Everything he did seemed to be done in a passion; all his actions betrayed the uneasiness of his mind. You know his general indifference to money; he seemed now to have become totally insensible to its value. Gold flowed through his hands like water. As he played without the slightest caution he lost almost invariably. He lost

immense sums, for he staked like a desperate gamester. Dearest O——, with an aching heart I write it, in four days he had lost above 12,000 zechins.

Do not reproach me. I blame myself sufficiently. But how could I prevent it? Could I do more than warn him? I did all that was in my power, and cannot find myself guilty. Civitella, too, lost not a little; I won about 600 zechins. The unprecedented ill luck of the Prince excited general attention, and, therefore, he would not leave off playing. Civitella, who is always ready to oblige him, immediately advanced him the required sum. The deficit is made up, but the Prince owes the Marquis 24,000 zechins. Oh! how I long for the savings of his pious sister! Are all sovereigns so, my dear friend? The Prince behaves as though he had done the Marquis a great honor, and he, at any rate, plays his part well.

Civitella sought to quiet me by saying, that this recklessness, this extraordinary ill luck, would be most effectual in bringing the Prince to his senses. The money, he said, was of no consequence. He himself would not feel the loss in the least, and would be happy to serve the Prince at any moment with three times the amount. The Cardinal also assured me that his nephew's intentions were honest, and that he should be ready to assist him in carrying them out.

The most unfortunate thing was, that these tremendous sacrifices did not even effect their object. One would have thought that the Prince would at least feel some interest in his play. But such was not the case. His thoughts were wandering far away, and the passion which we wished to stifle, by his ill luck in play, seemed, on the contrary, only to gather strength. When, for instance, a decisive stroke was about to be played, and every one's eyes were fixed full of expectation on the board, his were searching for Biondello, in order to catch the news he might have brought him, from the expression of his countenance. Biondello brought no tidings, and his master's losses continued.

The gains, however, fell into the needy hands. A few "*your Excellencies*," whom scandal reports to be in the habit of carrying home their frugal dinner from the market in their senatorial caps, entered our house as beggars, and left it with well-lined purses. Civitella pointed them out to me. "Look," said he, "how many poor devils make their

fortunes by one great man taking a whim into his head! This is what I like to see. It is princely and royal. A great man must, even by his failings, make some one happy, like a river, which, by its overflowing, fertilizes the neighboring fields."

Civitella has a noble and generous way of thinking, but—the Prince owes him 24,000 zechins!

At length the long-wished for Saturday arrived, and my master insisted upon going, directly after dinner, to the —— church. He stationed himself in the chapel where he had first seen the unknown, but in such a way as not to be immediately observed. Biondello had orders to keep watch at the church door, and to enter into conversation with the attendant of the ladies. I had taken upon myself to enter, like a chance passenger, into the same gondola with them on their return, in order to follow their track, if the other schemes should fail. At the spot where the gondolier said he had landed them the last time, two sedans were stationed; the Chamberlain Z—— was ordered to follow in a separate gondola, in order to trace the retreat of the unknown, if all else should fail. The Prince wished to give himself wholly up to the pleasure of seeing her, and, if possible, try to make her acquaintance in the church. Civitella was to keep out of the way altogether, as his reputation among the women of Venice was so bad that his presence could not have failed to excite the suspicions of the lady. You see, dear Count, it was not through any want of precaution on our part that the fair unknown escaped us.

Never, perhaps, were there offered up in any church such ardent prayers for success, and never were hopes so cruelly disappointed. The Prince waited till after sunset, starting in expectation at every sound which approached the chapel, and at every creaking of the church door. Seven full hours passed, and no Greek lady! I need not describe his state of mind. You know what hope deferred is—hope which one has nourished unceasingly for seven days and seven nights.

LETTER VII.

Baron von F—— to Count von O——.

July.

The mysterious unknown of the Prince reminded Marquis Civitella of a romantic inci-

238

dent, which happened to himself a short time since, and, to divert the Prince, he offered to relate it. I will give it you in his own words; but the lively spirit which he infuses into all he tells will be lost in my narration.

(Here follows the subjoined fragment, which appeared in the eighth part of the Thalia, and was originally intended for the second volume of the Ghost-Seer. It found a place here, after Schiller had given up the idea of completing the Ghost-Seer).

"In the spring of last year," began Civitella, "I had the misfortune to embroil myself with the Spanish ambassador, a gentleman who, in his 70th year, had been guilty of the folly of wishing to marry a Roman girl of eighteen. His vengeance pursued me, and my friends advised me to secure my safety by a timely flight, and to keep out of the way until the hand of nature, or an adjustment of differences, had secured me from the wrath of this formidable enemy. As I felt it too severe a punishment to quit Venice altogether, I took up my abode in a distant quarter of the town, where I lived in a lonely house, under a feigned name, keeping myself concealed by day, and devoting the night to the society of my friends, and to pleasure.

"My windows looked upon a garden, the west side of which was bounded by the walls of a convent, while towards the east it jutted out into the Laguna, in the form of a little peninsula. The garden was charmingly situated, but little frequented. It was my custom every morning, after my friends had left me, to spend a few moments at the window before retiring to rest, to see the sun rise over the Adriatic, and then to bid him good night. If you, my dear Prince, have not yet enjoyed this pleasure, I recommend exactly this station, the most eligible one, perhaps, in all Venice, to enjoy so splendid a prospect in perfection. A purple twilight hangs over the deep, and a golden mist on the Laguna announces the sun's approach. The heavens and the sea are wrapped in expectant silence. In two seconds the orb of day appears casting a flood of fiery light on the waves. It is an enchanting sight!

"One morning, when I was, according to custom, enjoying the beauty of this prospect, I suddenly discovered that I was not the only spectator of the scene. I fancied I heard voices in the garden, and turning to the quarter whence the sound proceeded, I perceived a gondola steering for the land. In a few moments I saw figures walking at a slow pace up the avenue. They were a man and a woman, accompanied by a little negro. The female was clothed in white, and had a brilliant on her finger; it was not light enough to perceive more.

"My curiosity was raised. Doubtless a rendezvous of a pair of lovers—but in such a place, and at so unusual an hour! It was scarcely three o'clock, and everything was still veiled in dusky twilight. The incident seemed to me novel, and proper for a romance, and I waited to see the end.

"I soon lost sight of them among the foliage of the garden, and some time elapsed before they again emerged to view. Meanwhile a delightful song was heard. It proceeded from the gondolier, who was in this manner shortening the time, and was answered by a comrade a short way off. They sang stanzas from Tasso; time and place were in unison, and the melody sounded sweetly in the profound silence around.

"Day in the mean time had dawned, and objects were discerned more plainly. I sought my people, whom I found walking hand-in-hand up a broad walk, often standing still, but always with their back turned towards me, and proceeding further from my residence. Their noble, easy carriage, convinced me at once that they were people of rank, and the splendid figure of the lady made me augur as much of her beauty. They appeared to converse little; the lady, however, more than her companion. In the spectacle of the rising sun, which now burst out in all its splendor, they seemed to take not the slightest interest.

"While I was employed in adjusting my glass, in order to bring them into view as closely as possible, they suddenly disappeared down a side path, and some time elapsed before I regained sight of them. The sun had now fully risen; they were approaching straight towards me, with their eyes fixed upon where I stood. What a heavenly form did I behold! Was it illusion, or the magic effect of the beautiful light? I thought I beheld a supernatural being, for my eyes quailed before the angelic brightness of her look.—So much loveliness, combined with so much dignity!—so much mind, and so much blooming youth! It is in vain I attempt to describe it. I had never seen true beauty till that moment.

"In the heat of conversation they lingered near me, and I had full opportunity to contemplate her. Scarcely, however, had I cast

my eyes upon her companion, but even her beauty was not powerful enough to fix my attention. He appeared to be a man still in the prime of life, rather slight, and of a tall, noble figure. Never have I beheld so much mind, so much noble expression in a human countenance. Though perfectly secured from observation, I was unable to meet the lightning glance that shot from beneath his dark eyebrows. There was a moving expression of sorrow about his eyes, but an expression of benevolence about the mouth which relieved the settled gravity spread over his whole countenance. A certain cast of features, not quite European, together with his dress, which appeared to have been chosen with inimitable good taste from the most varied costumes, gave him a peculiar air, which not a little heightened the impression produced by his appearance. A degree of wildness in his looks warranted the supposition that he was an enthusiast, but his deportment and carriage showed that his character had been formed by mixing in society."

Z——, who you know must always give utterance to what he thinks, could contain himself no longer. "Our Armenian!" cried he. "Our very Armenian, and nobody else."

"What Armenian, if one may ask?" inquired Civitella.

"Has no one told you of the farce?" replied the Prince. "But no interruption! I begin to feel interested in your hero. Pray continue your narrative."

"There was something inexplicable in his whole demeanor," continued Civitella. "His eyes were fixed upon his companion with an expression of anxiety and passion, but the moment they met hers, he looked down abashed. 'Is the man beside himself?' thought I. I could stand for ages and gaze at nothing else but her.

"The foliage again concealed them from my sight. Long, long did I look for their re-appearance, but in vain. At length I caught sight of them from another window.

"They were standing before the basin of a fountain, at some distance apart, and both wrapped in deep silence. They had, probably, remained some time in the same position. Her clear and intelligent eyes were resting inquiringly on his, and seemed as if they would imbibe every thought from him as it revealed itself in his countenance. He, as if he wanted courage to look directly into her face, furtively sought its reflection in the watery

mirror before him, or gazed steadfastly at the dolphin which bore the water to the basin. Who knows how long this silent scene might have continued could the lady have endured it? With the most bewitching grace, the lovely girl advanced towards him, and passing her arm round his neck, raised his hand to her lips. Calmly and unmoved the strange being suffered her caresses, but did not return them.

"This scene moved me strangely. It was the man that chiefly excited my sympathy and interest. Some violent emotion seemed to struggle in his breast; it was as if some irresistible force drew him towards her, while an unseen arm held him back. Silent, but agonizing, was the struggle, and beautiful the temptation. 'No,' I thought, 'he attempts too much; he will, he must yield.'

"At his silent intimation the young negro disappeared. I now expected some touching scene—a prayer on bended knees, and a reconciliation sealed with glowing kisses. But no! nothing of the kind occurred. The incomprehensible being took from his pocket-book a sealed packet, and placed it in the hands of the lady. Sadness overcast her face as she looked at it, and a tear bedewed her eye.

"After a short silence they separated. At this moment an elderly lady advanced from one of the side walks, who had remained at a distance, and whom I now first discovered. She and the fair girl slowly advanced along the path, and, while they were earnestly engaged in conversation, the stranger took the opportunity of remaining behind. With his eyes turned towards her he stood irresolute, at one instant making a rapid step forward, and in the next retreating. In another moment, he had disappeared in the copse.

"The women at length look around, seem uneasy at not finding him, and pause as if to await his coming. He comes not! Anxious glances are cast around, and steps are redoubled. My eyes aid in searching through the garden; he comes not, he is nowhere to be seen.

"Suddenly I hear a plash in the canal, and see a gondola moving from the shore. It is he, and I scarcely can refrain from calling to him. Now the whole thing is clear—it was a parting.

"She appears to have a presentiment of what has happened. With a speed that her companion cannot use, she hastens to the shore. Too late! Quick as the arrow in its flight,

the gondola bounds forward, and soon nothing is visible but a white handkerchief fluttering in the air from afar. Soon after this, I saw the fair *incognita* and her companion cross the water.

"When I awoke from a short sleep I could not help smiling at my delusion. My fancy had incorporated these events in my dreams, until truth itself seemed a dream. A maiden, fair as a houri, wandering beneath my windows at break of day with her lover—and a lover who did not know how to make a better use of such an hour! Surely these supplied materials for the composition of a picture which might well occupy the fancy of a dreamer! But the dream had been too lovely for me

not to desire its renewal again and again; nay, even the garden had become more charming in my sight since my imagination had peopled it with such attractive forms. Several cheerless days that succeeded this eventful morning drove me from the window, but the first fine evening involuntarily drew me back to my post of observation. Judge of my surprise, when, after a short search, I caught sight of the white dress of my *incognita*! Yes, it was she herself. I had not dreamed!

"Her former companion was with her, and led by the hand a little boy; but the fair girl herself walked apart, and seemed absorbed in thought. All spots were visited that had been

rendered memorable by the presence of her friend. She paused for a long time before the basin, and her fixed gaze seemed to seek on its crystal mirror the reflection of one beloved form.

"Although her noble beauty had attracted me when I first saw her, the impression produced was even stronger on this occasion; although, perhaps, at the same time more conducive to gentler emotions. I had now ample opportunity of considering this divine form; the surprise of the first impression gradually gave place to softer feelings. The glory that seemed to invest her had departed, and I saw before me the loveliest of women, and felt my senses inflamed. In a moment the resolution was formed that she must be mine.

"While I was deliberating whether I should descend and approach her, or whether, before I ventured on such a step, it would not be better to obtain information regarding her, a door opened in the convent wall, through which there advanced a Carmelite monk. The sound of his approach roused the lady, and I saw her advance with hurried steps towards him. He drew from his bosom a paper, which she eagerly grasped, while a vivid color instantaneously suffused her countenance.

"At this moment I was called from the window by the arrival of my usual evening visitor. I carefully avoided approaching the spot again, as I had no desire to share my conquest with another. For a whole hour I was obliged to endure this painful constraint before I could succeed in freeing myself from my importunate guest, and when I hastened to the window all had disappeared.

"The garden was empty when I entered it; no vessel of any kind was visible in the canal; no trace of people on any side; I neither knew whence she had come, or whither she had gone. While I was looking round me in all directions, I observed something white upon the ground. On drawing near, I found it was a piece of paper folded in the shape of a note. What could it be but the letter which the Carmelite had brought? 'Happy discovery!' I exclaimed; 'this will reveal the whole secret, and make me master of her fate.'

"The letter was sealed with a sphinx—had no superscription, and was written in ciphers; this, however, did not discourage me, for I have some knowledge of this mode of writing. I copied it hastily, as there was every reason

to expect that she would soon miss it and return in search of it. If she should not find it, she would regard its loss as an evidence that the garden was resorted to by different persons, and such a discovery might easily deter her from visiting it again. And what worse fortune could attend my hopes?

"That which I had conjectured actually took place, and I had scarcely ended my copy when she re-appeared with her former companion, anxiously intent on the search. I attached the note to a tile which I had detached from the roof, and dropped it at a spot which she would pass. Her gracefully expressed joy at finding it rewarded me for my generosity. She examined it in every part with keen searching glances, as if she were seeking to detect the unhallowed hand that might have touched it; but the contented look with which she hid it in her bosom showed that she was free from all suspicion. She went, and the parting glance she threw on the garden seemed expressive of gratitude to the guardian deities of the spot, who had so faithfully watched over the secret of her heart.

"I now hastened to decipher the letter. After trying several languages, I at length succeeded by the use of English. Its contents were so remarkable that my memory still retains a perfect recollection of them ——"

I am interrupted, and must give you the conclusion on a future occasion.

LETTER VIII.

BARON VON F—— TO COUNT VON O——.

August.

In truth, my dearest friend, you do the good Biondello injustice. The suspicion you entertain against him is unfounded, and, while I allow you full liberty to condemn all Italians generally, I must maintain that *this* one at least is an honest man.

You think it singular that a person of such brilliant endowments and such exemplary conduct should debase himself to enter the service of another if he were not actuated by secret motives, and these, you further conclude, must necessarily be of a suspicious character. But where is the novelty of a man of talent and of merit endeavoring to win favor with a Prince who has the power of establishing his fortune? Is there anything

derogatory in serving the Prince? and has not Biondello clearly shown that his devotion is purely personal by confessing that he earnestly desired to make a certain request of the Prince? The whole mystery will, therefore, no doubt be revealed when he acquaints him with his wishes. He may certainly be actuated by secret motives, but why may these not be innocent in their nature?

You think it strange that this Biondello should have kept all his great talents concealed, and in no way have attracted attention during the early months of our acquaintance with him, when you were still with us. This I grant; but what opportunity had he then of distinguishing himself? The Prince had not yet called his powers into requisition, and chance, therefore, could alone aid us in discovering his talents.

He very recently gave a proof of his devotion and honesty of purpose, which must at once annihilate all your doubts. The Prince was watched; measures were being taken to gain information regarding his mode of life, associates and general habits. I know not with whom this inquisitiveness originated. Let me beg your attention, however, to what I am about to relate:

There is a house in St. George's which Biondello is in the habit of frequenting. He probably finds some peculiar attractions there, but of this I know nothing. It happened, a few days ago, that he there met assembled together a party of civil and military officers in the service of the Government, old acquaintances and jovial comrades of his own. Surprise and pleasure were expressed on all sides at this meeting. Their former good fellowship was re-established; and after each in turn had related his own history up to the present time, Biondello was called upon to give an account of his life: this he did in a few words. He was congratulated on his new position; his companions had heard accounts of the splendid footing on which the Prince of ——'s establishment was maintained; of his liberality, especially to persons who showed discretion in keeping secrets; the Prince's connection with the Cardinal A——i was well known, he was said to be addicted to play, etc. Biondello's surprise at this is observed, and jokes are passed upon the mystery which he tries to keep up, although it is well known that he is the emissary of the Prince of ——. The two lawyers of the party make him sit down between them; their glasses are re-

peatedly emptied, he is urged to drink, but excuses himself on the ground of his inability to bear wine; at last, however, he yields to their wishes, in order that he may the better pretend intoxication.

"Yes!" cried one of the lawyers, "Biondello understands his business, but he has not yet learned all the tricks of the trade; he is but a novice."

"What have I still to learn?" asked Biondello.

"You understand the art of keeping a secret," remarked the other; "but you have still to learn that of parting with it to advantage."

"Am I likely to find a purchaser for any that I may have to dispose of?" asked Biondello.

On this the other guests withdrew from the apartment, and left him alone with his two neighbors, who continued the conversation in the same strain. The substance of the whole was, however, briefly as follows: Biondello was to procure them certain information regarding the intercourse of the Prince with the Cardinal and his nephew, acquaint them with the sources from whence the Prince derived his money, and to intercept all letters written to Count O——. Biondello put them off to a future occasion, but he was unsuccessful in his attempts to draw from them the name of the person by whom they were employed. From the splendid nature of the proposals made to him, it was evident, however, that they emanated from some influential and extremely wealthy party.

Last night he related the whole occurrence to the Prince, whose first impulse was without further ceremony to secure the manœuverers at once, but to this Biondello strongly objected. He urged that he would be obliged to set them at liberty again, and that, in this case, he should endanger not only his credit among this class of men, but even his life. All these men were connected together, and bound by one common interest, each one making the cause of the others his own; in fact, he would rather make enemies of the Senate of Venice than be regarded by these men as a traitor—and, besides, he could no longer be useful to the Prince if he lost the confidence of this class of people.

We have pondered and conjectured much as to the source of all this. Who is there in Venice that can care to know what money my master receives or pays out, what passes

between Cardinal A——i and himself, and what I write to you? Can it be some scheme of the Prince of —d—, or is the Armenian again on the alert?

LETTER IX.

BARON VON F—— TO COUNT VON O——.

August.

The Prince is revelling in love and bliss. He has recovered his fair Greek. I must relate to you how this happened.

A traveller, who had crossed from Chiozza, gave the Prince so animated an account of the beauty of this place, which is charmingly situated on the shores of the gulf, that he became very anxious to see it. Yesterday was fixed upon for the excursion; and, in order to avoid all restraint and display, no one was to accompany him but Z—— and myself, together with Biondello, as my master wished to remain unknown. We found a vessel ready to start, and engaged our passage at once. The company was very mixed but not numerous, and the passage was made without the occurrence of any circumstance worthy of notice.

Chiozza is built like Venice, on a foundation of wooden piles, and is said to contain about forty thousand inhabitants. There are but few of the higher classes resident there, but one meets sailors and fishermen at every step. Whoever appears in a peruke, or a cloak, is regarded as an aristocrat—a rich man; the cap and overcoat are here the insignia of the poor. The situation is certainly very lovely, but it will not bear a comparison with Venice.

We did not remain long, for the captain, who had more passengers for the return voyage, was obliged to be in Venice at an early hour, and there was nothing at Chiozza to make the Prince desirous of remaining. All the passengers were on board when we reached the vessel. As we had found it so difficult to place ourselves on a social footing with the company on the outward passage, we determined on this occasion to secure a cabin to ourselves. The Prince inquired who the new comers were, and was informed that they were a Dominican and some ladies, who were returning to Venice. My master evincing no curiosity to see them, we immediately betook ourselves to our cabin.

The Greek was the subject of our conversa-

tion throughout the whole passage, as she had been during our former transit. The Prince dwelt with ardor on her appearance in the church; and whilst numerous plans were in turn devised and rejected, hours passed like a moment of time, and we were already in sight of Venice. Some of the passengers now disembarked, the Dominican amongst the number. The captain went to the ladies, who, as we now first learned, had been separated from us by only a thin wooden partition, and asked them where they wished to land. The island of Murano was named in reply to his inquiry, and the house indicated ——. " The island of Murano!" exclaimed the Prince, who seemed suddenly struck by a startling presentiment. Before I could reply to his exclamation, Biondello rushed into the cabin. " Do you know," asked he eagerly, "who is on board with us?" The Prince started to his feet, as Biondello continued, " She is here ! she herself ! I have just spoken to her companion !"

The Prince hurried out. He felt as if he could not breathe in our narrow cabin, and I believe at that moment as if the whole world would have been too narrow for him. A thousand conflicting feelings struggled for the mastery in his heart; and his knees trembled, and his countenance was alternately flushed and pallid. I sympathized and participated in his emotion, but I cannot by words convey to your mind any idea of the state in which he was.

When we stopped at Murano, the Prince sprang on shore. She advanced from her cabin. I read in the face of the Prince that it was indeed the Greek. One glance was sufficient to dispel all doubt on that point. A more lovely creature I have never seen. Even the Prince's glowing descriptions fell far short of the reality. A radiant blush suffused her face when she saw my master. She must have heard all we said, and could not fail to know that she herself had been the subject of our conversation. She exchanged a significant glance with her companion, which seemed to say, "That is he ;" and then cast her eyes to the ground with diffident confusion. On placing her foot on the narrow plank, which had been thrown from the vessel to the shore, she seemed anxiously to hesitate, less, as it seemed to me, from the fear of falling than from her inability to cross the board without assistance, which was proffered her by the outstretched arm of the Prince. Necessity overcame her reluctance, and, accepting the aid of his hand, she stepped on shore. Excessive mental agita-

tion had rendered the Prince uncourteous, and he wholly forgot to offer his services to the other lady—but what was there that he would not have forgotten at this moment? My attention in atoning for the remissness of the Prince prevented my hearing the commencement of a conversation which had begun between him and the young Greek, while I had been helping the other lady on shore.

He was still holding her hand in his, probably from absence of mind, and without being conscious of the fact.

"This is not the first time, Signora, that —that—" He stopped short, unable to finish the sentence.

"I think I remember—" She faltered.

"We met in the church of ——," said he, quickly.

"Yes, it was in the church of ——," she rejoined.

"And could I have supposed that this day would have brought me—"

Here she gently withdrew her hand from his —he was evidently embarrassed; but Biondello, who had in the mean time been speaking to the servant, now came to his aid.

"Signor," said he, "the ladies had ordered sedans to be in readiness for them; they have not yet come, for we are here before the expected time. But there is a garden close by, in which you may remain until the crowd has dispersed."

The proposal was accepted; you may conceive with what alacrity on the part of the Prince! We remained in the garden till late in the evening; and, fortunately, Z—— and myself so effectually succeeded in occupying the attention of the elder lady, that the Prince was enabled, undisturbed, to carry on his conversation with the fair Greek. You will easily believe that he made good use of his time, when I tell you that he obtained permission to visit her. At the very moment that I am now writing he is with her; on his return I shall be able to give you further particulars regarding her.

When we got home yesterday, we found that the long expected remittances had arrived from our court; but, at the same time, the Prince received a letter which excited his indignation to the highest pitch. He has been recalled, and that in a tone and manner to which he is wholly unaccustomed. He immediately wrote a reply in a similar spirit, and intends remaining. The remittances are only just sufficient to pay the interest on the capital which he owes. We are looking with impatience for a reply from his sister.

———

LETTER X.

BARON VON F—— TO COUNT VON O——.

September.

The Prince has fallen out with his court, and all resources have consequently been cut off from home.

The term of six weeks, at the end of which my master was to pay the Marquis, has already elapsed several days; but still no remittances have been forwarded, either from his cousin, of whom he had earnestly requested an additional allowance in advance, or from his sister. You may readily suppose that Civitella has not reminded him of his debt; the Prince's memory is, however, all the more faithful. Yesterday morning at length brought an answer from the seat of government.

We had shortly before concluded a new arrangement with the master of our hotel, and the Prince had publicly announced his intention to remain here some time longer. Without uttering a word my master put the letter into my hand. His eyes sparkled, and I could read the contents in his face.

Can you believe it, dear O——? all my master's proceedings here are known at—and have been most calumniously misrepresented by an abominable tissue of lies. "Information has been received"—says the letter, amongst other things—"to the effect that the Prince has for some time past belied his former character, and adopted a mode of conduct totally at variance with his former exemplary manner of acting and thinking." "It is known," the writer says, "that he has addicted himself with the greatest excess to women and play; that he is overwhelmed with debts; puts his confidence in visionaries and charlatans, who pretend to have power over spirits; maintains suspicious relations with Roman Catholic prelates, and keeps up a degree of state which exceeds both his rank and his means. Nay, it is even said that he is about to bring this highly offensive conduct to a climax, by apostacy to the church of Rome! and, in order to clear himself from this last charge, he is required to return immediately. A banker at Venice, to whom he must make known the true amount of his debts, has received instructions to satisfy his creditors im-

mediately after his departure; for, under existing circumstances, it does not appear expedient to remit the money directly into his hands."

What accusations, and what a mode of preferring them! I read the letter again and again, in the hope of discovering some expression that admitted of a milder construction, but in vain; it was wholly incomprehensible.

Z—— now reminded me of the secret inquiries which had been made some time before of Biondello. The true nature of the inquiries and circumstances all coincide. He had falsely ascribed them to the Armenian; but now the source from whence they came was very evident. Apostacy! But who can have any interest in calumniating my master so scandalously? I should fear it was some machination of the Prince of —d—, who is determined on driving him from Venice.

In the mean time the Prince remained absorbed in thought, with his eyes fixed on the ground. His continued silence alarmed me. I threw myself at his feet. "For God's sake, your Highness," I cried, "moderate your feelings—you will—nay, you shall have satisfaction. Leave the whole affair to me. Let *me* be your emissary. It is beneath your dignity to reply to such accusations; but you will not, I know, refuse me the privilege of doing so for you. The name of your calumniator must be given up, and ——'s eyes must be opened."

At this moment we were interrupted by the entrance of Civitella, who inquired with surprise into the cause of our agitation. Z—— and I did not answer; but the Prince, who has long ceased to make any distinction between him and us, and who, besides, was too much excited to listen to the dictates of prudence, desired me to communicate the contents of the letter to him. On my hesitating to obey him, he snatched the letter from my hand, and gave it to the Marquis.

"I am in your debt, Marquis," said he, as Civitella gave him back the letter, after perusing it, with evident astonishment— "but do not let that circumstance occasion you any uneasiness—grant me but a respite of twenty days, and you shall be fully satisfied."

"Do I deserve this at your hands, gracious Prince?" exclaimed Civitella, with extreme emotion.

"You have refrained from pressing me, and I gratefully appreciate your delicacy. In twenty days, as I before said, you shall be fully satisfied."

"But how is this?" asked Civitella with agitation and surprise. "What means all this? I cannot comprehend it!"

We explained to him all that we knew, and his indignation was unbounded. The Prince, he asserted, must insist upon full satisfaction—the insult was unparalleled. In the meanwhile he implored him to make unlimited use of his fortune and his credit.

When the Marquis left us the Prince still continued silent. He paced the apartment with quick and determined steps, as if some strange and unusual emotion were agitating his frame. At length he paused, muttering between his teeth, "Congratulate yourself—he died at ten o'clock!"

We looked at him in terror.

"Congratulate yourself," he repeated; "did he not say that *I should congratulate myself?* What could he have meant!"

"What has reminded you of those words?" I asked; "and what have they to do with the present business?"

"I did not then understand what the man meant—but now I do. Oh! it is intolerable to be subject to a master!"

"Gracious Prince!"

"Who can make us feel our dependence! —ha!—it must be sweet, indeed."

He again paused. His looks alarmed me, for I had never before seen him thus agitated.

"Whether a man be poorest of the poor," he continued, "or the next heir to the throne, it is all one and the same thing. There is but *one* difference between men—TO OBEY OR TO COMMAND!"

He again glanced over the letter.

"You know the man," he continued, "who has dared to write these words to me! Would you salute him in the street, if fate had not made him your master? By heaven! there is something great in a crown!"

He went on in this strain, giving expression to many things which I dare not trust to paper. On this occasion the Prince confided a circumstance to me which alike surprised and terrified me, and which may be followed by the most alarming consequences. We have hitherto been entirely deceived regarding the family relations of the court of ——.

He answered the letter on the spot, notwithstanding my earnest entreaty that he should postpone doing so; and the strain in which he wrote leaves no ground to hope for a favorable settlement of these differences.

You are no doubt impatient, dear O——, to hear something definite with respect to the

THE GHOST-SEER.

THE DUEL.

Greek; but, in truth, I have very little to tell you. From the Prince I can learn nothing, as he has been admitted into her confidence; and is, I believe, bound to secrecy. The fact has, however, transpired that she is not a Greek as we supposed, but a German of the highest descent. From a certain report that has reached me, it would appear that her mother is of the most exalted rank, and that she is the fruit of an unfortunate amour which was once talked of all over Europe. A course of secret persecution to which she had been exposed, in consequence of her origin, compelled her to seek protection in Venice, and to adopt that concealment which had rendered it impossible for the Prince to discover her retreat. The respect with which the Prince speaks of her, and a certain deferential deportment which he maintains towards her, appear to corroborate the truth of this report.

He is devoted to her with a fearful intensity of passion, which increases day by day. In the earliest stage of their acquaintance but few interviews were granted; but after the first week the separations were of shorter duration, and now there is scarce a day on which the Prince is not with her. Whole evenings pass without our even seeing him, and, when he is not with her, she appears to form the sole subject of his thoughts. His whole being seems metamorphosed. He goes about as if wrapt in a dream, and nothing that formerly interested him has now power to arrest his attention even for a moment.

How will this end, my dear friend? I tremble for the future. The rupture with his court has placed my master in a state of humiliating dependence on one sole person—the Marquis Civitella. This man is now master of our secrets—of our whole fate. Will he always conduct himself as nobly as he does now? Are his good intentions to be relied upon? and is it expedient to confide so much weight and power to one person—even were he the best of men? The Prince's sister has again been written to—the result of this fresh appeal you shall learn in my next letter.

COUNT VON O—— IN CONTINUATION.

This letter never reached me. Three months passed without my receiving any tidings from Venice,—an interruption to our correspondence which the sequel but too clearly explained. All my friend's letters to me had been kept back and suppressed. My emotion may be conceived when, in the December of the same year, the following letter reached me by mere accident (as it afterwards appeared), owing to the sudden illness of Biondello, into whose hands it had been committed.

" You do not write ; you do not answer me.

Come! I entreat you, come on the wings of friendship! Our hopes are fled! Read the enclosed. All our hopes are at an end!

"The wounds of the Marquis are reported mortal. The Cardinal vows vengeance, and his bravos are in pursuit of the Prince. My master—Oh! my unhappy master! Has it come to this! Wretched, horrible fate! We are compelled to hide ourselves, like malefactors, from assassins and creditors.

"I am writing to you from the convent of ——, where the Prince has found an asylum. At this moment he is resting on his hard couch by my side, and is sleeping—but, alas! it is only the sleep of deadly exhaustion, that will but give him new strength for new trials. During the ten days that she was ill no sleep closed his eyes. I was present when the body was opened. Traces of poison were detected. To-day she is to be buried.

"Alas! dearest O——, my heart is rent. I have lived through scenes that can never be effaced from my memory. I stood beside her death-bed. She departed like a saint, and her last strength was spent in trying, with persuasive eloquence, to lead her lover into the path that she was treading in her way to heaven. Our firmness was completely gone—the Prince alone maintained his fortitude, and, although he suffered a triple agony of death with her, he yet retained strength of mind sufficient to refuse the last prayer of the pious enthusiast."

This letter contained the following enclosure:

To the Prince of ——, from his Sister.

"The one sole redeeming church which has made so glorious a conquest of the Prince of —— will surely not refuse to supply him with means to pursue the mode of life to which she owes this conquest. I have tears and prayers for one that has gone astray, but nothing further to bestow on one so worthless! Henriette—."

I instantly threw myself into a carriage—travelled night and day, and in the third week I was in Venice. My speed availed nothing. I had come to bring comfort and help to an unhappy one, but I found a happy one who needed not my weak aid. F—— was ill when I arrived, and unable to see me, but the following note was brought to me from him.

"Return, dearest O——, to whence you came. The Prince no longer needs you or me. His debts have been paid; the Cardinal is reconciled to him, and the Marquis has recovered. Do you remember the Armenian who perplexed us so much last year? In *his* arms you will find the Prince, who five days since attended mass for the first time."

Notwithstanding all this I earnestly sought an interview with the Prince, but was refused. By the bedside of my friend I learned the particulars of this strange story.

THE REVOLT OF THE UNITED NETHERLANDS

THE AUTHOR'S PREFACE.

SOME years ago, when I read the History of the Belgian Revolution in Watson's excellent description, I was impressed with a degree of enthusiasm which political events but rarely excite. On further reflection, I felt that this enthusiasm had arisen less from the book itself, than from the ardent workings of my own imagination, which had imparted to the imbibed materials the particular form that so fascinated me. These powers of imagination, therefore, I felt desirous to render permanent, to multiply, and to strengthen; these exalted sentiments I was anxious to extend, and to communicate to others. This was my first inducement to commence the present history, my only vocation to write it. The execution of this design carried me farther than I at first intended. A more intimate acquaintance with my materials, made me perceive defects, previously unnoticed, long waste tracts to be filled up, apparent contradictions to be removed, and isolated facts to be brought into connection with the rest of the subject. Not so much with the view of enriching my history with new facts, as to seek a key to old ones, I betook myself to the original sources, and thus what was at first intended to be only a general outline, expanded into an elaborate history. The first part, which concludes with the departure of the Duchess of Parma from the Netherlands, must be looked upon only as the introduction to the Revolution itself, which did not come to an open outbreak till the government of her successor. I devoted the more care and attention to this introductory period, because the generality of writers, who previously had treated of it, seemed deficient in these qualities; and because I was convinced that on this all the subsequent events depended. If, then, this first volume should appear but too meagre in important events, too prolix on trifles, or, rather, what at first sight seem profuse in reflections, and, in general, too tediously minute, it must be remembered that precisely out of all small beginnings the Revolution was gradually developed; and that all the subsequent great results sprung out of a countless number of small events.

Such a nation, as the one before us, ever takes its first steps with hesitation and uncertainty; to move afterwards so much the more rapidly. I have proposed to myself to follow the same method in describing this rebellion. The longer the reader delays on the introduction, the more he familiarizes himself with the actors, and the scene in which they took a part; and the more rapidly and surely shall I be able to conduct him through the subsequent periods, where the accumulation of materials forbids a slow pace, and minute attention.

As for authorities for our history, there is

251

not so much reason to complain of their paucity as of their extreme abundance ; since it is indispensable to read them all, to obtain that clear view of the subject, which is frequently disturbed by the perusal of a part, however large. From such unequal, partial, and often contradictory narratives of the same occurrences, it is often extremely difficult to seize the truth, which in all, is alike partly concealed, and to be found complete in none. In this first volume, besides de Thou, Strada, Reyd, Grotius, Meteren, Burgundius, Meursius, Bentivoglio and some moderns ; the Memoirs of Counsellor Hopperus, the life and correspondence of his friend Viglius, the records of the trials of the Counts of Hoorne and Egmont, the defence of the Prince of Orange, and some few others, have been my guides. I must here acknowledge my obligations to a work, compiled with much industry and critical acumen, and written with singular truthfulness and impartiality. Besides many original documents which I could not otherwise have had access to, it has abstracted all that is valuable in the excellent works of Bos, Hooft, Bandt, Le Clerc, which either were impossible for me to procure, or were not available to my use, as being written in Dutch, which I do not understand. I allude to the general history of the United Netherlands, which was published in Holland during the present century. An otherwise ordinary writer, Richard Dinoth, has also been

of service to me, by the many extracts he gives from the pamphlets of the day, which have been long lost. I have in vain endeavored to procure the Correspondence of Cardinal Granvella, which also would, no doubt, have thrown much light upon the history of these times. The lately published work on the Spanish Inquisition, by my excellent countryman, Professor Spittler of Göttingen, reached me too late for its sagacious and important contents to be available for my purpose.

The more I am convinced of the importance of the French history, the more I lament that it was not in my power to study, as I could have wished, its copious annals, in the original sources and contemporaneous documents, and to reproduce it, abstracted of the form in which it was transmitted to me by the more intelligent of my predecessors, and thereby emancipate myself from the influence which every talented author exercises more or less upon his readers. But to effect this, the work of a few years must have become the labor of a life. My aim in making this attempt will be more than attained, if it should convince a portion of the reading public of the possibility of writing a history with historic truth, without making a trial of patience to the reader ; and if it should extort from another portion the confession, that history can borrow from a cognate art, without thereby, of necessity, becoming a romance.

INTRODUCTION.

ONE of the most remarkable political events which have rendered the sixteenth century among the brightest of the world's epochs, appears to me to be the foundation of the freedom of the Netherlands. If the glittering exploits of ambition, and the pernicious lust of power, claim our admiration, how much more should an event, in which oppressed humanity struggles for its noblest rights, where with the good cause unwonted powers are united, and the resources of resolute despair triumph in unequal contest over the terrible arts of tyranny.

Great and encouraging is the reflection that there is a resource left us against the arrogant usurpations of regal power; that its best contrived plans against the liberty of mankind may be rendered abortive; that resolute opposition can weaken even the outstretched arm of a tyrant; and that heroic perseverance can eventually exhaust its fearful resources. Never did this truth penetrate me so sensibly as in the history of that memorable rebellion which for ever severed the United Netherlands from the Spanish Crown—and therefore I thought it not unworthy the attempt to exhibit to the world this grand memorial of social union, that it may awaken in the breast of my reader a spirit-stirring consciousness of his own powers, and give a new and irrefragable example of what men dare venture in a good cause, and what they may accomplish by union. It is not that which is extraordinary or heroic in this event which induces me to describe it. The annals of the world have recorded similar enterprises, which appear even bolder in the conception, and more brilliant in the execution. Some states have fallen with a more imposing convulsion, others have risen with more exalted strides. Nor are we here to look for prominent heroes, colossal personages, or those marvellous exploits which the history of past times presents in such rich abundance. Those times are gone, the men are no more. In the soft lap of refinement we have suffered the powers to relax which those ages exercised and made necessary. With admiring awe we wonder at these gigantic images, as a feeble old man gazes on the athletic sports of youth.

Not so, however, in the history before us. The people here presented to our notice were the most peaceful in this quarter of the globe, and less capable than their neighbors of that heroic spirit which imparts a higher character to the most insignificant actions. The pressure of circumstances surprised them with its peculiar power, and forced a transitory greatness upon them, which they never should have possessed, and may perhaps never possess again. It is, indeed, exactly the want of heroic greatness which makes this event peculiar and instructive ; and while others aim at showing the superiority of genius over chance, I present here a picture, where necessity created genius, and accident made heroes.

If, in any case, it be permitted to acknowledge the interference of Providence in human affairs, it is certainly allowable in the present history : so contradictory does its course appear to reason and experience. Philip II., the most powerful sovereign of his line—whose dreaded superiority menaced the independence of Europe—whose treasures surpassed the collective wealth of all the monarchs of Christendom besides—whose ambitious projects were backed by numerous and well - disciplined armies—whose troops, hardened by long and bloody wars, and in the recollection of their own past victories, and confident in the irresistible powers of the nation, were eager for any enterprise that promised glory and spoil, and to second with prompt and ready obedience the daring genius of their leaders—this dreaded potentate is here exhibited to us obstinately devoted to one favorite project, dedicating to it the unceasing efforts of a long reign, and bringing all these terrible resources to bear upon it ; but forced at last, in the evening of his days, to renounce it—the mighty Philip II. engaging in combat with a few weak and powerless adversaries, and retiring from it with disgrace.

And with what adversaries ? Here, a peaceful tribe of fishermen and shepherds, in an almost forgotten corner of Europe, which with difficulty they had rescued from the ocean ; the sea their profession, and at once their wealth and their plague ; poverty with freedom their highest blessing, their glory, their virtue. There, a harmless, moral, commercial people, revelling in the abundant fruits of thriving industry, jealous of the maintenance of laws which had proved their benefactors. In the happy leisure of affluence, they forsake the narrow circle of immediate wants, and learn to thirst after higher and nobler gratifications. The new views of truth, whose gladdening dawn now broke over Europe, cast a fertilizing beam on this favored clime, and the free burgher received with joy the light which oppressed and miserable slaves shut out. A spirit of independence, which is wont to accompany abundance and freedom, lured this people on to examine the authority of antiquated opinions, and to break an ignominious chain. The severe rod of despotism was held suspended over them ; an arbitrary power threatened to tear away the foundation of their happiness ; the guardian of their laws became their tyrant. Simple in their state-craft, as in their manners, they dared to appeal to ancient treaties, and to remind the Lord of both Indies of the rights of nature. A name decides the whole issue of things. In Madrid that was called rebellion which in Brussels was styled only a lawful remonstrance. The complaints of Brabant required a prudent mediator ; Philip II. sent an executioner, and the signal for war was given. An unparalleled tyranny assailed both property and life. The despairing citizens, to whom the choice of death was all that was left, chose the nobler one on the battlefield. A wealthy and luxurious nation loves peace, but becomes warlike as soon as it becomes poor. Then it ceases to tremble for a life which is deprived of everything that had made it desirable. In a moment. the rage of rebellion seized the most distant provinces ; trade and commerce are at a standstill. the ships disappear from the harbors, the artisan abandons his workshop, the rustic his uncultivated fields. Thousands fled to distant lands ; a thousand victims fell on the bloody field. and fresh thousands pressed on ; for divine, indeed, must that doctrine be for which men could die so joyfully. All that was wanting was the last achieving hand. the enlightened enterprising spirit, to seize on this great political crisis, and to mature the offspring of chance to the designs of wisdom. William the Silent devoted himself, a second Brutus, to the great cause of liberty. Superior to a timorous selfishness, he sent in to the throne his resignation of offices which devolved on him objectionable duties, and magnanimously divesting himself of all his princely dignities, he descended to a state of voluntary poverty, and became but a citizen of the world. The cause of justice was staked upon the hazardous game of battle ; but the sudden levies of mercenaries and peaceful husbandmen could not withstand the terrible onset of an experienced force. Twice did the brave William lead his dispirited troops against the tyrant, twice was he abandoned by them, but not by his courage.

Philip II. sent as many reinforcements as the dreadful importunity of his viceroy begged for. Fugitives, whom their fatherland rejected, sought a new country on the ocean, and turned to satisfy, on the ships of their enemy, the demon of vengeance and of want. Naval heroes were now formed out of corsairs, and a marine collected out of piratical vessels, and out of morasses arose a Republic. Seven provinces threw off the yoke at the same time, to form a new, youthful state, powerful by its waters, and its union, and despair. A solemn decree of the whole nation deposed the tyrant, and the Spanish name disappeared from all the laws.

For what had now been done, no forgiveness remained ; the Republic became formidable, because it was no longer possible for her to retrace her steps ; factions distracted her within ; her terrible element, the sea itself, leaguing with her oppressors, threatened her very infancy with a premature grave. She felt herself succumb to the superior force of the enemy, and cast herself a suppliant before the most powerful thrones of Europe, begging them to accept a dominion which she herself could no longer protect. At last, but with difficulty —so despised at first was this state, that even the rapacity of foreign monarchs spurned her opening bloom—a stranger deigned to accept their importunate offer of a dangerous crown. New hopes began to revive her sinking courage ; but in this new father of his country, destiny gave her a traitor ; and in the critical emergency, when the implacable foe was in full force before her very gates, Charles of Anjou invaded the liberties which he had been called to protect. The assassin's hand, too, tore the steersman from the rudder, and with

William of Orange the career, seemingly, of the infant Republic, and all her guardian angels, fled ; but the ship continued to scud along in the storm, and the swelling canvas carried her safe without the steersman's help.

Philip II. missed the fruits of a deed which cost him his royal honor, and, perhaps, also, his self-respect. Liberty struggled on still with despotism, in the obstinate and dubious contest ; sanguinary battles were fought ; a brilliant array of heroes succeeded each other on the field of glory ; and Flanders and Brabant were the schools which educated generals for the coming century. A long, devastating war laid waste the open country ; victor and vanquished alike were bathed in blood ; while the rising republic of the waters gave a welcome to fugitive industry, and out of the ruins erected the noble edifice of its own greatness. For forty years a war lasted, whose happy termination was not to bless the dying eye of Philip ; which destroyed one Paradise in Europe, to create a new one out of its shattered fragments ; which destroyed the choicest flower of military youth, and while it enriched more than a quarter of the globe, impoverished the possessor of the golden Peru. This monarch, who, even without oppressing his subjects, could expend nine hundred tons of gold, but who by tyrannical means extorted far more, heaped on his depopulated kingdom a debt of one hundred and forty millions of ducats. An implacable hatred of liberty swallowed up all these treasures, and consumed in fruitless labor his royal life. But the Reformation throve amidst the devastation of his sword, and over the blood of her citizens the banner of the new Republic floated victorious.

This improbable turn of affairs seems to border on a miracle ; much, however, combined to break the power of Philip, and to favor the progress of the infant state. Had the whole weight of his power fallen on the United Provinces, there had been no hope for their religion or their liberty. His own ambition came to the assistance of their weakness, by tempting him to divide his strength. The expensive policy of maintaining traitors in every cabinet of Europe ; the support of the League in France ; the revolt of the Moors in Granada ; the conquest of Portugal ; and the magnificent fabric of the Escurial, drained at last his apparently inexhaustible treasures, and prevented his acting in the field with spirit and energy. The German and Italian troops, who were allured to his banner only by the hope of

gain, mutinied when he could no longer pay them, and faithlessly abandoned their leaders in the decisive moment of action. These terrible instruments of oppression now turned their dangerous power against their employer, and wreaked their vindictive rage on the provinces which remained faithful to him. The unfortunate armament against England, on which, like a desperate gamester, he had staked the whole strength of his kingdom, completed his ruin; with the Armada sank the wealth of the two Indies, and the flower of Spanish chivalry.

But in the very same proportion that the Spanish power declined, the Republic acquired fresh vigor. The breaches which the new religion, the tyranny of the Inquisition, the furious rapacity of the soldiery, and the devastations of a long war, unbroken by any interval of peace, made in the provinces of Brabant, Flanders, and Hainault, at once the arsenals and the magazines of this expensive contest, naturally rendered it, every year, more difficult to support and recruit the royal armies. The Catholic Netherlands had already lost a million of citizens, and the trodden fields maintained their husbandmen no longer. Spain itself had but few more men to spare. That country, surprised by a sudden affluence, which brought idleness with it, had lost much of its population, and could not long support these continual drafts of men, both for the New World and the Netherlands. Of these conscripts, few ever saw their country again; and these few having left it as youths, returned to it infirm and old. Gold, which had become more common, made soldiers proportionately dearer; the growing charm of effeminacy enhanced the price of the opposite virtues. Wholly different was the posture of affairs with the rebels. The thousands whom the cruelty of the Viceroy expelled from the southern Netherlands, the war of the Huguenots from France as well as all whom the constraint of conscience drove from the other parts of Europe, all these flocked to unite themselves with them. The whole Christian world was their recruiting ground. The fanaticism both of the persecutor and the persecuted, worked in their behalf. The enthusiasm of a doctrine newly embraced, revenge, want, and hopeless misery, drew to their standard adventurers from every part of Europe. All whom the new doctrine had won, all who had already suffered, or had still cause to fear from despotism, linked their own fortunes with those of the new Republic. Every injury inflicted by a tyrant, gave a right of citizenship in Holland. Men pressed towards a country where liberty raised her inspiriting banner, where respect and security were ensured to a fugitive religion, and even revenge on the oppressors. If we consider the conflux of all people to Holland, in the present day, who on their entrance upon her territory are reinvested in their rights as men, what must it have been then, when the rest of Europe groaned under a heavy bondage, when Amsterdam was nearly the only free port for all opinions? Many hundred families sought a refuge for their wealth in a land which the ocean and domestic concord powerfully combined to protect. The republican army maintained its full complement, without the plough being stripped of hands to work it. Amid the clash of arms, trade and industry flourished; and the peaceful citizen enjoyed in anticipation all the fruits of liberty, which foreign blood must first purchase. At the very time when the Republic of Holland was struggling for existence, she extended her dominions beyond the ocean, and was quietly occupied in erecting her East Indian empire.

Moreover, Spain maintained this expensive war with dead, unfructifying gold, that never returned into the hand which gave it away, while it raised the price of all necessaries. The treasuries of the Republic were industry and commerce. Time lessened the one, whilst it multiplied the other. Exactly in the same proportion that the resources of the Spanish Government became exhausted by the long continuance of the war, the Republic began to reap a richer harvest. The field was sown sparingly with choice seed, and it bore fruit, though late, yet a hundred-fold; but the tree from which Philip gathered fruit was a fallen trunk, which never again became verdant.

Philip's adverse destiny decreed that all the treasures which he lavished for the oppression of the Provinces, contributed to enrich them. The incessant outlay of Spanish gold had diffused riches and luxury throughout Europe; but the increasing wants of Europe were supplied chiefly by the Netherlanders, who were masters of the commerce of the known world, and who, by their dealings, fixed the price of all merchandise. Even during the war, Philip could not prohibit his own subjects from trading with the Republic; nay, he could not even desire it. He himself paid the rebels the expenses of their own defence; for the very war

which was to ruin them, increased the sale of
their goods. The enormous sums expended
on his fleets and armies flowed, for the most
part, into the exchequer of the Republic,
which was more or less connected with the
commercial places of Flanders and Brabant.
Whatever Philip attempted against the rebels
operated directly in their favor.

The sluggish progress of this war did the
King as much injury as it brought advantage
to the rebels. His army was composed, for
the most part, of the remains of those victorious troops which had gathered their laurels
under Charles V. Old and long services entitled them to repose; many of them, whom
the war had enriched, impatiently longed for
their homes, and to end in ease a life of hard-
ship. Their former zeal, their heroic spirit,
and their discipline, relaxed in the same proportion as they thought they had redeemed
their honor and their duty, and as they began
to reap at last the reward of so many engage-
ments. Besides, the troops, which had been
accustomed, by their irresistible impetuosity,
to vanquish all opponents, were necessarily
wearied out by a war which was carried on,
not so much against men as against the elements; which exercised their patience more
than it gratified their love of glory; and where

there was less of danger than of difficulty and
want to contend with. Neither personal courage, nor long military experience, were of
avail in a country whose peculiar features
gave the most dastardly the advantage over
them. In fine, a single discomfiture on foreign
ground did them more injury than any victories gained over an enemy at home could
profit them. With the rebels, the case was
exactly the reverse. In so protracted a war,
in which no decisive battle took place, the
weaker party must naturally learn at last the
art of defence from the stronger; slight de-
feats accustomed him to danger, slight victories animated his confidence.

At the beginning of the civil war, the republican army scarce dared to show itself in
the field; the long continuance of the struggle
practised and hardened it. As the royal
armies grew wearied of victory, the confidence of the rebels rose with their improved
discipline and experience. At last, at the end
of half a century, master and pupil separated,
unsubdued, and equal in the fight.

Again, throughout the war the rebels acted
with more concord and unanimity than the
royalists. Before the former had lost their
first leader, the government of the Netherlands
had passed through as many as five hands.

The Duchess of Parma's indecision soon imparted itself to the cabinet of Madrid, which, in a short time, ran through nearly all the various systems of state policy. Duke Alva's inflexible sternness, the mildness of his successor Requesens, Don John of Austria's insidious cunning, and the active and imperious mind of the Prince of Parma, gave as many opposite directions to the war, while the plan of the rebellion remained the same in a single head, who, as he saw it clearly, pursued it with vigor. The greatest evil for the King was, that the right principles of action generally missed the right moment of application. In the commencement of the troubles, when the advantage was as yet clearly on the King's side, when prompt resolution and manly firmness might have crushed the rebellion in the cradle, the reins of government were allowed to hang loose in the hands of a woman. After the outbreak had come to an open revolt, and the strength of the factious and of the king stood more equally balanced, and when a skilful flexibility could alone have averted the impending civil war, the government devolved on a man, who was deficient in this necessary qualification. So watchful an observer as William the Silent, failed not to improve every advantage which the faulty policy of his adversary presented, and with silent industry he slowly advanced his great undertaking to its accomplishment.

But why did not Philip II. himself appear in the Netherlands? Why did he prefer to employ every other means, however improbable, rather than make trial of the only remedy which could ensure success? To curb the overgrown power and insolence of the nobility, there was no expedient more natural than the presence of their master. Before royalty itself, all secondary dignity must necessarily have sunk, all other splendor have dimmed. Instead of the truth flowing slowly and obscurely through impure channels to the distant throne, so that procrastinated measures of redress gave time to ripen ebullitions of the moment into acts of deliberation, his own penetrating glance would at once have been able to separate truth from error; and cold policy alone, not to speak of his humanity, would have saved the land a million of citizens. The nearer to their source, the more weighty would his edicts have been; the thicker they fell on their object, the weaker and the more dispirited the efforts of the rebels. It costs infinitely more to commit

an evil towards an enemy in his presence than in his absence. At first, the rebellion appeared to tremble at its own name, and long sheltered itself under the ingenious pretext of defending the cause of its sovereign against the arbitrary assumptions of his own viceroy. Philip's appearance in Brussels would have put an end at once to this juggling. In that case the rebels would have been compelled to act up to their pretence, or to cast aside the mask, and so, by appearing in their true shape, condemn themselves. And what a relief for the Netherlands if the King's presence had only spared them those evils which were inflicted upon them without his knowledge, and contrary to his will! What gain to himself, even if it had only enabled him to watch over the expenditure of the vast sums which, illegally raised on the plea of meeting the exigencies of the war, disappeared in the plundering hands of his deputies! What the latter were compelled to extort by the unnatural expedient of terror, the nation would have been disposed to grant to the sovereign Majesty. That which made his ministers detested would have rendered the monarch feared; for the abuse of hereditary power presses less painfully than the abuse of that which is delegated. His presence would have saved thousands had he been nothing more than an economical despot; and even had he been less, the awe of his person would have preserved a territory which was lost through hatred and contempt for his instruments.

In the same manner as the oppression of the people of the Netherlands excited the sympathy of all who valued their own rights, it might have been expected that their disobedience and defection would have been a call to all princes to maintain their own prerogatives in the case of their neighbors. But jealousy of Spain got the better of political sympathies, and the first powers of Europe arranged themselves more or less openly on the side of freedom.

Although bound to the house of Spain by the ties of relationship, the Emperor Maximilian II. gave it just cause to charge him with secretly favoring the rebels. By the offer of his mediation, he implicitly acknowledged the partial justice of their complaints, which could not but encourage them to a resolute perseverance in their demands. Under an Emperor sincerely devoted to the interests of the Spanish house, William of Orange would scarcely have drawn so many troops and so much money from Germany. France, without openly and formally breaking the peace, placed a Prince of the Blood at the head of the Netherlandish rebels; and it was with French gold and French troops that the operations of the latter were chiefly conducted. Elizabeth of England, too, did but exercise a just retaliation and revenge in protecting the rebels against their legitimate sovereign, and although her meagre and sparing aid availed no farther than to ward off utter ruin from the Republic, still even this was infinitely valuable at a moment when nothing but hope could have supported their exhausted courage. With both these powers, Philip at the time was at peace, but both betrayed him. Between the weak and the strong, honesty often ceases to appear a virtue; the delicate ties which bind equals are seldom beneficial to him whom all men fear. Philip had banished truth from political intercourse; he himself, between kings, had dissolved all morality, and had made artifice the divinity of cabinets. Without once enjoying the advantages of his superior power, he had, throughout his whole life, to contend with the jealousy which it awakened in others. Europe made him atone for the possible abuses of a power of which in fact he never had the full possession.

If against the disparity between the two combatants which, at first sight, is so astounding, we weigh all the incidental circumstances which were adverse to Spain, but befriended the Netherlands, that which is supernatural in this event will disappear, but that which is extraordinary remains—and a just standard is furnished by which to estimate the real merit of these republicans in working out their freedom. It must not, however, be thought that so accurate a calculation of the opposed powers could have preceded the undertaking itself, or that, on entering this unknown sea, they already knew the shore on which they would ultimately be landed. The work did not present itself to the mind of its originator in the mature form which it assumed when completed, any more than the mind of Luther foresaw the eternal separation of creeds, when he began to oppose the sale of indulgences. What a difference between the modest procession of those suitors in Brussels, who prayed for a more humane treatment as a favor, and the dreaded majesty of a free state, which treated with kings as equals, and in less than a century gave away the throne of its former

tyrant! The unseen hand of fate gave to the discharged arrow a higher flight and quite a different direction from that which it first received from the bowstring. In the womb of happy Brabant, that liberty had its birth which, torn from its mother in its earliest infancy, was to gladden the so despised Holland. But the enterprise must not be less thought of because its issue differed from the first design. Man works up, smooths and fashions the rough stone which the times bring to him; the moment and the instant may belong to him, but accident developes the history of the world. If the passions which co-operated actively in bringing about this event were only not unworthy of the great work to which they were unconsciously subservient—if the powers which aided in its accomplishment, and the single actions, out of whose concatenation it wonderfully arose, were but intrinsically noble powers, and the actions beautiful and great, then is the event grand, interesting and fruitful for us, and we are at liberty to wonder at the bold offspring of chance, or rather offer up our admiration to a higher Intelligence.

The history of the world, like the laws of nature, is consistent with itself, and simple as the soul of man. Like conditions produce like phenomena. On the same soil where now the Netherlanders were to resist their Spanish tyrants, their forefathers, the Batavi and Belgæ, fifteen centuries before, combated against their Roman oppressors. Like the former, submitting reluctantly to a haughty master, and misgoverned by rapacious satraps, they broke off their chain with like resolution, and tried their fortune in a similar unequal combat. The same pride of conquest, the same national grandeur marked the Spaniard of the sixteenth century and the Roman of the first; the same valor and discipline distinguished the armies of both, their battle array inspired the same terror. There, as here, we see stratagem in combat with superior force, and firmness, strengthened by unanimity, weary out a mighty power weakened by division; then, as now, private hatred arms a whole nation; a single man, born for his times, reveals to them the dangerous secret of their power, and brings their mute grief to a bloody announcement. "Confess, Batavians," cries Claudius Civilis to his fellow-citizens in the sacred grove, "we are no longer treated, as formerly, by these Romans, as allies, but rather as slaves. We are handed over to their præfects and centurions, who, when satiated with our plunder and with our blood, make way for others, who, under different names, renew the same outrages. If even at last Rome deigns to send us a legate, he oppresses us with an ostentatious and costly retinue, and with still more intolerable pride. The levies are again at hand which tear for ever children from their parents, brothers from brothers. Now, Batavians, is our time. Never did Rome lie so prostrate as now. Let not their names of legions terrify you, there is nothing in their camps but old men and plunder. Our infantry and horsemen are strong; Germany is allied to us by blood, and Gaul is ready to throw off its yoke. Let Syria serve them, and Asia and the East, who are used to bow before kings; many still live who were born among us before tribute was paid to the Romans. The gods are ever with the brave." Solemn religious rites hallow this conspiracy, like the league of the Gueux;

like that, it craftily wraps itself in the veil of submissiveness, in the majesty of a great name. The cohorts of Civilis swear allegiance on the Rhine to Vespasian in Syria, as the covenant did to Philip II. The same arena furnished the same plan of defence, the same refuge to despair. Both confided their wavering fortunes to a friendly element; in the same distress, Civilis preserves his island, as fifteen centuries after him, William of Orange did the town of Leyden—through an artificial inundation. The valor of the Batavi disclosed the impotency of the world's ruler, as the noble courage of their descendants revealed to the whole of Europe the decay of Spanish greatness. The same fecundity of genius in the generals of both times gave to the war a similarly obstinate countenance, and nearly as doubtful an issue; one difference, nevertheless, distinguishes them; the Romans and Batavians fought humanely, for they did not fight for religion.

FIRST BOOK

EARLIER HISTORY OF THE NETHERLANDS UP TO THE SIXTEENTH CENTURY.

RE we consider the immediate history of this great revolution, it will be advisable to go a few steps back into the ancient records of the country, and to trace the origin of that constitution of which we find it possessed at the time of this remarkable change.

The first appearance of this people in the history of the world is the moment of its fall; their conquerors first gave them a political existence. The extensive region which is bounded by Germany on the east, on the south by France, on the north and north-west by the North Sea, and which we comprehend under the general name of the Netherlands, was, at the time when the Romans invaded Gaul, divided amongst three principal nations, all originally of German descent, German institutions, and German spirit. The Rhine formed its boundaries. On the left of the river dwelt the Belgæ, on its right the Frisii, and the Batavi on the island which its two arms then formed with the ocean. All these several nations were sooner or later reduced into subjection by the

Romans, but their conquerors themselves give us the most glorious testimony to their valor. The Belgæ, writes Cæsar, were the only people amongst the Gauls who repulsed the invasion of the Teutones and Cimbri. The Batavi, Tacitus tells us, surpassed all the tribes on the Rhine in bravery. This fierce nation paid its tribute in soldiers, and was reserved by its conquerors, like arrow and sword, only for battle. The Romans themselves acknowledged the Batavian horsemen to be their best cavalry. Like the Swiss at this day, they formed for a long time the body-guard of the Roman Emperor; their wild courage terrified the Dacians, as they saw them, in full armor, swimming across the Danube. The Batavi accompanied Agricola in his expedition against Britain, and helped him to conquer that island. The Frieses were, of all, the last subdued, and the first to regain their liberty. The morasses among which they dwelt attracted the conquerors later, and enhanced the price of conquest. The Roman Drusus, who made war in these regions, had a canal cut from the Rhine into the Flevo, the present Zuyder Zee, through which the Roman fleet penetrated into the North Sea, and from thence, entering the mouths of the Ems and the Weser, found an easy passage into the interior of Germany.

Through four centuries, we find Batavian troops in the Roman armies, but after the time of Honorius, their name disappears from history. Presently we discover their island overrun by the Franks, who again lost themselves in the adjoining country of Belgium. The Frieses threw off the yoke of their distant and powerless rulers, and again appeared as a free, and even a conquering people, who governed themselves by their own customs and a remnant of Roman laws, and extended their limits beyond the left bank of the Rhine. Of all the provinces of the Netherlands, Friesland especially had suffered the least from the irruptions of strange tribes and foreign customs; and for centuries retained traces of its original institutions and of its national spirit and manners, which have not, even at the present day, entirely disappeared.

The epoch of the immigration of nations destroyed the original form of most of these tribes; other mixed races arose in their place, with other constitutions. In the general devastation, the towns and encampments of the Romans disappeared, and with them, the memorials of their wise government, which they had employed the natives to execute. The neglected dikes once more yielded to the violence of the streams, and to the encroachments of the ocean. Those wonders of labor and creations of human skill, the canals, dried up, the rivers changed their course, the continent and the sea confounded their olden limits, and the nature of the soil changed with its inhabitants. So, too, the connection of the two eras seems effaced, and with a new race a new history commences.

The monarchy of the Franks, which arose out of the ruins of Roman Gaul, had, in the sixth and seventh centuries, seized all the provinces of the Netherlands, and planted there the Christian faith. After an obstinate war, Charles Martel subdued to the French crown Friesland, the last of all the free provinces, and by his victories, paved a way for the gospel. Charlemagne united all these countries, and formed of them one division of the mighty empire, which he had constructed out of Germany, France, and Lombardy. As under his descendants, this vast dominion was again torn into fragments, so the Netherlands became at times German, at others French, or then again Lotheringian Provinces, and at last we find them under both the names of Friesland and Lower Lotheringia.

With the Franks, the feudal system, the offspring of the North, also came into these lands, and here, too, as in all other countries, it degenerated. The more powerful vassals gradually made themselves independent of the crown, and the royal governors usurped the countries they were appointed to govern. But the rebellious vassals could not maintain their usurpations without the aid of their own dependants, whose assistance they were compelled to purchase by new concessions. At the same time the church became powerful through pious usurpations and donations, and in its abbey lands and episcopal sees acquired an independent existence. Thus were the Netherlands, in the tenth, eleventh, twelfth and thirteenth centuries, split up into several small sovereignties, whose possessors did homage, at one time to the German Emperor, at another to the Kings of France. By purchase, marriages, legacies, and also by conquest, several of these provinces were often united under one suzerain, and thus in the fifteenth century, we see the house of Burgundy in possession of the chief part of the Netherlands. With more or less right, Philip the Good, Duke of Burgundy, had united as many as eleven provinces under his authority, and to these his son, Charles the Bold, added two others, acquired by force of arms. Thus imperceptibly a new state arose in Europe, which wanted nothing but the name to be the most flourishing kingdom in this quarter of the globe. These extensive possessions made the Dukes of Burgundy formidable neighbors to France, and tempted the restless spirit of Charles the Bold to devise a scheme of conquest, embracing the whole line of country from the Zuyder Zee and the mouth of the Rhine down to Alsace. The almost inexhaustible resources of this Prince justify in some measure this bold project. A formidable army threatened to carry it into execution. Already Switzerland trembled for her liberty; but deceitful fortune abandoned him in three terrible battles, and the infatuated hero was lost in the melee of the living and the dead.*

The sole heiress of Charles the Bold, Maria, at once the richest Princess and the unhappy Helen of that time, whose wooing brought misery on her inheritance, was now the centre

---

* A page who had seen him fall, a few days after the battle conducted the victors to the spot, and saved his remains from an ignominious oblivion. His body was dragged from a pool in which it was fast frozen, naked, and so disfigured with wounds, that with great difficulty he was recognized, by the well-known deficiency of some of his teeth, and by remarkably long finger-nails. But that, notwithstanding these marks, there were still incredulous people who doubted his death, and looked for his re-appearance, is proved by the missive in which Louis the Eleventh called upon the Burgundian States to return to their allegiance to the Crown of France. "If," the passage runs, "Duke Charles should still be living, you shall be released from your oath to me." Comines, t. iii., Preuves des Mémoires, 405, 407.

MARIA.

of attraction to the whole known world. Among her suitors appeared two great princes, King Louis XI. of France, for his son, the young Dauphin, and Maximilian of Austria, son of the Emperor Frederick III. The successful suitor was to become the most powerful prince in Europe; and now, for the first time, this quarter of the globe began to fear for its balance of power. Louis, the more powerful of the two, was ready to back his suit by force of arms; but the people of the Netherlands, who disposed of the hand of their Princess, passed by this dreaded neighbor, and decided in favor of Maximilian, whose more remote territories, and more limited power, seemed less to threaten the liberty of their country—a deceitful, unfortunate policy, which, through a strange dispensation of heaven, only accelerated the melancholy fate which it was intended to prevent.

To Philip the Fair, the son of Maria and Maximilian, a Spanish bride brought, as her portion, that extensive kingdom which Ferdinand and Isabella had recently founded; and Charles of Austria, his son, was born lord of the kingdoms of Spain, of the two Sicilies, of the New World, and of the Netherlands. In the latter country, the commonalty emancipated themselves much earlier than in other feudal states, and quickly attained to an independent political existence. The favorable situation of the country on the North Sea, and on great navigable rivers, early awakened the spirit of commerce, which rapidly peopled the towns, encouraged industry and the arts, attracted foreigners, and diffused prosperity and affluence among them. However contemptuously the warlike policy of those times looked down upon every peaceful and useful occupation, the rulers of the country could not fail altogether to perceive the essential advantages they derived from such pursuits. The increasing population of their territories, the different imposts which they extorted from natives and foreigners, under the various titles of tolls, customs, highway rates, escort money, bridge tolls, market fees, escheats and so forth, were too valuable considerations to allow them to remain indifferent to the sources from which they were derived. Their own rapacity made them promoters of trade, and, as often happens, barbarism itself rudely nursed it, until, at last, a healthier policy assumed its place. In the course of time they invited the Lombard merchants to settle among them, and accorded to the towns some valuable privileges and an independent jurisdiction, by which the latter acquired uncommon respectability and influence. The numerous wars which the counts and dukes carried on amongst one another, or with their neighbors, made them in some measure dependent on the good will of the towns, who, by their wealth, obtained weight and consideration, and for the subsidies which they afforded, failed not to extort important privileges in return. These privileges of the commonalties increased as the crusades with their expensive equipment augmented the necessities of the nobles; as a new road to Europe was opened for the productions of the

East; and as wide-spreading luxury created new wants to their princes. Thus as early as the eleventh and twelfth centuries we find in these lands a mixed form of government, in which the prerogative of the sovereign is greatly limited by the privileges of the States; that is to say, of the nobility, the clergy and the municipalities. These, under the name of States, assembled as often as the wants of the province required it. Without their consent no new laws were valid, no war could be carried on, and no taxes levied, no change made in the coinage, and no foreigner admitted to any office of government. All the provinces enjoyed these privileges in common; others were peculiar to the various districts. The supreme government was hereditary, but the son did not enter on the rights of his father before he had solemnly sworn to maintain the existing constitution.

Necessity is the first lawgiver: all the wants which had to be met by this constitution were originally of a commercial nature. Thus the whole constitution was founded on commerce, and the laws of the nation were adapted to their pursuits. The last clause, which excluded foreigners from all offices of trust, was a natural consequence of the preceding articles. So complicated and artificial a relation between the sovereign and his people, which in many provinces was further modified, according to the peculiar wants of each, and frequently to some single city, required for its maintenance the liveliest zeal for the liberties of the country, combined with an intimate acquaintance with them. From a foreigner, neither could well be expected. This law, besides, was enforced reciprocally in each particular province; so that in Brabant no Fleming, in Zealand no Hollander, could hold office; and it continued in force even after all these provinces were united under one government.

Above all others, Brabant enjoyed the highest degree of freedom. Its privileges were esteemed so valuable that many mothers from the adjacent provinces removed thither about the time of their accouchement, in order to entitle their children to participate, by birth, in all the immunities of that favored country; just as, says Strada, one improves the plants of a rude climate by removing them to the soil of a milder.

After the House of Burgundy had united several provinces under its dominion, the separate provincial assemblies which, up to that time, had been independent tribunals, were made subject to a supreme court at Malines, which incorporated the various judicatures into one body, and decided in the last resort all civil and criminal appeals. The separate independence of the provinces was thus abolished, and the supreme power vested in the senate at Malines.

After the death of Charles the Bold, the states did not neglect to avail themselves of the embarrassment of their Duchess, who, threatened by France, was consequently in their power. Holland and Zealand compelled her to sign a great charter, which secured to them the most important sovereign rights. The people of Ghent carried their insolence to such a pitch, that they arbitrarily dragged the favorites of Maria, who had the misfortune to displease them, before their own tribunals, and beheaded them before the eyes of that Princess. During the short government of the Duchess Maria, from her father's death to her marriage, the commons obtained powers which few free states enjoyed. After her death, her husband, Maximilian, illegally assumed the government as guardian of his son. Offended by this invasion of their rights, the states refused to acknowledge his authority, and could only be brought to receive him as viceroy for a stated period, and under conditions ratified by oath.

Maximilian, after he became Roman Emperor, fancied that he might safely venture to violate the constitution. He imposed extraordinary taxes on the provinces, gave official appointments to Burgundians and Germans, and introduced foreign troops into the provinces. But the jealousy of these republicans kept pace with the power of their regent. As he entered Bruges with a large retinue of foreigners, the people flew to arms, made themselves masters of his person, and placed him in confinement in the castle. In spite of the intercession of the Imperial and Roman courts, he did not again obtain his freedom until security had been given to the people on all the disputed points.

The security of life and property, arising from mild laws, and an equal administration of justice, had encouraged activity and industry. In continual contest with the ocean and rapid rivers, which poured their violence on the neighboring lowlands, and whose force it was requisite to break by embankments and canals, this people had early learned to observe the natural objects around them; by industry and perseverance to defy an element of

superior power; and like the Egyptian, instructed by his Nile, to exercise their inventive genius and acuteness in self-defence. The natural fertility of their soil, which favored agriculture and the breeding of cattle, tended at the same time to increase the population. Their happy position on the sea and the great navigable rivers of Germany and France, many of which debouched on their coasts; the numerous artificial canals which intersected the land in all directions, imparted life to navigation; and the facility of interior communication between the provinces, soon created and fostered a commercial spirit among these people.

The neighboring coasts, Denmark and Britain, were the first visited by their vessels. The English wool which they brought back, employed thousands of industrious hands in Bruges, Ghent and Antwerp; and as early as the middle of the twelfth century, cloths of Flanders were extensively worn in France and Germany. In the eleventh century we find ships of Friesland in the Belt, and even in the Levant. This enterprising people ventured, without a compass, to steer under the North Pole, round to the most northerly point of Russia. From the Wendish towns, the Netherlands received a share in the Levant trade, which, at that time, still passed from the Black Sea, through the Russian territories to the Baltic. When, in the thirteenth century, this trade began to decline, the Crusades having opened a new road through the Mediterranean for Indian merchandise, and after the Italian towns had usurped this lucrative branch of commerce, and the great Hanseatic League had been formed in Germany, the Netherlands became the most important emporium between the north and south. As yet, the use of the compass was not general, and the merchantmen sailed slowly and laboriously along the coasts. The ports on the Baltic were, during the winter months, for the most part frozen and inaccessible. Ships, therefore, which could not well accomplish within the year the long voyage from the Mediterranean to the Belt, gladly availed themselves of harbors which lay half way between the two. With an immense continent behind them, with which navigable streams kept up their communication, and towards the west and north open to the ocean by commodious harbors, this country appeared to be expressly formed for a place of resort for different nations, and for a centre of commerce. The

principal towns of the Netherlands were established marts. Portuguese, Spaniards, Italians, French, Britons, Germans, Danes and Swedes thronged to them with the produce of every country in the world. Competition ensured cheapness; industry was stimulated, as it found a ready market for its productions. With the necessary exchange of money, arose the commerce in bills, which opened a new and fruitful source of wealth. The princes of the country, acquainted at last with their true interest, encouraged the merchant by important immunities, and neglected not to protect their commerce by advantageous treaties with foreign powers. When, in the fifteenth century, several provinces were united under one rule, they discontinued their private wars, which had proved so injurious, and their separate interests were now more intimately reconciled by a common government. Their commerce and affluence prospered in the lap of a long peace, which the formidable power of their princes extorted from the neighboring monarchs. The Burgundian flag was feared in every sea, the dignity of their sovereign gave support to their undertakings, and the enterprise of a private individual became the affair of a powerful state. Such vigorous protection soon placed them in a position even to renounce the Hanseatic League, and to pursue this daring enemy through every sea. The Hanseatic merchants, against whom the ports of Spain were closed, were compelled at last, however reluctantly, to visit the Flemish fairs, and purchase their Spanish goods in the markets of the Netherlands.

Bruges, in Flanders, was, in the fourteenth and fifteenth centuries, the central point of the whole commerce of Europe, and the great market of all nations. In the year 1468, a hundred and fifty merchant vessels were counted entering the harbor of Sluys at one time. Besides the rich factories of the Hanseatic League, there were here fifteen trading companies, with their counting-houses, and many factories and merchants' families from every European country. Here was established the market of all northern products for the south, and of all southern and Levantine products for the north. These passed through the Sound, and up the Rhine, in Hanseatic vessels to Upper Germany, or were transported by land carriage to Brunswick and Luneburg.

As in the common course of human affairs, so here also, a licentious luxury followed prosperity. The seductive example of Philip the

Good could not but accelerate its approach. The court of the Burgundian dukes was the most voluptuous and magnificent in Europe, Italy itself not excepted. The costly dress of the higher classes, which afterwards served as patterns to the Spaniards, and eventually, with the Burgundian customs, passed over to the court of Austria, soon descended to the lower orders, and the meanest citizen nursed his person in velvet and silk.*

Comines, an author who travelled through the Netherlands, about the middle of the fifteenth century, tells us that pride had already attended their prosperity. The pomp and vanity of dress was carried by both sexes to extravagance. The luxury of the table had never reached so great a height among any other people. The immoral assemblage of both sexes at bathing places, and such other places of reunion for pleasure and enjoyment, had banished all shame—and we are not here speaking of the usual luxuriousness of the higher ranks; the females of the common class abandoned themselves to such extravagances without limit or measure.

But how much more cheering to the philanthropist is this extravagance, than the miserable frugality of want, and the barbarous virtues of ignorance, which at that time oppressed nearly the whole of Europe! The Burgundian era shines pleasingly forth from those dark ages, like a lovely spring day amid the showers of February. But this flourishing condition, tempted the Flemish towns at last to their ruin; Ghent and Bruges, giddy with liberty and success, declared war against Philip the Good, the ruler of eleven provinces, which

ended as unfortunately as it was presumptuously commenced. Ghent alone lost many thousand men in an engagement near Havre, and was compelled to appease the wrath of the victor by a contribution of 400,000 gold florins. All the municipal functionaries, and two thousand of the principal citizens, went, stripped to their shirts, bare-footed, and with heads uncovered, a mile out of the town to meet the Duke, and on their knees supplicated for pardon. On this occasion they were deprived of several valuable privileges, an irreparable loss for their future commerce. In the year 1482 they engaged in a war, with no better success, against Maximilian of Austria, with a view to deprive him of the guardianship of his son, which, in contravention of his charter, he had unjustly assumed. In 1487 the town of Bruges placed the Archduke himself in confinement, and put some of his most eminent ministers to death. To avenge his son, the Emperor Frederick III. entered their territory with an army, and blockading for ten years the harbor of Sluys, put a stop to their entire trade. On this occasion, Amsterdam and Antwerp, whose jealousy had long been roused by the flourishing condition of the Flemish towns, lent him the most important assistance. The Italians began to bring their own silk stuffs to Antwerp for sale, and the Flemish cloth-workers likewise, who had settled in England, sent their goods thither; and thus the town of Bruges lost two important branches of trade. The Hanse Union had long been offended at their overweening pride; and it now left them, and removed its factory to Antwerp. In the year 1516 all the foreign merchants left the town, except only a few Spaniards; but its prosperity faded as slowly as it had bloomed.

Antwerp received, in the sixteenth century, the trade which the luxuriousness of the Flemish towns had banished: and under the government of Charles V., Antwerp was the most stirring and splendid city in the Christian world. A stream like the Scheldt, whose broad mouth, in the immediate vicinity, shared with the North Sea the ebb and flow of the tide, and could carry vessels of the largest tonnage under the walls of Antwerp, made it the natural resort for all vessels which visited that coast. Its free fairs attracted men of business from all countries.* The industry

---

* Philip the Good was too profuse a Prince to amass treasures; nevertheless, Charles the Bold found accumulated among his effects, a greater store of table services, jewels, carpets, and linen than three rich princedoms of that time together possessed, and over and above all, a treasure of three hundred thousand dollars in ready money. The riches of this Prince. and of the Burgundian people, lay exposed on the battle fields of Granson, Murten, and Nancy. Here, a Swiss soldier drew from the finger of Charles the Bold that celebrated diamond, which was long esteemed the largest in Europe, which, even now, sparkles in the crown of France as the second in size, but which the unwitting finder sold for a florin. The Swiss exchanged the silver they found for tin, and the gold for copper, and tore into pieces the costly tents of cloth of gold. The value of the spoil of silver, gold, and jewels which was taken, has been estimated at three millions. Charles and his army had advanced to the combat, not like foes who purpose battle, but like conquerors who adorn themselves after victory.

* Two such fairs lasted forty days, and all the goods sold there were duty free.

of the nation had, in the beginning of this century, reached its greatest height. The culture of grain, flax, the breeding of cattle, the chase and fisheries enriched the peasant; arts, manufactures and trade brought wealth to burghers. Flemish and Brabantine manufactures were long to be seen in Arabia, Persia and India. Their ships covered the ocean, and, in the Black Sea, contended with the Genoese for supremacy. It was the distinctive characteristic of the seamen of the Netherlands that he made sail at all seasons of the year, and never laid up for the winter.

When the new route by the Cape of Good Hope was discovered, and the East India trade of Portugal undermined that of the Levant, the Netherlands did not feel the blow which was inflicted on the Italian Republics. The Portuguese established their mart in Brabant, and the spices of Calicut were displayed for sale in the markets of Antwerp. Hither poured the West Indian merchandise, with which the indolent pride of Spain repaid the industry of the Netherlands. The East Indian market attracted the most celebrated commercial houses from Florence, Lucca and Genoa; and the Fuggers and Welsers from Augsburg. Here the Hanse towns brought the wares of the north, and here the English company had a factory. Here art and nature seemed to expose to view all their riches; it was a splendid exhibition of the works of the Creator and of the creature.

Their renown soon diffused itself through the world. Even a company of Turkish merchants, towards the end of this century, solicited permission to settle here, and to supply the products of the East by way of Greece. With the trade in goods, they held also the exchange of money. Their bills passed current in the farthest parts of the globe. Antwerp, it is asserted, then transacted more extensive and more important business in a single month than Venice, at its most flourishing period, in two whole years.

In the year 1491 the Hanseatic League held its solemn meetings in this town, which had formerly assembled in Lubeck alone. In 1531 the exchange was erected, at that time the most splendid in all Europe, and which fulfilled its proud inscription. The town now reckoned 100,000 inhabitants. The tide of human beings which incessantly poured into it exceeds all belief. Between 200 and 250 ships were often seen loading at one time in its harbor; no day passed, on which the boats

entering inwards and outwards did not amount to more than 500; on market days the number amounted to 800 or 900. Daily, more than two hundred carriages drove through its gates; above two thousand loaded wagons arrived every week from Germany, France and Lorraine, without reckoning the farmers' carts and corn-vans, which were seldom less than 10,000 in number. Thirty thousand hands were employed by the English company alone. The market dues, tolls and excise brought millions to the government annually. We can form some idea of the resources of the nation from the fact that the extraordinary taxes which they were obliged to pay to Charles V., towards his numerous wars, were computed at forty millions of gold ducats.

For this affluence the Netherlands were as much indebted to their liberty as to the natural advantages of their country. Uncertain laws and the despotic sway of a rapacious prince would quickly have blighted all the blessings which propitious nature had so abundantly lavished on them. The inviolable sanctity of the laws can alone secure to the citizen the fruits of his industry, and inspire him with that happy confidence which is the soul of all activity.

The genius of this people, developed by the spirit of commerce and by the intercourse with so many nations, shone in useful inventions: in the lap of abundance and liberty all the noble arts were carefully cultivated and carried to perfection. From Italy, to which Cosmo de Medici had lately restored its golden age, painting, architecture and the arts of carving and of engraving on copper were transplanted into the Netherlands, where, in a new soil, they flourished with fresh vigor. The Flemish school, a daughter of the Italian, soon vied with its mother for the prize; and, in common with it, gave laws to the whole of Europe in the fine arts. The manufactures and arts, on which the Netherlanders principally founded their prosperity, and still partly base it, require no particular enumeration. The weaving of tapestry, oil painting, the art of painting on glass, even pocket-watches and sun-dials, were, as Guicciardini asserts, originally invented in the Netherlands. To them we are indebted for the improvement of the compass, the points of which are still known by Flemish names. About the year 1430 the invention of typography is ascribed to Laurence Koster, of Haarlem; and whether or not it is entitled to this honorable distinction, certain it is that

the Dutch were among the first to engraft this useful art among them; and fate ordained that a century later it should reward its country with liberty. The people of the Netherlands united, with the most fertile genius for inven- tions, a happy talent for improving the dis- coveries of others; there are probably few mechanical arts and manufactures which they did not either produce, or at least carry to a higher degree of perfection.

THE NETHERLANDS UNDER CHARLES THE FIFTH.

EFORE this time these provinces had formed the most enviable state in all Europe. Not one of the Burgundian dukes had ventured to indulge a thought of overturning the Constitution; it had remained sacred, even to the daring spirit of Charles the Bold, while he was preparing fetters for foreign liberty. All these princes grew up with no higher hope than to be heads of a republic, and none of their territories afforded them experience of a higher authority. Besides, these princes possessed nothing but what the Netherlands gave them; no armies but those which the nation sent into the field; no riches but what the states granted to them. Now all was changed. The Netherlands had fallen to a master who had at his command other instruments and other resources, who could arm against them a foreign power.*

Charles V. was an absolute monarch in his Spanish dominions; in the Netherlands he was no more than the first citizen. In the southern portion of his empire he might have learned contempt for the rights of individuals; here, he was taught to respect them. The rican campaigns; the desire of gain made the Belgians more inclined to peace, but not less sensitive of offence. No people were more free from the lust of conquest, but none defended its own more zealously. Hence, the numerous towns, closely pressed together in a confined tract of country; densely crowded with a foreign and native population; fortified near the sea and the great rivers. Hence, for eight centuries after the northern immigration, foreign arms could not prevail against them. Spain, on the contrary, often changed its masters; and when at last, it fell into the hands of the Goths, its character and its manners had suffered more or less from each new conqueror. The people thus formed, at last, out of these several admixtures, is described as patient in labor, imperturbable in danger, equally eager for riches and honor, proud of itself even to contempt of others, devout and grateful to strangers for any act of kindness, but also revengeful, and of such ungovernable passions in victory, as to regard neither conscience nor honor in the case of an enemy. All this is foreign to the character of the Belgian, who is astute but not insidious, who, placed midway between France and Germany, combines in moderation the faults and good qualities of both. He is not easily imposed upon, nor is he to be insulted with impunity. In veneration for the Deity, too, he does not yield to the Spaniard; the arms of the north-men could not make him apostatise from Christianity, when he had once professed it. No opinion which the church condemns had, up to this time, empoisoned the purity of his faith. Nay, his pious extravagance went so far, that it became requisite to curb by laws the rapacity of his clergy. In both people, loyalty to their rulers is equally innate, with this difference, that the Belgian places the law above kings. Of all the Spaniards, the Castilians require to be governed with the most caution; but the liberties which they arrogate for themselves, they do not willingly accord to others. Hence, the difficult task to their common ruler, so to distribute his attention and care between the two nations, that neither the preference shown to the Castilian should offend the Belgian, nor the equal treatment of the Belgian affront the haughty spirit of the Castilian." Grotii Annal. Belg. l. 1, 4, 5, seq.

* The unnatural union of two such different nations as the Belgians and Spaniards, could not possibly be prosperous. I cannot here refrain from quoting the comparison which Grotius, in energetic language, has drawn between the two. "With the neighboring nations," says he, "the people of the Netherlands could easily maintain a good understanding, for they were of a similar origin with themselves, and had grown up in the same manner. But the people of Spain and of the Netherlands differed in almost every respect from one another, and therefore, when they were brought together, clashed the more violently. Both had, for many centuries, been distinguished in war, only the latter had, in luxurious repose, become disused to arms, while the former had been inured to war in the Italian and Af-

more he there tasted the pleasures of unlimited power, and the higher he raised his opinion of his own greatness, the more reluctant he must have felt to descend elsewhere to the ordinary level of humanity, and to tolerate any check upon his arbitrary authority. It requires, indeed, no ordinary degree of virtue to abstain from warring against the power which imposes a curb on our most cherished wishes.

The superior power of Charles awakened, at the same time, in the Netherlanders, that distrust which always accompanies inferiority. Never were they so alive to their constitutional rights, never so jealous of the royal prerogative, or more observant in their proceedings. Under his reign we see the most violent outbreaks of republican spirit and the pretensions of the people carried to an excess, which nothing but the increasing encroachments of the royal power could in the least justify. A sovereign will always regard the freedom of the citizen as an alienated fief, which he is bound to recover. To the citizen, the authority of the sovereign is a torrent, which, by its inundation, threatens to sweep away his rights. The Belgians sought to protect themselves against the ocean by embankments and against their princes by constitutional enactments. The whole history of the world is a perpetually recurring struggle between liberty and the lust of power and possession; as the history of nature is nothing but the contest of the elements and organic bodies for space. The Netherlands soon found, to their cost, that they had become but a province of a great monarchy. So long as their former masters had no higher aim than to promote their prosperity, their condition resembled the tranquil happiness of a secluded family whose head is its ruler. Charles V. introduced them upon the arena of the political world. They now formed a member of that gigantic body which the ambition of an individual employed as his instrument. They ceased to have their own good for their aim; the centre of their existence was transported to the soul of their ruler. As his whole government was but one tissue of plans and manœuvres to advance his power, so it was, above all things, necessary that he should be completely master of the various limbs of his mighty empire, in order to move them effectually and suddenly. It was impossible, therefore, for him to embarrass himself with the tiresome mechanism of their interior political organization, or to extend to their

peculiar privileges the conscientious respect which their republican jealousy demanded. It was expedient for him to facilitate the exercise of their powers by concentration and unity. The tribunal at Malines had been, under his predecessor, an independent court of judicature; he subjected its decrees to the revision of a royal council, which he established in Brussels, and which was the mere organ of his will. He introduced foreigners into the most vital functions of their constitution and confided to them the most important offices. These men, whose only support was the royal favor, would be but bad guardians of privileges which, moreover, were little known to them. The ever increasing expenses of his warlike government compelled him as steadily to augment his resources. In disregard of their most sacred privileges, he imposed new and strange taxes on the provinces. To conserve their olden consideration, the states were forced to grant what he had been so modest as not to extort; the whole history of the government of this monarch, in the Netherlands, is almost one continued list of imposts demanded, refused and finally accorded. Contrary to the constitution, he introduced foreign troops into their territories, directed the recruiting of his armies in the provinces, and involved them in wars which could not advance, even if they did not injure, their interest, and to which they had not given their consent. He punished the offences of a free state as a monarch; and the terrible chastisement of Ghent announced to the other provinces the great change which their constitution had already undergone.

The welfare of the country was so far secured as was necessary to the political schemes of its master; the intelligent policy of Charles would certainly not violate the salutary regimen of the body, whose energies he found himself necessitated to exert. Fortunately, the opposite pursuits of selfish ambition and of disinterested philanthropy often bring about the same end; and the well-being of a state, which a Marcus Aurelius might propose to himself as a rational object of pursuit, is occasionally promoted by an Augustus or a Louis.

Charles V. was perfectly aware that commerce was the strength of the nation, and that the foundation of their commerce was liberty. He spared its liberty, because he needed its strength. Of greater political wisdom, though not more just than his son, he adapted his

CHARLES V.

principles to the exigencies of time and place, and recalled an ordinance in Antwerp and in Madrid, which he would under other circumstances have enforced with all the terrors of his power. That which makes the reign of Charles V. particularly remarkable, in regard to the Netherlands, is the great religious revolution which occurred under it; and which, as the principal cause of the subsequent rebellion, demands a somewhat circumstantial notice. This it was that first brought arbitrary power into the innermost sanctuary of the constitution; taught it to give a dreadful specimen of its might; and, in a measure, legalized it, while it placed republican spirit on a dangerous eminence. And as the latter sank into anarchy and rebellion, monarchical power rose to the height of despotism.

Nothing is more natural than the transition from civil liberty to religious freedom. Individuals, as well as communities, who, favored by a happy political constitution, have become acquainted with the rights of man, and accustomed to examine, if not also to create, the law which is to govern them; whose minds have been enlightened by activity and feelings

expanded by the enjoyments of life; whose natural courage has been exalted by internal security and prosperity; such men will not easily surrender themselves to the blind domination of a dull arbitrary creed, and will be the first to emancipate themselves from its yoke. Another circumstance, however, must have greatly tended to diffuse the new religion in these countries. Italy, it might be objected, the seat of the greatest intellectual culture, formerly the scene of the most violent political factions, where a burning climate kindles the blood with the wildest passions—Italy, among all the European countries, remained the freest from this change. But to a romantic people, whom a warm and lovely sky, a luxurious, ever young and ever smiling nature, and the multifarious witcheries of art, rendered keenly susceptible of sensuous enjoyment, that form of religion must naturally have been better adapted, which by its splendid pomp captivates the senses; by its mysterious enigmas opens an unbounded range to the fancy; and which, through the most picturesque forms, labors to insinuate important doctrines into the soul. On the contrary, to a people whom

271

the ordinary employments of civil life have drawn down to an unpoetical reality, who live more in plain notions than in images, and who cultivate their common sense at the expense of their imagination—to such a people, that creed will best recommend itself which dreads not investigation, which lays less stress on mysticism than on morals, and which is rather to be understood than to be dwelt upon in meditation. In few words: the Roman Catholic religion will, on the whole, be found more adapted to a nation of artists; the Protestant more fitted to a nation of merchants.

On this supposition, the new doctrine which Luther diffused in Germany, and Calvin in Switzerland, must have found a congenial soil in the Netherlands. The first seeds of it were sown in the Netherlands by the Protestant merchants who assembled at Amsterdam and Antwerp. The German and Swiss troops, which Charles introduced into these countries, and the crowd of French, German and English fugitives, who, under the protection of the liberties of Flanders, sought to escape the sword of persecution which threatened them at home, promoted their diffusion. A great portion of the Belgian nobility studied at that time at Geneva, as the University of Louvain was not yet in repute and that of Douai not yet founded. The new tenets publicly taught there were transplanted by the students to their various countries. In an isolated people, these first germs might easily have been crushed; but in the market-towns of Holland and Brabant, the resort of so many different nations, their first growth would escape the notice of Government, and be accelerated under the veil of concealment. A difference in opinion might easily spring up and gain ground among those who already were divided in national character, in manners, customs and laws. Moreover, in a country where industry was the most lauded virtue, mendicity the most abhorred vice, a slothful body of men, like that of the monks, must have been an object of long and deep aversion. Hence, the new religion, which opposed these orders, derived an immense advantage from having the popular opinion on its side. Occasional pamphlets, full of bitterness and satire, to which the newly discovered art of printing secured a rapid circulation, and several bands of strolling orators, called Rederiker, who at that time made the circuit of the provinces, ridiculing in theatrical representations or songs the abuses of their times contributed not a

little to diminish respect for the Romish Church, and to prepare the people for the reception of the new dogmas.

The first conquests of this doctrine were astonishingly rapid. The number of those who in a short time avowed themselves its adherents, especially in the northern provinces, was prodigious; but among these the foreigners far outnumbered the natives. Charles V., who, in this hostile array of religious tenets, had taken the side which a despot could not fail to take, opposed to the increasing torrent of innovation the most effectual remedies. Unhappily for the reformed religion, political justice was on the side of its persecutor. The dam which, for so many centuries, had repelled human understanding from truth, was too suddenly torn away for the outbreaking torrent not to overflow its appointed channel. The reviving spirit of liberty and of inquiry, which ought to have remained within the limits of religious questions, began also to examine into the rights of kings. While, in the commencement, iron fetters were justly broken off, a desire was eventually shown to rend asunder the most legitimate and most indispensable of ties. Even the Holy Scriptures, which were now circulated everywhere, while they imparted light and nurture to the sincere inquirer after truth, were the source also whence an eccentric fanaticism contrived to extort the virulent poison. The good cause had been compelled to choose the evil road of rebellion, and the result was what in such cases it ever will be, so long as men remain men. The bad cause, too, which had nothing in common with the good, but the employment of illegal means, emboldened by this slight point of connection, appeared in the same company, and was mistaken for it. Luther had written against the invocation of saints; every audacious varlet who broke into the churches and cloisters, and plundered the altars, called himself Lutheran. Faction, rapine, fanaticism, licentiousness, robed themselves in his colors; the most enormous offenders, when brought before the judges, avowed themselves his followers. The Reformation had drawn down the Roman prelate to a level with fallible humanity; an insane band, stimulated by hunger and want, sought to annihilate all distinction of ranks. It was natural that a doctrine, which to the state showed itself only in its most unfavorable aspect, should not have been able to reconcile a monarch who had already so many reasons to extirpate it; and it is no wonder, therefore, that he employed against it the arms it had itself forced upon him.

Charles must already have looked upon himself as absolute in the Netherlands, since he did not think it necessary to extend to these countries the religious liberty which he had accorded to Germany. While compelled by the effectual resistance of the German princes, he assured to the former country a free exercise of the new religion, in the latter he published the most cruel edicts for its repression. By these, the reading of the Evangelists and Apostles; all open or secret meetings to which religion gave its name in ever so slight a degree, all conversations on the subject at home or at the table, were forbidden, under severe penalties. In every province, special courts of judicature were established to watch over the execution of the edicts. Whoever held these erroneous opinions was to forfeit his office, without regard to his rank. Whoever should be convicted of diffusing heretical doctrines, or even of simply attending the secret meetings of the Reformers, was to be condemned to death; and if a male, to be executed by the sword; if a female, buried alive. Backsliding heretics were to be committed to the flames. Not even the recantation of the offender could annul these appalling sentences. Whoever abjured his errors gained nothing by his apostacy, but at farthest a milder kind of death.

The fiefs of the condemned were also confiscated, contrary to the privileges of the nation, which permitted the heir to redeem them for a trifling fine; and in defiance of an express and valuable privilege of the citizens of Holland, by which they were not to be tried out of their province, culprits were conveyed beyond the limits of the native judicature, and condemned by foreign tribunals. Thus did religion guide the hand of despotism to attack with its sacred weapon, and without danger or opposition, the liberties which were inviolable to the secular arm.

Charles V., emboldened by the fortunate progress of his arms in Germany, thought that he might now venture on everything, and seriously meditated the introduction of the Spanish Inquisition in the Netherlands. But the terror of its very name alone reduced commerce in Antwerp to a standstill. The principal foreign merchants prepared to quit the city. All buying and selling ceased. The value of houses fell, the employment of artisans stopped. Money disappeared from

the hands of the citizen. The ruin of that flourishing commercial city was inevitable, had not Charles V. listened to the representations of the Duchess of Parma, and abandoned this perilous resolve. The tribunal, therefore, was ordered not to interfere with the foreign merchants, and the title of Inquisitor was changed unto the milder appellation of Spiritual Judge. But in the other provinces that tribunal proceeded to rage with the inhuman despotism which has ever been peculiar to it. It has been computed that during the reign of Charles V., fifty thousand persons perished by the hand of the executioner for religion alone.

When we glance at the violent proceedings of this monarch, we are quite at a loss to comprehend what it was that kept the rebellion within bounds during his reign, which broke out with so much violence under his successor. A closer investigation will clear up this seeming anomaly. Charles's dreaded supremacy in Europe, had raised the commerce of the Netherlands to a height which it had never before attained. The majesty of his name opened all harbors, cleared all seas for their vessels, and obtained for them the most favorable commercial treaties with foreign powers. Through him, in particular, they destroyed the dominion of the Hanse towns in the Baltic. Through him, also, the New World, Spain, Italy, Germany, which now shared with them a common ruler, were, in a measure, to be considered as provinces of their own country, and opened new channels for their commerce. He had, moreover, united the remaining six provinces with the hereditary states of Burgundy, and thus given to them an extent and political importance which placed them by the side of the first kingdoms of Europe.*

By all this, he flattered the national pride of this people. Moreover, by the incorpora-

* He had, too, at one time the intention of raising it to a kingdom; but the essential points of difference between the provinces, which extended from constitution and manners to measures and weights, soon made him abandon this design. More important was the service which he designed them in the Burgundian treaty, which settled its relation to the German empire. According to this treaty, the seventeen provinces were to contribute to the common wants of the German empire twice as much as an electoral prince; in case of a Turkish war three times as much; in return for which, however, they were to enjoy the powerful protection of this empire, and not to be injured in any of their various privileges. The revolution which, under Charles's son, altered the political constitution of the provinces, again annulled this compact, which, on account of the trifling advantage that it conferred, deserves no further notice.

tion of Gueldres, Utrecht, Friesland and Groningen with these provinces, he put an end to the private wars which had so long disturbed their commerce; an unbroken internal peace now allowed them to enjoy the full fruits of their industry. Charles was therefore a benefactor of this people. At the same time the splendor of his victories dazzled their eyes; the glory of their sovereign, which was reflected upon them also, had bribed their republican vigilance; while the awe-inspiring halo of invincibility, which encircled the conqueror of Germany, France, Italy and Africa, terrified the factious. And then, who knows not on how much may venture the man, be he a private individual or a prince, who has succeeded in enchaining the admiration of his fellow creatures. His repeated personal visits to these lands, which he, according to his own confession, visited as often as ten different times, kept the disaffected within bounds; the constant exercise of severe and prompt justice maintained the awe of the royal power. Finally, Charles was born in the Netherlands, and loved the nation in whose lap he had grown up. Their manners pleased him, the simplicity of their character and social intercourse formed for him a pleasing recreation from the severe Spanish gravity. He spoke their language and followed their customs in his private life. The burdensome ceremonies, which form the unnatural barriers between king and people, were banished from Brussels. No jealous foreigner debarred natives from access to their prince, their way to him was through their own countrymen, to whom he entrusted his person. He spoke much and courteously with them; his deportment was engaging; his discourse obliging. These simple artifices won for him their love, and, while his armies trod down their corn-fields, while his rapacious imposts diminished their property, while his governors oppressed, his executioners slaughtered, he secured their hearts by a friendly demeanor.

Gladly would Charles have seen this affection of the nation for himself descend upon his son. On this account he sent for him in his youth from Spain, and showed him in Brussels to his future subjects. On the solemn day of his abdication, he recommended to him these lands as the richest jewel in his crown, and earnestly exhorted him to respect their laws and privileges.

Philip II. was in all the direct opposite of his father. As ambitious as Charles, but with less knowledge of men and of the rights of man, he had formed to himself a notion of royal authority, which regarded men as simply the servile instruments of despotic will, and was outraged by every symptom of liberty. Born in Spain, and educated under the iron discipline of the monks, he demanded of others the same gloomy formality and reserve as marked his own character. The cheerful merriment of his Flemish subjects was as uncongenial to his disposition and temper, as their privileges were offensive to his imperious will. He spoke no other language but the Spanish, endured none but Spaniards about his person, and obstinately adhered to all their customs. In vain did the royal ingenuity of the Flemish cities through which he passed vie with each other in solemnizing his arrival with costly festivities.* Philip's eye remained dark; all the profusion of magnificence, all the loud and hearty effusions of the sincerest joy, could not win from him one approving smile.

Charles entirely missed his aim by presenting his son to the Flemings. They might, eventually, have endured his yoke with less impatience if he had never set his foot in their land. But his look forewarned them what they had to expect; his entry into Brussels lost him all hearts. The Emperor's gracious affability with his people only served to throw a darker shade on the haughty gravity of his son. They read in his countenance the destructive purpose against their liberties, which, even then, he already revolved in his breast. Forewarned to find in him a tyrant, they were forearmed to resist him.

The throne of the Netherlands was the first which Charles V. abdicated. Before a solemn convention in Brussels he absolved the States-General of their oath, and transferred their allegiance to King Philip, his son. "If my death," addressing the latter as he concluded, "had placed you in possession of these countries, even in that case, so valuable a bequest would have given me great claims on your gratitude. But now that of my free will I transfer them to you, now that I die in order to hasten your enjoyment of them, I only require of you to pay to the people the increased obligation which the voluntary surrender of my dignity lays upon you. Other princes esteem it a peculiar felicity to bequeath to their children the crown which death is already ra-

---

* The town of Antwerp, alone, expended on an occasion of this kind 260,000 gold florins.

vishing from them. This happiness I am anxious to enjoy during my life—I wish to be a spectator of your reign. Few will follow my example, as few have preceded me in it. But this my deed will be praised, if your future life should justify my expectations, if you continue to be guided by that wisdom which you have hitherto evinced, if you remain inviolably attached to the pure faith which is the main pillar of your throne. One thing more I have to add: may Heaven grant you also a son, to whom you may transmit your power by choice, and not by necessity."

After the Emperor had concluded his address, Philip kneeled down before him, kissed his hand, and received his paternal blessing. His eyes, for the last time, were moistened with a tear. All present wept. It was an hour never to be forgotten.

This affecting farce was soon followed by another. Philip received the homage of the assembled states. He took the oath administered in the following words: "I, Philip, by the grace of God, Prince of Spain, of the two Sicilies, &c., do vow and swear that I will be a good and just lord in these countries,

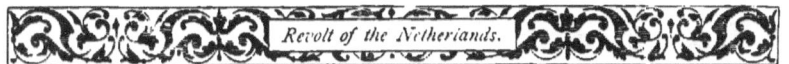

counties and duchies, &c.; that I will well and truly hold, and cause to be held, the privileges and liberties of all the nobles, towns, commons and subjects which have been conferred upon them by my predecessors, and also the customs, usages and rights which they now have and enjoy, jointly and severally, and moreover, that I will do all that by law and right pertains to a good and just prince and lord, so help me God and all His saints."

The alarm which the arbitrary government of the Emperor had inspired, and the distrust of his son, are already visible in the formula of this oath, which was drawn up in far more guarded and explicit terms than that which had been administered to Charles V. himself, and all the Dukes of Burgundy. Philip, for instance, was compelled to swear to the maintenance of their customs and usages, what before his time had never been required. In other obedience was promised than such as should be consistent with the privileges of the country. His officers were then only to reckon on submission and support, so long as they legally discharge the duties intrusted to them. Lastly, in this oath of allegiance, Philip is simply styled only the natural, the hereditary prince, and not, as the Emperor had desired, sovereign or lord; proof enough how little confidence was placed in the justice and liberality of the new sovereign.

PHILIP THE SECOND, RULER OF THE NETHERLANDS

PHILIP II. receiv- ed the lordship of the Netherlands in the brightest period of their prosperity. He was the first of their princes who united them all under his authority. They now consisted of seventeen provinces; the duchies of Brabant, Limburg, Luxembourg and Gueldres; the seven counties of Artois, Hainault, Flanders, Namur, Zütphen, Holland and Zealand; the margravate of Antwerp and the five lordships of Friesland, Mechlin (Malines), Utrecht, Overyssel and Gröningen, which, collectively, formed a great and powerful state able to contend with monarchies. Higher than it then stood, their commerce could not rise. The sources of their wealth were above the earth's surface, but they were more valuable and inexhaustible and richer than all the mines in America. These seventeen provinces which, taken together, scarcely comprised the fifth part of Italy, and do not extend beyond three hundred Flemish miles, yielded an annual revenue to their lord not much inferior to that which Britain formerly paid to its kings, before the latter had annexed so many ecclesiastical domains to their crown. Three hundred and fifty cities, alive with industry and pleasure, many of them fortified by their natural position, and secure without bulwarks or walls; 6,300 market towns of a larger size; smaller villages, farms and castles innumerable, imparted to this territory the aspect of one unbroken flourishing landscape. The nation had now reached the meridian of its splendor; industry and abundance had exalted the genius of the citizen, enlightened his ideas, ennobled his affections; every flower of the intellect had opened with the flourishing condition of the country. A happy temperament under a severe climate cooled the ardor of their blood, and modulated the rage of their passions; equanimity, moderation and enduring patience, the gifts of a northern climate; integrity, justice and faith, the necessary virtues of their profession; and the delightful fruits of liberty, truth, benevolence and a patriotic pride were blended in their character, with a slight admixture of human frailties in soft union with the vices of humanity. No people on earth was more easily governed by a prudent prince, and none with more difficulty by a charlatan or a tyrant. Nowhere was the popular voice so infallible a test of good government as here. True statesmanship could be tried in no nobler school, and a sickly artificial policy had none worse to fear.

A state constituted like this could act and endure with gigantic energy, whenever pressing emergencies called forth its powers and a skilful and provident administration elicited its resources. Charles V. bequeathed to his successor an authority in these provinces little inferior to that of a limited monarchy. The prerogative of the crown had gained a visible ascendancy over the republican spirit, and that complicated machine could now be set in motion almost as certainly and rapidly as the most absolutely governed nation. The numerous nobility, formerly so powerful, cheerfully accompanied their sovereign in his wars, or on the civil changes of the state courted the approving smile of royalty. The crafty policy of the crown had created a new and imaginary good, of which it was the exclusive dispenser. New passions and new ideas of happiness supplanted, at last, the rude simplicity of republican virtue. Pride gave place to vanity, true liberty to titles of honour, a needy independence to a luxurious servitude. To oppress or to plunder their native land, as the absolute satraps of an absolute lord, was a more powerful allurement for the avarice and ambition of the great, than, in the general assembly of the state, to share with the monarch a hundredth part of the supreme power. A large portion, moreover, of the nobility, were deeply sunk in poverty and debt. Charles V. had crippled all the most dangerous vassals of the crown by expensive embassies to foreign courts, under the specious pretext of honorary distinctions. Thus, William of Orange was despatched to Germany with the Imperial crown, and Count Egmont to conclude the marriage contract between Philip and Queen Mary. Both also afterwards accompanied the Duke of Alva to France, to negotiate the peace between the two crowns and the new alliance of their sovereign with Madame Elizabeth. The expenses of these journeys amounted to three hundred thousand florins, towards which the king did not contribute a single penny. When the Prince of Orange was appointed generalissimo, in the place of the Duke of Savoy, he was obliged to defray all the necessary expenses of his office. When foreign ambassadors or princes came to Brussels, it was made incumbent on the nobles to maintain the honor of their king, who himself always dined alone, and never kept open table. Spanish policy had devised a still more ingenious contrivance gradually to impoverish the richest families of the land. Every year, one of the Castilian nobles made his appearance in Brussels, where he displayed a lavish magnificence. In Brussels it was accounted an indelible disgrace to be distanced by a stranger in such munificence. All vied to surpass him, and exhausted their fortunes in this costly emulation, while the Spaniard made a timely retreat to his native country, and by the frugality of four years, repaired the extravagance of one year. It was the foible of the Netherlandish nobility to contest with every stranger the credit of superior wealth, and of this weakness the government studiously availed itself. Certainly these arts did not, in the sequel, produce the exact result that had been calculated on; for these pecuniary burdens only made the nobility the more disposed for innovation, since he

who has lost all can only be a gainer in the general ruin.

The Roman Church had ever been a main support of the royal power, and it was only natural that it should be so. Its golden time was the bondage of the human intellect, and like royalty, it had gained by the ignorance and weakness of men. Civil oppression made religion more necessary and more dear; submission to tyrannical power prepares the mind for a blind, convenient faith, and the hierarchy repaid with usury the services of despotism. In the states, the bishops and prelates were zealous supporters of royalty, and ever ready to sacrifice the welfare of the citizen to the temporal advancement of the church and the political interests of the sovereign. Numerous and brave garrisons also held the cities in awe, which were at the same time divided by religious squabbles and factions, and consequently deprived of their strongest support—union among themselves. How little, therefore, did it require to ensure this preponderance of Philip's power, and how fatal must have been the folly by which it was lost!

But Philip's authority in these provinces, however great, did not surpass the influence which the Spanish monarchy at that time enjoyed throughout Europe. No state ventured to enter the arena of contest with it. France, its most dangerous neighbor, weakened by a destructive war, and still more by internal factions, which boldly raised their heads during the feeble government of a child, was advancing rapidly to that unhappy condition which, for nearly half a century, made it a theatre of the most enormous crimes and the most fearful calamities. In England, Elizabeth could with difficulty protect her still tottering throne against the furious storms of faction and her new church establishment against the insidious arts of the Romanists. That country still awaited her mighty call before it could emerge from a humble obscurity, and had not yet been awakened by the faulty policy of her rival to that vigor and energy with which it finally overthrew him. The Imperial family of Germany was united with that of Spain by the double ties of blood and political interest; and the victorious progress of Soliman drew its attention more to the east than to the west of Europe. Gratitude and fear secured to Philip the Italian princes, and his creatures ruled the Conclave. The monarchies of the North still lay in barbarous darkness and ob-

scurity, or only just began to acquire form and strength, and were as yet unrecognized in the political system of Europe. The most skilful generals, numerous armies accustomed to victory, a formidable marine, and the golden tribute from the West Indies, which now first began to come in regularly and certainly— what terrible instruments were these in the firm and steady hand of a talented prince! Under such auspicious stars did King Philip commence his reign.

Before we see him act, we must first look hastily into the deep recesses of his soul, and we shall there find a key to his political life. Joy and benevolence were wholly wanting in the composition of his character. His temperament and the gloomy years of his early childhood denied him the former; the latter could not be imparted to him by men who had renounced the sweetest and most powerful of the social ties. Two ideas, his own self and what was above that self, engrossed his narrow and contracted mind. Egotism and religion were the contents and the title-page of the history of his whole life. He was a King and a Christian, and was bad in both characters; he never was a man among men, because he never condescended but only ascended. His belief was dark and cruel; for his divinity was a Being of terror from whom he had nothing to hope but everything to fear. To the ordinary man the divinity appears as a comforter, as a savior; before his mind it was set up as an image of fear, a painful, humiliating check to his human omnipotence. His veneration for this Being was so much the more profound and deeply rooted the less it extended to other objects. He trembled servilely before God because God was the only being before whom

he had to tremble. Charles V. was zealous for religion because religion promoted his objects. Philip was so because he had real faith in it. The former let loose the fire and the sword upon thousands for the sake of a dogma, while he himself, in the person of the Pope, his captive, derided the very doctrine for which he had sacrificed so much human blood. It was only with repugnance and scruples of conscience that Philip resolved on the most just war against the Pope; and resigned all the fruits of his victory as a penitent malefactor surrenders his booty. The Emperor was cruel from calculation, his son from impulse. The first possessed a strong and enlightened spirit, and was, therefore, perhaps, the worse man; the second was narrow-minded and weak, but the most upright.

Both, however, as it appears to me, might have been better men than they actually were, and still, on the whole, have acted on the very same principles. What we lay to the charge of personal character of an individual is very often the infirmity, the necessary imperfection of universal human nature. A monarchy so great and so powerful was too great a trial for human pride and too mighty a charge for human power. To combine universal happiness with the highest liberty of the individual, is the sole prerogative of infinite intelligence, which diffuses itself omnipresently over all. But what resource has man when placed in the position of omnipotence? Man can only aid his circumscribed powers by classification; like the naturalist, he establishes certain marks and rules by which to facilitate his own feeble survey of the whole, to which all individualities must conform. All this is accomplished for him by religion. She finds hope and fear planted in every human breast; by making herself mistress of these emotions, and directing their affections to a single object, she virtually transforms millions of independent beings into one uniform abstract. The endless diversity of the human will no longer embarrasses its ruler: now there exists one universal good, one universal evil, which he can bring forward or withdraw at pleasure, and which works in unison with himself even when absent. Now a boundary is established before which liberty must halt; a venerable, hallowed line, towards which all the various conflicting inclinations of the will must finally converge. The common aim of despotism and of priestcraft is uniformity, and uniformity is a necessary expedient of human poverty and imperfection. Philip became a greater despot than his father, because his mind was more contracted, or, in other words, he was forced to adhere the more scrupulously to general rules the less capable he was of descending to special and individual exceptions. What conclusion could we draw from these principles but that Philip II. could not possibly have any higher object of his solicitude than uniformity both in religion and in laws, because without these he could not reign?

And yet he would have shown more mildness and forbearance in his government if he had entered upon it earlier. In the judgment which is usually formed of this prince, one circumstance does not appear to be sufficiently considered in the history of his mind and heart, which, however, in all fairness, ought to be duly weighed. Philip counted nearly thirty years when he ascended the Spanish throne, and this early maturity of his understanding had anticipated the period of his majority. A mind like his, conscious of its powers, and only too early acquainted with his high expectations, could not brook the yoke of childish subjection in which he stood; the superior genius of the father and the absolute authority of the autocrat, must have weighed heavily on the self-satisfied pride of such a son. The share which the former allowed him in the government of the empire was just important enough to disengage his mind from petty passions and to confirm the austere gravity of his character; but also meagre enough to kindle a fiercer longing for unlimited power. When he actually became possessed of uncontrolled authority, it had lost the charm of novelty. The sweet intoxication of a young monarch in the sudden and early possession of supreme power; that joyous tumult of emotions which opens the soul to every softer sentiment, and to which humanity has owed so many of the most valuable and the most prized of its institutions; this pleasing moment had for him long passed by or had never existed. His character was already hardened when fortune put him to this severe test, and his settled principles withstood the collision of occasional emotion. He had had time, during fifteen years, to prepare himself for the change; and instead of youthfully dallying with the external symbols of his new station, or of losing the morning of his government in the intoxication of an idle vanity, he remained composed and serious enough to enter at once on the full possession of his power, so as to revenge himself through the most extensive employment of it for its having been so long withheld from him.

THE TRIBUNAL OF THE INQUISITION.

HILIP II. no sooner saw himself, through the peace of Chauteau-Cambray, in undisturbed enjoyment of his immense territory, than he directed his whole attention to the great work of purifying religion, and verified the fears of his Netherlandish subjects. The ordinances which his father had caused to be promulgated against heretics were renewed in all their rigor; and terrible tribunals, to whom nothing but the name of inquisition was wanting, were appointed to watch over their execution. But his plan appeared to him scarcely more than half fulfilled, so long as he could not transplant into these countries the Spanish Inquisition in its perfect form—a design in which the Emperor had already suffered shipwreck.

This Spanish Inquisition is an institution of a new and peculiar kind, which finds no prototype in the whole course of time, and admits of comparison with no ecclesiastical nor civil tribunal. Inquisition has existed from the time when reason meddled with what is holy and from the very commencement of skepticism and innovation; but it was in the middle of the thirteenth century, after some examples of apostasy had alarmed the hierarchy, that Innocent III. first erected for it a peculiar tribunal, and separated, in an unnat-

ural manner, ecclesiastical superintendence and instruction from its judicial and primitive office. In order to be the more sure that no human sensibilities or natural tenderness should thwart the stern severity of its statutes, he took it out of the hands of the bishops and secular clergy, who by the ties of civil life were still too much attached to humanity for his purpose, and consigned it to those of the monks, a half-denaturalized race of beings, who had abjured the sacred feelings of nature and were the servile tools of the Roman See. The Inquisition was received in Germany, Italy, Spain, Portugal and France; a Franciscan monk sat as judge in the terrible court which passed sentence on the Templars. A few states succeeded either in totally excluding or else in subjecting it to civil authority. The Netherlands had remained free from it until the government of Charles V.; their bishops exercised the spiritual censorship, and in extraordinary cases, reference was made to foreign courts of inquisition; by the French provinces to that of Paris, by the German to that of Cologne.

But the Inquisition which we are here speaking of came from the west of Europe, and was of a different origin and form. The last Moorish throne in Granada had fallen in the fifteenth century, and the false faith of the Saracen had finally succumbed before the fortunes of Christianity. But the gospel was still new, and but imperfectly established in this youngest of Christian kingdoms, and in the confused mixture of heterogeneous laws and manners, the religions had become mixed. It is true the sword of persecution had driven many thousand families to Africa, but a far larger portion, detained by the love of climate and home, purchased remission from this dreadful necessity by a show of conversion, and continued at Christian altars to serve Mohammed and Moses. So long as prayers were offered towards Mecca, Granada was not subdued; so long as the new Christian, in the retirement of his house, became again a Jew or a Moslem, he was as little secured to the throne as to the Romish See. It was no longer deemed sufficient to compel a perverse people to adopt the exterior forms of a new faith or to wed it to the victorious church by the weak bands of ceremonials; the object now was to extirpate the roots of an old religion and to subdue an obstinate bias, which by the slow operation of centuries had been implanted in their manners, their language and their laws, and by the enduring influence of a paternal soil and sky was still maintained in its full extent and vigor.

If the church wished to triumph completely over the opposing worship, and to secure her new conquest beyond all chance of relapse, it was indispensable that she should undermine the foundation itself on which the old religion was built. It was necessary to break to pieces the entire form of moral character to which it was so closely and intimately attached. It was requisite to loosen its secret roots from the hold they had taken in the innermost depths of the soul; to extinguish all traces of it, both in domestic life and in the civil world; to cause all recollection of it to perish; and, if possible, to destroy the very susceptibility for its impressions. Country and family, conscience and honor, the sacred feelings of society and of nature, are ever the first and immediate ties to which religion attaches itself; from these it derives while it imparts strength. This connection was now to be dissolved, the old religion was violently to be dissevered from the holy feelings of nature, even at the expense of the sanctity itself of these emotions. Thus arose that Inquisition which, to distinguish it from the more humane tribunals of the same name, we usually call the Spanish. Its founder was Cardinal Ximenes, a Dominican monk. Torquemada was the first who ascended its bloody throne, who established its statutes and for ever cursed his order with this bequest. Sworn to the degradation of the understanding and the murder of intellect, the instruments it employed were terror and infamy. Every evil passion was in its pay; its snare was set in every joy of life. Solitude itself was not safe from it; the fear of its omnipresence fettered

the freedom of the soul in its inmost and deepest recesses. It prostrated all the instincts of human nature before it, yielded all the ties which otherwise man held most sacred. A heretic forfeited all claims upon his race; the most trivial infidelity to his mother church divested him of the rights of his nature. A modest doubt in the infallibility of the pope met with the punishment of parricide and the infamy of sodomy; its sentences resembled the frightful corruption of the plague which turns the most healthy body into rapid putrefaction. Even the inanimate things belonging to a heretic were accursed; no destiny could snatch the victim of the Inquisition from its sentence; its decrees were carried in force on corpses and on pictures; and the grave itself was no asylum from its tremendous arm. The presumptuous arrogance of its decrees could only be surpassed by the inhumanity which executed them. By coupling the ludicrous with the terrible, and by amusing the eye with the strangeness of its processions, it weakened compassion by the gratification of another feeling; it drowned sympathy in derision and contempt. The delinquent was conducted with solemn pomp to the place of execution, a blood-red flag was displayed before him, the universal clang of all the bells accompanied the procession. First came the priests in the robes of the Mass and singing a sacred hymn; next followed the condemned sinner, clothed in a yellow vest covered with figures of black devils. On his head he wore a paper cap surmounted by a human figure, around which played lambent flames of fire and ghastly demons flitted. The image of the crucified Saviour was carried before but turned away from the eternally condemned sinner, for whom salvation was no longer available. His mortal body belonged to the material fire, his immortal soul to the flames of hell. A gag closed his mouth, and prevented him from alleviating his pain by lamentations, from awakening compassion by his affecting tale and from divulging the secrets of the holy tribunal. He was followed by the clergy in festive robes, by the magistrates and the nobility; the fathers, who had been his judges, closed the awful procession. It seemed like a solemn funeral procession, but on looking for the corpse on its way to the grave, behold it was a living body, whose groans are now to afford such shuddering entertainment to the people. The executions were generally held on the high festivals, for which a number of

such unfortunate sufferers were reserved in the prisons of the holy house, in order to enhance the rejoicing by the multitude of the victims; and on these occasions the king himself was usually present. He sat with uncovered head, on a lower chair than that of the Grand Inquisitor, to whom on such occasions he yielded precedence. Who, then, would not tremble before a tribunal at which majesty must humble itself?

The great revolution in the church accomplished by Luther and Calvin renewed the causes to which this tribunal owed its first origin, and that which, at its commencement, was invented to clear the petty kingdom of Granada from the feeble remnant of Saracens and Jews, was now required for the whole of Christendom. All the Inquisitions in Portugal, Italy, Germany and France adopted the form of the Spanish; it followed Europeans to the Indies, and established in Goa a fearful tribunal, whose inhuman proceedings make us shudder even at the bare recital. Wherever it planted its foot, devastation followed; but in no part of the world did it rage so violently as in Spain. The victims are forgotten whom it immolated; the human race renews itself, and the lands, too, flourish again which it has devastated and depopulated by its fury; but centuries will elapse before its traces dis-

appear from the Spanish character. A generous and enlightened nation has been stopped by it on its road to perfection; it has banished genius from a region where it was indigenous; and a stillness like that which hangs over the grave has been left in the mind of a people who, beyond most others of our world, were framed for happiness and enjoyment.

The first Inquisitor in Brabant was appointed by Charles V. in the year 1522. Some priests were associated with him as co-adjutors; but he himself was a layman. After the death of Adrian VI., his successor, Clement VII., appointed three Inquisitors for all the Netherlands; and Paul III. again reduced them to two, which number continued until the commencement of the troubles. In the year 1530, with the aid and approbation of the states, the edicts against heretics were promulgated, which formed the foundation of all that followed, and in which, also, express mention is made of the Inquisition. In the year 1550, in consequence of the rapid increase of sects, Charles V. was under the necessity of reviving and enforcing these edicts, and it was on this occasion that the town of Antwerp opposed the establishment of the Inquisition, and obtained an exemption from its jurisdiction. But the spirit of the Inquisition in the Netherlands, in accordance with the genius of

the country, was more humane than in Spain, and, as yet, had never been administered by a foreigner, much less by a Dominican. The edicts which were known to everybody served it as the rule of its decisions. On this very account it was less obnoxious; because, however severe its sentence, it did not appear a tool of arbitrary power, and it did not, like the Spanish Inquisition, veil itself in secrecy.

Philip, however, was desirous of introducing the latter tribunal into the Netherlands, since it appeared to him the instrument best adapted to destroy the spirit of this people and to prepare them for a despotic government. He began, therefore, by increasing the rigor of the religious ordinances of his father; by gradually extending the power of the Inquisitors; by making its proceedings more arbitrary and more independent of the civil jurisdiction. The tribunal soon wanted little more than the name, and the Dominicans, to resemble, in every point, the Spanish Inquisition. Bare suspicion was enough to snatch a citizen from the bosom of public tranquillity and from his domestic circle; and the weakest evidence was a sufficient justification for the use of the rack. Whoever fell into its abyss, returned no more to the world. All the benefits of the laws ceased for him; the maternal care of justice no longer noticed him; beyond the pale of his former world, malice and stupidity judged him according to laws which were never intended for man. The delinquent never knew his accuser, and very seldom his crime, a flagitious, devilish artifice, which constrained the unhappy victim to guess at his error, and in the delirium of the rack, or in the weariness of a long living interment, to acknowledge transgressions which, perhaps,

had never been committed, or, at least, had never come to the knowledge of his judges. The goods of the condemned were confiscated, and the informer encouraged by letters of grace and rewards. No privilege, no civil jurisdiction, was valid against the holy power; the secular arm lost for ever all whom that power had once touched. Its only share in the judicial duties of the latter was to execute its sentences with humble submissiveness. The consequences of such an institution were, of necessity, unnatural and horrible; the whole temporal happiness, the life itself, of an innocent man, was at the mercy of any worthless fellow. Every secret enemy, every envious person, had now the perilous temptation of an unseen and unfailing revenge. The security of property, the sincerity of intercourse, were gone; all the ties of interest were dissolved; all of blood and of affection were irreparably broken. An infectious distrust envenomed social life; the dreaded presence of a spy terrified the eye from seeing, and choked the voice in the midst of utterance. No one believed in the existence of an honest man, or passed for one himself. Good name, the ties of country, brotherhood, even oaths, and all that man holds sacred, were fallen in estimation. Such was the destiny to which a great and flourishing commercial town was subjected, where 100.000 industrious men had been brought together by the single tie of mutual confidence; every-one indispensable to his neighbor, and yet every one was now distrusted and distrustful; all attracted by the desire of gain, and repelled from each other by fear; all the props of society torn away, where social union was the basis of life and existence.

OTHER ENCROACHMENTS ON THE CONSTITU-
TION OF THE NETHERLANDS

ING PHILIP'S unnatural tribunal had proved so intolerable, even to the more submissive spirit of the Spaniard, that it is no wonder it drove a free state to rebellion. But the terror which it inspired was increased by the Spanish troops, which, even after the restoration of peace, were kept in the country, and, in violation of the constitution, garrisoned border towns. Charles V. had been forgiven for this introduction of foreign armies, so long as the necessity of it was evident, and his good intentions were less distrusted. But now men saw in these troops only the alarming preparations of oppression, and the instruments of a detested hierarchy. Moreover, a considerable body of cavalry, composed of natives, and fully adequate for the protection of the country, made these foreigners superfluous. The licentiousness and rapacity, too, of the Spaniards, whose pay was long in arrear, and who indemnified themselves at the expense of the citizens, completed the exasperation of the people, and drove the lower orders to despair. Subsequently, when the general murmur induced the government to move them from the frontiers, and transport them into the islands of Zealand, where ships were prepared for their deportation, their excesses were carried to such a pitch, that the inhabitants left off working at the embankments, and preferred to abandon their native country to the fury of the sea, rather than to submit any longer to the wanton brutality of these lawless bands.

Philip, indeed, would have wished to retain these Spaniards in the country, in order, by their presence, to give weight to his edicts, and to support the innovations which he had resolved to make in the constitution of the Netherlands. He regarded them as a guarantee for the submission of the nation, and as a chain by which he held it captive. Accordingly, he left no expedient untried to evade the persevering importunity of the states, who demanded the withdrawal of these troops; and for this end he exhausted all the resources of chicanery and persuasion. At one time he pretended to dread a sudden invasion by France; although torn by furious factions, that country could scarce support itself against a domestic enemy; at another time they were, he said, to receive his son Don Carlos on the frontiers; whom, however, he never intended should leave Castile. Their maintenance should not be a burden to the nation; he himself would disburse all their expenses from his private purse. In order to detain them with the more appearance of reason he purposely kept back from them their arrears of pay; for, otherwise, he would assuredly have preferred them to the troops of the country, whose demands he fully satisfied. To lull the fears of the nation and to appease the general discontent, he offered the chief command of these troops to the two favorites of the people, the Prince of Orange and Count Egmont. Both, however, declined his offer, with the noble-minded declaration that they could never make up their minds to serve contrary to the laws of the country. The more desire the king showed to have his Spaniards in the country the more obstinately the states insisted on their removal. In the following Diet at Ghent he was compelled, in the very midst of his courtiers, to listen to republican truth. "Why are foreign hands needed for our defence?" demanded the Syndic of Ghent. "Is it that the rest of the world should consider us too stupid or too cowardly to protect ourselves? Why have we made peace if the burdens of war are still to oppress us? In war necessity enforced endurance; in peace our patience is exhausted by its burdens. Or shall we be able to keep in order these licentious bands which thine own presence could not restrain? Here Cambray and Antwerp cry for redress; there Thionville and Marienburg lie waste; and, surely, thou hast not bestowed upon us peace that our cities should become deserts, as they necessarily must if thou freest them not from these destroyers? Perhaps thou art anxious to guard against surprise from our neighbors? This precaution is wise; but the report of their preparations will long outrun their hostilities. Why incur a heavy expense to engage foreigners, who will not care for a country which they must leave to-morrow? Hast thou not still at thy command the same brave Netherlanders to whom thy father intrusted the republic in far more troubled times? Why shouldst thou now doubt their loyalty, which, to thy ancestors, they have preserved for so many centuries inviolate? Will not they be sufficient to sustain the war long enough to give time to thy confederates to join their banners, or to thyself to send succor from the neighboring country?" This language was too new to the king, and its truth too obvious, for him to be able at once to reply to it. "I, also, am a foreigner," he at length exclaimed, "and they would like, I suppose, to expel me from the country!" At the same time he descended from the throne and left the assembly; but the speaker was pardoned for his boldness. Two days afterwards he sent a message to the states, that if he had been apprised earlier that these troops were a burden to them, he would have immediately made preparation to remove them, with himself, to Spain. Now it was too late, for they would not depart unpaid; but he pledged them his most sacred promise that they should not be oppressed with this burden more than four months. Nevertheless the troops remained in this country eighteen months, when the exigencies of the state made their presence indispensable in another part of the world.

The illegal appointment of foreigners to the most important offices of the country afforded further occasion of complaint against the government. Of all the privileges of the provinces none was so obnoxious to the Spaniards as that which excluded strangers from office, and none they had so zealously sought to abrogate. Italy, the two Indies, and all the provinces of this vast empire were indeed open to their rapacity and ambition; but from the richest of them all an inexorable fundamental law excluded them. They artfully persuaded their sovereign that his power in these countries would never be firmly established, so long as he could not employ foreigners as his instrument. The Bishop of Arras, a Burgundian by birth, had already been illegally forced upon the Flemings; and now the Count of Feria, a Castilian, was to receive a seat and voice in the council of state. But this attempt met with a bolder resistance than the king's flatterers had led him to expect, and his despotic omnipotence was this time wrecked by the politic measures of William of Orange and the firmness of the states.

WILLIAM OF ORANGE AND COUNT EGMONT.

UCH were the measures with which Philip ushered in his government of the Netherlands, and such were the grievances of the nation when he was preparing to leave them. He had long been impatient to quit a country where he was a stranger, where there was so much that opposed his secret wishes and where his despotic mind found such undaunted monitors to remind him of the laws of freedom. The peace with France, at last, rendered a longer stay unnecessary; the armaments of Soliman required his presence in the south, and the Spaniards also began to miss their long-absent king. The choice of a supreme Stadtholder for the Netherlands was the principal matter which still detained him. Emanuel Philibert, Duke of Savoy, had filled this place since the resignation of Mary, Queen of Hungary, which, however, so long as the king himself was present, conferred more honor than real influence. His absence would make it the most important office in the monarchy, and the most splendid aim for the ambition of a subject. It had now become vacant through the departure of the duke, whom the peace of Chateau Cambresis had restored to his dominions. The almost unlimited power with which the supreme Stadtholder would be intrusted, the capacity and experience which so extensive and delicate an appointment required, but, especially, the daring designs which the government had in contemplation against the freedom of the country, the execution of which would devolve on him, necessarily embarrassed the choice. The law, which excluded all foreigners from office, made an exception in the case of the supreme Stadtholder. As he could not be, at the same time, a native of all the provinces, it was allowable for him not to long to any one of them; for the jealousy of the man of Brabant would concede no greater right to a Fleming, whose home was half a mile from his frontier, than to a Sicilian, who lived in another soil and under a different sky. But here the interests of the crown itself seemed to favor the appointment of a native. A Brabanter, for instance, who enjoyed the full confidence of his countrymen, if he became a traitor, would have half accomplished his treason before a foreign governor could overcome the mistrust with which his most insignificant measures would be watched. If the government should succeed in carrying through its designs in one province, the opposition of the rest would then be a temerity, which it would be justified in punishing in the severest manner. In the common whole, which the provinces now formed, their individual constitutions were, in a measure, destroyed; the obedience of one would be a law for all, and the privilege which one knew not how to preserve was lost for the rest.

Among the Flemish nobles who could lay claim to the Chief Stadtholdership, the expectations and wishes of the nation were divided between Count Egmont and the Prince of Orange, who were alike entitled to this high dignity—by illustrious birth and personal merits, and by an equal share in the affections of the people. Their high rank placed them both near to the throne, and if the choice of

the monarch was to rest on the worthiest it
must necessarily fall upon one of these two.
As, in the course of our history, we shall often
have occasion to mention both names, the
reader cannot be too early made acquainted
with their characters.

William I., Prince of Orange, was descended from the princely German house of
Nassau, which had already flourished eight
centuries, had long disputed the pre-eminence
with Austria, and had given one Emperor to
Germany. Besides several extensive domains
in the Netherlands, which made him a citizen
of this Republic and a vassal of the Spanish
monarchy, he possessed also in France the independent princedom of Orange. William
was born in the year 1533. at Dillenburg, in
the country of Nassau, of a Countess Stolberg.
His father, the Count of Nassau, of the same
name, had embraced the Protestant religion
and caused his son also to be educated in it;
but Charles V., who early formed an attachment for the boy, took him when quite young
to his court, and had him brought up in the
Romish Church. This monarch, who already
in the child discovered the future greatness of
the man, kept him nine years about his person,

thought him worthy of his personal instruction
in the affairs of government and honored him
with a confidence beyond his years. He alone
was permitted to remain in the Emperor's
presence when he gave audience to foreign
ambassadors—a proof that, even as a boy, he
had already begun to merit the surname of the
Silent. The Emperor was not ashamed even
to confess openly on one occasion, that this
young man had often made suggestions which
would have escaped his own sagacity. What
expectations might not be formed of the intellect of a man who was disciplined in such a
school!

William was twenty-three years old when
Charles abdicated the government, and had
already received from the latter two public
marks of the highest esteem. The Emperor
had intrusted to him, in preference to all the
nobles of his court, the honorable office of
conveying to his brother Ferdinand the Imperial Crown. When the Duke of Savoy, who
commanded the Imperial army in the Netherlands, was called away to Italy by the exigency
of his domestic affairs, the Emperor appointed
him commander-in-chief against the united
representations of his military council. who

WILLIAM OF ORANGE.

declared it altogether hazardous to oppose so young a tyro in arms to the experienced generals of France. Absent and unrecommended by any, he was preferred by the monarch to the laurel-crowned band of his heroes, and the result gave him no cause to repent of his choice.

The marked favor which the prince had enjoyed with the father, was in itself a sufficient ground for his exclusion from the confidence of the son. Philip, it appears, had laid it down for himself as a rule to avenge the wrongs of the Spanish nobility, for the preference which Charles V. had on all important occasions shown to his Flemish nobles. Still stronger, however, were the secret motives which alienated him from the prince. William of Orange was one of those lean and pale men, who, according to Cæsar's words, "sleep not at night and think too much," and before whom the most fearless spirits quail. The calm tranquillity of a never varying countenance concealed a busy, ardent soul, which never ruffled even the veil behind which it worked, and was alike inaccessible to artifice and to love; a versatile, formidable, indefatigable mind, soft and ductile enough to be in-

stantaneously moulded into all forms; guarded enough to lose itself in none; and strong enough to endure every vicissitude of fortune. A greater master in reading and in winning men's hearts never existed than William. Not that, after the fashion of courts, his lips avowed a servility to which his proud heart gave the lie; but because he was neither too sparing nor too lavish of the marks of his esteem, and through a skilful economy of the favors which mostly bind men he increased his real stock in them. The fruits of his meditation were as perfect as they were slowly formed; his resolves were as steadily and indomitably accomplished as they were long in maturing. No obstacles could defeat the plan which he had once adopted as the best; no accidents frustrated it, for they all had been foreseen before they actually occurred. High as his feelings were raised above terror and joy they were, nevertheless, subject in the same degree to fear; but his fear was earlier than the danger, and he was calm in tumult because he had trembled in repose. William lavished his gold with a profuse hand, but he was a niggard of his moments. The hours of repast were the sole hours of relaxation, but these were exclusively devoted to his heart, his family and his friends; this the modest deduction he allowed himself from the cares of his country. Here his brow was cleared with wine, seasoned by temperance and a cheerful disposition; and no serious cares were permitted to enter this recess of enjoyment. His household was magnificent; the splendor of a numerous retinue, the number and respectability of those who surrounded his person, made his habitation resemble the court of a sovereign prince. A sumptuous hospitality, that master-spell of demagogues, was the goddess of his palace. Foreign princes and ambassadors found here a fitting reception and entertainment, which surpassed all that luxurious Belgium could elsewhere offer. A humble submissiveness to the government bought off the blame and suspicion which this munificence might have thrown on his intentions. But this liberality secured for him the affections of the people, whom nothing gratified so much as to see the riches of their country displayed before admiring foreigners, and the high pinnacle of fortune on which he stood enhanced the value of the courtesy to which he condescended. No one, probably, was better fitted by nature for the leader of a conspiracy than William the Silent. A comprehensive and intuitive glance into the past, the present and the future; the talent for improving every favorable opportunity; a commanding influence over the minds of men; vast schemes, which only when viewed from a distance show form and symmetry; and bold calculations, which were wound up in a long chain of futurity; all these faculties he possessed, and kept, moreover, under the control of that free and enlightened virtue, which moves with firm step, even on the very edge of the abyss.

A man like this might at other times have remained unfathomed by his whole generation; but not so by the distrustful spirit of the age in which he lived. Philip II. saw quickly and deeply into a character which, among good ones, most resembled his own. If he had not seen through him so clearly, his distrust of a man in whom were united nearly all the qualities which he prized highest and could best appreciate would be quite inexplicable. But William had another and still more important point of contact with Philip II. He had learned his policy from the same master, and had become, it was to be feared, a more apt scholar. Not by making Machiavelli's *Prince* his study, but by having enjoyed the living in-

struction of a monarch, who reduced the book to practice had he become versed in the perilous arts by which thrones rise and fall. In him Philip had to deal with an antagonist who was armed against his policy, and who, in a good cause, could also command the resources of a bad one. And it was exactly this last circumstance which accounts for his having hated this man so implacably above all others of his day, and his having had so supernatural a dread of him.

The suspicion which already attached to the prince was increased by the doubts which were entertained of his religious bias. So long as the Emperor, his benefactor, lived William believed in the pope; but it was feared, with good ground, that the predilection for the reformed religion, which had been imparted to his young heart, had never entirely left it. Whatever church he may at certain periods of his life have preferred, each might console itself with the reflection that none other possessed him more entirely. In later years he went over to Calvinism with almost as little scruple as, in his early childhood, he deserted the Lutheran profession for the Romish. He defended the rights of the Protestants rather than their opinions against Spanish oppression; not their faith, but their wrongs had made him their brother.

These general grounds for suspicion appeared to be justified by a discovery of his real intentions, which accident had made. William had remained in France as hostage for the peace of Chateau Cambresis, in concluding which he had borne a part; and here, through the imprudence of Henry II., who imagined he spoke with a confidant of the King of Spain, he became acquainted with a secret plot which the French and Spanish courts had formed against Protestants of both kingdoms. The prince hastened to communicate this important discovery to his friends in Brussels whom it so nearly concerned, and the letters which he exchanged on the subject fell, unfortunately, into the hands of the King of Spain. Philip was less surprised at this decisive disclosure of William's sentiments than incensed at the disappointment of his scheme; and the Spanish nobles, who had never forgiven the prince that moment when, in the last act of his life, the greatest of Emperors leaned upon his shoulders, did not neglect this favorable opportunity of finally ruining, in the good opinion of their king, the betrayer of a state secret.

Of a lineage no less noble than that of William was Lamoral, Count Egmont and Prince of Gavre, a descendant of the Dukes of Gueldres, whose martial courage had wearied out the arms of Austria. His family was highly distinguished in the annals of the country; one of his ancestors had, under Maximilian, already filled the office of Stadtholder over Holland. Egmont's marriage with the Duchess Sabina of Bavaria reflected additional lustre on the splendor of his birth and made him powerful through the greatness of this alliance. Charles V. had, in the year 1516, conferred on him at Utrecht the order of the Golden Fleece; the wars of this Emperor were the school of his military genius, and the battle of St. Quentin and Gravelines made him the hero of his age. Every blessing of peace, for which a commercial people feel most grateful, brought to mind the remembrance of the victory by which it was accelerated, and Flemish pride, like a fond mother, exulted over the illustrious son of their country who had filled all Europe with admiration. Nine children who grew up under the eyes of their fellow-citizens multiplied and drew closer the ties between him and his fatherland, and the people's grateful affection for the father was kept alive by the sight of those who were dearest to him. Every appearance of Egmont in public was a triumphal procession; every eye which was fastened upon him recounted his history; his deeds lived in the plaudits of his companions in arms; at the games of chivalry mothers pointed him out to their children. Affability, a noble and courteous demeanor—the amiable virtues of chivalry adorned and graced his merits. His liberal soul shone forth on his open brow; his frank-heartedness managed his secrets no better than his benevolence did his estate, and a thought was no sooner his than it was the property of all. His religion was gentle and humane but not very enlightened, because it derived its light from the heart and not from his understanding. Egmont possessed more of conscience than of fixed principles; his head had not given him a code of its own, but had merely learned it by rote; the mere name of an action, therefore, was often with him sufficient for its condemnation. In his judgment men were wholly bad or wholly good, and had either nothing bad or nothing good; in this system of morals there was no middle term between vice and virtue; and consequently a single good trait often decided his opinion of

men. Egmont united all the eminent qualities which form the hero; he was a better soldier than the Prince of Orange but far inferior to him as a statesman; the latter saw the world as it really was; Egmont viewed it in the magic mirror of an imagination that embellished all that it reflected. Men whom fortune has surprised with a reward for which they can find no adequate ground in their actions, are for the most part very apt to forget the necessary connection between cause and effect, and to insert in the natural consequences of things a higher miraculous power to which, as Cæsar to his fortune, they at last insanely trust. Such a character was Egmont. Intoxicated with the idea of his own merits, which the love and gratitude of his fellow-citizens had exaggerated, he staggered on in this sweet reverie as in a delightful world of dreams. He feared not, because he trusted to the deceitful pledge which destiny had given him of her favor in the general love of the people, and he believed in its justice because he himself was prosperous. Even the most terrible experience of Spanish perfidy could not afterwards eradicate this confidence from his soul, and on the scaffold itself his latest feeling was hope. A tender fear for his family kept his patriotic courage fettered by lower duties. Because he trembled for property and life he could not venture much for the republic. William of Orange broke with the throne because its arbitrary power was offensive to his pride; Egmont was vain, and therefore valued the favors of the monarch. The former was a citizen of the world; Egmont had never been more than a Fleming.

Philip II. still stood indebted to the hero of St. Quentin, and the supreme stadtholdership of the Netherlands appeared the only appropriate reward for such great services. Birth and high station, the voice of the nation and personal abilities, spoke as loudly for Egmont as for Orange; and if the latter was to be passed by. it seemed that the former alone could supplant him.

Two such competitors, so equal in merit, might have embarrassed Philip in his choice, if he had ever seriously thought of selecting either of them for the appointment. But the pre-eminent qualities by which they supported their claim to this office. were the very cause of their rejection; and it was precisely the ardent desire of the nation for their election to it, that irrevocably annulled their title to the appointment. Philip's purpose would not be answered by a stadtholder in the Netherlands who could command the good will and the energies of the people. Egmont's descent from the Duke of Gueldres made him an hereditary foe of the house of Spain, and it seemed impolitic to place the supreme power in the hands of a man to whom the idea might occur of revenging on the son of the oppressor the oppression of his ancestor. The slight put on their favorites could give no just offence either to the nation or to themselves, for it might be pretended that the king passed over both because he would not show a preference to either.

The disappointment of his hopes of gaining the regency did not deprive the Prince of Orange of all expectation of establishing more firmly his influence in the Netherlands. Among the other candidates for this office was also Christina, Duchess of Lorraine, and aunt of the king, who, as mediatrix of the peace of Chateau Cambresis, had rendered important service to the crown. William aimed at the hand of her daughter, and he hoped to promote his suit by actively interposing his good offices for the mother; but he did not reflect that, through this very intercession, he ruined her cause. The Duchess Christina was rejected, not so much for the reason alleged, namely, the dependence of her territories on France made her an object of suspicion to the Spanish court, as because she was acceptable to the people of the Netherlands and the Prince of Orange.

MARGARET OF PARMA. REGENT OF THE NETHERLANDS.

N the midst of the anxiety as to whom the future destinies of the prov-inces would be committed, there appeared on the frontiers of the country the Duchess Margaret of Parma, having been summon-ed by the king from Italy to assume the government.

Margaret was a natural daughter of Charles V. and of a noble Flemish lady named Van-geest, and born 1522. Out of regard for the honor of her mother's house, she was at first educated in obscurity; but her mother, who possessed more vanity than honor, was not very anxious to preserve the secret of her origin, and a princely education betrayed the daughter of the Emperor. While yet a child, she was intrusted to the Regent Margaret, her great aunt, to be brought up at Brussels under her eye. This guardian she lost in her eighth year, and the care of her education devolved on Queen Mary of Hungary, the successor of Margaret in the regency. Her father had already affianced her, while yet in her fourth year, to a Prince of Ferrara; but this alliance being subsequently dissolved, she was betrothed to Alexander de Medicis, the new Duke of Florence, which marriage was, after the victo-rious return of the Emperor from Africa, actually consummated in Naples. In the first year of this unfortunate union, a violent death removed from her a husband who could not love her, and for the third time her hand was disposed of to serve the policy of her father. Octavius Farnese, a prince of thirteen years of age, and nephew of Paul III., obtained, with her person, the duchies of Parma and Piacenza as her portion. Thus, by a strange destiny, Margaret at the age of maturity was contracted to a boy, as in the years of infancy she had been sold to a man. Her disposition, which was anything but feminine, made this last alliance still more unnatural, for her taste and inclinations were masculine, and the whole tenor of her life belied her sex. After the example of her instructress, the Queen of Hungary, and her great aunt, the Duchess Mary of Burgundy, who met her death in this favorite sport, she was passionately fond of hunting, and had acquired in this pursuit such bodily vigor that few men were better able to undergo its hardships and fatigues.

Her gait itself was so devoid of grace that one was far more tempted to take her for a disguised man than for a masculine woman; and Nature, whom she had derided by thus transgressing the limits of her sex, revenged itself finally upon her by a disease peculiar to men—the gout.

These unusual qualities were crowned by a monkish superstition, which was infused into her mind by Ignatius Loyola, her confessor and teacher. Among the charitable works and penances with which she mortified her vanity, one of the most remarkable was that during Passion week she yearly washed, with her own hands, the feet of a number of poor men (who were most strictly forbidden to cleanse themselves beforehand), waited on them at table like a servant and sent them away with rich presents.

Nothing more is requisite than this last feature in her character to account for the preference which the king gave her over all

her rivals; but his choice was at the same time justified by excellent reasons of state. Margaret was born and also educated in the Netherlands. She had spent her early youth among the people, and had acquired much of their national manners. Two regents (Duchess Margaret and Queen Mary of Hungary), under whose eyes she had grown up, had gradually initiated her into the maxims by which this peculiar people might be most easily governed; and they would also serve her as models. She did not want either in talents; and possessed, moreover, a particular turn for business, which she had acquired from her instructors, and had afterwards carried to greater perfection in the Italian school. The Netherlands had been, for a number of years, accustomed to female government; and Philip hoped, perhaps, that the sharp iron of tyranny, which he was about to use against them, would cut more gently if wielded by the hands of a woman. Some regard for his father, who at the time was still living, and was much attached to Margaret, may have in a measure, as it is asserted, influenced this choice; as it is also probable that the king wished to oblige the Duke of Parma, through this mark of attention to his wife, and thus to compensate for denying a request which he was just then compelled to refuse him. As the territories of the duchess were surrounded by Philip's Italian states, and at all times exposed to his arms, he could, with the less danger, intrust the supreme power into her hands. For his full security, her son, Alexander Farnese, was to remain at his court as a pledge for her loyalty. All these reasons were alone sufficiently weighty to turn the king's decision in her favor; but they became irresistible when supported by the Bishop of Arras and the Duke of Alva—the latter, as it appears, because he hated or envied all the other competitors; the former because, even then, in all probability, he anticipated, from the wavering disposition of this princess, abundant gratification for his ambition.

Philip received the new regent on the frontiers with a splendid cortege, and conducted her with magnificent pomp to Ghent, where the states general had been convoked. As he did not intend to return soon to the Netherlands, he desired, before he left them, to gratify the nation for once by holding a solemn Diet, and thus giving a solemn sanction and the force of law to his previous regulations. For the last time he showed himself to his Netherlandish people, whose destinies were, from henceforth, to be dispensed from a mysterious distance. To enhance the splendor of this solemn day, Philip invested eleven knights with the Order of the Golden Fleece, his sister being seated on a chair near himself, while he showed her to the nation as their future ruler. All the grievances of the people, touching the edicts, the Inquisition, the detention of the Spanish troops, the taxes and the illegal introduction of foreigners into the offices and administration of the country, were brought forward in this Diet, and were hotly discussed by both parties; some of them were skilfully evaded or apparently removed, others arbitrarily repelled. As the king was unacquainted with the language of the country, he addressed the nation through the mouth of the Bishop of Arras, recounted to them, with vainglorious ostentation, all the benefits of his government, assured them of his favor for the future, and once more recommended to the states, in the most earnest manner, the preservation of the Catholic faith and the extirpation of heresy. The Spanish troops, he promised, should in a few months evacuate the Netherlands, if only they would allow him time to recover from the numerous burdens of the last war, in order that he might be enabled to collect the means for paying the arrears of these troops; the fundamental laws of the nation should remain inviolate, the imposts should not be grievously burdensome, and the Inquisition should administer its duties with justice and moderation. In the choice of a supreme stadtholder, he added, he had especially consulted the wishes of the nation, and had decided for a native of the country, who had been brought up in their manners and customs, and was attached to them by a love to her native land. He exhorted them, therefore, to show their gratitude by honoring his choice and obeying his sister, the Duchess, as himself. Should, he concluded, unexpected obstacles oppose his return, he would send in his place his son, Prince Charles, who should reside in Brussels.

A few members of this assembly, more courageous than the rest, once more ventured on a final effort for liberty of conscience. Every people, they argued, ought to be treated according to their natural character, as every individual must in accordance to his bodily constitution. Thus, for example, the south may be considered happy under a certain degree of constraint, which would press intolerably on the north. Never, they added, would the Flemings consent to a yoke under which, perhaps, the Spaniards bowed with patience; and rather than submit to it, they would undergo any extremity if it was sought to force such a yoke upon them. This remonstrance was supported by some of the king's counsellors, who strongly urged the policy of mitigating the rigor of religious edicts. But Philip remained inexorable. Better not reign at all, was his answer, than reign over heretics!

According to an arrangement already made by Charles V., three councils or chambers were added to the regent to assist her in the administration of state affairs. As long as Philip was himself present in the Netherlands, these courts had lost much of their power, and the functions of the first of them, the state council, were almost entirely suspended. Now that he quitted the reins of government, they recovered their former importance. In the state council, which was to deliberate upon war and peace and security against external foes, sat the Bishop of Arras, the Prince of Orange, Count Egmont, the President of the Privy Council, Viglius Van Zuichem, Van Aytta, and the Count of Barlaimont, President of the Chamber of Finance. All knights of the Golden Fleece, all privy counsellors and counsellors of finance, as also the members of the great senate at Malines, which had been subjected by Charles V. to the Privy Council in Brussels, had a seat and vote in the Council of State if expressly invited by the regent. The management of the royal revenues and crown lands was vested in the Chamber of Finance, and the Privy Council was occupied with the administration of justice and the civil regulation of the country, and issued all letters of grace and pardon. The governments of the provinces which had fallen vacant were either filled up afresh or the former governors were confirmed. Count Egmont received Flanders and Artois; the Prince of Orange, Holland, Zealand, Utrecht and West Friesland; the Count of Aremberg, East Friesland, Overyssel and Gröningen; the Count of Mansfeld, Luxemburg; Barlaimont, Namur; the Marquis of Bergen, Hainault. Chateau Cambresis and Valenciennes; the Baron of Montigny, Tournay and its dependencies. Other provinces were given to some who have less claim to our attention. Philip of Montmorency, Count of Hoorn, who had been succeeded by the Count of Megen in the government of Gueldres and Zütphen, was confirmed as admiral of the Belgian navy.

Every governor of a province was, at the same time, a knight of the Golden Fleece and member of the Council of State. Each had. in the province over which he presided, the command of the military force which protected it, the superintendence of the civil administration and the judicature; the governor of Flanders alone excepted, who was not allowed to interfere with the administration of justice. Brabant, alone, was placed under the immediate jurisdiction of the regent, who, according to custom, chose Brussels for her constant residence. The induction of the Prince of Orange into his government was, properly speaking, an infraction of the constitution, since he was a foreigner; but several estates which he either himself possessed in the provinces or managed as guardian of his son, his long residence in the country, and above all, the unlimited confidence the nation reposed in him, gave him substantial claims in default of a real title of citizenship.

The military force of the Low Countries consisted, in its full complement, of three thousand horse. At present it did not much exceed two thousand, and was divided into fourteen squadrons, over which, besides the governors of the provinces, the Duke of Arschot, the Counts of Hoogstraten, Bostu, Roeur and Brederode held the chief command. This cavalry, which was scattered through all the seventeen provinces, was only to be called out on sudden emergencies. Insufficient as it was for any great undertaking, it was, nevertheless, fully adequate for the maintenance of internal order, in its courage had been approved in former wars, and the fame of its valor was diffused through the whole of Europe. In addition to this cavalry, it was also proposed to levy a body of infantry, but, hitherto, the states had refused their consent to it. Of foreign troops there were still some German regiments in the service which were waiting for their pay. The four thousand Spaniards, respecting whom so many complaints had been made, were under two Spanish generals, Mendoza and Romero, and were in garrison in the frontier towns.

Among the Belgian nobles, whom the king especially distinguished in these new appointments, the names of Count Egmont and William of Orange stand conspicuous. However inveterate his hatred was of both, and particularly of the latter, Philip nevertheless gave them these public marks of his favor because his scheme of vengeance was not yet fully ripe

and the people were enthusiastic in their devotion to them. The estates of both were declared exempt from taxes, the most lucrative governments were intrusted to them, and by offering them the command of the Spaniards, whom he left behind in the country, the king flattered them with a confidence which he was very far from really reposing in them. But at the very time when he obliged the prince with these public marks of his esteem, he privately inflicted the most cruel injury on him. Apprehensive lest an alliance with the powerful house of Lorraine might encourage this suspected vassal to bolder measures, he thwarted the negotiation for a marriage between him and a princess of that family, and crushed his hopes on the very eve of their accomplishment; an injury which the prince never forgave. Nay, his hatred to the prince on one occasion even got completely the better of his natural dissimulation, and seduced him into a step in which we entirely lose sight of Philip II. When he was about to embark at Flushing, and the nobles of the country attended him to the shore, he so far forgot himself as roughly to accost the prince and openly to accuse him of being the author of the Flemish troubles. The prince answered temperately that what had happened had been done by the states of their own suggestion and on legitimate grounds. "No," said Philip, seizing his hand and shaking it violently, "not the states, but You! You! You!" The prince stood mute with astonishment, and without waiting for the king's embarkation wished him a safe journey and went back to the town.

Thus the enmity which William had long harbored in his breast against the oppressor of a free people was now rendered irreconcilable by private hatred; and this double incentive accelerated the great enterprise which tore from the Spanish crown seven of its brightest jewels.

Philip had greatly deviated from his true character in taking so gracious a leave of the Netherlands. The legal form of a diet, his promise to remove the Spaniards from the frontiers, the consideration of the popular wishes, which had led him to fill the most important offices of the country with the favorites of the people, and finally the sacrifice which he made to the constitution in withdrawing the Count of Feria from the Council of State, were marks of condescension of which his magnanimity was never again guilty. But in fact he never stood in greater need of the good will of the states, that with their aid he might, if possible, clear off the great burden of debt which was still attached to the Netherlands from the former war. He hoped, therefore, by propitiating them through smaller sacrifices to win approval of more important usurpations. He marked his departure with grace, for he knew in what hands he left them. The frightful scenes of death which he intended for this unhappy people were not to stain the splendor of majesty which, like the Godhead, marks its course only with beneficence; that terrible distinction was reserved for his representatives. The establishment of the Council of State was, however, intended rather to flatter the vanity of the Belgian nobility than to impart to them any real influence. The historian Strada (who drew his information with regard to the regent from her own papers) has preserved a few articles of the secret instructions which the Spanish ministry gave her. Among other things it is there stated, if she observed that the councils were divided by factions, or, what would be far worse, prepared by private conferences before the session and in league with one another, then she was to prorogue all the chambers and dispose arbitrarily of the disputed articles in a more select council or committee. In this select committee, which was called the Consulta, sat the Archbishop of Arras, the President Viglius, and the Count of Barlaimont. She was to act in the same manner if emergent cases required a prompt decision. Had this arrangement not been the work of an arbitrary despotism it would perhaps have been justified by sound policy, and republican liberty itself might have tolerated it. In great assemblies, where many private interests and passions co-operate, where a numerous audience presents so great a temptation to the vanity of the orator and parties often assail one another with unmannerly warmth, a decree can seldom be passed with that sobriety and mature deliberation which, if the members are properly selected, a smaller body readily admits of. In a numerous body of men, too, there is, we must suppose, a greater number of limited than of enlightened intellects who through their equal right of vote frequently turn the majority on the side of ignorance. A second maxim which the regent was especially to observe, was to select the very members of council who had voted against any decree to carry it into execution. By this means not only would the people be kept in

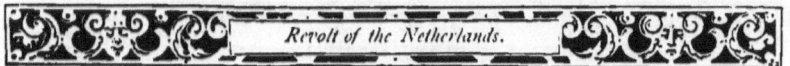

ignorance of the originators of such a law, but the private quarrels also of the members would be restrained and a greater freedom ensured in voting in compliance with the wishes of the court.

In spite of all these precautions Philip would never have been able to leave the Netherlands with a quiet mind, so long as he knew that the chief power in the council of state and the obedience of the provinces were in the hands of the suspected nobles. In order, therefore, to appease his fears from this quarter and also, at the same time, to assure himself of the fidelity of the regent, he subjected her and through her all the affairs of the judicature to the higher control of the Bishop of Arras. In this single individual he possessed an adequate counterpoise to the most dreaded

cabal. To him, as to an infallible oracle of majesty, the duchess was referred, and in him there watched a stern supervisor of her administration. Among all his contemporaries Granvella was the only one whom Philip II. appears to have excepted from his universal distrust; as long as he knew that this man was in Brussels he could sleep calmly in Segovia. He left the Netherlands in September, 1559, was saved from a storm which sank his fleet, and landed at Laredo in Biscay, and in his gloomy joy thanked the Deity who had preserved him by a detestable vow. In the hands of a priest and of a woman was placed the dangerous helm of the Netherlands; and the dastardly tyrant escaped in his oratory at Madrid the supplications, the complaints and the curses of the people.

SECOND BOOK

CARDINAL GRANVELLA.

NTHONY PEREN-OT, Bishop of Arras, subsequently Arch-bishop of Malines, and Metropolitan of all the Netherlands, who, under the name of Cardinal Granvella has been immortal-ized by the hatred of his contemporaries, was born in the year 1516, at Besancon, in Burgundy. His father, Nico-laus Perenot, the son of a blacksmith, had risen by his own merits to be the private secre-tary of Margaret, Duchess of Savoy, at that time Regent of the Netherlands. In this post he was noticed for his habits of business by Charles V., who took him into his own service and employed him in several important nego-tiations. For twenty years he was a member of the Emperor's cabinet and filled the offices of privy counsellor and keeper of the king's seal, and shared in all the state secrets of that monarch. He acquired a large fortune. His honors, his influence and his political know-ledge were inherited by his son Anthony Per-enot, who in his early years gave proofs of the great capacity which subsequently opened to him so distinguished a career. Anthony had cultivated, at several colleges, the talents with which nature had so lavishly endowed him, and in some respects had an advantage over his father. He soon showed that his own abilities were sufficient to maintain the advan-tageous position which the merits of another had procured him. He was twenty-fours years old when the Emperor sent him as his pleni-potentiary to the Ecclesiastical Council of Trent, where he delivered the first specimen of that eloquence which in the sequel gave him so complete an ascendancy over two kings. Charles employed him in several diffi-cult embassies, the duties of which he fulfilled to the satisfaction of his sovereign, and when finally that Emperor resigned the sceptre to his son, he made that costly present complete by giving him a minister who could help him to wield it.

Granvella opened his new career at once with the greatest masterpiece of political genius, in passing so easily from the favor of such a father into equal consideration with such a son. And he soon proved himself de-serving it. At the secret negotiations of which the Duchess of Lorraine had, in 1558, been the medium between the French and Spanish ministers at Peronne, he planned, conjointly with the Cardinal of Lorraine, that conspiracy against the Protestants which was afterwards matured but also betrayed at Cha-teau Cambresis, where Perenot likewise assisted in effecting the so-called peace.

A deeply penetrating, comprehensive intel-lect, an unusual facility in conducting great and intricate affairs, and the most extensive learning, were wonderfully united in this man, with persevering industry and never-wearying patience, while his enterprising genius was associated with thoughtful mechanical regularity. Day and night the state found him vigilant and collected; the most important and the most insignificant things were alike weighed by him with scrupulous attention. Not unfrequently he employed five secretaries at one time, dictating to them in different languages, of which he is said to have spoken seven. What his penetrating mind had slowly matured acquired in his lips both force and grace, and truth set forth by his persuasive eloquence irresistibly carried away all hearers. He was tempted by none of the passions which make slaves of most men. His integrity was incorruptible. With shrewd penetration he saw through the disposition of his master, and could read in his features his whole train of thought and, as it were, the approaching form in the shadow which outran it. With an artifice rich in resources he came to the aid of Philip's more inactive mind, formed into perfect thought his master's crude ideas while they yet hung on his lips, and liberally allowed him the glory of the discovery. Granvella understood the difficult and useful art of depreciating his own talents; of making his own genius the seeming slave of another; thus he ruled while he concealed his sway, and only in this manner could Philip II. be governed. Content with a silent but real power, he did not grasp insatiably at new and outward marks of it which, with lesser minds, are ever the most coveted objects; but every new distinction seemed to sit upon him as easily as the oldest. No wonder if such extraordinary endowments had alone gained him the favor of his master; but a large and valuable treasure of political secrets and experiences which the active life of Charles V. had accumulated, and had deposited in the mind of this man, made him indispensable to his successor. Self-sufficient as the latter was, and accustomed to confide in his own understanding, his timid and crouching policy was fain to lean on a superior mind, and to aid its own irresolution not only by precedent but also by the influence and example of another. No political matter which concerned the royal interest, even when Philip himself was in the Netherlands, was decided without the intervention of Granvella; and when the king embarked for Spain he made the new regent the same

valuable present of the minister which he himself had received from the Emperor, his father.

Common as it is for despotic princes to bestow unlimited confidence on the creatures whom they have raised from the dust, and of whose greatness they themselves are, in a measure, the creators, the present is no ordinary instance; pre-eminent must have been the qualities which could so far conquer the selfish reserve of such a character as Philip's as to gain his confidence, nay, even to win him into familiarity. The slightest ebullition of the most allowable self-respect which might have tempted him to assert, however slightly, his claim to any idea which the king had once ennobled as his own, would have cost him his whole influence. He might gratify, without restraint, the lowest passions of voluptuousness, of rapacity and of revenge, but the only one in which he really took delight, the sweet consciousness of his own superiority and power, he was constrained carefully to conceal from the suspicious glance of the despot. He voluntarily disclaimed all the eminent qualities, which were already his own, in order, as it were, to receive them a second time from the generosity of the king. His happiness seemed to flow from no other source, no other person could have a claim upon his gratitude. The purple, which was sent to him from Rome, was not assumed until the royal permission reached him from Spain. By laying it down on the steps of the throne, he appeared, in a measure, to receive it first from the hands of Majesty. Less politic, Alva erected a trophy in Antwerp, and inscribed his own name under the victory, which he had won as the servant of the crown—but Alva carried with him to the grave the displeasure of his master. He had invaded with audacious hand the royal prerogative, by drawing immediately at the fountain of immortality.

Three times Granvella changed his master, and three times he succeeded in rising to the highest favor. With the same facility with which he had guided the settled pride of an autocrat and the sly egotism of a despot, he knew how to manage the delicate vanity of a woman. His business between himself and the regent, even when they were in the same house, was, for the most part, transacted by the medium of notes, a custom which draws its date from the times of Augustus and Tiberius. When the regent was in any per-

plexity, these notes were interchanged from hour to hour. He probably adopted this expedient in the hope of eluding the watchful jealousy of the nobility, and concealing from them, in part at least, his influence over the regent. Perhaps, too, he also believed that by this means his advice would become more permanent; and, in case of need, this written testimony would be at hand to shield him from blame. But the vigilance of the nobles made this caution vain, and it was soon known in all the provinces that nothing was determined upon without the minister's advice.

Granvella possessed all the qualities requisite for a perfect statesman in a monarchy governed by despotic principles, but was absolutely unqualified for republics which are governed by kings. Educated between the throne and the confessional, he knew of no other relation between man and man than that of rule and subjection; and the innate consciousness of his own superiority gave him a contempt for others. His policy wanted pliability, the only virtue which was here indispensable to its success. He was naturally overbearing and insolent, and the royal authority only gave arms to the natural impetuosity of his disposition and the imperiousness of his order.

He veiled his own ambition beneath the interests of the crown, and made the breach between the nation and the king incurable, because it would render him indispensable to the latter. He revenged on the nobility the lowliness of his own origin; and, after the fashion of all those who have risen by their own merits, he valued the advantages of birth below those by which he had raised himself to distinction. The Protestants saw in him their most implacable foe; to his charge were laid all the burdens which oppressed the country, and they pressed the more heavily because they came from him. Nay, he was even accused of having brought back to severity the milder sentiments to which the urgent remonstrances of the states had at last disposed the monarch. The Netherlands execrated him as the most terrible enemy of their liberties, and the originator of all the misery which subsequently came upon them.

1559. Philip had evidently left the provinces too soon. The new measures of the government were still strange to the people, and could receive sanction and authority from his presence alone; the new machines, which he had brought into play, required to be set in motion by a dreaded and powerful hand,

and to have their first movements watched and regulated. He now exposed his minister to all the angry passions of the people, who no longer felt restrained by the fetters of the royal presence; and he delegated to the weak arm of a subject the execution of projects, in which Majesty itself, with all its powerful supports, might have failed.

The land, indeed, flourished; and a general prosperity appeared to testify to the blessings of the peace which had so lately been bestowed upon it. An external repose deceived the eye, for within raged all the elements of discord. If the foundations of religion totter in a country, they totter not alone; the audacity which begins with things sacred ends with things profane. The successful attack upon the hierarchy had awakened a spirit of boldness, and a desire to assail authority in general, and to test laws as well as dogmas—duties as well as opinions. The fanatical boldness with which men had learned to discuss and decide upon the affairs of eternity might change its subject-matter; the contempt for life and property which religious enthusiasm had taught could metamorphose timid citizens into foolhardy rebels. A female government of nearly forty years had given the nation room to assert their liberty; continual wars, of which the Netherlands had been the theatre, had introduced a license with them, and the right of the stronger had usurped the place of law and order. The provinces were filled with foreign adventurers and fugitives—generally men bound by no ties of country, family, or property, who had brought with them, from their unhappy homes, the seeds of insubordination and rebellion. The repeated spectacles of torture and of death had rudely burst the tenderer threads of moral feeling, and had given an unnatural harshness to the national character.

Still the rebellion would have crouched timorously and silently on the ground if it had not found a support in the nobility. Charles V. had spoiled the Flemish nobles of the Netherlands by making them the participators of his glory, by fostering their national pride, by the marked preference he showed for them over the Castilian nobles, and by opening an arena to their ambition in every part of his empire. In the late war with France they had really deserved this preference from Philip; the advantages which the king reaped from the peace of Chateau Cambresis were, for the most part, the fruits of

their valor, and they now sensibly missed the gratitude on which they had so confidently reckoned. Moreover, the separation of the German empire from the Spanish monarchy, and the less warlike spirit of the new government, had greatly narrowed their sphere of action, and except in their own country, little remained for them to gain. And Philip now appointed his Spaniards, where Charles V. had employed the Flemings. All the passions which the preceding government had raised and kept employed still survived in peace; and in default of a legitimate object, these unruly feelings found, unfortunately, ample scope in the grievances of their country. Accordingly, the claims and wrongs which had been long supplanted by new passions were now drawn from oblivion. By his late appointments the king had satisfied no party; for those even who obtained offices were not much more content than those who were entirely passed over, because they had calculated on something better than they got. William of Orange had received four governments (not to reckon some smaller dependencies which, taken together, were equivalent to a fifth), but William had nourished hopes of Flanders and Brabant. He and Count Egmont forgot what had really fallen to their share, and only remembered that they had lost the regency. The majority of the nobles were either plunged into debt by their own extravagance, or had willingly enough been drawn into it by the government. Now that they were excluded from the prospect of lucrative appointments, they at once saw themselves exposed to poverty, which pained them the more sensibly when they contrasted the splendor of the affluent citizens with their own necessities. In the extremities to which they were reduced, many would have readily assisted in the commission even of crimes; how then could they resist the seductive offers of the Calvinists, who liberally repaid them for their intercession and protection? Lastly, many whose estates were past redemption placed their last hope in a general devastation, and stood prepared, at the first favorable moment, to cast the torch of discord into the Republic.

This threatening aspect of the public mind was rendered still more alarming by the unfortunate vicinity of France. What Philip dreaded for the provinces was there already accomplished. The fate of that kingdom prefigured to him the destiny of his Netherlands, and the spirit of rebellion found there a seductive example. A similar state of things had, under Francis I. and Henry II., scattered the seeds of innovation in that kingdom; a similar fury of persecution and a like spirit of faction had encouraged its growth. Now, Huguenots and Catholics were struggling in a dubious contest; furious parties disorganized the whole monarchy, and were violently hurrying this once powerful state to the brink of destruction. Here, as there, private interest, ambition and party feeling might veil themselves under the names of religion and patriotism, and the passions of a few citizens drive the entire nation to take up arms. The frontiers of both countries merged in Walloon Flanders; the rebellion might, like an agitated sea, cast its waves as far as this: would a country be closed against it, whose language, manners and character wavered between those of France and Belgium? As yet, the government had taken no census of its Protestant subjects in these countries, but the new sect, it was aware, was a vast, compact republic, which extended its roots through all the monarchies of Christendom, and the slightest disturbance in any of its most distant members vibrated to its centre. It was, as it were, a chain of threatening volcanoes, which, united by subterraneous passages, ignite at the same moment with alarming sympathy. The Netherlands were, necessarily, open to all nations, because they derived their support from all. Was it possible for Philip to close a commercial state as easily as he could Spain? If he wished to purify these provinces from heresy, it was necessary for him to commence by extirpating it in France.

It was in this state that Granvella found the Netherlands at the beginning of his administration (1560).

To restore to these countries the uniformity of papistry, to break the co-ordinate power of the nobility and the states, and to exalt the royal authority on the ruins of republican freedom, was the great object of Spanish policy, and the express commission of the new minister. But obstacles stood in the way of its accomplishment; to conquer these demanded the invention of new resources, the application of new machinery. The Inquisition, indeed, and the religious edicts appeared sufficient to check the contagion of heresy; but the latter required superintendence, and the former able instruments, for its now extended jurisdiction. The church constitution continued the same as it had been in earlier times, when the provinces were less populous, when the church still enjoyed universal repose, and could be more easily overlooked and controlled. A succession of several centuries, which changed the whole interior form of the provinces, had left the form of the hierarchy unaltered, which, moreover, was protected from the arbitrary will of its ruler by the particular privileges of the provinces. All the seventeen provinces were parcelled out under four bishops, who had their seats at Arras, Tournay, Cambray and Utrecht, and were subject to the primates of Rheims and Cologne. Philip the Good, Duke of Burgundy, had, indeed, meditated an increase in the number of the bishops to meet the wants of the increasing population, but, unfortunately, in the excitement of a life of pleasure had abandoned the project. Ambition and lust of conquest withdrew the mind of Charles the Bold from the internal concerns of his kingdom, and Maximilian had already too many subjects of dispute with the states to venture to add to their number by proposing this change. A stormy reign prevented Charles V. from the execution of this extensive plan, which Philip II. now undertook as a bequest from all these princes. The moment had now arrived when the urgent necessities of the church would excuse the innovation, and the leisure of peace favored its accomplishment. With the prodigious crowd of people from all the countries of Europe who were crowded together in the towns of the Netherlands, a multitude of religious opinions had also grown up; and it was impossible that religion could any longer be effectually superintended by so few eyes as were formerly sufficient. While the number of bishops was so small, their districts must, of necessity, have been proportionably extensive, and four men could not be adequate to maintain the purity of the faith through so wide a district.

The jurisdiction which the Archbishops of Cologne and Rheims exercised over the Netherlands had long been a stumbling-block to the government, which could not look on this territory as really its own property so long as such an important branch of power was still wielded by foreign hands. To snatch this prerogative from the alien archbishops, by new and active agents to give fresh life and vigor to the superintendence of the faith, and, at the same time, to strengthen the number of the partisans of government at the diet, no

more effectual means could be devised than to
increase the number of bishops. Resolved
upon doing this, Philip II. ascended the
throne; but he soon found that a change in
the hierarchy would inevitably meet with warm
opposition from the states, without whose consent, nevertheless, it would be vain to attempt
it. Philip foresaw that the nobility would
never approve of a measure which would so
strongly augment the royal party and take
from the aristocracy the preponderance of
power in the diet. The revenues, too, for
the maintenance of these new bishops, must
be diverted from the abbots and monks, and
these formed a considerable part of the states
of the realm. He had, besides, to fear the
opposition of the Protestants, who would not
fail to act secretly in the diet against him.
On these accounts, the whole affair was discussed at Rome with the greatest possible
secrecy. Instructed by, and as the agent of,
Granvella, Francis Sonnoi, a priest of Louvain, came before Paul IV., to inform him
how extensive the provinces were, how thriving and populous, how luxurious in their prosperity. But, he continued, in the immoderate
enjoyment of liberty the true faith is neglected,
and heretics prosper. To obviate this evil,
the Romish See must have recourse to extraordinary measures. It was not difficult to prevail on the Romish pontiff to make a change,
which would enlarge the sphere of his own
jurisdiction.

Paul IV. appointed a tribunal of seven cardinals to deliberate upon this important matter; but death called him away, and he left to
his successor, Pius IV., the duty of carrying
their advice into execution. The welcome
tidings of the pope's determination reached
the king in Zealand, when he was just on the
point of setting sail for Spain, and the minister was secretly charged with the dangerous
reform. The new constitution of the hierarchy was published in 1560; in addition to the
then existing four bishoprics, thirteen new
ones were established, according to the number of seventeen provinces, and four of them
were raised into archbishoprics. Six of these
episcopal sees, viz., in Antwerp, Herzogenbusch, Ghent, Bruges, Ypres and Ruremonde,
were placed under the archbishopric of Malines; five others, Haarlem, Middelburg, Leuwarden, Deventer and Gröningen, under the
archbishopric of Utrecht; and the remaining
four, Arras, Tournay, St. Omer and Namur,
which lie nearest to France, and have lan-

guage, character and manners in common
with that country, under the archbishopric of
Cambray. Malines, situated in the middle of
Brabant, and in the centre of all the seventeen
provinces, was made the primacy of all the
rest, and was, with several rich abbeys, the
reward of Granvella. The revenues of the
new bishoprics were provided by an appropriation of the treasures of the cloisters and abbeys, which had accumulated from pious
benefactions during centuries. Some of the
abbots were raised to the episcopal throne,
and with the possession of their cloisters and
prelacies, retained also the vote and the diet
which was attached to them. At the same
time, to every bishopric nine prebends were
attached, and bestowed on the most learned
jurisconsultists and theologians, who were to
support the Inquisition and the bishop in his
spiritual office. Of these, the two who were
most deserving by knowledge, experience and
unblemished life were to be constituted actual
inquisitors, and to have had the first voice in
the Synods. To the Archbishop of Malines,
as metropolitan of all the seventeen provinces,
the full authority was given to appoint, or at
discretion depose, archbishops and bishops,
and the Romish See only to give its ratifica-
tion to his acts.

At any other period the nation would have
received with gratitude and approved of such
a measure of church reform, since it was fully
called for by circumstances, was conducive to
the interests of religion, and absolutely indispensable for the moral reformation of the
monkhood. Now the temper of the times saw
in it nothing but a hateful change. Universal
was the indignation with which it was received.
A cry was raised that the constitution was
trampled under foot, the rights of the nation
violated, and that the Inquisition was already
at the door, and would soon open here, as in
Spain, its bloody tribunal. The people beheld
with dismay these new servants of arbitrary
power and of persecution. The nobility saw
in it nothing but a strengthening of the royal
authority by the addition of fourteen votes in
the states' assembly and a withdrawal of the
firmest prop of their freedom, the balance of
the royal and the civil power. The old bishops
complained of the diminution of their incomes
and the circumscription of their sees; the abbots and monks had not only lost power and
income, but had received in exchange rigid
censors of their morals. Noble and simple,
laity and clergy, united against the common

foe, and while all singly struggled for some petty private interest, the cry appeared to come from the formidable voice of patriotism. Among all the provinces, Brabant was loudest in its opposition. The inviolability of its church constitution was one of the important privileges which it had reserved in the remarkable charter of the " Joyful Entry "—statutes which the sovereign could not violate without releasing the nation from its allegiance to him. In vain did the university of Louvain assert that in disturbed times of the church a privilege lost its power which had been granted in the period of its tranquillity. The introduction of the new bishoprics into the constitution was thought to shake the whole fabric of liberty. The prelacies, which were now transferred to the bishops, must henceforth serve another rule than the advantage of the province of whose states they had been members. The once free patriotic citizens were to be instruments of the Romish See and obedient tools of the archbishop, who again, as first prelate of Brabant, had the immediate control over them. The freedom of voting was gone, because the bishops, as servile spies of the crown, made every one fearful. " Who," it was asked, " will after this venture to raise his voice in Parliament before such observers, or in their presence dare to protect the rights of the nation against the rapacious hands of the government? They will trace out the resources of the provinces, and betray to the crown the secrets of our freedom and our property. They will obstruct the way to all offices of honor; we shall soon see the courtiers of the king succeed the present men; the children of foreigners will, for the future, fill the Parliament, and the private interest of their patron will guide their venal votes." " What an act of oppression," rejoined the monks, " to pervert to other objects the pious designs of our holy institutions, to contemn the inviolable wishes of the dead, and to take that which a devout charity had deposited in our chests for the relief of the unfortunate and make it subservient to the luxury of bishops, thus inflating their arrogant pomp with the plunder of the poor!" Not only the abbots and monks, who really did suffer by this act of appropriation, but every family which could flatter itself with the slightest hope of enjoying, at some time or other, even in the most remote posterity, the benefit of this monastic foundation, felt this disappointment of their distant expectations as much as

if they had suffered an actual injury, and the wrongs of a few abbot prelates became the concern of a whole nation.

Historians have not omitted to record the covert proceedings of William of Orange during this general commotion, who labored to conduct to one end these various and conflicting passions. At his instigation the people of Brabant petitioned the regent for an advocate and protector, since they alone of all his Flemish subjects had the misfortune to unite in one and the same person their counsel and their ruler. Had the demand been granted their choice could fall on no other than the Prince of Orange. But Granvella, with his usual presence of mind, broke through the snare. "The man who receives this office," he declared in the state council, "will, I hope, see that he divides Brabant with the king!" The long delay of the papal bull, which was kept back by a misunderstanding between the Romish and Spanish courts, gave the disaffected an opportunity to combine for a common object. In perfect secrecy the states of Brabant despatched an extraordinary messenger to Pius IV. to urge their wishes in Rome itself. The ambassador was provided with important letters of recommendation from the Prince of Orange, and carried with him considerable sums to pave his way to the father of the church. At the same time a public letter was forwarded from the city of Antwerp to the King of Spain, containing the most urgent representations and supplicating him to spare that flourishing commercial town from the threatened innovation. They knew, it was stated, that the intentions of the monarch were the best, and that the institution of the new bishops was likely to be highly conducive to the maintenance of true religion; but the foreigners could not be convinced of this, and on them depended the prosperity of their town. Among them the most groundless rumors would be as perilous as the most true. The first embassy was discovered in time and its object disappointed by the prudence of the regent; by the second the town of Antwerp gained so far its point that it was to remain without a bishop, at least until the personal arrival of the king, which was talked of.

The example and success of Antwerp gave the signal of opposition to all the other towns for which a new bishop was intended. It is a remarkable proof of the hatred to the Inquisition and the unanimity of the Flemish towns

at this date, that they preferred to renounce all the advantages which the residence of a bishop would necessarily bring to their local trade rather than by their consent promote that abhorred tribunal, and thus act in opposition to the interests of the whole nation. Deventer, Ruremond and Leuwarden placed themselves in determined opposition, and (1561) successfully carried their point; in the other towns the bishops were, in spite of all remonstrances, forcibly inducted. Utrecht, Haarlem, St. Omer and Middelburg were among the first which opened their gates to them; the remaining towns followed their example; but in Malines and Herzogenbusch the bishops were received with very little respect. When Granvella made his solemn entry into the former town not a single nobleman showed himself, and his triumph was wanting in everything that could make it real, because those remained away over whom it was meant to be celebrated.

In the mean time, too, the period had elapsed within which the Spanish troops were to have left the country, and as yet there was no appearance of their being withdrawn. People perceived with terror the real cause of the delay, and suspicion lent it a fatal connection with the Inquisition. The detention of these troops, as it rendered the nation more vigilant and distrustful, made it more difficult for the minister to proceed with the other innovations, and yet he would fain not deprive himself of this powerful and apparently indispensable aid in a country where all hated him, and in the execution of a commission to which all were opposed. At last, however, the regent saw herself compelled by the universal murmurs of discontent to urge most earnestly upon the king the necessity of the withdrawal of the troops. "The provinces," she writes to Madrid, "have unanimously declared that they would never again be induced to grant the extraordinary taxes required by the government so long as word was not kept with them in this matter. The danger of a revolt was far more imminent than that of an attack by the French Protestants, and if a rebellion was to take place in the Netherlands these forces would be too weak to repress it, and there was not sufficient money in the treasury to enlist new." By delaying his answer the king still sought at least to gain time, and the reiterated representations of the regent would still have remained ineffectual if, fortunately for the provinces, a loss which he

had lately suffered from the Turks had not compelled him to employ these troops in the Mediterranean. He therefore at last consented to their departure; they were embarked, 1561, in Zealand, and the exulting shouts of all the provinces accompanied their departure.

Meanwhile Granvella ruled in the council of state almost uncontrolled. All offices, secular and spiritual, were given away through him; his opinion prevailed against the unanimous vote of the whole assembly. The regent herself was governed by him. He had contrived to manage so that her appointment was made out for two years only, and by this expedient he kept her always in his power. It seldom happened that any important affair was submitted to the other members, and if it really did occur it was only such as had been long before decided, to which it was only necessary for formality's sake to give their sanction. Whenever a royal letter was read Viglius received instructions to omit all such passages as were underlined by the minister. It often happened that this correspondence with Spain laid open the weakness of the government or the anxiety felt by the regent, with which it was not expedient to inform the members whose loyalty was distrusted. If, again, it occurred that the opposition gained a majority over the minister, and insisted with determination on an article which he could not well put off any longer, he sent it to the ministry at Madrid for their decision, by which he at least gained time, and in any case was certain to find support. With the exception of the Count of Barlaimont, the President Viglius and a few others, all the other counsellors were but superfluous figures in the senate, and the minister's behaviour to them marked the small value which he placed upon their friendship and adherence. No wonder that men whose pride had been so greatly indulged by the flattering attention of sovereign princes, and to whom as to the idols of their country their fellow-citizens paid the most reverential submission, should be highly indignant at this arrogance of a plebeian. Many of them had been personally insulted by Granvella. The Prince of Orange was well aware that it was he who had prevented his marriage with the Princess of Lorraine, and that he had also endeavored to break off the negotiations for another alliance with the Princess of Savoy. He had deprived Count Horn of the government of Gueldres and Zütphen, and had kept

for himself an abbey which Count Egmont had in vain exerted himself to obtain for a relation. Confident of his superior power, he did not even think it worth his while to conceal from the nobility his contempt for them and which, as a rule, marked his whole administration; William of Orange was the only one with whom he deemed it advisable to dissemble. Although he really believed himself to be raised far above all the laws of fear and of decorum, still, in this point, however, his confident arrogance misled him, and he erred no less against policy than he sinned against propriety. In the existing posture of affairs the government could hardly have adopted a worse measure than that of throwing disrespect on the nobility. It had it in its power to flatter the prejudices and feelings of the aristocracy, and thus artfully and imperceptibly win them over to its plans, and through them subvert the edifice of national liberty. Now it admonished them most inopportunely of their duties, their dignity and their power; calling upon them even to be patriots, and to devote to the cause of true greatness an ambition which hitherto it had

inconsiderately repelled. To carry into effect the ordinances it required the active co-operation of the lieutenant-governors; no wonder, however, that the latter showed but little zeal to afford this assistance. On the contrary, it is highly probable that they silently labored to augment the difficulties of the minister and to subvert his measures, and, through his ill success, to diminish the king's confidence in him and expose his administration to contempt. The rapid progress which, in spite of those horrible edicts, the Reformation made during Granvella's administration in the Netherlands is evidently to be ascribed to the lukewarmness of the nobility in opposing it. If the minister had been sure of the nobles he might have despised the fury of the mob, which would have impotently dashed itself against the dreaded barriers of the throne. The sufferings of the citizens lingered long in tears and sighs, until the arts and the example of the nobility called forth a louder expression of them.

Meanwhile, the inquisitions into religion were carried on with renewed vigor by the crowd of new laborers (1561, 1562), and the ediéts against heretics were enforced with fearful obedience. But the critical moment when this detestable remedy might have been applied was allowed to pass by; the nation had become too strong and vigorous for such rough treatment. The new religion could now be extirpated only by the death of all its professors. The present executions were but so many alluring exhibitions of its excellence, so many scenes of its triumphs and radiant virtue. The heroic greatness with which the viétims died made converts to the opinions for which they perished. One martyr gained ten new proselytes. Not in towns only, or villages, but on the very highways, in the boats and public carriages, disputes were held touching the dignity of the Pope, the Saints, Purgatory and Indulgences, and sermons were preached and men converted. From the country and from the towns the common people rushed in crowds to rescue the prisoners of the Holy Tribunal from the hands of its satellites, and the municipal officers who ventured to support it with the civil forces were pelted with stones. Multitudes accompanied the Protestant preachers whom the Inquisition pursued, bore them on their shoulders to and from church, and at the risk of their lives concealed them from their persecutors. The first province which was seized with the fanatical spirit of rebellion was, as had been expeéted, Walloon Flanders. A French Calvinist, by name Lannoi, set himself up in Tournay as a worker of miracles, where he hired a few women to simulate diseases and to pretend to be cured by him. He preached in the woods near the town, drew the people in great numbers after him, and scattered in their minds the seeds of rebellion. Similar teachers appeared in Lille and Valenciennes, but in the latter place the municipal funétionaries succeeded in seizing the persons of these incendiaries. While, however, they delayed to execute them, their followers increased so rapidly that they became sufficiently strong to break open the prisons and forcibly deprive justice of its viétims. Troops at last were brought into the town and order restored. But this trifling occurrence had, for a moment, withdrawn the veil which had hitherto concealed the strength of the Protestant party, and allowed the minister to compute their prodigious numbers. In Tournay alone five thousand at one time had been seen attending the sermons, and not many less in Valenciennes. What might not be expeéted from

the northern provinces, where liberty was greater and the seat of government more remote, and where the vicinity of Germany and Denmark multiplied the sources of contagion? One slight provocation had sufficed to draw from its concealment so formidable a multitude. How much greater was, perhaps, the number of those who, in their hearts, acknowledged the new seét and only waited for a favorable opportunity to publish their adhesion to it. This discovery greatly alarmed the regent. The scanty obedience paid to the ediéts, the wants of the exhausted treasury, which compelled her to impose new taxes, and the suspicious movements of the Huguenots on the French frontiers, still farther increased her anxiety. At the same time she received a command from Madrid to send off two thousand Flemish cavalry to the army of the Queen Mother in France, who in the distresses of the religious war had recourse to Philip II. for assistance. Every affair of faith, in whatever land it might be, was made by Philip his own business. He felt it as keenly as any catastrophe which could befall his own house, and in such cases always stood ready to sacrifice his means to foreign necessities. If it were interested motives that here swayed him, they were at least kingly and grand, and the bold support of his principles wins our admiration as much as their cruelty withholds our esteem.

The regent laid before the Council of State the royal will on the subjeét of these troops, but with a very warm opposition on the part of the nobility. Count Egmont and the Prince of Orange declared that the time was ill chosen for stripping the Netherlands of troops, when the aspeét of affairs rendered rather the enlistment of new levies advisable. The movements of the troops in France momentarily threatened a surprise, and the commotions within the provinces demanded, more than ever, the utmost vigilance on the part of the government. Hitherto, they said, the German Protestants had looked idly on during the struggles of their brethren in the faith; but will they continue to do so, especially when we are lending our aid to strengthen their enemy? By thus aéting, shall we not rouse their vengeance against us and call their arms into the northern Netherlands? Nearly the whole Council of State joined in this opinion, their representations were energetic and not to be gainsayed. The regent herself, as well as the minister, could not but feel their truth, and their own interests appeared to forbid obedience to the royal mandate. Would it not be impolitic to withdraw from the Inquisition its sole prop, by removing the larger portion of the army and in a rebellious country to leave themselves without defence, dependent on the arbitrary will of an arrogant aristocracy? While the regent, divided between the royal commands, the urgent importunity of her council and her own fears, could not venture to come to a decision, William of Orange rose and proposed the assembling of the States General. But nothing could have inflicted a more fatal blow on the supremacy of the Crown than by yielding to this advice to put the nation in mind of its power and its rights. No measure could be more hazardous at the present moment. The danger which was thus gathering over the minister did not escape him; a sign from him warned the regent to break off the consultation and adjourn the council. "The government," he writes to Madrid, "can do nothing more injurious to itself than to consent to the assembling of the states. Such a step is at all times perilous, because it tempts the nation to test and restrict the rights of the crown; but it is many times more objectionable, at the present moment, when the spirit of rebellion is already widely spread among us; when the abbots, exasperated at the loss of their income, will neglect nothing to impair the dignity of the bishops; when the whole nobility and all the deputies from the towns are led by the arts of the Prince of Orange, and the disaffected can securely reckon on the assistance of the nation." This representation, which at least was not wanting in sound sense, did not fail in having the desired effect on the king's mind. The assembling of the states was rejected once and forever, the penal statutes against the heretics were renewed in all their rigor, and the regent was directed to hasten the despatch of the required auxiliaries.

But to this the Council of State would not consent. All that she obtained was, instead of the troops, a supply of money for the Queen Mother, which at this crisis was still more welcome to her. In place, however, of assembling the states, and in order to beguile the nation with at least the semblance of republican freedom, the regent summoned the governors of the provinces and the knights of the Golden Fleece to a special congress at Brussels, to consult on the present dangers and necessities of the state. When the President Viglius had laid before them the matters on

which they were summoned to deliberate, three days were given to them for consideration. During this time the Prince of Orange assembled them in his palace, where he represented to them the necessity of coming to some unanimous resolution before the next sitting, and of agreeing on the measures which ought to be followed in the present dangerous state of affairs.

The majority assented to the propriety of this course. Only Barlaimont, with a few of the dependents of the cardinal, had the courage to plead for the interests of the crown and of the minister. "It did not behove them," he said, "to interfere in the concerns of the government, and this previous agreement of votes was an illegal and culpable assumption, in the guilt of which he would not participate." A declaration which broke up the meeting without any conclusion being come to. The regent, apprised of it by the Count Barlaimont, artfully contrived to keep the knights so well employed during their stay in the town that they could find no time for coming to any further secret understanding. In this session, however, it was arranged, with their concurrence, that Florence of Montmorency, Lord of Montigny, should make a journey to Spain, in order to acquaint the king with the present posture of affairs. But the regent sent before him another messenger to Madrid, who previously informed the king of all that had been debated between the Prince of Orange and the knights at the secret conference.

The Flemish ambassador was flattered in Madrid with empty protestations of the king's favor and paternal sentiments towards the Netherlands; while the regent was commanded to thwart to the utmost of her power the secret combinations of the nobility, and if possible to sow discord among their most eminent members. Jealousy, private interest and religious differences had long divided many of the nobles; their share in the common neglect and contempt with which they were treated, and a general hatred of the minister had again united them. So long as Count Egmont and the Prince of Orange were suitors for the regency it could not fail but that at times their competing claims should have brought them into collision. Both had met each other on the road to glory and before the throne; both again met in the Republic, where they strove for the same prize—the favor of their fellow-citizens. Such opposite characters soon became estranged, but the powerful sympathy of necessity as quickly reconciled them. Each was now indispensable to the other, and the emergency united these two men together with a bond which their hearts would never have furnished. But it was on this very uncongeniality of disposition that the regent based her plans; if she could fortunately succeed in separating them, she would at the same time divide the whole Flemish nobility into two parties. Through the presents and small attentions by which she exclusively honored these two, she also sought to excite against them the envy and distrust of the rest, and by appearing to give Count Egmont a preference over the Prince of Orange she hoped to make the latter suspicious of Egmont's good faith. It happened that at this very time she was obliged to send an extraordinary ambassador to Frankfort, to be present at the election of a Roman Emperor; she chose for this office the Duke of Arschot, the avowed enemy of the prince, in order, in some degree, to show in his case how splendid was the reward which hatred against the latter might look for.

The Orange faction, however, instead of suffering any diminution had gained an important accession in Count Horn, who, as admiral of the Flemish marine, had convoyed the king to Biscay and now again took his seat in the Council of State. Horn's restless and republican spirit readily met the daring schemes of Orange and Egmont, and a dangerous triumvirate was soon formed by these three friends, which shook the royal power in the Netherlands, but which terminated very differently for each of its members.

(1562.) Meanwhile Montigny had returned from his embassy, and brought back to the Council of State the most gracious assurance of their monarch. But the Prince of Orange had, through his own secret channels of intelligence, received more credible information from Madrid which entirely contradicted this report. By this means he learned all the ill services which Granvella had done him and his friends with the king, and the odious appellations which were there applied to the Flemish nobility. There was no help for them so long as the minister retained the helm of government, and to procure his dismissal was the scheme, however rash and adventurous it appeared, which wholly occupied the mind of the prince. It was agreed between him and Counts Horn and Egmont to despatch a joint letter to the king, and in the name of the whole nobility formally to accuse the minister and press energetically for his removal. The Duke of Arschot, to whom this proposition was communicated by Count Egmont, refused to concur in it, haughtily declaring that he was not disposed to receive laws from Egmont and Orange, that he had no cause of complaint against Granvella, and that he thought it very presumptuous to prescribe to the king what ministers he ought to employ. Orange received a similar answer from the Count of Aremberg. Either the seeds of distrust which the regent had scattered among the nobility had already taken root, or the fear of the minister's power outweighed the abhorrence of his measures; at any rate the whole nobility shrunk back timidly and irresolutely from the proposal. This disappointment did not, however, discourage them; the letter was written and subscribed by all three (1563).

In it Granvella was represented as the prime cause of all the disorders in the Netherlands. So long as the highest power should be intrusted to him it would, they declared, be impossible for them to serve the nation and the king effectually; on the other hand all would revert to its former tranquillity, all opposition be discontinued, and the government regain the affections of the people as soon as his majesty should be pleased to remove this man from the helm of the state. In that case, they added, neither exertion nor zeal would be wanting on their part to maintain in these countries the dignity of the king and the purity of the faith, which was no less sacred to them than to the Cardinal Granvella.

Secretly as this letter was prepared, still the duchess was informed of it in sufficient time to anticipate it by another despatch, and to counteract the effect which it might have had on the king's mind. Some months passed ere an answer came from Madrid. It was mild but vague. "The king," such was its import, "was not used to condemn his ministers unheard on the mere accusations of their enemies. Common justice alone required that the accusers of the cardinal should descend from general imputations to special proofs, and if they were not inclined to do this in writing one of them might come to Spain, where he should be treated with all respect. Besides this letter, which was equally directed to all three, Count Egmont farther received an autograph letter from the king, wherein his

COUNT HORN.

majesty expressed a wish to learn from him in particular what in the common letter had been only generally touched upon. The regent, also, was specially instructed how she was to answer the three collectively and the count singly. The king knew his man. He felt it was easy to manage Count Egmont alone; for this reason he sought to entice him to Madrid, where he would be removed from the commanding guidance of a higher intellect. In distinguishing him above his two friends by so flattering a mark of his confidence, he made a difference in the relation in which they severally stood to the throne; how could they, then, unite with equal zeal for the same object when the inducements were no longer the same? This time, indeed, the vigilance of Orange frustrated the scheme; but the sequel of the history will show that the seed which was now scattered was not altogether lost.

(1563.) The king's answer gave no satisfaction to the three confederates; they boldly determined to venture a second attempt. "It had," they wrote, "surprised them not a little that his majesty had thought their representations so unworthy of attention. It was not as accusers of the minister but as counsellors of his majesty, whose duty it was to inform their master of the condition of his states, that they had despatched that letter to him. They sought not the ruin of the minister, indeed it would gratify them to see him contented and happy in any other part of the world than here in the Netherlands. They were however fully persuaded of this, that his continued presence there was absolutely incompatible with the general tranquillity. The present dangerous condition of their native country would allow none of them to leave it, much less to take so long a journey as to Spain on Granvella's account. If therefore his majesty did not please to comply with their written request, they hoped to be excused for the future from attendance in the senate, where they were only exposed to the mortification of meeting the minister, and where they could be of no service either to the king or the state, but only appeared contemptible in their own sight. In conclusion they begged his majesty would not take ill the plain simplicity of their language, since persons of their character set more value on acting well than on speaking finely." To the same purport was a separate letter from Count Egmont, in which he returned thanks for the royal autograph. This second address was followed by an answer to the effect that, "Their representations should be taken into consideration; meanwhile they were requested to attend the Council of State as heretofore."

It was evident that the monarch was far from intending to grant their request; they therefore from this time forth absented themselves from the State Council, and even left Brussels. Not having succeeded in removing the minister by lawful means, they sought to accomplish this end by a new mode, from which more might be expected. On every occasion they and their adherents openly showed the contempt which they felt for him, and con-

310

trived to throw ridicule on everything he undertook. By this contemptuous treatment they hoped to harass the haughty spirit of the priest, and to obtain through his mortified self-love what they had failed in by other means. In this, indeed, they did not succeed; but the expedient on which they had fallen led, in the end, to the ruin of the minister.

The popular voice was raised more loudly against him as soon as it was perceived that he had forfeited the good opinion of the nobles, and that men whose sentiments they had been used blindly to echo, preceded them in detestation of him. The contemptuous manner in which the nobility now treated him devoted him in a measure to the general scorn, and emboldened calumny, which never spares even what is holiest and purest, to lay its sacrilegious hand on his honor. The new constitution of the church, which was the great grievance of the nation, had been the basis of his fortunes—this was a crime that could not be forgiven. Every fresh execution, and with such spectacles the activity of the inquisitors was only too liberal, kept alive and furnished dreadful exercise to the bitter animosity against him, and at last custom and usage inscribed his name on every act of oppression. A stranger in a land into which he had been introduced against its will; alone among millions of enemies; uncertain of all his tools; supported only by the weak arm of distant royalty; maintaining his intercourse with the nation, which he had to gain, only by means of faithless instruments, all of whom made it their highest object to falsify his actions and misrepresent his motives; lastly, with a woman for his coadjutor who could not share with him the burden of the general execration—thus he stood exposed to the wantonness, the ingratitude, the faction, the envy and all the evil passions of a licentious, insubordinate people. It is worthy of remark that the hatred which he had incurred far outran the demerits which could be laid to his charge; that it was difficult, nay impossible, for his accusers to substantiate by proof the general condemnation which fell upon him from all sides. Before and after him fanaticism dragged its victims to the altar; before and after him civil blood flowed, the rights of men made a mock of and men themselves rendered wretched. Under Charles V. tyranny ought to have pained more acutely through its novelty—under the Duke of Alva it was carried to far more unnatural lengths, in so much that Granvella's adminis-

tration in comparison with that of his successor was even merciful; and yet we do not find that his contemporaries ever evinced the same degree of personal exasperation and spite against the latter, in which they indulged against his predecessor. To cloak the meanness of his birth in the splendor of high dignities, and by an exalted station to place him, if possible, above the malice of his enemies, the regent had made interest at Rome to procure for him the cardinal's hat; but this very honor, which connected him more closely with the Papal court, made him so much the more an alien in the provinces. The purple was a new crime in Brussels and an obnoxious detested garb which, in a measure, publicly held forth to view the principles on which his future conduct would be governed. Neither his honorable rank, which alone often consecrates the most infamous caitiff, nor his talents which commanded esteem, nor even his terrible omnipotence, which daily revealed itself in so many bloody manifestations, could screen him from derision. Terror and scorn, the fearful and the ludicrous were, in this instance, unnaturally blended.[*] Odious rumors branded his honor; murderous attempts on the lives of Egmont and Orange were ascribed to him; the most incredible things found credence; the most monstrous, if they referred to him or were said to emanate from him, surprised no longer. The nation had already become uncivilized to that degree where the most contradictory sentiments prevailed side by side, and the finer boundary lines of decorum and moral feeling are erased. This belief in extraordinary crimes is almost invariably their immediate precursor.

But, with this gloomy prospect, the strange destiny of this man opens at the same time a grander view, which impresses the unprejudiced observer with pleasure and admiration.

---

[*] The nobility, at the suggestion of Count Egmont, caused their servants to wear a common livery on which was embroidered a fool's cap. All Brussels interpreted it for the cardinal's hat, and every appearance of such a servant renewed their laughter; this badge of a fool's cap, which was offensive to the court, was subsequently changed into a bundle of arrows—an accidental jest which took a very serious end and probably was the origin of the arms of the republic. Vit. Vigl. T. II. 35 Thuan. 489. The respect for the cardinal sunk at last so low that a caricature was publicly placed in his own hand, in which he was represented seated on a heap of eggs out of which bishops were crawling. Over him hovered a devil with the inscription, "This is my son, hear ye him!"

Here he beholds a nation dazzled by no splendor and restrained by no fear, firmly, inexorably and unpremeditatedly unanimous in punishing the crime which had been committed against its dignity by the violent introduction of a stranger into the heart of its political constitution. We see him ever aloof and ever isolated, like a foreign hostile body, hovering over a surface which repels its contact. The strong hand itself of the monarch, who was his friend and protector, could not support him against the antipathies of the nation which had once resolved to withhold from him all its sympathy. The voice of national hatred was all-powerful, and was ready to forego even private interest, its certain gains; his alms even were shunned, like the fruits of an accursed tree. Like pestilential vapor the infamy of universal reprobation hung over him. In his case gratitude believed itself absolved from its duties; his adherents shunned him; his friends were dumb in his behalf. So terribly did the people avenge the insulted majesty of their nobles and their nation on the greatest monarch of the earth.

History has repeated this memorable example only once, in Cardinal Mazarin; but the instance differed according to the spirit of the two periods and nations. The highest power could not protect either from derision; but if France found vent for its indignation in laughing at its pantaloon, the Netherlands hurried from scorn to rebellion. The former, after a long bondage under the vigorous administration of Richelieu, saw itself placed suddenly in unwonted liberty: the latter had passed from ancient hereditary freedom into strange and unusual servitude; it was as natural that the Fronde should end again in subjection as that the Belgian troubles should issue in republican independence. The revolt of the Parisians was the offspring of poverty: unbridled, but not bold; arrogant, but without energy; base and plebeian, like the source from which it sprang. The murmur of the Netherlands was the proud and powerful voice of wealth. Licentiousness and hunger inspired the former; revenge, life, property and religion were the animating motives of the latter. Rapacity was Mazarin's spring of action; Granvella's, lust of power. The former was humane and mild; the latter harsh, imperious, cruel. The French minister sought, in the favor of his queen, an asylum from the hatred of the magnates and the fury of the people; the Netherlandish minister provoked the hatred of a whole nation in order to please one man. Against Mazarin were only a few factions and the mob they could arm; an entire and united nation against Granvella. Under the former, parliament attempted to obtain by stealth a power which did not belong to them; under the latter, it struggled for a lawful authority which he insidiously had endeavored to wrest from them. The former had to contend with the princes of the blood and the peers of the realm, as the latter had with the native nobility and the states; but instead of endeavoring, like the former, to overthrow the common enemy, in the hope of stepping themselves into his place, the latter wished to destroy the place itself, and to divide a power which no single man ought to possess entire.

While these feelings were spreading among the people, the influence of the minister at the court of the regent began to totter. The repeated complaints against the extent of his power must at last have made her sensible how little faith was placed in her own; perhaps, too. she began to fear that the universal abhorrence which attached to him, would soon include herself also, or that his longer stay would inevitably provoke the menaced revolt. Long intercourse with him, his instruction and example, had qualified her to govern without him. His dignity began to be more oppressive to her as he became less necessary, and his faults, to which her friendship had hitherto lent a veil, became visible as it was withdrawn. She was now as much disposed to search out and enumerate these faults as she formerly had been to conceal them In this unfavorable state of her feelings towards the cardinal, the urgent and accumulated representations of the nobles began, at last, to find access to her mind, and the more easily as they contrived to mix up her own fears with their own. "It was matter of great astonishment," said Count Egmont to her, "that to gratify a man who was not even a Fleming, and of whom, therefore, it must be well-known that his happiness could not be dependent on the prosperity of this country, the king could be content to see all his Netherlandish subjects suffer, and this to please a foreigner, who if his birth made him a subject of the Emperor, the purple had made a creature of the court of Rome." "To the king alone," added the count, "was Granvella indebted for his being still among the living; for the future, however, he would leave that care of him to the regent, and he hereby gave her warning." As the majority of the nobles, disgusted with the contemptuous treatment which they met with in the Council of State, gradually withdrew from it, the arbitrary proceedings of the minister lost the last semblance of republican deliberation which had hitherto softened the odious aspect, and the empty desolation of the council chamber made his domineering rule appear in all its obnoxiousness. The regent now felt that she had a master over her, and from that moment the banishment of the minister was decided upon.

With this object she despatched her private secretary, Thomas Armenteros, to Spain, to acquaint the king with the circumstances in which the cardinal was placed, to apprise him of the intimations she had received of the intentions of the nobles, and in this manner to cause the resolution for his recall to appear to emanate from the king himself. What she did not like to trust to a letter, Armenteros was ordered ingeniously to interweave in the oral communication which the king would probably require from him. Armenteros fulfilled his commission with all the ability of a consummate courtier; but an audience of four hours could not overthrow the work of many years, nor destroy in Philip's mind his opinion of his minister, which was there unalterably established. Long did the monarch hold counsel with his policy and his interest, until Granvella himself came to the aid of his wavering resolution and voluntarily solicited a dismissal, which he feared could not much longer be deferred. What the detestation of all the Netherlands could not effect, the contemptuous treatment of the nobility accomplished; he was at last weary of a power which was no longer feared and exposed him less to envy than to infamy.

Perhaps, as some have believed, he trembled for his life, which was certainly in more than imaginary danger; perhaps he wished to receive his dismissal from the king under the shape of a boon rather than of a sentence, and after the example of the Romans, meet with dignity a fate which he could no longer avoid. Philip too, it would appear, preferred generously to accord to the nation a request rather than to yield at a later period to a demand, and hoped at least to merit their thanks by voluntarily conceding now what necessity would ere long extort. His fears prevailed over his obstinacy, and prudence overcame pride.

Granvella doubted not for a moment what

the decision of the king would be. A few days after the return of Armenteros, he saw humility and flattery disappear from the few faces which had, till then, still servilely smiled upon him; the last small crowd of base flatterers and eye-servants vanished from around his person; his threshold was forsaken; he perceived that the fructifying warmth of royal favor had left him.

Detraction, which had assailed him during his whole administration, did not spare him even in the moment of resignation. People did not scruple to assert that a short time before he laid down his office he had expressed a wish to be reconciled to the Prince of Orange and Count Egmont, and even offered, if their forgiveness could be hoped for on no other terms, to ask pardon of them on his knees. It was base and contemptible to sully the memory of a great and extraordinary man with such a charge, but it is still more so to hand it down uncontradicted to posterity. Granvella submitted to the royal command with a dignified composure. Already had he written, a few months previously, to the Duke of Alva in Spain, to prepare him a place of refuge in Madrid, in case of his having to quit the Netherlands. The latter long bethought himself whether it was advisable to bring thither so dangerous a rival for the favor of his king, or to deny so important a friend such a valuable means of indulging his old hatred of the Flemish nobles. Revenge prevailed over fear, and he strenuously supported Granvella's request with the monarch. But his intercession was fruitless. Armenteros had persuaded the king that the minister's residence in Madrid would only revive, with increased violence, all the complaints of the Belgian nation, to which his ministry had been sacrificed; for then, he said, he would be suspected of poisoning the very source of that power whose outlets only he had hitherto been charged with corrupting. He therefore sent him to Burgundy, his native place, for which a decent pretext fortunately presented itself. The cardinal gave to his departure from Brussels the appearance of an unimportant journey, from which he would return in a few days. At the same time, however, all the state counsellors, who, under his administration, had voluntarily excluded themselves from its sittings, received a command from the court to resume their seats in the senate at Brussels. Although the latter circumstance made his return not very credible, nevertheless the remotest possibility of it sobered the triumph which celebrated his departure. The regent herself appears to have been undecided what to think about the report; for, in a fresh letter to the king, she repeated all the representations and arguments which ought to restrain him from restoring this minister. Granvella himself, in his correspondence with Barlaimont and Viglius, endeavored to keep alive this rumor, and at least to alarm with fears, however unsubstantial, the enemies whom he could no longer punish by his presence. Indeed, the dread of the influence of this extraordinary man was so exceedingly great that, to appease it, he was at last driven even from his home and his country.

After the death of Pius IV., Granvella went to Rome, to be present at the election of a new pope, and at the same time to discharge some commissions of his master, whose confidence in him remained unshaken. Soon after, Philip made him viceroy of Naples, where he succumbed to the seductions of the climate, and the spirit which no vicissitudes could bend voluptuousness overcame. He was sixty-two years old when the king allowed him to revisit Spain, where he continued with unlimited powers to administer the affairs of Italy. A gloomy old age and the self-satisfied pride of a sexagenarian administration made him a harsh and rigid judge of the opinions of others, a slave of custom, and a tedious panegyrist of past times. But the policy of the closing century had ceased to be the policy of the opening one. A new and younger ministry were soon weary of so imperious a superintendent, and Philip himself began to shun the aged counsellor, who found nothing worthy of praise but the deeds of his father. Nevertheless, when the conquest of Portugal called Philip to Lisbon he confided to the cardinal the care of his Spanish territories. Finally, on an Italian tour, in the town of Mantua, in the seventy-third year of his life, Granvella terminated his long existence in the full enjoyment of his glory, and after possessing for forty years the uninterrupted confidence of his king.

THE COUNCIL OF STATE.

(1564.)

PON the departure of the minister, all the happy results which were promised from his withdrawal were immediately fulfilled. The disaffected nobles resumed their seats in the council, and again devoted themselves to the affairs of the state with redoubled zeal, in order to give no room for regret for him whom they had driven away, and to prove, by the fortunate administration of the state, that his services were not indispensable. The crowd round the duchess was great. All vied with one another in readiness, in submission and zeal in her service; the hours of night were not allowed to stop the transaction of pressing business of state: the greatest unanimity existed between the three councils, the best understanding between the court and the states. From the obliging temper of the Flemish nobility everything was to be had, as soon as their pride and self-will was flattered by confidence and obliging treatment. The regent took advantage of the first joy of the nation to beguile them into a vote of certain taxes, which, under the preceding administration, she could not have hoped to extort. In this, the great credit of the nobility effectually supported her, and she soon learned from this nation the secret so often verified in the German diet—that much must be demanded, in order to get a little.

With pleasure did the regent see herself emancipated from her long thraldom; the emulous industry of the nobility lightened for her the burden of business, and their insinuating humility allowed her to feel the full sweetness of power.

(1564). Granvella had been overthrown, but his party still remained. His policy lived in his creatures whom he left behind him in the Privy Council and in the Chamber of Finance. Hatred still smouldered among the factious, long after the leader was banished, and the names of the Orange and Royalist parties, of the Patriots and Cardinalists, still continued to divide the senate and to keep up the flames of discord. Viglius Van Zuichem Van Aytta, President of the Privy Council, State Counsellor and Keeper of the Seal, was now looked upon as the most important person in the senate and the most powerful prop of the crown and the tiara. This highly meritorious old man, whom we have to thank for some valuable contributions towards the history of the rebellion of the Low Countries, and whose confidential correspondence with his friends has generally been the guide of our narrative, was one of the greatest lawyers of his time, as well as a theologian and priest, and had already, under the emperor, filled the most important offices. Familiar intercourse with the learned men who adorned the age, and at the head of whom stood Erasmus of Rotterdam, combined with frequent travels in the Imperial service, had extended the sphere of his information and experience, and in many points raised him in his principles and opinions above his contemporaries. The fame of his erudition filled the whole century in which he lived, and has handed his name down to posterity. When, in the year 1548, the connection of the Netherlands with the German empire was to be settled at the Diet of Augsburg, Charles V. sent hither this statesman to manage the interests of the provinces; and his ability principally succeeded in turning the negotiations to the advantage of the

315

Netherlands. After the death of the emperor, Viglius was one of the many eminent ministers bequeathed to Philip by his father, and one of the few in whom he honored his memory. The fortune of the minister Granvella, with whom he was united by the ties of an early acquaintance, raised him likewise to greatness; but he did not share the fall of his patron, because he had not participated in his lust of power nor, consequently, the hatred which attached to him. A residence of twenty years in the provinces, where the most important affairs were intrusted to him, approved loyalty to his king and zealous attachment to the Roman Catholic tenets, made him one of the most distinguished instruments of royalty in the Netherlands.

Viglius was a man of learning, but no thinker; an experienced statesman, but without an enlightened mind; of an intellect not sufficiently powerful to break, like his friend Erasmus, the fetters of error, yet not sufficiently bad to employ it, like his predecessor, Granvella, in the service of his own passions. Too weak and timid to follow boldly the guidance of his reason, he preferred trusting to the more convenient path of conscience; a thing was just so soon as it became his duty. He belonged to those honest men who are indispensable to bad ones; fraud reckoned on his honesty. Half a century later he would have received his immortality from the freedom which he now helped to subvert. In the Privy Council at Brussels, he was the servant of tyranny; in the Parliament in London, or in the Senate at Amsterdam, he would have died, perhaps, like Thomas More or Olden Barneveldt.

In Count Barlaimont, the President of the Council of Finance, the opposition had a no less formidable antagonist than in Viglius. Historians have transmitted but little information regarding the services and the opinions of this man. In the first part of his career the dazzling greatness of the Cardinal Granvella seems to have cast a shade over him. After the latter had disappeared from the stage, the superiority of the opposite party kept him down, but still the little that we do find respecting him throws a favorable light over his character. More than once the Prince of Orange exerted himself to detach him from the interests of the cardinal and to join him to his own party—sufficient proof that he placed a value on the prize. All his efforts failed, which shows that he had to do with no

vacillating character. More than once we see him alone, of all the members of the council, stepping forward to oppose the dominant faction and protecting, against universal opposition, the interests of the crown, which were in momentary peril of being sacrificed. When the Prince of Orange had assembled the knights of the Golden Fleece in his own palace, with a view to induce them to come to a preparatory resolution for the abolition of the Inquisition, Barlaimont was the first to denounce the illegality of this proceeding and to inform the regent of it. Some time after the prince asked him if the regent knew of that assembly, and Barlaimont hesitated not a moment to avow to him the truth. All the steps which have been ascribed to him bespeak a man whom neither influence nor fear could tempt—who with a firm courage and indomitable constancy remained faithful to the party which he had once chosen; but who, it must at the same time be confessed, entertained too proud and despotic notions to select any other.

Among the adherents of the royal party at Brussels, we have further the names of the Duke of Arschot, the Counts of Mansfeld, Megen and Aremberg—all three native Netherlanders; and therefore, as it appeared, bound equally with the whole Netherlandish nobility to oppose the hierarchy and the royal power in their native country. So much the more surprised must we feel at their contrary behavior, and which is indeed the more remarkable since we find them on terms of friendship with the most eminent members of the faction, and anything but insensible to the common grievances of their country.

But they had not self-confidence nor heroism enough to venture on an unequal contest with so superior an antagonist. With a cowardly prudence they made their just discontent submit to the stern law of necessity, and imposed a hard sacrifice on their pride because their pampered vanity was capable of nothing better. Too thrifty and too discreet to wish to extort from the justice or the fear of their sovereign the certain good which they already possessed from his voluntary generosity, or to resign a real happiness in order to preserve the shadow of another, they rather employed the propitious moment to drive a traffic with their constancy, which from the general defection of the nobility had now risen in value. Caring little for true glory, they allowed their ambition to decide which party they should take; for the ambition of base minds prefers to bow beneath the hard yoke of compulsion, rather than submit to the gentle sway of a superior intellect. Small would have been the value of the favor conferred had they bestowed themselves on the Prince of Orange ; but their connection with royalty made them so much the more formidable as opponents. There their names would have been lost among his numerous adherents and the splendor of their rival ; on the almost deserted side of the court their insignificant merit acquired lustre.

The families of Nassau and Croi (to the latter belonged the Duke of Arschot) had for several reigns been competitors for influence and honor, and their rivalry had kept up an old feud between their families which religious differences finally made irreconcilable. The house of Croi from time immemorial had been renowned for its devout and strict observance of papistic rites and ceremonies ; the Counts of Nassau had gone over to the new sect—sufficient reasons why Philip of Croi, Duke of Arschot, should prefer a party which placed him the most decidedly in opposition to the Prince of Orange. The court did not fail to take advantage of this private feud, and to oppose so important an enemy to the increasing influence of the house of Nassau in the republic. The Counts Mansfeld and Megen had till lately been the confidential friends of Count Egmont. In common with him they had raised their voice against the minister ; had joined him in resisting the Inquisition and the edicts ; and had hitherto held with him as far as honor and duty would permit. But at these limits the three friends now separated— Egmont's unsuspecting virtue incessantly hurried him forwards on the road to ruin ; Mansfeld and Megen, admonished of the danger, began in good time to think of a safe retreat. There still exist letters which were interchanged between the Counts Egmont and Mansfeld, and which although written at a later period give us a true picture of their former friendship. "If," replied Count Mansfeld to his friend, who in an amicable manner had reproved him for his defection to the king, "if formerly I was of opinion that the general good made the abolition of the Inquisition, the mitigation of the edicts, and the removal of the Cardinal Granvella necessary, the king has now acquiesced in this wish and removed the cause of complaint. We have already done too much against the majesty of the sovereign and the authority of the church ; it is high time for us to turn, if we would wish

to meet the king when he comes with open brow and without anxiety. As regards my own person, I do not dread his vengeance ; with confident courage I would, at his first summons, present myself in Spain, and boldly abide my sentence from his justice and goodness. I do not say this as if I doubted whether Count Egmont can assert the same, but he will act prudently in looking more to his own safety and in removing suspicion from his actions." "If I hear," he says in conclusion, "that he has allowed my admonitions to have their due weight, our friendship continues ; if not, I feel myself in that case strong enough to sacrifice all human ties to my duty and to honor."

The enlarged power of the nobility exposed the republic to almost a greater evil than that which it had just escaped by the removal of the minister. Impoverished by long habits of luxury, which at the same time had relaxed their morals, and to which they were now too much addicted to be able to renounce them, they yielded to the perilous opportunity of indulging their ruling inclination and of again repairing the expiring lustre of their fortunes. Extravagance brought on the thirst for gain, and this introduced bribery. Secular and ecclesiastical offices were publicly put up to sale ; posts of honor, privileges and patents were sold to the highest bidder ; even justice was made a trade. Whom the Privy Council had condemned was acquitted by the Council of State ; and what the former refused to grant was to be purchased from the latter. The Council of State, indeed, subsequently retorted the charge on the two other councils ; but it forgot that it was its own example that corrupted them. The shrewdness of rapacity opened new sources of gain. Life, liberty and religion were insured for a certain sum like landed estates ; for gold, murderers and malefactors were free and the nation was plundered by a lottery. The servants and creatures of the state, counsellors and governors of provinces were, without regard to rank or merit, pushed into the most important posts ; whoever had a petition to present at court had to make his way through the governors of provinces and their inferior servants. No artifice of seduction was spared to implicate in these excesses the private secretary of the duchess, Thomas Armenteros, a man up to this time of irreproachable character. Through pretended professions of attachment and friendship, they contrived to insinuate themselves

317

MARGARET.

into his confidence, and by luxurious entertainments to undermine his principles; the
seductive example infected his morals, and
new wants overcame his hitherto incorruptible
integrity. He was now blind to abuses in
which he was an accomplice, and drew a veil
over the crimes of others in order at the same
time to cloak his own. In connection with
him they robbed the royal exchequer and de-
feated the objects of the government through
a corrupt administration of its revenues.
Meanwhile, the regent wandered on in a fond
dream of power and activity, which the flattery of the nobles artfully knew how to foster.
The ambition of the factions played with the
foibles of a woman, and with empty signs and
an humble show of submission, purchased real
power from her. She soon belonged entirely
to the faction, and had imperceptibly changed
her principles. Diametrically opposing all
her former proceedings, even in direct violation of her duty, she now brought before the
Council of State, which was swayed by the
faction, not only questions which belonged to
the other councils, but also the suggestions
which Viglius had made to her in private, in
the same way as formerly, under Granvella's

administration, she had improperly neglected
to consult it at all. Nearly all business and
all influence were now diverted to the governors of provinces. All petitions were directed to them; by them all lucrative appointments were bestowed. Their usurpations were
indeed carried so far that law proceedings
were withdrawn from the municipal authorities
of the towns and brought before their own
tribunals. The respectability of the provincial courts decreased as theirs extended, and
with the respectability of the municipal functionaries the administration of justice and civil
order declined. The smaller courts soon followed the example of the government of the
country. The spirit which ruled the council
of state at Brussels, soon diffused itself through
the provinces. Bribery, indulgences, robbery,
venality of justice, were universal in the courts
of judicature of the country; morals degenerated, and the new sects availed themselves
of this all-pervading licentiousness to propa-
gate their opinions. The religious indifference
or toleration of the nobles, who either themselves inclined to the side of the innovators
or at least detested the Inquisition as an instrument of despotism, had mitigated the

rigor of the religious edicts; and through the letters of indemnity which were bestowed on many Protestants, the holy office was deprived of its best victims. In no way could the nobility more agreeably announce to the nation its present share in the government of the country than by sacrificing to it the hated tribunal of the Inquisition, and to this inclination induced them still more than the dictates of policy. The nation passed in a moment from the most oppressive constraint of intolerance into a state of freedom, to which, however, it had already become too unaccustomed to support it with moderation. The inquisitors, deprived of the support of the municipal authorities, found themselves an object of derision rather than of fear. In Bruges, the town council caused even some of their own servants to be placed in confinement and kept on bread and water, for attempting to lay hands upon a supposed heretic. About this very time the mob in Antwerp, having made a futile attempt to rescue a person charged with heresy from the holy office, there was placarded in the public market-place an inscription written in blood to the effect that a number of persons were bound by oath to avenge the death of that innocent person.

From the corruption which pervaded the whole Council of State the Privy Council and the Chamber of Finance, in which Viglius and Barlaimont were presidents, had as yet for the most part kept themselves pure.

As the faction could not succeed in insinuating their adherents into those two councils, the only course open to them was, if possible, to render both inefficient and to transfer their business to the Council of State. To carry out this design the Prince of Orange sought to secure the co-operation of the other state counsellors. "They were called, indeed, senators," he frequently declared to his adherents, "but the others possessed the power. If gold was wanted to pay the troops; or when the question was, how the spreading heresy was to be repressed or the people kept in order, then they were consulted; although in fact they were the guardians neither of the treasury nor of the laws, but only the organs through which the other two councils operated on the state. And yet, alone, they were equal to the whole administration of the country, which had been uselessly portioned out amongst three separate chambers. If they would among themselves only agree to reunite to the Council of State these two important branches of government,

which have been dissevered from it, one soul might animate the whole body." A plan was preliminarily and secretly agreed on in accordance with which twelve new Knights of the Fleece were to be added to the Council of State, the administration of justice restored to the tribunal at Malines—to which it originally belonged—the granting of letters of grace, patents and so forth assigned to the President Viglius, while the management of the finances should be committed to it. All the difficulties, indeed, which the distrust of the court and its jealousy of the increasing power of the nobility would oppose to this innovation were foreseen and provided against. In order to constrain the regent's assent some of the principal officers of the army were put forward as a cloak, who were to annoy the court at Brussels with boisterous demands for their arrears of pay, and in case of refusal to threaten a rebellion. It was also contrived to have the regent assailed with numerous petitions and memorials complaining of the delays of justice, and exaggerating the danger which was to be apprehended from the daily growth of heresy. Nothing was omitted to darken the picture of the disorganized state of society, of the abuse of justice and of the deficiency in the finances, which was made so alarming that she awoke with terror from the delusion of prosperity in which she had cradled herself. She called the three councils together to consult them on the means by which these disorders were to be remedied. The majority were in favor of sending an extraordinary ambassador to Spain, who by a circumstantial and vivid delineation should make the king acquainted with the true position of affairs, and if possible prevail on him to adopt efficient measures of reform. This proposition was opposed by Viglius, who however had not the slightest suspicion of the secret designs of the faction. "The evil complained of," he said, "is undoubtedly great, and one which can no longer be neglected with impunity, but it is not irremediable by ourselves. The administration of justice is certainly crippled, but the blame of this lies with the nobles themselves; by their contemptuous treatment they have thrown discredit on the municipal authorities, who moreover are very inadequately supported by the governors of provinces. If heresy is on the increase it is because the secular arm has deserted the spiritual judges, and because the lower orders, following the example of the nobles, have thrown off all respect for those in authority. The provinces are undoubtedly oppressed by a heavy debt, but it has not been accumulated, as alleged, by any malversation of the revenues, but by the expenses of former wars and the king's present exigencies; still, wise and prudent measures of finance would in a short time remove the burden. If the Council of State would not be so profuse of its indulgences, its charters of immunity and its exemptions; if it would commence the reformations of morals with itself, show greater respect to the laws, and do what lies in its power to restore to the municipal functionaries their former consideration; in short, if the councils and the governors of provinces would only fulfil their own duties, the present grounds of complaint would soon be removed. Why, then, send an ambassador to Spain, when as yet nothing has occurred to justify so extraordinary an expedient? If however the council thinks otherwise, he would not oppose the general voice; only he must make it a condition of his concurrence that the principal instruction of the envoy should be to entreat the king to make them a speedy visit."

There was but one voice as to the choice of an envoy. Of all the Flemish nobles Count Egmont was the only one whose appointment would give equal satisfaction to both parties. His hatred of the Inquisition, his patriotic and liberal sentiments and the unblemished integrity of his character, gave to the republic sufficient surety for his conduct, while for the reasons already mentioned he could not fail to be welcome to the king. Moreover, Egmont's personal figure and demeanor were calculated, on his first appearance, to make that favorable impression which goes so far towards winning the hearts of princes; and his engaging carriage would come to the aid of his eloquence, and enforce his petition with those persuasive arts which are indispensable to the success of even the most trifling suits to royalty. Egmont himself, too, wished for the embassy, as it would afford him the opportunity of adjusting personally matters with his sovereign.

About this time the Council, or rather Synod, of Trent closed its sittings, and published its decrees to the whole of Christendom. But these canons, far from accomplishing the object for which the Synod was originally convened and satisfying the expectation of religious parties, had rather widened the breach between them and made the schism irremediable and eternal.

The labors of the Synod instead of purify-ing the Romish Church from its corruptions, had only reduced the latter to greater definiteness and precision and invested them with the sanction of authority. All the subtilties of its teaching, all the arts and usurpations of the Roman See, which had hitherto rested more on arbitrary usage, were now passed into laws and raised into a system. The uses and abuses which during the barbarous times of ignorance and superstition had crept into Christianity were now declared essential parts of its worship, and anathemas were denounced upon all who should dare to contradict the dogmas or neglect the observances of the Romish Communion. All were anathematised who should either presume to doubt the miraculous power of relics and refuse to honor the bones of martyrs, or should be so bold as to doubt the availing efficacy of the intercession of saints. The power of granting indulgences, the first source of the defection from the See of Rome, was now propounded in an irrefragable article of faith; and the principle of monasticism sanctioned by an express decree of the Synod, which allowed males to take the vows at sixteen and females at twelve. And while all the opinions of the Protestants were without exception condemned, no indulgence was shown to their errors or weaknesses, nor a single step taken to win them back by mildness to the bosom of the mother church. Amongst the latter, the wearisome records of the subtle deliberations of the Synod and the absurdity of its decisions increased, if possible, the hearty contempt which they had long entertained for Popery and laid open to their controversialists new and hitherto unnoticed points of attack. It was an ill-judged step to bring the mysteries of the church too close to the glaring torch of reason, and to fight with syllogisms for the tenets of a blind belief.

Moreover, the decrees of the Council of Trent were not satisfactory even to all the powers in communion with Rome. France rejected them entirely, both because she did not wish to displease the Huguenots and also because she was offended by the supremacy which the Pope arrogated to himself over the Council; some of the Roman Catholic princes of Germany likewise declared against it. Little, however, as Philip II. was pleased with many of its articles which trenched too closely upon his own rights, for no monarch was ever more jealous of his prerogative; highly as the Pope's assumption of control over the Council and its arbitrary precipitate dissolution had offended him, just as was his indignation at the slight which the Pope had put upon his ambassador, he nevertheless acknowledged the decrees of the Synod, even in its present form, because it favored his darling object—the extirpation of heresy. Political considerations were all postponed to this one religious object, and he commanded the publication and enforcement of its canons throughout his dominions.

The spirit of revolt which was diffused through the Belgian provinces scarcely required this new stimulus. There the minds of men were in a ferment, and the character of the Romish Church had sunk almost to the lowest point of contempt in the general opinion. Under such circumstances the imperious and frequently injudicious decrees of the Council could not fail of being highly offensive; but Philip II. could not belie his religious character so far as to allow a different religion to a portion of his subjects, even though they might live on a different soil and under different laws from the rest. The regent was strictly enjoined to exact in the Netherlands the same obedience to the decrees of Trent which was yielded to them in Spain and Italy.

They met, however, with the warmest opposition in the Council of State at Brussels. "The nation," William of Orange declared, "neither would nor could acknowledge them since they were, for the most part, opposed to the fundamental principles of their constitution; and for similar reasons they had even been rejected by several Roman Catholic princes." The whole counsel, nearly, was on the side of Orange; a decided majority were for entreating the king either to recall the decrees entirely or, at least, to publish them under certain limitations. This proposition was resisted by Viglius, who insisted on a strict and literal obedience to the royal commands. "The church," he said, "had in all ages maintained the purity of its doctrines and the strictness of its discipline by means of such general councils. No more efficacious remedy could be opposed to the errors of opinion which had so long distracted their country than these very decrees, the rejection of which is now urged by the Council of State. Even if they are occasionally at variance with the constitutional rights of the citizens, this is an evil which can easily be met by a judicious and temperate application of them. For the rest it redounds to the honor of our sovereign, the King of Spain, that he alone of all the princes of his time refuses to yield his better judgment to necessity, and will not, for any fear of consequences, reject measures which the welfare of the church demands and which the happiness of his subjects makes a duty."

But the decrees also contained several matters which affected the rights of the crown itself. Occasion was therefore taken of this fact to propose that these sections, at least, should be omitted from the proclamation. By this means the king might, it was argued, be relieved from these obnoxious and degrading articles by a happy expedient; the national liberties of the Netherlands might be advanced as the pretext for the omission, and the name of the Republic lent to cover this encroachment on the authority of the Synod. But the king had caused the decrees to be received and enforced in his other dominions unconditionally; and it was not to be expected that he would give the other Roman Catholic powers such an example of opposition, and himself undermine the edifice whose foundation he had been so assiduous in laying.

COUNT EGMONT IN SPAIN.

URING this period of discontent Count Egmont was despatched to Spain to make a forcible representation to the king on the subject of these decrees. To persuade him, if possible, to adopt a milder policy towards his Protestant subjects and to propose to him the incorporation of the three councils, was the commission he received from the malcontents. By the regent he was charged to apprise the monarch of the refractory spirit of the people; to convince him of the impossibility of enforcing these edicts of religion in their full severity; and lastly, to acquaint him with the bad state of the military defences and the exhausted condition of the exchequer.

The count's public instructions were drawn up by the President Viglius. They contained heavy complaints of the decay of justice, the growth of heresy and the exhaustion of the treasury. He was also to press urgently a personal visit from the king to the Netherlands. The rest was left to the eloquence of the envoy, who received a hint from the regent not to let so fair an opportunity escape of establishing himself in the favor of his sovereign.

The terms in which the count's instructions and the representations which he was to make to the king were drawn up, appeared to the Prince of Orange far too vague and general. "The president's statement," he said, "of our grievances comes very far short of the truth. How can the king apply the suitable remedies if we conceal from him the full extent of the evil? Let us not represent the number of the heretics inferior to what it is in reality. Let us candidly acknowledge that they swarm in every province and in every hamlet, however small. Neither let us disguise from him the truth that they despise the penal statutes and entertain but little reverence for the government. What good can come of this concealment? Let us rather openly avow to the king that the Republic cannot long continue in its present condition. The Privy Council, indeed, will perhaps pronounce differently, for to them the existing disorders are welcome. For what else is the source of the abuse of justice and the universal corruption of the courts of law but its insatiable rapacity? By what means can the pomp and scandalous luxury of its members, whom we have seen rise from the dust, be supported if not by bribery? Do not the people daily complain that no other key but gold can open an access to them; and do not even their quarrels prove how little they are swayed by a care for the common weal? Are they likely to consult the public good who are the slaves of their private passions? Do they think, forsooth, that we, the governors of the provinces, are with our soldiers to stand ready at the beck and call of an infamous lictor? Let them set bounds to their indulgences and free pardons, which they so lavishly bestow on the very persons to whom we think it just and expedient to deny them. No one can remit the punishment of a crime without sinning against society and contributing to the increase of the general evil. To my mind, and I have no hesitation to avow it, the distribution among

so many councils of the state secrets and the affairs of government has always appeared highly objectionable. The Council of State is sufficient for all the duties of the administration; several patriots have already felt this in silence, and I now openly declare it. It is my decided conviction that the only sufficient remedy for all the evils complained of is to merge the other two chambers in the Council of State. This is the point which we must endeavor to obtain from the king, or the present embassy, like all others, will be entirely useless and ineffectual." The prince now laid before the assembled senate the plan which we have already described. Viglius, against whom this new proposition was individually and mainly directed, and whose eyes were now suddenly opened, was overcome by the violence of his vexation. The agitation of his feelings was too much for his feeble body, and he was found on the following morning paralyzed by apoplexy and in danger of his life.

His place was supplied by Joachim Hopper, a member of the Privy Council at Brussels, a man of old-fashioned morals and unblamable integrity, the president's most trusted and worthiest friend.* To meet the wishes of the Orange party he made some additions to the instructions of the ambassador, relating chiefly to the abolition of the Inquisition and the incorporation of the three councils, not so much with the consent of the regent as in the absence of her prohibition. Upon Count Egmont taking leave of the president, who had recovered from his attack, the latter requested him to procure in Spain permission to resign his appointment. His day, he declared, was passed; like the example of his friend and predecessor Granvella, he wished to retire into the quiet of private life and to anticipate the uncertainty of fortune. His genius warned him of impending storm, by which he could have no desire to be overtaken.

Count Egmont embarked on his journey to Spain in January, 1565, and was received there with a kindness and respect which none of his rank had ever before experienced. The nobles of Castile, taught by the king's example to conquer their feelings, or rather true to his policy, seemed to have laid aside their ancient grudge against the Flemish nobility, and vied with one another in winning his heart by their affability. All his private matters were immediately settled to his wishes by the king, nay, even his expectations exceeded; and during the whole period of his stay he had ample cause to boast of the hospitality of the monarch. The latter assured him in the strongest terms of his love for his Belgian subjects, and held out hopes of his acceding eventually to the general wish and remitting somewhat of the severity of the religious edicts. At the same time, however, he appointed in Madrid a commission of theologians to whom he propounded the question, "Is it *necessary* to grant to the provinces the religious toleration they demand?" As the majority of them were of opinion that the peculiar constitution of the Netherlands and the fear of a rebellion might well excuse a degree of forbearance in their case, the question was repeated more pointedly. "He did not seek to know," he said, "if he might do so, but if he must?" When the latter question was answered in the negative he rose from his seat, and kneeling down before a crucifix prayed in these words, "Almighty Majesty, suffer me not at any time to fall so low as to consent to reign over those who reject thee!" In perfect accordance with the spirit of this prayer were the measures which he resolved to adopt in the Netherlands. On the article of religion this monarch had taken his resolution once forever; urgent necessity might, perhaps, have constrained him temporarily to suspend the execution of the penal statutes, but never formally to repeal them legally or even to modify them. In vain did Egmont represent to him that the public execution of the heretics daily augmented the number of their followers, while the courage and even joy with which they met their death filled the spectators with the deepest admiration, and awakened in them high opinions of a doctrine which could make such heroes of its disciples. This representation was not indeed lost upon the king, but it had a very different effect from what it was intended to produce. In order to prevent these seductive scenes without, however, compromising the severity of the edicts, he fell upon an expedient, and determined in future that the executions should take place in private. The answer of the king on the subject of the embassy was given to the count in writing and

* Vita Vigl. ᴣ. 89. The person from whose memoirs I have already drawn so many illustrations of the times of this epoch. His subsequent journey to Spain gave rise to the correspondence between him and the president, which is one of the most valuable documents for our history.

addressed to the regent. The king, when he
granted him an audience to take leave, did
not omit to call him to account for his behavior to Granvella, and alluded particularly to
the livery invented in derision of the cardinal.
Egmont protested that the whole affair had
originated in a convivial joke, and nothing
was further from their meaning than to dero-
gate in the least from the respect that was
due to royalty. "If he knew," he said,
"that any individual among them had en-

tertained such disloyal thoughts, he himself
would challenge him to answer for it with
his life."

At his departure the monarch made him a
present of fifty thousand florins, and engaged,
moreover, to furnish a portion for his daughter
on her marriage. He also consigned to his care
the young Farnese of Parma, whom, to gratify
the regent his mother, he was sending to
Brussels. The king's pretended mildness
and his professions of regard for the Belgian

nation deceived the open-hearted Fleming. Happy in the idea of being the bearer of so much felicity to his native country, when, in fact, it was more remote than ever, he quitted Madrid, satisfied beyond measure to think of the joy with which the provinces would welcome the message of their good king; but the opening of the royal answer in the Council of State at Brussels disappointed all these pleasing hopes. "Although in regard to the religious edicts," this was its tenor, "his resolve was firm and immovable, and he would rather lose a thousand lives than consent to alter a single letter of it; still, moved by the representations of Count Egmont, he was, on the other hand, equally determined not to leave any gentle means untried to guard the people against the delusions of heresy, and so to avert from them that punishment which must otherwise infallibly overtake them. As he had now learned from the count that the principal source of the existing errors in the faith was in the moral depravity of the clergy, the bad instruction and the neglected education of the young, he hereby empowered the regent to appoint a special commission of three bishops, and a convenient number of learned theologians, whose business it should be to consult about the necessary reforms, in order that the people might no longer be led astray through scandal, nor plunge into error through ignorance. As, moreover, he had been informed that the public executions of the heretics did but afford them an opportunity of boastfully displaying a foolhardy courage, and of deluding the common herd by an affectation of the glory of martyrdom, the commission was to devise means for putting in force the final sentence of the Inquisition with greater secrecy, and thereby depriving condemned heretics of the honor of their obduracy." In order, however, to provide against the commission going beyond its prescribed limits, Philip expressly required that the Bishop of Ypres, a man whom he could rely on as a determined zealot for the Romish faith, should be one of the body. Their deliberations were to be conducted, if possible, in secrecy, while the object publicly assigned to them should be the introduction of the Tridentine decrees. For this, his motive seems to have been twofold; on the one hand, not to alarm the court of Rome by the assembling of a private council; nor, on the other, to afford any encouragement to the spirit of rebellion in the provinces. At its sessions the duchess was to preside, assisted by some of the more loyally disposed of her counsellors, and regularly transmit to Philip a written account of its transactions. To meet her most pressing wants he sent her a small supply in money. He also gave her hopes of a visit from himself; first, however, it was necessary that the war with the Turks, who were then expected in hostile force before Malta, should be terminated. As to the proposed augmentation of the Council of State, and its union with the Privy Council and Chamber of Finance, it was passed over in perfect silence: the Duke of Arschot, however, who is already known to us as a zealous royalist, obtained a voice and seat in the latter. Viglius, indeed, was allowed to retire from the Presidency of the Privy Council, but he was obliged, nevertheless, to continue to discharge its duties for four more years, because his successor, Carl Tyssenaque, of the council for Netherlandish affairs in Madrid, could not sooner be spared.

SEVERE RELIGIOUS EDICTS—UNIVERSAL OPPOSI-
TION OF THE NATION.

GMONT was scarcely returned, when severer edicts against heretics, which, as it were, pursued him from Spain, contradicted the joyful tidings which he had brought of a happy change in the sentiments of the monarch; they were at the same time accompanied with a transcript of the decrees of Trent, as they were acknowledged in Spain, and were now to be proclaimed in the Netherlands also; with it came likewise the death-warrants of some Anabaptists and other kinds of heretics. "The count has been beguiled," William the Silent was now heard to say, "and deluded by Spanish cunning. Self-love and vanity have blinded his penetration; for his own advantage he has forgotten the general welfare." The treachery of the Spanish ministry was now exposed, and this dishonest proceeding roused the indignation of the noblest in the land. But no one felt it more acutely than Count Egmont, who now perceived himself to have been the tool of Spanish duplicity, and to have become unwittingly the betrayer of his own country. "These specious favors, then," he exclaimed loudly and bitterly, "were nothing but an artifice to expose me to the ridicule of my fellow-citizens and to destroy my good name. If this is the fashion after which the king purposes to keep the promises which he made to

me in Spain, let who will take Flanders; for my part, I will prove by my retirement from public business that I have no share in this breach of faith." In fact, the Spanish ministry could not have adopted a surer method of breaking the credit of so important a man than by exhibiting him to his fellow-citizens, who adored him, as one whom they had succeeded in deluding.

Meanwhile the commission had been appointed, and had unanimously come to the following decision: "Whether for the moral reformation of the clergy, or for the religious instruction of the people, or for the education of youth, such abundant provision had already been made in the decrees of Trent that nothing now was requisite but to put these decrees in force as speedily as possible. The imperial edicts against the heretics already, ought on no account to be recalled or modified; the courts of justice, however, might be secretly instructed to punish with death none but obstinate heretics or preachers, to make a difference between the different sects, and to show consideration to the age, rank, sex or disposition of the accused. If it were really the case, that public executions did but inflame fanaticism, then, perhaps, the unheroic, less observed, but still equally severe punishment of the galleys, would be well adapted to bring down all high notions of martyrdom. As to the delinquencies which might have arisen out of mere levity, curiosity and thoughtlessness, it would perhaps be sufficient to punish them by fines, exile or even corporal chastisement."

During these deliberations, which, moreover, it was requisite to submit to the king at Madrid, and to wait for the notification of his approval of them, the time passed away unprofitably, the proceedings against the sectaries being either suspended or, at least, conducted very supinely. Since the recall of

Granvella, the disunion which prevailed in the higher councils, and from thence had extended to the provincial courts of justice, combined with the mild feelings generally of the nobles on the subject of religion, had raised the courage of the sects, and allowed free scope to the proselyting mania of their apostles. The inquisitors, too, had fallen into contempt, in consequence of the secular arm withdrawing its support, and in many places even openly taking their victims under its protection. The Roman Catholic part of the nation had formed great expectations from the decrees of the Synod of Trent, as well as from Egmont's embassy to Spain ; but in the latter case their hopes had scarcely been justified by the joyous tidings which the count had brought back, and in the integrity of his heart left nothing undone to make known as widely as possible. The more disused the nation had become to severity in matters pertaining to religion, the more acutely was it likely to feel the sudden adoption of even still more rigorous measures. In this position of affairs, the royal rescript arrived from Spain, in answer to the proposition of the bishops and the last despatches of the regent. " Whatever interpretation (such was its tenor) Count Egmont may have given to the king's verbal communications, it had never, in the remotest manner, entered his mind to think of altering in the slightest degree the penal statutes which the emperor, his father, had five-and-thirty years ago published in the provinces. These edicts he therefore commanded should henceforth be carried rigidly into effect, the Inquisition should receive the most active support from the secular arm, and the decrees of the Council of Trent be irrevocably and unconditionally acknowledged in all the provinces of his Netherlands. He acquiesced fully in the opinion of the bishops and canonists, as to the sufficiency of the Tridentine decrees as guides in all points of reformation of the clergy or instruction of the people ; but he could not concur with them as to the mitigation of punishment which they proposed, in consideration either of the age, sex or character of individuals, since he was of opinion that his edicts were in no degree wanting in moderation. To nothing but want of zeal and disloyalty on the part of the judges could he ascribe the progress which heresy had already made in the country. In future, therefore, whoever among them should be thus wanting in zeal, must be removed from his office and make room for a

more honest judge. The Inquisition ought to pursue its appointed path firmly, fearlessly and dispassionately, without regard to or consideration of human feelings, and was to look neither before nor behind. He would always be ready to approve of all its measures, however extreme, if it only avoided public scandal."

This letter of the king, to which the Orange party have ascribed all the subsequent troubles of the Netherlands, caused the most violent excitement among the state counsellors, and the expressions which in society they either accidentally or intentionally let fall from them with regard to it, spread terror and alarm among the people. The dread of the Spanish Inquisition returned with new force, and with it came fresh apprehensions of the subversion of their liberties. Already the people fancied they could hear prisons building, chains and fetters forging, and see piles of fagots collecting. Society was occupied with this one theme of conversation, and fear kept no longer within bounds. Writings were affixed to houses of the nobles, in which they were called upon, as formerly Rome called on her Brutus, to come forward and save expiring freedom. Biting pasquinades were published against the new bishops—tormentors as they were called ; the clergy were ridiculed in comedies, and abuse spared the throne as little as the Romish See.

Terrified by the rumors which were afloat, the regent called together all the counsellors of state to consult them on the course she ought to adopt in this perilous crisis. Opinion varied and disputes were violent. Undecided between fear and duty, they hesitated to come to a conclusion, until at last the aged Senator Viglius rose and surprised the whole assembly by his opinion. " It would," he said, " be the height of folly in us to think of promulgating the royal edict at the present moment ; the king must be informed of the reception which, in all probability, it will now meet. In the mean time, the inquisitors must be enjoined to use their power with moderation and to abstain from severity." But if these words of the aged president surprised the whole assembly, still greater was the astonishment when the Prince of Orange stood up and opposed his advice. " The royal will," he said, " is too clearly and too precisely stated ; it is the result of too long and too mature deliberation for us to venture to delay its execution, without bringing on ourselves the re-

proach of the most culpable obstinacy."
"That I take on myself," interrupted Viglius; "I oppose myself to his displeasure. If
by this delay we purchase for him the peace
of the Netherlands, our opposition will eventually secure for us the lasting gratitude of the
king." The regent already began to incline
to the advice of Viglius, when the prince
vehemently interposing, "What," he demanded, "what have the many representations which we have already made effected?
of what avail was the embassy we so lately
dispatched? Nothing! And what then do
we wait for more? Shall we, his state counsellors, bring upon ourselves the whole weight
of his displeasure by determining, at our own
peril, to render him a service for which he
will never thank us?" Undecided and uncertain, the whole assembly remained silent;
but no one had courage enough to assent to
or reply to him. But the prince had appealed
to the fears of the regent, and these left her
no choice. The consequences of her unfortunate obedience to the king's command will
soon appear. But, on the other hand, if by a
wise disobedience she had avoided these fatal
consequences, is it clear that the result would
not have been the same? However, she had
adopted the most fatal of the two counsels;
happen what would, the royal ordinance was

to be promulgated. This time, therefore, faction prevailed, and the advice of the only true
friend of the government, who to serve his
monarch was ready to incur his displeasure,
was disregarded. With this session terminated
the peace of the regent; from this day the
Netherlands dated all the trouble which unin-
terruptedly visited their country. As the
counsellors separated, the Prince of Orange
said to one who stood nearest to him, "Now
will soon be acted a great tragedy."*

* The conduct of the Prince of Orange in this meeting of the council has been appealed to by historians
of the Spanish party as a proof of his dishonesty, and
they have availed themselves over and over again to
blacken his character. "He," say they, "who had invariably up to this period, both by word and deed,
opposed the measures of the court, so long as he had
any ground to fear that the king's measures could be
successfully carried out, supported them now for the
first time, when he was convinced that a scrupulous obedience to the royal orders would inevitably prejudice
him. In order to convince the king of his folly in dis-
regarding his warnings; in order to be able to boast,
'this I foresaw' and 'I foretold that,' he was willing to
risk the welfare of his nation, for which alone he had
hitherto professed to struggle. The whole tenor of his
previous conduct proved that he held the enforcement
of the edicts to be an evil; nevertheless, he at once becomes false to his own convictions and follows an opposite course; although, so far as the nation was concerned,
the same grounds existed as had dictated his former
measures; and he changed his conduct simply that the

328

An edict, therefore, was issued to all the governors of provinces, commanding them rigorously to enforce the mandates of the emperor against heretics, as well as those which had been passed under the present government, the decrees of the Council of Trent, and those of the episcopal commission, which had lately sat to give all the aid of the civil force to the Inquisition, and also to enjoin a similar line of conduct on the officers of government under them. More effectually to secure their object, every governor was to select from his own council an efficient officer, who should frequently make the circuit of the province and institute strict inquiries into the obedience shown by the inferior officers to these commands, and then transmit quarterly to the capital an exact report of their visitation. A copy of the Tridentine decrees, according to the Spanish original, was also sent to the archbishops and bishops, with an intimation that in case of their needing the assistance of the secular power, the governors of their diocese, with their troops, were placed at their disposal. Against these decrees no privilege was to avail; however, the king willed and commanded that in no case should any infringement be made upon the par-

result might be different to the king." "It is clear, therefore," continue his adversaries, "that the welfare of the nation had less weight with him than his animosity to his sovereign. In order to gratify his hatred to the latter he does not hesitate to sacrifice the former." But is it then true that by calling for the promulgation of these edicts he sacrificed the nation? or to speak more correctly, did he carry the edicts into effect by insisting on their promulgation? Can it not, on the contrary, be shown, with far more probability, that this was really the only way effectually to frustrate them? The nation was in a ferment, and the indignant people would (there was reason to think) show so decided a spirit of opposition as must compel the king to yield. "Now," says Orange, "my country feels all the impulse necessary for it to contend successfully with tyranny! If I neglect the present moment, the tyrant will, by secret negotiation and intrigue, find means to obtain by stealth what by open force he could not. The same object will be steadily pursued, only with greater caution and forbearance; but extremity alone can combine the people to unity of purpose and move them to bold measures." It is clear, therefore, that with regard to the king the prince did but change his language only; but that as far as the people was concerned, his conduct was perfectly consistent. And what duties did he owe the king apart from those he owed the Republic? Was he to oppose an arbitrary act in the very moment when it was about to entail a just retribution on its author? Would he have done his duty to his country if he had deterred its oppressor from a precipitate step, which alone could save it from its otherwise unavoidable misery?

ticular territorial rights of the provinces and towns.

These commands, which were publicly read in every town by a herald, produced an effect on the people which in the fullest manner verified the fears of the President Viglius and the hopes of the Prince of Orange. Nearly all the governors of provinces refused compliance with them, and threatened to throw up their appointments if the attempt should be made to compel their obedience. "The ordinance," they wrote back, "was based on a statement of the numbers of the sectaries, which was altogether false.* Justice was appalled at the prodigious crowd of victims which daily accumulated under its hands. To destroy by the flames fifty or sixty thousand persons from their districts was no commission for them." The inferior clergy, too, in particular, were loud in their outcries against the decrees of Trent, which cruelly assailed their ignorance and corruption, and which moreover threatened them with a reform they so much detested. Sacrificing therefore the highest interests of their church to their own private advantage, they bitterly reviled the decrees and the whole council, and with liberal hand scattered the seeds of revolt in the minds of the people. The same outcry was now revived which the monks had formerly raised against the new bishops. The Archbishop of Cambray succeeded at last, but not without great opposition, in causing the decrees to be proclaimed. It cost more labor to effect this in Malines and Utrecht, where the archbishops were at strife with their clergy, who, as they were accused, preferred to involve the whole church in ruin rather than submit to a reformation of morals.

Of all the provinces Brabant raised its voice the loudest. The states of this province appealed to their great privilege, which protected their members from being brought before a foreign court of justice. They spoke

* The number of the heretics was very unequally computed by the two parties, according as the interests and passions of either made its increase or diminution desirable, and the same party often contradicted itself, when its interest changed. If the question related to new measures of oppression, to the introduction of the inquisitorial tribunals, etc., the numbers of the Protestants were countless and interminable. If, on the other hand, the question was of lenity towards them, of ordinances to their advantage, they were now reduced to such an insignificant number that it would not repay the trouble of making an innovation for this small body of ill-minded people.

loudly of the oath by which the king had bound himself to observe all their statutes, and of the conditions under which they alone had sworn allegiance to him. Louvain, Antwerp, Brussels and Herzogenbusch solemnly protested against the decrees, and transmitted their protests in distinct memorials to the regent. The latter, always hesitating and wavering, too timid to obey the king and far more afraid to disobey him, again summoned her council, again listened to the arguments for and against the question and, at last, again gave her assent to the opinion which, of all others, was the most perilous for her to adopt. A new reference to the king in Spain was proposed at one moment; in the next, that the urgency of the crisis did not admit of so dilatory a remedy; it was necessary for the regent to act on her own responsibility, and either defy the threatening aspect of despair or to yield to it by modifying or retracting the royal ordinance. She finally caused the annals of Brabant to be examined in order to discover, if possible, a precedent for the present case in the instructions of the first Inquisitor whom Charles V. had appointed to the province. These instructions, indeed, did not exactly correspond with those now given; but had not the king declared that he introduced no innovation? This was precedent enough, and it was declared that the new edicts must also be interpreted in accordance with the old and existing statutes of the province. This explanation gave, indeed, no satisfaction to the states of Brabant who had loudly demanded the entire abolition of the Inquisition, but it was an encouragement to the other provinces to make similar protests and an equally bold opposition. Without giving the duchess time to decide upon their remonstrances they, on their own authority, ceased to obey the Inquisition and withdrew their aid from it. The Inquisitors, who had so recently been expressly urged to a more rigid execution of their duties, now saw themselves suddenly deserted by the secular arm and robbed of all authority; while, in answer to their application for assistance, the court could give them only empty promises. The regent by thus endeavoring to satisfy all parties had displeased all.

During these negotiations between the court, the councils and the states, a universal spirit of revolt pervaded the whole nation. Men began to investigate the rights of the subject and to scrutinize the prerogative of kings.

"The Netherlanders were not so stupid," many were heard to say with very little attempt at secrecy, "as not to know right well what was due from the subject to the sovereign, and from the king to the subject; and that, perhaps, means would yet be found to repel force with force, although at present there might be no appearance of it." In Antwerp a placard was set up in several places calling upon the town council to accuse the King of Spain before the supreme court at Spires, of having broken his oath and violated the liberties of the country; for Brabant, being a portion of the Burgundian circle, was included in the religious peace of Passau and Augsbourg. About this time, too, the Calvinists published their confession of faith, in a preamble addressed to the king declared that they, although a hundred thousand strong, kept themselves, nevertheless, quiet, and like the rest of his subjects contributed to all the taxes of the country; from which it was evident, they added, that of themselves they entertained no ideas of insurrection. Bold and incendiary writings were publicly disseminated, which depicted the Spanish tyranny in the most odious colors and reminded the nation of its privileges and occasionally also of its powers.*

The warlike preparations of Philip against the Porte, as well as those which, for no intelligible reason, Eric, Duke of Brunswick, about this time made in the vicinity, contributed to strengthen the general suspicion that the Inquisition was to be forcibly imposed on the Netherlands. Many of the most eminent merchants already spoke of quitting their houses and business, to seek in some other part of the world the liberty of which they were here deprived; others looked about for a leader and let fall hints of forcible resistance and of foreign aid.

That, in this distressing position of affairs, the regent might be left entirely without an adviser and without support, she was now deserted by the only person who was at the

* The regent mentioned to the king a number (3,000) of these writings. Strada 117. It is remarkable how important a part printing, and publicity in general, played in the rebellion of the Netherlands. Through this organ one restless spirit spoke to millions. Besides the lampoons, which for the most part were composed with all the low scurrility and brutality which was the distinguishing character of most of the Protestant polemical writings of the time, works were occasionally published which defended religious liberty in the fullest sense of the word.

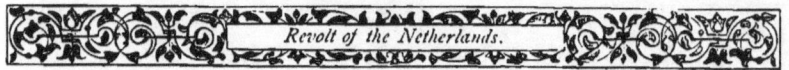

present moment indispensable to her, and who had contributed to plunge her into this embarrassment. "Without kindling a civil war," wrote to her William of Orange, "it was absolutely impossible to comply now with the orders of the king. If, however, obedience was to be insisted upon he must beg that his place might be supplied by another, who would better answer the expectations of his majesty and have more power than he had over the minds of the nation. The zeal which on every other occasion he had shown in the service of the crown would, he hoped, secure his present proceeding from misconstruction; for, as the case now stood, he had no alternative between disobeying the king and injuring his country and himself." From this time forth William of Orange retired from the Council of State to his town of Breda, where, in observant but scarcely inactive repose, he watched the course of affairs. Count Horn followed his example. Egmont, ever vacillating between the Republic and the throne, ever wearying himself in the vain attempt to unite the good citizen with the obedient subject—Egmont, who was less able than the rest to dispense with the favor of the monarch, and to whom therefore it was less an object of indifference—could not bring himself to abandon the bright prospects which were now opening for him at the court of the regent. The Prince of Orange had by his superior intellect gained an influence over the regent, which great minds cannot fail to command from inferior spirits. His retirement had opened a void in her confidence, which Count Egmont was now to fill by virtue of that sympathy which so naturally subsists between timidity, weakness and good nature. As she was so much afraid of exasperating the people by an exclusive confidence in the adherents of the crown, as she was fearful of displeasing the king by too close an understanding with the declared leaders of the faction, a better object for her confidence could now hardly be presented than this very Count Egmont, of whom it could not be said that he belonged to either of the two conflicting parties.

INDEX OF THE PLAYS, TALES, ETC.

VOLUME III.

TITLE	PAGE
THE BRIDE OF MESSINA	11
WILLIAM TELL	51
HOMAGE OF THE ARTS	112
WARBECK	120
THE MALTESE	131
THE CHILDREN OF THE HOUSE	138
DEMETRIUS	143
THE CRIMINAL FROM LOST HONOR	169
THE SPORT OF DESTINY	185
THE GHOST-SEER	193
THE REVOLT OF THE NETHERLANDS, BOOKS I. AND II.	251

Contents

INDEX

OF THE

WOOD ENGRAVINGS PRINTED WITH THE TEXT.

___

VOLUME III.

___

SUBJECT	PLAY	PAGE
Donna Isabella and the Elders	*Bride of Messina*	11
Meeting of Don Manuel and Don Cæsar	" "	17
Beatrice in the Garden	" "	23
Don Manuel and Beatrice	" "	33
Death of Don Manuel	" "	35
Donna Isabella and Beatrice	" "	39
The Remorse of Don Cæsar	" "	43
Death of Don Cæsar	" "	45
Donna Isabella and Beatrice	" "	47
The Fisherman's Boat	*William Tell*	51
Stauffacher and Gertrude	"	55
Gessler's Cap	"	57
Stauffacher, Furst and Von Melchthal	"	63
Baron of Attinghausen and Rudenz	"	65
The Rendezvous on the Lake	"	69
The Oath of the Confederates	"	74
William Tell and his Family	"	77
Hedwig and Child	"	79
Tell and Gessler's Cap	"	83
Tell and his Son	"	87
Arrest of Tell	"	88
The Storm on the Lake	"	89
William Tell waiting for Gessler	"	95
Death of Gessler	"	100

Contents

SUBJECT	PLAY	PAGE
The Horn of Uri	*William Tell*	101
Rescue of Bertha from the Burning Castle	"	103
Tell and Duke John	"	107
The Lion of Switzerland	"	109
Emblematical Head-piece	*Homage of the Arts*	112
Emblematical Tail-piece	" "	115
Warbeck and Lord Hereford	*Warbeck*	128
Emblematical Head-piece	*The Maltese*	131
La Valette and St. Priest	"	135
The Knights and the body of St. Priest	"	137
Saint Foix and Adelaide	*The Children of the House*	140
Demetrius at the Polish Diet	*Demetrius*	145
Tumult in the Polish Diet	"	149
Tail-piece. War	"	154
Marfa at the Convent	"	155
Demetrius receiving the Keys	"	163
The body of Demetrius	"	166
A Room in the Sun Inn	*The Criminal*	171
The Gamekeeper and Hannchen	"	172
The Sun keeper's Arrest	"	173
The Prisoners	"	174
The Murder	"	176
The Passport	"	181
The Magistrate's Office	"	183
The Arrest	*The Sport of Destiny*	187
The Prison Cell	" "	189
The Meeting with the Prince	" "	191
The Armenian	*The Ghost-Seer*	195
The Gondola	"	197
The Sicilian in Prison	"	204
Tail-piece. The Precipice	"	220
Assassination of Civitella	"	227
The Fair Greek in the Garden	"	241
The Prince by the body of the Fair Greek	"	247
Ornamental Head-piece. Belgica	*The Revolt of the Netherlands*	253
Crossing the Stream	" "	257
The Roman and Batavian Soldier	" "	260
Maria, Duchess of Burgundy	" "	263
Charles V. Portrait	" "	271
Charles V. and Philip	" "	275
The Oath of Philip	" "	276
Philip II. Portrait	" "	279
Auto-da-fe	" "	283
The Tribunal of the Inquisition	" "	284
Soldiers playing Dice	" "	286

Contents

SUBJECT	PLAY	PAGE
Egmont. Portrait	*The Revolt of the Netherlands* . . .	288
William of Orange. Portrait	" "	. . . 289
The Hero of St. Quentin and Gravelines	" "	. 292
King Philip and his Confessor	" "	. . . 297
Cardinal Granvella	" "	. 300
Deliverance of the Preachers from the Prisons . .	" "	. . . 306
Count Horn. Portrait	" "	. . . 310
Margaret, Duchess of Parma	" "	318
Philip II. at the Commission of Theologians . . .	" "	. . . 324
Viglius in the State Council	"	328
Emblematical Tail-piece	"	331

INDEX

OF

FULL-PAGE WOOD ENGRAVINGS.

VOLUME III.

SUBJECT	PLAY	ARTIST	PAGE
Don Manuel and Beatrice	*The Bride of Messina*	*Julius Benczur* . .	18
Don Cæsar and Beatrice	" "	"	22
Beatrice at the Bier of Don Manuel	" "	"	38
William Tell crossing the Lake .	*William Tell*	*A. Baur*	54
The Night Rendezvous on the Lake	"	"	68
Rudenz and Bertha	"	"	80
William Tell shooting the Apple .	"	"	88
Death of the Baron of Attinghausen	"	"	92
Death of Gessler	"	"	96
Hedwig and Duke John	"	"	106
Emblematical Illustration of the Fine Arts	*Homage of the Arts*	. . *Herm. Wislicenus*	112
The Duchess Margaret and War-beck	*Warbeck*	*H. Knadfusz*	120
The Captive	*The Maltese*	*Fr. Pecht* . .	132
The Criminal's Gift Refused	*The Criminal from Lost Honor* .	*F. Piloty*	174
The Sorcerer	*The Ghost-Seer*	. *F. Roeber*	200
The Fair Greek at Prayer . . .	"	"	234
The Duel	"	"	246

339

INDEX

OF THE

ENGRAVINGS ON STEEL.

VOLUME III.

SUBJECT	PLAY	PAGE
Queen Isabel . . . . From *Bride of Messina* . . .		Front
Don Manuel . . .	" "	16
Don Cæsar . .	" "	40
Beatrice .	" "	46
William Tell . . .	" *William Tell*	50
Bertha Von Bruneck	" "	77
Gessler	" "	84
Tell's Son	" "	86
Arnold of Melchthal	" "	102
Hedwig, Wife of Tell	" "	104
Demetrius	" *Demetrius*	143
The Prince	" *The Ghost-Seer*	193
The Fair Greek	" "	232

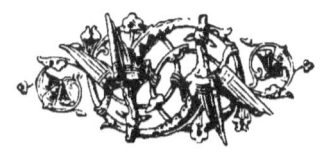

.